THE
PRIORY
OF THE
ORANGE
TREE

THE
PRIORY
OF THE
ORANGE
TREE

SAMANTHA SHANNON

BLOOMSBURY PUBLISHING
NEW YORK · LONDON · OXFORD · NEW DELHI · SYDNEY

BLOOMSBURY PUBLISHING
Bloomsbury Publishing Inc.
1385 Broadway, New York, NY 10018, USA

BLOOMSBURY, BLOOMSBURY PUBLISHING, and the Diana logo are trademarks of
Bloomsbury Publishing Plc

First published in 2019 in Great Britain
First published in the United States 2019

ISBN: HB: 978-1-63557-029-8; EBOOK: 978-1-63557-028-1

Library of Congress Cataloging-in-Publication Data is available

A catalogue record for this book is available from the British Library

12

Typeset by Integra Software Services Pvt. Ltd.
Printed and bound in India by Replika Press Pvt. Ltd.

To find out more about our authors and books visit www.bloomsbury.com
and sign up for our newsletters.

Bloomsbury books may be purchased for business or promotional use. For information on
bulk purchases please contact Macmillan Corporate and Premium Sales Department at
specialmarkets@macmillan.com.

Author's note

The fictional lands of *The Priory of the Orange Tree* are inspired by events and legends from various parts of the world. None is intended as a faithful representation of any one country or culture at any point in history.

Contents

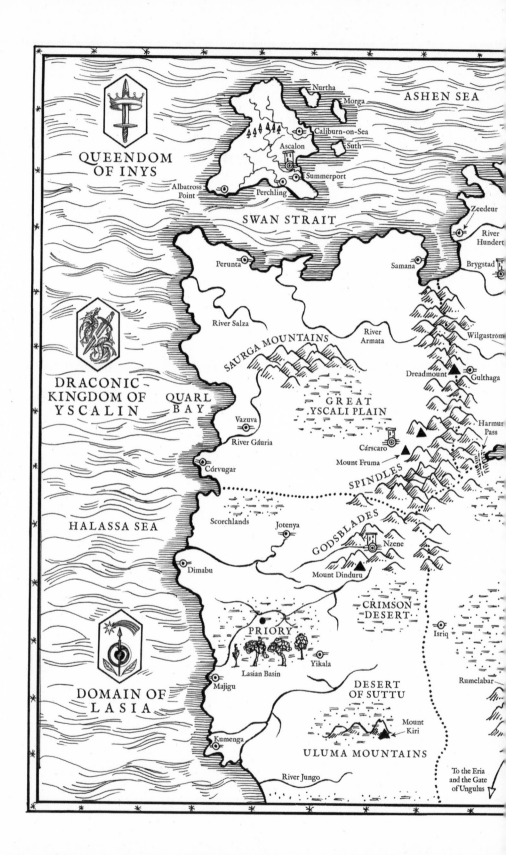

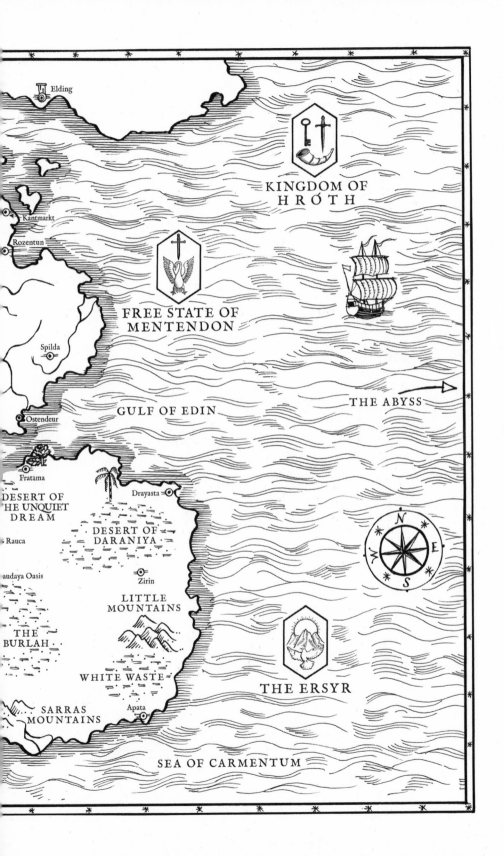

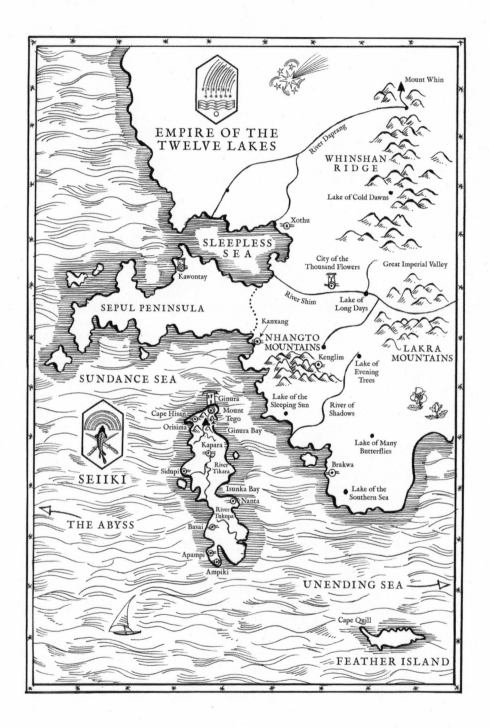

EMPIRE OF THE
TWELVE LAKES

River Daprang

Mount Whin

WHINSHAN
RIDGE

Lake of Cold Dawns

Xothu

SLEEPLESS
SEA

City of the
Thousand Flowers

Great Imperial Valley

Kawontay

SEPUL PENINSULA

River Shim

Lake of
Long Days

Kanxang

NHANGTO
MOUNTAINS

LAKRA
MOUNTAINS

Kenglim

Lake of
Evening
Trees

SUNDANCE SEA

Ginura

Cape Hisan

Mount
Tego

Orisima

Ginura Bay

Lake of the
Sleeping Sun

River of
Shadows

Kapara

Lake of Many
Butterflies

SEIIKI

Sidupi

River
Tikara

Brakwa

THE ABYSS

Isunka Bay

Lake of the
Southern Sea

Nanta

River
Tukupa

Basai

Apampi

Ampiki

UNENDING SEA

Cape Quill

FEATHER ISLAND

I
Stories of Old

And I saw an angel coming down out of heaven,
having the key to the Abyss and holding in his
hand a great chain. He seized the dragon, that
ancient serpent, who is the devil, or Satan, and
bound him for a thousand years.

He threw him into the Abyss, and locked and sealed
it over him, to keep him from deceiving the nations
any more until the thousand years were ended.

—Revelation 20.1–3

I

East

The stranger came out of the sea like a water ghost, barefoot and wearing the scars of his journey. He walked as if drunk through the haze of mist that clung like spidersilk to Seiiki.

The stories of old said water ghosts were doomed to live in silence. That their tongues had shriveled, along with their skin, and that all that dressed their bones was seaweed. That they would lurk in the shallows, waiting to drag the unwary to the heart of the Abyss.

Tané had not feared those tales since she was a small child. Now her dagger gleamed before her, its curve like a smile, and she fixed her gaze on the figure in the night.

When it called to her, she flinched.

The clouds released the moonlight they had hidden. Enough for her to see him as he was. And for him to see her.

This was no ghost. It was an outsider. She had seen him, and he could not be unseen.

He was sunburned, with hair like straw and a dripping beard. The smugglers must have abandoned him to the water and told him to swim the rest of the way. It was clear that he knew nothing of her language, but she understood enough of his to know that he was asking for help. That he wanted to see the Warlord of Seiiki.

Her heart was a fistful of thunder. She dared not speak, for to show she knew his language was to forge a link between them, and to betray herself. To betray the fact that just as she was now a witness to his crime, he was a witness to hers.

She should be in seclusion. Safe behind the walls of the South House, ready to rise, purified, for the most important day of her life. Now she was tainted. Soiled beyond redemption. All because she had wanted to immerse herself in the sea once more before Choosing Day. There were rumors that the great Kwiriki would favor those with the mettle to slip out and seek the waves during seclusion. Instead he had sent this nightmare.

All her life, she had been too fortunate.

This was her punishment.

She held the outsider at bay with the dagger. Faced with death, he began to shake.

Her mind became a whirlpool of possibilities, each more terrible than the last. If she turned this outsider over to the authorities, she would have to reveal that she had broken seclusion.

Choosing Day might not proceed. The honorable Governor of Cape Hisan—this province of Seiiki—would never allow the gods into a place that might be fouled with the red sickness. It could be weeks before the city was pronounced safe, and by then it would have been decided that the stranger arriving had been an ill omen, and that the next generation of apprentices, not hers, must be given the chance to be riders. It would cost her everything.

She could not report him. Neither could she abandon him. If he *did* have the red sickness, letting him roam unchecked would endanger the entire island.

There was only one choice.

She wrapped a strip of cloth around his face to keep him from breathing out the sickness. Her hands quaked. When it was done, she walked him from the black sand of the beach and up to the city, keeping as close as she dared, her blade pressed to his back.

Cape Hisan was a sleepless port. She steered the outsider through its night markets, past shrines whittled from driftwood, under the strings of blue and white lanterns that had been hung up for Choosing Day. Her prisoner stared at it all in silence. The dark obscured his features, but she tapped the flat of her blade on his head, forcing him to lower it. All the while, she kept him as far away from others as she could.

She had an idea of how to isolate him.

An artificial island clung to the cape. It was called Orisima, and it was something of a curiosity to the locals. The trading post had been constructed to house a handful of merchants and scholars from the Free State of Mentendon. Along with the Lacustrine, who were on the other side of the cape, the Ments alone had been granted permission to continue trading in Seiiki after the island had been closed to the world.

Orisima.

That was where she would take the outsider.

The torchlit bridge to the trading post was guarded by armed sentries. Few Seiikinese had permission to enter, and she was not one of them. The only other way past the fence was the landing gate, which opened once a year to receive goods from the Mentish ships.

Tané led the outsider down to the canal. She could not sneak him into Orisima herself, but she knew a woman who could. Someone who would know exactly where in the trading post to hide him.

It had been a long time since Niclays Roos had received a visitor.

He was rationing himself a little wine—a trickle of his paltry allowance—when the knock came at his door. Wine was one of his few remaining pleasures in the world, and he had been immersed in breathing in its aroma, savoring that golden moment before the first taste.

Now an interruption. Of course. With a sigh, he uprooted himself, grumbling at the sudden throb in his ankle. Gout was back once more to vex him.

Another knock.

"Oh, do shut *up*," he muttered.

Rain drummed on the roof as he groped for his cane. *Plum rain*, the Seiikinese called it at this time of the year, when the air hung thick and damp as cloud and fruit swelled on the trees. He limped across the mats, cursing under his breath, and opened the door a fraction of an inch.

Standing in the darkness outside was a woman. Dark hair fell to her waist, and she wore a robe patterned with salt flowers. Rain alone could not have made her as wet as she was.

"Good evening, learnèd Doctor Roos," she said.

Niclays raised his eyebrows. "I strongly dislike visitors at this hour. Or any hour." He ought to bow, but he had no reason to impress this stranger. "How do you know my name?"

"I was told it." No further explanation was forthcoming. "I have one of your countrymen with me. He will stay with you tonight, and I will collect him tomorrow at sunset."

"One of my countrymen."

His visitor turned her head a little. A silhouette parted ways with a nearby tree.

"Smugglers delivered him to Seiiki," the woman said. "I will take him to the honored Governor tomorrow."

When the figure came into the light from his house, Niclays turned cold.

A golden-haired man, just as drenched as the woman, was standing on his threshold. A man he had never seen in Orisima.

Twenty people lived in the trading post. He knew every one of their faces and names. And no Mentish ships would arrive with newcomers until later in the season.

Somehow, these two had entered unseen.

"No." Niclays stared. "Saint, woman, are you trying to involve me in a smuggling operation?" He fumbled for the door. "I *cannot* hide a trespasser. If anyone knew—"

"One night."

"One night, a year—our heads will be sliced from our shoulders regardless. Good evening."

As he made to shut the door, the woman jammed her elbow into the gap.

6

"If you do this," she said, now so close that Niclays could feel her breath, "you will be rewarded with silver. As much of it as you can carry."

Niclays Roos hesitated.

Silver *was* tempting. He had played one too many drunken games of cards with the sentinels and owed them more than he was likely to make in a lifetime. So far, he had stalled their threats with the promise of jewels from the next Mentish shipment, but he knew well that, when it came, there wouldn't be a single wretched jewel on board. Not for the likes of him.

His younger self urged him to accept the proposal, if only for the sake of excitement. Before his older, wiser self could intervene, the woman moved away.

"I will return tomorrow night," she said. "Do not let him be seen."

"Wait," he hissed after her, furious. "Who are you?"

She was already gone. With a glance down the street and a growl of frustration, Niclays dragged the frightened-looking man into his house.

This was madness. If his neighbors realized that he was harboring a trespasser, he would be hauled before a very angry Warlord, who was not known for his mercy.

Yet here Niclays was.

He locked the door. Despite the heat, the newcomer was shivering on the mats. His olive skin was burned across the cheeks, his blue eyes raw from salt. If only to calm himself, Niclays found a blanket he had brought from Mentendon and handed it to the man, who took it without speaking. He was right to look afraid.

"Where did you come from?" Niclays asked curtly.

"I'm sorry," his guest whispered. "I don't understand. Are you speaking Seiikinese?"

Inysh. That tongue was one he had not heard in some time.

"That," Niclays answered in it, "was not Seiikinese. That was Mentish. I assumed you were, too."

"No, sir. I am from Ascalon," came the meek reply. "May I ask your name, since I have you to thank for sheltering me?"

7

Typical Inysh. Courtesy first. "Roos," Niclays bit out. "Doctor Niclays Roos. Master surgeon. The person whose life you are currently endangering with your presence."

The young man stared at him.

"Doctor—" He swallowed. "Doctor Niclays Roos?"

"Congratulations, boy. The seawater has not impaired your ears."

His guest drew a shuddering breath. "Doctor Roos," he said, "this is divine providence. The fact that the Knight of Fellowship has brought me to *you*, of all people—"

"Me." Niclays frowned. "Have we met?"

He strained his memory to his time in Inys, but he was sure he had never clapped eyes on this person. Unless he had been drunk at the time, of course. He had often been drunk in Inys.

"No, sir, but a friend told me your name." The man dabbed his face with his sleeve. "I was sure I would perish at sea, but seeing you has brought me back to life. Thank the Saint."

"Your saint has no power here," Niclays muttered. "Now, what name do you go by?"

"Sulyard. Master Triam Sulyard, sir, at your service. I was a squire in the household of Her Majesty, Sabran Berethnet, Queen of Inys."

Niclays gritted his jaw. That name stoked a white-hot wrath in his gut.

"A squire." He sat down. "Did Sabran tire of you, as she tires of all her subjects?"

Sulyard bristled. "If you insult my queen, I will—"

"What will you do?" Niclays looked at him over the rims of his eyeglasses. "Perhaps I should call you Triam Dullard. Do you have any notion of what they do to outsiders here? Did Sabran send you to die a particularly drawn-out death?"

"Her Majesty does not know I am here."

Interesting. Niclays poured him a cup of wine. "Here," he said grudgingly. "All of it."

Sulyard drank it down.

"Now, Master Sulyard, this is important," Niclays continued. "How many people have seen you?"

8

"They made me swim to the shore. I came to a cove first. The sand was black." Sulyard was shivering. "A woman found me and led me into this city at knifepoint. She left me alone in a stable ... then a different woman arrived and bid me follow her. She took me to the sea, and we swam together until we came to a jetty. There was a gate at the end."

"And it was open?"

"Yes."

The woman must know one of the sentinels. Must have asked them to leave the landing gate open.

Sulyard rubbed his eyes. His time at sea had weathered him, but Niclays could see now that he was only young, perhaps not even twenty.

"Doctor Roos," he said, "I have come here on a mission of the utmost importance. I must speak to the—"

"I will have to stop you there, Master Sulyard," Niclays cut in. "I have no interest in why you are here."

"But—"

"Whatever your reasons, you came here to do it without permission from any authority, which is folly. If the Chief Officer finds you and they drag you away for interrogation, I wish to be able to say in all honesty that I have not the faintest idea why you turned up on my doorstep in the middle of the night, thinking you would be welcome in Seiiki."

Sulyard blinked. "Chief Officer?"

"The Seiikinese official in charge of this floating scrapyard, though he seems to think of himself as a minor god. Do you know what this place is, at least?"

"Orisima, the last Western trading post in the East. Its existence was what gave me the hope that the Warlord might see me."

"I assure you," Niclays said, "that under no circumstances will Pitosu Nadama receive a trespasser at his court. What he *will* do, should he get wind of you, is execute you."

Sulyard said nothing.

Niclays briefly considered telling his guest that his rescuer planned to come back for him, perhaps to alert the authorities to his presence. He decided against it. Sulyard might panic and try to flee, and there was nowhere for him to run.

Tomorrow. He would be gone tomorrow.

Just then, Niclays heard voices outside. Footsteps clattered on the wooden steps of the other dwellings. He felt a quiver in his belly.

"Hide," he said, and grasped his cane.

Sulyard ducked behind a folding screen. Niclays opened the door with shaking hands.

Centuries ago, the First Warlord of Seiiki had signed the Great Edict and closed the island to all but the Lacustrine and the Mentish, to protect its people from the Draconic plague. Even after the plague abated, the separation had endured. Any outsider who arrived without permission would be put to death. As would anyone who abetted them.

In the street, there was no sign of the sentinels, but several of his neighbors had gathered. Niclays joined them.

"What in the name of Galian is happening?" he asked the cook, who was staring at a point above their heads, mouth wide enough to catch butterflies in it. "I recommend not using that particular facial expression in the future, Harolt. People might think you a halfwit."

"Look, Roos," the cook breathed. "Look!"

"This had better be—"

He trailed off when he saw it.

An enormous head towered over the fence of Orisima. It belonged to a creature born of jewel and sea.

Cloud steamed from its scales—scales of moonstone, so bright they seemed to glow from within. A crust of gemlike droplets glistened on each one. Each eye was a burning star, and each horn was quicksilver, agleam under the pallid moon. The creature flowed with the grace of a ribbon past the bridge and took to the skies, light and quiet as a paper kite.

A dragon. Even as it rose over Cape Hisan, others were ascending from the water, leaving a chill mist in their wake. Niclays pressed a hand to the drumbeat in his chest.

"Now, what," he murmured, "are *they* doing here?"

2

West

He was masked, of course. They always were. Only a fool would trespass in the Queen Tower without ensuring his anonymity, and if he had gained access to the Privy Chamber, then this cutthroat was certainly no fool.

In the Great Bedchamber beyond, Sabran lay sound asleep. With her hair unbound and her lashes dark against her cheeks, the Queen of Inys would be a picture of repose. Tonight it was Roslain Crest who slept beside her.

Both were unaware that a shadow bent on slaughter moved closer by the moment.

When Sabran retired, the key to her most private space was left in the possession of one of her Ladies of the Bedchamber. Katryen Withy had it now, and she was in the Horn Gallery. The royal apartments were guarded by the Knights of the Body, but the door to the Great Bedchamber was not always watched. After all, there was only one key.

No risk of intrusion.

In the Privy Chamber—the last rampart between the royal bed and the outside world—the cutthroat looked over his shoulder. Sir Gules Heath had returned to his post outside, unaware of the threat that had stolen in while he was elsewhere. Unaware of Ead, concealed in the rafters, watching the cutthroat touch the door that would lead him to the queen. In silence, the intruder removed a key from his cloak and slid it into the lock.

It turned.

For a long time, he was still. Waiting for his chance.

This one was far more careful than the others. When Heath gave way to one of his coughing fits, the intruder cracked open the door to the Great Bedchamber. With the other hand, he unsheathed a blade. The same make of blade the others had used.

When he moved, so did Ead. She dropped in silence from the beam above him.

Her bare feet lit upon the marble. As the cutthroat stepped into the Great Bedchamber, dagger aloft, she covered his mouth and drove her blade between his ribs.

The cutthroat bucked. Ead held fast, careful not to let a drop of blood spill on to her. When the body stilled, she lowered it to the floor and lifted his silk-lined visard, the same as all the others had worn.

The face beneath was all too young, not quite out of boyhood. Eyes like pondwater stared at the ceiling.

He was nobody she recognized. Ead kissed his brow and left him on the marble floor.

Almost the moment she moved back into the shadows, she heard a shout for help.

———

Daybreak found her in the palace grounds. Her hair was held in a web of gold thread, studded with emerald.

Every morning she kept the same routine. To be predictable was to be safe. First she went to the Master of the Posts, who confirmed he had no letters for her. Then she went to the gates and gazed out at the city of Ascalon, and she imagined that one day she might walk through it, and keep walking until she reached a port and a ship that would take her home to Lasia. Sometimes she would glimpse someone she knew out there, and they would exchange the smallest of nods. Finally, she would go to the Banqueting House to break her fast with Margret, and then, at eight, her duties would begin.

Her first today was to trace the Royal Laundress. Ead soon found the woman behind the Great Kitchen, in a recess draped with ivy.

A stable hand seemed to be counting the freckles on her neckline with his tongue.

"Good morrow to you both," Ead said.

The pair sprang apart with gasps. Wild-eyed, the stable hand bolted like one of his horses.

"Mistress Duryan!" The laundress smoothed down her skirts and bobbed a curtsy, flushed to the roots of her hair. "Oh, please don't tell anyone, mistress, or I shall be ruined."

"You need not curtsy. I am not a lady." Ead smiled. "I thought it prudent to remind you that you must attend on Her Majesty *every* day. You have been lax of late."

"Oh, Mistress Duryan, I confess my mind has been elsewhere, but I have been so anxious." The laundress wrung her callused hands. "The servants have been whispering, mistress. They say a wyverling snatched some livestock from the Lakes not two days ago. A wyverling! Is it not frightening that the servants of the Nameless One are waking?"

"Why, you have hit upon the very reason you must be prudent in your work. Those servants of the Nameless One wish Her Majesty gone, for her death would bring their master back into this world," Ead said. "That is why your role is *vital*, goodwife. You must not fail to check her sheets each day for poison, and to keep her bedding fresh and sweet."

"Of course, yes. I promise I shall be more attentive to my duties."

"Oh, but you must not promise me. You must promise the Saint." Ead tilted her head toward the Royal Sanctuary. "Go to him now. Perhaps you could also ask forgiveness for your ... indiscretion. Go with your lover and pray for clemency. Make haste!"

As the laundress rushed away, Ead smothered a smile. It was almost too easy to fluster the Inysh.

The smile soon faded. A wyverling *had* dared to steal livestock from humans. Though Draconic creatures had been stirring from their long slumbers for years, sightings had remained uncommon— yet the last few months had seen several. It boded ill that the beasts were growing bold enough to hunt in settled areas.

Keeping to the shade, Ead took the long way to the royal apartments. She skirted the Royal Library, stepped around one of the white peacocks that roamed the grounds, and entered the cloisters.

Ascalon Palace—a climbing triumph of pale limestone—was the largest and oldest of the residences of the House of Berethnet, rulers of the Queendom of Inys. The damage wreaked upon it in the Grief of Ages, when the Draconic Army had mounted its year-long war against humankind, had long since been erased. Each window was fitted with stained glass in all colors of the rainbow. Its grounds were home to a Sanctuary of Virtues, gardens with shaded lawns, and the immense Royal Library with its marble-faced clock tower. It was the only place Sabran would hold court during the summer.

An apple tree stood in the middle of the courtyard. Ead stopped at the sight of it, chest aching.

Five days since Loth had disappeared from the palace in the dead of night, along with Lord Kitston Glade. Nobody knew where they had gone, or why they had left court without permission. Sabran had worn her disquiet like a cloak, but Ead had kept hers quiet and close.

She recalled the smell of woodsmoke at her first Feast of Fellowship, where she had first made the acquaintance of Lord Arteloth Beck. Every autumn, the court would come together to exchange gifts and rejoice in their unity in Virtudom. It was the first time they had seen one another in person, but Loth had told her later that he had long been curious about the new maid of honor. He had heard whispers of an eighteen-year-old Southerner, neither noble nor peasant, freshly converted to the Virtues of Knighthood. Many courtiers had seen the Ambassador to the Ersyr present her to the queen.

I bring no jewels or gold to celebrate the New Year, Your Majesty. Instead, I bring you a lady for your Upper Household, Chassar had said. *Loyalty is the greatest gift of all.*

The queen herself had only been twenty. A lady-in-waiting of no noble blood or title was a peculiar gift, but courtesy forced her to accept.

It was called the Feast of Fellowship, but fellowship only went so far. Nobody had approached Ead for a dance that night—nobody but Loth. Broad-shouldered, a head taller than she was, with deep black skin and a warm northern inflection. Everyone at court had known his name. Heir to Goldenbirch—the birthplace of the Saint—and close friend to Queen Sabran.

Mistress Duryan, he had said, bowing, *if you would do me the honor of a dance so I can escape from the Chancellor of the Exchequer's rather dull conversation, I would be in your debt. In return, I will fetch a flagon of the finest wine in Ascalon, and half will be yours. What say you?*

She had needed a friend. And a stronger drink. So, even though he was Lord Arteloth Beck, and even though she was a stranger to him, they had danced three pavanes and spent the rest of the night beside the apple tree, drinking and talking under the stars. Before Ead knew it, a friendship had blossomed.

Now he was gone, and there was only one explanation. Loth would never have left court of his own accord—certainly not without telling his sister or asking leave from Sabran. The only explanation was that he had been forced.

Both she and Margret had tried to warn him. They had told him that his friendship with Sabran—a friendship struck up in their childhood—would eventually make him a threat to her marriage prospects. That he must be less familiar with her now they were older.

Loth had never listened to reason.

Ead shook herself out of her reverie. As she left the cloisters, she stood aside for a group of retainers in the service of Lady Igrain Crest, the Duchess of Justice. Her livery badge was embroidered on their tabards.

The Sundial Garden drank in the morning light. Its paths were honeyed by the sun, and the roses that trimmed its lawns held a soft blush. It was watched over by the statues of the five Great Queens of the House of Berethnet, which stood on a lintel above the entrance to the nearby Dearn Tower. Sabran usually liked to take walks on days like this, arm in arm with one of her ladies, but today the paths were empty. The queen would be in no mood for a stroll when a corpse had been found so close to her bed.

Ead approached the Queen Tower. The woodvines that snaked up it were thick with purple blossom. She ascended the many stairs within and made her way to the royal apartments.

Twelve Knights of the Body, clad in gold-plated armor and green cloaks for the summer, flanked the doors to the Privy Chamber. Floriated patterns covered the vambraces, while the Berethnet badge took pride of place on their breastplates. They looked up sharply as Ead approached.

"Good morrow," she said.

The moment of caution waned, and they stood aside for a Lady of the Privy Chamber.

Ead soon found Lady Katryen Withy, niece to the Duke of Fellowship. At four and twenty, she was the youngest and tallest of the three Ladies of the Bedchamber, possessed of smooth brown skin, full lips, and tightly curling hair of such a deep red it was almost black.

"Mistress Duryan," she said. Like everyone else in the palace, she wore greens and yellows for summer. "Her Majesty is still abed. Did you find the laundress?"

"Yes, my lady." Ead curtsied. "It seems ... duties to her family have distracted her."

"No duty comes above our service to the crown." Katryen glanced toward the doors. "There has been another intrusion. This time, the knave was far less of a blunderer. Not only did he reach the Great Bedchamber itself—he had a key to it."

"The Great Bedchamber." Ead hoped she looked shocked. "Then someone in the Upper Household has betrayed Her Majesty."

Katryen nodded. "We think he came up the Secret Stair. That would have allowed him to avoid most of the Knights of the Body and get straight into the Privy Chamber. And given that the Secret Stair has been sealed since—" She sighed. "The Serjeant Porter has been dismissed for his laxity. From now on, the door to the Great Bedchamber must *never* be out of sight."

Ead nodded. "What would you have us do today?"

"I have a particular task for you. As you know, the Mentish ambassador, Oscarde utt Zeedeur, arrives today. His daughter has been rather slack in her manner of dress of late," Katryen said, pursing her lips. "Lady Truyde was always neat when she first came to court, but now— why, she had a *leaf* in her hair at orisons yesterday, and forgot her girdle the day before that." She took a long look at Ead. "You appear to know how to attire yourself in a manner befitting your position. See to it that Lady Truyde is ready."

"Yes, my lady."

"Oh, and Ead, do not speak of the intrusion. Her Majesty does not wish to sow unease at court."

"Of course."

As she passed the guards a second time, Ead sliced her gaze over the blank slates of their faces.

She had long known that someone in the household was letting cutthroats into the palace. Now that someone had given them a key to reach the Queen of Inys while she slept.

Ead meant to find out who.

The House of Berethnet, like most royal houses, had seen its fair share of premature deaths. Glorian the First had drunk from a poisoned cup of wine. Jillian the Third had ruled for only a year before being stabbed in the heart by one of her own servants. Sabran's own mother, Rosarian the Fourth, had been slain by a gown laced with basilisk venom. Nobody knew how the garment had entered the Privy Wardrobe, but foul play was suspected.

Now the cutthroats were back for the last scion of the House of Berethnet. They inched closer to the queen with every attempt on her life. One had given himself away when he knocked over a bust. Another had been spotted as she stole into the Horn Gallery, and another still had screamed hateful things at the doors of the Queen Tower until the guards had reached him. No connection had been found between the would-be murderers, but Ead was sure they shared the one master. Someone who knew the palace well. Someone who could have stolen the key, made a copy, and put it back in the space of a day. Someone who knew how to open the Secret Stair, which had been locked since the death of Queen Rosarian.

If Ead were one of the Ladies of the Bedchamber, a trusted intimate, protecting Sabran would be easier. She had waited for a chance at the position since her arrival in Inys, but she was beginning to accept that it would never be. An untitled convert was not a suitable candidate.

Ead found Truyde in the Coffer Chamber, where the maids of honor slept. Twelve beds sat cheek by jowl. Their quarters were more spacious here than they were at any of the other palaces, but uncomfortable for girls who had been born into noble families.

The youngest maids of honor were fooling about with pillows, laughing, but they stopped at once when Ead entered. The maid she sought was still abed.

Lady Truyde, Marchioness of Zeedeur, was a serious young woman, milk-pale and freckled, with eyes like bone black. She had been sent to Inys at fifteen, two years ago, to learn courtly ways until she inherited the Duchy of Zeedeur from her father. There was a watchfulness about her that put Ead in mind of a sparrow. She could often be found in the Reading Room, halfway up ladders or leafing through books with crumbling pages.

"Lady Truyde," Ead said, and curtsied.

"What is it?" the girl answered, sounding bored. Her accent was still thick as curds.

"Lady Katryen has asked me to help you dress," Ead said. "If it please you."

"I am seventeen years old, Mistress Duryan, and possessed of sufficient wit to dress myself."

There was an intake of breath from the other maids.

"I'm afraid Lady Katryen thinks otherwise," Ead said evenly.

"Lady Katryen is mistaken."

More gasps. Ead wondered that there was any air left in the room.

"Ladies," she said to the girls, "find a servant and ask for the washbasin to be filled, if you please."

They went. Not with curtsies. She outranked them in the household, but they were noble-born.

Truyde gazed at the leadlight for a few moments before rising. She deposited herself on to the stool beside the washbasin.

"Forgive me, Mistress Duryan," she said. "I am ill-humored today. Sleep has eluded me of late." She folded her hands in her lap. "If Lady Katryen wishes it, you may help me dress."

She did look tired. Ead went to warm some linen beside the fire. Once a servant had brought water, she stood behind Truyde and gathered her abundant curls. Cascading to her waist, they were the true red of madder. Such hair was common in the Free State of Mentendon, which lay across the Swan Strait, but unusual in Inys.

Truyde washed her face. Ead scrubbed her hair with creamgrail, then rinsed it clean and combed out every tangle. Throughout it all, the girl said nothing.

"Are you well, my lady?"

"Quite well." Truyde twisted the ring on her thumb, revealing the green stain beneath. "Only ... irritated with the other maids and their gossip. Tell me, Mistress Duryan, have you heard anything of Master Triam Sulyard, who was squire to Sir Marke Birchen?"

Ead patted Truyde's hair with the fire-warmed linen. "Not a great deal," she said. "Only that he left court in the winter without permission, and that he had gambling debts. Why?"

"The other girls talk ceaselessly of his absence, inventing wild stories. I hoped to silence them."

"I am sorry to disappoint you."

Truyde looked up from under auburn lashes. "You were a maid of honor once."

"Yes." Ead wrung out the linen. "For four years, after Ambassador uq-Ispad brought me to court."

"And then you were promoted. Perhaps Queen Sabran will make me a Lady of the Privy Chamber one day, too," Truyde mused. "Then I would not have to sleep in this cage."

"All the world is a cage in a young girl's eyes." Ead laid a hand on her shoulder. "I will fetch your gown."

Truyde went to sit beside the fire and finger-comb her hair. Ead left her to dry.

Outside the room, Lady Oliva Marchyn, Mother of the Maids, was rousing her charges with that crumhorn of a voice. When she saw Ead, she said stiffly, "Mistress Duryan."

She enunciated the name as if it were an affliction. Ead expected that from certain members of the court. After all, she was a Southerner, born outside of Virtudom, and that made the Inysh suspicious.

"Lady Oliva," she said calmly. "Lady Katryen sent me to help dress Lady Truyde. May I have her gown?"

"Hm. Follow me." Oliva led her down another corridor. A spring of gray hair had escaped her coif. "I wish that girl would eat. She'll wither away like a blossom in winter."

"How long has she had no appetite?"

"Since the Feast of Early Spring." Oliva tossed her a disdainful glance. "Make her look well. Her father will be angry if he thinks the child is being underfed."

"She is not sick?"

"I know the signs of sickness, mistress."

Ead smiled a little. "Lovesickness, then?"

Oliva pursed her lips. "She is a maid of honor. And I will have no gossip in the Coffer Chamber."

"Your pardon, my lady. It was a jest."

"You are Queen Sabran's lady-in-waiting, not her fool."

With a sniff, Oliva took the gown from the press and handed it over. Ead curtsied and retreated.

Her very soul abhorred that woman. The four years she had spent as a maid of honor had been the most miserable of her life. Even after her public conversion to the Six Virtues, still her loyalty to the House of Berethnet had been questioned.

She remembered lying on her hard bed in the Coffer Chamber, footsore, listening to the other girls titter about her Southern accent and speculate on the sort of heresy she must have practiced in the Ersyr. Oliva had never said a word to stop them. In her heart, Ead had known that it would pass, but it had hurt her pride to be ridiculed. When a vacancy had opened in the Privy Chamber, the Mother of the Maids had been only too happy to be rid of her. Ead had gone from dancing for the queen to emptying her washbasins and tidying the royal apartments. She had her own room and a better wage now.

In the Coffer Chamber, Truyde was in a fresh shift. Ead helped her into a corset and a summer petticoat, then a black silk gown with puffed sleeves and a lace partlet. A brooch showing the shield of her patron, the Knight of Courage, gleamed over her heart. All children of Virtudom chose their patron knight when they reached the age of twelve.

Ead wore one, too. A sheaf of wheat for generosity. She had received hers at her conversion.

"Mistress," Truyde said, "the other maids of honor say you are a heretic."

"I say my orisons at sanctuary," Ead said, "unlike some of those maids of honor."

Truyde watched her face. "Is Ead Duryan really your name?" she asked suddenly. "It does not sound Ersyri to my ear."

Ead picked up a coil of gold ribbon. "Do you speak Ersyri, then, my lady?"

"No, but I have read histories of the country."

"Reading," Ead said lightly. "A dangerous pastime."

Truyde looked up at her, sharp-eyed. "You mock me."

"By no means. There is great power in stories."

"All stories grow from a seed of truth," Truyde said. "They are knowledge after figuration."

"Then I trust you will use your knowledge for good." Ead skimmed her fingers through the red curls. "Since you ask—no, it is not my real name."

"I thought not. What *is* your real name?"

Ead eased back two locks of hair and braided them with the ribbon. "Nobody here has ever heard it."

Truyde raised her eyebrows. "Not even Her Majesty?"

"No." Ead turned the girl to face her. "The Mother of the Maids is concerned for your health. Are you quite sure you are well?" Truyde hesitated. Ead placed a sisterly hand on her arm. "You know a secret of mine. We are bound by a vow of silence. Are you with child, is that it?"

Truyde stiffened. "I am not."

"Then what is it?"

"It is none of your concern. I have had a delicate stomach, that's all, since—"

"Since Master Sulyard left."

Truyde looked as if she had struck her.

"He left in the spring," Ead said. "Lady Oliva says that you have had little appetite since then."

"You presume too much, Mistress Duryan. Far too much." Truyde pulled away from her, nostrils flared. "I am Truyde utt Zeedeur, blood of the Vatten, Marchioness of Zeedeur. The mere idea that I would stoop to rutting with some low-born squire—" She turned her back. "Get out of my sight, or I will tell Lady Oliva that you are spreading lies about a maid of honor."

Ead smiled briefly and retreated. She had been at court for too long to be rankled by a child.

Oliva watched her leave the corridor. As she stepped into the sunlight, Ead breathed in the smell of fresh-cut grass.

One thing was clear. Truyde utt Zeedeur had been secretly intimate with Triam Sulyard—and Ead made it her business to know the secrets of the court. If the Mother willed it, she would know this one, too.

3

East

Dawn cracked like a heron's egg over Seiiki. Pale light prowled into the room. The shutters had been opened for the first time in eight days.

Tané gazed at the ceiling with raw eyes. She had been restless all night, hot and cold by turns.

She would never wake in this room again. Choosing Day had come. The day she had awaited since she was a child—and risked, like a fool, when she decided to break seclusion. By asking Susa to hide the outsider in Orisima, she had also risked both their lives.

Her stomach turned like a watermill. She scooped up her uniform and wash bag, passed the sleeping Ishari, and stole out of the room.

The South House stood in the foothills of the Bear's Jaw, the mountain range that loomed over Cape Hisan. Along with the other three Houses of Learning, it was used to train apprentices for the High Sea Guard. Tané had lived in its halls since she was three.

Going outside was like stepping into a kiln. The heat varnished her skin and made her hair feel thicker.

Seiiki had a scent to it. The perfume of the heartwood in the trees, unlocked by rain, and the green on every leaf. Usually Tané found it calming, but nothing would comfort her today.

The hot springs steamed in the morning haze. Tané shed her sleep robe, stepped into the nearest pool, and scrubbed herself with a handful of bran. In the shade of the plum trees, she dressed in her uniform and combed her long hair to one side of her neck, so the blue dragon could be seen on her tunic. By the time she made her way indoors, there was movement in the rooms.

She took a small breakfast of tea and broth. A few apprentices wished her luck as they passed.

When the time came, she was first to leave.

Outside, the servants waited with horses. In unison, they bowed. As Tané mounted her steed, Ishari rushed from the house, looking flustered, and climbed into her saddle.

Tané watched her, a sudden thickness in her throat. She and Ishari had shared a room for six years. After the ceremony, they might never see each other again.

They rode to the gate that separated the Houses of Learning from the rest of Cape Hisan, over the bridge and past the stream that ran down from the mountains, joining the apprentices from elsewhere in the district. Tané caught sight of Turosa, her rival, sneering at her from his line. She kept hold of his gaze until he kicked his horse and set off at a gallop toward the city, shadowed by his friends.

Tané looked over her shoulder one last time, taking in the lush green hills and the silhouettes of larch trees against the pale blue sky. Then she stitched her gaze to the horizon.

It was a slow procession through Cape Hisan. Many citizens had woken early to see the apprentices ride to the temple. They threw salt flowers on to the streets and filled every pathway, craning for a glimpse of those who might soon be god-chosen. Tané tried to concentrate on the warmth of the horse, the clop of its hooves— anything to stop her thinking of the outsider.

Susa had agreed to take the Inysh man into Orisima. Of course she had. She would do anything for Tané, just as Tané would do anything for her.

As it happened, Susa had once had a liaison with one of the sentinels at the trading post, who was keen to win her back. With the landing gate unlocked, Susa had planned to swim to it with the outsider and deliver him to Orisima's master surgeon, with the empty promise of silver if he cooperated. The man apparently had gambling debts.

If the trespasser did have the red sickness, it would be trapped in Orisima. Once the ceremony was over, Susa would anonymously report him to the Governor of Cape Hisan. The surgeon would be whipped raw when they found the man in his home, but Tané doubted he would be killed—that would risk the alliance with the Free State of Mentendon. If torture loosened his tongue, the trespasser might tell the authorities about the two women who had intervened on the night of his arrival, but he would have little time to plead his case. He would be put to the sword to contain any risk of the red sickness.

The thought made Tané look at her hands, where the rash would appear first. She had not touched his skin, but going anywhere near him had been a terrible risk. A moment of true madness. If Susa had caught the red sickness, she would never forgive herself.

Susa had risked everything to make sure today was as Tané had always dreamed. Her friend had not questioned her scruples or her sanity. Just agreed that she would help.

The gates of the Grand Temple of the Cape were open for the first time in a decade. They were flanked by two colossal statues of dragons, mouths open in eternal roars. Forty horses trotted between them. Once made of wood, the temple had been burned to the ground during the Great Sorrow and later rebuilt with stone. Hundreds of blue-glass lanterns dripped from its eaves, exuding cold light. They looked like fishing floats.

Tané dismounted and walked beside Ishari toward the driftwood gateway. Turosa fell into line with them.

"May the great Kwiriki smile on you today, Tané," he said. "What a shame it would be if an apprentice of your standing were to be sent to Feather Island."

"That would be a respectable life," Tané said as she handed her horse to an ostler.

"No doubt you will tell yourself that when you live it."

"Perhaps you will, too, honorable Turosa."

The corner of his mouth twitched before he strode ahead to rejoin his friends from the North House.

"He should speak to you with more respect," Ishari murmured. "Dumu says you score better than him in most combat."

Tané said nothing. Her arms prickled. She was the best in her house, but so was Turosa in his.

A fountain carved into the image of the great Kwiriki—the first dragon ever to take a human rider—stood in the outer courtyard of the temple. Salt water poured from his mouth. Tané washed her hands in it and placed a drop on her lips.

It tasted clean.

"Tané," Ishari said, "I hope all goes as you desire."

"I hope the same for you." They all desired the same outcome. "You were last to leave the house."

"I woke late." Ishari performed her own ablutions. "I thought I heard the screens in our room opening last night. It unsettled me … I could not sleep again for some time. Did you leave the room at all?"

"No. Perhaps it was our learnèd teacher."

"Yes, perhaps."

They proceeded to the vast inner courtyard, where the sun brightened the rooftops.

A man with a long moustache stood atop the steps with a helm under his arm. His face was tanned and weathered. Clad in armored sleeves and gauntlets, a lightweight cuirass over a coat of darkest blue, and a high-collared surcoat of black velvet and gold-brocaded silk, he was clearly both a person of high rank and a soldier.

For a moment, Tané forgot her dread. She was a child again, dreaming of dragons.

This man was the honored Sea General of Seiiki. Head of Clan Miduchi, the dynasty of dragonriders—a dynasty united not by blood, but by purpose. Tané meant to have that name.

Upon reaching the steps, the apprentices formed two lines, knelt, and pressed their foreheads to the ground. Tané could hear Ishari breathing. Nobody rose. Nobody moved.

Scale rasped against stone. Every sinew in her body seemed to tighten.

She looked up.

There were eight of them. Years she had spent praying before statues of dragons, studying them, and observing them from a distance, but she had never seen them this close.

Their size was breathtaking. Most were Seiikinese, with silvery hides and lithe, whiplike forms. Impossibly long bodies held up their splendid heads, and they each had four muscular legs, ending in feet with three claws. Long barbels swirled from their faces and trailed like the lines of kites. The majority were quite young, perhaps four hundred years old, but several carried scars from the Great Sorrow. All were covered with scales and ringed with sucker marks—keepsakes from their quarrels with greatsquid.

Two of them possessed a fourth toe. These were dragons from the Empire of the Twelve Lakes. One of them—a male—had wings. Most dragons were wingless and flew by means of an organ on their heads, which scholars had named the *crown*. The few that did grow wings did so only after at least two thousand years of life.

The winged dragon was largest. If Tané had stretched to her full height, she might not even have been able to reach between his snout and his eyes. Though his wings looked fragile as spidersilk, they were strong enough to whip up a typhoon. Tané spied the pouch beneath his chin. Like oysters, dragons could make pearls, one in a lifetime. It never left the pouch.

The dragon beside the male, also Lacustrine, was close to his stature. Her scales were a pale, clouded green, like milk jade, her mane the golden-brown of riverweed.

"Welcome," the Sea General said.

His voice rang out like the call of a war conch.

"Rise," he said, and they obeyed. "You are here today to be sworn to one of two lives: that of the High Sea Guard, defending Seiiki from sickness and invasion, or a life of learning and prayer on Feather Island. Of the sea guardians, twelve of you will have the honor of becoming dragonriders."

Only twelve. Usually there were more.

"As you will know," the Sea General said, "there have been no hatchings of dragon eggs for the past two centuries. Several dragons have also been taken by the Fleet of the Tiger Eye, which continues its repulsive trade in dragonflesh under the tyranny of the so-called Golden Empress."

Heads bowed.

"To bolster our ranks, we are honored to receive these two great warriors from the Empire of the Twelve Lakes. I trust this will herald a closer friendship with our allies to the north."

The Sea General inclined his head toward the two Lacustrine dragons. They would not be quite as accustomed to the sea as Seiikinese dragons, since they preferred to live in rivers and other bodies of freshwater—but dragons from both countries had fought side by side in the Great Sorrow, and they had ancestors in common.

Tané sensed Turosa looking at her. If he became a rider, he would say his dragon was the greatest of them all.

"Today, you will learn your destinies." The Sea General took a scroll from his surcoat and unraveled it. "Let us begin."

Tané braced herself.

The first apprentice to be called forward was raised to the noble ranks of the High Sea Guard. The Sea General handed her a tunic the color of a summer sky. When she took it, a black Seiikinese dragon huffed smoke, making her startle. The dragon wheezed.

Dumusa of the West House also became a sea guardian. The granddaughter of two riders, she was of Southern descent as well as Seiikinese. Tané watched her accept her new uniform, bow to the Sea General, and take her place on his right side.

The next apprentice became the first to join the ranks of the scholars. His silk was the deep red of mulberry, and his shoulders trembled as he bowed. Tané sensed tension in the other apprentices, sudden as a rip current.

Turosa went to the High Sea Guard, of course. It seemed a lifetime before she heard her own name:

"The honorable Tané, of the South House."

Tané stepped forward.

The dragons watched her. It was said they could see the deepest secrets of a soul, for human beings were made of water, and all water was theirs.

What if they could see what she had done?

She concentrated on the placement of her feet. When she stood before the Sea General, he looked at her for what seemed like years. It took all her strength to remain standing.

At last, he reached for a blue uniform. Tané breathed out. Tears of relief pricked her eyes.

"For your aptitude and dedication," he said, "you are raised to the noble ranks of the High Sea Guard, and must swear to practice the way of the dragon until you draw your final breath." He leaned closer. "Your teachers speak very highly of you. It will be a privilege to have you in my guard."

She bowed low. "You honor me, great lord."

The Sea General smiled.

Tané joined the four apprentices on his right side in a stupor of bliss, blood rushing like water over pebbles. As the next candidate stepped forward, Turosa whispered against her ear, "So you and I will face each other in the water trials." His breath smelled of milk.

"Good."

"It will be a pleasure to fight against a warrior of your skill, honorable Turosa," Tané said calmly.

"I see through your mask, village chaff. I see what's in your heart. It's the same as what's in mine. Ambition." He paused as one of the men was sent to join the other side. "The difference is what I am, and what you are."

Tané glanced at him. "You stand on equal ground with whatever I am, honorable Turosa."

His laughter made her neck prickle.

"The honorable Ishari, of the South House," the Sea General called.

Ishari made her slow way up the steps. When she reached him, the Sea General handed her a roll of red silk.

"For your aptitude and dedication," he said, "you are raised to the noble ranks of the scholars, and must swear to devote yourself to the furtherance of knowledge until you draw your final breath."

Though she flinched at the words, Ishari took the parcel of cloth and bowed. "Thank you, great lord," she murmured.

Tané watched her go to the left.

Ishari must be distraught. Still, she might yet do well on Feather Island, and she could eventually return to Seiiki as a master teacher.

"Pity," Turosa said. "Wasn't she your friend?"

Tané bit her tongue.

The principal apprentice from the East House joined their ranks next. Onren was short and burly, her sun-browned face sprayed with freckles. Thick hair fell to her shoulders, stripped dry by salt water and brittle at the ends. Shellblood darkened her lips.

"Tané," she said, taking the place beside her. "Congratulations."

"And to you, Onren."

They were the only apprentices who rose without fail each dawn to swim, and a kind of friendship had risen from that foundation. Tané had no doubt that Onren had also hearkened to the rumors and stolen out to immerse herself once more before the ceremony.

The thought unsettled Tané. Cape Hisan was scalloped with small coves, but fate had made her choose the one the outsider had arrived in.

Onren looked down at her blue silk. Like Tané, she was from an impoverished home.

"They are marvelous," she whispered, nodding at the dragons. "I take it you hope to be one of the twelve."

"Aren't you too small to ride a dragon, little Onren?" Turosa drawled. "You might be able to perch on one's tail, I suppose."

Onren looked over her shoulder at him. "I thought I heard you talking. Have we met?" When he opened his mouth, she said, "Don't tell me. You're plainly a fool, and I have no interest in befriending fools."

Tané hid her smile behind her hair. For once, Turosa closed his mouth.

When the last apprentice had accepted his uniform, the two groups turned to face the Sea General. Ishari, whose cheeks were tear-stained, did not look up from the cloth in her arms.

"You are children no longer. Your paths are before you." The Sea General glanced to his right. "Four of the sea guardians have performed above expectations. Turosa, of the North House; Onren, of the East House; Tané, of the South House; and Dumusa, of the

West House—turn to face our elders, so they might know your names and faces."

They did. Tané stepped forward with the others and pressed her forehead to the floor again.

"Rise," one of the dragons said.

The voice made the ground quake. It was so deep, so low, that Tané hardly understood at first.

The four of them obeyed and straightened their backs. The largest Seiikinese dragon lowered his head until he was at eye level with them. A long tongue lashed from between his teeth.

With a great push of his legs, he suddenly took flight. The apprentices all threw themselves to the ground, leaving only the Sea General standing. He let out a booming laugh.

The milky-green Lacustrine dragon displayed her teeth in a grin. Tané found herself locked in those wild eddies of eyes.

The dragon rose with the rest of her kin over the rooftops of the city. Water made flesh. As a mist of divine rain streamed from their scales, soaking the humans below, a Seiikinese male reared up, gathered his breath, and expelled it in a mighty gust of wind.

Every bell in the temple rang out in answer.

———

Niclays woke with a dry mouth and a fearsome headache, as he had a thousand times before. He blinked and rubbed a knuckle in the corner of his eye.

Bells.

That was what had woken him. He had been on this island for years, but never heard a single bell. Niclays grasped his cane and stood, his arm trembling with the effort.

It must be an alarm. They were coming for Sulyard, coming to arrest them both.

Niclays turned on the spot, desperate. His only chance was to pretend the man had hidden in the house without his knowledge.

He peered past the screen. Sulyard was sound asleep, facing the wall. Well, at least he would die in peace.

The sun was sweating too much light. Close to the little house where Niclays lived, his assistant, Muste, was sitting under the plum tree with his Seiikinese companion, Panaya.

"Muste," Niclays shouted. "What in the world is that sound?"

Muste just waved. Cursing, Niclays jammed on his sandals and picked his way toward Muste and Panaya, trying to ignore the sense that he was walking to his doom.

"Good day to you, honorable Panaya," he said in Seiikinese, bowing.

"Learnèd Niclays." The corners of her eyes crinkled. She wore a light robe, white flowers on blue, the sleeves and collar embroidered in silver. "Did the bells wake you?"

"Yes. May I ask what they mean?"

"They are ringing for Choosing Day," she said. "The eldest apprentices at the Houses of Learning have completed their studies, and have been placed into the ranks of the scholars or the High Sea Guard."

Nothing to do with intruders, then. Niclays took out his handkerchief and mopped at his face.

"Are you well, Roos?" Muste asked, shading his eyes.

"You know how I loathe the summer here." Niclays stuffed the handkerchief back into his jerkin. "Choosing Day takes place once a year, does it not?" he said to Panaya. "I have never once heard bells."

Not bells, but he had heard the drums. The inebriating sounds of joy and revelry.

"Ah," Panaya said, her smile growing, "but this is a very special Choosing Day."

"It is?"

"Do you not know, Roos?" Muste chuckled. "You have been here longer than I have."

"This is not something Niclays would have been told," Panaya said gently. "You see, Niclays, it was agreed after the Great Sorrow that every fifty years, a number of Seiikinese dragons would take human riders, so we might always be prepared to fight together once again. Those who were chosen for the High Sea Guard this morning have been given this chance, and will now endure the water trials to decide which of them will be dragonriders."

"I see," Niclays said, interested enough to forget his terror about Sulyard for a moment. "And then they fly their steeds off to fight off pirates and smugglers, I presume."

"Not *steeds*, Niclays. Dragons are not horses."

"Apologies, honorable lady. A poor choice of word."

Panaya nodded. Her hand strayed to the pendant around her neck, carved into the shape of a dragon.

Such a thing would be destroyed in Virtudom, where there was no longer any distinction between the ancient dragons of the East and the younger, fire-breathing wyrms that had once terrorized the world. Both were deemed malevolent. The door to the East had been closed for so long that misunderstanding about its customs had flourished.

Niclays had believed it before he had arrived in Orisima. He had been half-convinced, on the eve of his departure from Mentendon, that he was being exiled to a land where people were in thrall to creatures just as wicked as the Nameless One.

How frightened he had been that day. All Mentish children knew the story of the Nameless One from the moment they could fathom language. His own dear mother had relished scaring him to tears with her descriptions of the father and overking of all fire-breathing creatures—he who had emerged from the Dreadmount bent on chaos and destruction, only to be grievously wounded by Sir Galian Berethnet before he could subjugate humankind. A thousand years later, the specter of him still lived in all nightmares.

Just then, hooves thundered across the bridge into Orisima, jolting Niclays from his musings.

Soldiers.

His bowels turned to water. They were coming for him—and now the moment was at hand, he found himself light-headed rather than afraid. If today was the day, so be it. It was either this, or death at the hands of the sentinels for his gambling debts.

Saint, he prayed, *let me not piss myself at the end.*

The soldiers wore green tunics beneath their coats. Leading them, of course, was the Chief Officer—handsome, ever-so-good-natured Chief Officer, who refused to tell anyone in Orisima his name. He was a foot taller than Niclays and always wore full armor.

The Chief Officer dismounted and strode toward the house where Niclays lived. He was surrounded by his sentinels, and one hand rested on the hilt of his sword.

"Roos!" A gauntlet-covered fist rapped on the door. "Roos, open this door, or I will break it down!"

"There is no need to break anything, honored Chief Officer," Muste called. "The learnèd Doctor Roos is here."

The Chief Officer turned on his heel. His dark eyes flashed, and he walked toward them.

"Roos."

Niclays liked to pretend that nobody had ever addressed him with such contempt, but that would be a lie. "You're very welcome to call me Niclays, honored Chief Officer," he said, with all the false cheer he could muster. "We've known each other long en—"

"Be *quiet*," the Chief Officer snapped. Niclays shut his mouth. "My sentinels found the door to the landing gate open last night. A pirate ship was seen nearby. If any of you are hiding trespassers or smuggled goods, speak now, and the dragon may show mercy."

Panaya and Muste said nothing. Niclays, meanwhile, did brief and violent battle with himself. There was nowhere for Sulyard to hide. Was it better to declare what he had done?

Before he could decide, the Chief Officer motioned to his sentinels. "Search the houses."

Niclays held his breath.

There was a certain bird in Seiiki with a call like a babe beginning to wail. To Niclays, it had become a torturous symbol of his life in Orisima. The whimper that never quite turned into a scream. The wait for a blow that never came. As the sentinels rummaged through his house, that wretched bird took up its cry, and it was all Niclays could hear.

When they returned, the sentinels were empty-handed. "Nobody there," one of them called.

It was all Niclays could do to stop himself sinking to his knees. The Chief Officer looked at him for a long time, his face a mask, before he marched to the next street.

And the bird kept calling. *Hic-hic-hic.*

4

West

Somewhere in Ascalon Palace, the black hands of a milk-glass clock were creeping toward noon.

The Presence Chamber was full for the Mentish visit, as it always was when foreign ambassadors came to Inys. The windows had been thrown open to let in a honeysuckle-scented breeze. It did little to flush out the heat. Brows were glazed with sweat and feather fans waved everywhere, so that it seemed as if the room were full of fluttering birds.

Ead stood in the crowd with the other Ladies of the Privy Chamber, Margret Beck on her right. The maids of honor faced them across the carpet. Truyde utt Zeedeur adjusted her carcanet. Why Westerners could not divest themselves of a few layers of clothing in the summer, Ead would never know.

Murmurs echoed through the cavernous hall. High above her subjects, Sabran the Ninth watched from her marble throne.

The Queen of Inys was the portrait of her mother, and her mother before that, and so on for generations. The resemblance was uncanny. Like her ancestors, she was possessed of black hair and eyes of a lucent green that seemed to fracture in the sunlight. It was said that while her bloodline endured, the Nameless One could never wake from his sleep.

Sabran took in her subjects with a detached gaze, lingering on nobody. She was eight and twenty, but her eyes held the wisdom of a much older woman.

Today she embodied the wealth of the Queendom of Inys. Her gown was black satin in deference to the Mentish fashion, laid open to the waist to show a stomacher, pale as her skin, glistering with silverwork and seed pearls. A crown of diamonds affirmed her royal blood.

Trumpets heralded the coming of the Mentish party. Sabran whispered something to Lady Arbella Glenn, Viscountess Suth, who smiled and laid a liver-spotted hand on hers.

The standard-bearers came first. They showed the Silver Swan of Mentendon displayed on a black field, with the True Sword pointed down, between its wings.

Next came the servants and the guards, the interpreters and the officials. Finally, Lord Oscarde, Duke of Zeedeur, walked briskly into the chamber, accompanied by the Resident Ambassador to Mentendon. Zeedeur was heavyset, and his beard and hair were red, as was the tip of his nose. Unlike his daughter, he had the gray eyes of the Vatten.

"Majesty." He bowed with a flourish. "What an honor it is to be received once more at your court."

"Welcome, Your Grace," Sabran said. Her voice was pitched low, rich with authority. She held out her hand to Zeedeur, who mounted the steps to kiss her coronation ring. "It lifts our heart to see you in Inys again. Was your journey an easy one?"

Ead still found the *our* jarring. In public, Sabran spoke for both herself and her ancestor, the Saint.

"Alas, madam," Zeedeur said, his expression grim, "we were set upon by a full-grown wyvern in the Downs. My archers felled it, but had it been more alert, there could have been a bloodbath."

Murmurs. Ead observed the looks of shock that swept across the hall.

"Again," Margret muttered to her. "Two wyverns in as many days."

"We are most concerned to hear this," Sabran said to the ambassador. "Our finest knights-errant will escort you back to Perchling. You will have a safer journey home."

"Thank you, Your Majesty."

"Now, you must desire to see your daughter." Sabran cut her gaze to the maid in question. "Come forward, child."

Truyde stepped on to the carpet and curtsied. When she rose, her father embraced her.

"Daughter." He took her by the hands, smiling as if his face would break. "You look radiant. And how you've grown. Tell me, how is Inys treating you?"

"Far better than I deserve, Father," Truyde said.

"And what makes you say that?"

"This court is so grand," she said, indicating the domed ceiling. "Sometimes I feel very small, and very dull, as if even the ceilings are more magnificent than I will ever be."

Riotous laughter filled the chamber. "So witty," Linora whispered to Ead. "Is she not?"

Ead closed her eyes. These *people*.

"Nonsense," Sabran said to Zeedeur. "Your daughter is well liked at court. She will be a worthy companion to whomsoever her heart chooses."

Truyde dipped her gaze with a smile. At her side, Zeedeur chuckled. "Ah, Your Majesty, I fear Truyde is too free-spirited to be wed just yet, much as I desire a grandchild. I thank you for taking such good care of my daughter."

"No thanks are necessary." Sabran held the arms of her throne. "We are always pleased to receive our friends in Virtudom at court. However, we are curious as to what brings you from Mentendon now."

"My lord of Zeedeur brings a proposition, Majesty." It was the Resident Ambassador to Mentendon who spoke. "A proposition we trust will interest you."

"Indeed." Zeedeur cleared his throat. "His Royal Highness, Aubrecht the Second, High Prince of the Free State of Mentendon, has long admired Your Majesty. He has heard tell of your courage, your beauty, and your stalwart devotion to the Six Virtues. Now his late grand-uncle has been entombed, he craves a firmer alliance between our countries."

"And how does His Royal Highness mean to forge such an alliance?" Sabran asked.

"Through marriage, Your Majesty."

Every head turned toward the throne.

There was always a period of fragility before a Berethnet sovereign got with child. Theirs was a house of daughters, one daughter for each queen. Their subjects called it proof of their sainthood.

It was expected of each Queen of Inys to marry and get with child as soon as possible, lest she die with no true heir. This would be dangerous in any country, since it would pitch the realm into civil war, but according to Inysh belief, the collapse of the House of Berethnet would also cause the Nameless One to rise again and lay waste to the world.

Yet Sabran had so far declined every offer of marriage.

The queen reclined into her throne, studying Zeedeur. Her face, as ever, betrayed nothing.

"My dear Oscarde," she said. "Flattered as we are, we seem to remember that you are already wed."

The court fell about laughing. Zeedeur had looked nervous, but now he grinned.

"Sovereign lady!" he said, chuckling. "It is my master who seeks your hand."

"Pray continue," Sabran said, with the faintest shadow of a smile.

The wyvern was forgotten. Clearly emboldened, Zeedeur took another step forward.

"Madam," he said, "as you know, your ancestor, Queen Sabran the Seventh, was wed to my own distant relation, Haynrick Vatten, who was Steward-in-Waiting to Mentendon while it was under foreign rule. Since the House of Lievelyn ousted the Vatten, however, there has been no formal knit between our countries, except our shared religion."

Sabran listened with a look of indifference that never quite touched on boredom or contempt.

"Prince Aubrecht is aware that his late grand-uncle's suit was declined by Your Majesty… and, ah, also by the Queen Mother"— Zeedeur cleared his throat again—"but my master believes he offers a different sort of companionship. He also believes there would be many advantages to a fresh alliance between Inys and Mentendon. We are the only country with a trading presence in the East, and with Yscalin fallen into sin, he believes an alliance that espouses our faith is vital."

Some murmuring followed this statement. Not long ago, the Kingdom of Yscalin to the south had also been part of Virtudom. Before it had taken the Nameless One as its new god.

"The High Prince offers you a token of his affection, if Your Majesty would be gracious enough to receive it," Zeedeur said. "He has heard of your love for pearls from the Sundance Sea."

He snapped his fingers. A Mentish servant approached the throne, carrying a velvet cushion, and knelt. On the cushion was an oyster, cracked open to reveal an iridescent black pearl, big as a cherry, tinged with green. It shone like folded steel under the sun.

"This is the finest dancing pearl in his possession, caught off the coast of Seiiki," Zeedeur said. "It is worth more than the ship that carried it over the Abyss."

Sabran leaned forward. The servant held the cushion higher.

"It is true that we have a fondness for dancing pearls, and a dearth of them," the queen said, "and we would accept this gladly. But to do so is not an acceptance of this suit."

"Of course, Majesty. A gift from a friend in Virtudom, no more."

"Very well."

Sabran's gaze flicked to Lady Roslain Crest, Chief Gentlewoman of the Privy Chamber, who wore a gown of emerald silk and a partlet of white needle lace. Her brooch showed a pair of goblets, like anyone who took the Knight of Justice as their patron, but hers was gilded, showing that she was the blood of that knight. Roslain made a barely perceptible sign to one of the maids of honor, who hastened to take away the cushion.

"Although we are touched by his gift, your master should know of our disdain for the heretical practices of the Seiikinese," Sabran said. "We desire no parlance with the East."

"Of course," Zeedeur said. "Even so, our master believes that the origin of the pearl does nothing to dull its beauty."

"Perhaps your master is right." Sabran settled back into her throne. "We hear His Royal Highness was training to be a sanctarian before he was High Prince of Mentendon. Tell us of his other ... qualities."

Titters.

"Prince Aubrecht is very clever and kind, madam, possessed of great political acumen," Zeedeur said. "He is four and thirty, with hair of a softer red than mine. He plays the lute beautifully, and dances with great vigor."

"With whom, we wonder?"

"Often with his noble sisters, Your Majesty. He has three: Princess Ermuna, Princess Bedona, and Princess Betriese. They are all eager to make your acquaintance."

"Does he pray often?"

"Three times a day. He is devoted most of all to the Knight of Generosity, who is his patron."

"Does your prince have *any* faults, Oscarde?"

"Ah, Majesty, we mortals all have faults—except for you, of course. My master's only flaw is that he tires himself with worry for his people."

Sabran grew serious again.

"In that," she said, "he is already one with us."

Whispers spread through the chamber like fire.

"Our soul is touched. We will consider this suit from your master." A smattering of tentative applause broke out. "Our Virtues Council will make arrangements to further this matter. Before that, however, we would be honored if you and your party would join us for a feast."

Zeedeur swept into another bow. "The honor would be ours, Majesty."

The court undulated with bows and curtsies. Sabran made her way down the steps, followed by her Ladies of the Bedchamber. The maids of honor walked in their wake.

Ead knew Sabran would never marry the Red Prince. This was her way. She strung her suitors along like fish on a line, accepting gifts and flattery, but never surrendered her hand.

As the courtiers dispersed, Ead left by another door with her fellow chamberers. Lady Linora Payling, blonde and rosy-cheeked, was one of the fourteen children of the Earl and Countess of Payling Hill. Her favorite pastime was dabbling in gossip. Ead found her a thorough vexation.

Lady Margret Beck, however, had been her dear friend for a long time now. She had joined the Upper Household three years ago and befriended Ead as quickly as her brother, Loth, who was six years her senior. Ead had soon discovered that she and Margret had the same sense of humor, knew from a look what the other was thinking, and shared the same opinions on most people at court.

"We must work fast today," Margret said. "Sabran will expect us to show our faces at the feast."

Margret looked so much like her brother, with her ebon skin and strong features. It had been a week since Loth had disappeared, and her eyelids were still swollen.

"A suit," Linora said as they walked down the corridor, out of earshot of the rest of the court. "And from Prince Aubrecht! I had thought him far too devout to be wed."

"No prince is too devout to marry the Queen of Inys," Ead said. "It is she who is too devout to wed."

"But the realm *must* have a princess."

"Linora," Margret said tightly, "a little temperance, if you please."

"Well, it must."

"Queen Sabran is not yet thirty. She has plenty of time."

It was clear to Ead that they had not heard about the cutthroat, else Linora would look more serious. Then again, Linora never looked serious. For her, tragedy was merely an occasion for gossip.

"I hear the High Prince is rich beyond measure," she continued, not to be put off. Margret sighed. "And we could take advantage of their trading post in the East. Just imagine—having all the pearls of the Sundance Sea, the finest silver, spices and jewels—"

"Queen Sabran scorns the East, as all of us should," Ead said. "They are wyrm-worshippers."

"Inys won't have to trade there, silly. We can buy from the Mentish."

It was still a tainted exchange. The Mentish traded with the East, and the East idolized wyrms.

"My worry is affinity," Margret said. "The High Prince was betrothed to the Donmata Marosa for a time. A woman who is now the crown princess of a Draconic realm."

"Oh, *that* betrothal is long since dissolved. Besides," Linora said, tossing her hair back, "I doubt he liked her overmuch. He must have been able to tell she had evil in her heart."

At the doors to the Privy Chamber, Ead turned to the other two women.

"Ladies," she said, "I will take care of our duties today. You should go to the feast."

Margret frowned. "Without you?"

"One chamberer will not be missed." Ead smiled. "Go, both of you. Enjoy the banquet."

"The Knight of Generosity bless you, Ead." Linora was already halfway down the corridor. "You are so good!"

As Margret made to follow, Ead caught her by the elbow. "Have you heard anything from Loth?" she murmured.

"Nothing yet." Margret touched her arm. "But something is afoot. The Night Hawk summons me this evening."

Lord Seyton Combe. The spymaster himself. Almost everyone called him the Night Hawk, for he snatched his prey under cover of darkness. Discontents, power-hungry lords, people who flirted too often with the queen—he could make any problem disappear.

"Do you think he knows something?" Ead asked quietly.

"I suppose we shall find out." Margret pressed her hand before she went after Linora.

When Margret Beck suffered, she suffered alone. She hated to burden anyone else. Even her closest friends.

Ead had never meant to be among those friends. When she had first arrived in Inys, she had resolved to keep to herself as much as she could, the better to protect her secret. Yet she had been raised in a close-knit society, and she had soon ached for company and conversation. Jondu, her sister in all but blood, had been by her side almost since she was born, and to be suddenly without her had left Ead bereft. So when the Beck siblings had offered their friendship, she had given in, and could not regret it.

She would see Jondu again, when she was finally called home, but she would lose Loth and Margret. Still, if the silence from the Priory was anything to go on, that day would not be soon.

The Great Bedchamber at Ascalon Palace was high-ceilinged, with pale walls, a marble floor, and a vast canopy bed at its heart. The bolsters and coverlet were brocaded ivory silk, the sheets were finest Mentish linen, and there were two sets of drapes, one light and one heavy, used according to how much light Sabran wanted.

A wicker basket waited at the foot of the bed, and the chamber-pot was absent from its cupboard. It seemed the Royal Laundress was back to work.

The household had been so busy preparing for the Mentish visit that the task of stripping the bed had been postponed. Opening the balcony doors to let out the stuffy heat, Ead removed the sheets and the coverlet and slid her hands over the featherbeds, checking for any blades or bottles of poison that might be stitched inside them.

Even without Margret and Linora to assist her, she worked fast. While the maids of honor were at the feast, the Coffer Chamber would be empty. Now was the perfect time to investigate the familiarity she suspected between Truyde utt Zeedeur and Triam Sulyard, the missing squire. It paid to know the affairs of this court, from the kitchens to the throne. Only with absolute knowledge could she protect the queen.

Truyde was noble-born, heir to a fortune. There was no reason she should take any great interest in an untitled squire. Yet when Ead had insinuated a connection between her and Sulyard, she had looked startled, like an oakmouse caught with an acorn.

Ead knew the scent of a secret. She wore it like a perfume.

Once the Great Bedchamber was secure, she left the bed to air and made her way to the Coffer Chamber. Oliva Marchyn would be at the Banqueting House, but she had a spy. Ead crept up the stair and stepped over the threshold.

"What ho," a voice croaked. "Who comes?"

She stilled. Nobody else would have heard her, but the spy had keen hearing.

"Trespasser. Who is it?"

"Wretched fowl," Ead whispered.

A bead of sweat trailed down her spine. She hitched up her skirts and drew a knife from the sheath at her calf.

The spy sat on a perch outside the door. As Ead approached him, he tilted his head.

"Trespasser," he repeated, in ominous tones. "Wicked maiden. Out of my palace."

"Listen carefully, sirrah." Ead showed him the knife, making him ruffle his feathers. "You may think you have the power here, but sooner or later, Her Majesty will be in the mood for pigeon pie. I doubt she would notice if I wrapped *you* in pastry instead."

In truth, he was a handsome bird. A rainbow mimic. His feathers blurred from blue to green to safflower, and his head was a brash pink. It would be a shame to cook him.

"Payment," he said, with a tap of one claw.

This bird had enabled many an illicit meeting when Ead had been a maid of honor. She tucked the knife away, lips pressed together, and reached into the silk purse on her girdle.

"Here." She placed three comfits on his dish. "I will give you the rest if you behave."

He was too busy hammering at the sweets to answer.

The Coffer Chamber was never locked. Young ladies were not supposed to have anything to hide. Inside, the drapes were drawn, the fire stanched, the beds made.

There was only one place for a clever maid of honor to conceal her secret treasures.

Ead lifted the carpet and used her knife to pry up the loose floorboard. Beneath it, in the dust, lay a polished oak box. She lifted it onto her knee.

Inside was a collection of items that Oliva would have merrily confiscated. A thick book, etched with the alchemical symbol for gold. A quill and a jar of ink. Scraps of parchment. A pendant carved from wood. And a sheaf of letters, held together with ribbon.

Ead unfurled one. From the smudged date, it had been written last summer.

The cipher took moments to break. It was a touch more sophisticated than the ones used in most love letters at court, but Ead had been taught to see through code since childhood.

For you, the letter said in an untidy hand. *I bought it from Albatross Point. Wear it sometimes and think of me. I will write again soon.* She picked up another, written on thicker paper. This one was from over a year before. *Forgive me if I am too forward, my lady, but*

I think of nothing but you. Another. *My love. Meet me beneath the clock tower after orisons.*

Without dwelling for too long, she could see that Truyde and Sulyard had been conducting a love affair, and that they had consummated their desire. The usual moonshine on the water. But Ead paused over some of the phrases.

Our enterprise will shake the world. This task is our divine calling. Two young people in love could not possibly describe such a passionate affair as a "task" (unless, of course, their lovemaking failed to match their poetry). *We must begin to make plans, my love.*

Ead leafed through pillow talk and riddles until she found a letter dated from early spring, when Sulyard had gone missing. The writing was smeared.

> *Forgive me. I had to leave. In Perchling I spoke to a seafarer, and she made me an offer I could not refuse. I know we planned to go together, and perhaps you will hate me for the rest of our lives, but it is better this way, my sweetheart. You can help where you are, at court. When I send word of my success, convince Queen Sabran to look kindly upon our enterprise. Make her realize the danger.*
>
> *Burn this letter. Let none of them know what we are doing until it is done. They will hail us as legends one day, Truyde.*

Perchling. The largest port in Inys, and its principal gateway to the mainland. Sulyard had fled on a ship, then.

There was something else beneath the floorboard. A thin book, bound in leather. Ead skirted one finger over its title, written in what was unquestionably an Eastern script.

Truyde could not have found this book in any Inysh library. Seeking knowledge of the East was heresy. She would get far worse than a scolding if anyone found it.

"Somebody coming," the mimic croaked.

A door closed below. Ead hid the book and letters beneath her cloak and returned the box to its nook.

Footsteps echoed through the rafters. She fitted the floorboard back into place. On her way past the perch, she emptied the rest of her comfits into the dish.

45

"Not a word," she whispered to the spy, "or I will turn those lovely feathers into quills."

The mimic chuckled darkly as Ead vaulted through the window.

They were lying side by side under the apple tree in the courtyard, as they often did in the high summer. A flagon of wine from the Great Kitchen sat beside them, along with a dish of spiced cheese and fresh bread. Ead was telling him about some prank the maids of honor had played on Lady Oliva Marchyn, and he was laughing so hard his belly ached. She was part poet and part fool when it came to telling stories.

The sun had lured out the freckles on her nose. Her black hair fanned across the grass. Past the glare of the sun, he could see the clock tower above them, and the stained-glass windows in the cloisters, and the apples on their branches. All was well.

"My lord."

The memory shattered. Loth looked up to see a man with no teeth.

The hall of the inn was full of country-dwellers. Somewhere, a lutenist was playing a ballad about the beauty of Queen Sabran. A few days ago, he had been hunting with her. Now he was leagues away, listening to a song that spoke of her as if she were a myth. All he knew was that he was on his way to near-certain death in Yscalin, and that the Dukes Spiritual loathed him enough to have set him on that path.

How suddenly a life could crumble.

The innkeeper set down a trencher. On it sat two bowls of pottage, rough-cut cheese, and a round of barley bread.

"Anything else I can do for you, my lords?"

"No," Loth said. "Thank you."

The innkeeper bowed low. Loth doubted it was every day that he hosted the noble sons of Earls Provincial in his establishment.

On the other bench, Lord Kitston Glade, his dear friend, tore into the bread with his teeth.

46

"Oh, for—" He sprayed it out. "Stale as a prayer book. Dare I try the cheese?"

Loth sipped his mead, wishing it was cold.

"If the food in your province is so vile," he said, "you should take it up with your lord father."

Kit snorted. "Yes, he does rather enjoy that sort of dullness."

"You ought to be grateful for this meal. I doubt there will be anything better on the ship."

"I know, I know. I'm a soft-fingered noble who sleeps on swansdown, loves too many courtiers, and gluts himself on sweetmeats. Court has ruined me. That's what Father said when I became a poet, you know." Kit poked gingerly at the cheese. "Speaking of which, I must write while I'm here—a pastoral, perhaps. Aren't my people charming?"

"Quite," Loth said.

He could not feign light-heartedness today. Kit reached across the table to grasp his shoulder.

"Stay with me, Arteloth," he said. Loth grunted. "Did the driver tell you the name of our captain?"

"Harman, I think."

"You don't mean Harlowe?" Loth shrugged. "Oh, Loth, you *must* have heard of Gian Harlowe. The pirate! Everyone in Ascalon—"

"I am patently not everyone in Ascalon." Loth rubbed the bridge of his nose. "Please, enlighten me as to what sort of knave is taking us to Yscalin."

"A legendary knave," Kit said in hushed tones. "Harlowe came to Inys as a boy from far-off shores. He joined the navy at nine and was captain of a ship by the time he turned eighteen—but he bit the hook of piracy, as so many promising young officers do." He poured more mead into their tankards. "The man has sailed every sea in the world, seas that no cartographer has ever named. By plundering ships, they say he had amassed wealth to rival the Dukes Spiritual by the time he was thirty."

Loth drank yet again. He had the feeling he would need another tankard before they left.

"I wonder, then, Kit," he said, "why this infamous outlaw is taking us to Yscalin."

"He may be the only captain brave enough to make the crossing. He is a man without fear," Kit replied. "Queen Rosarian favored him, you know."

Sabran's mother. Loth looked up, interested at last. "Did she?"

"She did. They say he was in love with her."

"I hope you are not suggesting that Queen Rosarian was ever unfaithful to Prince Wilstan."

"Arteloth, my surly northern friend—I never said she returned the love," Kit said equably, "but she liked the man enough to bestow on him the largest ironclad ship in her fleet, which he named the *Rose Eternal*. Now he calls himself *privateer* with impunity."

"Ah. Privateer." Loth managed a slight chuckle. "The most sought-after title in all the world."

"His crew has captured several Yscali ships in the last two years. I doubt they will take kindly to our arrival."

"I imagine the Yscals take kindly to very little nowadays."

They sat in silence for some time. While Kit ate, Loth gazed out of the window.

It had happened in the dead of night. Retainers wearing the winged book of Lord Seyton Combe had entered his chambers and ordered him to come with them. Before he knew it, he had been bundled into a coach with Kit—who had also been marched from his lodgings under cover of darkness—and shown a note to explain his circumstances.

Lord Arteloth Beck—

You and Lord Kitston are now Inysh ambassadors-in-residence to the Draconic Kingdom of Yscalin. The Yscals have been informed you are coming.

Make enquiries about the last ambassador, the Duke of Temperance. Observe the court of the Vetalda. Most importantly, find out what they are planning, and if they intend to mount an invasion of Inys.

For queen and country.

The note had been jerked out of his hands within moments, and presumably carried off to be burned.

What Loth could not work out was *why*. Why he, of all people, was being sent to Yscalin. Inys needed to know what was happening in Cárscaro, but he was no spy.

The hound of despair was on his back, but he could not let it buckle him. He was not alone.

"Kit," he said, "forgive me. You have been forced to join me in my exile, and I have been poor company."

"Don't you dare apologize. I've always rather fancied an adventure." Kit smoothed back his flaxen curls with both hands. "Since you're finally talking, though, we ought to speak about our ... situation."

"Don't. Not now, Kit. It's done."

"You must not think Queen Sabran ordered your banishment," Kit said firmly. "I tell you, this was arranged without her knowledge. Combe will have told her you left court of your own free will, and she will have doubts about her spymaster. You must tell her the truth," he urged. "Write to her. Disclose to her what they have done, and—"

"Combe reads every letter before it reaches her."

"Could you not use some cipher?"

"No cipher is safe from the Night Hawk. There is a reason why Sabran made him her spymaster."

"Then write to your family. Ask them for their help."

"They will not be granted an audience with Sabran unless they go through Combe. Even if they are," Loth said, "it will be too late for us by then. We will already be in Cárscaro."

"They should still know where you are." Kit shook his head. "Saint, I'm beginning to think you *want* to leave."

"If the Dukes Spiritual believe I am the best person to find out what has transpired in Yscalin, then perhaps I am."

"Oh, come, Loth. You know why this is happening. Everyone tried to warn you."

Loth waited, brow furrowed. With a sigh, Kit drained his tankard and leaned in closer.

"Queen Sabran is not yet married," he murmured. Loth tensed. "If the Dukes Spiritual favor a foreign match for her, your presence at her side ... well, it complicates things."

"You know Sab and I have *never*—"

49

"What I know is less important than what the world sees," Kit said. "Allow me to indulge in a little allegory. Art. Art is not one great act of creation, but many small ones. When you read one of my poems, you fail to see the weeks of careful work it took me to build it—the thinking, the scratched-out words, the pages I burned in disgust. All you see, in the end, is what I want you to see. Such is politics."

Loth puckered his brow.

"To ensure an heir, the Dukes Spiritual must paint a certain picture of the Inysh court and its eligible queen," Kit said. "If they believed your intimacy with Queen Sabran would spoil that picture—dissuade foreign suitors—it would explain why they chose you for this particular diplomatic mission. They needed you gone, so they ... painted you out."

Another silence fell. Loth clasped his ring-laden fingers and set his brow against them.

He was such a fool.

"Now, if my feeling is correct, the good news is that we may be allowed to sneak back to court once Queen Sabran is married," Kit said. "I say we weather the next few weeks, find poor old Prince Wilstan if we can possibly manage it, then return to Inys by whatever means needful. Combe will not stop us. Not once he has what he wants."

"You forget that if we return, we will be able to expose his scheming to Sabran. He would have considered that. We will not get near the palace gates."

"We will write to His Grace beforehand. Make him some offer. Our silence in exchange for him leaving us in peace."

"I cannot be silent about this," Loth bit out. "Sab must know if her Virtues Council machinates behind her back. Combe knows I will tell her. Trust me, Kit—he means for us to be in Cárscaro for good. His eyes in the most dangerous court in the West."

"Damn him. We will find a way home," Kit said. "Does the Saint not promise that all of us will?"

Loth drained his tankard.

"You can be very wise, my friend." With a sigh, he added, "I can only imagine how Margret must feel at this moment. She may have to inherit Goldenbirch."

"Meg must not burden that brilliant mind of hers. Goldenbirch will not need her as heir, because we will be back in Inys before you know it. This mission may not *seem* survivable," Kit said, back to his jocular self, "but you never know. We may return from it as princes of the world."

"I never thought you would have more faith than I do." Loth took in a deep breath through his nose. "Let us rouse the driver. We have tarried here for long enough."

5

East

The new soldiers of the High Sea Guard had been allowed to spend their last hours in Cape Hisan in whatever way they chose. Most of them had gone to bid farewell to friends. At the ninth hour of night, they would set off by palanquin to the capital.

The scholars had already left on the ship to Feather Island. Ishari had not stood on deck with the others to watch Seiiki disappear.

They had been close for years. Tané had nursed Ishari through a fever that had almost killed her. Ishari had been like a sister when Tané first bled, showing her how to make plugs out of paper. Now they might never see each other again. If only Ishari had studied harder—given more of herself to her training—they could have been riders together.

For now, Tané had to turn her mind toward another friend. She kept her head down as she wove through the clamor of Cape Hisan, where dancers and drummers were out to celebrate Choosing Day. Children skipped past, laughing, painted kites flying above them.

The streets heaved with people. They mopped at their faces with flat-woven linen. As Tané dodged merchants peddling trinkets, she breathed in the spice of incense, the scent of rain on sweat on skin, and the waft of sea-fresh fish. She listened to the tinsmiths and traders calling out and the gasps of delight as a tiny yellow bird warbled a song.

This might be the last time she walked in Cape Hisan, the only city she had ever known.

It had always been a risk to come here. The city was a dangerous place, where apprentices might be tempted to act in ways that would corrupt them. There were brothels and taverns, card games and cockfights, recruiters sent to press them into piracy. Tané had often wondered if the Houses of Learning had been built so close to all this as a test of will.

When she reached the inn, she let out her breath. There were no sentinels.

"Excuse me," she called through the bars.

A tiny girl came to the gate. When she saw Tané, and the blue tunic of the High Sea Guard, the child knelt at once and set her forehead between her hands.

"I am looking for the honorable Susa," Tané said gently. "Would you fetch her for me?"

The girl scurried back into the inn.

Nobody had ever bowed to Tané that way. She had been born in the impoverished village of Ampiki, on the southern tip of Seiiki, to a family of fisherfolk. One crisp winter day, a fire had sparked in the nearby forest and swallowed almost every house.

Tané had no memory of her parents. She had only avoided sharing their death because she had chased a butterfly out of the house, to the sea. Most foundlings and orphans washed up in the land army, but the butterfly had been interpreted by a holy woman as intervention from the gods, and it was decided that Tané must be trained as a rider.

Susa came to the gate in a robe of white silk, richly broidered. Her hair poured loose over her shoulders.

"Tané." She slid the gate aside. "We must speak."

Tané recognized the notch in her brow. They slipped into the alley beside the house, where Susa opened her umbrella and held it over them both.

"He is gone."

Tané wet her lips. "The outsider?"

"Yes." Susa looked nervous. She was never nervous. "There was gossip in the market earlier. A pirate ship was sighted off the coast of Cape Hisan. The sentinels looked all over the city for smuggled freight, but when they left, they had found nothing."

"They searched in Orisima," Tané realized, and Susa nodded. "Did they find the outsider?"

"No. But there is nowhere to hide there." Susa glanced toward the street, her eyes reflecting its lanternlight. "He must have escaped while the sentinels were distracted."

"No one could cross the bridge without the sentinels noticing. He *must* still be there."

"The man must be half ghost if he can hide himself so well." Susa tightened her grip on the umbrella. "Tané, do you think we should still tell the honored Governor about him?"

Tané had been asking herself the same question ever since the ceremony.

"I told Roos we would collect him, but ... perhaps if he stays hidden in Orisima, he will be able to avoid the sword and slip away on the next ship back to Mentendon," Susa went on. "They might mistake him for a legal settler. He was no older than us, Tané, and perhaps not here by choice. I have no desire to condemn him to death."

"Then let us not. Let him make his own way."

"What of the red sickness?"

"He had none of the signs. And if he *is* still in Orisima—and I cannot think it otherwise—the sickness cannot go far." Tané spoke quietly. "Further association with him is too much of a risk, Susa. You took him somewhere safe. What happens now is up to him."

"But if they find him, will he not tell them about us?" Susa whispered.

"Who would believe him?"

Susa took a deep breath, and her shoulders dropped. She looked Tané up and down.

"It seems all of the risk was worthwhile." Her smile made her eyes sparkle. "Was Choosing Day everything you imagined?"

The need to talk had been welling up for hours. "And more. The dragons were so beautiful," Tané said. "Did you see them?"

"No. I was asleep," Susa admitted. She must have been awake all night. "How many riders will there be this year?"

"Twelve. The honored Unceasing Emperor has sent two great warriors to raise our numbers."

"I have never seen a Lacustrine dragon. Are they very different to ours?"

"They have thicker bodies, and one more toe. It would be a privilege to ride with any of them." Tané pressed closer under the umbrella. "I *must* be a rider, Susa. I feel guilty for wanting so much when I have already received so many blessings, but—"

"It has been your dream since you were a child. You have ambition, Tané. Never apologize for that." Susa paused. "Are you afraid?"

"Of course."

"Good. Fear will make you fight. Don't let a little shit like Turosa get the better of you, whoever his mother is." Tané gave her a scolding look, but smiled. "Now, you must hurry. Remember, no matter how far from Cape Hisan you fly, I will always be your friend."

"And I yours."

The gate to the inn slid open, making them both start. "Susa," the girl called. "You need to come inside now."

Susa glanced toward the house. "I must go." She looked back at Tané, hesitated. "Will they let me write to you?"

"They must." Tané had never known any commoner to maintain a friendship with a sea guardian, but she prayed they would be the exception. "Please, Susa, be careful."

"Always." Her smile quivered. "You won't miss me so much. When you soar above the clouds, we will all seem very small down here."

"Wherever I am," Tané said, "I am with you."

Susa had risked everything for a dream that was not hers. That sort of friendship was something not found more than once in a lifetime. Some might not find it at all.

The space between them was fraught with memory, and their faces were no longer damp only from rain. Perhaps Tané would return to Cape Hisan to guard the eastern coast, or perhaps Susa could visit her, but for once in her life, nothing was certain. Their paths were about to pull apart, and unless the dragon willed it, they might never meet again.

"If anything happens—if anyone names you in relation to the outsider—come with all speed to Ginura," Tané said softly. "Come and find me, Susa. I will always keep you safe."

In a cramped excuse for a workroom in Orisima, a lantern guttered as Niclays Roos held a phial into its light. The stained label read KIDNEY ORE. It was all he could do to keep Sulyard from his mind, but the surest way to manage it was to lose himself in his great work.

Not that he was getting much work done, great or otherwise. He was perilously low on ingredients, and his alchemical equipment was as old as he was, but he wanted one more stab at this before he wrote yet again for supplies. The Governor of Cape Hisan was sympathetic, but often checked in his generosity by the Warlord, who seemed to know everything that happened in Seiiki.

The Warlord was almost mythical. His family had taken power after the imperial House of Noziken had been destroyed in the Great Sorrow. All Niclays really knew about the man was that he lived in a castle in Ginura. Every year, the Viceroy of Orisima would be taken there in a locked palanquin to pay tribute, offer gifts from Mentendon, and receive gifts in return.

Niclays was the only person in the trading post who had never been invited to join her on the journey. His fellow Ments were civil to his face, but unlike the rest of them, he was here because he was in exile. The fact that none of them knew why did not endear them to him.

Sometimes he wanted to unmask himself, just to see their faces. To tell them that *he* was the alchemist who had convinced the young Queen of Inys that he could brew her an elixir of life, removing any need for marriage or an heir. That he was the wastrel who had used Berethnet money to prop up years of guesswork, experiments, and debauchery.

How horrified they would be. How scandalized by his dearth of virtue. They would have no idea that even when he had made his way to Inys ten years ago, a walking tinderbox of pain and anger, he had remained faithful, in some hidden chamber of his heart, to the tenets of alchemy. Distillation, Ceration, Sublimation—these were the only deities that he would ever praise. They would have no idea that while he had sweated at the crucible, certain he could discover a way to set a body in the prime of its youth, he had also been trying to melt the knife of grief that had been buried in his side. A knife that had finally led him away from the crucible, back to the comfort and oblivion of wine.

He had not succeeded in either venture. And for that, Sabran Berethnet had made him pay.

Not with his life. Leovart had told him he ought to be grateful for that so-called kindness from Her Enmity. No, Sabran had not taken his head—but she had taken everything else. Now he was trapped on the edge of the world, surrounded by people who despised him.

Let them whisper. If this experiment worked, they would all be knocking at his door for the elixir. Tongue pinched between his teeth, he poured the kidney ore into the crucible.

It might as well have been gunpowder. Before he knew it, the draft was seething. It bubbled over, on to the table, and belched a thunderhead of evil-smelling smoke.

Niclays peered desperately into the crucible. All that was left was a tar-black residue. With a sigh, he rubbed the soot from his eyeglasses. His creation looked more like night soil than the elixir of life.

Kidney ore was not the answer. Then again, the powder may not have been kidney ore at all. Panaya had bought it from a merchant on his behalf, and merchants were not renowned for their honesty.

The Nameless One take all of this. He would have given up on making the damned elixir if not for the fact that he had no means of escaping this island but to buy his way back to the West with it.

Of course, he had no intention of giving it to Sabran Berethnet. She could hang. But if he made it known to any ruler that he had it, they would see to it that he was brought back to Mentendon and allowed to live out the rest of his life in luxury and wealth. And *he* would see to it that Sabran knew what he could do, and when she came to him, pleading for a taste of eternity, there would be no sweeter pleasure than denying it to her.

Still, he was a long way from that happy day. He needed the costly substances that long-dead Lacustrine rulers had sought to stretch their lives, like gold and orpiment and rare plants. Even though most of those rulers had poisoned themselves trying to live forever, there was a chance that their recipes for the elixir might spark a new flame of inspiration.

Time to write to Leovart yet again and ask him to flatter the Warlord with some pretty letter. Only a prince might be able to coax him into handing over his gold to be melted.

Niclays finished his cold tea, wishing it was stronger. The Viceroy of Orisima had barred him from the alehouse and limited him to two cups of wine each week. His hands had trembled for months.

They shook now, but not with the need for oblivion. There was still no sign of Triam Sulyard.

The bells clanged in the city again. The sea guardians must be on their way to the capital. The other apprentices would be packed off to Feather Island, a high isle in the Sundance Sea, where all known wisdom about dragonkind was stored. Niclays had written to the Governor of Cape Hisan several times, requesting permission to travel there, but had always been rebuffed. Feather Island was not for outsiders.

Dragons might yet be the key to his work. They could live for thousands of years. Something in their bodies must allow them to keep renewing themselves.

They were not what they had once been. In Eastern legend, dragons had possessed mystical abilities, like shape-shifting and dream-making. The last time they had exhibited these powers was in the years following the end of the Great Sorrow. That night, a comet had crossed the sky, and while wyrms the world over had fallen into a stonelike sleep, the Eastern dragons had found themselves stronger than they had been in centuries.

Now their powers had dwindled again. And yet they lived on. The elixir incarnate.

Not that the theory would help Niclays much. On the contrary, the realization had driven his work into a dead end. The islanders saw their dragons as sacred. Consequently, trade in any substance from their bodies was outlawed on pain of a particularly slow and hideous death. Only pirates risked it.

With gritted teeth and a pounding headache, Niclays limped from his workshop. As he stepped onto the mats, he gaped.

Triam Sulyard was sitting by the hearth. He was soaked to the skin.

"By the Saint's *codpiece*—" Niclays stared. "Sulyard!"

The boy looked wounded. "You should not take the Saint's intimate parts in vain."

"Hold your tongue," Niclays snapped, heart pounding. "My word, but you are a lucky wretch. If you've found a way out of this place, say it now."

"I tried to leave," Sulyard said. "I managed to evade the guards and slip out of the house, but more were by the gate. I got into the water and hid beneath the bridge until the Eastern knight left."

"The Chief Officer is no knight, you fool." Niclays let out a growl of frustration. "Saint, *why* did you have to come back? What did I do to deserve you turning up to threaten what little I have left of an existence?" He paused. "Actually, don't answer that."

Sulyard was silent. Niclays stormed past him and set about lighting a fire.

"Doctor Roos," Sulyard said, after a hesitation. "Why is Orisima so closely guarded?"

"Because outsiders cannot set foot in Seiiki on pain of death. And the Seiikinese, in turn, cannot leave." Niclays hooked the kettle over the hearth. "They let us stay here so they can trade with us and absorb odds and ends of Mentish knowledge, and so we can give the Warlord at least a hazy impression of the other side of the Abyss, but we cannot go beyond Orisima or speak heresy to the Seiikinese."

"Heresy like the Six Virtues?"

"Precisely. They also, understandably, suspect outsiders of carrying the Draconic plague—the red sickness, as they call it. If you had taken the trouble to do your *research* before you came here—"

"But they would surely listen if we asked for help," Sulyard said, with conviction. "Indeed, while I was hiding, I had a thought that

I might simply let them find me, so that they might take me to the capital." He seemed not to see the appalled look Niclays dealt him. "I *must* speak with the Warlord, Doctor Roos. If you would only hear what I have come to—"

"As I said," Niclays said tartly, "I have no interest in your mission, Master Sulyard."

"But Virtudom is in peril. The *world* is in peril," Sulyard pressed. "Queen Sabran needs our help."

"In terrible danger, is she?" He tried not to sound too hopeful. "Life-threatening?"

"Yes, Doctor Roos. And I know a way to save her."

"The richest woman in the West, venerated by three countries, needs a squire to save her. Fascinating." Niclays heaved a sigh. "All right, Sulyard. I will indulge you. Enlighten me as to how you plan to spare Queen Sabran from this unspecified peril."

"By interceding with the East." Sulyard looked determined. "The Warlord of Seiiki must send his dragons to help Her Majesty. I mean to persuade him to do this. He must help Virtudom put down the Draconic beasts before they fully wake. Before—"

"Wait," Niclays cut in. "Do you mean to say that you want ... an *alliance* between Inys and Seiiki?"

"Not just between Inys and Seiiki, Doctor Roos. Between Virtudom and the East."

Niclays let the words crystallize. The corner of his mouth twitched. And when Sulyard continued to look grave as a sanctarian, Niclays threw back his head and laughed.

"Oh, this is wonderful. Glorious," he declared. Sulyard stared at him. "Oh, Sulyard. I have had precious little entertainment in this place. Thank you."

"It is no *joke*, Doctor Roos," Sulyard said, indignant.

"Oh, but it is, dear boy. You think that you alone can overturn the Great Edict, a law that has stood for five *centuries*, just by asking nicely. You really are young." Niclays chuckled once more. "And who is your partner in this splendid endeavor?"

Sulyard huffed. "I know you are mocking me, sir," he said, "but you must not mock my lady. She is someone for whom I would die a thousand times, whose name I cannot tell. Someone who is the light in my life, the breath in my breast, the sun to my—"

"Yes, all right, that's quite sufficient. Did she not wish to come to Seiiki with you?"

"We planned to go together. But when I visited my mother in Perchling in the winter, I met a seafarer by chance. She offered me a place on a ship bound for Seiiki." His shoulders hunched inward. "I sent word to my love at court ... I pray she understands. That she forgives me."

It had been a while since Niclays had indulged in a bit of court gossip. It spoke volumes for his boredom that he was all but salivating for it. He poured two cups of willow tea and sat on the mats, stretching his sore leg in front of him. "This lady is your betrothed, I take it."

"My companion." A smile touched the cracked lips. "We took our vows."

"I assume Sabran gave her blessing to the match."

Sulyard flushed. "We ... did not ask Her Majesty for permission. No one knows of it."

He was braver than he looked. Sabran dealt harsh punishments to those who married in secret. It was where she differed from the late Queen Mother, who had been fond of a good love story.

"Your lady must be of a low station if *you* had to marry her in secret," Niclays mused.

"No! My lady is noble-born. She is as sweet as the richest honey, as beautiful as an autumn fore—"

"Saint, enough. You're giving me a headache." One had to wonder how Sabran had kept him around without having his tongue ripped out. "How old are you, exactly, Sulyard?"

"Eighteen."

"A grown man, then. Old enough to know that not all dreams should be pursued, especially not dreams conceived on the feather-bed of love. If the Chief Officer had found you, you would have been taken to the Governor of Cape Hisan. Not to the Warlord." Niclays sipped his tea. "I will humor you again, Sulyard. If you know Sabran to be in danger—so much danger that she needs assistance from Seiiki, which I doubt—then why not tell her?"

Sulyard hesitated.

"Her Majesty mistrusts the East, to her own detriment," he finally said, "and they are the only ones who can help us. Even when she is made aware of the danger she faces, which will no doubt be soon, her pride would never allow her to ask for Eastern aid. If I could *only* talk to the Warlord on her behalf, Truyde said she might realize the—"

"Truyde."

The cup shook in his hands.

"Truyde," he whispered. "Not—not Truyde utt Zeedeur. Daughter of Lord Oscarde."

Sulyard was frozen.

"Doctor Roos," he began, after an agony of stammering, "it must be a secret."

Before he could stop it, Niclays laughed again. This time it had an edge of madness.

"My, my," he cried, "but you are *quite* the companion, Master Sulyard! First you marry the Marchioness of Zeedeur without permission, an act that could destroy her reputation. Then you abandon her, and finally, you let slip her name to a man who knew her grandsire well." He dabbed his eyes on his sleeve. Sulyard looked as if he might faint. "Ah, how worthy you are of her love. What will you tell me next—that you left her great with child, too?"

"No, no—" Sulyard crawled toward him. "I beseech you, Doctor Roos, do not expose our transgression. I *am* unworthy of her love, but ... love her I do. It hurts my soul."

Niclays kicked him away, disgusted. It hurt *his* soul that Truyde had chosen such a pail of Inysh milk for a companion.

"I won't be exposing *her*, I assure you," he sneered, making Sulyard weep harder. "She is the heir to the Duchy of Zeedeur, blood of the Vatten. Let us pray that, one day, she weds someone with a backbone." He sat back. "Besides, even if I were to write to Prince Leovart to inform him that Lady Truyde has secretly wed beneath her station, it would take weeks for the ship to cross the Abyss. By that time, she will have forgotten you existed."

Sniffing, Sulyard managed to say, "Prince Leovart is dead."

The High Prince of Mentendon. The only person who had tried to help Niclays in Orisima.

"That would certainly explain why he ignores my letters." Niclays raised his cup to his lips. "When?"

"Less than a year ago, Doctor Roos. A wyvern burned his hunting lodge to ashes."

Niclays felt a pang of loss for Leovart. No doubt the Viceroy of Orisima had known the news, but chosen not to pass it on.

"I see," he said. "Who now rules Mentendon?"

"Prince Aubrecht."

Aubrecht. Niclays remembered him as a reserved young man who cared little for anything but prayer books. Though he had been of age when the sweat took his uncle, Edvart, it had been decided that Leovart—Edvart's own uncle—would rule first, to show tender-hearted Aubrecht the way. Of course, once Leovart was on the throne, he had found excuses not to vacate it.

Now Aubrecht had taken his rightful place. He would need a will of iron if he meant to control Mentendon.

Niclays pulled his thoughts away from home before he could fall into them for good. Sulyard was still looking at him, face blotched with pink.

"Sulyard," Niclays said, "go home. When the Mentish shipment arrives, stow away. Go back to Truyde and run away to the Milk Lagoon, or ... wherever lovers go these days." When Sulyard opened his mouth, he said, "Trust me. You can do nothing here but die."

"But my task—"

"Not all of us can finish our great works."

Sulyard fell silent. Niclays removed his eyeglasses and cleaned them on his sleeve.

"I have no love for your queen. In fact, I roundly despise her," he said, making Sulyard flinch, "but I doubt very much that Sabran would want an eighteen-year-old squire to die for her." A quake stole into his voice. "I want you to leave, Triam. And I want you to tell Truyde, from me, to stop involving herself in matters that could undo her."

Sulyard dropped his gaze.

"Forgive me, Doctor Roos, but I cannot," he said. "I must stay."

Niclays looked at him wearily. "And do what?"

"I will find a way to put my case before the Warlord ... but I shall not involve you any further."

"Having you in my house is involvement enough for me to lose my head."

Though Sulyard said nothing, his jaw was set. Niclays pursed his lips.

"You seem devout, Master Sulyard," he said. "I suggest you pray. Pray that the sentinels stay away from my house until the Mentish shipment arrives, so you have time to come to your senses on this subject. If we survive the next few days, I might just pray again myself."

6

West

When she shunned the Banqueting House, which was often, the Queen of Inys supped in her Privy Chamber. Tonight, Ead and Linora had been invited to break bread with her, an honor customarily reserved for her three bedfellows.

Margret had one of her headaches. *Skull-crushers*, she called them. Usually she refused to let them keep her from her obligations, but she must be sick with worry about Loth.

Despite the summer heat, a fire crackled in the Privy Chamber. So far, nobody had spoken to Ead.

Sometimes she felt as if they could smell her secrets. As if they sensed she had not come to this court to be a lady-in-waiting.

As if they knew about the Priory.

"What do you think of his eyes, Ros?"

Sabran gazed at the miniature in her hand. It had already been passed between the women and scrutinized from every angle. Now Roslain Crest took it and studied it again.

The Chief Gentlewoman of the Privy Chamber, heir apparent to the Duchy of Justice, had been born only six days before Sabran. Her hair was thick and dark as treacle. Pale and smalt-eyed, always fashionably dressed, she had spent almost her whole life with her queen. Her mother had been Chief Gentlewoman to Queen Rosarian.

"They are agreeable, Your Majesty," Roslain concluded. "Kind."

"I find them to be a trifle too close together," Sabran mused. "They put me in mind of a dormouse."

Linora tittered in her delicate way.

"Better a mouse than some louder beast," Roslain said to her queen. "Best he remembers his place if he weds you. He is not the one who is descended from the Saint."

Sabran patted her hand. "How are you always so wise?"

"I listen to you, Your Majesty."

"But not your grandmother, in this instance." Sabran looked up at her. "Lady Igrain thinks Mentendon will be a drain on Inys. And that Lievelyn should not trade with Seiiki. She has told me she will voice this at the next meeting of the Virtues Council."

"My lady grandmother worries about you. It makes her over-cautious." Roslain sat beside her. "I know she prefers the Chieftain of Askrdal. He is rich and devout. A safer candidate. I can also understand her concerns about Lievelyn."

"But?"

Roslain offered a faint smile. "I believe it would behoove us to give this new Red Prince a chance."

"I agree." Katryen lay on a settle, leafing through a book of poesy. "You have the Virtues Council to caution you, but your ladies to embolden you in matters such as these."

Beside Ead, Linora was drinking in the conversation in ravening silence.

"Mistress Duryan," Sabran said suddenly, "what is your opinion of Prince Aubrecht's countenance?"

All eyes turned to Ead. Slowly, she set down her knife. "You ask for *my* judgment, Majesty?"

"Unless there is another Mistress Duryan present."

Nobody laughed. The room was silent as Roslain delivered the miniature into her hands.

Ead considered the Red Prince. High cheekbones. Sleek copper hair. Strong brows arched over dark eyes, a hard contrast to his pallor. The set of his mouth was somewhat grave, but his face was pleasant.

Still, miniatures could lie, and often did. The artist would have flattered him.

"He is comely enough," she concluded.

"Faint praise indeed." Sabran sipped from her goblet. "You are a harder judge than my other ladies, Mistress Duryan. Are the men of the Ersyr more attractive than the prince?"

"They are different, Your Majesty." Ead paused, then added, "Less like dormice."

The queen gazed at her, expressionless. For a moment, Ead wondered if she had been too bold. A stricken look from Katryen only served to feed her misgiving.

"You have a quick tongue as well as light feet." The Queen of Inys reclined in her chair. "We have not spoken often since your coming to court. A long time has passed—six years, I think."

"Eight, Your Majesty."

Roslain shot her a warning glance. One did not correct the descendant of the Saint.

"Of course. Eight," was all Sabran said. "Tell me, does Ambassador uq-Ispad ever write to you?"

"Not often, madam. His Excellency is busy with other matters."

"Such as heresy."

Ead dropped her gaze. "The ambassador is a devout follower of the Dawnsinger, Majesty."

"But you, of course, no longer are," Sabran said, and Ead inclined her head. "Lady Arbella tells me you pray often at sanctuary."

How Arbella Glenn conveyed these things to Sabran was a mystery, since she never seemed to speak.

"The Six Virtues is a beautiful faith, Majesty," Ead said, "and impossible not to believe in, when the true descendant of the Saint walks among us."

It was a lie, of course. Her true faith—the faith of the Mother—blazed as strong as ever.

"They must tell tales of my ancestors in the Ersyr," Sabran said. "Of the Damsel, especially."

"Yes, madam. She is remembered in the South as the most right-wise and selfless woman of her time."

Cleolind Onjenyu was also remembered in the South as the greatest warrior of her time, but the Inysh would never believe that. They believed that she had needed to be saved.

To Ead, Cleolind was not the Damsel.

She was the Mother.

"Lady Oliva tells me that Mistress Duryan is a born storyteller," Roslain said, giving her a cool look. "Will you not tell us the tale of the Saint and the Damsel as you were taught it in the South, mistress?"

Ead sensed a trap. The Inysh seldom enjoyed hearing anything from a new perspective, let alone their most sacred tale. Roslain was expecting her to put a foot wrong.

"My lady," Ead said, "it cannot be told better than it is by the Sanctarian. In any case, we will hear it tomor—"

"We will hear it now," Sabran said. "As more wyrms stir, the story will comfort my ladies."

The fire crackled. Looking at Sabran, Ead felt a strange tension, as if there were a thread between them. Finally, she rose to take the chair beside the hearth. The place of the storyteller.

"As you wish." She smoothed her skirts. "Where shall I begin?"

"With the birth of the Nameless One," Sabran said. "When the great fiend came from the Dreadmount."

Katryen took the queen by the hand. Ead breathed in, steadying the roil within her. If she told the true story, she would doubtless face the pyre.

She would have to tell the tale she heard each day at sanctuary. The butchered tale.

Half a tale.

"There is a Womb of Fire that churns beneath this world," she began. "Over a thousand years ago, the magma within it came suddenly together, forming a beast of unspeakable magnitude—as a sword takes shape within the forge. His milk was the fire within the Womb; his thirst for it was quenchless. He drank until even his heart was a furnace."

Katryen shivered.

"Soon this creature, this wyrm, grew too large for the Womb. He longed to use the wings it had given him. Having torn his way upward, he broke through the peak of a mountain in Mentendon, which is called Dreadmount, and brought with him a flood of molten fire. Red lightning flashed at the summit of the mountain.

Darkness fell upon the city of Gulthaga, and all who lived there died choking on pernicious smoke.

"There was a lust in this wyrm to conquer all he saw. He flew south to Lasia, where the House of Onjenyu ruled a great kingdom, and settled close to their seat in Yikala." Ead took a sip of ale to wet her throat. "This nameless creature carried a terrible plague—a plague no humans had ever encountered. It made the very blood of the afflicted burn, driving them mad. To keep the wyrm at bay, the people of Yikala sent him sheep and oxen, but the Nameless One was never sated. He lusted after sweeter flesh—human flesh. And so, each day, the people cast their lots, and one was chosen as a sacrifice."

All was silent in the room.

"Lasia was ruled then by Selinu, High Ruler of the House of Onjenyu. One day, his daughter, Princess Cleolind, was chosen as the sacrifice." Ead spoke that name softly, reverently. "Though her father offered his subjects jewels and gold, and pleaded with them to choose another, they stood firm. And Cleolind went forth with dignity, for she saw that it was fair.

"On that very morning, a knight from the Isles of Inysca was riding for Yikala. At the time, these isles were riven by war and superstition, ruled by many overkings, and its people quaked in the shadow of a witch—but many good men dwelt there, sworn to the Virtues of Knighthood. *This* knight," Ead said, "was Sir Galian Berethnet."

The Deceiver.

That was the name he now had in many parts of Lasia, but Sabran had no idea of that.

"Sir Galian had heard of the terror that now abided in Lasia, and he wished to offer his services to Selinu. He carried a sword of extraordinary beauty; its name was Ascalon. When he was close to the outskirts of Yikala, he saw a damsel weeping in the shadow of the trees, and he asked why she was so afeared. *Good knight,* Cleolind answered, *thou art kind of heart, but for thine own sake, leave me to my prayers, for a wyrm doth come to claim my life.*"

It sickened Ead to speak of the Mother in this way, as if she were some swooning waif.

"The knight," she pressed on, "was moved by her tears. *Sweet lady*, he said, *I should sooner plunge my sword into my own heart than see thy blood water the earth. If thy people will give their souls to the Virtues of Knighthood, and if thou giveth me thy hand in marriage, I will drive this fell beast from these lands.* This was his promise."

Ead paused to gather her breath. And suddenly, an unexpected taste entered her mouth.

The taste of the truth.

"Cleolind told the knight to leave, insulted by his terms," she found herself saying, "but Sir Galian would not be deterred. Determined to win glory for himself, he—"

"No," Sabran cut in. "Cleolind *agreed* to his terms, and was grateful for his offer."

"This is as I heard it in the South." Ead raised her eyebrows, even as her heartbeat stumbled. "Lady Roslain asked me to—"

"And now your queen commands you otherwise. Tell the rest as the Sanctarian does."

"Yes, madam."

Sabran nodded for her to continue.

"As Sir Galian battled with the Nameless One," Ead said, "he was gravely wounded. Nonetheless, with the greatest courage of any man living, he found the strength to thrust his sword into the monster. The Nameless One slithered away, bleeding and weak, and tunneled back into the Womb of Fire, where he remains to this day."

She was too aware of Sabran observing her.

"Sir Galian returned with the princess to the Isles of Inysca, gathering a Holy Retinue of knights along the way. There he was crowned King of Inys—a new name for a new age—and for his first decree, he made the Virtues of Knighthood its true and sole religion. He built the city of Ascalon, named for the sword that had wounded the Nameless One, and it was there that he and Queen Cleolind were joyfully wed. Within a year, the queen gave birth to a daughter. And King Galian, the Saint, swore to the people that while his bloodline ruled Inys, the Nameless One could never return."

A neat story. One that the Inysh told again and again. But not the whole story.

What the Inysh did not know was that it was Cleolind, not Galian, who had banished the Nameless One.

They knew nothing of the orange tree.

"Five hundred years later," Ead said, softer, "the break in the Dreadmount widened again, and it let out other wyrms. First came the five High Westerns, the largest and cruelest of the Draconic creatures, led by Fýredel, he who was most loyal to the Nameless One. So too came their servants, the wyverns, each lit with fire from one of the High Westerns. These wyverns made their nests in the mountains and the caves, and they mated with fowl to birth the cockatrice, and with serpent to birth the basilisk and the amphiptere, and with ox to birth the ophitaur, and with wolf to birth the jaculus. And by means of these unions, the Draconic Army was born.

"Fýredel longed to do what the Nameless One had not, and conquer humankind. For more than a year, he turned the might of the Draconic Army on the world. Many great realms crumbled in that time, which we call the Grief of Ages. Yet Inys, led by Glorian the Third, was still standing when a comet passed over the world, and the wyrms fell suddenly into their age-old sleep, ending the terror and bloodshed. And to this day, the Nameless One remains in his tomb beneath the world, chained by the sacred blood of Berethnet."

Silence.

Ead folded her hands in her lap and looked straight at Sabran. That cold face was unreadable.

"Lady Oliva was right," the queen said eventually. "You do have the tongue of a storyteller—but I suspect you have heard too many stories, and not quite enough truth. I bid you listen well at sanctuary." She set down her goblet. "I am tired. Goodnight, ladies."

Ead rose, as did Linora. They curtsied and left.

"Her Majesty was displeased," Linora said crossly when they were out of earshot. "You told the story ever so beautifully at first. Why in the world did you say that the Damsel rejected the Saint? No sanctarian has *ever* said that. What a notion!"

"If Her Majesty was displeased, I am sorry for it."

"Now she might not invite us to sup with her again." Linora huffed. "You should have *apologized*, at least. Perhaps you should pray more often to the Knight of Courtesy."

Mercifully, Linora refused to speak after that. They parted ways when Ead reached her chamber.

Inside, she lit a few tapers. Her room was small, but it was her own.

She unlaced her sleeves and removed the stomacher from her gown. Once she was out of it, she cast away the petticoat and the farthingale, and, finally, off came the corset.

The night was young. Ead took a seat at her writing table. Inside was the book she had borrowed from Truyde utt Zeedeur. She could not read any Eastern script, but it bore the mark of a Mentish printer. It must have been published before the Grief of Ages, when Eastern texts were permitted in Virtudom. Truyde was a blossoming heretic, then, fascinated by the lands where wyrms basked in human idolatry.

At the end of the book, on a flyleaf, was a name in fresh ink, scribbled in a curling hand.

Niclays.

Ead thought back as she braided her hair. It was a common name in Mentendon, but there had been a Niclays Roos at court when she had first arrived. He had excelled in anatomy at the University of Brygstad and was rumored to practice alchemy. She remembered him as gorbellied and cheerful, kind enough to acknowledge her where others did not. There had been some trouble that had concluded in his departure from Inys, but the nature of the incident was a closely guarded secret.

In the silence, she listened to her body. Last time, the cutthroat had almost beaten her to the Great Bedchamber. She had not felt the flicker of her warding until it was almost too late.

Her siden was weak. The wardings she made with it had kept Sabran safe for years, but it was finally dying, like a candle at the end of its wick. Siden, the gift of the orange tree—a magic of fire and wood and earth. The Inysh in their witlessness would call it *sorcery*. Their ideas about magic were born of fear of what they could not understand.

It was Margret who had once explained to her why the Inysh had such a fear of magic. There was an ancient legend in these isles, still told to children in the north, of a figure known as the Lady of the Woods. Her name had been lost to time, but the fear of her enchantments, and her malice, had knitted itself into the bones of the Inysh and seeped through generations. Even Margret, level-headed in most things, had been reluctant to speak of it.

Ead raised a hand. She mustered her power, and golden light sputtered in her fingertips. In Lasia, when she had been close to the orange tree, siden had glowed like molten glass in her veins.

Then the Prioress had sent her here, to protect Sabran. If the years of distance extinguished her power for good, the queen would always be vulnerable. Sleeping at her side would be the only way to keep her safe, and only the Ladies of the Bedchamber did that. Ead was a long way from being a favorite.

Her restraint had cracked at supper, telling that story. She had learned to play a game over the years, to speak Inysh falsehoods and utter their prayers, but telling that butchered story herself had been difficult. And though her moment of defiance might have hurt her chances of rising any further at court, she could not quite regret it.

With the book and letters under one arm, Ead climbed onto the back of her chair and pressed at the strapwork on the ceiling, sliding a loose panel to one side. She stowed the items in the alcove beyond, where her longbow was hidden. When she was a maid of honor, she had buried the bow in the grounds of whatever palace the court occupied, but she was confident that even the Night Hawk could not find it in here.

Once she was ready for bed, she sat at her table and wrote a message to Chassar. In code, she told him there had been another attack on Sabran, and that she had stopped it.

Chassar had promised he would reply to her letters, but he never had. Not once in the eight years she had been here.

She folded the letter. The Master of the Posts would read it on behalf of the Night Hawk, but he would see nothing but courtesies. Chassar would know the truth.

A knock came at the door.

"Mistress Duryan?"

Ead put on her bedgown and undid the latch. Outside was a woman wearing a badge shaped like a winged book, marking her as a retainer in the service of Seyton Combe.

"Yes?"

"Mistress Duryan, good evening. I have been sent to inform you that the Principal Secretary wishes to see you at half past nine tomorrow," the girl said. "I will escort you to the Alabastrine Tower."

"Just me?"

"Lady Katryen and Lady Margret were both questioned today."

Ead's hand tightened on the door handle. "It is a questioning, then."

"I believe so."

With the other hand, Ead drew her bedgown closer. "Very well," she said. "Is that all?"

"Yes. Goodnight, mistress."

"Goodnight."

When the retainer walked away, darkness took back the corridor. Ead shut the door and set her brow against it.

She would have no sleep this night.

The *Rose Eternal* rocked on the water, tilted by the east wind. It was this ship that would bear them across the sea to Yscalin.

"This," Kit declared as they walked toward it, "is a fine ship. I believe that I would marry this ship, were I a ship myself."

Loth had to agree. The *Rose* was battle-scarred, but very handsome—and colossal. Even on his visits to see the navy with Sabran, he had never laid eyes upon such an immense ship as this ironclad man-of-war. She boasted one hundred and eight guns, a fearsome ram, and eighteen sails, all emblazoned with the True Sword, the emblem of Virtudom. The ensign attested that this was an Inysh vessel, and that the actions of its crew, however morally dubious they might appear, were sanctioned by its monarchy.

A figurehead of Rosarian the Fourth, lovingly polished, gazed down from the bow. Black hair and white skin. Eyes as green as sea glass. Her body tapered into a gilded tail.

Loth remembered Queen Rosarian fondly from the years before her death. The Queen Mother, as she was known now, had often watched him at play with Sabran and Roslain in the orchards. She had been a softer woman than Sabran, quick to laugh and gamesome in a way her daughter never was.

"She's a beauty, right enough," Gautfred Plume said. He was the quartermaster, a dwarf of Lasian descent. "Not half as great a beauty as the lady who gifted her to the captain, mind."

"Ah, yes." Kit doffed his feathered hat to the figurehead. "May she rest forever in the arms of the Saint."

Plume clicked his tongue. "Queen Rosarian had a merrow's soul. She should have rested in the arms of the sea."

"Oh, by the Saint, how beautifully put. Do merfolk really exist, incidentally? Did you ever see them when you crossed the Abyss?"

"No. Blackfish and greatsquid and baleens, I've seen, but nary the cap of a sea maid."

Kit wilted.

Seagulls circled in the cloud-streaked sky. The port of Perchling was ready for the worst, as always. The jetties rattled under the weight of soldiers armed with long-range muskets. Row upon row of mangonels and cannon bursting with chainshot, interspersed with stone mantlets, stood grimly on the beach. Archers occupied the watchtowers, ready to light their beacons at the *whump* of wings or the sight of an enemy ship.

Above it, a small city teetered. Perchling was so named because it perched on two great shelves that jutted halfway down the cliffside, joined to the top of the cliff, and to the beach, by a long and drunken stair. Buildings huddled like birds on a branch. Kit had been amused by its precariousness ("Saint, the architect must have been wondrous deep in the cups"), but it made Loth nervous. Perchling looked as if one good squall would blow it clean into the sea.

Still he drank it in, committing it to memory. This might be the last time he looked upon Inys, the only country he had ever known.

They found Gian Harlowe in his cabin, deep in letter-writing. The man the Queen Mother had favored was not quite what Loth had imagined. He was clean-shaven, his cuffs starched, but there was a bitten edge to him. His jaw was set like a sprung trap.

When they entered, he glanced up. Smallpox had pitted his deeply tanned face.

"Gautfred." A mane of pewter hair gleamed in the sunlight. "I take it these are our ... guests."

Though his accent was firmly Inysh, Kit had mentioned that Harlowe came from far-off shores. Rumor had it that he was descended from the people of Carmentum, once a prosperous republic in the South, that had fallen in the Grief of Ages. The survivors had scattered far and wide.

"Aye," Plume said, sounding jaded. "Lord Arteloth Beck and Lord Kitston Glade."

"Kit," came the prompt correction.

Harlowe put down his quill. "My lords," he said coolly. "Welcome aboard the *Rose Eternal.*"

"Thank you for finding cabins for us at such short notice, Captain Harlowe," Loth said. "This is a mission of the utmost importance."

"And the utmost secrecy, I'm told. Strange that no man but the heir to Goldenbirch could attend to it." Harlowe studied Loth. "We set sail for the Yscali port city of Perunta at dusk. My crew are not accustomed to having nobles under their feet, so it might well be more comfortable for us all if you keep to your cabins while you're with us."

"Yes," Kit said. "Good idea."

"I'm full of those," the captain said. "Either of you been to Yscalin before?" When they both shook their heads, he said, "Which of you offended the Principal Secretary?"

Loth sensed, rather than saw, Kit jab a thumb at him.

"Lord Arteloth." Harlowe barked a coarse laugh. "And you such a respectable fellow. Clearly you displeased His Grace to the point that he would rather not see you alive again." The captain leaned back in his chair. "I'm sure you're both aware that the House of Vetalda now openly declares its Draconic allegiance."

Loth shivered. The knowledge that a country could, within a few years, go from following the Saint to worshipping his enemy had shaken the whole of Virtudom.

"And all obey?" he said.

"The people do as their king commands, but they suffer. We hear from the dockworkers that plague is all over Yscalin." Harlowe picked up his quill again. "Speaking of which, my crew won't be escorting you ashore. You'll use a boat to reach Perunta."

Kit swallowed. "And then?"

"You'll be met by an emissary, who will take you to Cárscaro. No doubt its court is free of the sickness, since nobles have the luxury of barring themselves into their fortresses when this sort of thing occurs," Harlowe said, "but try to avoid touching anyone. The most common strain is passed from skin to skin."

"How do you know this?" Loth asked him. "The Draconic plague has not been seen in centuries."

"I have an interest in survival, Lord Arteloth. I recommend you nurture one, too." The captain stood. "Master Plume, ready the ship. Let's see to it that my lords reach the coast in one piece, even if they do die on arrival."

7

West

The Alabastrine Tower was one of the highest in Ascalon Palace. At the top of its winding staircase was the Council Chamber, round and airy, its windows framed by sheer drapes.

Ead was escorted through the doorway as the clock tower struck half past nine. As well as one of her finer gowns, she wore a modest ruff and her only carcanet.

A portrait of the Saint gazed down from a wall. Sir Galian Berethnet, direct ancestor to Sabran. Raised aloft in his hand was Ascalon, the True Sword, namesake of the capital.

Ead thought he looked a thorough dolt.

The Virtues Council comprised three bodies. Most powerful were the Dukes Spiritual, each from one of the families descended from a member of the Holy Retinue—the six knights of Galian Berethnet—and each of those was the guardian of one of the Virtues of Knighthood. Next were the Earls Provincial—the heads of the noble families who controlled the six counties of Inys—and the Knights Bachelor, who were born commoners.

Today, only four members of the council sat at the table that dominated the chamber.

The Lady Usher tapped her staff.

"Mistress Ead Duryan," she said. "An Ordinary Servant of Her Majesty's Privy Chamber."

The Queen of Inys was at the head of the table. Her lips were painted red as blood.

"Mistress Duryan," she said.

"Your Majesty." Ead gave her obeisance. "Your Graces."

"Do sit."

As she took a seat, Ead caught the eye of Sir Tharian Lintley, Captain of the Knights of the Body, who offered a reassuring smile from his post by the doors. Like most members of the Royal Guard, Lintley was tall, robust, and had no shortage of admirers at court. He had been in love with Margret since she had arrived, and Ead knew she returned his affection, but the difference in station had kept them apart.

"Mistress Duryan," Lord Seyton Combe said, eyebrows raised. The Duke of Courtesy was seated to the left of the queen. "Are you unwell?"

"Your pardon, my lord?"

"There are shadows under your eyes."

"I am very well, Your Grace. Only a little tired after the excitement of the Mentish visit."

Combe took the measure of her over the rim of his cup. Close to sixty, with eyes like storms, a sallow complexion, and a near-lipless mouth, the Principal Secretary was a formidable presence. It was said that if a plot was hatched against Queen Sabran in the morning, he would have the accomplices on the rack by noon. A pity the master of cutthroats still eluded him.

"Indeed. An unforeseen visit, but a pleasant one," Combe said, and a mild smile returned to his lips. All his expressions were mild. Like wine tempered with water. "We have already questioned many members of the royal household, but we thought it prudent to leave Her Majesty's ladies until last, busy as you were during the Mentish visit."

Ead held his gaze. Combe might speak the language of secrets, but he did not know hers.

Lady Igrain Crest, the Duchess of Justice, sat on the other side of the queen. She had been the chief influence on Sabran during her minority after the death of Queen Rosarian, and had apparently had a great hand in molding her into a paragon of virtue.

"Now that Mistress Duryan has arrived," she said, with a smile at Ead, "perhaps we can begin."

Crest had the same fine bone structure and azure eyes as her granddaughter, Roslain—though her hair, frizzled at the temples, had long since turned silver. Small lines were notched around her lips, which were nearly as pale as the rest of her face.

"Indeed," Lady Nelda Stillwater said. The Duchess of Courage was a full-figured woman, with skin of a deep brown and a head of dark curls. A carcanet of rubies glistered around her neck. "Mistress Duryan, a man was found dead at the threshold of the Great Bedchamber the night before last. He was holding an Yscali-made dagger."

A parrying dagger, specifically. In duels, they were used in place of a shield, to protect and defend the wielder, but they could also kill. Each cutthroat had carried one.

"It seems he meant to kill Her Majesty," Stillwater said, "but was himself killed."

"Terrible," the Duke of Generosity muttered. Lord Ritshard Eller, at least ninety, wore thick furs even in summer. From what Ead had observed, he was also a sanctimonious fool.

She schooled her features. "Another cutthroat?"

"Yes," Stillwater said, her brow creasing. "As you will no doubt have heard, this has happened more than once in the past year. Of the nine would-be killers that have gained entry to Ascalon Palace, five were slain before they could be apprehended."

"It is all very strange," Combe said, musingly, "but it seems sensible to conclude that someone in the Upper Household killed the knave."

"A noble deed," Ead said.

Crest snorted. "Hardly, my dear," she said. "This *protector*, whoever it is, is a killer as well, and they must be unmasked." Her voice was thin with frustration. "Like the cutthroat, this person entered the royal apartments unseen, somehow eluding the Knights of the Body. They then committed a murder and left the corpse for Her Majesty to find. Did they intend to frighten our queen to death?"

"I imagine they intended to stop our queen being *stabbed* to death, Your Grace."

Sabran lifted an eyebrow.

"The Knight of Justice frowns upon all bloodshed, Mistress Duryan," Crest said. "If whoever has been killing cutthroats had only come to us, we might have forgiven them, but their refusal to reveal themselves speaks of sinister intent. We *will* know who they are."

"We are relying on witnesses to help us, mistress. This incident happened the night before last, about midnight," Combe said. "Tell me, did you see or hear anything suspicious?"

"Nothing comes to mind, Your Grace."

Sabran had not stopped looking at her. The scrutiny made Ead a little warm under her ruff.

"Mistress Duryan," Combe said, "you have been a loyal servant at court. I sincerely doubt that Ambassador uq-Ispad would have presented Her Majesty with a lady who was not of faultless character. Nonetheless, I must warn you that silence now is an act of treason. Do you know *anything* about this cutthroat? Have you heard anyone expressing dislike for Her Majesty, or sympathy toward the Draconic Kingdom of Yscalin?"

"No, Your Grace," Ead said, "but if I should hear of any whispers, I will bring them to your door."

Combe exchanged a look with Sabran.

"Good day to you, mistress," the queen said. "Attend to your duties."

Ead curtsied and left the chamber. Lintley closed the doors behind her.

There were no guards here; they waited at the base of the tower. Ead made certain her footfalls were loud as she walked to the stair, but stopped after the first few steps.

She had sharper hearing than most. A perquisite of the lingering magic in her blood.

"—seems truthful," Crest was saying, "but I have heard that some Ersyris dabble in the forbidden arts."

"Oh, rot," Combe interjected. "You don't really believe in talk of alchemy and sorcery."

"As Duchess of Justice, I must consider *every* possibility, Seyton. We all know the cutthroats are an Yscali enterprise, of course—no one has stronger motivation than the Yscals to see Her Majesty slain—but we must also root out this *protector*, who kills with such manifest expertise. I would be very interested to speak with them about where they learned their ... craft."

"Mistress Duryan has always been a diligent lady-in-waiting, Igrain," Sabran said. "If you have no evidence that she was involved, perhaps we should move on."

"As you decree, Your Majesty."

Ead released a long-held breath.

Her secret was safe. No one had witnessed her entering the royal apartments that night. Moving unseen was another of her gifts, for with flame came the subtlety of shadow.

Sound from below. Armored feet on the stair. The Knights of the Body, carrying out their rounds.

She needed somewhere less open to eavesdrop. Swiftly, she descended to the next floor and slipped on to a balcony.

"... is of an age with you, by all accounts very pleasant and intelligent, and a sovereign of Virtudom." Combe. "As you know, Majesty, the last five Berethnet queens have taken Inysh consorts. There has not been a foreign match for more than two centuries."

"You sound concerned, Your Grace," Sabran said. "Do you have so little faith in the charms of Inysh men that you are surprised my ancestors chose them as consorts?"

Chuckles.

"As an Inysh man myself, I must protest that assessment," Combe said lightly, "but times have changed. A foreign match is critical. Now our oldest ally has betrayed the true religion, we *must* show the world that the remaining three countries who swear allegiance to the Saint will stand together, come what may, and that none will support Yscalin in its misguided belief that the Nameless One will return."

"There is danger in their claim," Crest said. "The Easterners venerate wyrms. They may be tempted by the idea of an alliance with a Draconic territory."

"I think you misjudge the danger of that, Igrain," Stillwater said. "Last I heard, the Easterners still feared the Draconic plague."

"So did Yscalin once."

"What is certain," Combe cut in, "is we cannot afford *any* signs of weakness. If you were to wed Lievelyn, Majesty, it would send a message that the Chainmail of Virtudom has never been tighter."

"The Red Prince trades with wyrm-worshippers," Sabran said. "Surely it would be unwise to give our implicit approval to such a practice. Especially now. Do you not agree, Igrain?"

As she listened, Ead had to smile. Already the queen had found an issue with her suitor.

"Though producing an heir as soon as possible is the bounden duty of a Berethnet, I do agree, Your Majesty. Wisely observed," Crest said, her tone motherly. "Lievelyn is unworthy of the scion of the Saint. His trade with Seiiki shames all Virtudom. If we imply our tolerance of this heresy, we may embolden those who love the Nameless One. Lievelyn was also—lest we forget—engaged to the Donmata Marosa, who is now the heir to a Draconic territory. An affection may remain."

A Knight of the Body walked past the balcony. Ead pressed herself flat to the wall.

"The engagement was broken off the moment Yscalin betrayed the faith," Combe spluttered. "As for the Eastern trade, the House of Lievelyn would not trade with Seiiki unless it were essential. The Vatten might have brought Mentendon into the faith, but they also beggared it. If we gave the Mentish favorable terms in an alliance, and if a royal match were on the horizon, perhaps the trade could be broken off."

"My dear Seyton, it is not necessity that compels the Mentish, but greed. They *enjoy* having a monopoly on trade with the East. Besides, we can hardly be expected to prop them up indefinitely," Crest said. "No, there is no need to discuss Lievelyn. A far stronger match—which I have *long* advocated to you, Majesty—is the High Chieftain of Askrdal. We must keep our links with Hróth strong."

"He is seventy years old," Stillwater said, sounding dismayed.

"And did Glorian Shieldheart not wed Guma Vetalda, who was four and seventy?" Eller piped up.

"Indeed she did, and he gave her a healthy child." Crest sounded pleased. "Askrdal would bring experience and wisdom that Lievelyn, prince of a young realm, would not."

After a pause, Sabran spoke. "Are there no other suits?"

There was a long silence. "Rumor of your familiarity with Lord Arteloth has spread, Majesty," Eller said, his voice tremulous. "Some believe you may be secretly *wed* to—"

"Spare me, Your Grace, from baseless gossip. And from talk of Lord Arteloth," Sabran said. "He has left court without reason or warning. I will not hear of him."

Another tense silence.

"Your Majesty," Combe said, "my intelligencers have informed me that Lord Arteloth has boarded a ship bound for Yscalin, accompanied by Lord Kitston Glade. Apparently, he discovered my intention to send a spy to find your lord father ... but believed himself to be the only man fit for a mission that touches Your Majesty so closely."

Yscalin.

For a terrible moment, Ead could not move or breathe.

Loth.

"It may be for the best," Combe continued into the stillness. "Lord Arteloth's absence will allow rumors of an affair between you to cool—and it is high time we knew what was happening in Yscalin. And whether your lord father, Prince Wilstan, is alive."

Combe was lying. Loth could not have just *stumbled* upon a plot to send a spy to Yscalin and decided to go himself. The idea was absurd. Not only would Loth never be so reckless, but the Night Hawk would never allow such plans to be discovered.

He had contrived this.

"Something is not right," Sabran finally said. "It is not like Loth to behave so rashly. And I find it exceedingly difficult to believe that none of you guessed his intentions. Are you not my councillors? Do you not have eyes in every corner of my court?"

The next silence was as thick as marchpane.

"I asked you to send someone to retrieve my father two years ago, Lord Seyton," the queen said, softer. "You told me the risk was too great."

"I feared it was, Majesty. Now I think a risk is needful if we are to know the truth."

"Lord Arteloth is *not* to be risked." There was marked strain in her voice. "You will send your retainers after him. To bring him back to Inys. You *must* stop him, Seyton."

"Forgive me, Majesty, but he will be in Draconic territory by now. It is quite impossible to send anyone to retrieve Lord Arteloth without betraying to the Vetalda that he is there on unsanctioned business, which they will already suspect. We would only endanger his life."

Ead swallowed the tightness in her throat. Not only had Combe sent Loth away, but he had sent him to a place where Sabran had lost all influence. There was nothing she could do. Not when Yscalin was now an unpredictable enemy, capable of destroying the fragile peace in a heartbeat.

"Your Majesty," Stillwater said, "I understand that this news has pained you, but we must make a final decision on the suit."

"Her Majesty has already decided *against* Lievelyn," Crest cut in. "Askrdal is the only—"

"I must insist upon further discussion, Igrain. Lievelyn is a better candidate, in many respects, and I would not see him dismissed." Stillwater spoke in clipped tones. "This is a delicate subject, Majesty, forgive me—but you must have a successor, and soon, to reassure your people and secure the throne for another generation. The need would not be half so urgent if not for the attempts on your life. If you *only* had a daughter—"

"Thank you for your concern, Your Grace," Sabran said curtly, "but I am not yet recovered enough from seeing a corpse by my bed to discuss its use for childing." A chair scraped on the floor, followed by four others. "You may question Lady Linora at your leisure."

"Majesty—" Combe began.

"I would break my fast. Good morrow."

Ead was back inside and descending before the doors to the Council Chamber opened. At the base of the tower, she walked down the path, her heart beating hard.

Margret would be devastated when she found out. Her brother was too naïve, too gentle, to be a spy in the court of the Vetalda.

He was not long for this world.

In the Queen Tower, the royal household danced to the dawn chorus. Grooms and maids crisscrossed between rooms. The scent of rising bread poured from the Privy Kitchen. Swallowing her bitterness as best she could, Ead edged her way through the Presence Chamber, where petitioners were packed tight, as always, waiting for the queen.

Ead sensed her warding as she approached the Great Bedchamber. They were laid like traps across the palace. For the first year at court, she had been a tattered nerve, unable to sleep as they rang with movement, but little by little, she had learned to recognize the sensations they sparked in her, and to shift them as if on a counting frame. She had taught herself to notice only when someone was out of place. Or when a stranger came to court.

Inside, Margret was stripping the bed, and Roslain Crest was shaking out plain-woven cloths. Sabran must be near her blood— the monthly reminder that she was not yet swollen with an heir.

Ead joined Margret in her work. She had to tell her about Loth, but it would have to wait until they were alone.

"Mistress Duryan," Roslain said, breaking the silence.

Ead straightened. "My lady."

"Lady Katryen has taken ill this morning." The Chief Gentlewoman hooked one of the cloths on to a silk girdle. "You will taste Her Majesty's food in her stead."

Margret frowned.

"Of course," Ead said calmly.

This was punishment for her deviation during the storytelling. The Ladies of the Bedchamber were rewarded in kind for the risks they took as food-tasters, but for a chamberer, it was a thankless and dangerous chore.

For Ead, it was also an opportunity.

On her way to the Royal Solarium, another opportunity presented itself. Truyde utt Zeedeur was walking behind two other maids of honor. When Ead passed, she took her by the shoulder and drew her aside, breathing into her ear, "Meet me after orisons tomorrow evening, or I will see to it that Her Majesty receives your letters."

When the other maids of honor looked back, Truyde smiled, as if Ead had told her a joke. Sharp little fox.

"Where?" she said, still smiling.

"The Privy Stair."

They parted ways.

The Royal Solarium was a quiet haven. Three of its walls jutted out from the Queen Tower, providing a peerless view of the Inysh capital, Ascalon, and the river that wound through it. Columns of stone and woodsmoke rose from its streets. Some two hundred thousand souls called the city their home.

Ead seldom went out there. It was not proper for ladies-in-waiting to be seen quibbling with merchants and toeing through filth.

The sun cast shadows on the floor. The queen was silhouetted at her table, alone but for the Knights of the Body in the doorway. Their partizans crossed in front of Ead.

"Mistress," one of them said, "you are not due to serve Her Majesty's meal today."

Before she could explain, Sabran called, "Who is that?"

"Mistress Ead Duryan, Your Majesty. Your chamberer."

Silence. Then: "Let her pass."

The knights stood aside at once. Ead approached the queen, the heels of her shoes making no sound.

"Good morrow, Your Majesty." She curtsied.

Sabran had already looked back at her gold-enameled prayer book. "Kate should be here."

"Lady Katryen has taken ill."

"She was my bedfellow last night. I would know if she was ill."

"Lady Roslain says it is so," Ead said. "If it please you, I will taste your food today."

When she received no reply, Ead sat. This close to Sabran, she could smell her pomander, stuffed with orris root and clove. The Inysh believed such perfumes could ward off illness.

They sat in silence for some time. Sabran's breast rose and fell steadily, but the set of her jaw betrayed her anger.

"Majesty," Ead finally said, "this may be too bold, but you seem not to be in high spirits today."

"It is far too bold. You are here to see that my food is not poisoned, not to remark upon my spirits."

"Forgive me."

"I have been too forgiving." Sabran snapped her book shut. "You clearly pay no heed to the Knight of Courtesy, Mistress Duryan. Perhaps you are no true convert. Perhaps you only pay empty service to my ancestor, while you secretly hold with a false religion."

She had been here for only a minute, and already Ead was walking on quicksand.

"Madam," she said carefully, "Queen Cleolind, your ancestor, was a crown princess of Lasia."

"There is no need for you to remind me of that. Do you think me a halfwit?"

"I meant no such insult," Ead said. Sabran set her prayer book to one side. "Queen Cleolind was noble and good of heart. It was through no fault of hers that she knew nothing of the Six Virtues when she was born. I may be naïve, but rather than punishing them, surely we should pity those in ignorance and lead them to the light."

"Indeed," Sabran said dryly. "The light of the pyre."

"If you mean to put me to the stake, madam, then I am sorry for it. I hear we Ersyris make very poor kindling. We are like sand, too used to the sun to burn."

The queen looked at her. Her gaze dipped to the brooch on her gown.

"You take the Knight of Generosity as your patron."

Ead touched it.

"Yes," she said. "As one of your ladies, I give you my loyalty, Majesty. To give, one must be generous."

"Generosity. The same as Lievelyn." Sabran said this almost to herself. "You may yet prove more giving than certain other ladies. First Ros insisted upon getting with child, so she was too tired to serve me, then Arbella could not walk with me, and now Kate feigns illness. I am reminded every day that none of *them* calls Generosity their patron."

Ead knew Sabran was angry, but it still took considerable restraint not to empty the wine over her head. The Ladies of the Bedchamber sacrificed a great deal to attend on the queen around the clock. They tasted her food and tried on her gowns, risking their own lives. Katryen, one of the most desirable women at court, would likely never take a companion. As for Arbella, she was seventy years old, had served both Sabran and her mother, and still would not retire.

Ead was spared from answering by the arrival of the meal. Truyde utt Zeedeur was among the maids of honor who would present it, but she refused to look at Ead.

Many Inysh customs had confounded her over the years, but royal meals were absurd. First, the queen was poured her choice of wine—then not one, not two, but *eighteen* dishes were offered to her. Wafer-thin cuts of brown meat. Currants stirred into frumenty. Pancakes with black honey, apple butter, or quail eggs. Salted fish from the Limber. Woodland strawberries on a bed of snow cream.

As always, Sabran chose only a round of goldenbread. A nod toward it was the only indication.

Silence. Truyde was gazing toward the window. One of the other maids of honor, looking panicked, jabbed her with her elbow. Jolted back to the task at hand, Truyde scooped up the goldenbread with a coverpane and set it on the royal plate with a curtsy. Another maid of honor served a whorl of buttersweet.

Now for the tasting. With a sly little smile, Truyde handed Ead the bone-handled knife.

First, Ead sipped the wine. Then she sampled the buttersweet. Both were unmeddled. Next, she cut off a piece of the bun and touched it with the tip of her tongue. A drop of the dowager would make the roof of the mouth prickle, dipsas parched the lips, and eternity dust—the rarest of poisons—gave each bite of food a cloying aftertaste.

There was nothing but dense bread inside. She slid the dishes before the queen and handed the tasting knife back to Truyde, who wiped it once and enclosed it in linen.

"Leave us," Sabran said.

Glances were exchanged. The queen usually desired amusement or gossip from the maids of honor at mealtimes. As one, they curtsied and quit the room. Ead rose last.

"Not you."

She sat again.

The sun was brighter now, filling the Royal Solarium with light. It danced in the jug of sweetbriar wine.

"Lady Truyde seems distracted of late." Sabran looked toward the door. "Unwell, perhaps, like Kate. I would expect such ailments to strike the court in winter."

"No doubt it is the rose fever, madam, no more. But Lady Truyde, I think, is more likely to be homesick," Ead said. "Or ... she may be sick in love, as young maids often are."

"You cannot yet be old enough to say such things. What is your age?"

"Six and twenty, Majesty."

"Not much younger than myself, then. And are *you* sick in love, as young maids often are?"

It might have sounded arch on different lips, but those eyes were as cold as the jewels at her throat.

"I fear an Inysh citizen would find it hard to love someone who was once sworn to another faith," Ead answered after a moment.

It was not a light question Sabran had asked. Courting was a formal affair in Inys.

"Nonsense," the queen said. The sun gleamed in her hair. "I understand you are close to Lord Arteloth. He told me the two of you have exchanged gifts at every Feast of Fellowship."

"Yes, madam," Ead said. "We are close. I was grieved to hear he had left the city."

"He will return." Sabran gave her an appraising glance. "Did he pay court to you?"

"No," Ead said truthfully. "I consider Lord Arteloth a dear friend, and want no more than that. Even if I did, I am not of a fit station to wed the future Earl of Goldenbirch."

"Indeed. Ambassador uq-Ispad told me that your blood was base." Sabran sipped her wine. "You are not in love, then."

A woman so quick to insult those beneath her must be vulnerable to flattery. "No, madam," Ead said. "I am not here to squander time in pursuit of a companion. I am here to attend the most gracious Queen of Inys. That is more than enough."

Sabran did not smile, but her face softened from its stern cast.

"Perhaps you would care to walk with me in the Privy Garden tomorrow," she said. "That is, if Lady Arbella is still indisposed."

"If it gives you pleasure, Majesty," Ead said.

The cabin was only just large enough for two berths. A burly Ment delivered them a supper of salted beef, a thumb-sized fish apiece, and raveled bread, stale enough to splinter their teeth. Kit managed half his beef before he fled to the deck.

Midway into his bread, Loth gave up. This was a far cry from the sumptuous offerings at court, but vile food was the least of his worries. Combe was sending him to his doom, and for naught.

He had always known that the Night Hawk could make people vanish. People he perceived as a threat to the House of Berethnet, whether they behaved in a manner that disgraced their positions or craved more power than their due.

Even before Margret and Ead had warned him that the court was talking, Loth had known about the rumors. Rumors that he had seduced Sabran, that he had wed her in secret. Now the Dukes Spiritual sought a foreign match for her, and the hearsay, however baseless, was an impediment. Loth was a problem, and Combe had solved him.

There had to be some way to get word to Sabran. For now, however, he would have to concentrate on the task at hand. Learning to be a spy in Cárscaro.

Rubbing the bridge of his nose, Loth thought of all he knew about Lord Wilstan Fynch.

As a child, Sabran had never been close to her father. Neat and bearded, military in his bearing, Fynch had always seemed to Loth to embody the ideals of his ancestor, the Knight of Temperance. The prince consort had never been given to displays of emotion, but he had plainly cherished his family, and had made Loth and Roslain, who were closest of all to his daughter, feel that they were part of it.

When Sabran was crowned, their relationship had changed. Father and daughter often read together in the Privy Library, and he had counseled her on the affairs of the queendom. The death of Queen Rosarian had left a space in both their lives, and it was in that space that they had finally befriended one another—but that had not been quite enough for Fynch. Rosarian had been his guiding star, and without her, he had felt lost in the vastness of the Inysh court. He had asked Sabran for permission to take up residence in Yscalin as her ambassador, and had been content in that role ever since, writing to her every season. She had always looked forward to his letters from Cárscaro, where the House of Vetalda ruled over a joyful court. Loth supposed it must have been easier for Fynch to bury his grief away from the home he had shared with Rosarian.

His final letter had been different. He had told Sabran, in as many words, that he believed the Vetalda had been involved in killing Rosarian. That was the last anyone in Inys had heard from the Duke of Temperance before rock doves had flown out from Cárscaro, declaring that Yscalin now took the Nameless One as its god and master.

Loth meant to find out what had happened in that city. What had caused the break from Virtudom, and what had become of Fynch. Any information could be invaluable if Yscalin ever declared war on the House of Berethnet, which Sabran had long feared it would.

He wiped his brow. Kit must be boiling like a coney on the deck. Come to think of it, Kit had been on the deck for rather a long time.

Heaving a sigh, Loth stood. There was no lock on the door, but he supposed there was nowhere for the pirates to lug the traveling chest of garments and other effects that had been on the coach. Combe must have sent his retainers to collect them while Loth was oblivious in the Privy Chamber, sharing a quiet supper with Sabran and Roslain.

The air was cool above. A breeze scuffed over the waves. As the crew moved hither and thither, they bellowed a song, too quick and drenched in sea cant for Loth to understand. Despite what Harlowe had said, nobody took any notice of him as he ascended to the quarterdeck.

The Swan Strait divided the Queendom of Inys from the great continent that held the West and the South. Even in high summer, perishing winds blew through it from the Ashen Sea.

He found Kit hanging over the side, wiping vomit from his chin. "Good evening to you, sirrah." Loth clapped him on the back. "Did you indulge in a little pirate wine?"

Kit was pale as a lily. "Arteloth," he said, "I don't think I'm at all well, you know."

"You need ale."

"I dare not ask them for it. They've been roaring like that for the whole time I've been up here."

"They're singing shanties," a husky voice said.

Loth started. A woman in a wide-brimmed black hat was leaning against the gunwale nearby.

"Work songs." She tossed Kit a wineskin. "Helps the swabbers pass the time."

Kit twisted off the stopper. "Did you say *swabbers*, mistress?"

"Them that clear the decks."

Going by her looks and accent, this privateer was from Yscalin. Deep olive skin, tanned and freckled. Hair like barley wine. Eyes of a clear amber, thinly outlined with black paint, the left eye underscored by a scar. She was well presented for a pirate, down to the sheen on her boots and her spotless jerkin. A rapier hung at her side.

"If I were you, I'd be back in my cabin before it gets dark," she said. "Most of the crew don't care overmuch for lordlings. Plume keeps them in check, but when he sleeps, so do their good manners."

"I don't believe we've made your acquaintance, mistress," Kit said.

Her smile deepened. "And what makes you think I wish to make *your* acquaintance, my lord nobleman?"

"Well, you did speak to us first."

"Perhaps I was bored."

"Perhaps we'll prove interesting." He bowed in his extravagant way. "I am Lord Kitston Glade, court poet. Future Earl of Honeybrook, to my father's chagrin. Delighted to make your acquaintance."

"Lord Arteloth Beck." Loth inclined his head. "Heir of the Earl and Countess of Goldenbirch."

93

The woman raised an eyebrow. "Estina Melaugo. Heir to my own gray hairs. Boatswain of the *Rose Eternal*."

It was clear from Kit's expression that he knew of this woman. Loth chose not to ask.

"So," Melaugo said, "you're heading for Cárscaro."

"Are you from that city, mistress?" Loth enquired.

"No. Vazuva."

Loth watched her drink from a glass bottle.

"Mistress," he said, "I wonder if you could tell us what to expect in the court of King Sigoso. We know so little about what has happened in Yscalin over the last two years."

"I know as much as you, my lord. I fled Yscalin, along with some others, the day the House of Vetalda announced its allegiance to the Nameless One."

Kit spoke again: "Did many of those who fled become pirates?"

"*Privateers*, if you please." Melaugo nodded to the ensign. "And no. Most exiles went to Mentendon or the Ersyr to start again, as best they could. But not everyone got out."

"Is it possible that the people of Yscalin do not *all* bow to the Nameless One, then?" Loth asked her. "That they are only afraid of their king, or trapped in the country?"

"Likely. Nobody goes out now, and very few go in. Cárscaro still accepts foreign ambassadors, as evidenced by your good selves, but the rest of the country could be dead from plague, for all I know." A curl blew across her eyes. "If you ever get out, you must tell me what Cárscaro is like now. I hear there was a great fire just before the birds flew out. Lavender fields used to grow near the capital, but they burned."

This was making Loth feel more uneasy than he had before.

"I'll confess to curiosity," Melaugo said, "as to why your queen is sending you into the snake pit. I had thought you were a favorite of hers, Lord Arteloth."

"It is not Queen Sabran who sends us, mistress," Kit said, "but the ghastly Seyton Combe." He sighed. "He never liked my poetry, you know. Only a soulless husk could hate poetry."

"Ah, the Night Hawk," Melaugo said, chuckling. "A suitable familiar for our queen."

Loth stilled. "What do you mean by that?"

"Saint." Kit looked fascinated. "A heretic as well as a pirate. Do you imply that Queen Sabran is some sort of witch?"

"*Privateer*. And keep your voice down." Melaugo glanced over her shoulder. "Don't misunderstand me, my lords. I've no personal dislike of Queen Sabran, but I come from a superstitious part of Yscalin, and there *is* something odd about the Berethnets. Each queen only having one child, always a daughter, and they all look so similar … I don't know. Sounds like sorcery to—"

"Shadow!"

Melaugo turned. The roar had come from the crow's nest.

"Another wyvern," she said under her breath. "Excuse me."

She vaulted onto the ropes and climbed. Kit ran to the side. "Wyvern? I've never seen one."

"We don't *want* to see one," Loth said. His arms were prickling. "This is no place for us, Kit. Come, back below deck before—"

"Wait." Kit shielded his eyes. His curls flew in the wind. "Loth, do you see that?"

Loth looked askance at the horizon. The sun was low and red, almost blinding him.

Melaugo was clinging to the ratlines, one eye to a spyglass. "Mother of—" She lowered it, then lifted it again. "Plume, it's— I can't believe what I'm seeing—"

"What is it?" the quartermaster called. "Estina?"

"It's a— a High Western." Her shout was hoarse. "A High Western!"

Those words were like a spark on kindling. Order splintered into chaos. Loth felt his legs become stone.

High Western.

"Ready the harpoons, the chainshot," a Mentish woman called. "Prepare for heat! Do not engage unless it attacks!"

When he saw it, Loth turned cold to the marrow of his bones. He could not feel his hands or face.

It was impossible, yet there it was.

A wyrm. A monstrous, four-legged wyrm, over two hundred feet long from its snout to the tip of its tail.

This was no wyverling prowling for livestock. This was a breed that had not been seen in centuries, since the last hours of the Grief of Ages. Mightiest of the Draconic creatures. The High Westerns, largest and most brutal of all the dragons, the dread lords of wyrmkind.

One of them had *woken*.

The beast glided above the ship. As it passed, Loth could *smell* the heat inside it, the reek of smoke and brimstone.

The bear-trap of its mouth. The hot coals of its eyes. They wrote themselves into his memory. He had heard stories since he was a child, seen the hideous illustrations that lurked in bestiaries—but even his most harrowing nightmares had never conjured such a soul-fearing thing.

"Do not engage," the Ment called again. "Steady!"

Loth pressed his back against the mainmast.

He could not deny what his eyes could see. This creature might not have the red scales of the Nameless One, but it was of his like.

The crew moved like ants fleeing water, but the wyrm appeared to have its mind set on another course. It soared over the Swan Strait. Loth could see the fire pulsing inside it, down the length of its throat to its belly. Its tail was edged with spines and ended in a mighty lash.

Loth caught the gunwale to hold himself upright. His ears were ringing. Close by, one of the younger seafarers was trembling all over, standing in a dark gold pool.

Harlowe had emerged from his cabin. He watched the High Western leave them behind.

"You had better start praying for salvation, my lords," he said softly. "Fýredel, the right wing of the Nameless One, appears to have woken from his sleep."

8

East

Sulyard snored. Yet another reason Truyde had been a fool to pledge herself to him. Not that Niclays would have been able to sleep even if his guest *had* shut up, for a typhoon had blown in.

Thunder rumbled, making a horse whinny outside. Drunk on a single cup of wine, Sulyard slept through it all.

Niclays lay on his bedding, slightly drunk himself. He and Sulyard had spent the evening playing cards and exchanging stories. Sulyard had told the gloomy tale of the Never Queen, while Niclays chose the more uplifting charms of Carbuncle and Scald.

He still had no liking for Sulyard, but he owed it to Truyde to protect her secret companion. He owed it to Jannart.

Jan.

The vise of grief snapped closed around his heart. He shut his eyes, and he was back to that autumn morning when they had met for the first time in the rose garden of Brygstad Palace, when the court of the newly crowned Edvart the Second was ripe with opportunity.

In his early twenties, when he was still Marquess of Zeedeur, Jannart had been tall and striking, with magnificent red hair that rippled to the small of his back. In those days, Niclays had been one of the few Ments to have a mane of fairest auburn, more gold than copper.

That was what had drawn Jannart to him that day. *Rose gold*, he had dubbed it. He had asked Niclays if he might paint his portrait, thus capturing the shade for posterity, and Niclays, like any vain young courtier, had been only too pleased to oblige.

Red hair and a rose garden. That was how it had begun.

They had spent the whole season together, with the easel and music and laughter for company. Even after the portrait was finished, they had stayed joined at the hip.

Niclays had never been in love before. It was Jannart who had been intrigued enough to paint him, but soon, Niclays had longed for the ability to paint him in return, so that he might capture the darkness of those lashes, and how the sun glowed in his hair, and the elegance of his hands on the harpsichord. He had gazed at his silken lips and the place where his neck met his jaw; he had watched his blood throbbing there, in that cradle of life. He had imagined, in exhilarating detail, how his eyes would look in the morning light, when sleep made their lids heavy. That exquisite dark amber, like the honey made by black bees.

He had lived to hear that voice, deep and mellow. Oh, he could sing ballads of its tenor, and the way it climbed to the height of passion when the conversation leaned toward art or history. Those subjects had set a fire in Jannart, drawing people to its warmth. With words alone, he could beautify the dullest object or bring civilizations rising from the dust. For Niclays, he had been a sunray, illuminating every facet of his world.

He had known there was no hope. After all, Jannart was a marquess, heir to a duchy, the dearest friend of Prince Edvart, while Niclays was an upstart from Rozentun.

And yet Jannart had seen him. He had seen him, and he had not looked away.

Outside the house, the waves crashed on the fence again. Niclays turned on to his side, aching all over.

"Jan," he said softly, "when did we get so old?"

The Mentish shipment was due any day now, and when it turned homeward, Sulyard would be with them. A few more days, and Niclays would be rid of this living reminder of Truyde and Jannart and the Saint-forsaken Inysh court. He would go back to tinkering with potions in his jailhouse at the edge of the world, exiled and unknown.

At last he dozed off, cradling the pillow to his chest. When he stirred awake, it was still dark, but the hairs on his neck stood to attention.

He sat up, peering into the black.

"Sulyard."

No reply. Something moved in the darkness.

"Sulyard, is that you?"

When the lightning cast the silhouette into relief, he stared at the face in front of him.

"Honored Chief Officer," he croaked, but he was already being towed out of bed.

Two sentinels bundled him toward the door. In the chokehold of terror, he somehow snatched his cane from the floor and swung with all his might. It cracked like a whip into one of their cheeks. He only had a moment to relish his accuracy before he was struck back with an iron truncheon.

He had never felt so much pain at once. His bottom lip split like fruit. Every tooth trembled in its socket. His stomach heaved at the coppery tang on his tongue.

The sentinel raised his truncheon again and dealt him a terrible blow to the knee. With a cry of "mercy," Niclays raised his hands over his head, dropping the cane. A leather boot snapped it in two. Blows rained down from all sides, striking his back and his face. He fell on to the mats, making weak sounds of submission and apology. The house was being pulled to shreds around him.

The din of breaking glass came from the workroom. His apparatus, worth more coin than he would ever have again.

"Please." Blood slavered down his chin. "Honored sentinels, please, you don't understand. The work—"

Ignoring his pleas, they marched him into the storm. All he wore was his nightshirt. His ankle was too tender to carry him, so they hauled him like a sack of millet. The few Ments who worked through the night were emerging from their dwellings.

"Doctor Roos," one of them called. "What's happening?"

Niclays gasped for breath. "Who's that?" His voice was lost to the sound of thunder. "Muste," he shouted thickly. "Muste, help me, you fox-haired fool!"

A hand covered his bloody mouth. He could hear Sulyard now, somewhere in the darkness, crying out.

"Niclays!"

He looked up, expecting to see Muste, but it was Panaya who ran into the fray. She somehow got between the sentinels and stood before Niclays like the Knight of Courage. "If he is under arrest," she said, "then where is your warrant from the honored Governor of Cape Hisan?"

Niclays could have kissed her. The Chief Officer was standing nearby, watching the sentinels ransack the house.

"Go back inside," he said to Panaya, not looking at her.

"The learnèd Doctor Roos deserves respect. If you harm him, the High Prince of Mentendon will hear of it."

"The Red Prince has no power here."

Panaya squared up to him. Niclays could only watch in awe as the woman in a sleep robe faced down the man in armor.

"While the Mentish live here, they have the all-honored Warlord's protection," she said. "What will he say when he hears that you spilled blood in Orisima?"

At this, the Chief Officer stepped closer to her. "Perhaps he will say that I was too merciful," he said, voice thick with contempt, "for this liar has been hiding a *trespasser* in his home."

Panaya fell silent, shock writ plain on her.

"Panaya," Niclays whispered. "I can explain this."

"Niclays," she breathed. "Oh, Niclays. You have defied the Great Edict."

His ankle throbbed. "Where will they take me?"

Panaya glanced nervously toward the Chief Officer, who was bellowing at his sentinels. "To the honored Governor of Cape Hisan. They will suspect you of having the red sickness," she murmured in Mentish. Suddenly she tensed. "Did you touch him?"

Niclays thought back, frantic. "No," he said. "No, not his bare skin."

"You must tell them so. Swear it on your Saint," she told him. "If they suspect you are deceiving them, they will do all they can to wrest the truth from you."

"Torture?" Sweat was beading on his face. "Not torture. You don't mean torture, do you?"

"Enough," the Chief Officer barked. "Take this traitor away!"

With that, the sentinels carried Niclays off like meat for the chop. "I want a lawyer," he shouted. "Damn you, there must be a decent bloody lawyer somewhere on this Saint-forsaken island!" When nobody responded, he called out desperately to Panaya, "Tell Muste to mend my apparatus. Continue the work!" She looked on, helpless. "And protect my books! For the love of the Saint, *save my books*, Panaya!"

9

West

"I suppose one cannot often go for walks like these in the Ersyr. The heat would be intolerable."

They were walking in the Privy Garden. Ead had never entered it before. This retreat was reserved for the pleasure of the queen, her Ladies of the Bedchamber, and the Virtues Council.

Lady Arbella Glenn was still confined to bed. The court was alive with whispers. If she died, then a new Lady of the Bedchamber would be needed. The other Ladies of the Privy Chamber were already striving to showcase their wit and talent to Sabran.

No doubt it was why Linora had been so vexed when Ead had, in her eyes, botched the storytelling. She had not wanted her chances dented by association.

"Not in winter. In the summer, we wear loose silks to stave off the heat," Ead answered. "When I lived in His Excellency's estate in Rumelabar, I would often sit by the pool in the courtyard and read. There were sweetlemon trees to shade the walkways and fountains to cool the air. It was a peaceful time."

In truth, she had only been there once. She had spent her childhood in the Priory.

"I see." Sabran held an ornate fan. "And you would pray to the Dawnsinger."

"Yes, madam. In a House of Silence."

They wandered into one of the orchards, where the greengage trees were in full bloom. Twelve Knights of the Body followed at a distance.

Over the last few hours, Ead had discovered that beneath her all-knowing exterior, the Queen of Inys had a circumscribed view of the world. Sealed behind the walls of her palaces, her knowledge of the lands beyond Inys came from wooden globes and letters from her ambassadors and fellow sovereigns. She was fluent in Yscali and Hróthi, and her tutors had educated her in the history of Virtudom, but she knew little of anywhere else. Ead could sense that she was straining not to ask questions about the South.

The Ersyr did not adhere to the Six Virtues. Neither did its neighbor, the Domain of Lasia, despite its important place in the Inysh founding legend.

Ead had undergone her public conversion to the Six Virtues not long after she came to court. One spring evening, she had stood in the Sanctuary Royal, proclaimed her allegiance to the House of Berethnet, and received the spurs and girdle of a worshipper of Galian. In return, she was promised a place in Halgalant, the heavenly court. She had told the Arch Sanctarian that before her arrival in Inys, she had believed in the Dawnsinger, the most widely followed deity in the Ersyr. No one had ever questioned it.

Ead had never followed the Dawnsinger. Though she had Ersyri blood, she had not been born in the Ersyr and had not often set foot in it. Her true creed was known only to the Priory.

"His Excellency told me that your mother was not from the Ersyr," Sabran said.

"No. She was born in Lasia."

"What was her name?"

"Zāla."

"I am sorry for your loss."

"Thank you, madam," Ead said. "It was a long time ago."

No matter the differences between them, they both knew what it was to lose a mother.

As the clock tower struck eleven, Sabran stopped beside her private aviary. She unlatched the door, and a tiny green bird hopped onto her wrist.

"These birds are from the Uluma Mountains," she said. Sunlight danced in the emeralds around her neck. "They often spend their winters there."

"Have you ever been to Lasia, Majesty?" Ead asked.

"No. I could never leave Virtudom."

Ead felt that familiar twist of irritation. It was hypocrisy at its finest for the Inysh to use Lasia as a cornerstone of their founding legend, only to deride its people as heretics.

"Of course," she said.

Sabran glanced at her. She took a pouch from her girdle and poured a few seeds into her palm.

"In Inys, this bird is called the lovejay," she said. The bird on her wrist gave a merry chirp. "They take only one partner all their lives, and will know their song even after many years apart. That is why the lovejay was sacred to the Knight of Fellowship. These birds embody his desire for every soul to be joined in companionship."

"I know them well," Ead said. The bird pecked up the seeds. "In the South, they are called peach-faced mimics."

"Peach-faced."

"A peach is a sweet orange fruit, madam, with a stone at its core. It grows in the Ersyr and some parts of the East."

Sabran watched the bird eat. "Let us not speak of the East," she said, and returned it to its perch.

The sun was hot as a stove, but the queen showed no sign of wanting to go inside. They continued their stroll down a path flanked by cherry trees.

"Do you smell smoke, mistress?" Sabran asked. "That is the smell of a fire in the city. This morning, two doomsingers were burned in Marian Square. Do you think that this is well?"

There were two kinds of heretic in Inys. A scattered few still followed the primordial religion of Inys, a form of nature worship that had been practiced before the foundation of the House of Berethnet, in the days when knighthood was still young and the country had been haunted by the Lady of the Woods. They could recant or be imprisoned.

Then there were those who prophesied the return of the Nameless One. For the last two years, these doomsingers had trickled to Inys from Yscalin and preached in the cities for as long as they could. They were burned by decree of the Duchess of Justice.

"It is a cruel death," Ead said.

"They would see Inys consumed by flame. They would have us open our arms to the Nameless One, to take him as our god. Lady Igrain says that we must do to our enemies what they would do to us."

"Did the Saint also say this, madam?" Ead asked calmly. "I am not as well versed in the Six Virtues as yourself."

"The Knight of Courage commands us to defend the faith."

"Yet you accepted a gift from Prince Aubrecht of Mentendon, who trades with the East. He even gave you an Eastern pearl," Ead said. "One might say that he is funding heresy."

It was out before she could stop it. Sabran gave her a glacial look.

"I am not a sanctarian, responsible for teaching you the complexities of the Six Virtues," she said. "If you wish to dispute those complexities, Mistress Duryan, I advise you to look elsewhere. In the Dearn Tower, perhaps, with others who question my judgment—which comes, as I am sure I need not remind you, from the Saint himself." She turned away. "Good morrow."

She strode away, shadowed by her Knights of the Body, leaving Ead alone beneath the trees.

When the queen was out of sight, Ead crossed the lawn and sat on the edge of a fountain, cursing herself. The heat was making her irrational.

She splashed her face with the water and then drank it from cupped palms, watched by a statue of Carnelian the First, the Flower of Ascalon, fourth queen of the House of Berethnet. Soon the dynasty would have ruled Inys for one thousand and six years.

Ead closed her eyes and let the runnels of water trickle down her neck. Eight years she had spent at the court of Sabran the Ninth. In all that time, she had never said anything to nettle her. Now she was like a viper, unable to keep her tongue in her mouth. Something made her want to *rile* the Queen of Inys.

She had to cut that something out, or this court would eat her whole.

Her duties that day went by in a haze. The warmth made their errands all the harder. Even Linora was subdued, her golden hair dampened by sweat, and Roslain Crest spent the afternoon fanning herself with rising fury.

After supper, Ead joined the other women in the Sanctuary of Virtues for orisons. The Queen Mother had ordered that blue stained-glass windows be set into the hall to make it look as if it had been built underwater.

There was one statue in the sanctuary, on the right side of the altar. Galian Berethnet, his hands folded on the hilt of Ascalon.

On the left, there was only a plinth in memory of the woman the Inysh knew as Queen Cleolind, the Damsel.

The Inysh had no record of what Cleolind had looked like. All images of her, if they had ever existed, had been destroyed after her death, and no Inysh sculptor had ever attempted to create a likeness since. Many believed it was because King Galian had been unable to bear seeing the woman he had lost to the childbed.

Even the Priory had only a few accounts of the Mother. So much had been destroyed or lost.

As the others prayed, so too did Ead.

Mother, I beg you, guide me in the land of the Deceiver. Mother, I implore you, let me comport myself with dignity in the presence of this woman who calls herself your descendant, who I have sworn to guard. Mother, I pray you, give me courage worthy of my cloak.

Sabran rose and touched the statue of her forebear. As she and her ladies filed from the sanctuary, Ead caught sight of Truyde. She was looking straight ahead, but her hands were clasped a little too tightly.

When night fell and she had seen to her duties in the Queen Tower, Ead descended the Privy Stair to the postern, where barges brought goods to the palace from the city, and waited in an alcove that held the well.

Truyde utt Zeedeur joined her, cloaked and hooded.

"I am forbidden to be out of the Coffer Chamber after dark without a chaperon." She tucked a wayward lock of red into her hood. "If Lady Oliva discovers I am gone—"

"You met your lover many times, my lady. Presumably," Ead said, "without a chaperon."

Dark eyes watched from beneath the hood. "What is it you want?"

"I want to know what you and Sulyard were planning. You reference a task in your letters."

"It is none of your concern."

"Permit me, then, to present a theory. I have seen enough to know that you take an unusual interest in the East. I think you and Sulyard meant to cross the Abyss together for some mischievous purpose, but he went ahead without you. Am I wrong?"

"You are. If you must continue to meddle, then you may hear the truth." Truyde sounded almost bored. "Triam is gone to the Milk Lagoon. We mean to live together as companions, where neither Queen Sabran nor my father can take issue with our marriage."

"Do not lie to me, my lady. You show an innocent face to the court, but I think you have another."

The postern opened. They pressed themselves deeper into the alcove as a guard came through with a torch, whistling. She marched up the Privy Stair without seeing them.

"I must go back to the Coffer Chamber," Truyde said under her breath. "I had to find *sixteen* comfits for that loathsome bird. It will raise a stink if I am gone for long."

"Tell me what you were plotting with Sulyard, then."

"And if I do not tell you?" Truyde let out a huff of laughter. "What will you do, Mistress Duryan?"

"Perhaps I will tell the Principal Secretary that I suspect you of conspiring against Her Majesty. Remember, child, that I have your letters. Or perhaps," Ead said, "I must use other means to make you talk."

Truyde narrowed her eyes.

"This is not courteous speech," she said softly. "Who are you? Why do you take such an interest in the secrets of the Inysh court?" Caution flashed across her face. "Are you one of Combe's intelligencers, is that it? I hear he makes spies of the basest sorts."

"All you need know is that I make it my business to protect Her Majesty."

"You are a chamberer, not a Knight of the Body. Haven't you some sheets to strip?"

Ead stepped closer. She was half a head taller than Truyde, whose hand now strayed to the knife on her girdle.

"I may not be a knight," Ead said, "but when I came to this court, I swore that I would protect Queen Sabran from her enemies."

"And I took the same oath," said Truyde hotly. "I am not her enemy—and neither are the people of the East. They despise the Nameless One, as we do. The noble creatures they worship are *nothing* like wyrms." She drew herself up. "Draconic things are waking, Ead. Soon they will rise—the Nameless One and his servants—and their wrath will be terrible. And when they rally against us, we will need help to fight them."

A chill went through Ead.

"You want to broker a military alliance with the East," she murmured. "You want to call *their* wyrms ... to help us deal with the awakenings." Truyde stared her out, her eyes bright. "Fool. Headstrong fool. When the queen discovers you wish to deal with *wyrms*—"

"They are not wyrms! They are *dragons*, and they are gentle creatures. I have seen pictures of them, read books about them."

"Eastern books."

"*Yes*. Their dragons are one with air and water, not with fire. The East has been estranged from us for so long that we have forgotten the difference." When Ead only looked at her in disbelief, Truyde tried a different tack: "As a fellow outsider in this country, hear me. What if the Inysh are wrong, and the continuation of the House of Berethnet is not what keeps the Nameless One at bay?"

"What are you prattling about, child?"

"You know something has changed. The Draconic creatures awakening, the breaking-away of Yscalin from Virtudom—these events are only the beginning." Her voice dropped low. "The Nameless One is coming back. And I believe he is coming *soon.*"

For a moment, Ead was speechless.

What if the continuation of the House of Berethnet is not what keeps the Nameless One at bay?

How had a young woman of Virtudom come to this heretical conclusion?

Of course, she might well be right. The Prioress had said as much to Ead before she came to Inys, explaining why a sister must be sent to guard Queen Sabran.

The House of Berethnet may protect us from the Nameless One, or it may not. There is no proof either way. Just as there is no proof to say whether the Berethnet queens are indeed descendants of the Mother. If they are, their blood is sacred, and it must be protected. She could see the Prioress now, clear as spring water. *That is the problem with stories, child. The truth in them cannot be weighed.*

That was why Ead had been sent to Inys. To protect Sabran, in case the myth was true and her blood would prevent the enemy rising.

"And you mean us to prepare for his ... second coming," Ead said, feigning amusement.

Truyde lifted her chin. "I do. The Easterners have many dragons that live alongside humans. That do not answer to the Nameless One," she said. "When he returns, we will need those Eastern dragons to defeat him. We must stand *together* to prevent a second Grief of Ages. Triam and I will not let humankind walk to its extinction. We may be small, and we may be young, but we will shake the world for our beliefs."

Whatever the truth, this girl had swallowed the torch of delusion.

"How is it you are so certain that the Nameless One will come?" Ead asked. "Are you not a child of Virtudom, born to believe that Queen Sabran keeps him chained?"

Truyde straightened.

"I love Queen Sabran," she said, "but I am no green child to believe what I am told without proof. The Inysh may have blind faith, but in Mentendon, we value evidence."

"And you have *evidence* that the Nameless One will return? Or is this guesswork?"

"Not guesswork. Hypothesis."

"Whatever your hypothesis, your plot is heresy."

"Do not speak to me of heresy," Truyde shot back. "Did you not once worship the Dawnsinger?"

"My beliefs are not in question here." Ead paused. "So that is where Sulyard is gone. On some mad-born quest in the East, trying to broker an impossible alliance on behalf of a queen who knows nothing about it." She sank onto the lip of the well. "Your lover will die in this attempt."

"No. The Seiikinese will listen—"

"He is not an official ambassador from Inys. Why ever should they hear him out?"

"Triam will persuade them. No one speaks from the heart as he does. And once the Eastern rulers are convinced of the threat, we will go to Queen Sabran. And she *will* see the necessity of an alliance."

The child was blinded by her passion. Sulyard would be executed the moment he set foot in the East, and Sabran would sooner cut off her own nose than strike up an alliance with wyrm-lovers, even if she *could* be persuaded to believe that the Nameless One might rise while she drew breath.

"The North is weak," Truyde ploughed on, "and the South is too proud to treat with Virtudom." Her cheeks were flushed. "You dare to judge me for seeking help elsewhere?"

Ead looked her in the eye.

"You may think yourself the only one who seeks to protect this world," she said, "but you have no idea of the foundation upon which you stand. None of you does." When Truyde knitted her brow, Ead said, "Sulyard asked for your help. What have you done to assist him from here? What plans have you made?" Truyde was silent. "If you have done *anything* to aid his mission, it is treason."

"I shall not speak another word." Truyde pulled away. "Go to Lady Oliva if you like. First you will have to explain what you were doing in the Coffer Chamber."

As she made to leave, Ead closed a hand around her wrist.

"You wrote a name in the book," she said. "*Niclays*. I think it refers to Niclays Roos, the anatomist." Truyde shook her head, but Ead saw the spark of recognition in her eyes. "What has Roos to do with all this?"

Before Truyde could answer, a wind rushed through the grounds.

Every branch quivered on every tree. Every bird in the aviary ceased its singing. Ead released her hold on Truyde and stepped out of the alcove.

Cannons were firing in the city. Muskets went off with sounds like chestnuts bursting on a fire. Behind her, Truyde stayed beside the well.

"What is that?" she said.

Ead breathed in as her blood pounded. It had been a long time since this feeling had swept through her body. For the first time in years, her siden had been kindled.

Something was coming. If it had got this far, it must have found a way through the coastal defenses. Or destroyed them.

A flare like the sun breaking through cloud, so hot it parched her eyes and lips, and a wyrm soared over the curtain wall. It burned away the archers and musketeers and smashed a line of catapults to splinters. Truyde sank to the ground.

Ead knew what it was from its magnitude alone. A High Western. A monster from its teeth to the bullwhip of its tail, where lethal spikes jutted. Its battle-scarred abdomen was rusted brown, but the bulk of it was black as tar. Arrows sliced from watchtowers and clattered off its scales.

Arrows were useless. Muskets were useless. It was not just any wyrm, not just any High Western. No one living had laid eyes on this creature, but Ead knew its name.

Fýredel.

He who had called himself the right wing of the Nameless One. Fýredel, who had bred and led the Draconic Army against humankind in the Grief of Ages.

He was awake.

The beast wheeled over Ascalon Palace, casting the lawns and orchards into shadow. Ead sickened, and her skin burned, as his smell enflamed the siden in her blood.

Her longbow was out of reach in her chamber. Years of routine had blunted her vigilance.

Fýredel landed on the Dearn Tower. His tail coiled serpentine around it, and his claws found purchase on its roof. Tiles crumbled away, forcing guards and retainers far below to scatter.

His head was crowned with two cruel horns. Eyes like pits of magma blazed out of the dark.

"SABRAN QUEEN."

The sky itself echoed his words. Half of Ascalon must be able to hear them.

"SEED OF THE SHIELDHEART." More stone fell from the tower. Arrows skittered off his armor. "COME FORTH AND FACE YOUR ENEMY OF OLD, OR WATCH YOUR CITY BURN."

Sabran would not answer his call. Someone would stop her. The Virtues Council would send a representative to treat with him.

Fýredel exposed his gleaming metal teeth. The Alabastrine Tower was too high for Ead to see its uppermost balcony, but her newly tuned ears picked up on a second voice: "I am here, abomination."

Ead froze.

The fool. The utter fool. By emerging, Sabran had signed her own death warrant.

Screams rang from every building. Courtiers and servants were leaning out of open windows to behold the evil in their midst. Others ran pell-mell for the palace gates. Ead charged up the Privy Stair.

"So you have awakened, Fýredel," Sabran said with contempt. "Why have you come here?"

"I come to give you warning, Queen of Inys. The time to choose your side is near." Fýredel let out a hiss that raised gooseflesh all over Ead. "My kin are stirring in their caves. My brother, Orsul, has already taken wing, and our sister, Valeysa, will soon follow. Before the year is out, all our followers will have awakened. The Draconic Army will be reborn."

"Damn your warnings," Sabran hit back. "I do not fear you, lizard. Your threats have as much weight as smoke."

Ead heard their words like thunder in her head. The fumes that rose from Fýredel were grindstones on her senses.

"My master stirs in the Abyss," he said, tongue flickering. "The thousand years are almost done. Your house was our great enemy before, Sabran Berethnet, in the days you call the Grief of Ages."

"My ancestor showed you Inysh mettle then, and I will show it to you now," Sabran retorted. "You speak of a thousand years, wyrm. What deceit does your forked tongue sell?"

Her voice was naked steel.

"That is for you to discover erelong." The wyrm stretched out his neck, so his head closed in on the other tower. "I offer you one chance to pledge your fidelity to my master and name yourself Flesh Queen of Inys." Fire roared behind his eyes. "Come with me now. Give yourself up. Choose the right side, as Yscalin has. Resist, and you will burn."

Ead looked to the clock tower. She could not reach her bow, but she had something else.

"Your lies will take root in no Inysh heart. I am not King Sigoso. My people know that your master will never wake while the bloodline of the Saint continues. If you think I will *ever* name this country the Draconic Queendom of Inys, you will be bitterly disappointed, wyrm."

"You claim your bloodline shields this realm," Fýredel said, "and yet you have stepped out to meet me." His teeth burned red-hot in his mouth. "Do you not fear my flame?"

"The Saint will protect me."

Even the most god-drunk fool could not believe Sir Galian Berethnet would extend a hand from the heavenly court and shield them from a bellyful of fire.

"You speak to one who knows the weakness of the flesh. I slew Sabran the Ambitious on the first day of the Grief. Your Saint," Fýredel said, mouth smoking, "did not protect *her*. Bow to me, and I will spare you the same end. Refuse, and you will join her now."

If Sabran answered, Ead did not hear it. Wind rushed in her ears as she tore across the Sundial Garden. The archers hit Fýredel with arrow after arrow, but not one pierced his scales.

Sabran would keep goading Fýredel until he torched her. The blockhead must really think the wretched Saint would protect her.

Ead ran past the Alabastrine Tower. Debris cascaded from above, and a guard fell dead before her. Cursing the weight of her gown, she reached the Royal Library, flung open its doors, and wove her way between the shelves until she hit the entrance to the clock tower.

She cast off her cloak, unbuckled her girdle. Up the winding steps she went, higher and higher.

Outside, Fýredel still taunted Sabran. Ead stopped in the belfry, where the wind howled through arched windows, and took in the impossible scene.

The Queen of Inys was on the uppermost balcony of the Alabastrine Tower. It stood just southeast of the Dearn Tower, where Fýredel was poised to kill. Wyrm on one building, queen on the other. In her hand was the ceremonial blade that represented Ascalon, the True Sword.

Useless.

"Leave this city, and harm no soul," she called, "or I swear by the Saint whose blood I carry, you will face a defeat beyond any the House of Berethnet has ever exacted on your kind." Fýredel bared his teeth again, but Sabran dared to take another step. "Before I leave this world, I will see your kind thrown down, sealed forever in the chasm in the mountain."

Fýredel reared up and opened his wings. Faced with this behemoth, the Queen of Inys was smaller than a poppet.

Still she did not balk.

The wyrm had bloodlust in his eyes. They burned as hot as the fire in his belly. Ead knew she had moments to decide what to do next.

It would have to be a wind-warding. Wardings like this used a great deal of siden, and she had so very little left—but perhaps, if she poured her last store of it into the effort, she could work one upon Sabran.

She held her hand toward the Alabastrine Tower, cast her siden outward, and twisted it into a wreath around the Queen of Inys.

As Fýredel unleashed his fire, so Ead broke the chains on her long-dormant power. Flame collided with ancient stone. Sabran vanished into light and smoke. Ead was distantly aware of Truyde coming into the belfry, but it was too late to hide what she was doing.

Her senses closed in on Sabran. She felt the strain on her braids of protection around the queen, the fire clawing for dominance, the pain in her own body as the warding gulped away her siden. Sweat soaked her corset. Her arm shook with the effort of keeping her hand turned outward.

When Fýredel closed his jaws, all was silent. Black vapors billowed from the tower, clearing slowly. Ead waited, heart tight as a drum, until she saw the figure in the smoke.

Sabran Berethnet was unscathed.

"It is my turn to give *you* a warning. A warning from my forebear," she said breathlessly, "that if you make war against Virtudom, this hallowed blood will quench your fire. And it will not return."

Fýredel did not acknowledge her. Not this time. He was looking at the blackened stone, and the spotless circle around Sabran.

A perfect circle.

His nostrils flared. His pupils thinned to slits. He had seen a warding before. Ead stood like a statue as his merciless gaze roved, searching for her, while Sabran remained still. When he looked toward the belfry, he sniffed, and Ead knew that he had caught her scent. She stepped out of the shadows beneath the clock face.

Fýredel showed his teeth. Every spine on his back flicked up, and a long hiss rattled on his tongue. Holding his gaze, Ead unsheathed her knife and pointed it at him across the divide.

"Here I am," she said softly. "Here I am."

The High Western let out a scream of rage. With a push of his hind legs, he launched himself off the Dearn Tower, taking part of the spire and most of its east-facing wall with him. Ead threw herself behind a pillar as a fireball exploded against the clock tower.

The cadence of his wings faded away. Ead lurched back to the balustrade. Sabran was still on the balcony, in her circle of pale stone. The sword had fallen from her hand. She had not looked toward the clock tower, or seen Ead watching her. When Combe reached her, she collapsed against him, and he carried her back into the Alabastrine Tower.

"What did you do?" came a quaking voice from behind Ead. Truyde. "I saw you. What did you do?"

Ead slid to the floor of the belfry, head lolling. Great shudders pushed through her body.

The essence in her blood was spent. Her bones felt hollow, her skin as raw as if she had been flayed. She needed the tree, just a taste of its fruit. The orange tree would save her ...

"You are a witch." Truyde stepped away, ashen-faced. "Witch. You practice sorcery. I saw it—"

"You saw nothing."

"It was aëromancy," Truyde whispered. "Now I know *your* secret, and it reeks far worse than mine. Let us see how far you can pursue Triam from the pyre."

She whirled toward the stair. Ead threw her knife.

Even in this state, she struck true. Truyde was pulled back with a strangled gasp, pinned by her cloak to the doorpost. Before she could escape, Ead was in front of her.

"My duty is to slay the servants of the Nameless One. I will also kill all those who threaten the House of Berethnet," she breathed. "If you mean to accuse me of sorcery before the Virtues Council, I bid you find some way to prove it—and find it quickly, before I make poppets of you and your lover and stab them in the heart. Do you think that because Triam Sulyard is in the East, I cannot smite him where he stands?"

Truyde breathed hard through her teeth.

"If you lay a finger on him," she whispered, "I will see you burn in Marian Square."

"Fire has no power over me."

She pulled the knife free. Truyde crumpled against the wall, panting, one hand at her throat.

Ead turned to the door. Her breath came swift and hot, and her ears rang.

She took one step before she fell.

10

East

Ginura was all that Tané had imagined. Ever since she was a child, she had pictured the capital in a thousand ways. Inspired by what she had heard from her learnèd teachers, her imagination had fashioned it into a dream of castles and teahouses and pleasure boats.

Her imagination had not failed her. The shrines were larger than any in Cape Hisan, the streets glistened like sand under the sun, and petals drifted along the canals. Still, more people meant more noise and commotion. Charcoal smoke thickened the air. Oxen pulled carts of goods, messengers ran or rode between buildings, stray hounds nosed at scraps of food, and here and there, a drunkard ranted at the crowds.

And *such* crowds. Tané had thought Cape Hisan busy, but a hundred thousand people jostled in Ginura, and for the first time in her life, she realized how little of the world she had seen.

The palanquins carried the apprentices deeper into the city. The season trees were as vivid as Tané had always been told, with their butter-yellow summer leaves, and the street performers played music that Susa would love. She spotted two snow monkeys perched on a roof. Merchants sang of silk and tin and sea grapes from the northern coast.

As the palanquins wound past canals and over bridges, people turned their backs, as if they were unworthy to look upon the sea guardians. Among them were the fish-people, as commoners disparagingly called them in Cape Hisan—courtiers who dressed as if they had just walked out of the ocean. Some of them were said to scrape the scales off rainbow fish and comb them through their hair.

When Tané saw Ginura Castle, her breath caught. The roofs were the color of sun-blanched coral, the walls like cuttlebone. It had been designed to resemble the Palace of Many Pearls, where the Seiikinese dragons entered their slumber each year and was said to bridge the sea and the celestial plane.

Once, in the days when they had possessed all their powers, the dragons had not needed a season of rest.

The procession came to a halt outside the Ginura School of War, where the sea guardians would be sorted for the last time. It was the oldest and most prestigious institute of its kind, where new soldiers lodged and continued their instruction in the arts of war. It was here that Tané would prove herself worthy of a place in Clan Miduchi. It was here that she would exhibit the skills she had honed since she was a child.

Thunder rumbled overhead. As she emerged from the palanquin, her legs buckled, sore from being scrunched up for so long. Turosa laughed, but a servant caught her.

"I have you, honored lady."

"Thank you," Tané said. Seeing that she was steady, he held an umbrella over her.

The first of the rain drenched her boots as she walked with the others through the gateway, drinking in the grandeur of its silver leaf and sea-blanched wood. Carvings of the great warriors of Seiikinese history clustered under its gable, as if hiding from the storm. Tané spotted the long-honored Princess Dumai and the First Warlord among them. Heroes of her childhood.

A woman was waiting for them in the hall, where they removed their boots. Her hair was sleeked into a coiffure.

"Welcome to Ginura," she said in a cool voice. "You have the morning to wash and rest in your quarters. At noon, you will begin the first of your water trials. In that time, you will be observed by the honored Sea General, and by those who may yet be your kin."

Clan Miduchi. Tané thrilled inside.

The woman led them deeper into the school, through courtyards and covered passageways. Each of the sea guardians was shown into a small room. Tané found herself installed on the upper floor, near the other three principal apprentices. Her room looked over a courtyard, where a fishpond was churned to bubbles by the downpour.

Her traveling clothes reeked. It had been three days since they had last stopped at a roadside inn.

She found a cypress bath behind a windwall. Scented oils and petals floated on the water. Her hair fanned out around her as she sank into it and thought back to Cape Hisan. To Susa.

She would be fine. Like a cat, Susa had a way of always landing on her feet. When they were young and Tané had still made frequent visits to the city, her friend would steal pan-fried lotus roots or salt plums, dashing away like a fox if she was spotted. They would hide somewhere and stuff themselves senseless, laughing all the while. The only time Susa had ever looked afraid was when Tané had first met her.

That winter had been long and harsh. One bitter evening, Tané had braved a blizzard with one of her teachers to buy firewood in Cape Hisan. While the teacher argued with a merchant, Tané had wandered away to warm her hands by a bowl of hot coals.

That was when she had heard the laughter, and the broken voice crying for help. In a nearby lane, she had found another child being kicked around in the snow by urchins. Tané had drawn her wooden sword with a shout. Even at eleven, she had known how to use it.

The urchins of Cape Hisan were hardened fighters. One of them had pulled his blade up her cheekbone, aiming for the eye, leaving a scar shaped just like a fishhook.

They had beaten Susa—a starving orphan—for eating a cut of meat from a shrine. Once Tané had frightened off the urchins, she had beseeched her teacher to help. At ten, Susa had been too old to begin an education in the Houses of Learning, but she was soon adopted by a tender-hearted innkeeper. Since then, she and Tané had always been friends. They had joked sometimes that they might be sisters, since Susa knew nothing of her parents.

Sea sisters, Susa had called them once. *Two pearls formed in the same oyster.*

Tané pushed herself from the bathwater.

How she had changed since that night in the snow. If it had happened now, she might have decided that brawling with urchins was no way for an apprentice to behave. She might even have decided that the girl deserved to be beaten for stealing what was meant for gods. At some point, she had started to realize how fortunate she was to have the chance to be a dragonrider. That was when her heart had grown harder, like a ship collecting barnacles.

And yet some part of her younger self remained. The part that had hidden the man from the beach.

There would be no second chances if she was tired during her first day of instruction. Tané dried herself with linen, threaded her arms into the unlined robe on the bed, and slept.

When she woke, it was still misty with rain, but a stream of sallow light had broken through the clouds. Her skin had dried, leaving her cooler and clear-headed.

A group of servants soon arrived. She had not been dressed by anyone since she was a child, but she knew better than to quarrel.

The first trial would take place in a courtyard at the center of the school, where the Sea General was waiting. The sea guardians took their seats on tiered stone benches. The dragons were already here, watching them from over the rooftops. Tané tried not to look.

"Welcome to your first water trial. You have been on the road for days, but soldiers of the High Sea Guard have little time for rest," the Sea General called. "Today, you will prove you can use a halberd. Let us begin with two apprentices whose learnèd teachers speak highly of their skills. Honorable Onren of the East House, honorable Tané of the South House—let us see who can best the other first."

Tané rose. Her throat felt small. When she reached the bottom of the steps, a man handed her a halberd: a light pole weapon, its handle made of white oak, with a curved steel blade at its end. She removed its lacquered sheath and ran a finger up to its tip.

In the South House, the blades had been wooden. Now, at last, she could use steel. Once Onren had received her halberd, they walked toward each other.

Onren grinned. Tané wiped her expression clean, even as her palms dampened. Her heart was a trapped butterfly. *The water in you is cold*, her teacher had once told her. *When you hold a weapon, you become a faceless ghost. You give nothing away.*

They bowed. A hush descended in her mind, like the quiet that came at twilight.

"Begin," the Sea General said.

At once, Onren closed the space between them. Tané whirled her halberd into both hands, the blades clashing together. Onren let out a short, loud shout.

Tané made no sound.

Onren broke the lock and paced backward, away from Tané, halberd pointed at her chest. Tané waited for her to make the next move. There had to be a reason Onren had been principal apprentice in the East House.

As if she could hear the thought, Onren began to spin her halberd around her body, passing it fluently over her arms and between her hands in a show of confidence. Tané tightened her grip, watching.

Onren favored one side. She avoided putting too much weight on her left knee. Tané recalled, distantly, that Onren had been kicked by a horse when she was younger.

Emboldened, Tané strode forward, halberd raised. Onren came to meet her. This time, they were faster. *One, two, three* clashes. Onren barked wordless threats with every attack. Tané parried her in silence.

Four, five, six. Tané snapped the halberd up and down, using the handle as well as the blade.

Seven, eight, nine.

When a downcut came, she wielded the halberd as if it were on a pivot—up at one end, then the other, shunting the blow aside and leaving her opponent exposed. Onren only just recovered in time to thwart the next strike—but when she thrust out her weapon again, wind hissed past Tané. One hand flew to her ear, seeking blood, but there was nothing.

Her distraction cost her. Onren came at her in a flurry of oak and steel, unleashing her considerable strength. They were fighting for honor, for glory, for the dreams they had nurtured since they were children. Tané clenched her teeth as she danced and dodged, sweat drenching her tunic, hair stuck to her nape. One of the dragons let out a huff.

The reminder of their presence stiffened her determination. To win this, she would have to take a hit.

She let Onren knock her arm with the handle, hard enough to bruise her. The pain went deep. Onren drove her weapon like a fish-spear. Tané leaped backward, giving her a wide berth—then, when Onren raised her arms for a final downcut, Tané rolled and swung hard for her weak knee. Wood snapped cleanly against bone.

Onren skidded with a gasp. Her knee gave way. Before she could rise, Tané had set her blade across her shoulders.

"Rise," said the Sea General, sounding pleased. "Well fought. Honorable Tané of the South House, victory is yours."

The spectators applauded. Tané handed the halberd to a servant and extended a hand to Onren.

"Did I hurt you?"

Onren let Tané help her up. "Well," she said, panting, "I suspect you've broken my kneecap."

A puff of briny air came from behind them. The green Lacustrine dragon was grinning at Tané over the rooftop, showing all her teeth. For the first time, Tané smiled back.

Distantly, she realized that Onren was still speaking.

"Sorry," she said, light-headed with joy. "What did you say?"

"I was only observing how the fiercest warriors can hide behind such gentle faces." They bowed to each other before Onren nodded to the benches, where the apprentices were still clapping. "Take a good look at Turosa. He knows he has a fight on his hands."

Tané followed her gaze. Turosa had never looked so angry—nor so determined.

I I

West

"There it is," Estina Melaugo said, with a sweeping gesture toward land. "Feast your eyes on the Draconic cesspit of Yscalin."

"No, thank you." Kit drank from the bottle they were sharing. "I would much rather my death was a surprise."

Loth peered through the spyglass. Even now, a day after seeing the High Western, his hands were unsteady.

Fýredel. Right wing of the Nameless One. Commander of the Draconic Army. If he had woken, then the other High Westerns would surely follow. It was from them that the rest of wyrmkind drew strength. When a High Western died, the fire in its wyverns, and in their progeny, burned out.

The Nameless One himself could not return—not while the House of Berethnet stood—but his servants could wreak destruction without him. The Grief of Ages had proven that.

There had to be a reason they were rising again. They had fallen into their slumber at the end of the Grief of Ages, the same night a comet had crossed the sky. Scholars had speculated for centuries as to why, and to when, they might wake, but no one had found an answer. Gradually, everyone had begun to assume that they never would. That the wyrms had become living fossils.

Loth returned his attention to what he could glimpse through the spyglass. The moon was a half-closed eye, and they floated on water as dark as his thoughts. All he could see was the nest of lights that was Perunta. A place that might be crawling with Draconic plague.

The sickness had first oozed from the Nameless One, whose breath, it was said, had been a slow-acting poison. A more fearsome strain had arrived with the five High Westerns. They and their wyverns carried it, the same way rats had once carried the pestilence. It had existed only in pockets since the end of the Grief of Ages, but Loth knew the signs from books.

It began with the reddening of the hands. Then a scalelike rash. As it tiptoed over the body, the afflicted would experience pain in the joints, fever and visions. If they were unlucky enough to survive this stage, the bloodblaze set in. They were at their most dangerous then, for if not restrained, they would run about screaming as if they were on fire, and anyone whose skin touched theirs would also be afflicted. Usually they died within days, though some had been known to survive longer.

There was no cure for the plague. No cure and no protection.

Loth snapped the spyglass closed and handed it to Melaugo.

"I suppose this is it," he said.

"Don't abandon hope, Lord Arteloth." Her gaze was detached. "I doubt the plague will be in the palace. It's those of us you call the commons who suffer most in times of need."

Plume and Harlowe were approaching the bow, the latter with a clay pipe in hand.

"Right, my lords," the captain said. "We've enjoyed having you, truly, but nothing lasts forever."

Kit finally seemed to grasp the danger they were in. Either he was cupshotten or he had lost his wits, but he clasped his hands. "I beseech you, Captain Harlowe—let us join your crew." His eyes were fevered. "You need not tell Lord Seyton. Our families have money."

"What?" Loth hissed. "Kit—"

"Let him speak." Harlowe motioned with his pipe. "Carry on, Lord Kitston."

"There is land in the Downs, good land. Save us, and it's yours," Kit continued.

"I have the high seas at my feet. Land is not what I need," Harlowe said. "What I need is seafarers."

"With your guidance, I wager we could be *outstanding* seafarers. I come from a long line of cartographers, you know." An outright lie. "And Arteloth used to sail on Elsand Lake."

Harlowe regarded them with dark eyes.

"No," Loth said firmly. "Captain, Lord Kitston is uneasy about our task, but we are duty-bound to enter Yscalin. To see that justice is done."

With a face like a skinned apple, Kit seized him by the jerkin and pulled him aside.

"Arteloth," he said under his breath, "I am trying to get us out of this. Because this"—he turned Loth toward the lights in the distance—"has *nothing* to do with justice. This is the Night Hawk sending us both to our deaths for a pennyworth of gossip."

"Combe may have exiled me for some ulterior purpose, but now I stand on the brink of Yscalin, I wish to find out what happened to Prince Wilstan." Loth placed a hand on his shoulder. "If you want to turn back, Kit, I will bear you no ill will. This was not your punishment."

Kit looked at him, frustration etched on to him. "Oh, Loth," he said, softer. "You're not the Saint."

"No, but he has got balls," Melaugo said.

"I've no time for this pious talk," Harlowe cut in, "but I do concur with Estina on the subject of your balls, Lord Arteloth." His gaze was piercing. "I need people with hearts like yours. If you think you could weather the seas, say it now, and I'll put it to my crew."

Kit blinked. "Really?"

Harlowe was expressionless. When Loth kept his peace, Kit sighed.

"I thought not." Harlowe dealt them a cold stare. "Now, get the fuck off my ship."

The pirates jeered. Melaugo, whose lips were pursed, beckoned to Loth and Kit. As his friend turned to follow, Loth gripped his arm.

"Kit," he murmured, "take the chance and stay behind. You are not a threat to Combe, not like I am. You could still go back to Inys."

Kit shook his head, a smile on his lips.

"Come now, Arteloth," he said. "What little piety I have, I owe to you. And he might not be my patron, but I know the Knight of Fellowship tells us not to leave our friends alone."

Loth wanted to argue with him, but he found himself smiling back at his friend. They walked side by side after Melaugo.

They had to descend on a rope ladder from the *Rose Eternal*. Their polished boots slipped on the rungs. Once they were settled in the rowing boat, where their traveling chests waited, Melaugo climbed in with them.

"Hand me the oars, Lord Arteloth." When Loth did, she whistled. "See you soon, Captain. Don't leave without me."

"Never, Estina." Harlowe leaned over the side. "Farewell, my lords."

"Keep those pomanders close, lordlings," Plume added. "Wouldn't want you catching anything."

The crew roared with laughter as Melaugo pushed away from the *Rose*.

"Don't mind them. They'd piss themselves before they ever did what you're doing." She glanced over her shoulder. "What made you offer up your services as a pirate, Lord Kitston? This life's not like it is in songs, you know. There's a little more shit and scurvy."

"A stroke of brilliance, I thought." Kit shot her a look of mock hurt. "I take the Knight of Courtesy as my patron, mistress. She commands poets to beautify the world—but how can I, unless I see it?"

"There's a question I'd need a few more drinks to answer."

As they drew closer to the shore, Loth took out his handkerchief and pressed it to his nose. Vinegar and fish and acrid smoke formed the rotten posy of Perunta. Kit kept up a smile, but his eyes were watering.

"How refreshing," he managed.

Melaugo did not smile. "Do keep those pomanders," she said. "Worth having, if only for comfort."

"Is there nothing we can do to protect ourselves?" Loth said.

"You can try not to breathe. Folk say the plague is everywhere, and no one is sure how it spreads. Some wear veils or masks to keep it out."

"Nothing else?"

"Oh, you'll see merchants peddling all sorts. Mirrors to deflect the foul vapors, countless potions and poultices—but you might as well swallow your gold. Best thing to do is put the afflicted out of their misery." She maneuvered the boat around a rock. "I can't imagine you two have seen much death."

"I resent your assumption," Kit objected. "I saw my dear old aunt upon her bier."

"Yes, and I suppose she wore a red gown for her meeting with the Saint. I suppose she was as clean as a licked kitten and smelled of rosemary." When Kit grimaced, Melaugo said, "You have not seen death, my lord. You have only seen the mask we put on it."

They sat in silence from then on. When the water was shallow enough to wade in, Melaugo stopped rowing.

"I'll go no closer." She nodded to the city. "You're to go to a tavern called the Grapevine. Someone should collect you." She pushed Kit with the toe of her boot. "Go, now. I'm a privateer, not a milk nurse."

Loth stood. "Our thanks to you, Mistress Melaugo. Your kindness will not be forgotten."

"Please forget it. I've a reputation to uphold."

They struck out from the boat with their chests. When they were both on the sand, dripping wet, Melaugo sculled back to the *Rose Eternal*, singing in quavering Yscali.

Harlowe might have taken them both. They could have seen places that no longer had names, oceans that had never been cross-stitched by trading routes. Loth could have found himself at the prow of his own ship one day—but he was not that man, and never would be.

"Not our most dignified entrance." Panting, Kit let his chest fall. "How do you suppose we find this tavern?"

"By ... relying on our instincts," Loth said, unsure. "The commons must get on well enough."

"Arteloth, we are courtiers. We have no useful instincts."

Loth had no counterstroke.

They made slow progress into the city. The chests were heavy, and they had neither map nor compass.

Perunta had once been known as the most beautiful port in the West. These mud-clotted streets, overflowing with fish bones and ashes and swill, were not what Loth had imagined. A dead bird writhed with maggots. Cesspits overflowed. In one unlit square, a sanctuary lay in ruins. Sabran had heard reports that King Sigoso had executed the sanctarians who would not renounce the Saint, but she had not wanted to believe them.

Loth tried not to breathe as he stepped over a rivulet of dark liquid. He dared not stray too far from Kit. People jostled around them, shrouding their faces with veils or cloth rags.

They saw their first plague house on the next street. Boards had been nailed over the windows, the oak door stained with scarlet wings. Yscali words were chalked above it.

"*Pity this house, for here we are cursed*," Kit read.

Loth looked askance at him. "You read Yscali?"

"I know. You're shocked," Kit said gravely. "After all, I am such a master of Inysh, such a prodigy of verse, it seems impossible that I could have room in my skull for another language, but—"

"Kit."

"Melaugo told me the translation."

The darkness was disorienting. Few candles were lit in Perunta, though braziers fumigated the broader streets. By dint of striding about with as much confidence as possible, Loth and Kit finally happened upon the tavern where they were to meet their escort to Cárscaro. Its sign displayed a bunch of succulent black grapes that had no business in this sump.

A coach waited outside. Built of what Loth was quite sure was iron, it terrified him even before he wondered what sort of horse could draw such a thing. Then he saw.

A great wolfish head turned to look at him, and a massive jaw, packed with teeth, slackened to let slip a rope of drool.

The creature was larger than a bear. Its thick neck tapered into a serpentine body, which could be moved by its muscular legs or a pair of bat wings. At its side was a second monster, this one furred with gray. Their eyes were identical. Embers from the Womb of Fire.

Jaculi.

The offspring of wyvern and wolf.

"Stay still," Kit whispered. "The bestiaries say that sudden movements make them pounce."

One of the jaculi growled. Loth wanted to make the sign of the sword, but he dared not move.

How many Draconic creatures were awake in Yscalin?

The driver of the coach was an Yscal with oiled hair. "Lord Arteloth and Lord Kitston, I presume," he said.

Kit made an incoherent noise. The driver pulled a lever, and a set of steps unfolded. "Leave the chests," he muttered. "Get in."

They obeyed.

Inside the coach, they found a woman awaiting them, dressed in a heavy crimson gown and a veil of black drum lace. She wore long velvet gloves, frilled at the elbow. A filigrain pomander hung at her side.

"Lord Arteloth. Lord Kitston," she said in a soft voice. Loth could just make out dark eyes through the veil. "Welcome to Perunta. I am Priessa Yelarigas, First Lady of the Bedchamber to Her Radiance, the Donmata Marosa of the Draconic Kingdom of Yscalin."

She was not afflicted. No one tortured by the plague could speak with so gentle a tongue.

"Thank you for meeting us here, my lady." Loth endeavored to steady his voice. Kit squeezed into the coach beside him. "We are honored to be received at the court of King Sigoso."

"His Majesty is honored to receive you."

A whip snapped outside, and the coach jolted forward.

"I confess myself surprised that Her Radiance would send such a high-ranking lady to meet us," Loth said. "Since this city is so full of the afflicted."

"If the Nameless One wishes me to surrender my life to his plague, so be it," was her even reply.

Loth clenched his jaw. To think that these people had once professed loyalty to Sabran, and to Virtudom.

"You will be used to horses drawing a coach, my lords," Lady Priessa continued, "but it would take many days to cross Yscalin that way. Jaculi are fleet-footed and never tire."

She folded her hands on her lap. Her fingers were home to several gold rings, fitted over the gloves.

"You should rest," she said. "However swift our coach, we have some way to go, my lords."

Loth attempted a smile. "I would prefer to watch the scenery."

"As you wish."

In truth, it was too dark to see a thing out of the window, but he would not sleep with a wyrm-lover so close.

This was Draconic territory. He would rise from the silk pillow of nobility and find the spy within. He would harden himself to the dangers of his mission. So while Kit nodded off, Loth sat as still as he could, eyes propped open by sheer force of will, and made a promise to the Saint.

He would accept the road he had been thrust on. He would seek out Prince Wilstan. He would reunite his queen with her father. And he would find his way home.

He could not tell if Priessa Yelarigas slept, or if she watched him all night long.

There was smoke in her hair. She could smell it.

"Where in Virtudom did you find her?"

"The belfry, of all places."

Footsteps. "Saint, it's Mistress Duryan. Send word to Her Majesty at once. And fetch a physician."

Her tongue was an ember in her mouth. When the strangers let go of her, she plunged into a fever dream.

She was a child again, shaded from the sun by the branches of the tree. The fruit hung above her head, too high for her to reach, and Jondu was calling *Come here, Eadaz, come and see.*

Then the Prioress was lifting a cup to her lips, saying it was the blood of the Mother. It tasted like sunlight and laughter and prayer. She had burned like this in the days that followed, burned until the fire melted away her ignorance. That day she had been born anew.

When she woke, a familiar woman was at her bedside, pouring water from a ewer to a bowl.

"Meg."

Margret turned to her so quickly she almost knocked the ewer over.

"Ead!" With a laugh of relief, she leaned in to kiss her brow. "Oh, thank the Saint. You've been insensible for days. The physicians said you had an ague, then the sweat, then the pestilence—"

"Sabran," Ead rasped. "Meg, is she well?"

"We must first establish if *you* are well." Margret felt her cheeks, her neck. "Does anything hurt? Should I fetch a physician?"

"No physicians. I am perfectly all right." Ead wet her lips. "Have you anything to drink?"

"Of course."

Margret filled a cup and held it up to her mouth. Ead swallowed a little of the ale inside.

"You were in the belfry," Margret said. "What were you doing up there?"

Ead pieced a lie together. "I took a wrong turn in the library. I found the door to the clock tower open and thought I would explore, and there I was when the beast came. I suppose its ... dreadful fumes gave me this fever." Before Margret could question this, she added, "Now, tell me if Sabran is all right."

"Sabran is as well as I have ever seen her, and all Inys knows that Fýredel himself could not touch her with his fire."

"Where is the wyrm now?"

Margret returned the cup to the nightstand and soaked a cloth in the bowl.

"Gone." Her brow pinched. "There were no deaths, but he did set fire to a few storehouses. Captain Lintley says the city is on edge. Sabran sent out heralds to reassure the people of her protection, but no one can believe that a High Western has woken."

"It was bound to happen," Ead said. "Smaller things have been stirring for some time."

"Aye, but never one of the overlords. Fortunately, most of the city has no idea that what they saw was the right wing of the Nameless One. All the tapestries depicting him are hidden away in here." Margret wrung out the cloth. "Him and his infernal kin."

"He said Orsul had already woken." Ead took another sip of ale. "And Valeysa soon."

"At least the others are long dead. And of course, the Nameless One himself cannot return. Not while the House of Berethnet endures."

When Ead tried to sit up, her arms shook, and she slumped back into the pillows. Margret went to the door to speak to a servant before returning.

"Meg," Ead said, while Margret dabbed her brow, "I know what happened to Loth."

Margret stilled. "He wrote to you?"

"No." Ead glanced toward the door. "I overheard the Dukes Spiritual speaking with Sabran. Combe claims Loth has gone to Cárscaro as a spy—to find out what is happening there, and to look for Wilstan Fynch. He said Loth went without permission ... but I think we both know the truth of it."

Slowly, Margret sat back. Her hand came to her middle.

"Saint save my brother," she murmured. "He is no spy. Combe has sentenced him to death."

Silence fell, broken only by the birds outside.

"I told him, Ead," Margret finally said. "I told him a friendship with a queen was not the same as any other, that he needed to be careful. But Loth never listens." She raised a sad, wry smile. "My brother thinks that everyone is just as good as he is."

Ead tried to find some words of comfort, but had none. Loth was in too much danger.

"I know. I tried to warn him, too." She took her friend by the hand. "He may yet find his way home."

"You know he will not last long in Cárscaro."

"You could petition Combe to bring him back. You are Lady Margret Beck."

"And Combe is the Duke of Courtesy. He has more influence and wealth than I ever will."

"Could you not tell Sabran yourself, then?" Ead asked. "She clearly has her suspicions about the story."

"I cannot accuse Combe or anyone without proof of a conspiracy. If he told Sab that Loth went by choice, and I can present no evidence to counter him, then even she can do nothing."

Ead knew Margret was right. She tightened her grip, and Margret released a shaking breath.

Someone tapped on the door. Margret murmured to whoever was outside. Now her siden was quiet, and her senses blunted, Ead could not hear what they said.

Her friend came back with a cup. "Caudle," she said. "Tallys made it specially. Such a kind girl."

The hot gruel, sweetened to the point of sickliness, was the answer to everything in Inys. Too weak to grip the handles, Ead let Margret spoon the awful stuff into her mouth.

Another knock. This time, when Margret opened it, she fell into a curtsy.

"Leave us a moment, Meg."

Ead knew that voice. With a glance in her direction, Margret left.

The Queen of Inys stepped into the room. Her riding habit was the dark green of holly.

"Call if you have need of us, Majesty," said a gruff voice from outside.

"I do not think a bedbound woman poses too great a danger to my person, Sir Gules, but thank you."

The door closed. Ead sat up as best she could, conscious of her sweat-soaked shift and the sour taste in her mouth.

"Ead," Sabran said, looking her over. A flush touched her cheeks. "I see you are at last awake. You have been absent from my lodgings for too long."

"Forgive me, Your Majesty."

"Your generosity has been missed. I intended to call upon you earlier, but the physicians feared you might have the sweat." The sun lightened her eyes. "You were in the clock tower the day the wyrm came. I would like to know why."

"Madam?"

"The Royal Librarian found you there. Lady Oliva Marchyn tells me that some courtiers and servants use the tower for ... venery."

"I have no lover, Majesty."

"I will brook no lewdness in this palace. Confess, and the Knight of Courtesy may show mercy."

Ead sensed the queen would not swallow the story about taking a wrong turn. "I went up to the belfry ... to see if I could distract the beast from Your Majesty." She wished she had the strength to speak with more conviction. "But I need not have feared for you."

It was the truth, stripped of its vital parts.

"I trust that Ambassador uq-Ispad would not ask for a person of loose morals to be accepted into my Upper Household," Sabran concluded, "but do not let me hear of you visiting the clock tower again."

"Of course, madam."

The queen walked to the open window. Setting a hand on the sill, she looked out at the palace grounds.

"Majesty," Ead said, "may I ask why you went out to face the wyrm?" A clement breeze floated in from outside. "Had Fýredel slain you, all would have been lost."

Sabran did not reply for a time.

"He threatened my people," she murmured. "I had stepped out before I had considered what else might be done." She looked back at Ead. "I have received another report about you. Lady Truyde utt Zeedeur has been telling my courtiers that you are a sorceress."

Damn that red-haired gurnet. Ead almost admired her mettle, ignoring the threat of a curse.

"Madam, I know nothing of sorcery," she said, tinging her words with a hint of scorn.

Sorcery was not a word the Prioress much liked.

"Doubtless," Sabran said, "but Lady Truyde has a notion that it was *you* who protected me from Fýredel. She claims she saw you in the clock tower, casting a spell toward me."

This time Ead was silent. There was no possible argument against the accusation.

"Of course," the queen said, "she is a liar."

Ead dared not speak.

"It was the Saint that drove back the wyrm. He held forth his heavenly shield to protect me from the fire. To imply that it was cheap sorcery comes very close to treason," Sabran stated, her voice flat. "I have half a mind to send her to the Dearn Tower."

All the tension rushed out of Ead. A laugh of relief bubbled in her, threatening to brim over.

"She is only young, Your Majesty," she said, forcing it down. "With youth comes folly."

"She is old enough to accuse you falsely," Sabran pointed out. "Do you not crave vengeance?"

"I prefer the taste of mercy. It lets me sleep at night."

Those stone-cold eyes ran her through. "Perhaps you imply that I should show mercy more often."

Ead was too exhausted to fear that look. "No. Only that I doubt Lady Truyde meant insult to Your Majesty. More likely she has a grudge against me, since I was promoted to a position she desires."

Sabran lifted her chin.

"You will return to your duties in three days. I will have the Royal Physician take care of you until then," she said. Ead raised her eyebrows. "I need you well," Sabran continued, rising to leave. "Once the announcement is made, I will need all my ladies by my side."

"Announcement, madam?"

Sabran had turned her back to her, but Ead saw her shoulders tense.

"The announcement," she said, "of my betrothal to Aubrecht Lievelyn, High Prince of the Free State of Mentendon."

12

East

The water trials passed like a long dream. Most citizens took shelter in their houses as the storm battered the west coast of Seiiki, but sea guardians were expected to endure the worst conditions.

"Rain is water, and so are we," the Sea General called over the thunder as he marched past the ranks. His hair was plastered to his skull, and raindrops rolled off the end of his nose. "If a little water can defeat you, you cannot hope to ride a dragon, or guard the sea, and this is not the place for you." He raised his voice. "Will water defeat you?"

"No, honored Sea General," the apprentices shouted.

Tané was already dripping. At least the rain was warm.

Archery and firearms were easy enough. Even in this downpour, Tané had sharp eyes and a steady hand. Dumusa was best with a bow—she could have done it blindfolded—but Tané came second. None of them, not even Dumusa, could best her with a pistol, but a sea guardian from the West House came close. Kanperu, the eldest and tallest, whose jaw looked as if a sword could be struck upon it, and whose hands seemed big enough to wrap around tree trunks.

Mounted archery was next. They each had to hit six glass floats that had been hung from a beam. Dumusa was not as skilled on horseback as she was on foot and only shattered five of them. Not being fond of horses, Onren, who gritted her teeth throughout the trial, lost control of her steed and missed three. Tané, however, struck true each time—until her horse stumbled and sent her final shot awry, allowing Turosa to steal first place.

They rode their horses back into the stables. "Bad luck, peasant," Turosa said to Tané as she slid from the saddle. "I suppose some things are in the blood. Perhaps one day, the honored Sea General will realize that dragonriders are born, not made."

Tané set her jaw as an ostler took her stallion. Its coat was dark with rain and sweat.

"Ignore him, Tané," Dumusa said, dismounting. Her hair coiled wetly about her shoulders. "The water runs the same in all of us."

Turosa curled his lip, but left. He never quarreled with the other descendants of riders.

When he was gone, Tané bowed to Dumusa. "You have great talent, honorable Dumusa," she said. "I hope to be as skilled an archer as you one day."

Dumusa bowed in return. "I hope to have the same mastery of firearms as you one day, honorable Tané."

They left the stables together. Tané had spoken to Dumusa before, but now they were alone, she found herself unsure of what to say. She had often wondered what it must have been like for her, growing up in a mansion in Ginura with her Miduchi grandparents.

When they reached the practice hall, they sat close to each other, and Tané set about cleaning the mud from her arrows. Kanperu, the tall and silent apprentice, was already there, furbishing his silver-mounted pistol.

As they worked, Onren entered the hall.

"That," she declared, "was the worst I have ever shot." She scraped back her drenched hair. "I must find a shrine and beg the great Kwiriki to wash away all horses. They have been out to thwart me since the day I was born."

"Peace." Dumusa did not look up from her bow. "You have plenty of time to show your skill to the Miduchi."

"Easy for you to say. You have the blood of the Miduchi. All of you become riders in the end."

"There is always a chance that I will be the first one who does not."

"A chance," Onren agreed, "but we all know that chance is very small."

Her knee was swollen from the duel. She would have to work hard if she meant to be a rider.

Kanperu returned his pistol to the wall-rack. As he left, he gave Onren an indecipherable look over his shoulder.

"I hear the honorable Kanperu has taken to visiting a tavern near the fruit market," Dumusa murmured to Onren when he was out of earshot. "He spends every evening there."

"What of it?"

"I thought we might go, too. When we become riders, we will all be spending a great deal of time together. It would behoove us to be well acquainted. Would you not agree?"

Onren smiled. "Dumu," she said, "are you trying to distract me so I won't outperform you?"

"You know very well that you outperform me in everything but archery." Dumusa inspected her bow once more. "Come. I need to get out of this place for a few hours."

"I should tell the honored Sea General what a bad influence you are." Onren stood and stretched. "Coming, Tané?"

It took Tané a moment to notice that they were both looking at her, waiting for an answer.

They were serious. In the middle of their water trials, they wanted to go to a tavern.

"Thank you," she said slowly, "but I must stay here and practice for the next water trial." She paused. "Should you not also be preparing for tomorrow, Onren?"

Onren snorted. "I have practiced for most of my life. Practicing last night did not help me today. No," she said, "what I need tonight is a stiff drink. And perhaps a stiff—" She glanced at Dumusa, and though their lips quaked in an effort to contain it, they both laughed.

They had lost their senses. Surely, at a time like this, no one could afford distractions.

"I hope you enjoy your evening," Tané said, rising. "Goodnight."

"Goodnight, Tané," Onren said. Her smile faded, and her brow furrowed. "Try to get some sleep, won't you?"

"Of course."

Tané crossed the hall and hung up her bow. Turosa, who was about to practice unarmed combat with his friends, caught her gaze and clapped his fist into his palm.

A damp breeze wafted through the corridors, warm as the steam off freshly made soup. The polished floor rattled beneath her as she strode back through the school.

She washed away the sweat and practiced alone in her room with her sword. When her arm finally tired, a worm of misgiving began to eat at her. There was no reason her horse should have stumbled during the trial. What if Turosa had impaired it somehow, just to spite her?

In the end, she went back to the stables. When she found the farrier, he assured her that there was nothing wrong. The ground had been wet. Most likely the horse had slipped.

Don't let a little shit like Turosa get the better of you, Susa had said, but her voice seemed very far away.

Tané spent what remained of the evening in the practice hall, pockmarking scarecrows with throwing knives. Only once she could hit every single one in the eye did she let herself return to her room, where she lit an oil lamp and began her first letter to Susa.

So far, the trials are as difficult as I feared. Today my horse slipped, and I paid the price for it.

Even though I feel as if I have bled myself dry practicing, some of the others seem to perform just as well as I do without working themselves to sleeplessness. They drink and smoke and laugh with one another, but all I can do is continue to refine my skill. After fourteen years of preparation, the water in me will not run true— and I am afraid, Susa.

Those fourteen years are nothing here. We are judged for today, not for yesterday.

She gave it to a servant to send to Cape Hisan, then lay on her bedding and listened to the cut of her own breath.

Outside, an owl hooted. After a short while, Tané got up and slipped back out of her room.

She could practice a little more.

The Governor of Cape Hisan was a slender fellow, neat as a parcel, who lived in an illustrious mansion in the middle of the city. Unlike the Chief Officer, he knew how to smile. He was gray-haired, with a kind face, and was rumored to be soft on petty criminals.

A pity that Niclays, having broken the cardinal rule of Seiiki, could by no stretch of the imagination be deemed a *petty criminal*.

"So," the Governor said, "the woman brought the outsider to your door."

"Yes," Niclays confirmed. His throat was almost too dry to form words. "Yes, indeed, honored Governor. I had been enjoying a cup of your remarkable Seiikinese wine just moments before their arrival."

They had held him in a room for several days. He had lost count in the darkness. When soldiers had finally marched him out, he had almost fainted, thinking they were taking him straight to the block. Instead they presented him to a physician, who had checked his hands and examined his eyes. The soldiers had then given Niclays fresh clothes and escorted him to the most powerful official in this region of Seiiki.

"So you took this man into your home," said official continued. "Did you believe he was a legal settler in Orisima?"

Niclays cleared his throat. "I, ah— no. I know everyone in Orisima. But the woman threatened me," he said, trying to appear haunted by the memory. "She . . . held a dagger to my throat, and sh-she said that if I did not take the outsider in, she would kill me."

Panaya had told him to be honest, but every good story needed a pinch of embellishment.

Two foot soldiers kept watch close by. Iron helms covered their heads and napes, secured by green cords that tied beneath their chins. In unison, they slid the screens aside, letting two more soldiers into the room. They held someone between them.

"Was it this woman?" the Governor asked.

Her hair clumped around her shoulders. One of her eyes was swollen closed. From the bloated lip on the soldier to her left, she had fought. Someone gallant would deny it.

"Yes," Niclays admitted.

She gave him a hateful look.

"Yes," the Governor echoed. "She is a musician in a theatre in Cape Hisan. The all-honored Warlord permits some Seiikinese artists to provide entertainment and conversation on certain days in Orisima." He raised his eyebrows. "Have you ever been visited?"

Niclays managed a strained smile. "I have generally been content with my own company."

"Good," the woman spat at him. "Then you can fuck yourself, silver-loving liar."

One of the soldiers struck her. "Quiet," she snapped.

Niclays flinched. The woman crumpled to the floor, where she drew in her shoulders and pressed a hand to her cheek.

"Thank you for confirming that this is the woman." The Governor drew his lacquered writing box toward him. "She will say nothing of how an outsider came to be on this island. Do you know?"

Niclays swallowed. His saliva felt as thick as pottage.

Honesty be damned. No matter how far away she was, he could not implicate Truyde.

"No," he lied. "He would not say."

The Governor glanced over the tops of his eyeglasses. His small, dark eyes had pouches beneath them.

"Learnèd Doctor Roos," he said, grinding an inkstick with water, "I respect your knowledge, so I will be frank. If you can tell me nothing more, this woman will be tortured."

The woman began to tremble.

"It is not our custom to use such methods except under the most serious circumstances. We have enough evidence to prove that she is involved in a conspiracy that may threaten the whole of Seiiki. If she brought the outsider to Orisima, she must know where he came from in the first place. Therefore, she must either be in league with smugglers, which is punishable by death . . . or she is protecting someone else, someone who has yet to be revealed." The Governor selected a brush from his box. "If she has been used, the all-honored Warlord may show mercy. Are you certain you know nothing more about Sulyard's purpose here, or who might have helped him enter?"

Niclays looked at the woman on the floor. One dark eye stared up from behind her hair.

"I am certain."

The moment he said it, he felt as if another truncheon had struck the breath from him.

"Take her to the jailhouse," the Governor said. As the soldiers hauled her up, the woman began to gasp in panic. For the first time, Niclays saw how young she was. No older than Truyde.

Jannart would have been ashamed. He bowed his head, disgusted at the feel of his own skin.

"Thank you, learnèd Doctor Roos," the Governor said. "I suspected this state of affairs, but I required your confirmation."

When the footsteps had receded from the corridor outside, the Governor spent several minutes with his head bent over his letter, during which Niclays dared not speak.

"Your Seiikinese is very good. I understand you taught anatomy in Orisima," the Governor finally remarked, making Niclays start. "How did you find our students?"

It was as if the woman had never existed.

"I learned as much from them as they did from me," Niclays said truthfully, and the Governor smiled. Seizing the opportunity, Niclays added, "I am, however, very short on ingredients for . . . other work, which the long-honored High Prince of Mentendon assured me would be provided. I also fear that the honored Chief Officer of Orisima has destroyed my apparatus."

"The honorable Chief Officer can be . . . overzealous." The Governor set down his brush. "You cannot return to Orisima until this matter is closed. It must not be known that a trespasser was able to breach its walls, and we must cleanse the trading post to ensure there is no trace of the red sickness. I'm afraid I must place you under house arrest in Ginura while we conduct our investigation."

Niclays stared at him.

He could not be this fortunate. Instead of torture, they were giving him freedom.

"Ginura," he repeated.

"For a few weeks. It is best if we remove you from the situation."

Niclays sensed the issue was diplomatic. He had sheltered a trespasser. A Seiikinese citizen in his position would be put to death for that crime, but the execution of a Mentish settler would sour the delicate alliance with the House of Lievelyn.

"Yes." He tried to look contrite. "Yes, honored Governor, of course. I understand."

"By the time you return, I pray all this will be resolved. To thank you for your information, I will make sure you receive the ingredients you need," the Governor said, "but you must be silent about all that has occurred." He dealt Niclays a penetrating look. "Is this acceptable to you, learnèd Doctor Roos?"

"Perfectly. I thank you for your kindness." Niclays hesitated. "And Sulyard?"

"The trespasser is in the jailhouse. We were waiting for him to display any symptoms of the red sickness," the Governor said. "If he does not reveal who helped him reach Seiiki, he will also be tortured."

Niclays wet his lips.

"Perhaps I could help you," he said, even as he wondered why he was willingly asking for deeper entanglement in this mess. "As a fellow man of Virtudom, I may be able to make Sulyard see the sense in confessing—if you would let me visit him before I go."

The Governor appeared to consider this.

"I do not like bloodshed where it can be avoided. Perhaps tomorrow," he conceded. "For now, I must send word of this unfortunate situation to the all-honored Warlord." He returned his attention to his writing. "Rest well this night, learnèd Doctor Roos."

13

East

The next trial was with knives. Like the others, it was observed by the Sea General and a group of strangers in blue robes. Other members of Clan Miduchi, who had undergone their own trials fifty years ago. The people whose legacy Tané might share if her body did not fail her.

Her eyes sat like pufferfish in her skull. As she picked up each knife, her hands felt slick and clumsy. She still performed better than all the apprentices but Turosa, whose skill with these blades was what had earned him such great renown at the North House.

Onren strode into the hall just after Turosa had achieved a perfect score. Her hair was loose and uncombed. The Sea General raised his eyebrows, but she only bowed to him and approached the knives.

Kanperu appeared next. The Sea General raised his eyebrows even higher. Onren took hold of a blade, found her stance, and threw it across the hall at the first scarecrow.

Every knife found its mark.

"A perfect score," the Sea General remarked, "but do not be late again, honorable Onren."

"Yes, honored Sea General."

That night, the sea guardians were woken by the servants and escorted, still in their sleep robes, to a line of palanquins. Ensconced in hers, Tané chewed her nails to the quick.

They emerged from their palanquins beside a vast spring-fed lake in the forest. Raindrops pinked its surface.

"Members of the High Sea Guard are often woken in the night to answer threats to Seiiki. They must swim better than fish, for they may be separated at any time from their ship, or from their dragon," the Sea General said. "Eight dancing pearls have been scattered in this lake. Should you retrieve one, it will encourage me to rank you higher."

Turosa was already undressing. Slowly, Tané removed her sleep robe and waded in up to her waist.

Six and twenty sea guardians and only eight pearls. They would be hard to find in the darkness.

She closed her eyes and released the thought. When the Sea General gave the order, she sliced into the lake.

Water enfolded her. Clear, sweet water, cool against her skin. Her hair rippled around her like seaweed as she turned, straining for a glimpse of silver-green.

Onren entered the lake with barely a splash. She dived, snatched her treasure, and glided upward in one graceful arc. She swam like a dragon.

Determined to be next, Tané ventured deeper. The spring, she reasoned, would waft the pearls west. Turning, she descended smoothly to the lakebed and swam using only her legs, ghosting her hands through the silt as she went.

Her chest was tight by the time her fingers brushed a tiny bead. She surfaced almost in unison with Turosa, who shook back his hair and held his pearl up to inspect it.

"Dancing pearls. Worn by the god-chosen," he said. "Once these were symbols of heritage, of history." He bared a knife of a smile. "Now they adorn so many peasants, they might as well be dirt."

Tané looked him in the eye and said, "You swam well, honorable Turosa."

That made him chuckle. "Oh, villager. I'm going to make such a fool of you that they'll never let a peasant soil Clan Miduchi again." He swam past. "Get ready to fall."

He struck out for the edge of the lake. Tané followed at a distance.

There was a rumor that in the final trial, each principal appren-tice would always fight another. She had already dueled Onren. Her opponent would either be Turosa or Dumusa.

If it was the former, he would do everything in his power to break her.

Niclays spent a restless night in the Governor of Cape Hisan's mansion. The bedding was far more luxurious than what he had in Orisima, but rain battered the tiled roof and would not give him peace. On top of that, it was insufferably humid, as it always was in the Seiikinese summer.

Sometime in the small hours, he rose from the clammy heap of bedding and moved the window screen aside. The breeze was warm and thick as caudle, but at least he could see the stars. And think.

No educated person could believe in ghosts. Quacks professed that the spirits of the dead lived in an element called *ether*—pure drivel. Yet there was a whisper in his ear that he knew to be Jannart, telling him that what he had done to that musician was a crime.

Ghosts were the voices the dead left behind. Echoes of a soul taken too soon.

Jannart would have lied to keep the musician safe. Then again, Jannart had been good at lying. Most of his life had been a perform-ance. Thirty years of lying to Truyde. To Oscarde.

And of course, to Aleidine.

Niclays shivered. A chill rumbled through his belly when he remembered the look in her eyes at the entombment. She had known all along. She had known and said nothing.

It is not her fault my heart belongs to you, Jannart had told him once, and he had spoken true. Like many unions among those of noble blood, theirs had been arranged by their families. The betrothal had been sealed the day Jannart turned twenty, a year before Niclays had met him.

He had not been able to face going to the wedding. The knot in the strings of their fates had tortured him. If only he had arrived at court sooner, they might have been companions.

He snorted. As if the Marquess of Zeedeur would have been allowed to wed a penniless nobody from Rozentun. Aleidine had been a commoner, but her hand in marriage had come with jewels on it. Niclays, fresh out of university, would have brought the family nothing but debt.

Aleidine must be past sixty by now. Her auburn hair would be laced with silver, her mouth framed by lines. Oscarde was at least forty. Saint, how the years flew.

The breeze did nothing to cool him down. Defeated, he closed the screen and lay back on the bedding.

The warmth basted his skin. He willed himself to sleep, but his mind refused to quiet, and a low fire burned in his ankle.

By morning, there was no sign of the storm ending. He watched it water the grounds of the mansion. The servants brought him bean curd, grilled loach, and barley tea to break his fast.

At noon, a servant informed him that the Governor had granted his request. He was to visit Triam Sulyard in the jailhouse and mine what information he could from the boy. The servants also provided him with a new walking cane, made of a stronger, lighter wood. He begged a little water of them. They brought it to him in a gourd.

A closed palanquin took him to the jailhouse at dusk. Safe inside his box, Niclays peered through the blinds.

In seven years, he had never taken a step into Cape Hisan. He had heard its music and its chatter, glimpsed its lights—like fallen stars—and longed to walk its streets, but it had remained a mystery to him. His world had been closed in a fist of high walls.

The lanternlight revealed a bustling city. In Orisima, he had been surrounded by reminders of Mentendon. Now he remembered just how far from home he was. No Western settlement smelled of cedarwood or sinking incense. No Western settlement sold squid ink or iridescent floats for fishing.

And of course, no Western city paid tribute to dragons. Signs of their presence were everywhere. Merchants touted amulets on every corner, promising luck and succor from the lords of sea and rain. Almost every street housed a driftwood shrine and a basin of salt water.

The palanquin stopped outside the jailhouse. Once it was unlocked, Niclays climbed out and slapped a gnat away from his face. A pair of prison sentinels hurried him through the gate.

The first thing that hit him was the eye-watering odor of shit and piss. He gathered one sleeve to his nose and mouth. When they passed the execution ground, the strength deserted his legs. Rotting heads were displayed on a stand, tongues swollen like curl grubs.

Sulyard had been hidden in an underground room. He lay prone in his cell, a cloth around his waist. The sentinels were good enough to hand Niclays a lantern before they left.

Their footsteps receded into the black. Niclays knelt and gripped one of the wooden bars.

"Sulyard." He rapped his cane on the floor. "Look lively."

Nothing. Niclays slotted his cane through the bars and gave Sulyard a firm prod. He stirred.

"Truyde," he murmured.

"Sorry to disappoint. It's Roos."

There was a pause. "Doctor Roos." Sulyard unfolded himself. "I thought I was dreaming."

"Would that you were."

Sulyard was in bad shape. His face had bloated like dough in the oven, and his brow had been inked with the characters for *trespasser*. Dried blood laddered his back and thighs.

Sulyard had no protection from a prince across the sea. Niclays might have been shocked by the brutality once, but the nations of Virtudom used crueler means to mangle the truth from prisoners.

"Sulyard," Niclays said, "tell me what you told the questioners."

"Only the truth." Sulyard coughed. "That I came ashore to beg the Warlord for help."

"Not about that. About how you reached Orisima." Niclays pressed closer. "The other woman—the first woman you saw, the one on the beach. Did you tell them about her?"

"No."

It was all Niclays could do not to wring the blockhead by the throat. Instead, he opened the gourd.

"Drink." He pushed it between the bars. "The first woman took you to the theatre district instead of reporting you. It was her crime that landed you in Orisima. You must be able to describe her—her face, her clothes, *something*. Help yourself, Sulyard."

A blood-streaked hand reached for the gourd. "She had long, dark hair, and a scar at the top of her left cheek. Like a fishhook." Sulyard drank. "I think . . . that she was of an age with me, or younger. She wore sandals and a coat of gray cloth over a black tunic."

"Offer this information to your captors," Niclays urged. "In exchange for your life. Help them find her, and they may show mercy."

"I beseeched them to listen to me." Sulyard seemed delirious. "I said I came from Her Majesty, that I was her ambassador, that my ship foundered. None of them would listen."

"Even if you *were* a real ambassador, which you clearly are not, they would not welcome you." Niclays glanced over his shoulder. The sentinels would soon come back for him. "Listen carefully now, Sulyard. The Governor of Cape Hisan is sending me to the capital while this matter is investigated. Let *me* take your message to the Warlord."

Fresh tears filled his eyes. "You would do that for me, Doctor Roos?"

"If you tell me more about your undertaking. Tell me why you believe Sabran needs an alliance with Seiiki."

He had no idea if he would be able to keep his word, but he needed to know exactly why this boy was here. What Truyde had conspired with him to do.

"Thank you." Sulyard reached between the bars and took Niclays by the hand. "Thank you, Doctor Roos. The Knight of Fellowship blessed me with your company."

"I'm sure," Niclays said dryly.

He waited. Sulyard squeezed his hand and lowered his voice to the barest whisper.

"Truyde and I," he began, "we— we believe the Nameless One will awaken very soon. That the endurance of the House of Berethnet was never what kept him imprisoned. That come what may, he will return, and that is why his servants have been stirring. They are answering his call."

His lips trembled as he spoke. Expressing the idea that the House of Berethnet was not what kept the Nameless One at bay was high treason in Virtudom.

"What led you to believe this?" Niclays asked, stumped. "What doomsinger has frightened you, boy?"

"Not a doomsinger. Books. Your books, Doctor Roos."

"*Mine?*"

"Yes. The books on alchemy you left behind," Sulyard whispered. "Truyde and I were planning to find you in Orisima. The Knight of Fellowship took me to your side. Do you not see that this is a divine mission?"

"No, I do not, you witless cabbage."

"But—"

"You really thought the rulers of the East would be more sympathetic to this mad-born proposal than Sabran?" Niclays sneered. "You thought you would cross the Abyss and risk your heads ... because the two of you leafed through a few books on alchemy. Books that take alchemists decades, if not lifetimes, to understand. If they ever do."

He almost pitied Sulyard for his folly. He was young and love-drunk. The boy must have convinced himself that he was like Lord Wulf Glenn or Sir Antor Dale, the romantic heroes of Inysh history, and must honor his lady by charging headlong into danger.

"Please, Doctor Roos, I beg you, hear me. Truyde *does* understand those books. She believes there is a natural balance in the world, as ancient alchemists did," Sulyard prattled on. "She *believes* in your work, and she believes she has found a way to apply it to our world. To our history."

Natural balance. He was referring to the words scored into the long-lost Tablet of Rumelabar, words that had fascinated alchemists for centuries.

> *What is below must be balanced by what is above,*
> *and in this is the precision of the universe.*
> *Fire ascends from the earth, light descends from the sky.*
> *Too much of one doth inflame the other,*
> *and in this is the extinction of the universe.*

"Sulyard," Niclays said through his teeth, "no one understands that wretched tablet. This is guesswork and folly."

"I was not convinced at first, either. I was in denial. But when I saw the passion in Truyde—" Sulyard tightened his grip. "She explained it to me. That when the wyrms lost their flame and fell into their long sleep, the Eastern dragons grew strong. Now they are losing their strength once more, and the Draconic breeds are awakening. Do you not see? It is a cycle."

Niclays looked again at that earnest face. Sulyard was not the author of this mission.

Truyde. It *was* Truyde. Her heart, and her mind, were the soil it had sprung from. How like her grandsire she had become. The obsession that had killed him had lived on in his blood.

"You are both fools," he said hoarsely.

"No."

"Yes." His voice cracked. "If you know the dragons are losing strength, why on earth do you want help from them?"

"Because they are stronger than *us*, Doctor Roos. And we have a better chance with them than we do alone. If we are to have a hope of victory—"

"Sulyard," Niclays said, softer, "stop. The Warlord will not hear this. Just as Sabran will not hear it."

"I wanted to try. The Knight of Courage t-teaches us to raise our voices when others fear to speak." Sulyard shook his head, tears welling. "Were we wrong to hope, Doctor Roos?"

Suddenly Niclays felt exhausted. This man was going to die in vain a world away from home. There was only one thing to do. Lie.

"It is true that they trade with Mentendon. Perhaps they will listen." Niclays patted the grimy hand that held his. "Forgive an old man his cynicism, Sulyard. I see your passion. I am convinced of your sincerity. I will ask for an audience with the Warlord and put your case to him."

Sulyard pushed his weight on to his elbow. "Doctor Roos—" His voice thickened. "Will they not kill you?"

"I will risk it. The Seiikinese respect my knowledge as an anatomist, and I am a lawful settler," Niclays said. "Let me try. I suspect the worst they will do to me is laugh."

Tears filled those bloodshot eyes. "I do not know how to thank you."

"I have a way." Niclays grasped his shoulder. "At least try to save yourself. When they come for you, tell them about the woman on the beach. Swear to me that you will tell them."

Sulyard nodded. "I swear it." He pressed a kiss to Niclays's hand. "The Saint bless you, Doctor Roos. There is a seat for you at his Great Table beside the Knight of Courage."

"He can keep it," Niclays muttered. He could envision no greater torment than feasting with a circle of dead braggarts for eternity.

As for the Saint, he would have his work cut out if he meant to save this wretch.

He heard the sentinels approaching and withdrew. Sulyard set his cheek on the floor.

"Thank you, Doctor Roos. For giving me hope."

"Good luck, Triam the Fool," Niclays said quietly, and allowed himself to be marched back into the rain.

Another palanquin was waiting at the jailhouse gates. It was far less grand than the one that had taken him to the Governor, borne by four new chair-carriers. One of them bowed to him.

"Learnèd Doctor Roos," she said, "we have orders to return you to the honored Governor of Cape Hisan, so you might report what you have learned. After that, we will take you to Ginura."

Niclays nodded, tired to his bones. He would tell the Governor of Cape Hisan only that the outsider wished to help identify a second person who had aided him. That was where his involvement ended.

As he hoisted himself into the palanquin, Niclays wondered if he would ever see Triam Sulyard again. For Truyde's sake, he hoped so.

For his own sake, he rather hoped not.

14

West

Shortly after the heralds took news of the betrothal across Inys, Aubrecht Lievelyn sent word that he was preparing to sail with his retinue, which comprised some eight hundred people. The days that followed were a round-wind of preparation such as Ead had never known.

Food came by the bargeload from the Leas and the Downs. The Glade family sent casks of wine from their vineyards. The Extraordinary Chamberers, who might be asked to serve in the Upper Household on special occasions—significant anniversaries, the Holy Feasts—took up residence at court. New gowns were made for the queen and her ladies. Every corner of Ascalon Palace was spruced and polished, down to the last candlestick. For the first time, it seemed Queen Sabran was serious about accepting a suit. Excitement burned through the palace like a ground fire.

Ead tried her utmost to keep pace. Though the fever had drained her, the Royal Physician had personally approved her return to duty. Yet more proof that Inysh physicians were quacks.

At least Truyde utt Zeedeur was keeping her head down. Ead had heard no more rumors about sorcery.

For now, she was safe.

There were nearly a thousand residents at court at any time of the year, but as Ead traversed the palace with baskets of flowers and armfuls of cloth-of-silver, she seemed to be passing more and more people. She watched every day for the golden banners of the Ersyr, and the man who would come under them, disguised as an ambassador to King Jantar and Queen Saiyma. Chassar uq-Ispad, who had brought her to Inys.

First came the guests from elsewhere in the queendom. The Earls Provincial and their families were among the most recognizable. As she entered the cloisters one morning, Ead spotted Lord Ranulf Heath the Younger, cousin to the late Queen Rosarian, on the other side of the garth. He was deep in conversation with Lady Igrain Crest. As she often did at court, Ead stopped to listen.

"And how is your companion, my lord?" Crest was saying.

"Sore disappointed not to be here, Your Grace, but he will join us soon," Heath replied. His skin was brown and freckled, his beard shot with gray. "How happy that Her Majesty will soon know the same joy I found in companionship."

"We can only hope. The Duke of Courtesy believes the alliance will serve to tighten the Chainmail of Virtudom," Crest said, "though whether his intuition is correct has yet to be seen."

"I would hope his intuition is unparalleled," Heath said, chuckling, "given his ... particular role."

"Oh, there are things that even Seyton misses," Crest remarked, a rare smile on her face. "How thin his hair is getting, for instance. Even a hawk cannot see the back of its own head." Heath stifled a laugh. "Of course, we all pray that Her Majesty will soon be delivered of a daughter."

"Aye, but she's young, Your Grace, and so is Lievelyn. Give them time to get to know each other first."

Ead had to agree. Few Inysh seemed to care whether Sabran and Lievelyn knew each other from a stuffed capon, so long as they were wed.

"It is vital that we have an heir as soon as possible," Crest said, as if on cue. "Her Majesty knows her duty on that front."

"Well, no one has guided Her Majesty in her duty better than you, Your Grace."

"You are too kind. She has been my pride and joy. Alas," Crest said, "that mine is no longer the only counsel she heeds. Our young queen is determined to go her own way."

"As we all must, Your Grace."

They parted. Ead scarcely had time to draw back before the duchess strode around the corner, almost headlong into her.

"Mistress Duryan." Crest recovered. "Good morrow, my dear."

Ead curtsied. "Your Grace." Crest nodded and left the cloisters. Ead walked in the opposite direction.

Crest might well quip about Combe, but in truth, the Night Hawk missed nothing. It struck Ead as extraordinary that he could have failed to see who was hiring the cutthroats.

She slowed as a possibility occurred to her. For the first time, she considered that Combe himself might be the architect behind the attacks. He would have had the means to arrange them. To bring people unseen into the court, just as he swept others out. He had also taken charge of interrogating the surviving cutthroats. And disposing of them.

There was no reason Combe should wish Sabran dead. He was a descendant of the Holy Retinue, his power tied to the House of Berethnet ... but perhaps he believed he could grasp even more if the Queen of Inys fell. If Sabran died childless, the people would give way to fear that the Nameless One was coming. In chaos like that, the Night Hawk could rise.

Yet each cutthroat had botched the job. Ead did not sense his hand in that. Neither was she convinced he would risk the instability of an Inys without the House of Berethnet. The spymaster did not work that way. He left nothing to chance.

It was when she was halfway across the Sundial Garden that it struck her.

That the blundering had been deliberate.

She thought back to how staged each attack had appeared. How each cutthroat had given the game away. Even the last one had not gone straight for the kill. He had taken his time.

In this she could find Combe. Perhaps he had never meant to kill Sabran, but to manipulate her. To remind her of her mortality, and the importance of the heir. To frighten her into accepting Lievelyn. It fitted with his way of arranging the court to look as he desired it.

Except that he had not anticipated Ead. She had stopped most of the cutthroats before they could get close enough to terrify Sabran.

That must be why he had given the last one the key to the Secret Stair. To bolster their chances of reaching the Great Bedchamber.

Ead permitted herself a smile. No wonder Combe wanted to find the anonymous protector. If she had it right, she was killing off *his* hirelings.

Of course, all this was speculation. She had no proof of it, just as she had no proof that Combe had exiled Loth. Yet she knew in her gut that she was on the right path.

The marriage to Lievelyn was all but sealed. Combe was satisfied. If no cutthroats returned, then her instinct was right, and Sabran was safe until the next time she vexed Combe. Then the Night Hawk would take flight again, dark wings spread over the throne.

Ead meant to clip them. All she needed was the evidence—and the opportunity.

Guests continued to pour in. The families of the Dukes Spiritual. Knights-errant, who handled petty crimes and sought out sleeping wyrms to slay. Sanctarians in long-sleeved herigauts. Barons and baronets. Mayors and magistrates.

Soon the long-awaited visitors from the Kingdom of Hróth began to arrive. King Raunus of the House of Hraustr had sent a host of high-born representatives to witness the union. Sabran welcomed them with genuine affection, and the palace was soon ringing with Northern songs and laughter.

Not long ago, there would have been Yscals here. Ead remembered well the last visit by representatives of the House of Vetalda, when the Donmata Marosa had come for the celebration of a thousand years of Berethnet rule. Now their absence was another reminder of the uncertain future.

On the morning Aubrecht Lievelyn was due to reach Ascalon Palace, the most important courtiers and guests crowded into the Presence Chamber. Most of the Virtues Council were here. Arbella Glenn had recovered from her illness, much to the regret of certain ambitious Ladies of the Privy Chamber, and now stood to the right of the throne.

Arbella looked frail at the best of times, with her rheumy eyes and fingers bent from needlework, but Ead was sure she ought not to have risen from bed today. Though she smiled like a proud mother at her queen, there was a quiet sadness about her.

The rest of the room was thrumming like a skep. Sabran waited for her betrothed in front of her throne, flanked by the six Dukes Spiritual, who were resplendent in their cloaks and livery collars. She wore a simple gown of crimson velvet and satin, a rich contrast to the nightfall of her hair. No ruff or jewels. Ead studied her from her position with the other Ladies of the Privy Chamber.

She was most beautiful like this. The Inysh seemed to think her trappings were her beauty, but in truth, they concealed it.

Sabran caught her gaze. Ead looked away.

"Where are your parents?" she said to Margret, who was standing on her right.

"They are pleading Papa's indisposition, but I think it is because Mama has no wish to see Combe." Margret spoke behind her peacock-feather fan. "He told her in a letter that Loth went to Cárscaro of his own free will. She will suspect otherwise."

Lady Annes Beck had been a Lady of the Bedchamber to Queen Rosarian. "She must know well the machinations of this court."

"Better than most. I see Lady Honeybrook has not come, either." Margret shook her head. "Poor Kit."

The Earl of Honeybrook stood with the other members of the Virtues Council. He did not look troubled by the absence of his son, who he resembled in every way but the mouth, which never smiled.

Trumpets proclaimed the coming of the High Prince. Even the fine tapestries that draped the Presence Chamber seemed to quiver with anticipation. Ead glanced toward Combe, who was smiling like a cat with a mouse pinned beneath its paw.

Her ribs clenched in revulsion at the sight of him. Even if he was not the architect behind the cutthroats, he had sent Loth into life-threatening peril to clear the way for this marriage to take place, based on rumors with not a whit of substance. He could rot.

Standard-bearers and trumpeters paraded into the Presence Chamber. Necks craned for a glimpse of the man who was to be prince consort of Inys. Linora Payling stood on her tiptoes, fanning herself as if she would swoon on the spot. Even Ead allowed herself a flutter of curiosity.

Sabran drew back her shoulders. The fanfare swelled, and the High Prince of the Free State of Mentendon appeared.

Aubrecht Lievelyn had the strong arms and broad shoulders Ead would have expected of a seasoned knight. Clean-shaven and even taller than Sabran, he had nothing of the dormouse about him. His waving hair gleamed like copper as he walked into a beam of sunlight. A cloak was slung over his shoulder, and he wore a black jerkin over a full-sleeved ivory doublet.

"Oh, he is *so* handsome," Linora breathed.

When he reached his betrothed, Lievelyn knelt before her and lowered his head.

"Your Majesty."

Her face was a mask. "Your Royal Highness," she said, and presented her hand. "Welcome to the Queendom of Inys."

Lievelyn kissed her coronation ring.

"Majesty," he said, "I am already enamored with your city, and humbled by your acceptance of my suit. It is the greatest honor to be in your presence."

His voice was quiet. Ead was surprised by his reserve. Usually a suitor would be piling unctuous praise on to the royal person the moment he opened his mouth, but Lievelyn just looked with dark eyes at the Queen of Inys, the figurehead of his religion.

Sabran, whose eyebrows were raised, took back her hand.

"The Dukes Spiritual, scions of the Holy Retinue," she said. They bowed to Lievelyn, and he dipped his head lower in return.

"You are most welcome here, Your Royal Highness," Combe said warmly. "We have long anticipated this meeting."

"Rise," Sabran said. "Please."

Lievelyn obeyed. There was a brief silence as the companions-to-be took the measure of each other.

"We understand Your Royal Highness has visited Ascalon once before," Sabran said.

"Yes, Majesty, for the marriage of your parents. I was only two years old, but my mother, who was also present, spoke often of how beautiful Queen Rosarian looked that day, and how the people were praying that she would soon be delivered of a daughter as gracious and resilient as she. And so you have proved to be. When I heard that Your Majesty had cowed the right wing of the Nameless One, it only confirmed what I knew of your strength."

Sabran did not smile, but her eyes shone. "We had expected to meet your noble sisters."

"They will come soon, Your Majesty. Princess Betriese was taken ill, and the others would not leave her side."

"We are sorry for it." Sabran held out her hand again, this time to the ambassador. "Welcome back, Oscarde."

"Majesty." The ambassador stooped to kiss the ring. "If I may, I would like to present my mother, Lady Aleidine Teldan utt Kantmarkt, Dowager Duchess of Zeedeur."

The Dowager Duchess curtsied. "Your Majesty." She was a striking woman, possessed of rich copper hair and hooded eyes. Crow's feet were etched into her olive skin. "What a great honor."

"You are welcome to Ascalon, Your Grace. As are you," Sabran added to someone behind her, "Your Excellency."

When Lievelyn stood aside, Ead drew a breath. The ambassador who had just entered the Presence Chamber wore a golden head-dress and a cloak of tinseled satin, dyed the rich blue of larkspur. Behind him were the Ersyri and Lasian delegations.

"Majesty." With a smile, Chassar uq-Ispad bowed. Faces turned to look at this mountain of a man, with his swathed head and his full black beard. "It has been a very long time."

He was here.

After all these years, he had come back.

"It has," Sabran said. "We began to think His Most High Majesty would send no representatives."

"My master would never insult Your Majesty in such a manner. King Jantar sends his congratulations on your betrothal, as does High Ruler Kagudo, whose delegation joined us in Perchling."

Kagudo was High Ruler of the Domain of Lasia, head of the oldest royal house in the known world. She was a direct descendant of Selinu the Oathkeeper, and was thus a blood relative of the Mother. Ead had never met her, but she often wrote to the Prioress.

"Fortunately," Chassar continued, "Prince Aubrecht had just docked when we came ashore, so I was able to enjoy his good company for the remainder of the journey."

"We hope to enjoy Prince Aubrecht's good company for the foreseeable future," Sabran said.

Some of the maids of honor hid their giggles behind their fans. Lievelyn smiled again.

The courtesies went on, Sabran never taking her eyes off her betrothed, and he never taking his eyes off her. Chassar glanced at Ead and gave her the very smallest of nods before looking away.

Once the audience had reached its end, Sabran invited her guests to the tiltyard to watch the lance games. Challengers would joust in view of a thousand citizens from the city. They just about lost their heads at the sight of Sabran, cheering for the queen who had banished a High Western. She was Glorian Shieldheart come again.

"Hail, Sabran the Magnificent," they shouted. "Long live the House of Berethnet!" The roars of appreciation loudened as Lievelyn sat beside her in the Royal Box.

"Protect us, Your Majesty!"

"Majesty, we take heart from your courage!"

Ead found a place on the shaded benches with the other ladies-in-waiting and watched the crowd, waiting for a crossbow or pistol to appear in the stands. Her siden was all but extinguished, but she had knives enough for a slew of cutthroats.

Chassar was on the other side of the Royal Box. She would have to wait until after Sabran had retired to speak with him.

"Saint, I thought that introduction would never end." Margret took a glass of strawberry wine from a page. Two knights-errant lowered their visors. "I do believe Sabran likes her Red Prince. She tried to hide it, but I think she is already smitten."

"Lievelyn certainly is," Ead said, distracted.

Combe was in the Royal Box. She scoured him with her gaze, trying to work out whether he looked at Sabran as though she were his queen, or a piece to be moved on a gameboard.

Margret followed her line of sight. "I know," she said quietly. "He has gotten away with murder." She sipped her wine. "I detest his retainers, too. For abetting him."

"Sabran *must* know," Ead murmured. "Can she not think of some way to be rid of him?"

"Much as it pains me to admit it, Inys needs his intelligencers. And if Sab ousted him without very good reason, other nobles might feel that their positions were just as fragile. She cannot afford malcontent, not when there is such uncertainty about the threat of Yscalin." Margret grimaced as the knights-errant broke their lances on each other, drawing a roar from the stands. "Nobles have revolted in the past, after all."

Ead nodded. "The Gorse Hill Rebellion."

"Aye. At least there are laws to lessen the danger of it happening again. Once, you would have seen Combe's retainers strutting about in *his* livery, as if their first loyalty were not to their queen. All they can do now is wear his badge." She pursed her lips. "I *hate* that the symbol of his virtue is a book, you know. Books are too good for him."

The two challengers wheeled to face each other again. Igrain Crest, who had been talking to a baron, now crossed to the Royal Box and sat in the row behind Sabran and Lievelyn. She leaned down to say something to the queen, who smiled at her.

"I hear Igrain is against this marriage," Margret said, "though pleased it might yield the long-awaited heir." She lifted an eyebrow. "She was Protector of the Realm in all but name when Sab was a child. A second mother. And yet if rumor has it right, she would prefer her to be wed to someone with one foot on the corpse road."

"She may yet get her wish," Ead said.

Margret looked at her. "You think Sab will change her mind about the Red Prince."

"Until the ring is on her finger, I think there is every chance of it."

"Court has made you cynical, Ead Duryan. We might be about to witness a romance to rival that of Rosarian the First and Sir Antor Dale." Margret linked an arm through hers. "You must be pleased to see Ambassador uq-Ispad after all these years."

Ead smiled. "You have no idea."

The games went on for several hours. Ead stayed under the awnings with Margret, never taking her gaze off the stands. Finally, Lord Lemand Fynch, the acting Duke of Temperance, was declared the champion. After giving her cousin a ring as a prize, Sabran retired to escape the heat.

At five of the clock, Ead found herself ensconced in the Privy Chamber, where Sabran was playing the virginals. While Roslain and Katryen whispered to one another, and poor Arbella fumbled her needlework, Ead pretended to be absorbed in a prayer book.

The queen had paid more attention to her than usual since her fever. She had been invited several times to play cards and listen to the Ladies of the Bedchamber as they kept Sabran abreast of goings-on at court. Ead had noticed that they sometimes spoke well of certain people and advised Sabran to show them greater favor than she had. If there was no bribery involved in these recommendations, then Ead was Queen of the Ersyr.

"Ead."

She looked up. "Majesty?"

"Come to me."

Sabran patted a stool. When Ead sat, the queen leaned toward her conspiratorially. "It seems the Red Prince is less like a dormouse than we thought. What do you make of him?"

Ead felt Roslain watching her.

"He seemed courteous and gallant, madam. If he is a mouse," she said lightly, "then we may rest assured that he is a prince among mice."

Sabran laughed. A rare sound. Like a vein of gold hidden in rock, loath to show itself.

"Indeed. Whether he will make me a good consort has yet to be seen." She ghosted a finger over the virginals. "I am not yet wed, of course. A betrothal can always be annulled."

"You should do as you see fit. There will always be voices telling you what to do, and how to act, but it is you who wears the crown," Ead said. "Let His Royal Highness prove that he is worthy of a place by your side. He must earn that honor, for it is the greatest one of all."

Sabran studied her.

"You do speak comely words," she remarked. "I wonder if you mean them."

"Mine are honest words, madam. All courts will fall prey to affectation and deceit, often veiled as courtesy," Ead said, "but I like to believe that I speak from the heart."

"We all speak from the heart to Her Majesty," Roslain snapped. Her eyes were bright with anger. "Are you implying that courtesy is a kind of artifice, Mistress Duryan? Because the Knight of Courtesy would—"

"Ros," Sabran said, "I was not addressing you."

Roslain fell silent, plainly stunned.

In the tense period that followed, one of the Knights of the Body entered the Privy Chamber.

"Majesty." He bowed. "His Excellency, Ambassador uq-Ispad, asks if you might spare Mistress Duryan for a short while. If it please you, he is waiting for her on the Peaceweaver Terrace."

Sabran brought her cascade of hair to one side of her neck.

"I think she can be spared," she said. "You are excused, Ead, but be back in time for orisons."

"Yes, madam." Ead rose at once. "Thank you."

As she left the Privy Chamber, she avoided looking at the other women. She ought not to make an enemy of Roslain Crest if she could help it.

Ead made her way out of the Queen Tower and ascended to the south-facing battlements of the palace, where the Peaceweaver Terrace overlooked the River Limber. Her heart chirred like a bee-moth. For the first time in eight years, she was going to speak to someone from the Priory. Not just anyone, but Chassar, who had raised her.

The evening sun had transfigured the river to molten gold. Ead crossed the bridge and stepped onto the tiled floor of the terrace. Chassar was waiting at the balustrade. At the sound of her footsteps, he turned and smiled, and she went to him like a child to a father.

"Chassar."

She buried her face against his chest. His arms encircled her.

"Eadaz." He placed a kiss on the top of her head. "There, light of my eyes. I am here."

"I have not heard that name in so long," she said thickly in Selinyi. "For the love of the Mother, Chassar, I thought you had abandoned me for good."

"Never. You know that leaving you here was like having a rib wrenched from my side." They walked together to a canopy of sweetbriar and honeysuckle. "Sit with me."

Chassar must have reserved the terrace for his private use. Ead sat at a table, where a platter was piled high with sun-dried Ersyri fruit, and he poured her a glass of pale Rumelabari wine.

"I had all this brought across the sea for you," he said. "I thought you might like a small reminder of the South."

"After eight years, it would be easy to forget that the South even existed." She gave him a hard look. "I had no word. You did not answer *one* of my letters."

His smile faded. "Forgive my long silence, Eadaz." He sighed. "I would have written, but the Prioress decided that you should be left alone to learn Inysh ways in peace."

Ead wanted to be angry, but this was the man who had sat her on his lap when she was small and taught her to read, and her relief at seeing him outweighed her vexation.

"The task you were given was to protect Sabran," Chassar said, "and you have honored the Mother by keeping her alive and unharmed. It cannot have been easy." He paused. "The cutthroats that stalk her. You said in your letters that they carried Yscali-made blades."

"Yes. Parrying daggers, specifically, from Cárscaro."

"Parrying daggers," Chassar repeated. "A strange choice of weapon for murder."

"I thought the same. A weapon used for defense."

"Hm." Chassar stroked his beard, as he often did when he was thinking. "Perhaps this is as simple as it looks, and King Sigoso is hiring Inysh subjects to kill a queen he despises . . . or perhaps these blades are a rotten fish. Covering the scent of the true architect."

"I think the latter. Someone at court is involved," Ead said. "Finding the daggers would have been possible on the shadow market. And someone let the cutthroats into the Queen Tower."

"And you have no sense of who in the Upper Household might want Sabran dead?"

"None. They all think she keeps the Nameless One chained." Ead swilled her wine. "You always told me to trust my instinct."

"Always."

"Then I tell you now that something does not sit right with me about these attempts on Sabran. Not just the choice of weapon," she said. "Only the last incursion seemed ... serious. All the others have botched the thing. As if they wanted to be caught."

"Most likely they are simply untrained. Desperate fools, bribed with a pittance."

"Perhaps. Or perhaps it is deliberate," she said. "Chassar, do you remember Lord Arteloth?"

"Of course," he replied. "I was surprised that he was not with Sabran when I arrived."

"He is not here. Combe exiled him to Yscalin for stepping too close to her, to clear the way for the marriage to Lievelyn."

Chassar raised his eyebrows. "The rumors," he murmured. "I heard them even in Rumelabar."

Ead nodded. "Combe was willing to send Loth to his death. And now I fear the Night Hawk is moving the pieces once more. That by making Sabran fear for her life, he drove her to Lievelyn."

"So she would beget an heir as soon as possible." Chassar seemed to consider this. "In a way, this would be good news, were it true. Sabran is safe. She has done as he wants."

"But what if she does not in future?"

"I do not think he would go any further than he has. His power dissolves without her."

"I am not sure he believes that. And I do not think it well that Sabran remains unaware of his scheming."

Chassar stilled at this. "You must not voice these suspicions to her, Eadaz. Not without evidence," he said. "Combe is a powerful man, and he would find a way to hurt you."

"I would not. All I can do is continue to watch." She caught his gaze. "Chassar, my wardings are beginning to fail."

"I know." He kept his voice down. "When word reached us that Fýredel had shown himself, and that Sabran had banished him from

Ascalon, we knew the truth at once. We also knew it would have burned through your siden. You have been away from the tree for too long. You are a root, beloved. You must drink, or you will wither."

"It may not matter. I might have a chance, finally, to be a Lady of the Bedchamber," Ead said. "To protect her with my own blade."

"No, Eadaz."

Chassar placed a big hand over hers. An orange blossom, cut from glass-like sunstone, was mounted on a silver ring on his forefinger. The symbol of their shared and true allegiance.

"Child," he murmured, "the Prioress is dead. She was old, as you know, and passed in peace."

The news pained Ead, but it was no surprise. The Prioress had always seemed ancient, her skin as gnarled and furrowed as an olive tree. "When?"

"Three months ago."

"May her flame ascend to light the tree," Ead said. "Who has taken up her mantle?"

"The Red Damsels elected Mita Yedanya, the *munguna*," Chassar said. "Do you remember her?"

"Yes, of course." From what little Ead could remember of her, Mita had been a quiet and serious woman. The *munguna* was the presumed heir to the Priory, though the Red Damsels would occasionally elect someone else if they deemed her unfit for the position. "I wish her well in her new role. Has she chosen her own *munguna* already?"

"Most of the sisters wager it will be Nairuj, but in truth, Mita has not yet decided."

Chassar leaned closer. In the faint light that remained, Ead noticed lines around his mouth and eyes. He looked so much older than when she had last seen him.

"Something has changed, Eadaz," he said. "You must feel it. Wyrms have been stirring from their slumber, and now a High Western has risen. The Prioress fears that these are the first steps toward the Nameless One himself awakening."

Ead took a moment to let the words settle inside her. "You are not alone in fearing this," she said. "A maid of honor, Truyde utt Zeedeur, sent a messenger to Seiiki."

"The young heir to the Duchy of Zeedeur." Chassar frowned. "Why would she want to parley with the East?"

"The girl has taken it into her head to call their wyrms to protect us from the Nameless One. She is convinced he will return—whether the House of Berethnet stands or not."

Chassar let a soft hiss escape between his teeth. "What has led her to believe this?"

"The Draconic awakenings. And her own imaginings, I suppose." Ead poured them both more wine. "Fýredel said something to Sabran. *The thousand years are almost done.* He also said his master stirred in the Abyss."

The ocean that yawned between one side of the world and the other. Black water that sunlight could not penetrate. A vault of darkness that seafarers had always feared to cross.

"Ominous words indeed." Chassar contemplated the horizon. "Fýredel must believe, as Lady Truyde does, and as the Prioress does, that the Nameless One is poised to return."

"The Mother defeated him more than a thousand years ago," Ead said. "Did she not? If that were the date the wyrm meant, the Nameless One should have risen already."

Chassar took a thoughtful sip of wine. "I wonder," he said, "if this threat has anything to do with the Mother's lost years."

All sisters knew about the lost years. Not long after vanquishing the Nameless One and founding the Priory, the Mother had left on unknown business and perished before she could make her way home. Her body had been returned to the Priory. No one knew who had sent it.

One small faction of sisters believed that the Mother had gone to join her suitor, Galian Berethnet, and had a child with him, establishing the House of Berethnet. This idea, unpopular in the Priory, was the founding legend of Virtudom—and what had landed Ead in Inys.

"How could it?" she asked.

"Well," Chassar said, "most sisters believe that the Mother left to protect the Priory from some unnamed threat." He pressed his lips together. "I will write to the Prioress and tell her what Fýredel said. She may be able to solve this riddle."

They fell into a brief silence. Now twilight had drawn in, candles began to flicker to life in the windows of the palace.

"I must go soon," Ead murmured. "To pray to the Deceiver."

"Eat a little first." Chassar moved the bowl of fruit toward her. "You look tired."

"Well," Ead said dryly, "banishing a High Western alone, as it turns out, *is* a tiring affair."

She picked at the honey-sweet dates and cherries. Tastes of a life she had never forgotten.

"Beloved," Chassar said, "forgive me, but before you go, there is something else I must tell you. About Jondu."

Ead looked up.

"Jondu." Her mentor, her beloved friend. Something twisted in her gut. "Chassar, what is it?"

"Last year, the Prioress decreed we must resume our efforts to find Ascalon. With Draconic stirrings on the rise, she believed we should do everything we could to find the sword the Mother used to vanquish the Nameless One. Jondu began her search in Inys."

"Inys," Ead said, chest tight. "Surely she would have come to see me."

"She was ordered not to approach the court. To leave you to your task."

Ead closed her eyes. Jondu was headstrong, but she would never have disobeyed a direct order from the Prioress.

"We last heard from her when she was in Perunta," Chassar continued, "presumably making her way home."

"When was this?"

"The end of winter. She did not find Ascalon, but she wrote to tell us she carried an object of importance from Inys and urgently required a guard. We sent sisters to find her, but there was no trace. I fear the worst."

Ead stood abruptly and walked to the balustrade. Suddenly the sweetness of the fruit was cloying.

She remembered Jondu teaching her how to yoke the raw flame that scorched in her blood. How to hold a sword and string a bow. How to open a wyvern from gizzard to tail. Jondu, her dearest friend—who, along with Chassar, had made her all she was.

"She may still be alive." Her voice was hoarse.

"The sisters are searching. We will not give up," Chassar said, "but someone must take her place among the Red Damsels. That is the message I bring from Mita Yedanya, our new Prioress. She commands you to return, Eadaz. To wear the cloak of blood. We shall need you in the days to come."

A shiver caressed Ead from her scalp to the base of her spine, chill and warm at once.

It was all she had ever wanted. To be a Red Damsel, a slayer-in-waiting, was the dream of every girl born into the Priory.

And yet.

"So," Ead said, "the new Prioress does not care to protect Sabran."

Chassar joined her at the balustrade. "The new Prioress is more skeptical of the Berethnet claim than the last," he admitted, "but she will not leave Sabran undefended. I have brought one of your younger sisters with me to Inys, and I mean to present her to Queen Sabran in exchange for you. I will tell her one of your relatives is dying, that you must return to the Ersyr."

"That will look suspicious."

"We have no choice." He looked at her. "You are Eadaz du Zāla uq-Nāra, a handmaiden of Cleolind. You should not stay any longer in this court of blasphemers."

Her name. It had been so long. As she digested his words, his face grew taut with worry.

"Eadaz," he said, "do not tell me now that you wish to stay. Have you become attached to Sabran?"

"Of course not," Ead said flatly. "The woman is arrogant and over-indulged—but, whatever she is, there is a chance, however small, that she *is* the Mother's true descendant. Not only that: if she dies, the country with the greatest naval strength in the West will collapse—and that will not do any of us a whit of good. She needs protection."

"And she will have it. The sister I have brought is gifted—but you have a different path to follow now." He placed a hand on her back. "It is time to come home."

A chance to be close to the orange tree again. She could speak her own tongue and pray to the true image of the Mother without being cooked in Marian Square.

Yet she had spent eight years learning about the Inysh—their customs, their religion, the intricacies of this snare of a court. She could not waste that knowledge.

"Chassar," Ead said, "I want to leave this place with you, but you are calling me away just as Sabran is beginning to trust me. All my years here will have been for nothing. Do you think you could persuade the new Prioress to give me a little more time?"

"How long?"

"Until the royal succession is assured." Ead turned to him. "Let me guard her until she bears a daughter. Then I will come home."

He mulled this over for some time, his mouth a thin line in the thicket of his beard.

"I will try," he concluded. "I will try, beloved. But if the Prioress refuses, you must submit."

Ead kissed his cheek. "You are too good to me."

"I can never be too good to you." He took her by the shoulders. "But be mindful, Eadaz. Do not lose your focus. It is the Mother who compels you, not this Inysh queen."

She looked back at the towers of the city. "Let the Mother compel us in all that we do."

15

West

Cárscaro.

Capital of the Draconic Kingdom of Yscalin.

The city sat high in the mountains above a vast plain. It was scarped into a ridge in the Spindles, the snow-capped range that stood between Yscalin and the Ersyr.

Loth gazed through the window of the coach as it approached the mountain path. He had heard stories about Cárscaro all his life, but had never thought to lay eyes on it.

Yscalin had become the second link in the Chainmail of Virtudom when King Isalarico the Fourth had wed Queen Glorian the Second. For love of his bride, he had abjured the old gods of his country and pledged it to the Saint. In those days, Cárscaro had been famed for its masques, its music, and the red pear trees that grew along its streets.

No longer. Since Yscalin had renounced its age-old devotion to the Saint and taken the Nameless One as its god, it had been doing all it could to undermine Virtudom.

As dawn broke, bright threads of cloud appeared over the Great Yscali Plain. Once upon a time, this expanse of land had been carpeted with lavender, and when the wind blew, it had carried its scent up to the city.

Loth wished he could have seen it then. All that remained was a charred waste.

"How many souls live in Cárscaro?" he asked Lady Priessa, if only to distract himself.

"Fifty thousand, or thereabouts. Ours is a small capital," she replied. "When you arrive, you will be shown to your chambers in the ambassadorial gallery. You will have an audience with Her Radiance at her earliest convenience to present your credentials."

"Will we also meet King Sigoso?"

"His Majesty is indisposed."

"I am sorry to hear it."

Loth pressed his brow to the window and stared at the city in the mountains. Soon he would be at the heart of the mystery of what had happened to Yscalin.

A blur of movement caught his attention. He reached for the latch so that he might get a better look at the sky, but a gloved hand snapped it shut.

"What was that?" Loth asked, unnerved.

"A cockatrice." Lady Priessa folded her hands in her lap. "You would do well not to wander far from the palace, Lord Arteloth. Many Draconic beings dwell in the mountains."

Cockatrices. The spawn of bird and wyvern. "Do they harm the people in the city?"

"If they are hungry, they will harm anything that moves, except those who already have the plague. We keep them fed."

"How?"

No reply.

The coach began its trundle up the mountain path. Across from Loth, Kit stirred from his doze and rubbed his eyes. He hitched up his smile at once, but Loth could tell he was afraid.

Night had fallen by the time the Gate of Niunda came into view. Colossal as the deity it was named after, carved from green and black granite and lit by torches, it was the sole entrance to Cárscaro. As they grew closer, Loth could make out shapes below its lintel.

"What is that, up there?"

Kit understood first.

"I would look away, Arteloth." He sat back. "Unless you want this hour to haunt your nights forever."

It was too late. He had seen the men and women chained by their wrists to the gate. Some looked dead or half-dead already, but others were alive and bloody, fighting their restraints.

"*That* is how we keep them fed, Lord Arteloth," Lady Priessa said. "With our criminals and traitors."

For a terrible moment, Loth thought he was going to cast up his last meal right here in the coach.

"I see." His mouth flooded with saliva. "Good."

He ached to make the sign of the sword, but here that would condemn him.

As the coach approached, the Gate of Niunda opened. No fewer than six wyverns guarded it. They were smaller than their High Western overlords and had only two legs, but their eyes scorched with the same fire. Loth looked away until they were past.

He was in a nightmare. The bestiaries, the stories of old, had come to life in Yscalin.

A tower of volcanic rock and glass rose from the middle of the city. That must be the Palace of Salvation, seat of the House of Vetalda. The mountain Cárscaro sat on was one of the lowest in the Spindles, but vast enough that its summit was hidden by the haze above the plateau.

The palace was a fearful thing, but it was the river of lava that unsettled Loth. It flowed in six forks around and through Cárscaro before merging into one pool and cascading onto the lower slopes of the mountain, where it cooled to volcanic glass.

The lava falls had appeared in Cárscaro a decade ago. It had taken the Yscals some time to build channels for the flaming river. In Ascalon, people now whispered that the Saint had sent it as a warning to the Yscals—a warning that the Nameless One would one day be the false god of their country.

Streets wound like rat tails around the buildings. Loth could see now that they were linked by high stone bridges. Stalls with red awnings were surrounded by people in heavy robes. Many wore veils over their faces. Fortifications against the plague could be seen everywhere, from charms in doorways to masks with glass eyes and long beaks, but some dwellings were still marked with red writing.

The coach brought them to the vast doors of the Palace of Salvation, where a line of servants waited. Lifelike carvings of Draconic creatures formed an arch around the entrance. It looked like the neck of the Womb of Fire.

Loth stepped from the coach and stiffly held out a hand to Lady Priessa, who declined it. It had been foolish to offer in the first place. Melaugo had told him to keep his distance.

The jaculi growled as their small party walked away from the coach. Loth fell into step beside Kit, and they followed the servants into a high-ceilinged vestibule, where a chandelier hung. He could have sworn its candles were burning with red flames.

Lady Priessa disappeared through a side door. Loth and Kit exchanged baffled glances.

Two braziers flanked a grand staircase. A servant lit a torch from one of them. He led Loth and Kit through deserted corridors and passages hid behind tapestries and trick walls, up cramped and tapering stairs that left Loth feeling even more nauseated, past oil paintings of former Vetalda monarchs, and finally into a gallery with a vaulted ceiling. The servant pointed first to one door, then another, and handed each of them a key.

"Perhaps we could have some—" Kit began, but the man had already vanished behind a tapestry. "Food."

"We can eat tomorrow," Loth said. Every word echoed in this corridor. "Who else do you think is here?"

"I am no expert on the subject of foreign ambassadors, but we must assume there are some Ments about." Kit rubbed his grumbling stomach. "They have their fingers in every pie."

That was true. It was said there was no place in the world the Ments refused to go.

"Meet me here at noonday," Loth said. "We ought to discuss what to do."

Kit clapped him on the back and went into one of the chambers. Loth slotted his key into the other door.

It took his eyes a moment to attune to the shadows in his bedchamber. The Yscals might have declared their allegiance to the Nameless One, but they clearly spared no expense in the upkeep of their ambassadors-in-residence. Nine windows lined the west-facing wall, one smaller than the others. On closer inspection, this turned out to be a door to an enclosed balcony.

A canopy bed dominated the north end of the room. An iron candle holder stood beside it. The candles were formed of a pearlescent wax, and their flames *were* red. True red. His chest had been set down nearby. On the south end, he swept aside a velvet curtain to discover a stone bath, full to the brim with steaming water.

The windows made him feel as if all Yscalin could see in. He closed the drapes and snuffed all but a handful of the candles. They released a puff of black smoke when extinguished.

He sank into the water and lay there for a long while. When his aches had dulled, he found a cake of olive soap and set about getting the ash from his hair.

Wilstan Fynch might have slept in this very chamber while he investigated the murder of Queen Rosarian, the woman he had loved. He might have been here when the lavender fields burned, and when the birds flew out with news that the Chainmail of Virtudom had lost a link.

Loth poured water over his head. If someone in Cárscaro had arranged for Queen Rosarian to die, that same person might be trying to kill Sabran. To remove her before she gave Virtudom an heir. To resurrect the Nameless One.

With a shiver, Loth rose from the bath and reached for the folded linen beside it. He used his knife to shave, leaving a patch of hair on his chin and a little on his upper lip. As he worked, his mind lingered on Ead.

He was sure Sabran was safe with her. From the moment he had first seen her in the Banqueting House—a woman with acorn skin and watchful eyes, whose posture had been almost regal—he had sensed an inner warmth. Not the heat of wyrmfire, but something soft and golden, like the first light of a summer morning.

Margret had been telling him for a year that he should marry Ead. She was beautiful, she made him laugh, and they could talk for hours. He had brushed his sister off—not only because the future Earl of Goldenbirch could not take a commoner as a bride, as she knew full well, but because he loved Ead as he loved Margret, as he loved Sabran. As a sister.

He had not yet experienced the all-consuming love reserved for a companion. At thirty, he was more than old enough to be wed, and he longed to honor the Knight of Fellowship by partaking in that most sacred institution.

Now he might never have a chance.

A silk nightshirt was laid out on the bed, but he donned his own, crumpled from travel, before stepping on to the balcony.

The air was cooling. Loth rested his arms on the balustrade. Below him, Cárscaro sprawled toward the sheer drop to the plateau. The glow from the lava stained every street. Loth watched a silhouette plummet from above and drink from the river of fire.

At midnight, he gingerly climbed into the bed and drew the coverlet to his chest.

When he slept, he dreamed his sheets were poisoned.

———

Close to noonday, Kit found him sitting by his table in the shade of the balcony, gazing down at the plateau.

"Well met, sirrah," Loth said.

"Ah, sirrah, 'tis a beautiful day in the land of death and evil." Kit was carrying a trencher. "These people might worship the Nameless One, but what fine beds! I never slept better."

Kit could never be serious, and Loth could never help but smile at his outlook, even here. "Where did you find food?"

"The first place I look for in any new building is the kitchen. I hand-signed at the servants until they understood that I was famished. Here." He set the trencher on the table. "They will bring us something more filling later."

The board was piled with fruit and toasted nuts, a jug of straw wine and two goblets.

"You ought not to have wandered off alone, Kit," Loth said.

"My belly waits for no man." When he saw his expression, Kit sighed. "All right."

The sun was an open wound, the sky a thousand variations on pink. A pale mist hung over the plain. Loth had never seen a view quite like it. They were shielded from the brunt of the heat, but their collarbones were jeweled with sweat.

It must have been unspeakably beautiful when the lavender still grew. Loth tried to imagine walking through the open-air corridors in the summer, warmed by a perfumed breeze.

Was it fear or evil that had seized King Sigoso, to corrupt this place the way he had?

"So," said Kit, through a mouthful of almonds, "how are we to approach the Donmata?"

"With the greatest courtesy. As far as she knows, we are here as permanent ambassadors-in-residence. I doubt she will think it suspicious if we ask what became of the last one."

"If they did something to Fynch, she will lie."

"Then we will ask for evidence that he is alive."

"You do not demand *evidence* from a princess. Her word is law." Kit peeled a blood orange. "We are spies now, Loth. You had better stop listening to that trusting nature of yours."

"What shall we do, then?"

"Blend into the court, act like good ambassadors, and find out what we can. There may be other foreign diplomats here. Someone must know something useful." He gave Loth a sunny smile. "And if all else fails, I shall flirt with the Donmata Marosa until she opens her heart to me."

Loth shook his head. "Knave."

A rumble passed through Cárscaro. Kit caught his cup before the wine could spill.

"What was that?"

"A quake," Loth said, unsettled. "Papa told me once that fire mountains can cause such things."

The Yscals would not have built a city here if it could be razed by a quake. Trying not to think about it, Loth took a sip of his wine, still haunted by the thought of what Cárscaro must once have been. Humming, Kit took out his quill and a small knife.

"Poesy?" Loth asked.

"Inspiration has yet to strike. Terror and creativity, in my experience, do not often walk hand in hand." Kit set about sharpening the quill. "No, this is a letter. For a certain lady."

Loth clicked his tongue. "Why you haven't told Kate how you feel is beyond me."

"Because though I am charming in person, I am Sir Antor Dale on the page." Kit shot him an amused look. "Do you think they send their letters by bird or basilisk nowadays?"

"Cockatrice, most likely. It combines the qualities of both." Loth watched his friend remove an inkwell from a pouch. "You know Combe will burn any letters we send."

"Oh, I have no intention of trying. If Lady Katryen never reads this, so be it," Kit said lightly, "but when the heart grows too full, it overflows. And mine, inevitably, overflows on to a page."

A knock rang out in the chamber behind them. Loth glanced at Kit before he went to open the door, ready to use his baselard.

Outside was a servant in a black doublet and breeches.

"Lord Arteloth." He wore a pomander. "I am come to tell you that Her Radiance, the Donmata Marosa, will see you in due course. For now, you and Lord Kitston must go to the physician, so Her Radiance may be assured that you do not carry any sickness to her door."

"Now?"

"Yes, my lord."

The last thing Loth wanted was to be prodded at by a physician with Draconic sympathies, but he doubted they had a choice.

"Then please," he said, "do lead the way."

16

East

The rest of the water trials passed in a haze. The night when they were told to swim against the current in the swift-flowing river. The duel with nets. Demonstrating competence in signaling to other riders. Sometimes there would be a day between them, and sometimes many days. And before Tané knew it, the final trial was on top of her.

Midnight found her in the practice hall again, coating the blade of her sword with clove oil. The smell of it cleaved to her fingers. Her shoulders ached and her neck was rigid as a tree stump.

This sword could win or lose her everything tomorrow. She could see her own bloodshot eyes in its flat.

Rain drizzled from the rooftops of the school. On her way back to her quarters, she heard a muffled laugh.

The door to a small balcony was open. Tané glanced over the balustrade. In the courtyard below, where pear trees grew, Onren and Kanperu were sitting together, heads bowed over a game board, fingers intertwined.

"Tané."

She startled. Dumusa was looking out from her own quarters, dressed in a short-sleeved robe, holding a pipe. She joined Tané on the balcony and followed her gaze.

"You must not be envious of them," she said after a long silence.

"I am not—"

"Peace. I envy them too, sometimes. How easy they seem to find it. Onren, especially."

Tané hid her face behind her hair.

"She excels," she said, "with so little—" The words lodged in her throat. "With so little."

"She excels because she trusts in her skill. I suspect you fear that yours will slip between your fingers if you loosen your grip for even a moment," Dumusa said. "I was born a descendant of riders. That was a great blessing, and I always wanted to prove to myself that I was worthy of it. When I was sixteen, I stopped everything but my studies. I stopped going to the city. I stopped painting. I stopped seeing Ishari. All I did was practice until I became principal apprentice. I forgot how to possess a skill. Instead, the skill possessed me. All of me."

Tané felt a chill.

"But—" She hesitated. "You do not look the way I feel."

Dumusa blew out a mouthful of smoke.

"I realized," she said, "that if I am fortunate enough to become a rider, I will be expected to answer the moment Seiiki calls. I will not have days of practice beforehand. Remember, Tané, that a sword does not need to be whetted at all hours to keep it sharp."

"I know."

Dumusa gave her a look. "Then stop sharpening. And go to sleep."

The final trial would take place in the courtyard. Tané broke her fast early and found a spot on the benches.

Onren came to sit beside her at dawn. They listened to the distant rumble of the thunder.

"So," Onren said, "are you ready?"

Tané nodded, then shook her head.

"Me, too." Onren turned her face into the heavy rain. "You will ride, Tané. The Miduchi judge us based on our performance across all of the water trials, and you have done enough."

"This is the most important," Tané murmured. "We will use swords more than any other weapon. If we cannot win a fight in a school—"

"We all know how good you are with a blade. You're going to be fine."

Tané twisted her hands between her knees.

The others trickled outside. When everyone was present, the Sea General emerged. The servant beside him craned on tiptoe to hold an umbrella over his head.

"Your final trial is with swords," the Sea General told them all. "First, the honorable Tané, of the South House."

She stood.

"Honorable Tané," he said, "this day you will face the honorable Turosa, of the North House."

Turosa rose from the benches without hesitation.

"First blood wins."

They walked to separate ends of the courtyard to collect their swords. Gazes locked, blades unsheathed, they walked toward each other.

She would show him what village chaff could do.

Their bows were small and stiff. Tané gripped her sword with both hands. All she could see was Turosa, his hair dripping, nostrils flared.

The Sea General called out, and Tané ran at Turosa. Sword clashed on sword. Turosa shoved his face so close to hers that she could feel his breath and smell the tang of sweat on his tunic.

"When I command the riders," he hissed, "I will see to it that no peasant ever rides a dragon again." A clangor of blades. "Soon you will be back in that hovel they pulled you from."

Tané thrust at him. He stopped her blade just shy of his waist.

"Remind me," he said, so only she could hear, "where it was you came from?" He shoved her sword away. "Do they even give names to shit-heap villages?"

If he thought to provoke her by insulting the family she had never known, he would be waiting a thousand years.

He swung at her. Tané parried, and the duel began in earnest.

This was no dance with wooden swords. There was no lesson to be learned here, no skill to be refined. In the end, her confrontation with her rival was as quick and ruthless as having a tooth pulled.

Her world was a torrent of rain and metal. Turosa sprang high. Tané sliced up, deflecting his downcut, and he landed in a crouch. He was on her again before she could breathe, sword flashing like a fish through water. She matched every blow until he feinted and punched her in the chin. A brutal kick to the stomach sent her sprawling.

She should have seen that feint from leagues away. Her exhaustion had been her undoing. Through the droplets on her lashes, she glimpsed the Sea General, observing them without expression.

"That's right, villager," Turosa sneered. "Stay on the ground. Just where chaff belongs."

Like a prisoner awaiting execution, Tané lowered her head. Turosa looked her over, as if to decide where it would hurt most to cut her. Another step brought him within reach.

That was when her head snapped up, and she swung her legs toward Turosa, forcing him into a leap to avoid them. She impelled her body away from the ground and whirled like a windstorm back to her feet. Turosa repulsed her first blow, but she had caught him off his guard. She saw it in his eyes. His footwork turned clumsy on the wet stone, and when her blade thrummed toward him again, his arm came up too slowly to block it.

It shaved his jaw, soft as a blade of grass.

A heartbeat later, his sword gashed open her shoulder. She gasped as he jerked away from her, teeth bared and slick with spittle.

The other sea guardians were straining to see. Tané watched her opponent, breathing hard.

If she had not broken the skin, this fight was lost.

Slowly, rubies welled from the line she had drawn. Trembling and drenched, Turosa touched one finger to his jaw and found a smear, bright as a quince blossom.

First blood.

"The honorable Tané of the South House," the Sea General announced, and he was smiling, "victory is yours."

No words had ever sounded sweeter.

When she bowed to Turosa, blood oozed like molten copper from her shoulder. His face wheeled from the shallows to the depths of anger. He had fallen for the trick—a trick that should have fooled no one—because he had expected weakness. As he looked her in the face, Tané knew, at last, that he would never call her village chaff again. To call her that would prove that chaff could grow taller than grass.

The only way to save face was to treat her as his equal.

Under the cracked-open sky, the descendant of riders bowed to her, lower than he ever had.

17

West

Having been declared free of plague, Loth and Kit were admitted into the presence of the Donmata Marosa several days after their arrival. During those days, they had kept to their rooms, unable to leave with guards keeping watch in the gallery. Loth still shuddered at the memory of the Royal Physician, who had placed leeches where leeches should never be placed.

So it was that Loth found himself walking with Kit into the cavernous throne room of the Palace of Salvation. The space was awash with courtiers and nobles, but there was no sign of Prince Wilstan.

The Donmata Marosa, crown princess of the Draconic Kingdom of Yscalin, sat on a throne of volcanic glass beneath a canopy of state. Her head was encased in a horned mask of iron, shaped like the head of a High Western. The weight of it must have been enormous.

"Saint," Kit whispered, so low that only Loth could hear. "She wears the face of Fýredel."

Guards in golden armor stood in front of the throne. The canopy showed the badge of the House of Vetalda. Two black wyvems and a sword, broken in twain.

Not just any sword, but Ascalon. The symbol of Virtudom.

The ladies-in-waiting had folded back their plague veils, which hung from small but ornate coronets. Lady Priessa Yelarigas stood to the right of the throne. Now her face was revealed, Loth could see her pale, freckled cheeks, her deep-set eyes, and the proud bearing of her chin.

The purr of conversation dwindled when they stopped in front of the throne.

"Radiance," the steward called, "I present to you two Inysh gentlemen. Here is Lord Arteloth Beck, son of the Earl and Countess of Goldenbirch, and here is Lord Kitston Glade, son of the Earl and Countess of Honeybrook. Ambassadors from the Queendom of Inys."

Silence fell in the throne room, followed swiftly by hissing. Loth got down on one knee and bowed his head.

"Your Radiance," he said, "we thank you for receiving us at your court."

The hissing tapered off when the Donmata raised her hand.

"Lord Arteloth and Lord Kitston," she said. The iron helm made her voice echo strangely. "My beloved father and I bid you welcome to the Draconic Kingdom of Yscalin. My sincere apologies for delaying this audience—I had business elsewhere."

"You need not justify it, Radiance," was all Loth said. "You have the right to see us at your pleasure." He cleared his throat. "Lord Kitston has our letters of credence, if you will accept them."

"Of course."

Lady Priessa nodded to a servant, who took the letters from Kit.

"When the Duke of Courtesy wrote to my father, we were delighted that Inys wishes to strengthen its diplomatic ties to Yscalin," the Donmata continued. "We would hate to think that Queen Sabran would endanger our long friendship over ... religious differences."

Religious differences.

"Speaking of Sabran, it has been *such* a long time since I last heard from her," the Donmata remarked. "Tell me, is she yet with child?"

A muscle flinched beneath Loth's eye. That she could sit beneath that blasphemous device and proclaim friendship to Sabran was repulsive.

"Her Majesty is not wed, madam," Kit said.

"But soon." She laid a hand on each arm of her throne. When neither of them answered her, she said, "I think you do not yet know the happy tidings, my lords. Sabran is lately promised to Aubrecht Lievelyn, High Prince of the Free State of Mentendon. My one-time betrothed."

Loth could only stare at her.

Of course, he had known Sabran would eventually choose a companion—a queen had no choice in that—but he had always assumed that it would be someone from Hróth, the more established of the two other countries in Virtudom. Instead she had chosen Aubrecht Lievelyn, grand-nephew to the late Prince Leovart, who had also courted Sabran despite the decades between them.

"Sadly," the Donmata said, "I was not asked to attend the ceremony." She leaned back. "You look troubled, Lord Arteloth. Come, speak your mind. Is the Red Prince not worthy of bedding your mistress?"

"Queen Sabran's heart is a private matter," Loth bit out. "It is not to be discussed in such a place as this."

Laughter shattered the hush in the throne room, making his spine tingle. The Donmata joined in merrily from behind her terrible mask. "Her Majesty's heart may be a private matter, but her bed is not. After all, they say the day the Berethnet bloodline ends, the Nameless One will return to us. If she means to keep him bound, had Sabran better not get on with the business of opening her ... country to Prince Aubrecht?"

More laughter.

"I pray the Berethnet bloodline continues to the end of time," Loth said, before he quite knew what he was doing, "for it stands between us and chaos."

In one smooth movement, the guards unsheathed their rapiers. The laughter stopped.

"Careful, Lord Arteloth," the Donmata said. "Do not say anything that could be construed as speaking ill of the Nameless One." She held a hand toward the guards, who put away their blades. "Do you know, I heard tell that *you* were to become prince consort. Did you prove too low to love a queen?" Before he could protest, she clapped. "Never mind. We can remedy your lack of companion here in Yscalin. Musicians! Play the thirty turns! Lady Priessa will dance with Lord Arteloth."

At once, Lady Priessa stepped down to the marble floor. Loth steeled himself and walked toward her.

The dance of thirty turns had once been taught in many courts. It had been outlawed in Inys by Jillian the Fifth, who had deemed it lewd, but later queens had been more lenient. Most courtiers learned it in one way or another.

Lady Priessa curtsied as the consort struck up a sprightly tune. Loth bowed to his partner before they both turned to face the Donmata and took hands.

At first his legs moved stiffly. Lady Priessa was light on her feet. He skipped in a circle about her, never letting his heels touch the floor.

She shadowed him. Hither and thither they pranced and sprang, side to side and face to face—then the music surged, and with one hand on the small of her back and the other on her waist, Loth raised his partner off the floor. Over and over he lifted her, until his arms ached and sweat welled on his face and nape.

He could hear Lady Priessa catching her breath. A coil of dark hair came loose as they spun around each other, slowing with each step, until at last they joined hands to face the Donmata Marosa again.

Something crunched between their palms. Loth dared not look at her as he took whatever she had slipped into his hand. The Donmata and her court applauded.

"You are tired, Lord Arteloth," came the voice from the mask. "Was Lady Priessa too heavy for you?"

"I think the gowns in Yscalin weigh more than the ladies, Radiance," Loth said, breathing hard.

"Oh, no, my lord. It *is* the ladies, the gentlemen, all. Our hearts are heavy with grief that the Nameless One has not yet returned to guide us." The Donmata rose. "A long and peaceful night to you." The helm tilted. "Unless there is anything you wish to ask me."

Loth was painfully aware of the paper in his hand, but this was an opportunity.

187

"One thing, Radiance." He cleared his throat. "There is another ambassador-in-residence at your court, who has served Queen Sabran here for many years. Wilstan Fynch, the Duke of Temperance. I was wondering where in the palace he lodges, so we might speak to him."

No one moved or spoke.

"Ambassador Fynch," the Donmata finally said. "Well, Lord Arteloth, you and I are both in the dark on that front. His Grace left several weeks ago, heading for Córvugar."

"Córvugar," Loth echoed. It was a port in the far south of Yscalin. "Why would he go there?"

"He said he had business elsewhere, the nature of which he did not disclose. I am surprised he did not write to Sabran to tell her."

"I am also surprised, Your Radiance. In fact," Loth said, "I find it difficult to believe."

There was a brief silence as his implication settled over the throne room.

"I hope, Lord Arteloth," the Donmata said, "that you are not accusing me of lying."

The courtiers had pressed closer. Like hounds with the scent of blood. Kit gripped Loth by the shoulder, and he closed his eyes.

If they were ever to find out the truth, they had to survive this court, and to survive, they would have to play along with its rules.

"No, Your Radiance," he said. "Of course not. Forgive me."

Without speaking again, the Donmata Marosa glided out of the throne room with her ladies.

The courtiers began to murmur. Jaw clenched, Loth turned his back on the line of guards and strode through the doors, Kit hurrying at his heels.

"She could have had your tongue ripped out for that," his friend muttered. "Saint, man, what possessed you to all but accuse a princess of lying in her own throne room?"

"I cannot *stomach* it, Kit. The blasphemy. The deceit. The bare-faced contempt for Inys."

"You can't let them see that their taunting has worked. Your patron is the Knight of Fellowship. At least give these people the impression of that virtue." Kit caught his arm, stopping him in his tracks. "Arteloth, *listen* to me. We are no use to Inys dead."

Sweat was beading on his face, and his pulse was distinct in his neck. Loth had never seen him look this worried.

"The Knight of Courtesy is your patron, Kit." Loth sighed. "Let us hope she will help me to mask my intentions."

"Even with her help, it will not be easy."

Kit walked to the windows of the gallery.

"I masked my anger with my father all my life," he said softly. "I learned to smile as he sneered at my poetry. As he called me a hedonist and a milksop. As he cursed his lack of other heirs, and cursed my poor mother for not giving them to him." He breathed in. "You helped me to do that, Loth. For as long as I had someone I could be myself with, I could bear to be someone else with him."

"I know," Loth murmured. "And I promise you that from now on, I will show my true face only to you."

"Good." Kit turned back to him with a smile. "Have faith, as you always do, that we will survive this. Queen Sabran is to be wed. Our exile will not be long." He clapped Loth on the shoulder. "In the meantime, let me find us some supper."

They parted ways. Only when Loth had secured the door to his chamber did he look at the scrap of parchment Priessa Yelarigas had pressed into his hand.

The Privy Sanctuary at three of the clock.
The door is beside the library. Come alone.

The Privy Sanctuary. Now the House of Vetalda had abandoned the Six Virtues, it would have been left to gather dust.

This could be a trap. Perhaps Prince Wilstan had received a note like this before he disappeared.

Loth ran his palms over his head. The Knight of Courage was with him. He would see what Lady Priessa had to say.

Kit returned at eleven that night with lamb drenched in wine, a block of spiced cheese, and plaits of olive bread with garlic. They sat on the balcony to eat while the torches of Cárscaro flickered below.

"What I would not pay for a food-taster," Loth said, picking through the meal.

"Tastes superb to me," Kit said, his mouth full of oil-dipped bread. He wiped his mouth. "Now, we must assume that Prince Wilstan is not sunning himself in Córvugar. Nobody with a wit goes to Córvugar. Nothing there but graves and crows."

"You think His Grace is dead?"

"I fear it."

"We must know for certain." Loth glanced toward the door and lowered his voice. "Lady Priessa passed me a note during the dance, asking me to meet her tonight. Perhaps she has something to tell me."

"Or perhaps she has a dagger, and means to introduce it to your back." Kit raised an eyebrow. "Wait. You're not *going*, are you?"

"Unless you have any other leads, I must. And before you ask, she stipulated that I must go alone."

Kit grimaced and drank. "The Knight of Courage has lent you his sword, my friend."

Somewhere in the mountains, a wyvern screamed a war cry. A deathly chill scraped through Loth.

"So," Kit said, and cleared his throat, "Aubrecht Lievelyn. The former betrothed of our wyrm-headed Donmata."

"Aye." Loth gazed at the starless firmament. "Lievelyn seems a respectable choice. From what I've heard, he is kind and virtuous. He will make Sab a fine companion."

"Doubtless, but now she will have to marry him without her dearest friend beside her."

Loth nodded, lost in memory. He and Sabran had always promised that when they wed, they would give each other away. That he would miss the ceremony was the final twist of the knife.

Seeing his face, Kit let out a theatrical sigh. "Pity us both," he said. "I made a solemn promise to myself that if Queen Sabran ever married, I would ask Kate Withy to dance with me and unmask myself as the man who has been sending her lovelorn poems these past three years. Now I shall never discover if I have the mettle."

Loth allowed Kit to distract him while they finished their supper. Fortunate indeed that his friend had come with him on this journey, or he would have gone mad by now.

At midnight, the palace grew quiet as the Yscals began to retire. Kit returned to his chamber after exacting a promise that Loth would knock on his door on his return from meeting the lady.

A bell tolled somewhere in Cárscaro every hour. Close to three of the clock, Loth rose and slid his baselard into the sheath at his side. He took a red-flamed candle from one of the holders and left the colonnade.

The Library of Isalarico formed the heart of the Palace of Salvation. As Loth walked toward its doors, he almost missed the corridor on his left. He approached the door at its end, found the key in its lock, and stepped into the darkness of the Privy Sanctuary.

The glow from his candle flickered on a vaulted ceiling. Prayer books and broken statues were strewn across the floor. A portrait of Queen Rosarian was among the ruins, the face knifed almost beyond recognition. All evidence of Virtudom had been stashed in here and locked away.

A figure stood before the stained-glass window at the end of the sanctuary. She held a candle with a natural flame. When he was close enough to touch her, Loth broke the silence.

"Lady Priessa."

"No, Lord Arteloth." She lowered her hood. "You look upon a princess of the West."

In the clean flame of her candle, her features were made plain to him. Brown skin and dark, heavy brows. An eagle nose. Her hair was black velvet, so long that it reached past her elbows, and her eyes were such a striking amber that they looked like topaz. The eyes of the House of Vetalda.

"Donmata," Loth murmured.

She held his gaze.

The sole heir of King Sigoso and the late Queen Sahar. He had seen Marosa Vetalda once before, when she had come to Inys to celebrate the thousand-year anniversary of the Foundation of Ascalon. She had still been engaged to Aubrecht Lievelyn then.

"I don't understand." He tightened his grip on the candle. "Why are you dressed as your lady-in-waiting?"

"Priessa is the only person I trust. She lends me her livery so I can move about the palace undetected."

"Were you the one who came to collect us from Perunta?"

"No. That *was* Priessa." When Loth started to speak, she held a gloved finger to her lips. "Listen well, Lord Arteloth. Yscalin does not only worship the Nameless One. We are also under Draconic rule. Fýredel is the true king of Yscalin, and his spies lurk everywhere. It was why I had to act the way I did in the throne room. It is all a performance."

"But—"

"You seek the Duke of Temperance. Fynch is dead, and has been for months. I sent him to carry out a task for me, in the name of Virtudom, but ... he never returned."

"Virtudom." Loth stared at her. "What do you want from me?"

"I want your help, Lord Arteloth. I want you to do for me what Wilstan Fynch could not."

Summer was on its way out. A chill was on the breeze, and the days were growing shorter. In the Privy Library, Margret had shown Ead a knot of ladybeetles nestled in the scrollwork of a bookshelf, and they had known it was almost time to travel downriver.

A day later, Sabran had decreed that the court would move to Briar House, one of the oldest royal palaces in Inys. Built during the reign of Marian the Second, it sprawled in the outskirts of Ascalon and backed onto the ancient hunting ground of Chesten Forest. The court usually journeyed to it in the autumn, but since Sabran had elected to marry Lievelyn in its sanctuary, it would take up residence there earlier than usual.

The moving of the court was always a chaos of folding and packing. Ead had departed with Margret and Linora in one of many coaches. Their possessions, locked in trunks, had followed.

Sabran had ridden with Lievelyn in a coach with gilded wheels. As the procession trundled down Berethnet Mile—the sweeping thoroughfare that divided the capital—the people of Ascalon had waved and cheered for their queen and their soon-to-be prince consort.

Briar House was cosier than Ascalon Palace. Its windows were forest glass, its corridors laid with honey-colored stone in a checkered pattern, and its walls blackbrick, which held in warmth like nothing else. Ead liked it well.

Two days after the court had arrived, she found herself at a dance in the candlelit Presence Chamber. Tonight, the queen had told her chamberers and maids of honor to go and enjoy themselves while she played cards with her Ladies of the Bedchamber.

A viol consort played gentle music. Ead sipped her mulled wine. It was strange, but she was almost sorry that she was here, and not with the queen. The Privy Chamber at Briar House was inviting, with its bookshelves and fireplace and Sabran playing the virginals. Her music had grown melancholy as the days went by, her laughter tapering into silence.

Ead looked to the other side of the room. Lord Seyton Combe, the Night Hawk, was watching her.

She turned away as if she had not seen him, only for him to approach. Like a shadow crossing a patch of sunlight.

"Mistress Duryan," he said. He wore a livery collar with a pendant shaped like a book of manners. "Good evening."

Ead dipped a small curtsy and spruced her face into a mask of indifference. She could bite down her loathing, but she would give him no smiles. "Good evening, Your Grace."

There was a long silence. Combe studied her with his peculiar gray eyes.

"I have a sense," he said, "that you do not think well of me, Mistress Duryan."

"I do not think of you often enough to have formed any opinion of you, Your Grace."

The corner of his mouth flinched. "A fine hit."

She made no apology.

A page offered them wine, but Combe refused it with a gesture. "Do you not partake, my lord?" Ead asked civilly, even as she imagined stretching him on one of his own racks.

"Never. My ears and eyes must always be open for danger to the crown, and drink works hard to close them both." Combe softened his voice. "Whether you think of me or not, I wanted to reassure you that you have a friend in me at court. Others may whisper about you, but I see that Her Majesty values your counsel. As she values mine."

"That is kind of you to say."

"Not kind. Merely truth." He made a polite bow. "Excuse me."

He walked away, parting the crowd, and Ead was left wondering. Combe did nothing without purpose. Perhaps he had talked to her because he needed a new intelligencer. Perhaps he thought she could wring knowledge about the Ersyr from Chassar and pass it on to him.

Over my dead body, bird of prey.

Aubrecht Lievelyn occupied one of the high seats. While Sabran hid in her apartments, her betrothed was always among her subjects, flattering the Inysh with his enthusiasm. At present, he was talking to his sisters, who were fresh off the ship from Zeedeur.

The twins, Princess Bedona and Princess Betriese, were twenty. They seemed to spend their days laughing at secrets known only to those who had grown together in the womb.

Princess Ermuna, the eldest sister and heir apparent, was half a year older than Sabran. She was the spit of her brother, tall and arresting, with the same pallid complexion. Thick crimson hair rippled to her hips. Her sleeves were slashed to reveal a lining of gold silk, then pulled in with six brocaded cuffs apiece, each cuff representing a virtue. The Inysh maids of honor were already tying ribbons around their own sleeves to imitate her.

"Mistress Duryan."

Ead turned, then curtsied low. "Your Grace."

Aleidine Teldan utt Kantmarkt, Dowager Duchess of Zeedeur and grandmother of Truyde, had come to stand beside her. Coin-sized rubies dripped from her ears.

"I was most curious to meet you." Her voice was silvery and mellow. "Ambassador uq-Ispad says you are his pride and joy. A paragon of virtue."

"His Excellency is too kind."

"Queen Sabran also speaks well of you. It pleases me to see that a convert can live in peace here." Her gaze flicked toward the high seats. "We are more free-minded in Mentendon. I hope our influence will soften the treatment of skeptics and apostates in this country."

Ead drank.

"May I ask how you know His Excellency, Your Grace?" she asked, steering for a safer topic.

"We met in Brygstad many years ago. He was a friend of my companion, the late Duke of Zeedeur," the Dowager Duchess said. "His Excellency was at Jannart's entombment."

"My condolences."

"Thank you. The Duke was a kind man, and a tender father to Oscarde. Truyde takes after him." As she looked toward her granddaughter, who was deep in conversation with Chassar, her face tightened with sudden grief. "Forgive me, Mistress Duryan—"

"Sit with me, Your Grace." Ead guided her to a settle. "Child, bring my lady some more wine," she added to a page, who sprang to obey.

"Thank you." As Ead perched beside her, the Dowager Duchess patted her hand. "I am well." She accepted the wine from the page. "As I was saying, Truyde— Truyde really is the very image of Jannart. She has inherited his love of books and language, too. He had so many maps and manuscripts in his library, I could hardly think where to put them all after his death. Of course, he left most of them to Niclays."

That name again. "Would that be Doctor Niclays Roos?"

"Yes. He was a great friend to Jannart." She paused. "And to me. Even if he did not know it."

"He was here during my first year at court. I was sorry that he left."

"It was not by choice." The Dowager Duchess leaned closer, so Ead could smell the rosemary in her pomander. "I should not say this to most, mistress . . . but Ambassador uq-Ispad is an old friend, and he seems to trust you." She opened a folding fan and hid her lips with it. "Niclays was exiled from court because he failed to make Queen Sabran an elixir of life."

Ead tried not to change her expression. "Her Majesty *asked* him to do this?"

"Oh, yes. He arrived in Inys on her eighteenth birthday, not long after Jannart died, and offered her his services as an alchemist."

"In exchange for her patronage, I assume."

"Indeed."

Many royals had sought the water of life. Playing on the fear of death must be a lucrative business—and there had long been rumors at court that Sabran feared the childbed. Roos had preyed on a young queen, dazzling her with his knowledge of science. A charlatan.

"Niclays was no fraud," the Dowager Duchess said, as if she could read Ead's mind. "He truly believed he could make it for her. The elixir was his passion for decades." There was a note of sadness in her voice. "Her Majesty gave him great lodgings and a workshop at Ascalon Palace—but from what I understand, he lost himself to wine and gambling. And used his royal pension to pay for it." She paused to let a page top up her glass. "After two years, Sabran decided that Niclays had swindled her. She banished him from Inys and decreed that no country that craved her friendship could give him refuge. The late High Prince Leovart elected to send him to Orisima."

The trading post. "I assume Her Majesty has not relented on the subject of his exile."

"No. He has been there for seven years."

Ead raised her eyebrows. "Seven?"

From what she understood, Orisima was a tiny island (if *island* were not too grand a word for it) that clung to the Seiikinese port of Cape Hisan. Seven years there would drive a person mad.

"Yes," the Dowager Duchess said, seeing her face. "I beseeched Prince Aubrecht to have him brought home, but he will only do so if Queen Sabran pardons him."

"Do you . . . not believe he deserves to be in exile, Your Grace?" Ead ventured.

After a hesitation, the reply came: "I believe he has been punished enough. Niclays is a good man. If he had not been so deep in mourning for Jannart, I do not think he would have behaved the way he did. He wanted to lose himself."

Ead thought of the name on Truyde's little book of heresy. *Niclays.* Had the girl intended to use Roos in her plan?

"I suppose your granddaughter also knows Doctor Roos," she said.

"Oh, yes. Niclays was like an uncle to her when she was young." The Dowager Duchess paused again. "I understand you have some sway with Her Majesty. As one of her ladies, she must hold your opinion in high regard."

Now Ead understood why this noblewoman had come to speak to her.

"The Teldan of Kantmarkt understand commerce," the Dowager Duchess said, her voice soft. There was a lit cinder of hope in her gaze. "If you speak for Niclays, I can make you a rich woman, Mistress Duryan."

This must be what happened to Roslain and Katryen. A hushed request, a sweetener, a whisper to Sabran. What Ead could not understand was why it was happening to her.

"I am not one of the Ladies of the Bedchamber," she said. "I do not presume to have Her Majesty's ear."

"I think you are far too modest." The Dowager Duchess smiled a little. "I saw her walking with you in the Knot Gardens just this morning."

Ead took a sip of wine, buying herself a moment.

She could not get involved in dealings like these. It would be folly to speak for someone Sabran despised when the queen had only just shown an interest in her.

"I cannot help you, Your Grace," Ead said. "You would be better served asking Lady Roslain or Lady Katryen." She stood and curtsied. "Excuse me. I have duties elsewhere."

Before the Dowager Duchess could press her on the matter, she made her way toward the doors.

The Royal Bedchamber in Briar House was much smaller than its counterpart at Ascalon Palace. The ceiling was set low, the walls paneled with dark linenfold oak, and crimson drapes surrounded the bed. Ead was early, but she found Margret sitting inside.

"Ead," she said. Her voice was thick with the cold that had buckled half the court. "Now you've spoiled the surprise. I hoped to have arrayed the bed before you got here."

"So I could continue making idle conversation with nobles I scarcely know?"

"So you could dance. You used to love to dance."

"That was when the sight of the Night Hawk did not make me as bilious as it does now."

With a sound of distaste, Margret rose, a letter in her hand. "Is it from home?" Ead asked.

"Aye. Mama says that Papa has been asking to see me for weeks. Apparently, he has something important to tell me, but I can hardly go to him in the middle of all this."

"Sabran would let you."

"I know she would, but Mama insists I stay here. She says Papa most likely has no idea what he is saying, and that it is my duty to remain— but in truth, I think she is living through me." With a sigh, Margret tucked the letter into her bodice. "You know … I was fool enough to think the Master of the Posts would have something from Loth."

"He may have written." Ead helped her lift a fustian. "Combe intercepts every letter."

"Then perhaps I shall write a letter saying what a cur he is," Margret muttered.

Ead smiled. "I would pay to see his face. Speaking of which," she added, quieter, "I was just offered payment of my own. In exchange for petitioning the queen."

Margret looked up at her, eyebrows raised. "Who from?"

"The Dowager Duchess of Zeedeur. She wants me to speak for Niclays Roos."

"That will do you no good. Loth told me Sabran hates that man with a passion." Margret glanced at the door. "You be careful, Ead. She lets Ros and Kate get away with it, but Sab is no fool. She knows when the whispers in her ear are too sweet."

"I have no intention of playing those games." Ead touched her elbow. "I think Loth will be all right, Meg. He knows now that the world is more dangerous than it seems."

Margret snorted. "You think too highly of his wits. Loth will trust anyone who smiles at him."

"I know." Ead took her by the shoulders and steered her to the door. "Now, go and drink some hot wine at the dance. I am sure Captain Lintley would be pleased to see you."

"Captain Lintley?"

"Yes. The very gallant Captain Lintley."

Margret was a little bright-eyed as she left.

Linora was nowhere to be seen. No doubt she was still dancing. Ead secured the Royal Bedchamber alone. Unlike the room at Ascalon Palace, it had two entrances. The Great Door was for the queen, the Little Door for her consort.

There had been no attempts on Sabran since the betrothal was announced, but Ead knew it must only be a matter of time. She checked the featherbed, looked behind the curtains, searched every wall and tapestry and floorboard. There was no secret third way in, she was sure, but the possibility that she had missed something nudged at her. At least Chassar had laid new wardings on the threshold, stronger than her own. He had recently eaten of the fruit.

Ead plumped the little pillows and replenished the closet. She was closing a hot coal into a bedwarmer when Sabran stepped into the room. Ead stood and curtsied.

"Majesty."

Sabran looked her up and down with half-lidded eyes. She wore a sleeveless rail over her nightgown, and a blue sash around her waist. Ead had never seen her so undressed.

"Forgive me," Ead said, to fill the silence. "I thought you would not retire until later."

"I have slept ill of late. Doctor Bourn tells me I should try to retire by ten of the clock to promote a quiet mind, or some such," Sabran said. "Do you know some cure for sleeplessness, Ead?"

"Do you take anything presently, madam?"

"Sleepwater. Sometimes caudle, if the night is cold."

Sleepwater was the Inysh name for a decoction of setwall. While it had some medicinal properties, it was clearly doing little good.

"I would recommend lavender, earthapple, and creamgrail root, simmered in milk," Ead said, "with one spoonful of rosewater."

"Rosewater."

"Yes, madam. In the Ersyr, they say the scent of the rose brings sweet dreams."

Slowly, Sabran unfastened her sash.

"I will taste your remedy. Nothing else has worked," she said. "When Kate comes, you may tell her what to bring."

Ead approached with the barest nod and took the sash from her. Sabran's eyes were circled with shadow.

"Does something trouble Your Majesty?" Ead helped her out of the rail. "Something that disquiets your sleep?"

It was meant in courtesy, with no expectation of an answer. To her surprise, Sabran gave one.

"The wyrm." Her gaze was on the fire. "He said the thousand years were almost done. It has been just over a thousand years now since my ancestor vanquished the Nameless One."

There was a furrow in her brow. Standing there in her night-gown, she seemed as vulnerable as she would have looked when the cutthroat had beheld her.

"Wyrms have forked tongues for duplicity, madam." Ead hung the rail over the back of a chair. "Fýredel is still weak from his slumber, his fire not yet fully lit. He fears the union of Berethnet and Lievelyn. He speaks in riddles to sow misgiving in your mind."

"He has succeeded." Sabran sank onto the bed. "It seems that I must wed. For Inys."

Ead did not know the acceptable way to reply to this.

"Do you not wish to wed, madam?" she finally asked.

"That matters not."

Sabran had power in all things but this. To conceive a legitimate heir, she must wed.

Roslain or Katryen should be here. They would soothe her fears while they combed her hair for bed. They knew the right things to say, the right way to comfort her while keeping her in the state of mind necessary to her union with Prince Aubrecht.

"Do you dream, Ead?"

It came from nowhere, but Ead kept her composure. "I dream of my childhood," she replied, "and things I have seen around me by daylight, woven into new tapestries."

"I long for that. I dream of—of terrible things," Sabran murmured. "I do not tell my Ladies of the Bedchamber, for I think they would be afraid of me, but ... I will tell them to you, Ead Duryan, if you will hear them. You are made of firmer stuff."

"Of course."

She curled up on the rug beside the fire, close to Sabran, who sat with a taut back.

"I dream of a shaded bower in a forest," she began, "where sunlight dapples the grass. The entrance is a gateway of purple flowers—sabra flowers, I think."

They grew at the end of the known world. It was said that their nectar glowed like starlight. This far north, they were legendary.

"Everything in the bower is beautiful and pleasing to the ear. Birds sing charming songs, and the breeze is warm, yet the path that leads me on is jeweled with blood."

Ead nodded her reassurance, even as something glinted in the back of her mind.

"At the end of the path, I find a great rock," Sabran continued, "and I reach out to touch it with a hand I do not think is mine. The rock breaks in two, and inside—" Her voice wavered. "Inside—"

A chamberer did not have leave to touch the royal person. And yet, seeing that drawn face, Ead found herself reaching for Sabran and clasping one of her hands between her own.

"Madam," Ead said, "I am here."

Sabran looked up. A moment passed. Slowly, she moved her other hand to cup the braid of their fingers.

"Blood overflows from within the cleft, and my arms, my belly, are awash with it. I step through the rock, into a standing circle, like those in the north. And scattered all around me are bones. Small bones." Her eyes closed, and her lips quaked. "I hear terrible laughter, and I realize the laughter is mine. And then I wake."

Ead kept the queen in her gaze.

Sabran had been right. Roslain and Katryen would have been frightened.

"It is not real." Ead tightened her grasp. "None of it is real."

"There is a story in this country of a witch," Sabran said, too far into her memory to hear. "She stole children and took them into the forest. Do you know it, Ead?"

After a moment, Ead said, "The Lady of the Woods."

"I suppose Lord Arteloth told you, as he did me."

"Lady Margret."

Sabran nodded, her gaze distant. "They tell it to all children in the north. Warn them to stay away from the haithwood, where she walked. She lived long before my ancestor, and yet the fear of her lingers among my subjects." Gooseflesh stippled her neckline. "My mother told me stories of the sea, not the land. I never believed in a Lady of the Woods. Now I fear there *was* a witch, and that she lives still, working her sorcery upon me."

Ead said nothing.

"That is but one dream," Sabran said. "On other nights, I dream of the childbed. As I have since I had my first blood. I lie dying while my daughter struggles out of me. I feel her tearing my body, like a knife through silk. Between my legs, waiting to devour her, is the Nameless One."

For the first time in the eight years Ead had been at court, she saw tears bead on Sabran's eyelids.

"The blood keeps flowing, hot as iron in the forge. It clings to my thighs, sticks them together. I know I am crushing my child, but if I let her breathe ... she will fall into the jaws of the beast." Sabran closed her eyes. When she opened them, they were dry. "That nightmare torments me the most."

The weight of the crown had taken its toll on her. "Dreams reach deep into our pasts," Ead said quietly. "Lord Arteloth told you the story of the Lady of the Woods, and it has come back to haunt you now. The mind often wanders to strange places."

"I might agree with you," Sabran said, "had I not had both dreams since long before Lord Arteloth shared that tale with me."

Loth had told Ead once that Sabran could not sleep without a candle. Now she knew why.

"So you see, Ead," the queen said, "I do not sleep because I am not only afraid of the monsters at my door, but also of the monsters my own mind can conjure. The ones that live within."

Ead held her hand a little tighter.

"You are Queen of Inys," she said. "All your life, you have known that you would one day wear the crown." Sabran watched her face. "You fear for your people, but cannot show it to your court. You wear so much armor by daylight that, by night, you can carry it no longer. By night, you are only flesh. And even the flesh of a queen is prone to fear."

Sabran was listening. Her pupils were large enough to almost blot the green from her eyes.

"In darkness, we are naked. Our truest selves. Night is when fear comes to us at its fullest, when we have no way to fight it," Ead continued. "It will do everything it can to seep inside you. Sometimes it may succeed—but never think that you *are* the night."

The queen seemed to mull this over. She looked to their hands and slowly circled her thumb in Ead's palm.

"More of your comely words," she said. "I like them well, Ead Duryan."

Ead looked her in the eye. She imagined two gemstones falling to the ground, shattering from within. Those were the eyes of Sabran Berethnet.

Footsteps just beyond the threshold. Ead stood and clasped her hands in front of her just as Katryen came in with her arm around Lady Arbella Glenn, who was in her nightgown. Sabran reached out to her oldest bedfellow.

"Bella," she said, "come to me. I want to discuss the marriage preparations with you."

Arbella smiled and hobbled to her queen, who took her by the hand. With dewy eyes and a serene expression, Arbella stroked Sabran's black hair behind her ear, like a mother tending to a child.

"Bella," Sabran murmured, "never weep. I can't bear it."

Ead slipped away.

Once Sabran and Arbella were abed, Ead told Katryen about the decoction, and though the Mistress of the Robes looked skeptical, she sent for it. Once it was tasted and delivered, the royal apartments were sealed, and Ead took her position for night duty.

Kalyba.

That was the name the Lady of the Woods had gone by in Lasia. Little did the Inysh know that the witch was very much alive, though far away. And that the entrance to her lair was guarded with sabra flowers.

Sabran had never seen the Bower of Eternity. If she was dreaming of it, something was afoot.

Hours tiptoed by. Ead remained still, watching for any movement between shadow and moonbeam.

Siden allowed her to cloak herself in darkness. A cutthroat, no matter how skilled, did not have that gift. If another one came to either of the doors, she would see them.

Close to one of the clock, Roslain Crest, who was also on night duty, appeared with a candle.

"Mistress Duryan," she said.

"Lady Roslain."

They stood in silence for some time.

"Do not think me unaware of your intentions," Roslain said. "I know full well what you are doing. As does Lady Katryen."

"I was not aware that I had given you offense, my—"

"Do not take me for a fool. I see you moving closer to the queen. I see you trying to curry favor with her." Her eyes were dark as sapphires in the gloom. "Lady Truyde has said that you are a sorceress. I cannot think that she would make such an accusation without reason."

"I took the spurs and the girdle. I renounced the false faith of the Dawnsinger," Ead said. "The Knight of Fellowship tells us to embrace the converts. Perhaps you should listen to him better, my lady."

"I am the blood of the Knight of Justice. Be careful how you address me, Mistress Duryan."

Another silence rang between them.

"If you truly care for her," Roslain said, softer, "I take no issue with your new standing. Unlike many Inysh, I have nothing against converts. We are all equal in the eyes of the Saint. But if you only seek gifts and riches, I will see to it that you are cut from her side."

"I seek no gifts or riches. Only to serve the Saint as best I may," Ead said. "Can we not both agree that no more of her friends should be cut from her side?"

Roslain looked away.

"I know Loth was fond of you," she said, with what Ead could see was a degree of difficulty. "For that, I must think the best of you." With still more difficulty, she continued: "Forgive my caution. It is wearisome to watch the spiders that surround her, who only think to climb the—"

A cry rose from the Royal Bedchamber. Ead spun to face the door, heart thumping.

She had no movement from the wardings. No cutthroat could have entered that chamber.

Roslain stared at her, lips parted, eyes wide. Ead took the key from Roslain's frozen hand and ran up the steps.

"Hurry, Ead, open it," Roslain shouted. "Captain Lintley! Sir Gules!"

Ead turned the key in the lock and flung open the door. The fire burned low in the hearth.

"Ead." A shape moved on the bed. "Ead, Ros, please, you *must* wake Arbella." Sabran, ravels of hair escaping her braid. "I woke and reached for her hand, and it was so cold—" She sobbed. "Oh, Saint, say it is not so—"

Captain Lintley and Sir Gules Heath appeared at the door, swords drawn. "By the Saint, Lady Roslain, is she hurt?" Heath barked.

While Roslain hastened to her queen, Ead circled to the other side of the bed, where a small figure lay beneath the coverlet. Even before Ead searched in vain for a pulse, she knew. A terrible hush descended as she moved away.

"I am sorry, Your Majesty," she said.

The two men bowed their heads. Roslain began to weep, one hand over her mouth.

"She did not see me wed," Sabran said faintly. A tear ran down her cheek. "I promised her she would."

18

East

The journey to the capital was hideous. Niclays was jounced along for days in the stuffy palanquin with little to do but doze, or squint at bits of scenery between the wooden blinds.

Ginura lay north of the Bear's Jaw, the mountain range that guarded Cape Hisan. The trade road cleaved to the foothills before it struck a crossway.

Ever since the day Niclays had arrived in Seiiki, it had been his dream to visit Ginura. Back then, he had been grateful for the chance to live in a place few Westerners would ever see.

He remembered being called to Brygstad Palace, where Leovart had broken the news that Sabran had ordered his expulsion from Virtudom. He had thought her rage quenched after Seyton Combe had questioned him at length in the Dearn Tower about his misuse of Berethnet money. Naïvely, he had believed it would be a short exile.

Only after the third year had he understood that the tiny house on the edge of the world was to be his final resting place. That was when he had stopped dreaming of discovery, and had dreamed only of home. Now he could feel his old curiosity in the world awakening.

On the first night of the journey, they stopped at an inn in the foothills, where Niclays bathed in a hot spring. He looked at the far-off lights of Cape Hisan, and the ember that was Orisima, and for the first time in close to seven years, he started to feel as if he could breathe again.

The feeling did not last. The next morning, the chair-carriers began to complain about the owl-faced Ment they were lugging north, the spy of a prince who spat upon dragons, who must have the red sickness in his breath. Certain words were said in return, and from that point on, the jolting grew worse. The chair-carriers also began to sing about an insolent man no one liked, who was left crying on the side of the road for the mountain cats to take away.

"Yes, yes, very funny," Niclays barked at them in Seiikinese. "Shall I sing about the four chair-carriers who fell down a cliff and into the river, never to be seen again?"

All that did was make them laugh.

Countless things went wrong following that incident. A hand-hold broke off the palanquin ("Great Kwiriki wash away this owl man!") and they were forced to delay their journey while a carpenter was fetched to repair it. Once they were on their way again, the chair-carriers finally let Niclays sleep.

When he heard voices, his eyes cracked open. The chair-carriers were singing a lullaby from the Great Sorrow.

Hush, my child, the wind is rising.
Even the birds are quiet.
Stop your tears. The fire-breathers will hear us.
Sleep now, sleep, or you will see them coming.
Hold on to me and close your eyes.

There were cradle songs like this in Mentendon. Niclays strained his memory to when he was small enough for his mother to sit him on her lap and croon to him while his father drank himself into rages that had left them both quaking in fear of his belt. Fortunately, he had drunk himself into such a fury on one occasion that he had been good enough to stumble off a cliff, and that was the end of that.

For a time, all had been peaceful. Then was when Helchen Roos had convinced herself that her son would grow up to be a sanctarian and atone for the many sins of his father. She had prayed for that outcome every day. Instead, Niclays had become, in her view, a morbid hedonist who spent his time either slicing open dead bodies or tinkering with potions like a sorcerer, all while drinking himself sodden. (This was not, Niclays conceded, a baseless impression.) To her, science was the greatest sin of all, anathema to virtue.

Of course, she had still written to him at once when she had discovered his unexpected friendships with the Marquess of Zeedeur and Prince Edvart, demanding he invite her to court, as if the years she had tormented him about every facet of his existence were nothing. He and Jannart had made a sport out of finding ways to destroy her letters.

Thinking of that made him smile for the first time in days. The trill of insects in the forest sent him back to sleep.

After two more painful days, during which he thought he might die of the heat and boredom and confinement, the palanquin stopped. A bang on the roof shunted him from a doze.

"Out."

The door slid open, letting in a glare of sunlight. Niclays got down blearily from the palanquin, straight into a puddle.

"Galian's *girdle*—"

One of the chair-carriers lobbed his cane after him. They hefted the palanquin on to their shoulders and turned back to the road.

"Hold a moment," Niclays shouted after them. "I said *hold*, damn you! Where am I to go?"

Laughter was his only reply. Niclays cursed, picked up his cane, and trudged toward the west gate of the city. By the time he reached it, the hem of his robe was soaked and sweat dripped down his face. He had expected soldiers, but there was nobody in armor to be seen. The sun burned on the crown of his head as he entered the ancient capital of Seiiki.

Ginura Castle was a behemoth. The white-walled complex bestrode a great hill in the middle of the city. A friend had told Niclays that the paths in its gardens were made of seashells, and its salt-water moat sparkled with fish, their bodies clear as crystal.

He walked past the bustling markets of what he assumed was Seabed Town, the outermost district of the city. Its stone-paved streets billowed with oil-paper umbrellas and fans and hats. This close to court, people wore cooler shades than they did in Cape Hisan—green and blue and silver—and their hair was waxed and wound into ostentive styles, adorned with sea-glass ornaments, salt flowers, and cowry shells. Robes here were slippery and lustrous, so when the wearer moved, they glistened in the sun. Niclays dimly remembered that it was the height of fashion in Ginura to appear as if you had just emerged from the sea. Some courtiers even oiled their eyelashes.

Necks were encircled by branching coral or tiny plates of steel arranged to look like overlapping fish scales. Lips and cheeks sparkled with crushed pearl. Most citizens were forbidden to wear dancing pearls, as they were symbols of the royal and god-chosen, but Niclays had heard that misshapen ones without a core were often powdered and sold to the wealthy.

In the shade of a maple, two women batted a featherball to one another. The sun sparkled on the canals, where merchants and fishers unloaded their wares from graceful cedar boats. It was difficult to imagine that most of this city had burned down in the Great Sorrow five centuries ago.

As Niclays walked, unease eclipsed his wonder. The chair-carriers, damn them to the Womb of Fire, had taken the letter from the Governor, along with all his other possessions. That meant he could now be mistaken for an outsider, and he could hardly go up to Ginura Castle to explain himself in this state. The sentinels would think him a cutthroat.

Still, he had no other choice. People were catching on to his presence. Nervous looks came at him from all directions.

"Doctor Roos?"

The voice spoke in Mentish. Niclays turned.

When he saw who had hailed him, he beamed. A fine-boned man in tortoiseshell eyeglasses was weaving his way through the crowd. His black hair, cut short, was gray at the temples.

"Doctor Moyaka," Niclays called, delighted. "Oh, Eizaru, how marvelous to see you!"

Finally, some good fortune. Eizaru was a gifted surgeon Niclays had taught for a year in Orisima. He and his daughter, Purumé, had been among the first to sign up for anatomy lessons, and never in his life had Niclays seen two people so willing to learn. They had taught him a great deal about Seiikinese medicine in exchange for his knowledge. Meeting them had been a bright spot in his exile.

Eizaru broke free of the throng, and they bowed to one another before embracing. Seeing that the outsider was with someone, people returned to their business.

"My friend," Eizaru said warmly, still in Mentish. "I was just thinking of writing to you. What are you doing in Ginura?"

"Due to various disagreeable circumstances, I have some respite from Orisima," Niclays said in Seiikinese. "The honored Governor of Cape Hisan decided to send me here to be placed under house arrest."

"Whoever brought you here should not have abandoned you in the street. Did you come by palanquin?"

"Sadly."

"Ah. Those who carry them are often mischief-makers." Eizaru grimaced. "Please, come to my house, before someone wonders why you are here. I will let the honored Governor of Ginura know what happened."

"You are too kind."

Niclays followed Eizaru over a bridge, into a much wider street that led straight to the main gate of Ginura Castle. Musicians played in pools of shade while vendors touted fresh clams and sea grapes.

He had never thought to lay eyes upon the famous season trees of Ginura. Their branches formed a natural pavilion over the street. At present, they wore dazzling yellow for the summer.

Eizaru lived in a modest house near the silk market, which backed onto one of the many canals that latticed Ginura. He had been widowed for a decade, but his daughter had stayed with him so that they could pursue their passion for medicine together. Rainflowers frothed over the exterior wall, and the garden was redolent of mugwort and purple-leaved mint and other herbs.

It was Purumé who opened the door to them. A bobtail cat snaked around her ankles.

"Niclays!" Purumé smiled before bowing. She favored the same eyeglasses as her father, but the sun had tanned her skin to a deeper brown than his, and her hair, held back with a strip of cloth, was still black at the roots. "Please, come in. What an unexpected pleasure."

Niclays bowed in return. "Please forgive me for disturbing you, Purumé. This is unexpected for me, too."

"We were your honored guests in Orisima. You are always welcome." She took one look at his travel-soiled clothes and chuckled. "But you will need something else to wear."

"I quite agree."

When they were inside, Eizaru sent his two servants to the well. "Rest for a while," he told Niclays. "You may have the sun quake after that journey. I will go at once to White River Castle and ask to speak to the honored Governor. Then we can eat."

Niclays sighed with relief. "That would be wonderful."

When the servants had returned from the well and filled a tub, Niclays divested himself of his garments and laved away the mud and sweat. The cold water was bliss.

Damned if he was ever traveling in a palanquin again. They could drag him back to Orisima.

Reinvigorated, he donned the summer robe the servants had left in the guest room. A cup of tea steamed on the balcony. He sat drinking it in the shade, watching boats glide past on the canal. After years of imprisonment, Orisima had never seemed farther away.

"Learnèd Doctor Roos."

He stirred from a contented doze. One of the servants had appeared on the balcony.

"The learnèd Doctor Moyaka is back," she said. "He requests your presence."

"Thank you."

Downstairs, Eizaru awaited him.

"Niclays." There was a hint of mischief in his smile. "I spoke to the honored Governor. She has agreed to my request that you remain with Purumé and myself while you are in the city."

"Oh, Eizaru." Perhaps it was the heat or his exhaustion, but the good news almost brought Niclays to tears. "Are you quite sure it's no trouble?"

"Of course not." Eizaru ushered him into the next room. "Come, now. You must be famished."

The servants had done what they could to keep the heat out. Every door had been opened, screens blocked the sunlight, and bowls of ice waited on the table. Niclays knelt with Purumé and Eizaru, and they dined on marbled beef and salt-pickled vegetables and sweetfish and sea lettuce and little cups of toasted seaweed, each bursting with roe. While they ate, they spoke of what they had all been doing since last they had met.

It had been a long time since Niclays had been allowed the pleasure of a conversation with like-minded people. Eizaru was still running his medical practice, which now offered both Seiikinese and Mentish remedies for ailments. Purumé, meanwhile, was working on a herbal concoction that brought on a deep sleep, allowing a surgeon to remove carnosities from the body without causing pain.

"I call it blossom sleep," she said, "as the final ingredient was a flower from the South Mountains."

"She trekked for days to find that flower in the spring," Eizaru said, with a proud smile at his daughter.

"It sounds revolutionary," Niclays said, stunned. "You could use it to study the interior of *living* bodies. In Mentendon, all we can do is cut open corpses." His heart thumped. "Purumé, you must publish these findings. Think of how anatomy would change."

"I would," she said, with a weary smile, "but there is one problem, Niclays. Firecloud."

"Firecloud?"

"A restricted substance. Alchemists make it from the bile of fire-breathers," Eizaru explained. "The bile is smuggled into the East by Southern pirates, treated in some way, then stuffed into a ceramic orb with a dab of gunpowder. When the wick is lit, the orb explodes and releases a smoke as black and thick as tar. If a dragon breathes it in, it falls asleep for many days. The pirates can then sell its body parts."

"An evil practice," Purumé said.

Niclays shook his head. "What has that to do with blossom sleep?"

"If the authorities believe my creation might be used for similar means, they will stop my research. They may even close down our practice."

Niclays was speechless.

"It is very sad," Eizaru said heavily. "Tell us, Niclays—are any Seiikinese medical documents translated in Mentendon? Perhaps Purumé could publish her findings there."

Niclays sighed. "Unless things have changed dramatically in the years I have been away, I doubt it. Pamphlets change hands in some circles, but they are not approved by the crown. Virtudom does not hold with heresy, or with the knowledge of heretics."

Purumé shook her head. As Niclays helped himself to some prawns, a young man appeared in the doorway, dewy from the heat.

"Learnèd Doctor Roos." He bowed, panting. "I come from the honored Governor of Ginura."

Niclays braced himself. She must have changed her mind about letting him stay here.

"She asks me to inform you," the servant said, "that you will be expected at Ginura Castle for an audience when it pleases the all-honored Warlord."

Niclays raised his eyebrows. "The all-honored Warlord wishes to see *me*? Are you quite sure?"

"Yes."

The servant bowed out of the room.

"So you will be received at court." Eizaru looked amused. "Be ready. They say it is like a reef of sea flowers. Beautiful, but everything you touch will sting."

"I can hardly wait," Niclays said, but his brow knitted. "I wonder why he wants to see me."

"The all-honored Warlord likes to hear from the Mentish settlers. Sometimes he will ask to hear a song or a story from your country. Or he may wish to know what sort of work you are doing," Eizaru said. "It will be nothing to worry about, Niclays, truly."

"And until then, you are free," Purumé pointed out, eyes twinkling. "Let us show you our city while you are out of Orisima. We could visit the theatre, speak about medicine, see the dragons in flight—anything you have wanted to do since you arrived."

Niclays could have wept with gratitude.

"Truly, my friends," he said, "I should like nothing better."

19

West

Loth followed the Donmata Marosa through yet another passageway. Torchlight baked his eyes as he edged between the sweating walls.

Days after he had last heard from her, she had told him to meet her again in a darkened solar. Now they were in a warren of tunnels behind the walls, where a clever system of copper pipes conducted water from the hot springs to the bedchambers.

At the end of the passage was a spiraling stair. The Donmata began to ascend.

"Where are you taking me?" Loth said stiffly.

"We are going to meet the one who plotted the murder of Queen Rosarian."

His hand grew clammy on the torch.

"I am sorry, incidentally," she said, "for making you dance with Priessa. It was the only way to get you the message."

"Could she not have given it to me in the coach?" he muttered.

"No. She was searched before she left the palace, and the coach driver was a spy, there to ensure she could not flee. No one is permitted to leave Cárscaro for long."

The Donmata detached a key from her girdle. When Loth followed her through the door she unlocked, he coughed on the dust in the chamber beyond, where the only light stemmed from his torch. The furniture stank of sickness and decay, with a mordant edge of vinegar.

The Donmata lifted her veil and draped it over a chair. Loth followed her toward a four-poster bed, hardly breathing for fear, and held up his torch.

A blindfolded figure sat in the bed. Loth made out waxen skin, charcoal lips, and chestnut hair that straggled to the collar of a crimson bedgown. Chains bound two emaciated arms. Red lines branched down them, following the tracery of his veins.

"What is this?" Loth murmured. "This is the killer?"

The Donmata folded her arms. Her jaw was a steady line, her eyes bereft of emotion.

"Lord Arteloth," she said, "I present to you my lord father, Sigoso the Third of the House of Vetalda, Flesh King of the Draconic Kingdom of Yscalin. Or what is left of him."

Loth looked back at the man in disbelief.

Even before the betrayal of Yscalin, he had not seen King Sigoso, but in his portraits, he had always looked hale and handsome, if cold, with the amber eyes of the Vetalda. Sabran had invited him to court several times, but he had always preferred to send representatives.

"A flesh king rules as the puppet of a wyrm. A title Fýredel hopes to bestow on every ruler in the world." The Donmata walked around the bed. "Father has a rare form of the Draconic plague. It allows Fýredel to ... commune with him, somehow. To see and hear into the palace."

"You mean at this very moment—"

"Peace. I put a sedative in his evening drink," she said. "I cannot do it often, or Fýredel becomes suspicious, but it keeps the wyrm from using him. For a short while."

At the sound of her voice, Sigoso stirred.

"I had no idea wyrms could do such a thing." Loth swallowed. "Control a body."

"When High Westerns die, the fire goes out in the wyverns who serve them, and in the progeny those wyverns sired. Perhaps this is a similar kind of connection."

"How long has he been like this?"

"Two years."

He had fallen ill when Yscalin had betrayed Virtudom. "How did he *become* this?"

"First you must hear the truth," the Donmata said. "My father remembers enough to tell you."

"Marosa," Sigoso croaked. "Marosssssa."

Loth flinched at his voice. It was as if a knot of rattlesnakes were nesting in his throat.

"Where are you, daughter?" the king asked very softly. "Must I come and find you?"

Expressionless, the Donmata turned to him and set about removing the blindfold. Though she wore velvet gloves that covered her to the elbow, Loth could not breathe while she was so close to her father, fearing Sigoso might bite through the velvet or make a grab for her face. When the blindfold came away, Sigoso bared his teeth. His eyes were no longer topaz, but gray all the way through. Hollows of cold ash.

"I hope you slept well, Father," the Donmata said in Inysh.

"I dreamed of a clock tower and a woman with a fire within her. I dreamed she was my enemy." King Sigoso stared at Loth, flexing his arms in their chains. "Who is this?"

"This is Lord Arteloth Beck of Goldenbirch. He is our new ambassador from Inys." The Donmata forced a smile. "I wondered if you would care to tell him how Queen Rosarian died."

Sigoso breathed like a bellows. His gaze darted between them, a hunter sizing up two morsels.

"I ended Rosarian."

The way he spoke that name, rolling it about on his tongue like a comfit, gave Loth a chill.

"Why?" the Donmata said.

"That venereal slut refused my hand. The hand of *royalty*," Sigoso spat out. The cords in his neck strained. "She would rather whore herself for pirates and lordlings than unite with the blood of the House of Vetalda—" Spittle ran from his mouth. "Daughter, I am burning."

With a glance at Loth, the Donmata went to his nightstand, where a cloth lay beside a bowl of water. She soaked the cloth and set it on his brow.

"I had her a gown made," Sigoso continued. "A gown of such beauty that a vain harlot like Rosarian could never resist it. I had it laced with basilisk venom I bought from a merchant prince, and I sent it to Inys to be hid among her garments."

Loth was shivering. "Who hid it?" he whispered. "Who hid the gown?"

"He will not speak to anyone but me," the Donmata murmured. "Father, who hid the gown?"

"A friend in the palace."

"In the palace," Loth echoed. "By the Saint. Who?"

The Donmata repeated his question. Sigoso chuckled, but it splintered into a cough.

"The cupbearer," he said.

Loth stared. The position of cupbearer had been defunct for centuries.

The gown would have been planted in the Privy Wardrobe. The Mistress of the Robes at the time had been Lady Arbella Glenn, and she would never have hurt her queen.

"I hope," Sigoso said, "that there was some of the strumpet left to bury. Basilisk venom is so strong." He hacked up a laugh. "Even bone yields before its bite."

At this, Loth drew his baselard.

"Forgive my lord father." The Donmata gazed soullessly at the Flesh King. "I would say that he is not himself, but I think he is as much himself as he has ever been."

Disgusted, Loth took a step toward the bed. "The Knight of Courage turns his back to you, Sigoso Vetalda," he said, voice quaking. "Her hand was hers to give to whomever she desired. Damn you to the Womb of Fire."

Sigoso smiled. "I am there," he said, "and it is paradise."

The gray in his eyes flickered. Red flecks ignited inside them, like embers.

"Fýredel." The Donmata snatched a cup from the nightstand. "Father, drink this. It will ease the pain."

She pressed it to his lips. Never taking his gaze from Loth, Sigoso drank what was inside. Overcome by what he had heard, Loth let the Donmata usher him out.

His mother, Lady Annes Beck, had been with the Queen Mother when she died. Now he understood why neither she nor Sabran had ever been able to utter a word to him about the day Rosarian had been laced into that lovely gown. Why Lady Arbella Glenn, who had loved her like her own child, had never uttered a word again.

Loth sank onto the steps. As he shook, he became aware of the Donmata behind him.

"Why have me listen to him?" he asked. "Why not just tell me?"

"So that you could see and hear the truth," she said, "and deliver it to Sabran. And so that you would believe it, and not leave thinking that a mystery still lies in Yscalin."

The Donmata sat on the step behind his, so their heads were level. She placed a silk-wrapped bundle into her lap.

"Can he hear us?" Loth asked her.

"No. He sleeps again." She sounded tired. "I pray Fýredel will not realize that I stopped him. He may think Father is dying. Which I think he is." Her chin lifted. "I have no doubt the wyrm intends for me to replace him. His manikin to be controlled."

"Does Fýredel not take issue with your keeping the king like this, chained in a dark room?"

"Fýredel understands that my father does not look ... *kingly* in his present state, his body rotting even as it continues to draw breath," the Donmata said dryly, "but I must lead him from his rooms when ordered. So our lord and master can see into the palace whenever he desires. So he can issue orders to the Privy Council. So he can ensure we are not mounting a rebellion. So he can stop us calling for aid."

"If you killed your father, Fýredel would know," Loth realized. "And punish you."

"The last time I defied him, he had one of my ladies put on the Gate of Niunda." Her face tightened. "I had to watch as his cockatrices pecked her to shreds."

They were quiet and still for a time.

"Queen Rosarian died fourteen years ago," Loth stated. "Then ... Sigoso did not do it under Draconic control."

"Not all evil comes from wyrms."

The Donmata turned to face him on the stair, so her back was against the wall.

"I do not remember a great deal about my father from my child-hood. Just his cold gaze," she murmured. "When I was sixteen, my mother came to my bedchamber in the middle of the night. Their marriage had always been strained, but now she looked afraid. And angry. She said we were going to join her brother, King Jantar, in Rauca. We dressed as servants and stole through the palace.

"Of course, the guards stopped us. Confined us both to our bedchambers and forbade us from speaking. I have never cried so hard in my life. Mama bribed a guard to pass me a letter, telling me to remain strong." She touched the pendant at her throat, set with emeralds. "A week later, Father came to inform me of her death. He told the court that she took her own life, shamed by her attempt to abandon her king ... but I know otherwise. She would never have left me alone with him."

"I am sorry," Loth said.

"Not as sorry as I am." Disgust tightened her face. "Yscalin does not deserve this, but my father does. He deserves to look as corrupt on the outside as he always was within."

Sahar Taumargam and Rosarian Berethnet, both dead by the hand of the same king. All while Inys had considered him a friend in Virtudom.

"I wanted to tell Sabran the truth. I wanted to call for aid, for troops ... but this palace is a dungeon. The Privy Council has fallen utterly to Fýredel, too afraid to anger him. They have families in the city who would die if we stoked his wrath."

Loth lifted his sleeve to his face to blot the sweat.

"Sabran was my friend. Prince Aubrecht was my betrothed for a long while," the Donmata reminded him. "I know they must think ill of me now."

Guilt pricked at Loth. "Forgive us," he murmured. "We should not all have assumed—"

"You could never have known Fýredel was awake. Or that we were under his wing."

"Tell me how Cárscaro fell. Help me understand."

The Donmata breathed out through her nose.

"Two years ago, there was a quake in the Spindles," she said. "Fýredel had awakened in a chamber in Mount Fruma, where he had gone to sleep after the Grief of Ages. We were on his doorstep. Ripe for the seizing.

"The lavender fields burned first. Black smoke choked the evening sky." She shook her head. "It all happened so quickly. Wyverns had surrounded Cárscaro before the city guards could reach the old defenses. Fýredel appeared for the first time in centuries. He said he would set us all afire if my father did not come to him to pay tribute."

"And did he?"

"He sent a decoy at first, but Fýredel sensed the deception. He burned the man alive, and my father was forced to emerge," she said. "Fýredel took him into the mountains. For the rest of that night, Cárscaro descended into chaos. People thought a second Grief of Ages had begun—which, in a way, it had." A terrible sadness darkened her eyes. "Panic reigned. Thousands tried to flee, but the only way out is through the Gate of Niunda, and the wyverns guarded it." Her mouth pinched. "Father returned at dawn. The people saw that their king was alive and unharmed and did not know what to think. He told them they would be the first to witness the rise of the Draconic world—if they obeyed.

"Behind the walls of this palace, Father ordered his Privy Council to announce our allegiance to the Nameless One. They sent word to every nation, too craven to challenge him. Too craven when he ordered our defenses be torn down. Too craven when he burned down the aviary, and every bird left in it. I tried to organize a counterstroke, to no avail. I could do no more without endangering my life."

"But the rest of the country did not know the truth," Loth said.

"Cárscaro became a fortress that night. No one could get word out." Her head dropped back against the wall. "Wyrms are weak when they first stir. For a year, Fýredel remained under Mount Fruma, regaining his strength. I watched as he used my father to turn my country into the base of his power. I watched him destroy the Six Virtues. I watched the plague awaken and spread among my people. And my home became my prison."

That was when Arteloth Beck did exactly what Gian Harlowe had warned him not to do.

He took Marosa Vetalda by the hand.

She wore velvet gloves. It was still a risk, and yet he did it without a second thought.

"You are the very embodiment of courage," he told her. "And your friends in Virtudom have failed you."

The Donmata looked at their hands with a notch in her brow. Loth wondered when it was that she had last been touched.

"Tell me how I can help you," he said.

Slowly, she placed her other hand over his. "You can go back into that bedchamber," she said, lifting her gaze to his, "and lay your uncovered hands upon my father."

It took him a moment to understand. "You want me to ... afflict myself?"

"I will explain," she said, "but if you do it, I offer you a chance to escape Cárscaro in return."

"You said it was a fortress."

"My mother knew one way out." She set a hand on the bundle in her lap. "I want you to journey across the Spindles and deliver this to Chassar uq-Ispad, the Ersyri ambassador. You must entrust it only to him."

The man who had raised Ead, and who had presented her to court eight years ago. The Donmata unwrapped the silk. Inside was an iron box, engraved with symbols.

"In the spring, a woman was captured near Perunta, trying to find a ship that would take her on to Lasia. The torturers had her for days, but she never spoke. When my father set eyes on the red cloak she had with her, Fýredel was enraged. He ordered that she must spend her last hours in agony."

Loth was not sure if he could stand to hear this.

"That night, I sought her out." The Donmata skimmed her fingers over the box. "I thought they had torn her tongue out at first, but when I gave her wine, she told me her name was Jondu. She told me that if I valued human life, I would get the object she had been carrying to Chassar uq-Ispad." She paused. "I killed Jondu myself. Told Fýredel she had died of her wounds. Better that than the gate. The box that had been taken from Jondu was locked. No one could open it, and eventually they lost interest. It was easy for me to steal it. I am sure that it is vital in our fight, and that Ambassador uq-Ispad will know more."

She traced the patterns on its lid.

"He is most likely in Rumelabar. To reach the Ersyr and avoid the guarded borders, you must cross the Spindles. The safest way to do that without harm from the Draconic creatures that now live there is to become afflicted, so that when they smell you, they will not attack," she continued. "Jondu swore the ambassador knows a cure for the plague. If you reach him in time, you may live to tell the tale."

Loth understood then. "You sent Prince Wilstan to do this," he said. "Or tried."

"I did everything the same. I showed him my father and had him hear from his own lips how Rosarian died. And then I gave him the box. But Fynch had been waiting for his opportunity to flee, and to return to his daughter with news of this place," she said. "He assured me he had given himself the plague. When I realized he had not, I went after him with all haste. He had abandoned the box in the secret tunnel that leads to the mountains. He clearly never meant to honor my request ... but I can hardly blame him for thinking he could get back to Sabran."

"Where is he now?" Loth asked quietly.

"I found him not far from the end of the tunnel," she said. "It was an amphiptere."

Loth rested his brow against his clasped hands.

Amphipteres were vicious Draconic creatures without limbs. They had strong jaws, and were said to shake their prey like poppets until they were too weak to run.

"I would have retrieved his remains, but I was attacked the moment I ventured too close. I said the necessary prayers."

"Thank you."

"Despite appearances, I am still faithful to the Saint. And he needs us now, Lord Arteloth." The Donmata placed a hand on his forearm. "Will you do as I ask?"

He swallowed. "What of Lord Kitston?"

"He can remain here, and I will watch over him. Or he can go with you—but he must be afflicted, too."

Even the Knight of Fellowship would not expect Kit to do this for him. He had already done too much.

"Will Fýredel see through me?" Loth asked.

"No. You will have the usual kind of plague," she said. "I have tested the theory."

He elected not to ask how. "Surely there are others in the palace who are loyal to the Saint," he said. "Why not send one of your own servants?"

"I trust only Priessa, and her disappearance would raise alarm. I would go myself, but I cannot leave my people without a sane Vetalda. Even if I am powerless to save them, I must stay and do what I can to undermine Fýredel."

He had misjudged the Donmata Marosa. She was a true woman of Virtudom, imprisoned in the shell of a home she must once have loved.

"It is too late for me, my lord," she said, "but not for Virtudom. What has happened here in Yscalin must not be allowed to happen elsewhere."

Loth looked away from those fire-opal eyes, to the patron brooch on his doublet. Two hands joined in affinity. The self-same twine of fingers that graced a love-knot ring.

If the Knight of Fellowship were here, Loth knew what she would do.

"If you consent," the Donmata said, "I will take you back to the Flesh King, and you will lay your hands on him. Then I will show you the way out of Yscalin." She rose. "If you refuse, I advise you to prepare yourself for a long life in Cárscaro, Lord Arteloth Beck."

20

East

While the other sea guardians celebrated the end of the trials in the banquet hall, Tané lay exhausted in her quarters. She had not emerged since her fight with Turosa. A surgeon had cleaned and stitched her shoulder, but moving drained her, and the throb was ceaseless.

Tomorrow, she would find out if she was to ride.

She gnawed the nail on her little finger until she tasted blood. If only for something less painful to do with her hands, she found her copy of *Recollections of the Great Sorrow*. The book had been a gift from one of her teachers for her fifteenth birthday. It had been some time since she had opened it, but its illustrations would distract her.

Close to the twelfth hour, when the song of the tree crickets was swelling outside, she was still awake, reading.

One image portrayed a Seiikinese woman with the red sickness. Her hands and eyes were crimson. On another page were the fire-breathers. Their bat wings had frightened Tané when she was fifteen, and they still gave her a chill. The next image showed the people of Cape Hisan standing on the coast, watching a great battle. Dragons twisted and thrashed among the waves. Their jaws snapped at the demons as they rained fire upon Seiiki.

The final image showed the comet that had come on the last night of the Great Sorrow—Kwiriki's Lantern—weeping meteors into the sea. The winged demons fled from it, while the dragons of Seikii rose from the waves, painted in coin-bright silvers and blues.

A knock interrupted her reflections. Tané shifted painfully to her feet. When she slid open the door, she found Onren, clad in a dark green robe, hair bedecked with salt flowers. She was holding a tray.

"I brought supper," she said.

Tané stood aside. "Come in."

She returned to her bedding. Her candles had burned low, stretching every shadow. Onren set the tray down, revealing a small feast. Tender cuts of sea bream, bean curd rolled in roe, and salt-pickled kelp in a fragrant broth, as well as a jar of spiced wine and a cup.

"The honored Sea General let us taste his famous sea-aged wine," Onren said with a brief smile. "I would have saved you some, but it ran out almost as quickly as it arrived. This is a touch less special"— she poured from the jar—"but it might dampen your pain."

"Thank you," Tané said. "It was kind of you to think of me, but I never had a taste for wine. You have it."

"The trials are over, Tané. You can let go. But . . . I suppose I could use it." Onren knelt on the mats. "We missed you at the banquet hall."

"I was tired."

"I thought you might say that. Not to insult you, but you look as if you haven't slept in years. And you've earned a rest." She picked up the cup. "You did well against Turosa. Perhaps the bastard's finally realized that he is not so high above the peasants he despises."

"We are not peasants now." Tané studied her. "You look worried."

"I think I lost the chance to ride today. Kanperu fights as well as he—" She sipped the wine. "Well."

So she had fought Kanperu. Tané had been taken to the surgeon before she could see the other trials.

"You excelled on all the other days," Tané reminded her. "The honored Sea General will judge us fairly."

"How do you know?"

"He is a rider."

"Turosa will be a rider tomorrow, yet he has spent years picking on those of us who came from peasant stock. I heard he beat a servant once for not bowing low enough. Either of us would have been exiled from the Houses of Learning for behaving that way … but blood still holds power."

"You do not know that he will be a rider just because of that."

"I wager you all I own that he will."

Silence fell. Tané picked at the bean curd.

"I was scolded once, when I was sixteen, for gambling in the city," Onren said. "Because it was disreputable, I was barred from lessons and told I would have to earn back my place in the East House. I was scrubbing the outhouses for the rest of the season. Meanwhile, Turosa can almost murder a servant and have a sword in his hand a few days later."

"Our learnèd teachers had their reasons. They understand the true meaning of justice."

"Their reason was that he is the grandson of a rider, and I am not. And that will be their reason tomorrow if I am cast off in favor of him."

"That will not be the reason," Tané bit out.

It had leaped from her tongue before she could catch it, like a slippery fish eluding her grasp.

Onren raised her eyebrows. The silence hung, an unstruck bell, as Tané wrestled with herself.

"Come, Tané. Speak your mind." Onren raised a cautious smile. "We are friends, after all."

It was too late now to take it back. The trials, the outsider, her exhaustion and guilt—all of it came together violently, like bubbles in boiling water, and Tané could no longer hold it in.

"You seem to think that if you are not made a rider tomorrow, it will not be through any fault of yours," she heard herself say. "I have worked every day and night during our time here. You, in the meantime, have shown no respect. You arrive *late* to your trials, in front of the Miduchi. You spend your nights in taverns when you ought to be practicing, then wonder why you fight poorly against your opponent. Perhaps *that* will be the reason that you do not become a rider."

Onren was no longer smiling.

"So," she said curtly, "you think I don't deserve it. Because ... I went to the tavern." She paused. "Or is it because I went to the tavern and still outperformed you in the knife trial?"

Tané stiffened.

"Your eyes were bloodshot that morning. They still are. You stayed up all night practicing."

"Of course I did."

"And you resent me because I didn't." Onren shook her head. "Balance is necessary in all things, Tané—it does not equate to disrespect. This position is the chance of a lifetime, and not to be squandered."

"I know that," Tané said, her tone clipped. "I only hope that you do, too."

At this, Onren smiled thinly, but Tané glimpsed the hurt in her eyes.

"Well," she said, rising, "in that case, I had better leave you. I have no wish to drag you down with me."

As quickly as the anger had brimmed inside Tané, it cooled. She sat very still, her hands pressed on the bedding, trying to swallow the tang of shame. Finally, she rose and bowed.

"I apologize, honorable Onren," she murmured. "I should not have said any of that. It was inexcusable."

After a pause, Onren softened. "Forgiven. Truly." She sighed. "I have been worried about you." Tané kept her gaze down. "You have always worked hard, but throughout these trials, it seems to me as if you have been punishing yourself, Tané. Why?"

When she spoke like that, it was like having Susa again. A kind face and an open mind. Just for a moment, Tané was tempted to tell Onren everything. Perhaps she would understand.

"No," she said at last. "I have only been afraid. And tired." She sank back onto the bedding. "I will be better tomorrow. When I know my fate."

Onren laughed at that. "Oh, Tané. You make it sound as if the jailhouse is the alternative."

Tané flinched, but managed a smile.

"I will leave you. We both need rest." Onren drained the cup. "Goodnight, Tané."

"Goodnight."

As soon as Onren was gone, Tané quenched the oil lamp and crawled under her bedding. Exhaustion and pain engulfed her at last, and she plunged into a dreamless sleep.

When she woke, the light was golden. For a moment, she could not understand why the room was so bright. It seemed as if it had been dark for an eternity.

She slid open the window. The sun gleamed on the rooftops of Ginura, even as the rain kept sheeting.

A sunshower. A good omen.

The servants would come soon with her new uniform. If the dragon on the back of the surcoat was silver, she would remain a sea guardian and serve as a leader in the navy.

If it was gold, she was god-chosen.

She paced the room and lit the incense in the shrine for one last prayer. She asked forgiveness for her impoliteness toward Onren, and again for what she had done on the night before the ceremony. If the great Kwiriki would only absolve her, she would prove her devotion for the rest of her life.

The servants came as afternoon ended. Tané waited, eyes closed, before she turned to face them.

The tunic was watersilk. Blue as sapphires. And on the back of the surcoat was the dragon emblem, embroidered in gold thread.

———

Her new attendants skinned her hair into a military style. The scar on her cheek looked more prominent, and her shoulder ached, but her eyes were as bright as fresh ink.

As the sun took its leave, she emerged from her palanquin and stepped on to the pale sand of Ginura Bay. The choosing always took place at the end of the day, for her old life ended here. She wore new leather boots with a thick heel, the better to grip the stirrups of a saddle.

A night rainbow burned against the smoky purple of the sky, daubed across the horizon in intensities of red. People were gathering on the cliffs to stare at this peculiar sign from the great Kwiriki, and to watch the twelve new dragonriders walk toward the water.

Turosa was among them. So were all the other relatives of dragonriders. Tané fell into step beside Onren, who smiled at her. She had earned a place in Clan Miduchi.

The last time Tané had been on a beach, the stranger had stepped from the dark like a curse. Yet the tides within her, which had pushed her toward this day from the cradle, were strangely calm and still.

Ten Seiikinese dragons waited in the sea, lithe and beautiful. The sun and the rainbow lit the waves that lapped against their bodies. The two Lacustrine warriors, it seemed, had yet to arrive.

When he was called, Kanperu bowed to the Sea General, who lifted a string of dancing pearls around his neck. He handed Kanperu a helm and a padded saddle. Next, the Sea General bestowed on him a mask to keep the elements off his face and a sword quenched with salt water, its scabbard inlaid with mother-of-pearl, made by the finest bladesmith in Seiiki.

Kanperu passed the cords of the helm around his neck, then hefted the saddle under his arm and strode into the water. Once he was up to his waist, he held out his right hand, palm turned upward.

A blue-gray dragon extended her neck and considered him with eyes like full moons. When she dipped her head farther, Kanperu hooked his fingers into her mane and clambered onto her, mindful of her spines. No sooner were he and the saddle in place than his dragon let out a haunting call and plunged into the sea, drenching everyone on the beach.

Onren approached the shore next, cheeks full of her smile. She had only held out her hand for a moment before the largest of the dragons—a hulking Seiikinese with a black mane, his scales like beaten silver—came gliding toward the beach. Onren tensed at first, but once she had made contact, she relaxed and climbed his neck like a ladder.

"The honorable Miduchi Tané," the Sea General called. "Step forward."

Onren lowered her mask over her face. The dragon lowered his head and swam away.

Tané bowed to the Sea General and let him lock the pearls at the base of her neck, the sign that she was god-chosen. She took the helmet and the saddle and, finally, the sword in its scabbard. It already felt like a part of her arm. She fastened it to her sash and waded into the sea.

As warm salt water swilled around her calves, her breath came short. She reached out a hand. Head down. Eyes shut. Her hand was steady, but the rest of her was quaking.

Cold scale brushed her fingers. She dared not look. She must. When she did, two eyes, as bright as fireworks, stared back from the face of a Lacustrine dragon.

21

West

Loth left his rooms in the Palace of Salvation for the last time in the dead of night.

The Draconic plague was inside him. One touch to the brow of the Flesh King, a prickle in his hand, and an hourglass had turned over in his mind. Soon enough, the fine grains of his sanity would begin to course between his fingers.

Slung over his shoulder was a leather sack, filled with supplies for the journey through the mountains. His baselard and sword were at his side, concealed beneath a winter cloak.

Kit followed him down the winding stairs. "I do hope this is a good idea, Arteloth," he said.

"It is the opposite of a good idea."

"Piracy was the better option."

"Undeniably."

They were entering the bowels of Cárscaro. The Donmata Marosa had told him how to access a hidden stair from the Privy Sanctuary, which tapered as they descended. Loth dried the cold sweat from his brow. He had pleaded with Kit to stay behind, but his friend had insisted on coming with him.

An eternity passed before their boots hit flat ground. Loth held his torch up.

The Donmata Marosa was waiting at the foot of the stair, her face cast into shadow by her hood. She stood before a great crack in the wall.

"What is this place?" Loth asked.

"A forgotten escape route. For use in sieges, I suppose," she said. "It was how Mama and I meant to flee."

"Why did you not use it to get word out?"

"I tried." She lowered her hood. "Lord Kitston. Are you now afflicted?"

Kit bowed. "Yes, Radiance. I believe I am sufficiently plague-ridden."

"Good." Her gaze snapped back to Loth. "I sent one of my ladies. That was before I knew how many Draconic creatures were in the mountains."

The inference was clear.

The Donmata reached behind her and held out matching wooden staffs, each capped with a hook. "Ice staves. They will help you find your balance."

They took them. To Loth she handed another sack, heavy with the iron box.

"I bid you not abandon this task I have set for you, Lord Arteloth." Her eyes were jewel-like in the firelight. "I trust that you will do this for me. And for Virtudom."

With these words, she stood aside.

"We will send help." Loth spoke quietly. "Keep your father alive for as long as you can. If he dies, hide yourself from Fýredel. When this task is done, we will tell the sovereigns of Virtudom what has happened here. You will not die alone in this place."

At last, the Donmata Marosa smiled, just a little. As if she had forgotten how.

"You have a kind heart, Lord Arteloth," she said. "If you do get back to Inys, give Sabran and Aubrecht my regards."

"I will." He bowed to her. "Goodbye, Your Radiance."

"Goodbye, my lord."

Their gazes held for a song of heartbeats. Loth dipped his head once more and stepped into the passage.

"May the Knight of Courage bring you cheer in these dark hours," Kit said to Marosa.

"And you, Lord Kitston."

Her footsteps echoed as she left. Loth felt a sudden regret that they could not take her with them. Marosa Vetalda, Donmata of Yscalin, imprisoned in her tower.

The passageway was unspeakably dark. A breeze drew Loth on like a beckoning hand. He snared his boot on the uneven ground at once, almost robbing himself of an eye with his torch. They were surrounded by the glimmer of volcanic glass and the porous swell of pumice. The glass mirrored the light of his torch, casting a hundred different reflections.

They walked for what seemed like hours, sometimes turning a corner, but otherwise moving in a straight line. Their staves tapped out a rhythm.

Once Kit coughed, and Loth tensed. "Hush," he said. "I would rather not wake whatever dwells down here."

"A man must cough when need be. And *nothing* dwells down here."

"Tell me these walls don't look as if a basilisk carved them."

"Oh, stop being such a doomsinger. Think of this as another adventure."

"I never wanted an adventure," Loth said wearily. "Not even one. At this moment, I want to be at Briar House with a cup of mulled wine, preparing to walk my queen to the altar."

"And I should like to be waking up beside Kate Withy, but alas, we cannot have everything."

Loth smiled. "I'm glad you're here, Kit."

"I should think so," Kit said, his eyes shining.

This place made Loth think of the Nameless One, and how he had torn through the earth until he found his way into the world above. His mother had often told him the story when he was a child, using different voices to frighten him and make him laugh.

He took another step. The ground underfoot gave a hollow rumble, like the belly of a giant.

Loth stopped dead, clutching the torch. Its flame guttered as another cold wind feathered through the tunnel.

"Is it a quake?" Kit murmured. When Loth did not reply, his voice grew tense. "Loth, is it a quake?"

"Hush. I don't know."

Another rumble came, louder this time, and the earth seemed to tilt. Loth lost his footing. No sooner had he caught himself than a terrific shuddering began—first soft, like a shiver of fear, then more and more violent, until his teeth rattled in their sockets.

"It's a quake," he shouted. "Run. Kit, *run*, man. Run!"

The iron box pounded against his back. They barreled through the darkness, desperately searching for any glint of daylight ahead. It was as if the very mantle of the earth was convulsing.

"Loth!" Kit, his voice shot through with terror. "The torch—my torch is out!"

Loth turned on his heel, winded, and thrust out his torch. His friend had fallen far behind.

"Kit!" He ran back. "On your feet, man, hurry. Follow my voice!"

A creak. Like weak ice underfoot. Small rocks, like gravel, peppering his back. He threw his hands over his head as the roof of the tunnel came pouring down.

For a long time, he expected to die. The Knight of Courage fled from him, and he whimpered like a child. The darkness blinded him. Rock smashed. Glass shattered and rang. He coughed on foul-tasting dust.

And then, just like that, it stopped.

"Kit," Loth bellowed. "Kit!"

Panting, he reached for his torch—still lit, miraculously—and swung it toward the place he had heard Kit calling out to him. Rock and volcanic glass filled the tunnel.

"Kitston!"

He could not be dead. He *must* not be dead. Loth shoved at the wall of debris with all his might, threw his shoulder against it time and again, struck at it with the ice staff and pounded his fists bloody. When at last it gave way, he reached into the rubble and hauled at the rocks with his bare hands, and the air down here was like half-set honey, sticky in his throat . . .

His fingers closed around a limp hand. He shoved more glass aside, his muscles straining with the effort.

And there, at last, was Kit. There were the eyes Loth knew, their laughter gone. The mouth, so quick to smile, that would never smile again. There was the tablet about his neck, twin to the one he had given Loth at their last Feast of Fellowship. The rest of him was out of sight. All Loth could see was the blood that seeped between the rocks.

A desperate sob heaved out of him. His cheeks were wet with sweat and tears, his knuckles bled, and his mouth tasted of iron.

"Forgive me," he said thickly. "Forgive me, Kitston Glade."

22

West

The marriage of Sabran the Ninth and Aubrecht the Second took place as summer turned to autumn. It was customary for the vows to be taken at midnight, during the new moon, for it was in the darkest hours that companionship was needed most.

And a dark hour it was. Never in Berethnet history had a marriage come so soon after a burial.

The Great Sanctuary of Briar House, like most sanctuaries, was round, modeled on the shields used by the early knights of Inys. After the Grief of Ages, when its roof had caved in, Rosarian the Second had ordered red stained-glass windows be set into the arches in memory of those whose blood had been spilled.

Over the centuries, three scoundrel trees had broken through the floor and pleached their branches over the walkway. Their leaves already burned with gold and umber. Six hundred people had gathered beneath them for the ceremony, including the Most Virtuous Order of Sanctarians.

When the Queen of Inys appeared at the south-facing doors, the witnesses fell silent. Her hair was brushed to an ebony gloss, threaded with white flowers. A partlet latticed her neckline. She wore a crown of filigrain gold, inlaid with rubies that caught the light of every candle.

The choir began to sing, their voices fluting high and rich. Sabran took one step, then stopped.

From her position among the candle-bearers, Ead watched the queen as she stayed there, rooted to the spot. Roslain, her giver, pressed her arm.

"Sab," she whispered.

Sabran drew herself up. In the darkness of the sanctuary, few would be able to see the rigid set of her shoulders, or the shiver that might have been put down to the chill.

A moment later, she was on her way.

Seyton Combe observed her approach from where the Dukes Spiritual and their families stood. The candlelight revealed the pinch of satisfaction at the corner of his mouth.

He had sent Loth to his death for this night. Loth, who should be with Sabran. It was traditional in Inys for the closest friends of the betrothed to lead them into the state of companionship.

Nearby, Igrain Crest was impenetrable. Ead supposed this was both a victory and a defeat for her. She wanted an heir, but not by this father. It was also proof that Sabran was no longer the grief-stricken girl who had needed so much guidance in her minority.

The Red Prince entered on the other side of the sanctuary. His eldest sister was his giver. He wore a cloak to match his betrothed, lined with crimson silk and ermine, and a doublet with gold fastenings. Like Sabran, he wore gloves with ostentive cuffs, the better to draw the eye during the ceremony. A circlet of gilded silver declared his royalty.

Sabran walked with poise toward him. Her wedding gown was something to behold. Deep crimson, like cherry wine, and a black forepart, rich with goldwork and pearls. Her ladies, Ead included, were her inverse, their black gowns set off by red stomachers.

The marriage party met on the boss of the sanctuary, beneath a gilded baldachin that stood on ornate columns. The witnesses formed a circle around it. Now Sabran was lit by the candles on the boss, close enough to Lievelyn for him to see her clearly, he swallowed.

Sabran took Roslain by the hand, while Lievelyn locked fingers with his eldest sister, and the four of them knelt on hassocks. Everyone else fanned away. As she snuffed her candle, Ead spied Chassar in the crowd.

The Arch Sanctarian of Inys was spindle-fingered, so pale that traceries of blue veins could be seen about his temples. The True Sword was figured in silver on the front of his herigaut.

"Friends." He spoke into the silence. "We meet tonight, in this haven from the world, to bear witness to the union of these two souls in the sacred state of companionship. Like the Damsel and the Saint, they seek to meet in soul and in flesh for the preservation of Virtudom. Companionship is a great service, for Inys itself was built on the love between Galian, a knight of Inysca, and Cleolind, a heretic woman of Lasia."

Moments in, and someone had already called the Mother a heretic. Ead exchanged a brief look with Chassar across the aisle.

After clearing his throat, the Arch Sanctarian opened a silver-fronted prayer book and read the story of the Knight of Fellowship, who had been first to join the Holy Retinue. Ead only half-listened. Her gaze was fixed to Sabran, who was perfectly still. Lievelyn glanced at her.

When the story was finished, Roslain and Ermuna, their duties as givers complete, stepped away from the royal couple. Roslain went to stand by her companion, Lord Calidor Stillwater, who drew her close. She never pulled her gaze from Sabran, who in turn watched her friend leave her under the baldachin with an all-but stranger.

"Let us begin." The Arch Sanctarian nodded to Lievelyn. The High Prince removed the glove from his left hand and held it out. "Sabran the Ninth of the House of Berethnet, Queen of Inys, your betrothed extends to you the hand of fellowship. Will you accept, and be his faithful companion, from this day to the end of days?"

Lievelyn gave Sabran a smile that barely creased his eyes. The shadows made it hard to tell if she was smiling back as she took a love-knot ring from the Arch Sanctarian.

"Friend," she said, "I will."

She paused, jaw tight, and Ead saw the slight rise of her breast.

"Aubrecht Lievelyn," she continued, "I take you now as my companion." She slid the ring onto his forefinger. Gold, reserved for sovereigns. "My friend, my bedfellow, my constant partner in all things." Pause. "I swear to love you with my soul, defend you with my sword, and give nobody else my favor. This I vow to you."

The Arch Sanctarian nodded again. Now it was Sabran who removed her left glove.

"Aubrecht the Second of the House of Lievelyn, High Prince of the Free State of Mentendon," came the exhortation, "your betrothed extends to you the hand of fellowship. Will you accept, and be her faithful companion, from this day to the end of days?"

"Friend," Lievelyn said, "I will."

When he took Sabran's ring from the Arch Sanctarian, her hand gave a barely visible quake. This was her last chance to withdraw from the marriage before it was legally binding. Ead glanced toward Roslain, whose lips were moving just a little, as if in encouragement. Or in prayer.

Sabran looked up at Lievelyn and, at last, gave him a subtle nod. He took her left hand, as gently as if it were a butterfly, and placed the ring. It gleamed on her finger.

"Sabran Berethnet," he said, "I take you now as my companion. My friend, my bedfellow, my constant partner in all things. I swear to love you with my soul, defend you with my sword, and give nobody else my favor." He pressed her hand. "This I vow to you."

There was a brief silence as their gazes locked. Then the Arch Sanctarian opened his arms as if to embrace the witnesses, shattering the moment.

"I now pronounce these two souls joined in the holy state of companionship in the eyes of the Saint," he called out, "and through him, all of Virtudom."

Cheers erupted across the sanctuary. That sound of shared joy seemed loud enough to bring down the roof again. As she clapped, Ead took stock of the Dukes Spiritual within her sight. Nelda Stillwater and Lemand Fynch looked pleased. Crest stood like a scepter, her mouth a lipless stripe, but tapped her fingertips on her palm in a game attempt at applause. Behind them, the Night Hawk was all smiles.

Companions usually kissed once they were wed, but for royals, such a display was not seemly. Sabran instead took the arm Lievelyn proffered, and they descended from the platform together. And Ead saw that, though her face was drawn, the Queen of Inys smiled for her people.

Ead traded a glance with Margret, who took a teary-eyed Linora by the elbow. Like ghosts, the three of them walked away.

———

In the Royal Bedchamber, they arrayed the bed and checked every nook for danger. A cast-bronze figurine of the Knight of Fellowship had been placed beneath the leadlight. Ead lit the candles on the mantelpiece, drew the curtains, and knelt to start a fire. The Arch Sanctarian had insisted upon a great deal of warmth. A prayer book was on the nightstand, turned to the tale of the Knight of Fellowship. A red apple sat on top of it. A symbol of fertility, Linora told Ead as they worked. "It is an old heathen tradition," she explained, "but Carnelian the Second liked it so much that she asked the Order of Sanctarians to include it in the consummation."

Ead wiped her forehead. The Arch Sanctarian clearly meant for an heir to be baked into existence like a loaf of bread.

"I must fetch something for them to drink." Margret touched Ead on the arm and left. Linora filled two warming pans with coals, humming, and slid them under the coverlet.

"Linora," Ead said to her, "go and join in with the celebrations. I will finish here."

"Oh, you *are* good, Ead."

When Linora was gone, Ead made sure the leadlight was fastened. The Royal Bedchamber had been locked and guarded all day, the key held only by Roslain, but she trusted no one in this court.

After a long moment, during which she reflected on whether this was a wise decision, Ead took out the rose she had cut that afternoon and tucked it behind the pillow on the right side of the bed. The pillow embroidered with the Berethnet badge.

Let her have sweet dreams tonight, at least.

The wardings rang with a footstep Ead recognized. A shadow appeared in the doorway, and Roslain Crest surveyed the room, her chin pinched.

A thread of hair had escaped her heart-shaped coiffure. She looked around the chamber as if it were unfamiliar to her, and not where she had slept beside her queen on countless occasions.

"My lady." Ead curtsied. "Are you well?"

"Yes." Roslain let out a breath through her nose. "Her Majesty requests your presence, Ead."

This was unexpected. "Surely only the Ladies of the Bedchamber can disrobe her on—"

"As I said," Roslain interrupted, "she has asked for you. And you appear to have completed your duties in here." With a last glance at the room, she returned to the corridor, and Ead followed her. "A chamberer is not permitted to touch the royal person, as you know, but I will overlook it tonight. In so far as is necessary."

"Of course."

The Withdrawing Chamber, where Sabran was washed and dressed each day, was a square room with an ornate plaster ceiling, the smallest in her royal apartments. Its curtains were shut.

Sabran stood barefoot beside the fire, gazing into the flames as she took off her earrings. Her gown had doubtless been locked away in the Privy Wardrobe, leaving her in her shift. Katryen was removing the padded roll from about her waist.

Ead went to the queen and moved her hair aside to reach her nape, where her carcanet was clasped.

"Ead," Sabran said. "Did you enjoy the ceremony?"

"Yes, Your Majesty. You looked magnificent."

"Do I not still?"

She asked it lightly, but Ead heard the trace of doubt in her voice.

"You are always beautiful, madam." Ead worked the hook free and slipped the jewels from about her throat. "But in my eyes . . . never more so than you are now."

Sabran looked at her.

"Do you suppose," she said, "that Prince Aubrecht will find me so?"

"His Royal Highness is mad or a fool if he does not."

Their gazes pulled apart when Roslain returned to the chamber. She approached Sabran and set about unlacing her corset.

"Ead," she said, "the nightgown."

"Yes, my lady."

While Ead found a pan to warm the garment, Sabran raised her arms, allowing Roslain to slip her shift over her head. The two

Ladies of the Bedchamber took their queen to the washbasin, where they cleaned her from head to toe. As she smoothed the nightgown, Ead stole a glance.

Divested of her regalia, Sabran Berethnet did not look like the scion of any saint, false or true. She was mortal. Still imposing, still graceful, but softer, somehow.

Her body was a sandglass. Round hips, a small waist, and full breasts, the nipples whetted. Long legs, strong from riding. When she saw the dusk between them, a chill flickered through Ead.

She wrenched her attention back to her task. The Inysh were squeamish about nakedness. She had not seen a disrobed body that was not her own in years.

"Ros," Sabran said, "will it hurt?"

Roslain patted her skin dry with clean linen. "It can a little, at first," she said, "but not for long. And not if His Royal Highness is … attentive."

Sabran stared into the room without seeming to see it. She turned her love-knot ring.

"What if I cannot conceive?"

In the silence that followed that question, a mouse could not have breathed unheard.

"Sabran," Katryen said gently, taking her arm, "of course you will."

Ead kept quiet. This seemed like a conversation only for the intimates, but no one had ordered her to leave.

"My grandmother could not for many years," Sabran murmured. "High Westerns are on the wing. Yscalin has betrayed me. If Fýredel and Sigoso invade Inys and I have no heir—"

"You will have an heir. Queen Jillian gave birth to a beautiful daughter, your lady mother. And soon enough, you will be a mother, too." Roslain rested her chin on Sabran's shoulder. "After it is done, lie still for a time, and sleep on your back."

Sabran leaned into her.

"I wish Loth had been here," she said. "He was to be my giver. I promised him." Now the powder was gone, the bruise-like marks under her eyes had never looked starker. "Now he is … lost. Somewhere in Cárscaro. And I am powerless to reach him."

"Loth will be all right. I have faith that he will come home soon." Roslain held her closer. "And when he does, he will bring news of your lord father."

"Another missing face. Loth and Father … and Bella, too. Loyal Bella, who served three queens." Sabran closed her eyes. "It bodes ill that she died so near to this day. In the bed where—"

"Sabran," Roslain said, "this is your wedding night. You must not have these dark thoughts, or they will taint the seed."

Ead emptied the pan back into the hearth. She wondered if the Inysh knew anything useful about childing, or if their physicians dealt in naught but guesswork.

As the hour approached, the queen grew quiet. Roslain whispered guidance in her ear, and Katryen combed every petal from her hair.

They dressed her in the nightgown and a fur-lined rail. Katryen lifted her hair from under the collar.

"Ead," Sabran said as they faced the door, "is this how it is done in the Ersyr?"

A furrow had appeared in her brow. The same furrow that had been there when she had described her nightmare. Ead found herself wanting to smooth it.

"Something like this, madam," she said.

Somewhere outside, a firework whistled skyward. The celebrations were beginning in the city.

They led Sabran from the Withdrawing Chamber. She was shivering, but she kept her head up.

A queen could not show fear.

When the doors of the Royal Bedchamber came into sight, Roslain and Katryen pressed closer to their sovereign. Sir Tharian Lintley and two of his Knights of the Body, who had been standing guard, now knelt before her.

"Your Majesty," Lintley said, "for the sake of courtesy, I cannot guard your chamber on this, your wedding night. I entrust your protection to your companion, and your Ladies of the Bedchamber."

Sabran laid a hand on his head. "Good Sir Tharian," she said, "the Knight of Courtesy smiles on you."

He stood, and he and his knights bowed to her. As they left, Katryen took the key from Roslain and opened the doors.

At the foot of the bed, the Arch Sanctarian stood with a prayer book in hand, murmuring. Aubrecht Lievelyn waited with his Grooms of the Inner Chamber. His nightshirt, edged with black-work, fell open to show his collarbones.

"Your Majesty," he said. In the firelight, his eyes were inkwells.

Sabran gave just the barest dip of her head. "Your Royal Highness."

The Arch Sanctarian made the sign of the sword.

"The Saint blesses this bed. Let it bear the fruit of his unend-ing vine." He closed his prayer book. "And now it is time for friends to take their leave, so that these new friends might come to know each other. Saint give us all goodnight, for he watches us in darkness."

"He watches us in darkness," came the echo. Ead did not say it with the others.

The ladies and the grooms all curtsied. As Roslain straightened, Sabran whispered, "Ros."

Roslain looked her in the eye. Out of sight of the men, she grasped Sabran so tightly by the hand that both their fingers blanched.

Katryen led Roslain out. As Ead followed them back through the door, she looked back at the queen, and their gazes touched.

For the first time, she saw Sabran Berethnet for who she was beneath the mask: a young and fragile woman who carried a thousand-year legacy on her shoulders. A queen whose power was absolute only so long as she could produce a daughter. The fool in Ead wanted to take her by the hand and get her away from this room, but that fool was too much of a coward to act. She left Sabran alone, like all the others had.

Margret and Linora were waiting. The five of them gathered in the dark.

"Did she seem all right?" Margret asked softly.

Roslain ran her hands down the front of her gown. "I don't know." She paced back and forth. "For the first time in my life, I cannot tell."

"It is natural for her to be nervous." Katryen spoke in a whisper. "How did you feel with Cal?"

"That was different. Cal and I were betrothed as children. He was not a stranger," Roslain said. "And the fate of nations did not rest upon the fruit of our union."

They kept their vigil, ears pricked for any changes in the Royal Bedchamber. When quarter of an hour had passed, Katryen pressed her ear to the doors.

"He is talking about Brygstad."

"Let them talk," Ead said, keeping her voice low. "They hardly know one another."

"But what will we do if the union is not consummated?"

"Sabran will see it done." Roslain looked into nothing. "She knows it is her bounden duty."

The waiting continued for some time. Linora, who had settled on the floor, dozed off against the wall. Finally, Roslain, who had been still as stone, began to pace again.

"What if—" She wrung her fingers. "What if he is a monster?"

Katryen stepped toward her. "Ros—"

"You know, my lady mother told me that Sabran the Eighth was ill-used by her companion. He drank and whored and said cruel things to her. She never told anyone. Not even her ladies-in-waiting. Then, one night"—she pressed a hand flat to her stomacher—"the despicable knave *struck* her. Cracked her cheekbone and broke her wrist—"

"And he was executed for it." Katryen gathered her close. "Listen, now. Nothing is going to happen to Sab. I have seen how Lievelyn is with his sisters. He has the heart of a lambkin."

"He might be the very picture of a lambkin," Ead said, "but monsters often have soft faces. They know how to mask themselves." She looked them both in the eye. "We will watch her. We will listen well. Remember why we wear blades as well as jewels."

Roslain held her gaze, and slowly she nodded. A moment later, so did Katryen. Ead saw then that they would do anything for Sabran. They would take a life, or lay down theirs. Anything.

At the turn of the hour, something changed in the Royal Bedchamber. Linora stirred awake and clapped a hand over her mouth.

Ead moved closer to the door. Thick as it was, she could hear enough to understand well what was happening within. When it was over, she nodded to the Ladies of the Bedchamber.

Sabran had done her duty.

———————

In the morning, Lievelyn left the Royal Bedchamber at just past nine of the clock. Only when the Little Door had closed behind him could the ladies-in-waiting go to their queen.

Sabran lay in bed, the sheets gathered over her breasts. She or Lievelyn had opened the curtains, but the sky was overcast, offering scant light.

She looked over her shoulder when they entered. Roslain rushed to her side.

"Are you well, Majesty?"

"Yes." Sabran sounded tired. "I believe I am, Ros."

Roslain pressed a kiss to her hand.

When Sabran rose, Katryen was there at once with a mantle. While Ead stepped toward the bed with Margret and Linora, the two Ladies of the Bedchamber guided Sabran to the chair beside the fire.

"Today, I will keep to my apartments." Sabran tucked a lock of hair behind her ear. "I have a hankering for fruit."

"Lady Linora," Katryen said, "fetch Her Majesty some blackberries and pears. And a cup of caudle, if you please."

Linora left, looking peeved to be dismissed. As soon as the door shut, Roslain knelt in front of Sabran, making her skirts puff around her.

"Oh, Sab, I was so—" She shook her head. "Was everything well with His Royal Highness?"

"Perfectly," Sabran said.

"Truly?"

"Truly. It felt strange, but His Royal Highness was ... attentive." She placed a hand on her belly. "Might I be with child already?"

A pregnancy was unlikely from one night, but the Inysh knew little of the body and its workings. "You must wait until the usual time of your courses," Roslain said as she rose, always forbearing. "If no blood comes, you are with child."

"Not necessarily," Ead said. When Sabran and both Ladies of the Bedchamber looked at her, she bobbed a curtsy. "Sometimes the body is a trickster, Majesty. They call it a false pregnancy." Margret nodded at this. "It is hard to be sure until the child quickens."

"But of course," Katryen added, "we have every faith that you will be with child very soon."

Sabran held the arms of her chair.

"Then I should lie with Aubrecht again," she said. "Until I am sure."

"A child will come when the time is right." Roslain dropped a kiss on her head. "For now, you must think only to make your marriage a happy one. Perhaps you and Prince Aubrecht could take a honey month. Glowan Castle is lovely at this time of year."

"I cannot leave the capital," Sabran said. "Not with a High Western on the wing."

"Let us not speak of High Westerns." Roslain smoothed her hair. "Not now."

Margret rose to the occasion. "Since we are seeking a new subject," she said, a teasing sparkle in her eye, "will you tell us about *your* wedding night, Ros?"

Katryen tittered, and Roslain smiled a little as Sabran gave her a knowing look.

Linora returned with the fruit as Roslain recounted her marriage to Lord Calidor Stillwater. When the bed was made, they all moved to the Withdrawing Chamber, where Sabran sat beside the washbasin. She was silent while Katryen worked creamgrail into her hair and gave her rosewater to rinse her mouth. At her request, Margret played the virginals.

"Mistress Duryan," Katryen said, "help rinse Her Majesty's hair, if you please. I must go to the Lord Chamberlain."

"Of course."

Katryen scooped up the wicker basket and left. Ead, in the meantime, joined Roslain at the washbasin.

She poured water from the ewer, washing away the sweet-smelling lather. As she reached for the linen, Sabran caught her wrist.

Ead grew very still. An Ordinary Chamberer did not have leave to touch the queen, and this time Roslain had made no promises to overlook it.

"The rose smelled beautiful, Mistress Duryan."

Sabran slid her fingers between hers. Thinking she meant to say more, Ead leaned down to hear—but instead, Sabran Berethnet kissed her on the cheek.

Her lips were soft as swansdown. Gooseflesh whispered all over Ead, and she fought the need to let out all her breath.

"Thank you," Sabran said. "It was generous."

Ead glanced at Roslain, who looked stricken.

"It was my pleasure, madam," she said.

Outside, the grounds were wreathed in mist. Rain slithered down the clouded windows of the Withdrawing Chamber. The queen reclined into her seat as if it were her throne.

"Ros," she said, "when Kate returns, bid her go back to the Lord Chamberlain. She will tell him that Mistress Ead Duryan has been raised to the position of Lady of the Bedchamber."

II

Declare I Dare Not

Consider the way she had to go,
Think of the hungry snare,
The net she herself had woven,
Aware or unaware ...

—Marion Angus

23

South

The hook of the ice staff bit into snow, and Lord Arteloth Beck bowed his head against the wind that bellowed through the Spindles. Beneath his gloves, his fingers were as red as if he had dipped them in madder. Draped over his shoulder was the carcass of a mountain ewe.

The tears had frozen on his cheeks for days, but now the cold had entered him. He could not think of Kit for long when every step was agony. A mercy from the Saint.

Night had fallen. Snow starched his beard. He crossed a rill of lava, which oozed from a cleft in the mountainside, and crawled into the cave, where he coasted in and out of sleep. When he had the strength, he forced himself to arrange the firewood and kindling he had gathered. He struck the flint and blew, urging the flame to grow. Then, steeling his nerves, he set about excoriating the ewe. When he had skinned his first animal on the third night, he had vomited and sobbed himself hoarse. Now his hands were well versed in the motions of survival.

Once it was done, he fashioned himself a spit. He had feared, at first, that the wyrms would see his fires and fly to them like moths to a taper, but they never had.

He cleaned his hands in the snow outside the cave, then heaped more of it over the blood, muffling the scent. In his shelter, he tore into the mutton and beseeched the Knight of Courtesy to look away. Once he had eaten as much as he could and stripped the remaining edible parts, Loth buried the carcass and sheathed his hands in gloves again. The sight of his red-tipped fingers made him queasy.

The rash was already crawling down his back—at least, he thought it was. He had no way of knowing if the itch was real, or his imagination. The Donmata Marosa had not told him exactly how long he had, doubtless to stop him counting down the days.

Chilled, he returned to the fire and cushioned his head on his pack. He would rest for a few hours and strike out again.

As he lay there, swaddled in his cloak, he checked the compass that hung from a cord around his neck. The Donmata had instructed him to move southeast until he reached the desert. He would cross it to the Ersyri capital of Rauca and join a caravan to Rumelabar, where Chassar uq-Ispad lived on a vast estate. Ead had grown up there as his ward.

It would be a hard journey, and if he meant to avoid joining the afflicted, he would have to make better time. There was no map in his pack, but he had discovered a purse of gold and silver suns. Each coin bore the image of Jantar the Splendid, King of the Ersyr.

Loth tucked the compass back into his shirt. A fever torched his brow. Ever since his hands had flushed, his dreams had left him drenched in sweat. He dreamed of Kit, entombed in bloodstained glass, trapped forever between one world and the next. He dreamed of Sabran in her childbed, dying, and his being powerless to stop it. And he dreamed, inexplicably, of the Donmata Marosa dancing in Ascalon, before she had been yoked to her tower, at the mercy of the manikin her father had become.

He came around to a rustling at the mouth of the cave. Ears pricked, he lay still and waited.

Talon rang on stone. The fire had dwindled to a dusting of embers, but there was just enough light for Loth to catch a glimpse of the monstrosity.

Bone-white plumage and scaled pink legs. Three toes on each foot. A comb of flesh above a beak. Loth had never laid eyes on anything so hideous, so *wrong*. He called on the Knight of Courage, but all he found was a pit of dread.

It was a cockatrice.

A guttural sound clacked from deep in its throat, and wattle slobbered. Its eyes were two blood blisters in its head. Unmoving in the shadows, Loth observed its torn and bloodied wing and the dirt across its plumage. A slug of a tongue rasped over the lesions.

Butterfingered with fear, Loth eased the strap of his pack across his chest and took hold of the ice staff. As the cockatrice licked its wounds, he drew his sword and crept toward the mouth of the cave, cleaving to the closest wall.

The cockatrice jerked up its head. It let out a deafening screech and clawed itself upright. Loth charged forward and hurdled its tail, and then he ran as he never had, out of the cave and down the slopes, boots scudding on ice. In his blind haste, he lost his footing and rolled, holding on to his pack as if it were the hand of the Saint himself.

Talons punched into his shoulders from above. He shouted as the ground tumbled away. His sword slipped from his grasp, but he clung to the staff by his fingertips.

The cockatrice flapped skyward, over a ravine. Its body listed toward its broken wing. Loth kicked and thrashed until he realized, through the fumes of panic, that the cockatrice was all that kept him from a fatal plunge. He let himself fall limp in its clutches, and it crowed in triumph.

Solid ground lurched up to greet them. The moment the talons relaxed, Loth flung out his shoulder and rolled. The collision jarred every bone in his body.

The beast had taken him to the summit of a low mountain. Panting, Loth shoved off the ground and snatched up the ice staff. He had often hunted with Sabran on horseback, but he had not been the quarry then.

A scaled white tail caught him hard across the midriff. He flew backward and cracked his head against a burl of rock, belly clenched in protest, but kept hold of his weapon.

Let him die here if he must, but he would take this monster with him.

Sick from the blow, he thrust out the staff. The cockatrice stamped its feet, raised its hackle feathers, and thundered toward him. Loth hurled the ice staff like a spear. The cockatrice flattened itself to avoid it, and his only weapon skittered into the ravine.

This time, the swing from its tail almost threw Loth over the precipice. The cockatrice bore down on him with a shudder of wet clucks. Talons *click-click*ed. He knotted himself into a ball and clenched his teeth so hard his jaw ached. Warmth soaked into his breeches.

A heavy foot crashed down on his back. A beak savaged his cloak. He tried, as a sob heaved through him, to cling on to a kernel of joy. The first memory that came to him was the day Margret was born, and how lovely she had been, with her huge eyes and tiny hands. His dances with Ead at every Feast of Fellowship. Hunting from dawn until dusk with Sabran. Sitting in the Royal Library with Kit, reading his poems back to him.

A new sound came, and the foot was gone. Loth cracked open his eyes to see the cockatrice blundering like a sodden-witted giant. It was fighting off another creature, furred where the cockatrice was scaled and feathered. The Draconic beast yawped and shrieked and lashed its tail, but its labors were in vain—the newcomer ripped out its throat.

The cockatrice crumpled. Blood throbbed from its carcass. Its vanquisher let out a bark and shunted it into the canyon.

Now it was still, Loth could see what his savior was. It had the shape of a mongoose, with a sweep of tail, coated in alder-brown fur that paled to white around its paws and muzzle—but it was *giant*, big as a Northern bear. Its chops were dark with gore.

An ichneumon. The natural archenemy of wyrms. They were the champions of many an Inysh legend, but he had never dreamed that they still existed.

The Saint had met one of these creatures on the road to Inys from Lasia. It had carried the Damsel on its back when she was too tired to carry on.

The ichneumon licked its teeth clean. When it looked at him, it bared them anew.

Its eyes were round and amber, wolflike, ringed by black skin. White markings striped the end of its tail. At present, its face was covered in bloody tufts of feather. It stalked toward Loth, impossibly light-footed for its bulk, and sniffed at his cloak.

Tentatively, Loth held out a hand. Once it had nosed his glove, the ichneumon growled. It must smell the plague in him, the scent of its age-old foe. Loth held still as hot breath dampened his cheek. After some time, the ichneumon bent its front legs and let out a bark.

"What is it, friend?" Loth asked. "What do you want me to do?"

He could have sworn it sighed. It pushed its head under his arm.

"No. I have the plague." His voice was weak with exhaustion. "Don't come near."

It occurred to him that he had never heard of an animal catching the Draconic plague. Warmth exuded from its fur—a gentle, animal warmth, not the red-hot scorch of wyrmfire.

His strength reborn, Loth shouldered his pack. He knotted his fingers into thick fur and climbed on to the ichneumon.

"I would go to Rauca," he said, "if you will show me the way."

The ichneumon barked again and sprang down the mountainside. As it ran, its paws swift as the winds, Loth whispered a prayer of gratitude to the Damsel and the Saint. He knew now that they had put him on this path, and he meant to follow it to the bitter end.

At dawn, the ichneumon prowled to a stop on a crag of rock. Loth smelled sunbaked earth and the spice of flowers. Before them lay the dusty foothills of the Spindles—and beyond those, a desert sprawled as far as the eye could see, powdered gold beneath the sun. It could almost be a mirage in the heat, but he knew that it was real.

Against all odds, he looked upon the Desert of the Unquiet Dream.

24

West

Early autumn was bittersweet. Ead awaited word from Chassar as to whether the Prioress would permit her to stay in Inys for a little longer, but no messages came.

As the winds blew colder and the fashions of summer were exchanged for fur-trimmed reds and browns, the court fell in love with the prince consort. To the surprise of all and sundry, he and Sabran began to watch masques and plays in the Presence Chamber together. Such entertainment had always occurred, but the queen had not attended in several years, except for the betrothal celebrations. She would call for her fools and laugh at their capers. She would bid the maids of honor dance for her. Sometimes she would take her companion by the hand, and they would smile at each other as if there were nobody else in the world.

Ead stood close throughout it all. Nowadays, she was seldom far from the queen.

Not long after the marriage, Sabran woke to find blood on her sheets. It sent her into a rage that left Roslain wringing her hands and the rest of the Upper Household cowering. Even Prince Aubrecht retreated for the day to hunt in Chesten Forest.

Ead supposed it was to be expected. Sabran was a queen, born with the expectation that the world had a duty to provide what she wanted, *when* she wanted it—but she could not command her own womb to bear fruit.

"I woke today with a great craving for cherries," Sabran remarked to Ead one morning. "What do you suppose it means?"

"Cherries are no longer in season, madam," Ead had answered. "Perhaps you miss the bounty of summer."

The queen had bridled, but said nothing more. Ead had continued brushing her cloak.

She would not indulge Sabran in this. Katryen and Roslain told Sabran what she wished to hear, but Ead was resolved to tell her what she needed to know.

Sabran had never been a patient woman. She soon became reluctant to join her companion at night, staying with her ladies to play cards into the small hours. By day, she was tired and captious. Katryen fretted to Roslain that this frame of mind could make a womb less welcoming, which made Ead want to dash her head until her teeth fell out.

It was not just the dearth of a child that must trouble the queen. Defending Mentendon from the wyrms in the Spindles was already proving to be a greater financial burden than anticipated. Lievelyn had brought a dowry, but it would soon run dry.

Ead was privy to this sort of knowledge now. Intimate, secret knowledge. She knew Sabran would sometimes lie in bed for hours, held there by a sorrow that ran in her bloodline. She knew she had a scar on her left thigh, gained when she had fallen from a tree when she was twelve. And she knew how she both hoped for a pregnancy and feared it more than anything.

Sabran might call Briar House her nest, but at present it was more of a cage. Rumors haunted its corridors and cloisters. The very walls seemed to hold their breath.

Ead herself was no stranger to rumors. Nobody could stop speculating on what a baseborn convert had done to become a Lady of the Bedchamber. Even she had no notion of why Sabran had chosen her over the many noble women in the Upper Household. Linora flung her many a sour look, but Ead paid her little mind. She had stomached these beef-witted courtiers for eight years.

One morning, she dressed in one of her autumn gowns and left to take the air before Sabran woke. Nowadays she had to be up with the lark if she meant to have any time alone with her thoughts. She spent most of each day with Sabran, her access to the queen almost unbounded.

The dawn was fresh and crisp, the cloisters mercifully silent. The only sound was the coo of a wood pigeon. Ead burrowed into the fur collar of her cloak as she passed the statue of Glorian the Third, the queen who had led Inys through the Grief of Ages. It depicted her riding in armor, full to bursting with child, sword raised in defiance.

Glorian had come to power on the day Fýredel slew her parents. The war had been unexpected, but Glorian Shieldheart had not balked. She had married the elderly Duke of Córvugar and betrothed their unborn child to Haynrick Vatten of Mentendon, all while leading the defense of Inys. On the day her daughter was born, she had taken the babe onto the battlefield to show her armies that there was hope. Ead could not decide if that was madness or mettle.

There were other stories like hers. Other queens who had made great sacrifices for Inys. These were the women whose legacy Sabran Berethnet carried on her shoulders.

Ead turned right through a passage and onto a gravel path flanked by horse-chestnut trees. At its end, beyond the walls of the palace grounds, stood Chesten Forest, as ancient as Inys itself.

There was a hothouse in the grounds, built of cast iron and glass. A redbreast took off from the roof as Ead stepped into its brothy warmth.

Jewel lilies floated in a pool. When she found the autumn crocus, she crouched and unhooked a pair of scissors from her girdle. In the Priory, a woman would take saffron for days before she tried to get with child.

"Mistress Duryan."

She looked up, startled. Aubrecht Lievelyn stood close by, wrapped in a russet cloak.

"Your Royal Highness." She stood and curtsied, slipping the crocus into her cloak. "Forgive me. I did not see you."

"On the contrary, I am sorry to disturb you. I did not think anyone else rose this early."

"Not always, but I enjoy the light before sunrise."

"I enjoy the quiet. This court is so busy."

"Is court life so different in Brygstad?"

"Perhaps not. There are eyes and whispers in every court, but the whispers here are— well, I must not complain." He offered a kind smile. "May I ask what you are doing?"

Her instinct was to be wary of his interest, but Lievelyn had never struck her as the conniving sort. "I am sure you know that Her Majesty suffers from night terrors," she said. "I was looking for some lavender to grind down and put beneath her pillow."

"Lavender?"

"It promotes a quiet sleep."

He nodded. "You may wish to look in the Apothecary Garden," he said. "May I join you?"

The offer surprised her, but she could hardly refuse. "Yes, of course, Your Highness."

They left the hothouse just as the upper limb of the sun reached over the horizon. Ead wondered if she should make a stab at conversation, but Lievelyn seemed content to take in the frosted beauty of the grounds as they walked side by side. His Royal Guard followed them at a distance.

"It is true that Her Majesty does not sleep well," he finally said. "Her duties weigh on her."

"As yours must weigh on you."

"Ah, but I have it easier. It is Sabran who will carry our daughter. Sabran who will give her life." Hoisting up another smile, he motioned toward Chesten Forest. "Tell me, Mistress Duryan. Was the Lady of the Woods ever said to walk among those trees?"

A chill darted through Ead. "That is a very old legend, Highness. I confess myself surprised you have heard of it."

"One of my new Inysh attendants told it to me. I asked if he would enlighten me on some of the stories and customs of the country. We have our wood-elves and red wolves and suchlike in Mentendon, of course—but a witch who murdered children does seem a particularly bloody tale."

"Inys was a bloody country once."

"Indeed. Thank the Saint it no longer is."

Ead looked toward the forest. "The Lady of the Woods was never known to be here, to my knowledge," she said. "Her haithwood is in the north, close to Goldenbirch, where the Saint was born. The only time anyone enters it is to make pilgrimage in the spring."

"Ah." He chuckled. "What a relief. I almost fancied I might look out of my window one morning and see her standing there."

"There is nothing to fear, Highness."

They soon came to the Apothecary Garden. It lay in a courtyard by the Great Kitchen, where the furnaces were being lit.

"Might I do the honor?" Lievelyn asked.

Ead handed him her scissors. "Of course."

"Thank you."

They knelt beside the lavender, and Lievelyn removed his gloves, a boyish smile on his lips. Perhaps he found it exasperating to be able to do so little with his own hands. His Grooms of the Inner Chamber must take care of everything, from serving his food to washing his hair.

"Your Royal Highness," Ead said, "pardon my ignorance, but who rules Mentendon in your absence?"

"Princess Ermuna is acting as steward while I am in Inys. Of course, I hope that Queen Sabran and I will eventually come to an arrangement whereby I am able to spend more of my time at home. Then I can be both consort and ruler." He ran a stem between his fingers. "My sister is a force of nature, but I fear for her. Mentendon is a fragile realm, and ours is a young royal house."

Ead watched his face while he spoke. His gaze was on his love-knot ring.

"This is also a fragile realm, Highness," she said.

"As I am learning."

He cut the lavender and passed it to her. Ead rose and dusted off her skirts, but Lievelyn seemed in no hurry to leave.

"I understand you were born in the Ersyr," he said.

"Yes, Highness. I am a distant relation of Chassar uq-Ispad, ambassador to King Jantar and Queen Saiyma, and grew up as his ward."

It was the lie she had told for eight years, and it came easily.

"Ah," Lievelyn said. "Rumelabar, then."

"Yes."

Lievelyn pulled his gloves back on. He looked over his shoulder, to where his Royal Guard waited by the entrance to the garden.

"Mistress Duryan," he said, softer, "I am glad I happened upon you this morning, for I would have your counsel on a private matter, if you would be good enough to give it."

"In what capacity, Highness?"

"As a Lady of the Bedchamber." He cleared his throat. "I should like to take Her Majesty into the streets, to give alms to the people of Ascalon, with the view to going on a longer progress in the summer. I understand she has never made a formal visit to any of her provinces. Before I raise it with her . . . I wondered if you might know why."

A prince seeking her counsel. How things had changed.

"Her Majesty has not walked among her people since she was crowned," Ead said. "Because of . . . Queen Rosarian."

Lievelyn frowned at this. "I know the Queen Mother was cruelly murdered," he said, "but that was in her own palace, not on the streets."

Ead considered his earnest face. There was something about him that compelled her to honesty.

"There are wrong-headed people in Ascalon, drunk on the same evil that has tainted Yscalin, who long for the Nameless One to return," she told him. "They would bring down the House of Berethnet to ensure it. Some of these people have been able to enter Ascalon Palace. Cutthroats."

Lievelyn was quiet for a short while. "I did not know of this." He sounded troubled, and Ead wondered what Sabran did talk to him about. "How close did they get to her?"

"Close. The last came in the summer, but I have no doubt that their master continues to plot against Her Majesty."

His jaw firmed.

"I see," he murmured. "Of course, I have no wish to put Her Majesty in danger. And yet—to the people of Virtudom, she is a beacon of hope. Now a High Western has returned, they *must* be reminded of her love for them, her devotion to them. Especially if she is forced to, say, raise taxes for the creation of new ships and weapons."

He was serious.

"Highness," Ead said, "I beg you, wait until you have a daughter before you put this idea to Her Majesty. A princess will give the commons all the comfort and reassurance they need."

"Alas that children cannot be called into being merely by our wishing hard enough for them. It may be a long time yet before an heir arrives, Mistress Duryan." Lievelyn breathed out through his nose. "As her companion, I should know her best, but my bride is the blood of the Saint. What mortal can ever know her?"

"You will," Ead said. "I have never seen her look at anyone the way she does at you."

"Not even Lord Arteloth Beck?"

The name stilled her. "Highness?"

"I heard the rumors. Whispers of a love affair," Lievelyn continued, after a hesitation. "I made my offer to Queen Sabran in spite of them ... but from time to time, I wonder if—" He cleared his throat, looking abashed.

"Lord Arteloth is very dear to Her Majesty," Ead told him. "They have been friends since they were children, and they love each other as brother and sister. That is all." She did not break his gaze. "No matter what rumor might have you believe."

His face softened into a smile again. "I suppose I ought to know better than to pay heed to gossip. Doubtless there is plenty about me," he said. "Lord Seyton tells me Lord Arteloth is now in Yscalin. He must be a man of great courage, to go so boldly into danger."

"Yes, Highness," Ead said softly. "He is."

There was a brief silence between them, peppered by birdsong.

"Thank you for your counsel, Mistress Duryan. It was generous of you to give it." Lievelyn touched a hand on his patron brooch, the mirror of hers. "I see why Her Majesty speaks so highly of you."

Ead curtsied. "You are too kind, Your Royal Highness. As is Her Majesty."

With a courteous bow, he took his leave.

Aubrecht Lievelyn was no dormouse. He was ambitious enough to want to effect change, and he possessed what appeared to be an intrinsic Mentish fondness for dangerous ideas. Ead prayed he would heed her counsel. It would be madness for Sabran to show herself in public when her life was under threat.

In the royal apartments, Ead found the queen awake and calling for a hunt. Not having a swift horse of her own, Ead was given a high-bred steed from the Royal Mews.

Truyde utt Zeedeur, who had taken Ead's position as an Ordinary Chamberer, would be among the hunting party. When they came face to face, Ead raised her eyebrows. The girl turned away, expressionless, and climbed on to her chestnut horse.

She must be losing hope in her lover. If Sulyard had written to her, she would not look so sullen.

Sabran refused to hunt with hounds. They were bound to kill their quarry cleanly, or not at all. As the party rode into Chesten Forest, Ead felt a sudden thirst for this hunt. She relished the wind in her hair. Her fingers itched to draw a bowstring.

Restraint was paramount. Too many kills would raise the question of where she had learned to shoot so well. She hung back at first, watching the others.

Roslain, who was said to have a flair for hawking, was all thumbs when it came to archery. She lost her temper within the hour. Truyde utt Zeedeur struck down a woodcock. Margret was the best shot of the ladies-in-waiting—she and Loth were both keen hunters—but no one could best the queen. It was all the beaters could do to keep up with her as she careered through the forest. She had a fine batch of conies by noon.

When she spied a hart between the trees, Ead almost let it go. A sensible lady-in-waiting would allow the queen to take the prize, but perhaps she could make *one* kill without arousing suspicion.

Her arrow flew. The hart collapsed. Margret, seated on her gelding, was the first to reach it.

"Sab," she called.

Ead followed the queen at a trot to the clearing. The arrow had taken the hart through its eye.

Just where she had aimed it.

Truyde utt Zeedeur reached the hart next. She took in the carcass with taut features.

"It appears we will have venison for dinner." Sabran was pink-cheeked with cold. "I was under the impression you had not hunted often, Ead."

Ead inclined her head. "Some of us have innate skill, Your Majesty." Sabran smiled. Ead found herself smiling back.

"Let us see if you have any other *innate skills*." Sabran wheeled her mount around. "Come, ladies—we will have a race back to Briar House. A purse for the victor."

With cheers, the women spurred their horses after her, leaving the grooms to gather their kills.

They broke from the forest and thundered across the grass. Soon Ead was neck and neck with the queen, and they were breathless with laughter, neither able to gain on the other. With her wind-spun hair and eyes bright from the hunt, Sabran Berethnet looked almost carefree—and for the first time in years, Ead felt her own cares lifted from her shoulders. Like seeds from a dandelion clock.

Sabran was in high spirits for the rest of the day. In the evening, she permitted all the ladies-in-waiting to retire so she could attend to matters of state in her Privy Library.

Ead had inherited a double lodging from Arbella Glenn, closer to the royal apartments than her old quarters. The lodging was made up of two adjoining rooms, wood-paneled and hung with tapestries, and boasted a four-poster bed. Mullion windows looked out over the grounds.

The servants had already lit a fire. Ead removed her riding habit and patted the sweat away with a cloth.

A knock came on the door at eight. Outside was Tallys, the sweet young scullion.

"Supper for you, Mistress Duryan." She bobbed a curtsy. No matter how many times Ead had told her it was unnecessary, she always insisted. "The bread is good and hot. They say a dread frost is on its way."

"Thank you, Tallys." Ead took the plate of food. "Tell me, child, how do your parents do?"

"Things do not go so well with my mother," Tallys admitted. "She broke her arm and cannot work for a time, and the landlord is so harsh. I send all my wages, but … for a scullion, it is not much." She hastened to add, "I don't complain, of course, mistress. I am so fortunate to work here. It's just a hard month, is all."

Ead reached into her purse.

"Here." She handed some coins to Tallys. "That should pay the rent until high winter."

Tallys stared at them. "Oh, Mistress Duryan, I couldn't—"

"Please. I have plenty saved, and little need to spend it. Besides, are we not taught to practice generosity?"

Tallys nodded, mouth quaking. "Thank you," she whispered.

When she was gone, Ead ate her supper at her table. Fresh bread, buttered ale, and a pottage garnished with fresh sage.

Something tapped the window.

A sand eagle sat outside, its yellow eye fixed on her. His plumage was the gold of almond butter, his wingtips darkening to chestnut. Ead hastened to the window and opened it.

"Sarsun."

He hopped inside and cocked his head. She smoothed his ruffled feathers with her fingertips.

"It has been a long time, my friend," she said in Selinyi. "I see you avoided the Night Hawk." He chirruped. "Hush. You'll end up in the aviary with those silly doves."

He butted his head against her palm. Ead smiled and stroked his wings until he stuck out one leg. Gently, she took the scroll attached to it. Sarsun soared onto her bed.

"By all means, make yourself comfortable."

He ignored her, preening.

The scroll was unbroken. Combe could intercept anything that arrived by postrider or rock dove, but Sarsun was clever enough to elude him. Ead read the coded message.

The Prioress grants you leave to remain in Inys until the queen is delivered of a daughter. Once news of the birth reaches us, I will come to you.

Do not argue next time.

Chassar had done it.

Exhaustion lapped over her again. She dropped the letter into the fire. When she was under the covers, Sarsun burrowed into the crook of her arm like a nestling. Ead stroked his head with one finger.

Reading that message had filled her with both sorrow and relief. An opportunity to go home had presented itself to her on a platter—yet here she was, by choice, in the same place she had longed for years to escape. On the other hand, this meant her years at court would not go to waste. She would be able to see Sabran through her childing.

In the end, it mattered not how long she stayed. It was her destiny to take the red cloak. Nothing would alter that.

She thought of Sabran's cool touch on her hand. When she slept, she dreamed of a bloodred rose against her lips.

Ead was dressed and on her way to the royal apartments by dawn, ready for the Feast of Early Autumn. Sarsun had taken off during the night. He had a long journey ahead of him.

When she had passed the Knights of the Body and stepped into the Privy Chamber, Ead found Sabran already up. The queen was arrayed in a gown of chestnut silk with sleeves of cloth-of-gold, her hair a contrivance of topaz and plaiting.

"Majesty." Ead curtsied. "I did not know you had risen."

"The birdsong woke me." Sabran put her book to one side. "Come. Sit with me."

Ead joined her on the settle.

"I am pleased you have come," Sabran said. "I have something of a private nature to tell you before the feast." Her smile gave it away. "I am with child."

Caution was what came to Ead first. "Are you certain, Majesty?"

"More than certain. I am long past the proper time for my courses."

At last. "Madam, this is wonderful," Ead said warmly. "Congratulations. I am so very pleased for you and Prince Aubrecht."

"Thank you."

As Sabran looked down at her belly, her smile faltered. Ead watched the crease appear in her brow.

"You must not tell anyone yet," the queen said, recovering. "Even Aubrecht has no idea. Only Meg, the Dukes Spiritual, and my Ladies of the Bedchamber know of my condition. My councillors have agreed that we will announce it when I begin to show."

"When will you tell His Royal Highness?"

"Soon. I mean to surprise him."

"Be sure there is a settle for him nearby when you do."

Sabran smiled again at that. "I will," she said. "I shall have to be gentle with my dormouse."

A child would secure his position at court. He would be the happiest man alive.

―――――――

At ten of the clock, Lievelyn met the queen at the doors to the Banqueting House. A silver thaw made the grounds shine. The prince consort wore a heavy surcoat, trimmed with wolf fur, that made him seem broader than he was. He bowed to Sabran, but there, in sight of them all, she took his nape in hand and kissed him.

Ead grew suddenly cold. She watched Lievelyn wrap his arms around Sabran and draw her flush against him.

The maids of honor were all titters. When the couple broke apart at last, Lievelyn smiled and kissed Sabran on the brow.

"Good morrow, Majesty," he said, and they walked arm in arm, Sabran leaning into her companion, so their cloaks blended like ink.

"Ead," Margret said. "Are you well?"

Ead nodded. The feeling in her chest had already dulled, but it had left a nameless shadow in her.

When Sabran and Lievelyn entered the Banqueting House, a throng of courtiers rose to meet them. The royals went to the High Table with the Dukes Spiritual, while the ladies-in-waiting pared away to the benches. Ead had never seen the Dukes Spiritual so pleased. Igrain Crest was smiling, and Seyton Combe, who usually darkened every doorway he entered, looked as if he could hardly keep from rubbing his hands together.

The Feast of Early Autumn was an extravagant affair. Black wine flowed, thick and heavy and sweet, and Lievelyn was presented with a huge rum-soaked fruit cake—his childhood favorite—which had been re-created according to a famous Mentish recipe.

On the tables, the bounty of the season filled copper-gilt platters. White peacock with a gold-leaf beak, roasted and soaked in a honey and onion sauce, then stitched back into its feathers, so it gave an impression of life. Damsons plumped in rosewater. Apple halves in a crimson jelly. Spiced blackberry pie with a fluted crust and tiny venison tartlets. Ead and Margret made sympathetic noises as Katryen lamented the loss of her secret admirer, whose love letters had stopped coming.

"Did Sabran tell you the news?" Katryen asked, voice low. "She wanted you both to know."

"Yes. Thank the Damsel for her mercies," Margret said. "I was beginning to think I would die of irritation if one more person remarked that Her Majesty was looking *very well* of late."

Ead glanced behind her to make sure no one was eavesdropping.

"Katryen," she murmured, "are you quite sure Sabran missed her blood?"

"Yes. Don't trouble yourself, Ead." Katryen sipped her bramble wine. "Her Majesty will have to begin putting together a household for the princess in due course."

"Saint. That will set off more peacocking than poor Arbella's death," Margret said dryly.

"A household." Ead raised an eyebrow. "Does a child need its own household?"

"Oh, yes. A queen has not the time to rear a child. Well," Katryen added, "Carnelian the Third insisted on nursing her daughter herself, come to think of it, but it is not often done.

The princess will need milk nurses, a governess, tutors, and so on."

"How many people will be in this household?"

"Two hundred or so."

A household that large seemed excessive. Then again, everything in Inys was excessive.

"Tell me," Ead said, still curious, "what would happen if Her Majesty had a son?"

Katryen tilted her head at that. "I suppose it would not matter," she mused, "but it has never happened, not in all Berethnet history. Clearly the Saint meant for this isle to be a queendom."

When the dishes were finally cleared and chatter had begun, the steward tapped his staff on the floor.

"Her Majesty," he called, "Queen Sabran."

Lievelyn stood and extended a hand to his companion. She took it and rose, and the court rose with her.

"People of the court," she said, "we bid you welcome to the Feast of Early Autumn. The time of the harvest, loved above all by the Knight of Generosity. From this day forth, winter begins its slow approach toward Inys. It is a time that wyrms despise, for it is heat that sustains the fire within them."

Applause.

"Today," she continued, "we announce another reason to celebrate. This year, to mark the Feast of Generosity, we will be making a progress into Ascalon."

Murmurs rang up to the roof. Seyton Combe choked on his mulled wine.

"During this visit," Sabran said, her gaze taut with resolve, "we will pray at the Sanctuary of Our Lady, give alms to the poor, and comfort those whose homes and livelihoods were damaged by Fýredel. In showing ourselves to the people, we will remind them that we stand united under the True Sword, and that no High Western will break our spirits."

Ead looked to Lievelyn. He avoided her eyes.

Her counsel had not been strong enough. She should have done more to hammer the danger into that copper saucepan of a head.

He was a fool, and so was Sabran. Fools in crowns.

"That is all." The queen returned to her seat. "Now, I believe there is one more course."

Cheers erupted across the Banqueting House. At once, the servants came with yet more platters, and all concern was lost to feasting.

Ead touched nothing else. She was no diviner, but anyone with half a wit could see that this would end in blood.

25

East

Following his inglorious arrival in Ginura, Niclays Roos was an honored guest in the Moyaka household. Until the Warlord deigned to see him, he was free to do as he pleased, so long as he had his Seiikinese chaperons. Happily, Eizaru and Purumé were pleased to fulfill that role.

The three of them joined a great throng in the streets for the festival of Summerfall, which celebrated the beginning of autumn. Many Seiikinese citizens traveled to Ginura for what was commonly agreed to be the most spectacular of the four tree festivals. Peddlers grilled bladefish over their stoves, simmered bites of sweet pumpkin in broth, and handed out hot wine and tea to keep the chill at bay. People took their meals outside, crowned with the golden leaves that whiffled like maple seeds from the branches, and when the final leaf had fallen, they watched new ones bud and spring forth, red as dawn, throughout the night.

For Niclays, every day was a new lease of life. His friends took him for strolls across the beach. They pointed out the Grieving Orphan, the largest volcanic stack in the East, which formed a sole tooth in the mouth of the bay. They used a spyglass to watch mereswine in the sea.

And slowly, *perilously*, Niclays allowed himself to dream of a future in this city. Perhaps the Seiikinese authorities would forget he existed. Perhaps, since he had been so well behaved, they would decide to let him live out the rest of his exile beyond Orisima. It was a sliver of hope, and he clung to it like a drowning sailor to flotsam.

Panaya sent his books from Orisima with a note from Muste, who told him that his friends at the trading post gave him their warmest regards and hoped he would return soon. Niclays might have been touched had he considered any of them friends, or been interested in their regards, warm or otherwise. Now he had tasted freedom, the thought of returning to Orisima, to the same twenty faces and the same grid of streets, was intolerable.

The Mentish ship *Gadeltha* docked at the landing gate, bringing with it a stack of letters from home. Niclays had received two.

The first letter was closed with the seal of the House of Lievelyn. He fumbled it open and read the lines of neat handwriting.

From Brygstad, Free State of Mentendon,
by way of Ostendeur Port Authority
Late Spring, 1005 CE

Sir,

I gather from my late grand-uncle's records that you remain in a state of exile in our trading post of Orisima, and that you have petitioned for clemency from the House of Lievelyn. Having reviewed your case, I regret to conclude that I cannot give you permission to return to Mentendon. Your conduct caused some great affront to Queen Sabran of Inys, and to invite you back to court presently may serve to foster her rancor.

If you can devise some way to appease Queen Sabran, I will be delighted to reconsider this unhappy conclusion.

Your servant,

Aubrecht II, High Prince of the Free State of
Mentendon, Archduke of Brygstad, Defender of the Virtues,
Protector of the Sovereignty of Mentendon, &c.

Niclays crushed the letter into his hand. There must be some political reason that the new High Prince was wary of provoking Sabran. At least he was courteous, and willing to return to the matter if Niclays could find some way of pacifying Her Acrimony. Or Lievelyn himself. Even he might be tempted by the elixir of life.

He opened the second letter, heart thumping. This one had been written over a year ago.

From Ascalon, Queendom of Inys,
by way of Zeedeur Custom House
Early Summer, 1004 CE

Dearest Uncle Niclays,

Forgive me for not writing for some time. Duties in Upper Household keep me occupied & seldom allowed to go anywhere without a chaperon. Inysh court concerns itself most deeply with the private time of its young ladies! I pray this reaches Ostendeur before the next shipment eastward.

  I do bid you send me word how that you do in Orisima. Have been occupying myself in the meantime with remembering the books you left to me, which are presently held in the Silk Hall. I believe I have a theory & am certain the significance of a certain object has been overlooked. Will you write with all you know of the Tablet of Rumelabar? Have you an answer to its riddle?

All my love, Truyde

(Note to Zeedeur Custom House: I would appreciate your due haste in conferring this to Ostendeur Port Authority. Regards, your Marchioness.)

Niclays read the words again, half-smiling, eyes hot.

He was supposed to have received this letter long before Sulyard arrived. She might have warned him to expect the boy, but Lord

Seyton Combe, the spymaster of Inys, would have seen through any code.

He had sent replies to her earlier letters, but he suspected they had been destroyed. Exiles were not permitted to write home. Even if he *had* been able to reach her, he had no good tidings.

That evening, Purumé and Eizaru took him to the river to spot night-flying herons. The day after, Niclays elected to keep to his room and ice his ankle. While he nursed an excitement-induced headache, he found himself thinking of Sulyard.

He ought to feel shame for enjoying himself while the boy rotted in jail, especially when he believed that Niclays was finishing his quest for him. A quest based on an unsolved riddle and the dangerous passion Truyde had inherited from Jannart.

A passion for truth. A riddle that now refused to leave Niclays alone. At midday, he asked the servants for a writing box and painted out the words, just so he could see them on the page.

What is below must be balanced by what is above,
and in this is the precision of the universe.
Fire ascends from the earth, light descends from the sky.
Too much of one doth inflame the other,
and in this is the extinction of the universe.

Niclays thought back to what he had learned about the riddle at university. It was from the Tablet of Rumelabar, found many centuries ago in the Sarras Mountains.

Ersyri miners had discovered a subterranean temple in those mountains. Stars had been carved on its ceiling, flaming trees onto its floor. A block of skystone had stood at its heart, and the words scored into it, written in the script of the first Southern civilization, had captivated academic minds the world over.

Niclays underlined one part of the riddle and contemplated its meaning.

Fire ascends from the earth.

Wyrms, perhaps. The Nameless One and his followers were said to have come from the Womb of Fire in the core of the world.

He underlined again.

Light descends from the sky.

The meteor shower. The one that had ended the Grief of Ages, weakened the wyrms, and granted strength to the Eastern dragons.

Too much of one doth inflame the other, and in this is the extinction of the universe.

A warning of disparity. This theory posited the universe as yoked to the balance of fire and starlight, weighed on a set of cosmic scales. Too much of either would tip them.

The extinction of the universe.

The closest the world had ever come to ending was the arrival of the Nameless One and his followers. Had some sort of imbalance in the universe *created* these beasts of fire?

The sun beat hard on the back of his head. He found himself drowsing. When Eizaru woke him, his cheek was stuck to the parchment, and he felt as heavy as a sack of millet.

"Good afternoon, my friend." Eizaru chuckled. "Were you working on something?"

"Eizaru." Clearing his throat, Niclays peeled himself free. "No, no. Merely a trifle."

"I see. Well," Eizaru said, "if you are finished, I wondered if you might like to come with me into the city. The fisherfolk have brought a haul of silver crab from the Unending Sea, but it sells out quickly at the market. You must try it before you return to Orisima."

"I fondly hope that I never *will* return to Orisima."

His friend hesitated.

"Eizaru," Niclays said, wary. "What is it?"

Eizaru reached into his robe, tight-lipped, and pulled out and handed him a scroll. The seal was broken, but Niclays could see it belonged to the Viceroy of Orisima.

"I received this today," Eizaru said. "After your audience with the all-honored Warlord, you are to return to Orisima. A palanquin will collect you."

Suddenly the scroll weighed more than a boulder. It might have been his death warrant.

"Do not despair, Niclays." Eizaru laid a hand on his shoulder. "The honored Queen Sabran will relent. Until then, Purumé and I will seek permission to visit you in Orisima."

It took Niclays all his strength to swallow his disappointment. It went down like a mouthful of thorns.

"That would be wonderful." He dredged up a smile. "Come, then. I suppose I had better enjoy the city while I can."

Purumé was absorbed in setting a bone, so once he was dressed, Niclays set out alone with Eizaru to the fish market. The sea lashed a stinging wind across the city, fogging his eyeglasses, and in his jaundiced state, the gazes he received seemed more suspicious than ever. As they passed a robe shop, its owner scowled at him. "Sickness-bearer," she snapped.

Niclays was too downcast to respond. Eizaru directed a stern look at the woman over his eyeglasses, and she turned away.

In the moment his attention was diverted, Niclays trod on a booted foot.

He heard an intake of breath. Eizaru clutched him in time to break his fall, but the young Seiikinese woman whose foot he had squashed was not so fortunate. Her elbow knocked into a vase, which shattered on the paving stones.

Damn it all, he was like an olyphant in a teahouse.

"Excuse me, honorable lady," Niclays said, and bowed deep. "I was not paying attention."

The merchant stared glumly at the shards. Slowly, the woman turned to face Niclays.

Black hair was wrapped into a knot at the crown of her head. She wore pleated trousers, a tunic of deep blue silk, and a velvet surcoat. A fine sword hung at her side. When he saw the sheen on the tunic, Niclays was unable to stop his mouth popping open. Unless he was mistaken, that was *water*silk. Erroneously named—it was not a silk at all, but hair. The manehair of dragons, to be precise. It repelled moisture like oil.

The woman took a step toward him. Her face was angular and brown, her lips chapped. Dancing pearls adorned her throat.

But what seared itself into his memory, in the few moments their gazes held, was the scar. It whipped across her left cheekbone before curling toward the corner of her eye.

Exactly like a fishhook.

"Outsider," she murmured.

Niclays realized that the crowd around them had fallen almost silent. The back of his neck prickled. He had the sense that he had just committed a greater transgression than blundering.

"Honorable citizen, what is this man doing in Ginura?" the woman asked Eizaru curtly. "He should be in Orisima, with the other Mentish settlers."

"Honored Miduchi." Eizaru bowed. "We humbly apologize for interrupting your day. This is the learnèd Doctor Roos, an anatomist of the Free State of Mentendon. He is here to see the all-honored Warlord."

The woman cut her gaze between them. There was a rawness in her eyes that spoke of disturbed nights.

"What is your name?" she asked Eizaru.

"Moyaka Eizaru, honored Miduchi."

"Do not let this man out of your sight, honorable Moyaka. He must always have an escort."

"I understand."

She tossed Niclays a final look before she strode away. As she turned, he caught sight of a golden dragon on the back of her jacket.

She had long, dark hair, and a scar at the top of her left cheek. Like a fishhook.

By the Saint, it *had to be* her.

Eizaru paid the merchant for his loss and hurried Niclays into a cobbled lane. "Who was that, Eizaru?" Niclays asked in Mentish.

"The honored Lady Tané. She is Miduchi. Rider of the great Nayimathun of the Deep Snows." Eizaru dabbed his neck with a cloth. "I should have bowed lower."

"I will repay you for the vase. At, er, some point."

"It is only a few coins, Niclays. The knowledge you gave me in Orisima is worth far more."

Eizaru, Niclays decided, was as close as anyone could get to being flawless.

The two of them reached the fish market in the nick of time. Silver crabs spilled from nets of wheatstraw, gleaming like the steel armor of knights. Niclays almost lost Eizaru in the ensuing scramble, but his friend emerged triumphant, his eyeglasses askew.

It was almost sunset by the time they got back to the house. Niclays feigned another headache and retreated to his room, where he sat beside the lantern and rubbed his brow.

He had always prided himself on his brain, but it had been idle of late. It was high time he set it to work.

Tané Miduchi was, without question, the woman Sulyard had seen on the beach. Her scar betrayed her. She had brought an outsider into Cape Hisan on that fateful night and then handed him over to a musician, who was now languishing in prison. Or headless.

The bobtail cat jumped into his lap, purring. Niclays absently scratched between its ears.

The Great Edict required islanders to report trespassers to the authorities without delay. Miduchi should have done that. Why, instead, had she enlisted a friend to hide him in the Mentish trading post?

When he realized, Niclays let out such a loud "ha!" that the cat sprang off his lap in fright.

The *bells*.

The bells had been ringing the next day, heralding the ceremony that would open the way for Miduchi to become a dragonrider. If an outsider had been discovered in Cape Hisan the night before, the port would have been closed to ensure there was no trace of the red sickness. Miduchi had hidden Sulyard in Orisima—isolated from the rest of the city—so as not to disturb the ceremony. She had put her ambition above the law.

Niclays weighed his options.

Sulyard had agreed to tell his questioners about the woman with the fishhook scar. Perhaps he had, but no one had realized who it was. Or taken a trespasser at his word. Niclays, however, was protected by the alliance between Seiiki and Mentendon. That had shielded him against punishment before, and it might just aid him now.

He might still save Sulyard. If he could muster the courage to accuse Miduchi during his audience with the Warlord, before witnesses, the House of Nadama would have to act upon it, or risk appearing to dismiss their Mentish trading partners.

Niclays was quite sure there was some way to turn this to his advantage. If only he knew what it was.

Purumé came home at nightfall with bloodshot eyes, and the servants prepared the silver crab with fine-cut vegetables and rice steamed with chestnuts. The flaky white meat was delectable, but Niclays was too deep in thought to appreciate it. When they were finished, Purumé retired, while Niclays stayed at the table with Eizaru.

"My friend," Niclays said, "please pardon me if this is an ignorant question."

"Only ignorant men do *not* ask questions."

Niclays cleared his throat. "This dragonrider, Lady Tané," he began. "From what I can tell, the riders are almost as esteemed as the dragons. Is that correct?"

His friend considered for some time.

"They are not gods," he said. "There are no shrines in their honor—but they are revered. The all-honored Warlord is descended from a rider who fought in the Great Sorrow, as you know. The dragons see their riders as their equals among humankind, which is the greatest honor."

"With that in mind," Niclays said, trying to sound casual, "if you knew that one of them had committed a crime, what would you do?"

"If I knew beyond all possible doubt that it was true, I would report it to their commander, the honored Sea General, at Salt Flower Castle." Eizaru tilted his head. "Why do you ask, my friend? Do you believe one of them *has* committed a crime?"

Niclays smiled to himself.

"No, Eizaru," he said. "I was only speculating." He changed the subject: "I have heard that the moat around Ginura Castle is full of fish with bodies like glass. That when they glow at night, you can see right the way to their bones. Tell me, is that true?"

He did love the delicious onset of a good idea.

Tané found a foothold and pushed with all her strength, reaching for an overhang. Beneath her, the sea crashed against a smattering of rocks.

She was halfway up the volcanic stack that rose from the sea at the mouth of Ginura Bay. It was called the Grieving Orphan, for it stood alone, like a child whose parents had been shipwrecked. As her fingertips touched stone, her other hand slipped on sea moss.

Her stomach lurched. For a moment, she thought she would fall and shatter every bone—then she shoved herself upward, snatched the overhang, and clung to it like a barnacle. With a last, tremendous effort, she got on to the ledge above and lay there, breathing hard. It had been reckless to climb without her gloves, but she had wanted to prove to herself that she could.

Her mind kept returning to that Ment in the street, and the way he had stared at her. As if he had *recognized* her. It was impossible, of course—she had never seen him before. But why that look of shock?

He was a large man. Wide in the shoulders, broad in the chest, paunchy in the stomach. Eyes like clove, hooded with age, set in a sallow and blunt-edged face. Gray hair that held glints of copper. A mouth with a history of laughter etched around it. Round eyeglasses.

Roos.

Finally, it came to her.

Roos. A name Susa had whispered to her so briefly, it had almost been carried away by the wind.

He was the one who had hidden the outsider.

There was no reason he should be in Ginura. Not unless he was here to testify about that night. The thought locked her chest. She recalled his perceptive look in the street, and it sent a shudder through her.

With a clenched jaw, she stretched toward the next handhold. Whatever Roos thought he knew about her or Susa, he had no proof. And the outsider would be dead by now.

When she reached the top, she stood, palms bloody. The watersilks worked like feathers—one quick shake and they were dry.

She could see the whole of Ginura from here. Salt Flower Castle shone in the last of the sunlight.

The dragon awaited her in a natural shelter. Her true name was impossible for humans to pronounce, so she was known to them as Nayimathun. Hatched long ago in the Lake of Deep Snows, she now bore countless scars from the Great Sorrow. Every night, Tané would climb to the shelter and sit beside her dragon until the sun rose. It was just as she had always dreamed.

Talking had been hard at first. Nayimathun would not hear of Tané using the sort of respectful language that befitted a god. They were to be as kin, she said. As sisters. Anything else, and they would not be able to fly together. Dragon and rider had to share one heart.

Tané had not known how to cope with this rule. All her life she had spoken to her elders with respect, and now a *god* wished for them to speak as if they were the closest of friends. Gradually, haltingly, she had told the dragon about her childhood in Ampiki, the fire that had taken her parents, and her years of training in the South House. Nayimathun had listened patiently.

Now, as the ocean swallowed the sun, Tané walked barefoot to the dragon, whose head was curled against her neck. The position reminded Tané of a sleeping duck.

She knelt beside Nayimathun and placed a hand flat on her scales. Dragons did not hear in quite the same way humans did. Touch helped them to feel the vibrations of a voice.

"Good evening, Nayimathun."

"Tané." Nayimathun half-opened one eye. "Sit with me."

Her voice was war conch and whale song and the distant rumble of a storm, all smoothed into words like glass shaped by the sea. Listening to it made Tané drowsy.

She sat down and leaned against the ever-damp scales of her dragon. They were wonderfully cool.

Nayimathun sniffed. "You are wounded."

Blood was still leaking from her hand. Tané closed it. "Only a little," she said. "I left in haste and forgot my gloves."

"No need for haste, small one. The night is newborn." A rattling breath passed through the dragon, right down the length of her body. "I thought we might talk about stars."

Tané looked to the sky, where tiny eyes of silver were starting to peer out. "Stars, Nayimathun?"

"Yes. Do they teach the lore of stars in your Houses of Learning?"

"A little. In the South House, our teachers told us the names of the constellations, and how to find our way with them." Tané hesitated. "In the village I was born in, they say stars are the spirits of people who fled from the Nameless One. They climbed up ladders and hid in the heavens to await the day when every fire-breather lies dead in the sea."

"Villagers can be wiser than scholars." Nayimathun looked down at her. "You are my rider now, Tané. You are therefore entitled to the knowledge of my kind."

Not one of her teachers had ever told her this would happen.

"It would be my honor to receive it," she said.

Nayimathun turned her gaze skyward. Her eyes grew brighter, as if they were mirrors for the moon.

"Starlight," she said, "is what birthed us. All dragons of the East came first from the heavens."

As she sat beside the dragon, Tané admired her bright horns, the fringe of spines beneath her jaw, and her crown, blue as a fresh bruise. That was the organ that allowed her to fly.

Nayimathun saw her looking. "That part of me marks the place where my ancestors fell from the stars and struck their heads against the seabed," she said.

"I thought—" Tané wet her lips. "Nayimathun, forgive me, but I thought dragons came from eggs."

She knew they did. Eggs like clouded glass, smooth and wet, each with an iridescent shine. They could sit for centuries in water before a dragon wriggled out as a tiny, fragile being. Still, questioning a god made her voice quake.

"Now, yes," Nayimathun said. "But it was not always so." She raised her head to face the sky again. "Our ancestors came from the comet you call Kwiriki's Lantern, before there were any children of the flesh. It rained light into the water, and from that water, dragonkind came forth."

Tané stared at her. "But, Nayimathun," she said, "how can a comet make a dragon?"

"It leaves behind a substance. Molten starlight that falls into the sea and the lakes. As to how the substance grew into dragons, that is knowledge I do not possess. The comet comes from the celestial plane, and I have yet to occupy it.

"When the comet passes," Nayimathun continued, "we are at full strength. We lay eggs, and they hatch, and we regain every gift that we once possessed. But slowly, our strength fades. And we must await the next coming of the comet to return it."

"Is there no other way to regain your strength?"

Nayimathun looked at her with those ancient eyes. Tané felt very small under her gaze.

"Other dragons may not share this with their riders, Miduchi Tané," she rumbled, "but I will make you a gift of another piece of knowledge."

"Thank you."

Shivers twitched through her. Surely no one living was worthy of so much wisdom from a god.

"The comet ended the Great Sorrow, but it has come to this world many times before," Nayimathun said. "Once, many moons ago, it left behind two celestial jewels, each infused with its power. Solid fragments of itself. With them, our ancestors could control the waves. Their presence allowed us to hold on to our strength for longer than we could before. But they have been lost for almost a thousand years."

Sensing the sadness in the dragon, Tané stroked a hand over her scales. Though they gleamed like the scales of a fish, they were hatched with scars, rent by teeth and horns.

"How were such precious objects lost?" she asked.

Nayimathun let out the softest rattle through her teeth. "Almost a thousand years ago, a human used them to fold the sea over the

Nameless One," she said. "That was how he was defeated. After that, the two jewels passed out of history, as if they never were."

Tané shook her head. "A human," she repeated. She remembered the legends from the West. "Was he called Berethnet?"

"No. It was a woman of the East."

They sat in silence. Water dripped from the rock above their heads.

"We had many ancient powers once, Tané," Nayimathun said. "We could shed our skins like snakes, and change our forms. You have heard the Seiikinese legend of Kwiriki and the Snow-Walking Maiden?"

"Yes." Tané had heard it many times in the South House. It was one of the oldest stories in Seiiki.

Long ago, when they had first emerged from the waves, the dragons of the Sundance Sea had agreed among themselves to befriend the children of the flesh, whose fires they had seen on a nearby beach. They had brought them gifts of golden fish to show their good intent—but the islanders, suspicious and afraid, threw spears at the dragons, and they disappeared sadly to the depths of the sea, not to be seen again for years.

One young woman, however, had witnessed the coming of the dragons and mourned their absence. Every day she would wander into the great forest and sing of her sorrow for the beautiful creatures that had come to the island for such a brief time. In the story, she had no name, like too many women in stories of old. She was only *Snow-Walking Maiden*.

One bitter morning, Snow-Walking Maiden came across a wounded bird in a stream. She mended its wing and fed it with drops of milk. After a year in her care, the bird grew strong, and she carried it to the cliffs to let it fly away.

That was when the bird had transformed into Kwiriki, the Great Elder, who had been wounded at sea and taken a new form to escape. Snow-Walking Maiden was filled with joy, and so was the great Kwiriki, for he knew now that the children of the flesh had good in them.

To thank Snow-Walking Maiden for caring for him, the

great Kwiriki carved her a throne out of his own horn, which was called the Rainbow Throne, and made her a handsome consort, Night-Dancing Prince, out of sea foam. Snow-Walking Maiden became the first Empress of Seiiki, and she flew over the island with the great Kwiriki, teaching the people to love the dragons and harm them no more. Her bloodline had ruled Seiiki until they had perished in the Great Sorrow, and the First Warlord had taken up arms to avenge them.

"The story is true. Kwiriki did take the form of a bird. With time, we could learn to take many shapes," Nayimathun said. "We could change our size, weave illusions, bestow dreams—such was our power."

But no longer.

Tané listened to the sea below. She imagined herself as a conch, carrying that roar in her belly. As her eyelids grew heavier, Nayimathun looked down at her.

"Something troubles you."

Tané tensed.

"No," she said. "I was just thinking how happy I am. I have everything I ever wanted."

Nayimathun rumbled, and mist puffed from her nostrils. "There is nothing you cannot tell me."

Tané could not meet her gaze. Every grain of her being told her not to lie in the presence of a god, but she could *not* tell the truth about the outsider. For that crime, her dragon would cast her aside.

She would sooner die than have that happen.

"I know," was all she said.

The pupil of the dragon's eye grew to a pool of darkness. Tané could see her own face inside it. "I meant to fly you back to the castle," Nayimathun said, "but I must rest tonight."

"I understand."

A low growl rolled through Nayimathun. She spoke as if to herself. "He is stirring. The shadow lies heavy on the West."

"Who is stirring?"

The dragon closed her eyes and lowered her head back on to her neck. "Stay with me until sunrise, Tané."

"Of course."

Tané lay on her side. Nayimathun shifted closer and coiled around her.

"Sleep," she said. "The stars will watch over us."

Her body shut out the wind. As Tané drowsed against the dragon she had always dreamed about, lulled by her heartbeat, she had the curious sense that she was in the womb again.

She also had the sense that something was closing in on her. Like a net around a writhing fish.

26

West

News of the royal progress to Ascalon spread across Inys, from the Bay of the Balefire to the misty cliff-lined reaches of the Fells. After fourteen long years, Queen Sabran would show herself to the people of the capital, and the capital prepared to welcome her. Before Ead knew it, the day was upon them.

As she dressed, she concealed her blades. Two went beneath her skirts, another she tucked behind her stomacher, a fourth into one of her boots. The ornamental dagger carried by all Ladies of the Bedchamber was the only one she could display.

At five of the clock, she joined Katryen in the royal apartments and went with her to rouse Sabran and Roslain.

For her first public appearance since her coronation, the ladies-in-waiting had to make the queen more than beautiful. They had to make her divine. She was arrayed in midnight velvet, a girdle of carnelians, and a stole of bodmin fur, making her stand out against the bronze tinseled satin and brown furs around her. This way, she would invoke memories of Queen Rosarian, who had loved to wear blue.

A sword-shaped brooch was pinned to her bodice. She alone, in all Virtudom, took the Saint himself as her patron.

Roslain, whose hair was adorned with amber and cranberry glass, took charge of choosing the jewels. Ead picked up a comb. Holding Sabran by the shoulder, she grazed its teeth through the cascade of black hair until each lock glided between her fingers.

Sabran stood like a stanchion. Her eyes were raw with sleeplessness.

Ead gentled her brushing. Sabran tilted her head into her touch. With each stroke of the comb, her stance lost some of its tension, and the cast of her jaw softened. As she worked, Ead set her fingertips on the naked place behind Sabran's ear, holding her still.

"You look very beautiful today, Ead," Sabran said.

It was the first time she had spoken since rising.

"Your Majesty is kind to say so." Ead teased at a stubborn knot. "Are you looking forward to your visit to the city?"

Sabran did not answer for some time. Ead kept combing.

"I look forward to seeing my people," Sabran finally said. "My father always encouraged me to walk among them, but ... I could not."

She must be thinking of her mother. The reason she had seen little but the gleaming interiors of her palaces for fourteen years.

"I wish I could tell them I am with child." She touched her jewel-encrusted stomacher. "The Royal Physician has advised me to wait until my daughter quickens."

"What they desire is to see *you*. Whether your belly is big or not," Ead said. "In any case, you will be able to tell them in a few weeks. And think how pleased they will be then."

The queen studied her face. Then, quite unexpectedly, she took her by the hand.

"Tell me, Ead," she said, "how is it you always know what to say to comfort me?"

Before Ead could answer, Roslain approached. Ead stepped away, and Sabran's hand slipped from hers, but she still felt the ghost of it against her palm. Its fine-spun bones. The scallops of her knuckles.

Sabran let her ladies guide her to the washbasin. Katryen took charge of reddening her lips, while Ead braided six sections of her hair and wound them into a rosette at the back of her head, leaving the rest loose and waving. Last came a silver crown.

Once she was ready, the queen beheld herself in the glass. Roslain straightened the crown.

"Just one last touch," she said, and slipped a necklace around Sabran's throat. Graduated sapphires and pearls, and a pendant shaped like a seahorse. "You remember."

"Of course." Sabran traced the pendant, her expression distant. "My mother gave it to me."

Roslain placed a hand on her shoulder. "Let her be with you now. She would be so proud."

The Queen of Inys studied the glass a moment longer. Finally, she gathered her breath and turned.

"My ladies," she said, with a faint smile, "how do I look?"

Katryen tucked a strand of hair into her crown and nodded. "Like the blood of the Saint, Your Majesty."

By ten of the clock, the sky was blinding in its blueness. The ladies-in-waiting escorted Sabran to the gates of Briar House, where Aubrecht Lievelyn was waiting in a greatcloak with the six Dukes Spiritual. Seyton Combe, as usual, had a clement smile on his lips. Ead itched to swipe it away.

He might look pleased with himself, but he had clearly made no progress on the matter of the cutthroats. Neither, to her frustration, had Ead. Much as she wanted to investigate, her duties left her with so little time.

If the killers were to strike again, it would be today.

While Sabran was given a hand into the royal coach, Igrain Crest held out a hand to her granddaughter.

"Roslain," she said, smiling. "How lovely you are today, child. The jewel of my world."

"Oh, Grandmother, you are too generous." Roslain curtsied and kissed her on the cheek. "Good day."

"We can only hope it *will* be a good day, Lady Roslain," Lord Ritshard Eller muttered. "I mislike the queen walking among the commons."

"Everything will be fine," Combe said. His livery collar reflected the sunlight. "Her Majesty and His Royal Highness are well protected. Are they not, Sir Tharian?"

"Never more so than they will be today, Your Grace," Lintley said, with a smart bow.

"Hm." Eller looked unconvinced. "Very good, Sir Tharian."

Ead shared a coach with Roslain and Katryen. As they trundled away from the palace, into the thick of the city, she gazed out of the window.

Ascalon was the first and only capital of Inys. Its cobbled streets were home to thousands of people from all corners of Virtudom and beyond. Before Galian had returned to these isles, they had been a patchwork of ever-warring territories, ruled by a surfeit of overlords and princelings. Galian had united them all under one crown. His crown.

The capital he built, named after his sword, was said to have been a paradise once. Now it was as rife with knavery and filth as any other city.

Most of the buildings were stone. After the Grief of Ages, when fire had raged across Inys, a law had been passed to ban thatched roofs. Only a handful of wooden houses, designed by Rosarian the Second, had been allowed to remain, for their beauty. Dark timber-work, arranged in opulent designs, formed a striking contrast to the white of their filling.

The richer wards were rich indeed. Queenside boasted fifty goldsmiths and twice as many silversmiths. Hend Street was for workshops, where inventors devised new weapons to defend Inys. On the Isle of Knells, Pounce Lane was for poets and playwrights, Brazen Alley for booksellers. Goods from elsewhere in the world were sold at the great market in Werald Square. Bright Lasian copper and ceramic and gold jewelry. Mentish paintings and marquetry and salt-glazed pottery. Rare cranberry glass from the old Serene Republic of Carmentum. Perfume burners and skystone from the Ersyr.

In the poorer wards the royal party would visit today, like Kine End and the Setts, life was less beautiful. In these wards were the shambles, the brothels—disguised as inns to avoid the Order of Sanctarians—and alehouses where footpads counted stolen coin.

Tens of thousands of Inysh were out in force, waiting for a glimpse of their queen. The sight of them struck disquiet into

Ead. There had been no cutthroats since the marriage, but she was certain the threat had not yet diminished.

The royal procession stopped outside the Sanctuary of Our Lady, which was believed to house the tomb of Cleolind. (Ead knew that it did not.) It was the highest building in Inys, taller even than the Alabastrine Tower, made of a pale stone that shone beneath the sun.

Ead stepped from the coach, into the light. It had been a long time since she had walked the streets of Ascalon, but she knew them well. Before Chassar had presented her to Sabran, she had spent a month learning every vein and sinew of the city so she would find her way if she ever had to flee from court.

A concourse had gathered at the steps of the sanctuary, hungry for attention from their sovereign. They had scattered queenflower and jewel lilies over the cobblestones. While the maids of honor and the Extraordinary Chamberers emerged from their coaches with Oliva Marchyn, Ead took stock of the crowd.

"I don't see Lady Truyde," she said to Katryen.

"She has a headache." Katryen pursed her lips. "A fine day for it."

Margret came to stand beside them. "I expected a great many people," she said, breath clouding, "but by the Saint, I think the whole city has come." She nodded to the royal coach. "Here we go."

Ead braced herself.

When Lievelyn emerged, the Inysh cheered as if the Saint himself had returned. Unfazed, he raised a hand in greeting before extending it to Sabran, who climbed out with poise.

The roar of the crowd grew so loud, so fast, that it seemed to Ead to transcend sound and attain a physicality. It wrenched out her breath and dealt a blow to her insides. She felt Katryen shiver with exhilaration beside her, and saw Margret stare, as the Inysh went to their knees before their queen. Hats were removed, tears were shed, and she thought the cheers would lift the Sanctuary of Our Lady from the ground. Sabran stood like one stricken by a thunderbolt. Ead watched her take it all in. Since the day she was crowned, she had hidden in her palaces. She had forgotten what she was to her people. The living embodiment of hope. Their shield and their salvation.

She recovered quickly. Though she did not wave, she smiled and joined hands with Lievelyn. They remained side by side for a time and allowed their subjects to adore them.

Captain Lintley walked first, one hand resting on his basket-hilted sword. The Knights of the Body and some three hundred guards, posted along the route they would take, had been mustered to protect the queen and the prince consort on their tour of the city.

As she followed Sabran, Ead watched the crowd, her gaze darting from face to face, hand to hand. No good killer would ignore an opportunity like this.

The Sanctuary of Our Lady was as magnificent inside as it was on the exterior, with a vaulted ceiling. Trefoil windows towered, scattering the party with splinters of purple light. The guards waited outside.

Sabran and Lievelyn walked toward the tomb. It was a stately block of marble, set into an alcove behind the altar. The Damsel was thought to rest incorrupt in a locked vault beneath it. There was no effigy.

The royal couple knelt on the hassocks in front of it and bowed their heads. After a while, Lievelyn stepped back to allow Sabran to say a prayer in private. The Ladies of the Bedchamber came to kneel around her.

"Blessèd Damsel," Sabran said to the tomb, "I am Sabran the Ninth. Mine is your crown, mine is your queendom, and every day I long to bring glory to the House of Berethnet. I long to be possessed of your compassion, your courage, and your forbearance."

She closed her eyes, and her voice became a ghost of a breath.

"I confess," she said, "that I am not much like you. I have been impatient and arrogant. For too long I forswore my duty to this realm, refusing to gift unto my people a princess, and instead sought errant means of prolonging my own life."

Ead glanced at her. The queen took off her fur-trimmed glove and laid her hand upon the marble.

She was praying to an empty tomb.

"I ask you this, as your loving scion. Let me carry my daughter to term. Let her be hale and spirited. Let me give the people of

Virtudom hope. I will do anything for this. I will die to give my daughter life. I will sacrifice all else for her—but let our house not end with me."

Her voice was steady, but her face was an ode to fatigue. Ead considered, then reached for her.

At first, Sabran stiffened. A moment later, she twined their fingers and held on.

No woman should be made to fear that she was not enough.

When Sabran rose, so did her ladies. Ead steeled herself. The next part of the journey would be the most dangerous. Sabran and Lievelyn were to meet the unfortunate of Ascalon and give them purses of gold. As they descended the steps of the sanctuary, Sabran stayed close to her companion.

The party would go on foot from here. They followed Berethnet Mile through the city, flanked by city guards. Halfway down it, they crossed Marian Square, and a tinker called, "Get her with child, or get back to Mentendon!" Lievelyn remained impassive, but Sabran clenched her jaw. As the man was dragged away by the guards, she took Lievelyn by the hand.

To reach Kine End, they had to pass through the ward of Sylvan-by-the-River, where the streets were shaded by evergreens, and the Carnelian Theatre loomed over the stalls. The noise was thunderous, the air heady with excitement.

As Sabran paused to admire a bolt of cloth, something made Ead glance toward the bakehouse across the street. Crouched on its balcony was a figure with a rag over his nose and mouth. As Ead watched, he raised his arm.

A pistol gleamed in the sunlight.

"Death to the House of Berethnet," he shouted.

It was as if time slowed. Sabran looked up sharply, and someone let out a cry of horror, but Ead was already there. She collided with Sabran and hooked an arm around her waist, and they dropped to the cobblestones as the pistol discharged with a sound like the world splitting. Screams erupted from the crowd as an old man buckled, hit by the bullet meant for the queen.

Ead landed hard on her hip, curled around Sabran, who clutched her in return, one arm crossed over her belly. Ead scooped her up and handed her to Lievelyn. He wheeled her away from the direction of the gunfire. "The queen," Captain Lintley bellowed. "All swords to the queen!"

"Up there." Ead pointed. "Kill him!"

The shooter had already hurdled to the next balcony. Lintley took aim with his crossbow, but the quarrel missed by an inch. He cursed and loaded another.

Ead put herself in front of Sabran. Lievelyn drew his broadsword and guarded her back. The other ladies-in-waiting fanned out around their queen. As her gaze shadowed the shooter, who was now leaping like an antelope between rooftops, Ead grew cold all over. She looked to the other side of the street.

They did not wear visards. Not like the cutthroats in the palace. Instead, their faces were hidden by plague masks, the sort physicians had used to protect themselves in the Grief of Ages. As the first of them burst out of the crowd and bore down on the royal party, Ead hurled the dagger from her girdle. It hit the nearest attacker in the throat.

The crowd splintered. In the chaos, the next attacker was suddenly on top of them. "Fuck the House of Berethnet," he screamed at Sabran. He slammed into one of the Knights of the Body, who threw him off and thrust her sword at him. "Hail the Nameless One!"

"The God of the Mountain!" The invocation went up nearby. "His kingdom will come!"

Doomsingers. In a heartbeat, Lintley had traded crossbow for sword and cut down the nearest threat. The gallant knight was gone, replaced by a man who had been hand-picked to protect the Queen of Inys. The next attacker stopped in her tracks, and when Lintley bore down on her, she turned and fled. A musket fired and blew her guts across the cobblestones.

In the chaos, Ead looked for the Night Hawk, but there was too much panic, too many bodies. Sabran stayed rooted in place, fists clenched at her side, unbowed.

A preternatural calm descended on Ead. As she drew two blades, she forgot that Ladies of the Bedchamber were not educated in combat. She let fall the cloak of secrecy she had worn for all these years. All she knew was her duty. To keep Sabran alive.

The war dance was calling to her. As it had the first time she had hunted a basilisk. Like wind on fire, she flashed into the next wave of attackers, wheeling her blades, and they fell dead around her.

She pulled herself back from the brink. Lintley was staring at her, his face dappled with blood. A scream made his head turn. Linora. She keened in terror, pleading, as two of the doomsingers wrestled her to the ground. Ead and Lintley both ran toward her at once, but a knife opened her throat, spraying blood, and it was too late, she was lost.

Ead tried to temper her shock, but bile scalded her gorge. Sabran stared at her dying lady. The Knights of the Body encircled their queen, but they were surrounded, the threat everywhere. Another masked figure charged at the royals, but Roslain, with a ferocity Ead had never seen in her, thrust her knife into his thigh. A shout came from behind the mask.

"The Nameless One will rise," a voice said, panting. "We pledge our allegiance." Fog obscured the eyeholes. "Death to the House of Berethnet!"

Roslain went for his throat, but he smashed his fist into her head, snapping it back. Sabran cried out in anger. Ead pulled out of the fray and ran toward her just as the knave slashed with a knife at Lievelyn, who raised his sword just in time to parry.

The tussle that followed was short and violent. Lievelyn was the stronger, years of tutelage behind every movement. With one brutal downcut, it was over.

Sabran backed away from the corpse. Her companion beheld his own sword and swallowed. Blood dripped from its blade.

"Your Majesty, Your Royal Highness, follow me." A Knight of the Body had broken free of the fray. His copper-plated armor was redder than before. "I know a safe place in this ward. Captain Lintley commanded me to take you hence. We must go now."

Ead pointed one of her knives at him. Most Knights of the Body wore close helms outdoors, and the voice beneath this one was muffled. "Come no farther," she said. "Who are you?"

"Sir Grance Lambren."

"Take off your helm."

"Peace, Mistress Duryan. I recognize his voice," Lievelyn said. "It is not safe for Sir Grance to remove his helm."

"Ros—" Sabran was straining to reach her Chief Gentlewoman. "Aubrecht, carry her, please."

Ead looked for Margret and Katryen, but they were nowhere to be seen. Linora lay in her lake of blood, eyes glazed in death.

Lievelyn gathered Roslain into his arms and followed Sir Grance Lambren, who was rushing Sabran away. Roundly cursing Lievelyn for his trust, Ead chased after them. The other Knights of the Body strove to join their queen, but they were overwhelmed.

How had someone orchestrated such a swarm?

She caught up to Sabran and Lievelyn just as Lambren was leading them around a corner, out of sight of Berethnet Mile. He took them through an overgrown charnel garden on Quiver Lane, to a sanctuary that had fallen into ruin. He shepherded his royal charges inside, but when Ead reached the doors, he barred her way.

"You ought to find the other ladies, mistress."

"I will follow the queen, sir," Ead said, "or you will not."

Lambren did not move. She tightened her grip on her knives.

"Ead." Sabran. "Ead, where are you?"

The knight was as a statue for a moment longer before he stood aside. Once Ead had passed, he sheathed his sword and bolted the doors behind them. When he removed his helm, Ead beheld the ruddy face of Sir Grance Lambren. He shot her a look of intense dislike.

The interior of the sanctuary was as wild as the charnel garden. Weeds fingered through the shattered windows. Roslain lay on the altar, still but for the rise and fall of her breast. Sabran, who had covered her with her own cloak, stood beside her with outward composure, holding her limp hand.

Lievelyn paced back and forth, his face pinched. "Those poor souls outside. Lady Linora—" Blood smeared his cheek. "Sabran, I must return to the street and assist Captain Lintley. You stay with Sir Grance and Mistress Duryan."

At once, Sabran went to him. "No." She grasped his elbows. "I command you to stay."

"Mine is as good a sword as any," Lievelyn told her. "My Royal Guard—"

"My Knights of the Body are also outside," Sabran cut in, "but if we die, their labors to protect us will be in vain. They will have to think of us as well as themselves."

Lievelyn framed her face in his hands.

"Sweeting," he said, "I will be all right."

For the first time, Ead saw how deeply in love with Sabran he was, and it shook her. "Damn you, you are my companion. You have shared my bed. My flesh. My—my heart," Sabran snapped at him. Her face was taut, her voice ragged. "And you will not leave our daughter fatherless, Aubrecht Lievelyn. You will not leave us here to mourn you."

His face twitched from one expression to another. Hope kindled a light in his eyes.

"Is it true?"

Holding his gaze, Sabran took his hand in hers and guided it to her belly.

"It is true," she said very softly.

Lievelyn released a breath. A smile pulled at his mouth, and he stroked a thumb over her cheek.

"Then I am the most fortunate of all princes," he whispered. "And I swear to you, our child will be the most beloved princess who ever lived." Breathing out, he gathered Sabran to his chest. "My queen. My blessing. I will love you both until I am worthy of my good fortune."

"You are already worthy." Sabran kissed his jaw. "Do you not wear my love-knot ring?"

She set her chin on his shoulder. Her hands stroked up and down his back, and her eyes fluttered shut as he touched his lips to her temple. Whatever tension had been there was erased. A flame pressed into nonexistence as the rift between their bodies closed.

Fists hammered on the doors.

"Sabran," a voice called. "Majesty, it's Kate, with Margret! Please, let us in!"

"Kate, Meg—" Sabran pulled away from Lievelyn at once. "Let them in," she barked at Lambren. "Make haste, Sir Grance."

Too slow, Ead heard the trick. It was not Lady Katryen Withy behind that door. It was an imitation. The mockery of a mimic.

"No," she said sharply. "Stop."

"How dare you countermand my orders?" Sabran rounded on her. "Who gave you authority?"

She was flushed with anger, but Ead kept her nerve. "Majesty, it is not Katryen—"

"I think I should know her voice." Sabran nodded to Lambren. "Let my ladies in. Now."

He was a Knight of the Body, so he obeyed.

Ead wasted no time. One of her knives was already slicing through the air when Lambren unlocked the doors and someone crashed into the sanctuary. The intruder avoided whirling death with one deft turn, fired a pistol at Lambren, then pointed it at Ead.

Lambren collapsed with a peal of armor on stone. The bullet was buried between his eyes.

"Don't move, Ersyri," a voice said. The pistol smoked. "Put down that knife."

"So you can kill the Queen of Inys?" Ead remained still. "I would sooner you kept that pistol on *my* heart—but I suspect you only have one bullet, else all of us would be dead."

The cutthroat gave no answer.

"Who sent you?" Sabran squared her shoulders. "Who conspires to end the bloodline of the Saint?"

"The Cupbearer wishes you no ill, Your Majesty, except when you do not listen to reason. Except when you lead Inys down paths it should not tread."

Cupbearer.

"Paths," the woman continued, her voice muffled by the plague mask, "that will lead Inys toward sin."

As the pistol snapped toward the royals, Ead threw her last knife. It struck the cutthroat through the heart just as the pistol fired.

Sabran flinched. Ead closed the space between them and felt for moisture on her bodice, sick with dread, but there was no blood. The gown was still pristine.

Behind them, Aubrecht Lievelyn dropped to one knee. His hands were at his doublet, where darkness was spreading.

"Sabran," he murmured.

She turned.

"No," she rasped. "Aubrecht—"

Ead watched, as if from a great distance, as the Queen of Inys ran to her companion and lowered him to the floor with her, gasping out his name as his heart's blood soaked into her skirts. As she held him close and pleaded with him to stay with her, even as he slipped away. As she doubled over him, cradling his head.

As he grew still.

"Aubrecht." Sabran looked up, her eyes overflowing. "Ead. Ead, help him, please—"

Ead had no time to go to her. The doors opened again, and a second cutthroat stumbled into the sanctuary, heaving. At once, Ead divested the dead Lambren of his sword and pinned the cutthroat to the wall.

"Take off your mask," she bit out, "or I swear to you, I will take off the face beneath it."

Two gloved hands revealed a pale countenance. Truyde utt Zeedeur stared at the lifeless High Prince of Mentendon.

"I never meant for him to die," she whispered. "I only wanted to help you, Your Majesty. I only wanted you to listen."

27

East

Niclays Roos was *conniving*. And it was a plan so dangerous and unflinching that he almost wondered if he really had come up with it, eternal coward that he was.

He was going to make the elixir and buy his way back to the West if it killed him. And it very well might. To escape Orisima for good, and to breathe life back into his work, he needed to take a risk. He needed what Eastern law had denied him.

He needed blood from a dragon, to see how gods renewed themselves.

And he knew just where to start.

The servants were busy in the kitchen. "What help can we be, learnèd Doctor Roos?" one asked when Niclays appeared in the doorway.

"I need to send a message." Before Niclays could lose the speck of courage that remained to him, he held out the letter. "It must reach the honored Lady Tané at Salt Flower Castle before sunset. Will you take it to the postriders for me?"

"Yes, learnèd Doctor Roos. It will be done."

"Do not tell them who sent it," he added quietly. She looked uncertain, but promised she would not. He handed her money enough to pay a postrider, and she left.

All he could do now was wait.

Fortunately, waiting meant more time to read. While Eizaru was at the market and Purumé was tending to patients, Niclays sat in his room, the bobtail cat purring beside him, and perused *The Price of Gold*, his favorite text on alchemy. His copy was well worn.

As he turned to a new chapter that afternoon, a sliver of delicate silk fluttered out.

His breath caught. He retrieved the fragment from the floor and smoothed it out before the cat could claw it to shreds. It had been years since he had last brought himself to look at the greatest mystery of his life.

Most of the books and documents in his possession had once belonged to Jannart, who had bequeathed half of his library to Niclays, as well as his armillary sphere, a Lacustrine candle clock, and a host of other curiosities. There had been many beautiful tomes in the collection—illuminated manuscripts, rare tracts, miniature prayer books—but nothing had obsessed Niclays more than this tiny scrap of silk. Not because it was brushed with a language he could not decipher, and not because it was clearly very old—but because in attempting to unlock its secret, Jannart had lost his life.

Aleidine, his widow, had given it to Truyde, who had mourned for her grandfather by fixating on his possessions. The child had kept the fragment in a locket for a year.

Just before Niclays had left for Inys, Truyde had come to his house in Brygstad. She had worn a little ruff, and her hair—Jannart's hair—had curled around her shoulders.

Uncle Niclays, she had said gravely, *I know you are leaving soon. My lord grandsire was holding this piece of paper when he died. I have tried to work out what it says, but the petty school has not taught me enough.* She had offered it with a gloved hand. *Papa says you are very clever. I think you will be able to work out what the writing means.*

This belongs to you, child, he had said, even as he had ached to take it. *Your lady grandmother gave it to you.*

I think it was supposed to be for you. I would like you to have it. Only write to me and tell me if you work out what it means.

He had never been able to send her good news. Based on the script and material, the fragment was certainly from the ancient East, but that was all Jannart had gleaned from it at the time of his death. Years had passed, and still Niclays did not know why he had been clutching it on his deathbed.

He rolled it now, carefully, and slotted it into the ornate case Eizaru had gifted him. He dried his eyes, breathed in deeply, and opened *The Price of Gold* once again.

That evening, Niclays supped with Eizaru and Purumé before feigning sleep. As night fell, he crept from his room and put on a hat that belonged to Eizaru. Then he stole into the dark.

He knew his way to the beach. Evading the sentinels, he hurried past the night markets, head down and cane in hand.

There were no lanterns to betray his arrival on the beach. It was empty of everyone but her.

Tané Miduchi waited beside a rock pool. The brim of a helm cast her face into shadow. Niclays sat at a distance.

"You honor me with your presence, Lady Tané."

It was some time before she answered. "You speak Seiikinese."

"Of course."

"What do you want?"

"A favor."

"I owe you no favors." Her voice was cold and soft. "I could kill you here."

"I suspected you might threaten me, which is why I left a note about your crime with the learnèd Doctor Moyaka." A lie, but she had no way of knowing that. "His household is asleep now—but if I do not return to burned that note, all of them will know what you have done. I doubt the Sea General will allow you to keep your place among the riders—you, who might have let the red sickness into Seiiki."

"You misjudge what I would do to keep that place."

Niclays chuckled. "You left an innocent man and a young woman to die in the shit and piss of a jailhouse, all so your special ceremony would go just as you wanted," he reminded her. "No, Lady Tané. I have not misjudged you. I feel as if I know you very well."

She was quiet for some time. Then: "You said *young woman*."

Of course, she could have no idea. "I doubt you care for poor Sulyard," Niclays said, "but your friend from the theatre was arrested, too. I shudder to think of what they might have done to try to draw your name from her."

"You are lying."

Niclays watched her lips press together. They were all he could see of her face.

"I offer you a fair bargain," he said. "I will leave here tonight and say nothing of your involvement with Sulyard. In exchange for my silence, you will bring me blood and scale from your dragon."

She moved like a bird taking wing. Suddenly a keen-edged blade was pressed against his throat.

"Blood," she whispered, "and scale."

Her hand was shaking. Instinct screamed at Niclays to recoil, but he found himself anchored in place.

"You would have me mutilate a dragon. Defile the flesh of a god," the dragonrider said. He could see her eyes now, and they cut deeper than her blade. "The authorities will do worse to you than beheading. You will be burned alive. The water in you is too polluted to cleanse."

"I wonder if they will burn *you* for your crimes. Abetting a trespasser. Contempt of the sea ban. Putting the whole of Seiiki at risk." Niclays gritted his teeth when her knife bit into his neck. "Sulyard will confirm what I say. He remembered your face in great detail, I'm afraid, down to that scar of yours. No one listened, of course, but if I join my voice to his . . ."

She was shivering now.

"So," she said, "you are threatening me." She withdrew the knife. "But not to save Sulyard. You use the suffering of others for your own gain. You are a servant of the Nameless One."

"Oh, nothing as exciting as that, Lady Tané. Just a lonely old man, trying to get off this island so I can die in my own country." Warmth dampened his collar. "I understand you may need some time to obtain what I need. I will be on this beach four days from now, at dusk. If you do not come, I advise you to leave Ginura with all speed."

He bowed deeply and left her there, alone beneath the stars.

The sun welled up like blood from a wound. Tané sat on the cliff that overlooked Ginura Bay, watching the waves shatter into white crystal on the rocks below.

Her shoulder throbbed where Turosa had sliced into it. She drank the wine she had taken from the kitchens, and it burned her from the roof of her mouth to her chest.

These were her last hours as Lady Tané of Clan Miduchi. Only a few days after receiving her new name, she would be stripped of it.

Tané traced the scar on her cheek, the scar that had made her memorable to Sulyard. The scar from saving Susa. It was not her only scar—she had another, deeper mark on her side. She had no memory of receiving that one.

She thought of Susa, languishing in jail. And then she thought of what Roos wanted her to do, and her stomach flopped like a fish on dry land.

Even disfiguring an image of a dragon was forbidden on pain of death. To steal the blood and armor of a god was more than criminal. There were pirates who used firecloud to put dragons to sleep, haul them into stolen treasure ships, and strip them of everything they could sell on the shadow market in Kawontay, from their teeth to the blubber under their scales. It was the gravest of all crimes in the East, and past Warlords had been known to punish those involved with brutal public executions.

She would have no part in that cruelty. After all the battles Nayimathun must have fought in the Great Sorrow, all the scars she already had, Tané would not mutilate her also. Whatever Roos wanted with her sacred blood, it did not bode well for Seiiki.

And yet she could not gamble with Susa's life—not when she had been the one to drag her friend into this morass.

Tané scraped her fingers over her scalp, pulling at her hair in the way she sometimes had when she was younger. Her teachers had always slapped her hands to stop her.

No. She would not do what Roos wanted. She would go to the Sea General and confess what she had done. It would cost her Nayimathun and her place among the riders. It would cost her everything she had worked for since she was a child—but it was what she deserved, and it might save her only friend from the sword.

"Tané."

She looked up.

Nayimathun was drifting at the edge of the cliff. Her crown pulsed with light.

"Great Nayimathun," Tané rasped.

Nayimathun tilted her head. Her body drifted with the wind, as though she were as light as paper. Tané placed her hands in front of her and pressed her brow into the ground.

"You did not come to the Grieving Orphan tonight," Nayimathun said.

"Forgive me." Since she could not touch the dragon, Tané signed the words with her hands as she spoke them. "I cannot see you any more. Truly, great Nayimathun, I am sorry." Her voice was breaking, like rotted wood under strain. "I must go to the honored Sea General. I have something to confess."

"I would like you to fly with me, Tané. We will talk about what troubles you."

"I would dishonor you."

"Do you also disobey me, child of flesh?"

Those eyes were blazing rings of fire, and that mouthful of teeth invited no argument. Tané could not disobey a god. Her body was a vessel of water, and all water was theirs.

It was dangerous, but possible, to ride on dragonback without a saddle. She rose and stepped toward the edge of the cliff. Shivers flickered up her sides as Nayimathun lowered her head, allowing Tané to grip her mane, plant a boot on her neck, and sit astride her. Nayimathun flowed away from the castle—

—and dived.

A thrill sang through Tané as they plummeted toward the sea. She could not breathe for dread and joy. It was as if her heart had been hooked from her mouth, caught like a fish on a line.

A spine of rocks rushed up to meet them. The wind roared in her ears. Just before they hit the water, instinct pushed her head down.

The impact almost unseated her. Water flooded her mouth and nose. Her thighs ached and her fingers cramped with the effort of holding on as Nayimathun swam, tail sweeping, legs clawing, graceful as a blackfish. Tané forced her eyes open. Her shoulder burned with the healing fire only the sea could light.

Bubbles drifted like sea-moons around her. Nayimathun broke the surface, and Tané followed.

"Up," Nayimathun said, "or down?"

"Up."

Scale and muscle flexed beneath Tané. She tightened her hands in the slick of mane. With one great leap, Nayimathun was high over the bay, raining water down upon the waves.

Tané turned to see over her shoulder. Ginura was already far below. It looked like a painting, real and unreal, a floating world on the verge of the sea. She felt alive, *truly* alive, as if she had never breathed until now. Here, she was no longer Lady Tané of Clan Miduchi, or anyone at all. She was faceless in the gloaming. A breath of wind over the sea.

This was what her death would feel like. Jeweled turtles would come to escort her spirit to the Palace of Many Pearls, and her body would be given to the waves. All that would be left of it was foam.

At least, that was what would have happened if she had not transgressed. Only riders could rest with their dragons. Instead, she would haunt the ocean for eternity.

The drink was heavy in her blood. Nayimathun soared higher, singing in an ancient language. The breath of both human and dragon came like cloud.

The sea was vast below them. Tané nestled into Nayimathun's mane, where the wind could hardly touch her. Countless stars glistened above, crystal-clear without cloud to obscure them. Eyes of dragons never born. When she slept, she dreamed of them, an army falling from the skies to drive away the shadows. She dreamed she was small as a seedling, and that all her hopes grew branches, like a tree.

She stirred, warm and listless, with a light ache in her temples.

It took her some time to wake fully, so deep was she in dreaming. As she remembered everything, her skin turned cold again, and she realized she was lying upon rock.

She rolled on to her hip. In the darkness, she could just make out the shape of her dragon.

"Where are we, Nayimathun?"

Scale hissed on rock.

"Somewhere," the dragon rumbled. "Nowhere."

They were in a tidal cave. Water washed in from outside. Where it broke against the rock, pale lights bloomed and dwindled, like the tiny glowing squid that had sometimes washed up on the beaches of Cape Hisan.

"Tell me," Nayimathun said, "how you have dishonored us."

Tané wrapped one arm around her knees. If there was any courage left in her, there was not enough to refuse a dragon twice.

She spoke softly. Nothing was secret. As she recounted everything that had happened since the outsider had blundered onto that beach, Nayimathun made no sound. Tané pressed her brow to the ground and waited for judgment.

"Rise," Nayimathun said.

Tané obeyed.

"What has happened does not dishonor me," the dragon said. "It dishonors the world."

Tané ducked her head. She had promised herself she would not cry again.

"I know I cannot be forgiven, great Nayimathun." She kept her gaze on her boots, but her jaw trembled. "I will go to the honored Sea General in the morning. You c-can choose another rider."

"No, child of flesh. You are my rider, sworn to me before the sea. And you are right that you cannot be forgiven," Nayimathun said, "but only because there was no crime."

Tané stared up at her. "There *was* a crime." Her voice quaked. "I broke seclusion. I hid an outsider. I disobeyed the Great Edict."

"No." A hiss echoed through the cave. "West or East, North or South—it makes no difference to the fire. The threat comes from beneath, not from afar." The dragon lay flat on the ground, so her eyes were as close as possible to Tané. "You hid the boy. Spared him the sword."

309

"I did not do it out of kindness," Tané said. "I did it because—" Her stomach twisted. "Because I wanted my life to run a smooth course. And I thought that he would ruin that."

"That disappoints me. That dishonors you. But not beyond forgiveness." Nayimathun tilted her head. "Tell me, little kin. Why did the Inysh man come to Seiiki?"

"He wanted to see the all-honored Warlord." Tané wet her lips. "He seemed desperate."

"Then the Warlord must see him. The Emperor of the Twelve Lakes must also hear his words." The quills on her back stiffened. "The earth will shake beneath the sea. He stirs."

Tané dared not ask who she meant. "What must I do, Nayimathun?"

"That is not the question you must ask. You must ask what *we* must do."

28

South

Rauca, capital of the Ersyr, was the largest remaining settlement in the South. As he threaded his way through its jumble of high-walled pathways, Loth found himself at the mercy of his senses. Mounds of rainbow spices, flower gardens that perfumed the streets, tall windcatchers accented with blueglass—all of it was unlike anything he knew.

In the moil of the city, only glances were spared for the ichneumon at his side. They must not be as rare in the Ersyr as they were farther north. Unlike the creature of legend, this one seemed not to be able to speak.

Loth edged through the crowds. Despite the heat, he had covered himself to the neck with his cloak, but it still made panic coil in him when someone came too close.

The Ivory Palace, seat of the House of Taumargam, loomed over the city like a silent god. Doves waffed around it, carrying messages between the people of the city. Its domes shone gold and silver and bronze, as bright as the sun they mirrored, and the walls were spotless white, arched windows cut into them like patterns into lace.

It was for the House of Taumargam that Chassar uq-Ispad worked as an ambassador. Loth tried to go toward the palace, but the ichneumon had other ideas. He led Loth into a covered market, where the air was sweet as pudding.

"I really don't know where you think you're going," Loth said, through cracked lips. He was sure the animal could understand him. "Could we stop for water, please, sirrah?"

He might as well have held his tongue for all the good it did him. When they passed a trove of saddle flasks, each crystalline with water, he could bear it no longer. He fumbled the purse of coins from his bag. The ichneumon looked back at him and growled.

"Please," Loth said wearily.

The ichneumon let out a huff, but sat on its haunches. Loth turned to the merchant and pointed to the smallest bottle, spun from iridescent glass. The man replied in his own tongue.

"I speak no Ersyri, sir," Loth said ruefully.

"Ah, you are Inysh. My apologies." The merchant smiled, crinkling the corners of his eyes. Like most Ersyris, he had golden skin and dark hair. "That will be eight suns."

Loth hesitated. Being rich, he had no experience of wrangling with merchants. "That . . . seems very expensive," he muttered, conscious of his paltry store.

"My family are the best glassblowers in Rauca. I can hardly taint our good name, my friend, by underselling my skills."

"Very well." Loth wiped his brow, too hot to gainsay. "I have seen people wearing cloths about their faces. Where can I buy one?"

"You came without a *pargh*— why, you are lucky not to be sand-blind." With a click of his tongue, the merchant shook out a square of white cloth. "Here. This will be my gift to you."

"You are too kind."

Loth extended a hand for the cloth. He was so afraid the plague might seep through his glove that he almost dropped it. Once the *pargh* covered all but his eyes, he gave the man a handful of the gold coins from his purse.

"The dawn shines on you, friend," the merchant said.

"And on you," Loth said awkwardly. "You have already been so generous, but I wonder if you could help me. I am in the Ersyr to find His Excellency, Chassar uq-Ispad, who is an ambassador to King Jantar and Queen Saiyma. Might he be in residence at the Ivory Palace?"

"Ha. You will be fortunate to find him. His Excellency is often abroad," the merchant said, chuckling, "but if he is anywhere at this time of year, he will be at his estate in Rumelabar." He handed Loth the flask. "Caravans leave from the Place of Doves at dawn."

"Could I send a letter from there, too?"

"Of course."

"Thank you. Good day to you, sir."

Loth stepped away and drained the flask in three long swallows. Panting, he wiped his mouth.

"The Place of Doves," he remarked to the ichneumon. "How beautiful it sounds. Will you take me there, my friend?"

The ichneumon took him to what must be the central hall of the market, where stalls offered sacks of dried rose petals, bowls of spun sugar, and sapphire tea, fresh from the kettle. By the time they emerged, the sun had dipped toward the horizon and stained-glass lanterns were being lit.

The Place of Doves was impossible to miss. Overlaid with square pink tiles, it was surrounded by a wall that connected four towering dovecotes, shaped like beehives. Loth soon worked out that the nearest was for mail heading to the West. He stepped into the cool honeycomb, where thousands of white rock doves nestled in alcoves.

On his last night in Cárscaro, he had written Margret a letter. And he had an idea of how to get it past Combe. A bird-keeper took it now, along with his coin, and promised it would be sent at dawn.

Weary to his bones, Loth let the ichneumon lead him from the dovecote and nudge him toward a building with the same lattice-work windows as the palace. Though the Ersyri woman inside could not speak Inysh, they somehow conveyed to one another, by dint of fervent gesturing and jaw-breaking smiles, that he wanted to stay for one night.

The ichneumon remained outside. Loth reached up to scratch between its ears.

"Do wait for me, my friend," he murmured. "I would treasure your company in another desert."

A short bark was his only answer. The last he saw of the ichneumon was its tail disappearing into an alley.

Beside that alley stood a woman. She was leaning against a pillar, her arms folded. Her face was hidden by a bronze mask. She wore belled trousers, tucked into boots with open toes, and a thigh-length brocade coat. Unnerved by her gaze, Loth turned away and went back into the inn.

He found a small room overlooking a courtyard, where sweet-lemon trees surrounded a pool. Dizziness wafted through him at the cloying scent. He took in the unfamiliar bed, piled with bolsters and corncockle silk, and wanted nothing but to sleep.

Instead, he went to his knees beside the window, and he wept for Kitston Glade.

The Saint gave him slumber when he could sob no more. He woke in the small hours, puffy-eyed and aching, with a swollen bladder that wanted his attention. Once he had relieved himself, he groped his way back to his room.

Thinking of Kit split his chest open. Grief was a swallet in him, draining all good thoughts.

Outside, the doves had gone to roost. The burnished domes of the Ivory Palace drank in the lights and flickered like candles. Above them, stars wound across the darkness.

He was not in the West any longer. This was a land sworn not to Virtudom, but to a false prophet. Ead had confessed to finding the teachings of the Dawnsinger beautiful as a child, but Loth had shivered. He could not imagine what it must be like to live without the comfort and structure of the Six Virtues. He was glad she had converted when she came to court.

A breeze cooled his skin. He longed for a bath, but feared the plague would poison the water. He would burn the sheets when he rose in the morning and pay the innkeeper for her loss.

Fire itched along his back. His hands were becoming scaled, and he could only wear gloves for so long without raising suspicions. He prayed Chassar uq-Ispad would indeed have the cure.

The Knight of Fellowship had sent the ichneumon to him. He could not be meant to die that way.

He slept again, dreamlessly, until he was awake.

His limbs were shaking uncontrollably. Fever roared through him, but he was certain something else had made him stir. He fumbled for his sword, only to remember it was lost.

"Who is that?" He tasted salt on his lips. "Ead?"

A shadow moved into the moonlight. A bronze mask loomed over him, and then all was dark.

29

East

Rain was falling on the capital again. Tané knelt at her table in her private rooms at Salt Flower Castle.

After her confession, Nayimathun had delivered her to the castle, where she remained. The dragon had said she would return to Cape Hisan for Sulyard. If he had the protection of a god, his petition would have to be heard at court. Nayimathun would also order that Susa be released at once from the jailhouse. They were to meet on the beach at sunrise, and then go together to the Sea General to tell him everything.

Tané tried to eat her supper, but her hands shook. Most of the dragonriders had been called away to assist the High Sea Guard in the coastal settlement of Sidupi. The Fleet of the Tiger Eye had attacked with a hundred-strong force of pirates, who were looting at will.

She called for tea. It was brought to her by one of her personal attendants, who now stayed close to serve her when she needed it.

Her bedchamber in the inner quarter was more beautiful than she had ever dreamed it would be, with a coffered lattice ceiling and sweet-smelling mats. Gold foil shone from the ornately painted walls, and the softest of bedding was waiting to embrace her.

At the heart of all this finery, she could not eat or sleep.

Her hands shook as she finished the tea. If she could only sleep, Nayimathun would be there when she woke up.

Tané had taken one step toward the bedding when the floor shunted and thunder rolled beneath the castle. She pitched into the wall. The force of the quake knocked her legs from under her, sprawling her across the mats.

The lantern flickered. Three of her attendants came running into the chamber. One of them knelt beside her while the others took her by the elbows and lifted her to her feet. She gasped when she put weight on her left ankle, and they hurried her to the bedding.

"Lady Tané, are you hurt?"

"A sprain," Tané said. "Nothing more."

"We will bring you something for your pain," the youngest attendant said. "Wait here, honored Miduchi." The three of them retreated.

Distant, confused shouts drifted through the open window. Earthshakes did happen in Seiiki, but there had not been one in a long time.

The attendants brought her a bowl of ice. Tané wrapped some in cloth and pressed it to her tender ankle. The fall had kindled the pain in her shoulder, and in her left side, where her old scar was.

When the ice was almost melted, she blew out the lantern and lay down, trying to find a comfortable position. Her side ached as if a horse had kicked it. Even as she succumbed to sleep, it was throbbing, like a second heart.

A knock jolted her awake. For a moment, she thought she was back in the South House, late for her class.

"Lady Tané."

It was not the voice of any of her attendants.

The pain in her side was raging now. Blear-eyed, she rose, trying not to jar her ankle.

Six masked foot soldiers waited outside her room. All wore the green tunics of the land army.

"Lady Tané," one of them said with a bow, "forgive us for disturbing you, but you must come with us at once."

It was unusual for any soldier of the land army to set foot in Salt Flower Castle. "It is the middle of the night." Tané tried to sound imperious. "Who summons me, honorable soldier?"

"The honored Governor of Ginura."

The most powerful official in the region. Chief magistrate of Seiiki, responsible for administering justice to those of high rank.

Tané was suddenly aware of every drop of blood in her veins. Her body felt untethered from the ground, and her mind gleamed with terrible possibilities, the foremost being that Roos had already gone to the authorities. Perhaps it was best to go softly, to play innocent. If she ran now, they would consider it an admission of her guilt.

Nayimathun would be back soon. Whatever happened, wherever she was taken, her dragon would come for her.

"Very well."

The soldier relaxed his stance. "Thank you, Lady Tané. We will send your servants to help you dress."

Her attendants brought her uniform. They lifted the surcoat on to her shoulders and tied a blue sash around her waist. As soon as she was dressed and they turned their backs to leave, she took a blade from under her pillow and slipped it into her sleeve.

The soldiers escorted her down the corridor. Every time her left foot touched the floor, pain arrowed up her calf. They took her through the near-deserted castle, into the night.

A palanquin awaited her at the gateway. She stopped. Every instinct was telling her not to get inside.

"Lady Tané," one of the soldiers said, "you cannot refuse this summons from the honored Governor."

Movement caught her eye. Onren was returning to the castle with Kanperu. Seeing Tané, they strode toward her.

"As a member of Clan Miduchi," Tané said to the soldier, emboldened, "I believe I can do as I choose."

Deep in the eyeholes of his mask, his gaze flickered.

Onren and Kanperu had reached her now. "Honorable Tané," the latter said, "is something wrong?"

His voice was a rasp and a ring. A sword eased from its scabbard. Faced with two more riders, the soldiers shifted their weight.

"These soldiers wish to take me to White River Castle, honorable Kanperu," Tané said. "They cannot tell me why I am summoned."

Kanperu looked at the captain with a rimple in his brow. He was almost a head taller than all the soldiers. "By what right do you summon a dragonrider without warning?" he asked. "Lady Tané is god-chosen, yet you take her from this castle as though she were a thief."

"The honored Sea General has been informed, Lord Kanperu."

Onren raised her eyebrows. "Indeed," she said. "I will be sure to confirm that with him when he returns."

The soldiers said nothing. Casting them a stern look, Onren took Tané aside.

"You must not worry," she said quietly. "It will be some trivial matter. I've heard the honored Governor likes to make her authority known even to Clan Miduchi." She paused. "Tané, you look unwell."

Tané swallowed.

"If I am not back within the hour," she said, "will you send word to the great Nayimathun?"

"Of course." Onren smiled. "Whatever it is will soon be resolved. See you tomorrow."

Tané nodded and tried to smile back. Onren watched as she climbed into the palanquin, as it left the castle grounds.

She was a dragonrider. There was nothing to fear.

The soldiers carried her through the streets, past the evening market, and under the season trees. Laughter rolled from crowded taverns. It was only when they passed the Imperial Theatre that Tané realized they were not going to White River Castle, where the honored Governor of Ginura lived. They were heading into the southern outskirts of the city.

Fear clenched her chest. She reached for the door of the palanquin, but it was bolted from the outside.

"This is not the right way," she called. "Where are you taking me?"

No answer.

"I am a Miduchi. I am the rider of the great Nayimathun of the Deep Snows." Her voice cracked. "How dare you treat me in this way."

All she heard was footsteps.

When the palanquin finally stopped, and she saw where they were, her stomach dropped. The door unlocked and slid open. "Honored Miduchi," one of the soldiers said, "please follow me."

"You dare," Tané whispered. "You *dare* bring me to such a place."

A rotten smell curdled in her nostrils, sharpening her fear. She had squandered her opportunity to run. Even a dragonrider could not fight all the sentinels here, not without a sword, and in any case, there was nowhere to go. She got down from the palanquin and walked, chin raised, side throbbing with every step, hands clenched.

They could not have brought her here to kill her. Not without a trial. Not without Nayimathun. She was god-chosen, protected, safe.

As the soldiers led her toward Ginura Jailhouse, the hum of insects snatched her gaze upward. Three flyblown heads, bloated with decay, watched the street from the gate above.

Tané stared at the freshest of them. The thatch of hair, taut with blood, the tongue puffy in death. His features had already slackened, but she recognized him. Sulyard. She tried to keep her grip on her composure, but her spine tightened and her stomach churned and her mouth turned dry as salt.

She had heard that far away in Inys, where the water ghost had come from, people gathered in public to witness executions. Not so in Seiiki. Most of the city was unaware that in the grounds of the jailhouse, a young woman of seventeen was on her knees by a ditch, her arms roped behind her back, waiting for the end. Her long hair had been shaved away.

The soldiers marched Tané toward the prisoner and held her in place. An official was speaking, but she could not hear through the swash of blood in her ears. The woman had looked up at the sound of footsteps, and Tané wished she had not, for she knew her.

"No," Tané said, voice cracking. "No. I order you to stop this!"

Susa stared back at her. Hope had rushed into her eyes, but now grief quenched it.

"I am god-chosen," Tané screamed at the executioner. "She is under my protection. The great Nayimathun will bring the sky down on your heads for this!" He might as well have been made of stone. "It was not her. It was me. It is *my* fault, my crime—"

Susa shook her head, lips quivering. Rain beaded on her lashes.

"Tané," she said thickly, "look away."

"Susa—"

Sobs clotted in her throat. *It was a mistake. Stop this.* Fingertips bit into her arms as she struggled, all her self-possession gone, more and more hands grasping her. *Stop this.* All she could see was Susa as a child, crowned with snowflakes, and her smile when Tané had taken her hand.

The executioner raised his sword. When the head rolled into the ditch, Tané slid to her knees.

I will always keep you safe.

When the dragonrider did not arrive at the beach at the agreed-upon time, Niclays generously assumed that she had been unavoidably delayed and made himself comfortable. He had brought with him a satchel containing some of his books and scrolls, including the fragment Truyde had given him, which he perused by the light of an iron lantern.

His pocket watch was open beside him. The clock—the modern symbol of the Knight of Temperance. A symbol of regulation, measurement, restraint. It was the virtue of dullards, but also of scholars and philosophers, who believed it encouraged self-examination and the pursuit of wisdom. Certainly it was the closest of the Six Virtues to rational thought.

It should have been his patron virtue. Instead, on his twelfth birthday, he had chosen the Knight of Courage.

His brooch now rusted somewhere in Brygstad. He had torn it off the day he was exiled.

An hour passed, and then another. The truth was indisputable.

Lady Tané had called his bluff.

The promise of dawn was on the horizon. Niclays snapped his watch shut. There went his chance of a glorious return to Ostendeur with a freshly brewed elixir of life.

Purumé and Eizaru would be horrified if they knew what he had asked the dragonrider to do. It made him no better than a pirate, but creating the damned elixir was the only way he would ever get home, his only potential sway with the royal houses over the Abyss.

He sighed. To save Sulyard, he needed to tell the Warlord about Tané Miduchi and her crime against Seiiki. It was what he would have done at once, were he a better man.

As he trudged back up the beach, he stopped. For a moment, he thought the stars had been rubbed out. When he looked harder, and made out the flicker of light, he froze.

Something was descending.

Something vast.

It moved as if it were sinking through water. A banner of scarred, iridescent green. A bladder-shaped organ dominated its head, glowing lambent blue. The same glow throbbed under its scales.

A Lacustrine dragon. Niclays watched hungrily as it landed on the sand, graceful as a bird.

A great weathered rock hunched like a shoulder from the sand. He retreated behind it, never taking his gaze off the dragon. From the way it turned its head, it was looking for something.

Niclays hunkered down and blew out his lantern. He watched as the creature snaked toward the shore, closer to his hiding place. The creature spoke.

"Tané."

Its massive front legs waded into the sea. Niclays was almost near enough to touch one of its scales. The key to his work, almost at his fingertips. He stayed crouched beneath the rock, craning his neck to look. Its eyes were pinwheels.

"Tané, the boy is dead," it said in Seiikinese. "So is your friend." It bared its teeth. "Tané, where are you?"

So this was her beast. The dragon sniffed, its nostrils flaring.

That was when a blade chilled his throat, and a hand covered his mouth. Niclays made a muffled sound.

The dragon jerked its head toward the rock.

Niclays trembled. He heard nothing of his own body, not his heartbeat or his breath, but he could picture the sword at his throat in meticulous detail. A curved blade. An edge sharp enough to spill his life if he moved a fraction of an inch.

A *hiss* came through the night. Then another.

And another.

The dragon let out a snarl. Claw rang against rock, like sword on sword.

Black smoke consumed the beach. The smell of it was acrid, like burning hair and brimstone. And gunpowder. *Firecloud.* Abruptly Niclays was wrenched to his feet—then he was stumbling through the billows of smoke, choking on them, hauled by a figure shrouded in cloth. The sand slithered beneath his feet, sending each footstep awry.

"Wait," he panted at his captor. "Wait, damn you—"

A tail lashed out of the smoke and caught him a terrific blow in the gut. He was thrown back on to the sand, where he lay, benumbed and winded, his eyeglasses dangling off one ear.

He drifted, drunk on the black cloud. It rushed into his nostrils and plumed out again.

A mournful sound, like a dying baleen. A thud that shook the earth. He saw Jannart walking barefoot on the beach, a faint smile on his lips. "Jan," he breathed, but he was gone.

Two booted feet pressed into the sand.

"Give me a reason," a voice said in Seiikinese, "and I may not gut you." A bone-handled knife flashed in front of him. "Do you have something to offer the Fleet of the Tiger Eye?"

He tried to speak, but his tongue felt bee-stung. *Alchemist,* he wanted to say. *I am an alchemist. Spare me.*

Someone lifted his satchel. Time splintered as scarred hands rummaged through his books and scrolls. Then the hilt of the knife clipped his temple, and a dark wave swept away his cares.

30

West

Truyde utt Zeedeur was imprisoned in the Dearn Tower. Under threat of the rack, she had confessed to many crimes. After the royal visit had been announced, she had approached a playing company called the Servants of Verity, a so-called masterless troupe, bereft of the patronage of a noble and treated as vagabonds by the authorities. Truyde had promised her own patronage, and money for their families, in exchange for their help.

The staged attack had been intended to convince Sabran that she was in mortal danger, both from Yscalin and the Nameless One. Truyde had meant to use it as grounds to petition her to open negotiations with the East.

It had not taken much wit to piece together what had happened next. Those with true hatred toward the House of Berethnet had infiltrated the performance. One of those—Bess Weald, whose home in Queenside had been stuffed with pamphlets written by doomsingers—had murdered Lievelyn. Several innocent members of the Servants of Verity had also been slain in the fray, along with a number of city guards, two of the Knights of the Body, and Linora Payling, whose grief-stricken parents had already come for her.

Truyde might not have meant to kill anyone, but her good intentions had been for naught.

Ead had already written to Chassar to tell him what had happened. The Prioress would not be pleased that Sabran and her unborn child had come so close to death.

Briar House was draped in the gray samite of mourning. Sabran shut herself into the Privy Chamber. Lievelyn was laid in state in the Sanctuary of Our Lady until a ship arrived to bear him home. His sister Ermuna was to be crowned, with Princess Bedona as heir apparent.

A few days after Lievelyn had been taken, Ead made her way to the royal apartments. Usually the early morning was peaceful, but she could not shake the tension in her back.

Tharian Lintley had watched her take four lives during the ambush. He must have realized she was trained. She doubted anyone else had seen in that bloody clash, and it was clear Lintley had not reported her affinity for blades, but she intended to keep her head down.

Easier said than done as a Lady of the Bedchamber. Especially when the queen had also seen her kill.

"Ead."

She turned to see a breathless Margret, who caught her by the arm. "It's Loth," her friend whispered. "He sent me a letter."

"What?"

"Come with me, quick."

Heart pounding, Ead followed her into an unused room. "How did Loth get a letter past Combe?"

"He sent it to a playwright Mama supports. He managed to pass it to me during the visit to Ascalon." Margret withdrew a crumpled note from her skirts. "Look."

Ead recognized his writing at once. Her heart swelled to see it again.

Dearest M, I cannot say much for fear this note will be intercepted. Things are not as they seem in Cárscaro. Kit is dead, and I fear Snow is in danger. Beware the Cupbearer.

"Lord Kitston is dead," Ead murmured. "How?"

Margret swallowed. "I pray he is mistaken, but ... Kit would do anything for my brother." She touched the handstamp. "Ead, this was sent from the Place of Doves."

"Rauca," Ead said, stunned. "He left Cárscaro."

"Or *escaped*. Perhaps that was how Kit—" Margret pointed to the last line. "Look at this. Did you not say the woman who shot Lievelyn invoked a cupbearer?"

"Yes." Ead read the note again. "Snow is Sabran, I assume."

"Aye. Loth used to call her Princess Snow when they were children," Margret said, "but for the life of me, I cannot understand this web of intrigue. There *is* no official cupbearer to the queen."

"Loth was sent to find Prince Wilstan. Wilstan was investigating the death of Queen Rosarian," Ead said under her breath. "Perhaps they are connected."

"Perhaps," Margret said. Sweat dewed her brow. "Oh, Ead, I want so badly to tell Sab he is alive, but Combe will find out how I got the note. I fear to close that door to Loth."

"She is mourning Lievelyn. Do not give her false hope that her friend will return." Ead squeezed her hand. "Leave the Cupbearer to me. I mean to root them out."

With a deep breath, Margret nodded.

"Another letter from Papa, too." She shook her head. "Mama says he is becoming agitated. He keeps saying he has something of the utmost importance to impart to the heir to Goldenbirch. Unless Loth returns—"

"Do you think it is the mind fog?"

"Perhaps. Mama says I should not indulge it. I will go back soon, but not yet." Margret tucked the letter into her skirts. "I must go. Perhaps we could meet for supper."

"Yes."

They parted ways.

It had been a terrible risk for Loth to send that note. Ead meant to heed his warning. Sabran had come all too close to death in the city, but never again.

Not on her watch.

The pregnancy was making Sabran sick. Roslain was up with the lark to hold back her hair while she retched over a chamberpot.

On some nights, Katryen would sleep beside them on a truckle bed.

Still only a handful of people knew about the child. Now was not the time, in these early days of mourning.

Each day, the queen would emerge from the Royal Bedchamber, where she had spent her wedding night, looking more careworn than the day before. Each day, the shadows below her eyes seemed grimmer. On the rare occasions she talked, she was curt.

So when she spoke one evening without being coaxed, Katryen almost dropped her embroidery.

"Ead," the Queen of Inys said, "you will be my bedfellow this night."

At nine of the clock, the Ladies of the Bedchamber disrobed her, but for the first time, Ead also changed into her nightgown. Roslain took her to one side.

"There must be light in the room all night," she told her. "Sabran will be afraid if she wakes in darkness. I find it easiest to keep a candle burning on the nightstand."

Ead nodded. "I will make sure."

"Good."

Roslain looked as if she wanted to say more, but refrained. Once the Royal Bedchamber was secure, she shepherded the other ladies-in-waiting out and locked the doors.

Sabran was recumbent in the bed. Ead climbed in beside her and drew the coverlet over herself.

For a long time, they were silent. Katryen knew how to keep Sabran in good spirits, while Roslain knew how to counsel her. Ead wondered what her role ought to be. To listen, perhaps.

Or to tell her the truth. Perhaps that was what Sabran valued most.

It had been years since she had slept so close to someone else. She was too aware of Sabran. The flicker of sooty lashes. The warmth of her body. The rise and sink of her breast.

"I have had many nightmares of late." Her voice broke the silence. "Your remedy helped, but Doctor Bourn tells me I must take nothing while I am with child. Not even sleepwater."

327

"I have no wish to contest Doctor Bourn," Ead said, "but perhaps you could use the rosewater in an ointment. It will soothe your skin, and may still help fend off the nightmares."

Nodding, Sabran laid a hand on her belly. "I will ask for it tomorrow. Perhaps your presence will keep the nightmares at bay tonight, Ead. Even if roses cannot."

Her hair was unbound, parted like drapes where her shoulders peeked through.

"I never thanked you. For everything you did in Quiver Lane," she said. "Pained though I was, I did notice how well you fought to protect me." She lifted her chin. "Was it you who slew the other cutthroats? Are you the watcher in the night?"

Her expression was impenetrable. Ead wanted to do as she had resolved—tell the truth—but the risk was too great. If word got back to Combe, she would be forced out of court.

"No, madam," she said. "Perhaps they could have protected Prince Aubrecht, as I could not."

"It was not your duty to protect the prince," Sabran said. Her profile was half shadow and half gold. "It is my fault that Aubrecht is dead. You told me not to open that door."

"The cutthroat would have found a way to him, that day or another," Ead said. "Somebody paid Bess Weald handsomely to ensure Prince Aubrecht died. His fate was sealed."

"That may be true, but I should have listened. You have never deceived me. I cannot ask Aubrecht for his forgiveness, but ... I will ask yours, Ead Duryan."

It took effort to hold her gaze. She had no idea just how greatly Ead *had* deceived her.

"Granted," Ead said.

Sabran released her breath through her nose. For the first time in eight years, Ead felt a stab of remorse for the lies she had told.

"Truyde utt Zeedeur must pay the price for her treachery, no matter her youth," Sabran stated. "By rights I should demand that High Princess Ermuna sentences her to death. Or perhaps you would prefer me to offer mercy, Ead, since you find its taste so comforting."

"You must do as you will with her."

In truth, Ead did not want the girl dead. She was a dangerous fool, and her stupidity had caused a slew of deaths, but she was seventeen. There was time for her to make amends.

Another silence passed before the queen turned to face her. This close, Ead could see the thick black rings that surrounded her irises, dark against their startling green.

"Ead," she said, "I cannot speak with Ros or Kate of this, but I will speak with you. I feel that you will think no less of me. That you will ... understand."

Ead interlaced their fingers.

"You can always speak freely to me," she said.

Sabran shifted closer. Her hand was cold and delicate, the fingers bare without their jewels. She had buried her love-knot ring in the Sunken Gardens to mark a place for a memorial.

"You asked me, before I took Aubrecht to consort, if I wanted to wed," she said, almost too softly to hear. "I confess now, to you alone, that I did not. And ... still do not."

The revelation hung between them. This was dangerous talk. With the threat of invasion, the Dukes Spiritual would soon be exhorting Sabran to take another companion, even with the heir inside her.

"I never thought I would say those words aloud." Her breath verged on a laugh. "I know that Inys faces war. I know that Draconic things are waking the world over. I know that my hand would strengthen any of our existing alliances, and that the other countries of Virtudom were brought into the fold through the sacred institution of companionship."

Ead nodded. "But?"

"I fear it."

"Why?"

Sabran was still for a time. One hand sat on her belly, while Ead kept hold of the other.

"Aubrecht was kind to me. Tender and good," she finally said, voice low in her throat, "but when he was inside me, even when I found pleasure in it, it felt—" She closed her eyes. "It felt as if my body were not wholly my own. It ... still feels that way now."

Her gaze dipped to the barely visible bump, swathed by the silk velvet of her nightgown.

"Alliances have ever been forged and strengthened through royal marriages," she said. "While Inys has the greatest navy in the West, we lack a well-trained standing army. Our population is small. If we are invaded, we will need as much support as we can muster ... but each nation in Virtudom will consider itself duty-bound to defend its own shores first. A marriage, however, would come with legal stipulations. Guarantees of military support."

Ead kept her silence.

"I have never had any great inclination toward marriage, Ead. Not the sort of marriage those of royal blood must make—born not of love, but fear of isolation," Sabran murmured. "Yet if I refrain, the world will stand in judgment. Too proud to wed my country to another. Too selfish to give my daughter a father to love her if I should perish. This is how I will be seen. Who would rise in defense of such a monarch?"

"Those who call her Sabran the Magnificent. Those who saw her vanquish Fýredel."

"They will soon forget that deed when enemy ships darken the horizon," Sabran said. "My blood cannot deter the armies of Yscalin." Her eyelids were sinking. "I do not expect you to say anything to comfort me, Ead. You have let me unburden myself, even though my fears are selfish. The Damsel has granted me the child I begged of her, and all I can do is ... quake."

Even though a fire roared in the hearth, gooseflesh flecked her skin.

"Where I come from," Ead said, "we would not call it *selfish* to do as you have done."

Sabran looked at her.

"You have just lost your companion. You are carrying his child. Of course you feel vulnerable." Ead pressed her hand. "Childing is not always easy. It seems to me that this is the best-kept secret in all the world. We speak of it as though there were nothing sweeter, but the truth is more complex. No one talks openly about the difficulties. The discomfort. The uncertainty. So now you feel the weight of your condition, you believe yourself alone in it. And you have turned the blame upon yourself."

At this, Sabran swallowed.

"Your fear is natural." Ead held her gaze. "Let no one convince you otherwise."

For the first time since the ambush, the Queen of Inys smiled.

"Ead," she said, "I am not quite sure what I did without you."

31

East

White River Castle was named not for a river, but for the moat of seashells that surrounded its grounds. Behind it was the ageless Forest of the Wounded Bird, and beyond that, the bleak and brutal Mount Tego. A year before their Choosing Day, all apprentices had been challenged to climb to the top of that peak, where the spirit of the great Kwiriki was said to descend to bless the worthy.

Of all the apprentices from the South House, Tané alone had made it to the summit. Half-frozen, beset with mountain sickness, she had crawled up the last slope, retching blood on to the snow.

She had not been human in that final hour. Just a paper lantern, thin and wind-torn, clinging to the flickering remnants of a soul. Yet when there was no more to climb, and she had looked up and seen nothing but the terrible beauty of the sky, she had found the strength to rise. And she had known the great Kwiriki was with her, with*in* her.

At this moment, that feeling had never felt so far away. She was the tattered lantern again. Barely alive.

She was not sure how long they had kept her in the jailhouse. Time had become a bottomless pool. She had lain with her hands cupped over her ears, so all she could hear was the sea.

Then other hands had loaded her into a palanquin. Now she was escorted past a guardhouse, into a room with a high ceiling and walls painted with scenes from the Great Sorrow, and then on to a roofed balcony.

The Governor of Ginura dismissed her soldiers. She stood tall, her gaze crisp with distaste.

"Lady Tané," she said coolly.

Tané bowed and knelt on the mats. The title already sounded like something from another life.

Outside, a sorrower called out. Its *hic-hic-hic*, like a grizzling child, was said to have driven an empress mad. Tané wondered if it would break her, too, if she listened hard enough.

Or perhaps her mind was already lost.

"Several days ago," the Governor said, "a prisoner incriminated you in a most serious crime. He was smuggled into Seiiki from Mentendon. In accordance with the Great Edict, he was put to death."

A head on the gate, hair stiff with blood.

"The prisoner told magistrates in Cape Hisan that when he arrived here, a woman found him on the beach. He described the scar beneath her eye."

Tané pressed her clammy palms to her thighs.

"Tell me," the Governor continued, "why an apprentice with a spotless record, who was raised from nothing, who was given the rare opportunity to be god-chosen, would risk everything—including the safety of every citizen of this island—by doing this."

It took Tané a long time to find her voice. She had left it in a bloodstained ditch.

"There were whispers. That those who broke seclusion would be rewarded. Just once, I wanted to be fearless. To take a risk." She sounded nothing like herself. "He ... came out of the sea."

"Why did you not report it to the authorities?"

"I thought the ceremony would not proceed. I thought the port would be closed, the gods kept out. That I would never ride."

How craven it sounded. How selfish and senseless. When she had explained it to Nayimathun, her dragon had understood. Now the shame of it was crushing.

"He seemed like a message. Sent from the gods." She could hardly speak. "I was too fortunate. All my life, the great Kwiriki was too good to me. Every day, I have waited for his favor to disappear. When the outsider came, I knew it was time. But I was not ready. I had to ... sever his connection to me. Hide him away until I had what I wanted."

All she could see was her hands, fingernails bitten raw, knurled with faint scars.

"The great Kwiriki *has* favored you, Lady Tané." The Governor sounded almost pitying. "Had you made a different choice that night, that favor might still be yours."

The bird outside, *hic-hic-hic*. A child that could never be soothed.

"Susa was innocent, honored Governor," Tané said. "I forced her to help me."

"No. We interrogated the sentinel she convinced to let her into Orisima. She was a willing participant. Loyal to you above Seiiki." The Governor pressed her lips together. "I am aware that a dragon requested clemency for her. Unfortunately, the news reached me too late."

"Nayimathun," Tané whispered. "Where is she?"

"That brings me to the second, even more serious matter. Close to dawn, a group of hunters landed in Ginura Bay."

"Hunters?"

"The Fleet of the Tiger Eye. The great Nayimathun of the Deep Snows was ... taken."

All sensation drained from Tané. Her hands clammed into fists.

"The High Sea Guard will do its utmost to retrieve her, but it is rare that our gods are spared the butchery that awaits them in Kawontay." The Governor tightened her jaw for a moment. "It pains me to say it, but the great Nayimathun is most likely beyond our reach."

Tané trembled.

Her stomach was a poison in her. She tried not to imagine what Nayimathun must be suffering. The thought of it was so unbearable that her vision swam and her lips quaked.

She was doomed, and she had nothing and no one left to lose. Perhaps, in this final act, she could leach some of the corruption out of Seiiki with her.

"There is someone else involved," she said quietly. "Roos. A surgeon from Orisima. He tried to blackmail me. Told me to bring him dragon scales and blood for his work. He has nothing moral or good in him." Heat pricked her eyes. "He must have helped them take the great Nayimathun. Let him hurt no other dragons. Let him face justice."

The Governor considered her for some time.

"Roos has been reported as missing," she finally said. Tané stared. "He went to the beach last night, according to his friends. We think he may have escaped the island."

If Roos was with the Fleet of the Tiger Eye, he was already dead. A man like him would soon cross the wrong person.

It brought Tané no comfort. Her enemy was gone, but so was her dragon. So was her friend. And so was the dream she had never deserved.

"I made a mistake." It was all she had left. "A terrible mistake."

"You did."

Silence gaped between them.

"By rights, you should be executed," the Governor told her. "Your self-interest and greed could have destroyed Seiiki. Out of respect for the great Nayimathun, however, and for what you could have been, I will show mercy on this day. You will live out your days on Feather Island. There, you may learn to serve the great Kwiriki well."

Tané stood and bowed, and the soldiers took her back to the palanquin. She had thought she would beg or weep or ask forgiveness, but in the end, she felt nothing.

32

South

The reflection of water danced on an arched ceiling. The air was cool, but not so cool as to raise gooseflesh. Loth became aware of these things shortly after realising he was naked.

He lay on a woven rug. To his right was a four-sided pool, and to his left, a recess scooped into the rock, where an oil lamp shone.

Sudden pain clawed up his back. He turned on to his belly and vomited, and then it was upon him.

The bloodblaze.

It had been a far-off nightmare in Inys. A fireside story for dark nights. Now he knew what all the world had faced in the Grief of Ages. He knew why the East had locked its doors.

His very blood was boiling oil. He screamed into the darkness of his cauldron, and the darkness screamed back. A skep broke open somewhere inside him, and a swarm of enraged bees disgorged into his organs, setting them aflame. And as his bones cracked in the heat, as tears melted down his cheeks, all he desired in the world was to be dead.

A flash of memory. Through the crimson haze, he knew he must reach the pool he had seen and douse the fire within. He started to get up, moving as if on a bed of hot coals, but a cool hand graced his brow.

"No."

A voice spoke, a voice like sunlight. "Who are you?"

His lips burned. "Lord Arteloth Beck," he said. "Please, st-stay away. I have the plague."

"Where did you find the iron box?"

"The Donmata Marosa." He shuddered. "Please—"

Fear made him sob, but someone else was soon beside him, urging a jug to his lips. He drank.

When he woke next, he was in a bed, though still quite naked, in the same underground chamber as before.

It was a long time before he dared to move. There was no pain, and the red had vanished from his hands.

Loth made the sign of the sword over his chest. The Saint, in his mercy, had seen fit to spare him.

He lay still for a time, listening for footsteps or voices. At last, he stood on quaking legs, so weak his head swam. His bruises from the cockatrice were coated in ointment. Even the memory of the agony was draining, but some good soul had treated him and given him their hospitality, and he meant to be presentable when he greeted them.

He sank into the pool. The smooth floor was bliss against his weary soles.

He remembered nothing after his arrival in Rauca. A vague recollection of a market returned to him, and a sense of being on the move, and then the inn. After that, a void.

His beard had grown too thick for his liking, but there was no sign of a razor. When he was refreshed, he rose and drew on the bedgown that had been left on the nightstand.

He startled when he saw her. A woman in a green cloak, holding a lamp in her palm. Her skin was a deep brown, like her eyes, and her hair spiraled around her face.

"You must come with me."

She spoke Inysh with a Lasian accent. Loth shook himself. "Who are you, mistress?"

"Chassar uq-Ispad invites you to his table."

So the ambassador had found him, somehow. Loth wanted to ask more, but he had not the boldness in him to question this woman, who looked at him with a cool, unblinking gaze.

He followed her through a series of windowless passages, carved out of rosy stone and lit with oil lamps. This must be where the ambassador lived, though it was nothing like the place Ead had described growing up in. No open-air walkways or striking views of the Sarras Mountains. Just alcoves here and there, each framing a bronze statuette of a woman holding a sword and an orb.

His guide stopped outside an archway, which was hung with a translucent curtain.

"Through here," she said.

She walked away, taking her light with her.

The chamber beyond the veil was small, with a low ceiling. A tall Ersyri man sat at a table. He wore a silver wrap around his head. When Loth entered, he glanced up.

Chassar uq-Ispad.

"Lord Arteloth." The ambassador motioned to another seat. "Please, do sit down. You must be very tired."

The table was piled with fruit. Loth sat in the opposite chair.

"Ambassador uq-Ispad," he said a little hoarsely. "Is it you I should thank for saving my life?"

"I did vouch for you," was the reply, "but no. This is not my estate, and the remedy you took was not mine. In the spirit of Ersyri hospitality, however, you may call me Chassar."

His voice was not as Loth remembered it. The Chassar uq-Ispad he had known at court had been full of laughter, not this unnerving calm.

"You are very lucky to be at this table," Chassar said. "Few men seek the Priory and live to see it."

Another man poured Loth a cup of pale wine.

"The Priory, Your Excellency?" Loth asked, perplexed.

"You are in the Priory of the Orange Tree, Lord Arteloth. In Lasia."

Lasia. Surely not. "I was in Rauca," he said, still more perplexed. "How is that possible?"

"The ichneumon." Chassar poured himself a drink. "They are old allies of the Priory."

Loth was none the wiser.

"Aralaq found you in the mountains." He put down his cup. "He summoned one of the sisters to collect you."

The Priory. The sisters.

"Aralaq," Loth repeated.

"The ichneumon."

Chassar sipped his drink. Loth noticed for the first time that a sand eagle was perched nearby, its head cocked. Ead had praised these birds of prey for their intelligence.

"You look confused, Lord Arteloth," Chassar said lightly. "I will explain. To do that, I must first tell you a tale."

This was the strangest greeting in the world.

"You know the story of the Damsel and the Saint. You know how a knight rescued a princess from a dragon and took her away to a kingdom across the sea. You know that they founded a great city and lived happily ever after." He smiled. "Everything you know is false."

It was so quiet in the room that Loth heard the sand eagle ruffle its feathers.

"You are a follower of the Dawnsinger, Your Excellency," he finally said, "but I ask that you not blaspheme in front of me."

"The Berethnets are the blasphemers. *They* are the liars."

Loth was stunned into silence. He had known Chassar uq-Ispad was an unbeliever, but this came as a shock.

"When the Nameless One came to the South, to the city of Yikala," Chassar said, "High Ruler Selinu attempted to placate him by organizing a lottery of lives. Even children were sacrificed if their lot was drawn. His only daughter, Princess Cleolind, swore to her father that she could kill the beast, but Selinu forbade it. Cleolind was forced to watch as her people suffered. One day, though, she was chosen as the sacrifice."

"This is as the Sanctarian tells it," Loth said.

"Be silent and learn something." Chassar selected a purple fruit from the bowl. "On the day that Cleolind was meant to die, a Western knight rode through the city. He carried a sword named Ascalon."

"Precisely—"

"Hush, or I will cut out your tongue."

Loth closed his mouth.

"This *gallant* knight," Chassar said, voice soaked in disdain, "promised to kill the Nameless One with his enchanted sword. But he had two conditions. The first was that he would have Cleolind as his bride, and she would return to Inysca with him as his queen consort. The second was that her people would convert to the Six Virtues of Knighthood—a code of chivalry that he had decided to turn into a religion, with himself as its godhead. An invented faith."

To hear the Saint described like some roaming madman was too much to bear. *Invented faith*, indeed. The Six Virtues had been the code all Inysh knights had lived by at that time. Loth opened his mouth, remembered the warning, and shut it again.

"Despite their fear," Chassar continued, "the Lasian people did not *want* to convert to this new religion. Cleolind told the knight as much and refused both his terms. Yet Galian was so overcome with greed and lust that he fought the beast nonetheless."

Loth almost choked. "There was no lust in his heart. His love for Princess Cleolind was chaste."

"Try not to be irritating, my lord. Galian the Deceiver was a brute. A power-hungry, selfish brute. To him, Lasia was a field from which to reap a bride of royal blood and adoring devotees of a religion he had founded, all for his own gain. He would make himself a god and unite Inysca under his crown." Chassar poured more wine while Loth seethed. "Of course, your beloved Saint fell almost instantly with a trifling injury and pissed himself. And Cleolind, a woman of courage, took up his sword.

"She followed the Nameless One deep into the Lasian Basin, where he had made his lair. Few had ever dared enter the forest, for its sea of trees was vast and uncharted. She tracked the beast until she found herself in a great valley. Growing in this valley was an orange tree of astonishing height and untold beauty.

"The Nameless One was wrapped like a snake about its trunk. They fought across the valley, and though Cleolind was a powerful warrior, the beast set her afire. In agony, she crawled to the tree. The Nameless One crowed in triumph, certain of his victory, and opened his mouth to burn her once more—but while she was beneath the branches, his fire could not touch her.

"Even as Cleolind wondered at the miracle, the orange tree yielded its fruit. When she ate of it, she was healed—not only healed, but *changed*. She could hear the whispers in the earth. The dance of the wind. She was reborn as a living flame. She fought the beast once more and plunged Ascalon beneath one of his scales. Grievously injured, the Nameless One slithered away. Cleolind returned in triumph to Yikala and banished Sir Galian Berethnet from her land, returning his sword to him so he would never come back for it. He fled to the Isles of Inysca, where he told a false version of events, and they crowned him King of—"

Loth slammed his fist down. The sand eagle shrieked in protest.

"I will not sit at your table and listen to you sully my faith," Loth said quietly. "Cleolind went *with* him to Inys, and the Berethnet queens are their descendants."

"Cleolind cast away her riches," Chassar said, as if Loth had not spoken, "and journeyed back into the Lasian Basin with her handmaidens. There, she founded the Priory of the Orange Tree, a house of women blessed with the sacred flame. A house, Lord Arteloth, of mages."

Sorcery.

"The Priory's purpose is to slay wyrms, and to protect the South from Draconic power. Its leader is the Prioress—she who is most beloved of the Mother. And I'm afraid, Lord Arteloth, that this great lady believes you may have murdered one of her daughters." When Loth looked blank, Chassar leaned forward, his eyes intent. "You were in possession of an iron box that was last held by a woman named Jondu."

"I am no murderer. Jondu was captured by the Yscals," Loth insisted. "Before she died, she entrusted the box to the Donmata of Yscalin, who gave it to me." He groped for the back of the chair and stood up. "She begged me to bring it to you. You have it now," he said, desperate. "I must leave this place."

"So Jondu is dead. Sit down, Lord Arteloth," Chassar said coolly. "You will stay."

"So you can insult my faith still further?"

"Because whomsoever seeks the Priory can never leave its walls." Loth turned cold.

"This is a difficult thing to tell you, Lord Arteloth. I am acquainted with your lady mother, and it pains me to know that she will never see her son again ... but you cannot leave. No outsider may. There is too great a risk that you could tell someone about the Priory."

"You—" Loth shook his head. "You cannot— this is *madness*."

"It is a comfortable life. Not as comfortable as your life in Inys," Chassar admitted, "but you will be safe here, away from the eyes of the world."

"I am the heir to Goldenbirch. I am a friend to Queen Sabran the Ninth. I will not be mocked like this!" His back hit the wall. "Ead always said you were a man of good humor. If this is some jest, Your Excellency, say it now."

"Ah." Chassar sighed. "Eadaz. She told me of your friendship."

Something shifted inside Loth. And, slowly, he began to understand.

Not Ead, but *Eadaz*. The feeling of sunlight. Her secrets. Her obscure childhood. But no, it could *not* be true ... Ead had converted to the Six Virtues. She prayed at sanctuary twice a day. She could not, *could* not be a heretic, a practitioner of the forbidden arts.

"The woman you knew as Ead Duryan is a lie, Arteloth. I devised that identity for her. Her true name is Eadaz du Zāla uq-Nāra, and she is a sister of the Priory. I planted her in Inys, on the orders of the last Prioress, to protect Sabran the Ninth."

"No."

Ead, who had shared his wine and danced with him at every Feast of Fellowship since he was two and twenty. Ead, the woman his father had told him he should marry.

Ead Duryan.

"She is a mage. One of the most gifted," Chassar said. "She will return here as soon as Sabran births her child."

Every word drove the knife of betrayal deeper. He could take no more. He pushed through the curtain and blundered into the passages, only to come face to face with the woman in green. And he saw, then, that she was not holding an oil lamp.

She was *holding fire*.

"The Mother is with you, Arteloth." She smiled at him. "Sleep."

33

East

They were ensconced in the highest room of Brygstad Palace, where they often stole a night alone when the High Prince was away. The walls were hung with tapestries, the window clammy with the heat of the fire. This was where the royals would give birth. Beneath a starry vault.

On other nights, they would abscond to the Old Quarter, to a room Jannart held at an inn called the Sun in Splendor, which was known for its discretion. It sheltered many lovers who had fled from the laws of the Knight of Fellowship. Some, like Jannart, were locked in marriages they had not chosen. Others were unwed. Others had fallen for people who were far above or below their station. All loved in a way that would see them pay a price in Virtudom.

That day, Edvart had set off with half the court, his daughter, and his nephew to the summer residence in the Bridal Forest. Jannart had promised Edvart they would join him soon to hunt the fabled Sangyn Wolf that stalked the north of Mentendon.

Niclays had never been sure if Edvart knew the truth about his relationship with Jannart. Perhaps he had closed his eyes to it. If the matter became public, the High Prince would have no choice but to banish Jannart, his closest friend, for breaking his vow to the Knight of Fellowship.

A log collapsed in the fire. Beside it, Jannart was poring over his manuscripts, which were fanned across the rug in front of him. For the past few years, he had forsaken his art to pursue his passion for history. He had always been troubled by the calamitous loss of knowledge in the Grief of Ages—the burning of libraries, the destruction of archives, the irrevocable ruin of ancient buildings—and now that his son, Oscarde, was taking on some duties in the duchy, he could finally lose himself in knitting the holes in history together.

Niclays lay naked in the bed, gazing at the painted stars. Someone had gone to a great deal of effort to make them mirror the true sky.

"What is it?"

Jannart had not even needed to look up to know something was wrong. Niclays heaved a sigh. "A wyvern on the edge of our capital should dampen even your spirits."

Three days before, two men had ventured into a cave west of Brygstad and happened upon a slumbering wyvern. It was well known that Draconic beings had found places to sleep all over the world after the Grief of Ages, and that if you looked hard enough in any country, you might be able to find one.

In the Free State of Mentendon, the law declared that, if discovered, these beasts should be left alone on pain of death. There was an ubiquitous fear that waking one could wake others—but these men had thought themselves above the law. Drunk on dreams of knighthood, they had drawn their swords and tried to kill the beast. Not best pleased with the rude awakening, it had eaten its attackers and clawed its way out of the cave in a fury. Too listless from its sleep to breathe fire, it had still managed to maul several residents of a nearby town before some brave soul put an arrow through its heart.

"Clay," Jannart said, "it was two arrogant boys playing the fool. Ed will ensure it does not happen again."

"Perhaps dukes are naïve to such things, but there are arrogant fools the world over." Niclays poured himself a glass of black wine. "There was an abandoned mine not far from Rozentun, you know. Rumor had it among children that there was a cockatrice in there that had laid a clutch of golden eggs before it went to sleep. A girl I knew broke her back trying to get to it. A boy got himself lost in the darkness. He was never found. Arrogant fools, both."

"It amazes me that after all these years, I am still learning things about your childhood." Jannart arched an eyebrow, mouth quirked. "Did you ever seek the golden clutch?"

Niclays snorted. "The notion. Oh, I tiptoed to the entrance once or twice, but the love of your life was an abject coward even as a boy. I fear death too much to seek it."

"Well, I can only be grateful for the softness of your spine. I confess to fearing your death, too."

"I remind you that you are two years my senior, and that the arithmetic of death is against you."

Jannart smiled. "Let us not speak of death when there is still so much life to be lived."

He stood, and Niclays drank in the powerful delineation of his body, sculpted by years of fencing. At fifty, he was as striking as he had been on the day they had first met. His hair reached his waist, and it had darkened over time to a rich garnet, silvered at the roots. Niclays still had no notion of how he had held on to this man's heart for all these years.

"Very soon, I mean to whisk you away to the Milk Lagoon, and there we shall live without name or title." Jannart climbed onto the bed, hands on either side of Niclays, and kissed him. "Besides, you are likely to die before me at this rate. Perhaps if you would stop cuckolding me with Ed's wine—" His hand snuck toward the glass.

"You have your dusty books. I have wine." Chuckling, Niclays held it out of reach. "We agreed."

"I see." Jannart made another, half-playful swipe for it. "And when did we agree this?"

"Today. You may have been asleep."

Jannart gave up and rolled onto the bed beside him. Niclays tried to ignore the tug of remorse.

They had quarreled about his weakness for wine many times over the years. He had curbed his drinking enough to stop him losing hours of memory, as he often had in his youth, but his hands shook if he went too long without a cup. Jannart seemed too weary of the subject to fight him on it these days. It hurt Niclays to disappoint the one person who loved him.

346

Black wine was his comfort. Its thick sweetness filled the hollow that opened whenever he looked at his finger, empty of a love-knot ring. It blunted the pain of living a lie.

"Do you really think the Milk Lagoon exists?" he murmured.

A place of lore and lullaby. The haven for lovers.

Jannart circled his navel with one finger. "I do," he said. "I have gathered enough evidence to believe it existed before the Grief of Ages, at least. Ed has heard that the remaining scions of the family of Nerafriss know where it is, but they will tell only the worthy."

"That rules me out, then. You had better go alone."

"You are not getting away from me that easily, Niclays Roos." Jannart shifted his head closer, so their noses brushed. "Even if we never find the Milk Lagoon, we can go elsewhere."

"Where?"

"Somewhere else in the South, perhaps. Anywhere the Knight of Fellowship has no sway," Jannart said. "There are uncharted places beyond the Gate of Ungulus. Perhaps other continents."

"I'm no explorer."

"You could be, Clay. You could be anything, and you should never think otherwise." Jannart rolled a thumb over Niclays's cheekbone. "If I had convinced myself I was no sinner, I would never have kissed the lips I longed to kiss. The lips of a man with rose-gold hair, whose birth, by the laws of a long-dead knight, made him unworthy of my love."

Niclays tried not to stare like a fool into those gray Vatten eyes. Even now, after all these years, looking at this man took his breath away.

"What of Aleidine?" he said.

He tried to sound curious rather than sour. It was difficult for Jannart, who had spent decades stealing between companion and lover, at great risk to his standing at court. Niclays had no such care. He had never wed, and nobody had tried to force him.

"Ally will be fine," Jannart said, even as his brow crinkled. "She will be the Dowager Duchess of Zeedeur, wealthy and powerful in her own right."

Jannart cared about Aleidine. Even if he had never loved her as companions loved, they had fostered a close friendship in their thirty-year marriage. She had handled his affairs, carried his child, run the Duchy of Zeedeur at his side, and throughout it all, she had loved him unconditionally.

When they left, Niclays knew Jannart would miss her. He would miss the family they had made—but in his eyes, he had given them his youth. Now he wanted to live out his last years with the man he loved.

Niclays reached for his hand, the one that bore a silver love-knot ring.

"Let's go soon," he said lightly, to distract him. "Hiding like this is beginning to age me."

"Age becomes you, my golden fox." Jannart kissed him. "We will be gone. I promise."

"When?"

"I want to spend a few more years with Truyde. So she has some memory of her grandsire."

The child was only five years old, and already she would leaf ham-fisted through whatever tome Jannart set in front of her, bottom lip stuck out in determination. She had his hair.

"Liar," Niclays said. "You want to make sure she carries on your legacy as a painter, since Oscarde has no artistic skill."

Jannart laughed richly. "Perhaps."

They lay still for a while, fingers intertwined. The sunlight washed the room in gold.

They would be alone together soon. Niclays told himself that it was true, as he had every day for year after year. Another year, perhaps two, until Truyde was a little older. Then they would leave Virtudom behind.

When Niclays turned to look at him, Jannart smiled—that roguish smile that teased at one corner of his mouth. Now he was older, it made his cheek crease in a way that somehow only served to make him more beautiful. Niclays raised his head to meet the kiss, and Jannart cradled his face in both hands as if he were framing one of his portraits. Niclays drew a line down the white canvas of Jannart's stomach, making his body arch closer and quicken. And even though they knew each other by heart, the strength of this embrace felt new.

By the time dusk fell, they lay entwined in front of the fire, heavy-eyed and slippery with sweat. Jannart skimmed his fingers through Niclays's hair.

"Clay," he murmured, "I must go away for a while."

Niclays looked up. "What?"

"You wonder what I do in my study all day," Jannart said. "A few weeks ago, I inherited a fragment of text from my aunt, who was Viceroy of Orisima for forty years."

Niclays sighed. Once Jannart was in pursuit of a mystery, he was like a crow on a carcass, driven by his nature to pick every bone clean. As Niclays craved alchemy and wine, Jannart craved the restoration of knowledge.

"Do tell me more," Niclays said, as gamely as he could.

"The fragment is many centuries old. I almost fear to handle it in case it falls apart. According to her journal, my aunt received it from a man who told her to carry it far from the East and never bring it back."

"How mysterious." Niclays couched his head on his arms. "What has this to do with your going away?"

"I cannot read the text. I must go to the University of Ostendeur to see if anyone knows the language. I think it is an ancient form of Seiikinese, but something about the characters sits oddly with me. Some are larger, others smaller, and they are spaced in a strange manner." His gaze was distant. "There is a hidden message in it, Clay. Intuition tells me that it is a vital piece of history. Something of more importance than anything I have studied before. I *must* understand it. I have heard of a library that might help me do that."

"Where is this place, exactly?" Niclays asked. "Is it part of the University?"

"No. It is ... rather isolated. A few miles from Wilgaström."

"Oh, *Wilgaström*. Thrilling." It was a sleepy town on the River Lint. No wyverns there. "Well, come back soon. The moment you leave, Ed tries to involve me in hunting or battledore or some other pastime that involves *talking to courtiers*."

Jannart pressed closer. "You will survive." His smile faded and, just for a moment, there was darkness in his eyes. "I would never leave you without reason, Clay. On my oath."

"I will hold you to it, Zeedeur."

———

There existed a realm between dreaming and waking, and Niclays was imprisoned in it. As he stirred, a tear squeezed from the corner of his eye.

Rain dusted his face. He was in a rowing boat, swayed like an infant in a cradle. Figures hunkered around him, trading words, and a fearsome thirst blazed in his throat.

Dim memories swam at the back of his mind. Hands dragging him. Food being shoveled between his lips, almost choking him. A cloth over his nose and mouth.

He groped for the side of the boat and retched. All around the vessel were green waves, clear as forest glass.

"Saint—" His voice was dry. "Water," he said in Seiikinese. "Please."

Nobody answered.

It was twilight. Or dawn. The sky was bruised with cloud, but the sun had left a finger-smear of honey. Niclays blinked the rain from his eyes and beheld the fire-orange sails that loomed over the boat, illuminated by scores of lanterns. A ghost ship, wreathed in sea mist. One of his captors slapped him across the head and barked something in Lacustrine.

"All right," Niclays murmured. "All right."

He was heaved up by the ropes that bound his wrists and forced at knifepoint to a ladder. The sight of the ship undid his jaw and shook the last of the drowse from him.

A nine-masted galleon, its hull banded with iron, at least twice the length of a High Western. Niclays had never seen a ship as colossal as this, not even in Inysh waters. He placed his bare feet on the wooden slats and climbed, chased by shouts and jeers.

He was among pirates, undoubtedly. From the jade-green of the waves, this was most likely the Sundance Sea, which bled into the Abyss—the dark ocean that separated East from West and North and South. This was the sea he had crossed when he had sailed toward Seiiki all those years ago.

It would also be the sea he died in. Pirates were not known for their mercy, or their civil treatment of hostages. It was a wonder he had made it this far without having his throat slit.

At the top, he was led by his ropes across the deck. All around him were Eastern men and women, with a handful of Southerners scattered among them. Several of the pirates nailed suspicious looks on Niclays, while others ignored him. Many had a Seiikinese word inked on to their brows: *murder, theft, arson, blasphemy*—the crimes for which they had been punished.

Niclays was lashed to one of the masts, where he reflected on the misery of his condition. This had to be the largest ship in existence, which meant he had been snatched by the Fleet of the Tiger Eye: pirates who specialized in the shadow-market trade in parts taken from dragons. They also, like all pirates, indulged in many other crimes.

They had taken all his possessions, including the text Jannart had died for—the fragment that was never supposed to have come back to the East. It was the last piece of him Niclays still possessed and, damn his soul, he had lost it. The thought made him want to weep, but he had to convince these pirates that they needed an old man. Sobbing in terror was not the way to achieve that end.

It felt like months before somebody approached him. By that time, the sun was rising.

A Lacustrine woman came to stand before him. Paint darkened her lips. Over her grizzled hair was a headdress, golden and heavy with razor-sharp ornaments, each a little work of art. At her side was a sword just as golden and twice as sharp. The lines etched into her brown skin spoke of many years spent under the sun.

She was flanked by six pirates, including a moustachioed giant of a Sepuli fellow, whose bare chest was so smothered in tattoos that there was no virgin skin left on him. Giant tigers ripped dragons apart across his torso, and the blood swirled amid sea foam to his shoulders. A pearl sat right over his heart.

The leader—for leader she unquestionably was—wore a long coat of black watersilk. Her missing right arm had been replaced by an articulated wooden substitute, complete with an elbow, fingers, and a thumb, fitted with a cage over her shoulder and secured with a leather strap across her chest. Niclays doubted it was much use to her in the heat of battle, but it was a remarkable innovation, quite unlike anything he had seen in the West.

The woman regarded Niclays, then marched back into the crowd of pirates, who parted to let her through. The giant unraveled the ropes and bundled Niclays into her cabin, which was decorated with swords and bloody flags.

Two people stood in the corner. A thickset woman with freckled brown skin and lines around her mouth, and a bone-thin man, tall and pale, who frankly looked ancient. A tunic of tattered red silk came past his knees.

The pirate sprawled on a throne, accepted a wood-and-bronze pipe from the man, and inhaled whatever vapors were within. She considered Niclays through a blue-tinged haze before addressing him in Lacustrine. Her voice was deep and measured.

"My pirates do not usually take hostages," the freckled woman translated into Seiikinese, "except when we are short of seafarers." She arched an eyebrow at Niclays. "You are special."

He knew better than to speak without permission, but inclined his head. The interpreter waited while the captain spoke again.

"You were found on the beach in Ginura, carrying certain documents," the interpreter continued. "One of them is part of an ancient manuscript. How did you come into possession of this item?"

Niclays bowed low. "Honored captain," he said, addressing the Lacustrine woman, "it was bequeathed to me by a dear friend after his death. I brought it with me when I came to Seiiki from the Free State of Mentendon, hoping to find some meaning behind it."

His words were passed back to the woman in Lacustrine.

"And did you?" came the reply.

"Not yet."

Her eyes were shards of volcanic glass.

"You have had this item for a decade and carry it on your person like a talisman, but you say you know nothing about it. A fascinating claim," the interpreter said, once the captain had spoken. "Perhaps a beating will inspire you to tell the truth. When a person vomits blood, secrets often spill out with it."

Sweat soaked his back.

"Please," he said, "it *is* the truth. Have mercy."

She laughed softly as she answered.

"I did not become the lord of all pirates by showing mercy to thieving liars."

Lord of all pirates.

This was not just any pirate captain. This was the dread sovereign of the Sundance Sea, the conqueror of myriad ships, a mistress of chaos with forty thousand pirates under her command. This was the Golden Empress, the enemy of order, who had clawed herself from poverty to construct her own nation on the waves—a nation beyond the dominion of dragons.

"All-honored Golden Empress." Niclays prostrated himself. "Forgive me for not showing you the appropriate respect. I did not know who you were." His knees screamed, but he kept his brow against the floor. "Let me sail with you. I will give you my skills as an anatomist, my knowledge, my loyalty. I will do anything you ask. Only spare my life."

The Golden Empress took up her pipe again. "I would have asked your name, had you proven the existence of your backbone," was her answer, "but you shall be called Sea-Moon now."

The pirates at the door roared with laughter. Niclays winced. *Sea-moon*—the Seiikinese term for a quarl. A spineless jelly in the clutches of the current.

"You say you are an anatomist," the interpreter said to Niclays, pausing every few moments to listen to the captain. "It so happens that I need a surgeon on this ship. My last one thought herself a cunning poisoner. She wanted vengeance for the ruin of her shit-heap of a village, so she dropped the gold silkworm into my wine." The Golden Empress sipped from the pipe again, then breathed out a curl of smoke. "She learned that salt water is just as deadly."

Niclays swallowed.

"I do not like to waste what I can use. Prove your skill," the Golden Empress told him, "and we may talk again."

"Thank you." His voice split. "Thank you, all-honored captain. For your mercy."

"This is not mercy, Sea-Moon. This is business." She reclined in her seat and spoke again. "Be sure to be loyal to me," the interpreter continued. "There are no second chances in the Fleet of the Tiger Eye."

"I understand." Niclays mustered his courage. "All-honored Golden Empress, I have one more question to ask, if I may." She glanced at him. "Where is the dragon you took from the beach?"

"Below decks," came the translation. "Drunk on firecloud. But not for long." She raked her gaze over him. "We will speak again soon, Sea-Moon. For now, you have your first surgery to perform."

34

West

When it was formally proclaimed that Queen Sabran was with child, the people of Inys ceased their mourning and celebrated in the streets. Prince Aubrecht was dead, but by gifting them the next ruler of Virtudom, he had bought them another generation of safety from the Nameless One.

Though she would traditionally stay in Briar House for half the year, no one grumbled when Sabran decreed that the court would return to Ascalon Palace for the remainder of her pregnancy. Every corridor in the winter residence was choked with memories of the prince consort, and it was commonly agreed that it was best for Queen Sabran to have a fresh outlook.

New gowns were made to accommodate her condition. The lying-in chamber was aired for the first time in decades. The palace was a butterfly house of chatter, and with every meal, courtiers raised their cups to the queen. Laughter rang bright and loud as a bell.

They did not see what the Ladies of the Bedchamber saw. The sickness that racked her at all hours. The relentless exhaustion. The way she lay awake at night, ill at ease with the change in her body.

Now, Roslain had told the ladies-in-waiting in private, was the most dangerous time in the pregnancy. Sabran was not to exert herself. She was not to hunt, or to go on vigorous walks, or to harbor unhappy thoughts. They would all have to work together to keep her calm and in good spirits.

The life of the child took precedence over that of the mother, since there was no evidence that the women of the House of Berethnet could conceive more than once. Little wonder Sabran had been withdrawn of late. The childbed was the one place where her divine authority would not protect her, and every day now brought her closer to it.

If she needed further confirmation of the dangers that surrounded her, the Dukes Spiritual saw fit to remind her daily.

"It is vital that we decide on our course. Yscalin could mount an invasion any day now," Igrain Crest said to her one morning. "Our coastal defenses have been strengthened since Fýredel came, in accordance with your orders, but more is necessary. We have received word that the Flesh King has been constructing a new fleet in Quarl Bay. Some fifty ships are already built."

It was a moment before Sabran spoke. "An invasion fleet."

There were horseshoes of shadow under her eyes.

"I fear so, Majesty," Crest said, gentler. "As does your cousin, the Lord Admiral."

The Duchess of Justice had arrived while Sabran was breaking her fast. She stood in a bar of sunlight, which glinted off her patron brooch.

"We will open negotiations with Hróth immediately," she said. "The wolfcoats will strike fear into Sigoso. To strengthen the chances of aid, we will, of course, take word that Your Majesty has at last accepted the long-standing offer from the Chieftain of Askrdal. Once King Raunus hears—"

"There will be no acceptance of Askrdal," Sabran cut in. "King Raunus is a sovereign of Virtudom, and my distant relative. Let us see how many troops he offers *us* before we make any offers to him."

Katryen pulled in a slow breath. It was unlike Sabran to interrupt Crest.

Crest, too, looked as if she had been caught off-guard. Nonetheless, she smiled.

"Majesty," she said, "I do understand that this must be difficult, given the recent death of Prince Aubrecht. But I trust you will remember what I told you the day before your coronation. As a sword must be oiled, so a fellowship must be renewed. Best that you are not a distant relative to Raunus, but a near and dear one. You must wed again."

Sabran gazed at the window. "I do not see the need for it now."

Crest let her smile fall this time. Her attention darted first to Katryen, then to Ead.

"Majesty," she said, in a reasonable tone, "perhaps we could continue this conversation in private."

"Why, Igrain?" Sabran asked evenly.

"Because this is a sensitive diplomatic issue." After a delicate pause, she said, "If you will forgive us, Lady Katryen, Mistress Duryan. I would like to speak to Queen Sabran alone."

Ead curtsied and made to leave, as did Katryen, but Sabran said, "No. Ead, Kate, stay where you are."

After a moment, they both stepped back into place. Sabran drew herself up in her chair and laid her hands on its arms.

"Your Grace," she said to Crest, "whatever you wish to say of this matter, you may say in front of my ladies. They would not be standing in this chamber if I did not trust them absolutely."

Ead exchanged a glance with Katryen.

Crest forced another smile. "Regarding King Raunus," she continued, "we *must* have confirmation that His Majesty will commit to the defense of Inys. I will send Ambassador Sterbein to Elding at once, but it would strengthen his hand if he carried an acceptance of this suit."

At this, Sabran laid a hand on her belly.

"Igrain," she said, her voice quiet, "you have long stressed to me the need for an heir. My bounden duty. To honor that, I will not take another companion, or even consider it, while I am still with child, lest the strain of the matter harm my daughter." Her gaze was piercing. "Offer Raunus anything else. And we will see what he offers us in return."

The evasion was clever. Crest could not dispute it without appearing to dismiss the well-being of the heir.

"Majesty," she said, disappointment etched on her face, "I can only advise. The choice, and its consequences, are yours."

She curtsied and left the Privy Chamber. Sabran looked after her, expressionless.

"She pushes too hard," she said softly, once the doors were shut. "I never saw, when I was younger. I revered her too much to see how much she hates to be denied."

"It is only that Her Grace believes she knows best," Katryen said. "And she has a will to rival yours."

"My will was not always what it is now. Once I was as molten glass, yet to be spun into shape. I sense I have taken a shape she mislikes."

"Don't be silly." Katryen sat on the arm of her throne. "Let Her Grace drink her sour wine for a few days. She will come around, just as she did after you chose Prince Aubrecht." She gave Sabran the gentlest pat on the belly. "You must think only of this now."

Two days later, a signal beacon was fired in Perchling, warning of danger to the coast. Sabran received Lord Lemand Fynch, her cousin, while she was still in her bedgown.

"Majesty, I regret to inform you that the *Anbaura* was sighted in the Swan Strait this morning," he said. "Though it did not attack, the House of Vetalda is clearly taking the measure of our coastal defenses. As Lord Admiral, I have commanded your navy to keep any further scouts at bay—but I beg you, coz, to ask King Raunus for support. His ships would be of great use in guarding our eastern coast."

"Ambassador Sterbein is already on his way to Elding. I have also requested hellburners from High Princess Ermuna in exchange for Inysh support on her border with Yscalin," Sabran said. "Should the Flesh King flick his tongue at our coast again, I bid you remind him why the Inysh navy is known as the greatest in the world."

"Yes, Majesty."

"You will also send mercenaries to Quarl Bay. I expect them to be hand-chosen by you, and indisputably loyal to Inys." Her eyes were hard as emeralds. "I want his fleet torched."

Her cousin considered this. "A foray into Draconic territory could incite an armed response."

"The Knight of Courage bids us go forth into even the greatest danger in the interest of defending Virtudom, Your Grace. I see no reason why I should wait for bloodshed before I defend this isle,"

Sabran said. "Send Sigoso a message. If he wants to dance with fire, it is he who will burn."

Fynch bowed. "Majesty, I will see it done."

He marched back out. Two of the Knights of the Body closed the doors behind him.

"If Yscalin courts war, I will oblige, but we must be ready," Sabran murmured. "If Raunus is not in a generous mood, it may be my fate to make this marriage to the Chieftain of Askrdal. For Inys."

Marriage to a man old enough to be her grandsire. Even Katryen, who was practiced in courtesy, creased her nose in distaste. Sabran crossed her arms over her midriff.

"Come." Ead laid a hand on her back. "Let us take the air while the snow is untouched."

"Oh, *yes*." Katryen rose to the occasion with relish. "We could pick some damsons and blackberries. And do you know, Sabran, Meg said she saw a dear little hedgepig a few days ago. Perhaps we can help the servants to chase the poor things from under the balefires."

Sabran nodded, but her face was a mask. And Ead knew that, in her mind, she was trapped under a balefire of her own, waiting for an unseen hand to set light to the kindling.

———

Not long after the announcement, Ead found herself once more in the Privy Chamber, embroidering roses on a baby cap. Since the scent of roses had kept her nightmares at bay, Sabran wanted them on everything her daughter would wear in the first days of her life.

The queen lay on a couch in her padded bedgown. She had shed weight in the days following the ambush in Ascalon, making her belly impossible to miss.

"I feel nothing," she said. "Why does she not move?"

"That is natural, Majesty." Roslain was bordering one end of a swaddle blanket. Katryen worked on the other. "You may not feel her quicken for some time."

Sabran kept exploring the little round in her belly with her fingers.

"I believe," she said, "that I have a name for my daughter."

The Chief Gentlewoman looked up so quickly, she must have given herself a cricked neck. The blanket was forgotten as she and Katryen rushed to sit on either side of Sabran. Only Ead remained where she was.

"This is wonderful news, Sab." Smiling, Katryen laid a hand over hers. "What have you chosen?"

There were six historical names for Berethnet monarchs, Sabran and Jillian being the most popular.

"Sylvan. After Sylvan-by-the-River," the queen said, "where her lord father died."

That name was not one of them.

Roslain and Katryen exchanged a worried glance. "Sabran," Roslain said, "it is not traditional. I do not think your people would take well to it."

"And am I not their queen?"

"Superstition knows no rulers."

Sabran looked coldly toward the window. "Kate?"

"I agree, Your Majesty. Let the child not have the shadow of death over her head."

"And you, Ead?"

Ead wanted to support her. She should have the right to name her own child as she pleased, but the Inysh did not take kindly to change.

"I agree." She pulled her needle through the cloth. "Sylvan is a beautiful name, Majesty, but it may serve to make your daughter melancholy. Better to name her after one of your royal ancestors."

At this, Sabran looked exhausted. She turned on to her side and pressed her cheek into the cushion.

"Glorian, then."

A grand name indeed. Since the death of Glorian Shieldheart, it had never been bestowed on any princess.

Katryen and Roslain both made approving sounds. "Her Royal Highness, Princess Glorian," Katryen said, with the air of a steward announcing her entrance. "It already suits her. What hope and heart it will give to your subjects."

Roslain nodded sagely. "It is high time such a magnificent name was resurrected."

Sabran stared at the ceiling as if it were a bottomless chasm.

Within a day, the news had seeped into the capital. Celebrations were planned for the day the princess was born, and the Order of Sanctarians prophesied the might of Glorian the Fourth, who would lead Inys into a Golden Age.

Ead watched it all with weary detachment. Soon the Prioress would call her home. Part of her longed to be among her sisters, united with them in praise of the Mother. Another part wanted nothing but to remain.

She had to crush it.

———————

There was something Ead had to do before she left. One evening, when the other ladies were occupied and Sabran was resting, she made her way to the Dearn Tower, where Truyde utt Zeedeur remained imprisoned.

The guards were on high alert, but she needed no siden to get into forbidden places. As the clock tower struck eleven, she reached the highest floor.

Dressed in naught but a soiled petticoat, the Marchioness of Zeedeur was a shadow of the beauty she had been. Her curls were twisted and heavy with grease, and her cheekbones strained against her skin. A chain snaked between her ankle and the wall.

"Mistress Duryan." Her gaze was as intense as ever. "Have you come to crow over me?"

She had wept when she saw her prince lying dead. It seemed her grief had cooled.

"That would not be courteous," Ead said. "And only the Knight of Justice can judge you."

"You know no Saint, heretic."

"Rich words, traitor." Ead took in the piss-soaked straw. "You do not look afraid."

"Why should I be afraid?"

"You are responsible for the death of the prince consort. That is high treason."

"You will find I am protected here, as a Mentish citizen," Truyde said. "The High Princess will try me in Brygstad, but I am confident I will not be executed. I am *so* young, after all."

Her lips were split. Ead took a wineskin from her bodice, and Truyde, after a moment, drank.

"I came to ask," Ead said, "what you thought you would achieve."

Truyde swallowed the ale. "You know." She wiped her mouth. "I will not tell you again."

"You wanted Sabran to fear for her life. You wanted her to feel as if there were too many battles for her to fight alone. You imagined that this would cause her to seek help from the East," Ead said. "Was it also you who let the cutthroats into Ascalon Palace?"

"Cutthroats?"

As a maid of honor, she would not have been told.

"Has someone tried to kill her before?" Truyde pressed.

Ead nodded. "Do you know the identity of this Cupbearer the shooter invoked?"

"No. As I told the Night Hawk." Truyde looked away. "He says he will have the name from me, one way or another."

Ead found that she believed in her ignorance. Whatever her faults, the girl did appear to want to protect Inys.

"The Nameless One will rise, as his servants have," Truyde said. "Whether there is a queen in Inys or a sun in the sky, he will rise." The chain had rubbed her ankle bloody. "You are a sorceress. A heretic. Do *you* believe the House of Berethnet is all that binds the beast?"

Ead stoppered the wineskin and sat.

"I am not a sorceress," she said. "I am a mage. A practitioner of what you might call magic."

"Magic is not real."

"It is," Ead said, "and its name is *siden*. I used it to protect Sabran from Fýredel. Perhaps that will confirm to you that we are on the same side, even if our methods differ. And even if you are a dangerous fanatic whose folly killed a prince."

"I never meant for him to die. It was all a masque. Wrong-headed outsiders poisoned it." Truyde paused to cough pitifully. "Still,

Prince Aubrecht's death *does* open a new avenue for an Eastern alliance. Sabran could marry an Eastern noble—the Unceasing Emperor of the Twelve Lakes, perhaps. Give her hand and claim an army to kill every wyrm."

Ead huffed a laugh. "She would sooner swallow poison than share a bed with a wyrm-lover."

"Wait until the Nameless One shows himself in Inys. Wait until her people see that the House of Berethnet is built on a lie. Some of them must already believe it," Truyde raised her eyebrows. "They have seen a High Western. They see that Yscalin is emboldened. Sigoso knows the truth."

Ead held out the wineskin again.

"You have risked a great deal for this ... belief of yours," she said as Truyde swallowed. "There must be more to it than mere suspicion. Tell me what planted the seed."

Truyde withdrew, and for a long time, Ead thought she would not answer.

"I tell you this," she finally said, "only because I know no one will listen to a traitor. Perhaps it will plant a seed in you as well." She curled an arm around her knees. "You are from Rumelabar. I trust you have heard of the ancient skystone tablet that was unearthed in its mines."

"I know of it," Ead said. "An object of alchemical interest."

"I first read about it in the library of Niclays Roos, the dearest friend of my grandsire. When he was banished, he entrusted most of his books to me," Truyde said. "The Tablet of Rumelabar speaks of a balance between fire and starlight. Nobody has ever been able to interpret it. Alchemists and scholars have theorized that the balance is symbolic of the worldly and the mystic, of anger and temperance, of humanity and divinity—but I think the words should be taken literally."

"You *think*." Ead smiled. "And are you so much cleverer than the alchemists who have puzzled over it for centuries?"

"Perhaps not," Truyde granted, "though history boasts many so-called scholars of only middling ability. No, not cleverer ... but more disposed to take risks."

"What risk did you take?"

"I went to Gulthaga."

The city that had once lain in the shadow of the Dreadmount, now buried under ash.

"My grandsire told us he was going to visit Wilgastrōm," Truyde said, "but he died of the Draconic plague, contracted in Gulthaga. My father told me the truth when I was fifteen. I rode to the Buried City myself. To see what had driven my grandsire there."

The world believed that the late Duke of Zeedeur had died of the pox. Doubtless the family had been commanded to uphold the lie to avoid creating panic.

"Gulthaga has never been excavated, but there is a way through the tuff, to the ruins," Truyde said. "Some ancient texts have survived. I found the ones my grandsire had been studying."

"You went to Gulthaga *knowing* the Draconic plague was there. You are mad, child."

"It is why I was sent to Inys. To learn temperance—but as you have seen, Mistress Duryan, Temperance is not my patron knight." Truyde smiled. "Mine is Courage."

Ead waited.

"My ancestor was Viceroy of Orisima. From her journals, I learned that the comet that ended the Grief of Ages—that came the hour the wyrms fell—also gave strength to the Eastern dragons." Her eyes were bright. "My grandsire knew a little of the ancient language of Gulthaga. He had translated some of the astronomical writings. They revealed that this comet, the Long-Haired Star, causes a starfall each time it passes."

"And what has *this* to do with anything else, pray tell?"

"I think it connects to the Tablet of Rumelabar. I think the comet is supposed to keep the fire beneath the world in check," Truyde said. "The fire builds over time, and then a starfall cools it. Before it can grow too strong."

"Yet it grows strong now. Where is your comet?"

"That is the problem. I believe that at some point in history, something upset the cycle. Now the fire grows too strong, too fast. Too fast for the comet to subdue it."

"You *believe*," Ead said, frustrated.

364

"As others believe in gods. Often with less proof," Truyde pointed out. "We were lucky in the Grief of Ages. The coming of the Long-Haired Star coincided with the rise of the Draconic Army. It saved us then—but by the time it comes again, Fýredel will have conquered humankind." She grabbed Ead by the wrist, eyes flashing. "The fire will rise as it did before, when the Nameless One was born into this world. Until it has consumed us all."

Her face was wrought with conviction, her jaw tight with it.

"*That*," she finished, with an air of triumph, "is why I believe he will return. And why I think the House of Berethnet has naught to do with it."

They locked gazes for a long moment. Ead pulled her wrist free.

"I want to pity you, child," she said, "but I find my heart cold. You have fished in the waters of history and arranged some fractured pieces into a picture that gives your grandsire's death some meaning—but your determination to make it truth does not mean it is so."

"It is *my* truth."

"Many have died for your truth, Lady Truyde. I trust," Ead said, "that you can live with that."

A draft shivered through the arrow-slit. Truyde turned away from the chill, rubbing her arms.

"Go to Queen Sabran, Ead. Leave me to my beliefs, and I will leave you to yours," she said. "We will see soon enough whose truth is correct."

As she walked back to the Queen Tower, Ead winnowed her memories for the exact words that had been scored into the Tablet of Rumelabar. The first two lines eluded her, but she recalled the rest.

> ... *Fire ascends from the earth, light descends from the sky.*
> *Too much of one doth inflame the other,*
> *and in this is the extinction of the universe.*

A riddle. The sort of nonsense alchemists bickered over for want of anything more useful to do. Bored with her privileged existence, the girl had parsed her own meaning from the words.

And yet Ead found herself dwelling on it. After all, fire *did* ascend from the earth—through wyrms, and through the orange tree. Mages ate of its fruit, becoming vessels of the flame.

Had the Southerners of ancient times known some truth that had disappeared from history?

Uncertainty threw shadows on her mind. If there *was* some connection between the tree and the comet and the Nameless One, surely the Priory would know of it. But so much knowledge had been lost over the centuries, so many records destroyed . . .

Ead cast the thought aside as she entered the royal apartments. She would think on the girl in the tower no more.

In the Great Bedchamber, the Queen of Inys sat upright in her bed, nursing a cup of almond milk. As Ead sat beside the fire, braiding her hair, she felt Sabran's gaze like the tip of a knife.

"You took their side."

Ead stopped. "Madam?"

"You agreed with Ros and Kate about the name."

Days had passed since that discussion. This must have been curdling inside her ever since.

"I wanted my child to carry some part of her father," Sabran said bitterly. "Morose it might be, but it is the place where we were last together. Where he learned that we would have a daughter. Where he vowed that she would be beloved."

Compunction waxed in Ead.

"I wanted to support you," she said, "but I thought Lady Roslain was right, about not breaking with tradition. I still do." She tied off her braid. "Forgive me, Majesty."

With a sigh, Sabran patted the bed. "Come. The night is cold."

Ead stood with a nod. Ascalon Palace did not hold in warmth so well as Briar House. She blew out all but two of the candles before she got under the coverlets.

"You are not yourself." Sabran inferred. "What troubles you, Ead?"

A girl with a skullful of dangerous ideas.

"Only the talk of invasion," Ead answered. "These are uncertain times."

"Times of treachery. Sigoso has betrayed not only the Saint, but humankind." Sabran exerted a stranglehold on her cup. "Inys survived the Grief of Ages, but barely. Villages were turned to ash, cities set afire. Our population was decimated, and even centuries later, any armies I can muster will not be as large as those we had before." She put the cup aside. "I cannot think of this now. I must ... deliver Glorian. Even if all three High Westerns lead their forces to my queendom, the Nameless One cannot join them."

Her nightgown was drawn back to bare her belly, as if to let the child breathe. Blue veins traced her sides.

"I prayed to the Damsel, asking her to fill my womb." Sabran released her breath. "I can be no good queen. No good mother. Today, for the first time, I ... almost resented her."

"The Damsel?"

"Never. The Damsel does what she must." One pale hand came to rest on the bump. "I resent ... my unborn child. An innocent." Her voice strained. "The people already turn to her as their next queen, Ead. They speak of her beauty and her magnificence. I did not expect that. The suddenness of it. Once she is born, my purpose is served."

"Madam," Ead said gently, "that is not true."

"Is it not?" Sabran circled a hand on her belly. "Glorian will soon come of age, and I will be expected, sooner or later, to abdicate in her favor. When the world considers me too old."

"Not all Berethnet queens have abdicated. The throne is yours for as long as you desire."

"It is considered an act of greed to hold it for too long. Even Glorian Shieldheart abdicated, despite her popularity."

"Perhaps by the time your child is grown, you will be ready to relinquish the throne. To lead a quieter life."

"Perhaps. Or perhaps not. Whether I live or die in childbed, I will be cast aside. Like an eggshell."

"Sabran."

Before she knew it, Ead had reached to touch her cheek. Sabran looked at her.

"There will be fools and flatterers," Ead said, "who forsake your side to fawn over a newborn. Let them. See them for what they are." She kept Sabran's gaze prisoner. "I told you fear was natural, but you must not let it consume you. Not when there is so much at stake."

The skin against her palm was cool and petal-soft. Warm breath caressed her wrist.

"Be at my side for the birth. And onward," Sabran murmured. "You must always stay with me, Ead Duryan."

Chassar would be back for her in half a year. "I will stay with you for as long as I can," Ead said. It was all that she could promise.

With a nod, Sabran shifted closer and rested her head on Ead's shoulder. Ead held still—allowing herself to grow used to her nearness, to the shape of her.

Her skin was all chills. She could smell the milky sweetness of creamgrail in her hair, feel the swell of her belly. Ead sensed she would jostle the child as they slept, so she rotated their bodies until Sabran faced away from her, and they fitted together like acorn and cup. Sabran reached for Ead's hand and brought it around her middle. Ead drew the coverlets over both of their shoulders. Soon the queen was fast asleep.

Her grasp was soft, but Ead still felt a heartbeat in her fingers. She imagined what the Prioress would say if she could see her now. No doubt she would scorn her. She was a sister of the Priory, destined to slay wyrms, and here she was, giving succor to a sad Berethnet.

Something was changing in her. A feeling, small as a rosebud, was opening its petals.

She had never been meant to harbor anything more than indifference toward this woman. Yet she knew now that when Chassar returned, it would be hard to go. Sabran would need a friend more than ever. Roslain and Katryen would be preoccupied with the newborn, and would talk of nothing but blankets and cradles and milk nurses for months. Sabran would not weather that time well. She would go from being the sun of her court to the shadow behind a child.

Ead fell asleep with her cheek against a wash of black hair. When she woke, Sabran was quiet beside her.

A drumbeat pounded at her temple. Her siden lay dormant, but her instincts had woken.

Something was wrong.

The fire was low, the candles almost burned out. Ead rose to trim the wicks.

"No," Sabran breathed. "The blood."

From the tortured look on her face, she was dreaming. Dreaming, so it seemed, of the Lady of the Woods.

Kalyba was no ordinary mage. From what little Ead remembered about her, she had possessed gifts unknown to the Priory, including immortality. Perhaps dream-giving was another. But why should Kalyba be concerned with tormenting the Queen of Inys?

Ead went back to Sabran and laid a hand on her brow. She was sodden. Her nightgown was stuck fast, and strands of hair clung to her face. Chest tight, Ead felt her brow for the heat of a fever, but her skin was icy cold. Incoherent words escaped her.

"Hush." Ead reached for the goblet and tipped it to her lips. "Drink, Sabran."

Sabran took a swallow of milk and sank back into the pillows, twisting like a kitten caught by the scruff of its neck. As if she were trying to escape from her nightmare. Ead sat beside her and stroked her lank hair.

Perhaps it was because Sabran was so cold that Ead noticed at once when her own skin heated.

A Draconic thing was near.

Ead strove to remain calm. When Sabran was still, she sponged the sweat from her and arranged the bedclothes so only her face was exposed to the night. She could alert no one, for it would betray her gifts.

All she could do was wait.

The first warning was the shouts from the palace walls. At once, Ead was on her feet.

"Sabran, quickly." She scooped an arm around the queen. "You must come with me now."

Her eyes flickered open. "Ead," she said, "what is it?"

Ead helped her into her slippers and bedgown. "You must get to the wine cellars at once."

The key turned in the door. Captain Lintley appeared, armed with his crossbow.

"Majesty," he said, with a rigid bow, "there is a flock of Draconic creatures approaching, led by a High Western. Our forces are ready, but you must come with us now, before they breach the walls."

"A flock," Sabran repeated.

"Yes."

Ead watched her waver. This was the woman who had gone out to meet Fýredel.

It was not in her nature to hide.

"Your Majesty," Lintley urged. "Please. Your safety is paramount."

Sabran nodded. "Very well."

Ead wrapped the heaviest coverlet around her shoulders. Roslain appeared at the doors, her face lit stark by the taper in her hand.

"Sabran," she said, "hurry, you must hurry—"

Throwing a final, unreadable look at Ead, Sabran was escorted away by Lintley and Sir Gules Heath, who kept a reassuring hand at the small of her back. Ead waited for them to vacate the Great Bedchamber before she ran.

In her own rooms, she changed and threw on a hooded cloak before grabbing her longbow. She would have to aim true. Only certain parts of a High Western could be pierced.

The arrows were vast things. She took them and sheathed her arm in a leather bracer. It had been twelve years since she had fought a wyrm without her siden, but she, of all the people in this city, had the greatest chance of driving off the High Western.

She needed a vantage point. Carnelian House, where many of the courtiers lodged, would give her a clear view.

She took the Florell Stair, which connected on the third floor to the main stair of the Queen Tower. She could hear the Knights of the Body coming down it.

She quickened her pace. The stairs spiraled in a rush beneath her. Soon she emerged into the biting chill of the night. Fleet-footed, unseen by the guards, she skirted the edge of the Sundial Garden and, with a great leap, caught hold of a blind arch on the north-facing side of Carnelian House. Each adornment on the walls gave her a handhold.

A bitter wind pulled at her hair as she climbed. Her body was no longer as strong as it had been in Lasia, and she had not tested her limbs like this in months. She ached all over by the time she hitched herself on to the roof.

The Knights of the Body and the ladies-in-waiting emerged from the Queen Tower and gathered into a protective knot around Sabran and Heath. The party struck out from the vestibule and across the Sundial Garden.

When they were halfway across, Ead beheld a sight that would have been unthinkable a year ago.

Wyverns coming toward Ascalon Palace, screaming like crows surrounding a carcass.

She had seen nothing like this in all her years. These were no blear-eyed creatures jarred from their sleep, scavenging for live-stock. This was a declaration of war. Not only were these wyverns bold enough to show themselves in the capital, but they were *flocking*. As dread threatened to freeze her, she thought back to her lessons in the Priory.

Wyverns would only fly in these numbers if they were united by a High Western. If she killed the master, they would scatter.

Her breath clouded before her. The High Western had not yet shown itself, but she caught its foul stench on the wind, like the fumes from a fire mountain. She slid an arrow from her quiver.

The Mother had designed these arrows. Long enough to pierce the thickest Draconic armor, made of metal from the Dreadmount, they froze at the lightest touch of ice or snow.

Her fingers prickled. The reek of brimstone blew through the courtyard, and the snow thawed around her boots.

She knew the cadence of wings when she heard it. Thunderous as the footsteps of a giant.

With every *whump*, the ground quaked. A drumbeat of impending grief.

The High Western tore through the night. Almost as large as Fýredel, its scales were pale as bone. It crashed down next to the clock tower and, with a bone-shattering lash of its tail, threw a group of palace guards across the courtyard. More charged at it with swords and partizans. With this monstrosity blocking the way, Lintley and the Knights of the Body could no longer reach the entrance to the cellars.

In the days after Fýredel had come, several weapons on the walls of Ascalon Palace had been set on rounds of wood, allowing them to be revolved. Cannons flung gunstones at the intruder. Two hit it in the flank, another in the thigh—hard enough to break bone on a wyvern—but they only served to incense the High Western. It scoured the walls with its spiked tail, sweeping away the guards who had been trying to load a harpoon. Their screams died as quickly as they began.

Ead dragged the arrow through the snow, freezing it, and fitted it to her bow. She had seen Jondu fell a wyvern with one well-placed shot, but this was a High Western, and her arm was no longer strong enough to make a full draw. Years of needlework had milked her strength. Without that, and without her siden, her chances of a hit were slim.

A breath left her. She released the bow and, with a *thrwang*, the arrow skirred toward the wyrm. It moved at the last, and the arrow just missed its flank. Ead glimpsed Lintley at the northwest corner of the Sundial Garden, hurrying his charges into the cover of the Marble Gallery.

Retreating to the Queen Tower would now take Sabran into full view of the wyrm. They were trapped. If Ead could distract the beast, and if they were quick, they might be able to slip past unnoticed and make a break for the cellars.

Another arrow was in her hand a moment later, nocked and drawn. This time, she angled it toward a softer part of the face before she let go. It clanked off a scaled eyelid.

The slit of the pupil constricted, and the High Western turned its head to face her. Now its attention was all hers.

She iced a third arrow.

Hurry, Lintley.

"Wyrm," she called in Selinyi. "I am Eadaz du Zāla uq-Nāra, a handmaiden of Cleolind. I carry the sacred flame. Leave this city untouched, or I will see you brought down."

The Knights of the Body had reached the end of the Marble Gallery. The wyrm gazed at her with eyes as green as willow. She had never seen that eye color in a Draconic thing.

"Mage," it said in the same tongue, "your fire is spent. The God of the Mountain comes."

Its voice churned like a millstone through the palace. Ead did not flinch.

"Ask Fýredel if my fire is spent," she answered.

The wyrm hissed.

Most Draconic creatures were easy to distract. Not this one. Its gaze snapped to where the Knights of the Body had emerged. Their copper-plated armor reflected the flames, drawing its eye.

"Sabran."

Ead felt a chill in her bones. The wyrm said that name with a softness. A familiarity.

That softness did not last. Teeth bared, the beast threw back its head and spoke in the Draconic tongue. As fireballs rained from the wyverns, the Knights of the Body, in terror, divided. Half retreated into the Marble Gallery, while the others ran for the Banqueting House. Lintley was one of the latter. So was Margret. So was Heath, ever fearless. Ead could see him with his shield raised high, cradling Sabran with his sword arm. She was bent over her belly.

The wyrm opened its jaws. The Marble Gallery melted beneath its fiery breath, cooking the knights inside.

Ead released the bowstring. With punishing force, her arrow seared across the space between mage and wyrm.

It found its mark.

The bay of agony was deafening. She had struck it in the place Jondu had shown her, the supple armor under the wing. Blood poured down its scales and bubbled around the spit of ice.

One green eye burned into Ead. She felt herself etched into that eye. Into its memory.

Then it happened. As it took off, bleeding and enraged, the wyrm swung his spiked tail—and the vestibule of the Dearn

Tower, its foundations already weakened by Fýredel, collapsed into the courtyard. So did the statues of the Great Queens atop it. Ead looked down in time to see Heath struck by a block of masonry, and Sabran falling from his arms, before a cloud of dust swallowed them both.

The silence was a held breath. It rang with a secret that could not be spoken.

Ead dropped like a shadow from the roof, and she ran as she never had in her life.

Sabran.

She was curled, like a feather shaken from a bird, by the body of Sir Gules Heath. Eyes closed. Still breathing. Just breathing. Ead wrapped the Queen of Inys in her arms and gathered her up as darkness stole into her nightgown, stemming from between her thighs.

The stone head of Glorian Shieldheart watched her bleed.

35

East

All things considered, his first surgery aboard the *Pursuit*—the flagship of the Fleet of the Tiger Eye—had gone better than Niclays had anticipated. He had been presented with a Lacustrine fellow who had been stung by a frilled and glowing quarl, rarely seen in these waters. The poor man had shrieked in agony while his leg took on the appearance of rawhide.

By a stroke of luck, Eizaru had once told Niclays exactly how to soothe a sting from this quarl. Niclays had cobbled together the ingredients and, lo and behold, the pirate was free of pain, if mutilated for life. He would be back to pillaging and killing again soon.

Having received word that the Seiikinese had sent the High Sea Guard to reclaim the dragon, the Golden Empress had ordered the fleet to scatter in all directions. The *Pursuit* would skirt the Abyss before sailing to the Sleepless Sea and unloading its forbidden cargo in the lawless city of Kawontay. The Eastern dragons were afraid of the Abyss, slow to enter it.

That night, Niclays found himself shivering in the rain on the three-foot stretch of the deck he had been allotted to sleep on. A few pirates had kicked him in the shins as they passed. He wondered dimly if anyone had ever felt worse than he did at this moment.

This was his life now. He should have been grateful for his little house in Orisima. Suddenly he missed the sunken hearth and the pothook, the bedding he left to air in the sun, the dark walls, and woven mats. It had not belonged to him, but it had kept a roof over his head.

A pair of booted feet appeared in front of him. He shrank away, expecting another kick.

"Gods lie weeping. Look at the state of you."

The interpreter was standing over him, one hand on her hip. This time she wore a shawl and gloves that made him weak with envy. A cloud of dark hair, marbled with gray, sprang in tiny curls around her face. A band of silk kept it out of her eyes.

"No sea legs yet, I see, Old Red," she said.

Niclays blinked. She spoke his language impeccably. Few but the Mentish spoke Mentish.

"I don't suppose you feel well enough for supper, but I thought I'd bring it." With a broad smile, she handed him a bowl. "The Golden Empress bids me tell you that you are now her master surgeon. You're to be ready at all hours to tend her seafarers."

"The quarl was a test, then," he said gloomily.

"I'm afraid so." She bent to kiss his cheek. "Laya Yidagé. Welcome aboard the *Pursuit*."

"Niclays Roos. Would that I could greet you in a more dignified state, dear lady." He squinted at the food. Rice and globs of pinkish meat. "Saint. Is that raw eel?"

"Be glad it's not still wriggling. The last hostage had to bite its head off. That was before *his* head came off, of course." Laya squeezed in beside him. "Cure a few more pirates and you might get it cooked. And somewhere a little more hospitable to sleep."

"You realize I'm more likely to kill one of them. I have a degree in anatomy, but a master surgeon I am not."

"I suggest you keep pretending otherwise." She threw some of her cloak around him. "Here. It's warm."

"Thank you." Niclays pulled it close and smiled wearily at her. "I beg you to distract me from this supposed meal. Tell me how you came to sail with the dreaded Golden Empress."

While he winnowed the clean grains from the bloodstained rice, she did.

Laya had been born in the beautiful city of Kumenga, famous for its academies, sun wine, and limpid waters. As a child, she had thirsted for knowledge of the world, her interest fed by her father, an explorer, who had taught her several languages.

"One day, he set off for the East, determined to be the first Southerner to set foot in it in centuries," she said. "He never came back, of course. No one does. Years later, I paid the pirates of the Sea of Carmentum to take me over the Abyss to find him." Rain seeped down her cheek. "We came under fire by a ship in this fleet. Everyone was slain, but I pleaded for my life in Lacustrine, which surprised the captain. He took me to the Golden Empress, and I became her interpreter. It was that or the sword."

"How long have you worked for her?"

She sighed. "Too long."

"You must wish to go back to the South."

"Of course," she said, "but I would be a fool to try an escape. I am no navigator, Old Red, and the Abyss is wide."

She had a point.

"Do you suppose, Mistress Yidagé—"

"Laya."

"Laya. Do you suppose the Golden Empress would allow me to see the dragon below decks?"

Laya raised her eyebrows. "And why would you want to do that, pray tell?"

Niclays hesitated.

It would be safest to hold back. After all, many feared or mocked alchemy—but he imagined that Laya, having spent years on a pirate ship, would not be easily daunted.

"I am an alchemist," he told her under his breath. "Not a great one—an amateur, really—but I have been trying, for the last decade, to create an elixir of immortality." Her eyebrows crept higher. "I have so far failed in this endeavor, mostly thanks to a scarcity of decent ingredients. Given that the dragons can live for centuries, I was hoping to ... study the one below. Before we reach Kawontay."

"Before every part of its body is sold." Laya nodded. "Usually I would advise you against mentioning this."

"But?"

"The Golden Empress has a vested interest in immortality. Your alchemy may endear her to you." She leaned closer, so their breath formed one plume. "There is a reason this ship is called the *Pursuit*, Niclays. Did you ever hear the story of the mulberry tree?"

Niclays knitted his eyebrows. "*The* mulberry tree?"

"It's a little-known legend in the East. More myth than history." Laya leaned against the gunwale. "Centuries ago, a sorceress was said to rule over an island called Komoridu. Black doves and white crows flocked to her, for she was mother to the outcasts.

"The story is told from the perspective of an unnamed woman, who is shunned by the people of Ginura. She hears whispers of Komoridu, where all are welcome, and decides she must get there by any means necessary. When she finally does, she goes to visit the fabled sorceress, whose power comes from a mulberry tree. A source of eternal life."

Now his heart was pounding like a tabor.

"Although the legend has survived," Laya said, "no one has ever been able to find Komoridu. For centuries, the scroll containing its story was kept on Feather Island. Someone stole it from the sacred archives and gave it to the Golden Empress ... but it soon became apparent that part of it was missing. A part she believes is vital."

Niclays was as raw as if he had been struck by lightning.

My aunt received it from a man who told her to carry it far from the East and never bring it back.

"Yes. You brought it to her." Seeing his astonished expression, Laya smiled at him. "The final piece of the puzzle."

The puzzle.

Jannart.

A sound grumbled through the belly of the ship. The *Pursuit* listed, shunting Niclays against Laya.

"Is it a storm?" he asked, his voice a notch higher than usual.

"Shh."

The next sound was an echo of the first. Frowning, Laya got to her feet. Niclays rubbed some feeling back into his legs and followed. The Golden Empress was on the quarterdeck.

They were at the threshold of the Abyss, the place where even dragons feared to go, where the water deepened from green to black. And not a ripple marred the surface.

Within this impossible sea, every star, every constellation, every fold and spiral of the cosmos was reflected. As if there were two firmaments, and their ship was a ghost ship, adrift between worlds. The sea had turned itself to glass, so the heavens might finally look upon themselves.

"Did you ever see such a thing?" Niclays murmured.

Laya shook her head. "This is no natural thing."

Not a single wave broke against the fleet. Each ship was as steady as if it were on land. The crew of the *Pursuit* stood in restless silence, but Niclays Roos was tranquil, entranced by the vision of the double universe. A balanced world, like the one described in the Tablet of Rumelabar.

What is below must be balanced by what is above, and in this is the precision of the universe.

Words that no one living understood. Words that had made Truyde send her lover across the sea with a plea for help that would go unheard. A lover who must now be dead.

Voices shouted in myriad languages. Niclays staggered back as spray exploded over the deck, drenching his hair in hot water. His moment of calm dissolved.

Bubbles swarmed around the hull. Laya clutched his arm. She ran with him to the nearest mast and seized the ropes.

"Laya," he called to her, "what is happening?"

"I don't know. Hold on!"

Niclays blinked away salt water, gasping. He shouted out as water roiled into the fleet, destroying a rowing boat and sweeping pirates off the decks. Their shrieks were lost to a sound he thought at first was thunder.

And then, as the sea crested the side of the *Pursuit*, it appeared. A mass of red-hot scale. Niclays stared in disbelief at the tail that ended in cruel spikes, at the wings that could have bridged the River Bugen. Amid the roar of the sea and the howl of the wind, a High Western swooped low over the fleet and screamed in triumph.

"MASTER," it screamed. "SOON. SOON. SOON."

36

West

The nightingales had forgotten how to sing. Ead lay on her side on the truckle bed, listening to Sabran breathe.

Oftentimes since the wyrm had come, she had drowned in dreams of what had happened that night. How she had carried Sabran to the Royal Physician. The hideous barb he had drawn from her belly. The blood. The cloth-wrapped form they had carried away. Sabran unmoving on the bed, looking as if she were on her bier.

A breeze wafted through the Great Bedchamber. Ead turned over.

Though she had watched Doctor Bourn and his assistants to ensure they first boiled everything that touched Sabran, it had not been enough. Inflammation had taken root. Fever had ravaged her, and she had lain on the brink of death for days—but she had fought. She had fought for her life like Glorian Shieldheart.

In the end, she had clawed herself from the edge of the grave, drained in body and soul. Once her fever had broken, the Royal Physician had concluded that the barb he had pulled from her had come from the High Western. Fearful that it might have given her the plague, he had sent for a Mentish expert in Draconic anatomy. What she had concluded was the unutterable.

The Queen of Inys did not have the plague, but she would never bear a living child.

Another draft rushed into the room. Ead rose from bed and shut the window.

Stars dotted the midnight sky. Beneath them, Ascalon flickered with torchlight. Some of its people would be awake now, praying for protection from what the commons were calling the White Wyrm.

They did not carry the same knowledge that haunted the Dukes Spiritual and the Ladies of the Bedchamber. Aside from the Royal Physician, only they knew the most dangerous secret in the world.

The House of Berethnet would end with Sabran the Ninth.

Ead trimmed the wick on one of the candles and lit it again. Since the White Wyrm had come, Sabran had only grown more fearful of the dark.

Fragments of historical evidence from the world over agreed that there had been five High Westerns. There were likenesses of them in the caves of Mentendon and the bestiaries made after the Grief of Ages.

According to that evidence, none of those High Westerns had possessed green eyes.

"Ead."

She glanced over her shoulder. Sabran was a silhouette behind the see-through drapes around her bed.

"Majesty," Ead said.

"Open the window."

Ead placed the candle on the mantelpiece. "You will catch a chill."

"I may be barren," Sabran bit out, "but until I breathe my last, I am your queen. Do as I say."

"You are still healing. If you perish from cold, the Principal Secretary will have my head."

"Damn you, obstinate bitch. I will have your head *myself* if you do not do as I command."

"By all means. I doubt I will have much use for it once it has bid my neck farewell."

Sabran twisted to face her.

"I will kill you." The cords in her neck were straining. "I despise all of you, overweening crows. All any of you think about is what you can peck from me. A pension, estates, an heir—" Her voice broke.

"Damn you all. I would sooner throw myself off the Alabastrine Tower than I would swallow another spoonful of your pity."

"Enough," Ead snapped. "You are not a child. Cease this wallowing."

"Open the window."

"Come and open it yourself."

Sabran let out a small, dark laugh. "I could have you burned for this insolence."

"If it rouses you from that bed, I would gladly dance upon the pyre."

The clock tower chimed once. Shuddering, Sabran lapsed back into the pillows.

"I was meant to die in childbed," she whispered. "I was meant to give Glorian life. And yield my own."

Her breasts had leaked for days after her loss, and her belly was still round. Even as she tried to heal, her own body kept opening the wound.

Ead lit two more candles. She pitied Sabran, so much so that she thought her ribs would break apart with it, but could not pander to her fits of self-hatred. Berethnet sovereigns were prone to what the Inysh called *grievoushead*—periods of sadness, with or without a discernible root. Carnelian the Fifth had been known as the Mourning Dove, and it was rumored at court that she had taken her own life by walking into a river. Combe had charged the Ladies of the Bedchamber with ensuring Sabran did not wander down the same path.

To be a moth on the window of the Council Chamber tonight. Some of the Dukes Spiritual would be arguing that the truth should never come out. Padding under gowns. An orphan child with black hair and jade eyes. Some of the council might contemplate such notions, but most of them would not brook the idea of bowing to anyone but a Berethnet.

"I was certain—" Sabran clenched her fists in her hair. "I must be beloved of the Saint. I drove away Fýredel. Why am I abandoned now?"

Ead forced down a surge of guilt. Her warding had fed into the lie.

"Madam," she said, "you must maintain your faith. It does not do to dwell on—"

Another joyless laugh interrupted her. "You sound like Ros. I do not need another Ros." Sabran tightened her hands. "Perhaps I should think of lighter things. Ros would tell me so. What shall I think of, Ead? My dead companion, my barren womb, or the knowledge that the Nameless One is coming?"

Ead made herself kneel and stoke the fire.

Sabran had spoken little for days, but what she had said had been meant to hurt. She had barked at Roslain for being too quiet. She had taunted the maids of honor when they served her meals. She had told a page to get out of her sight, reducing her to tears.

"I will be the last Berethnet. I am the destroyer of my house." She gripped the sheets. "This is my doing. For spurning the childbed for so long. For trying to avoid it."

Her head dropped forward.

Ead went to the Queen of Inys. She moved the drape aside and sat on the edge of the bed. Sabran was half-sitting, huddled over her bruised abdomen.

"I was selfish. I wanted—" Sabran breathed out through her nose. "I asked Niclays Roos to make me an elixir, something that would preserve my youth, so I would never have to get with child. When he could not," she whispered, "I banished him to the East."

"Sabran—"

"I turned my back on the Knight of Generosity for all that he had given me. I resented having to give just once in return."

"Stop this," Ead said firmly. "You had a great burden to bear, and you bore it bravely."

"It is a divine calling." Her cheeks glinted. "Over a thousand years of the same rule. Thirty-six women of the House of Berethnet bore daughters in the name of Inys. Why could I not?" She pressed a hand to her belly. "Why did this have to happen?"

At this, Ead took her gently by the chin.

"It is *not* your fault," she said. "Remember it, Sabran. None of this is on your head."

Sabran shied from her touch. "The Virtues Council will try everything, but my people are not fools," she said. "The truth will out. Virtudom will collapse without its foundation. Faith in the Saint will be destroyed. The sanctuaries will be empty."

The prophecy had the ring of truth. Even Ead knew that the collapse of Virtudom would cause turmoil. It was part of why she had been sent here. To preserve order.

She had failed.

"I have no place in the heavenly court," Sabran said. "When I lie rotting in the soil, the Dukes Spiritual, whose blood comes from the Holy Retinue, will each lay claim to my throne." A breath of humorless laughter escaped her. "Perhaps they will not even wait for me to die before the infighting begins. They believed in my power to keep the Nameless One shackled, but that power will now end with my death."

"Then surely it is in their interest to keep you safe." Ead tried to sound reassuring. "To buy themselves time to prepare for his coming."

"Safe, perhaps, but not enthroned. Some of them will be asking themselves, at this very moment, if they should act at once. To choose a new ruler before Fýredel returns to destroy us." Sabran narrated this in hollow tones. "They will all be asking themselves if the story of my divinity was ever true. I have been asking myself the same question." Her hand slid back to her belly. "I have shown that I am only flesh."

Ead shook her head.

"They will press me to name one of them my successor. Even if I do, the others may challenge it," Sabran said. "The nobles will each raise their banners for one of the claimants. Inys will divide. While it is weak, the Draconic Army will return. And Yscalin stands poised to aid it." She closed her eyes. "I cannot see it, Ead. I cannot see this queendom fall."

She must have feared this outcome from the beginning.

"She was so ... delicate. Glorian," Sabran rasped. "Like the tracery of a leaf. The frail after the green has left it." She gazed into nothing. "They tried to hide her from me, but I saw."

A different lady-in-waiting would have told her that her child was safe in the heavenly court. Roslain would have painted her a picture of a black-haired baby swaddled in the arms of Galian Berethnet, smiling forever in a castle in the sky.

Ead did not. Such an image would not comfort Sabran in her grief. Not yet.

She reached for one icy hand and warmed it between hers. Shivering in the vastness of the bed, Sabran seemed more of a lost child than a queen.

"Ead," she said, "there is a pouch of gold in the coffer." She nodded to the chest her jewels were stored in. "Go into the city. The shadow market. They sell a poison there called the dowager."

The breath went out of Ead.

"Don't be a fool," she whispered.

"You dare call the last Berethnet a fool."

"Of course, when you speak like one."

"I ask you this," Sabran said, "not as your queen, but as a penitent." Her face was taut, and her jaw trembled. "I cannot live knowing my people are doomed to death by the Nameless One or civil war. I could never be at peace with myself." She took back her hand. "I thought you would understand. I thought you would help me."

"I understand more than you know." Ead cupped her cheek. "You have tried to turn yourself to stone. Do not be afeared to find that you are not. Queen you may be, but you are flesh and blood."

Sabran smiled in a way that broke her heart.

"That is what it is to be a queen, Ead," she said. "Body and realm are one and the same."

"Then you cannot kill the body for the realm." Ead held her gaze. "So no, Sabran Berethnet. I will not bring you poison. Not now. Not ever."

The words came from a place she had tried to lock. The place where a rose had grown.

Sabran looked at her with an expression Ead had never seen. All the melancholy faded, leaving her curious and intent. Ead could see every splinter of green in her eyes, every lash, the candles trapped inside her pupils. The firelight danced on her shoulder. As Ead chased it with her fingertips, Sabran leaned into her touch.

"Ead," she said, "stay with me."

Her voice was almost too soft to hear, but Ead felt each word in her very flesh.

Their lips were close now, a breath apart. Ead dared not move for fear that she would shatter this moment. Her skin was tender, aching at the feel of Sabran pressed against her.

Sabran framed her face between her hands. In her gaze was both a question and her fear of the answer.

As black hair brushed her collarbone, Ead thought of the Prioress and the orange tree. She thought of what Chassar would say if he knew how her blood sang for the pretender, who prayed to the empty tomb of the Mother. Scion of Galian the Deceiver. Sabran drew her close, and Ead kissed the Queen of Inys as she would kiss a lover.

Her body was spun glass. A flower just opened to the world. When Sabran parted her lips with her own, Ead understood, with an intensity that wrenched the breath from her, that what she had wanted for months now was to hold her like this. When she had lain beside Sabran and listened to her secrets. When she had stowed the rose behind her pillow. It was a realization that pierced her to the core.

They were still. Their lips lingered, just touching.

Her heart was too fast, too full. At first, she dared not breathe—even the smallest movement could sunder them—but then Sabran embraced her, voice breaking on her name. Ead felt the flutter of a heart against her own. Soft and quick as a butterfly.

She was lost and found and wandering, all at once. At the cusp of dreaming, yet somehow never more awake. Her fingers mapped Sabran, drawn across her skin by instinct. They followed the scar up her thigh, coursed in her hair, traced beneath her swollen breasts.

Sabran drew back to look at her. Ead caught a glimpse of her face in the candlelight—brow smooth, eyes dark and resolute—before they came together again, and the kiss was hot and new and world-forming, the flare of starbirth on their lips. They were honeycombs of secret places, fragile and intricate. Ead shivered as the night welcomed her skin.

She felt the wash of gooseflesh on Sabran. The nightgown slipped from her shoulder, farther, until it came to rest around her hips, so Ead could trace the pathway of her spine and fold her hands at the arch in her back. She kissed her neck and the naked place behind her ear, and Sabran breathed her name, head tilting back to bare the hollow of her throat. Moonlight filled it up like milk.

The silence of the Great Bedchamber was vast. Vast as night and all its stars. Ead heard each rustle of silk, each brush of hand on skin on sheets. Their breaths were hushed, held in anticipation of a knock on the door, a key in the lock, and a torch to bare their union. It would light a flame of scandal, and the fire would rise until it scorched them both.

But Ead called fire her friend, and she would plunge into the furnace for Sabran Berethnet, for just one night with her. Let them come with their swords and their torches.

Let them come.

Later, they lay in the light of the blood moon. For the first time in many years, the Queen of Inys slept without a candle.

Ead gazed at the canopy. She knew one thing now, and it blotted all else out of her mind.

Whatever the Priory desired, she could not abandon Sabran.

As she stirred in the depths of sleep, Ead breathed in the scent of her. Creamgrail and lilacs, laced with the clove from her pomander. She imagined stealing her away to the Milk Lagoon, that fabled land, where her name would never find her.

It could never be.

Slant light glowed through the Great Bedchamber. Gradually, Ead became aware of herself, and of Sabran. Black hair draped across the pillow. Skin on skin on skin. The sunlight had not yet reached the bed, but she felt as warm as if it had.

She felt no regret. Confusion, yes, and birds in her belly, but no desire to turn back time.

A knock came then, and it was as if a cloud had passed over the sun.

"Your Majesty."

Katryen.

Sabran lifted her head. She looked first at Ead, heavy-eyed, then toward the doors.

"What is it, Kate?" Her voice was thick with sleep.

"I wondered if you might like to have a bath this morning. The night was so cold."

She had been trying to coax her queen out for two days. "Draw the bath," Sabran said. "Ead will knock when I am ready."

"Yes, madam."

The footsteps withdrew. Sabran turned back, and Ead met her unsure gaze. Now the sun was up, they took the measure of each other, as if they were meeting for the first time.

"Ead," Sabran said softly, "you need not feel obliged to continue as my bedfellow." Slowly, she sat up. "The duties of a Lady of the Bedchamber do not extend to what we did last night."

Ead raised her eyebrows. "You think I did it out of duty?"

Sabran drew her knees to her chest and looked away. Nettled, Ead got out of bed.

"You are wrong," she said, "Your Majesty." She pulled on her nightgown and retrieved a mantle from the chair. "You ought to get up. Kate is waiting."

Sabran gazed at the window. The sun turned her eyes to the pale green of beryl.

"It is almost impossible for a queen to tell what comes from deference, and what from the heart." Those eyes sought hers. "Tell me the truth of it, Ead. Was it your own choice to lie with me last night, or did you feel compelled because of my rank?"

Her hair was a tangle about her shoulders. Ead softened.

"Fool," she said. "I would not be compelled by you or anyone. Have I not always given you truth?"

Sabran smiled at that. "Too much of it," she said. "You are the only one who does."

Ead leaned in to kiss her brow, but before she could, Sabran caught her face between her hands and pressed her parted lips to hers. When they broke apart at last, Sabran smiled a true smile, rare as a desert rose.

"Come." Ead draped the mantle over her shoulders. "I would see you walk under the sun today."

Court life stirred again that morning. Sabran summoned the Dukes Spiritual to her Privy Chamber. She would show them that, though she was bruised in body and spirit, she was very much alive. She would arrange the conscription of new soldiers, hire mercenaries, and increase her funding to inventors in the hope that they could create better weapons. When the High Westerns returned, Inys would bite back.

As far as Ead could tell, the Dukes Spiritual had not yet broached the subject of a successor, but it was only a matter of time. They would be looking to the future now, to war with Yscalin and the two High Westerns that stood poised to wake and unite the Draconic Army. There was no heir and no chance of one. The Nameless One was coming.

Ead returned to her duties. But the nights were for Sabran. Their secret was like wine in her. When they were behind the drapes of the bed, all else was forgotten.

In the Privy Chamber, Sabran played the virginals. She was too weak to do a great deal else, and there was little else for her to occupy her time. Doctor Bourn had said she would not be fit to hunt for at least a year.

Ead sat close by, listening. Roslain and Katryen were silent beside her, absorbed in needlework. They were making favors stitched with the royal initials, to be handed out in the city to reassure the people.

"Majesty."

Heads turned. Sir Marke Birchen, one of the Knights of the Body, was at the door in his copper-plated armor.

"Good evening, Sir Marke," Sabran said.

"The Duchess of Courage has requested an audience, Majesty. She has state papers that require your signature."

"Of course."

Sabran rose. As she did, she swayed dangerously and caught the virginals.

"Majesty—" Sir Marke started toward her, but Ead, the closest, had already steadied her. Roslain and Katryen rushed to join them.

"Sabran, are you not well?" Roslain felt her brow. "Let me fetch Doctor Bourn."

"Peace." Sabran placed a hand on her midriff and breathed in. "Ladies, let me alone to sign these papers for Her Grace, but be back by eleven to help me disrobe."

Roslain pursed her lips. "I will bring Doctor Bourn when I return," she said. "Just let him look at you, Sab, please."

Sabran nodded. As they all left, Ead looked back, and their gazes touched.

On most days, the Presence Chamber would be packed with courtiers, all waiting for Sabran to come forth so they could petition her. Now it was silent, as it had been since Sabran had taken to her rooms. Roslain went to pay a visit to her grandmother, while Katryen returned to her own rooms for supper. Not yet hungry, and with nothing to distract her from her worry about Sabran, Ead found a table in the Royal Library.

As darkness encroached, she considered, for the first time in days, what to do.

She had to tell Chassar the truth. If Sabran was right about what would happen next in Inys, Ead needed to remain here to protect her, and she needed to explain to Chassar in person. After much deliberation, she lit a candle, dipped her quill, and wrote:

From Ascalon, Queendom of Inys,
by way of Zeedeur Custom House
Late Autumn, 1005 CE

Your Excellency,

It has been far too long since I last heard from you. Doubtless
you are preoccupied with your diligent work for King Jantar and
Queen Saiyma. Will you be visiting Inys again soon?

Your assured friend and most humble ward,

Ead Duryan

She addressed it to Ambassador uq-Ispad. A courteous enquiry
from his ward.

The office of the Master of the Posts was adjacent to the library.
Ead found it deserted. She slotted the letter into a box for sorting,
along with enough coin for postage by bird. If Combe deemed it
free of suspicious words, one bird would take the letter to Zeedeur,
another to the Letter Office in Brygstad. Next it would go to the
Place of Doves, and, finally, with a postrider across the desert.

Chassar would receive her summons by high winter. The Prioress
would not be pleased when she heard her request, but once she
knew the danger, she would understand.

It was dark by the time Ead left the Royal Library, just as Sir
Tharian Lintley was coming in.

"Mistress Duryan." He dipped his head. "Good evening. I hoped
to find you here."

"Captain Lintley." Ead returned the gesture. "How do you fare?"

"Well enough," he said, but there was a notch of worry between
his brows. "Forgive me for disturbing you, Ead, but Lord Seyton
Combe asked that I bring you to him."

"Lord Seyton." Her heart raced. "Her Majesty did ask me to
return to the royal apartments by eleven."

"Her Majesty has already retired for the night. Orders from
Doctor Bourn." Lintley gave her a rueful look. "And ... well, I do
not think it was a request."

Of course. The Night Hawk did not make requests.

"Very well," Ead said, and forced a smile. "Lead on."

37

West

The Principal Secretary kept a well-ordered study on the floor below the Council Chamber. His *lair*, some called it, though the room was almost disappointing in its mundanity. A far cry from the splendor Combe must enjoy in his ancestral home of Strathurn Castle.

The corridor leading to it had been lined with retainers. All of them wore the brooch of the Knight of Courtesy, with the wings that marked them as servants of her bloodline.

"Mistress Ead Duryan, Your Grace." Lintley bowed. "A Lady of the Bedchamber."

Ead sank into a curtsy.

"Thank you, Sir Tharian." Combe was writing at a table. "That will be all."

Lintley closed the door behind him. Combe looked up at Ead and removed his spectacles.

The silence continued until a log crumbled into the fire.

"Mistress Duryan," Combe said, "I regret to inform you that Queen Sabran no longer requires your services as a Lady of the Bedchamber. The Lord Chamberlain has formally discharged you from the Upper Household and revoked its associated privileges."

Her neck prickled.

"Your Grace," she said, "I was not aware that I had given Her Majesty any offense."

Combe dredged up a smile. "Come, now, Mistress Duryan," he said. "I see you. How clever you are, and how you loathe me. You know why you are here." When she said nothing, he continued: "This afternoon, I received a report. That you were in … an inappropriate state of undress last night in the Great Bedchamber. As was Her Majesty."

Even as the feeling drained from her legs, Ead kept her composure.

"Who reported this?" she asked.

"I have eyes in every room. Even the royal apartments," Combe said. "One of the Knights of the Body, dedicated as he is to Her Majesty, nonetheless reports to me."

Ead closed her eyes. She had been so drunk on Sabran that her caution had failed her.

"Tell me, Combe," she said, "what can it possibly matter to you now what happens in her bed?"

"Because her bed is the stability of this realm. Or the undoing of that stability. Her bed, Mistress Duryan, is all that stands between Inys and chaos."

Ead stared him out.

"Her Majesty must wed again. To give the impression that she is trying to conceive the heir that will save Inys," Combe continued. "It could buy her many more years on the throne. As such, she cannot afford to make lovers of her ladies-in-waiting."

"I suppose you summoned Lord Arteloth like this," Ead said. "In the dead of night, while Sabran slept."

"Not in person. I am fortunate to have a loyal affinity of retainers, who act on my behalf. Still," Combe added wryly, "reports of my night-time arrangements have flourished. I am aware of my name at court."

"It suits you."

The fireplace flickered to his right, casting the other side of his face into shadow.

"I have rid the court of several people in my years as Principal Secretary. My predecessor would pay off those she wanted gone, but I am not so wasteful. I prefer to make use of my exiles. They become my intelligencers, and if they provide what I require, I may invite them home. Under circumstances that benefit us all."

Combe clasped his thick-knuckled fingers. "And so my web whispers to me."

"Your web has whispered lies before. I have known Sabran in body," Ead said, "but Loth never did."

Even as she spoke, she began to calculate her way out. She had to reach Sabran.

"Lord Arteloth *was* different," Combe conceded. "A virtuous man. Loyal to Her Majesty. For the first time, I was pained by what I had to do."

"Forgive me if I find my compassion wanting."

"Oh, I expect no compassion, mistress. We who are the hidden dagger of the crown—the rack-masters, the rat-catchers, the spies, and the executioners—do not often receive it."

"And yet," Ead said, "you are a descendant of the Knight of Courtesy. That sits oddly on you."

"By no means. It is my work in the shadows that allows courtesy to maintain its face at court." Combe observed her for a few moments. "I meant what I said to you at the dance. You had a friend in me. I admired the way you ascended without treading on others, and how you comported yourself . . . but you crossed a line that cannot be crossed. Not with her." He looked almost sorry. "I wish it were otherwise."

"Strip me from her side, and she *will* know. And she will find some means to be rid of you."

"I hope you are mistaken, Mistress Duryan, for her sake. I fear you misjudge how fragile her rule has become now there is no hope of an heir." Combe held her gaze. "She needs me more than ever. I am faithful to her for her qualities as a ruler, and for the legacy of her house, but some of my fellow Dukes Spiritual will not brook her on that throne. Not now she has failed in her chief duty as a Berethnet queen."

Ead kept her expression carefully blank, but a wardrum beat within her breast. "Who?"

"Oh, I have my suspicions as to who will act first. I mean to be her shield in the days to come," Combe said. "You, unhappily, do not factor into my plans. You threaten them."

Perhaps they will not even wait for me to die before the infighting begins.

"Falden," Combe said, louder, "would you come in?" The door opened, and one of his retainers entered. "If you would be so kind as to see Mistress Duryan to the coach."

"Yes, Your Grace."

The man took Ead by the shoulder. As he steered her toward the door, Combe said, "Wait, Master Falden. I have changed my mind." His face was expressionless. "Kill her."

Ead stiffened. At once, the retainer grabbed her by the hair and pulled, baring her throat to his blade.

Heat flared in her hands. She twisted the arm that held her, and in a welter of limbs, the retainer was on the floor and crying in agony, his shoulder thrust out of the joint.

"There," Combe said softly.

The retainer panted, clutching his arm. Ead looked at her hands. Reacting to a threat, the very last of her siden, her deepest reserve, had forced itself to the surface.

"Lady Truyde spread rumors of your sorcery some time ago." Combe took in the glow in her fingertips. "I ignored them, of course. The jealous spite of a young courtier, no more. Then I heard of your ... *curious* skill with blades during the ambush."

"I taught myself to protect Queen Sabran," Ead said, outwardly calm, but her blood hammered.

"So I see." Combe sighed through his nose. "You are the watcher in the night."

She had revealed her true nature. There could be no return from this.

"I do not believe in sorcery, Mistress Duryan. Perhaps it is alchemy in your hands. What I do believe is that you never came here out of a desire to serve Queen Sabran, as you claimed. More likely Ambassador uq-Ispad placed you here as a spy. Even greater reason for me to send you far away from court."

Ead took a step toward him. The Night Hawk did not move or flinch.

"I have wondered," Ead said, her voice low, "if you are the Cupbearer. If you arranged those cutthroats to come ... to frighten her into marrying Lievelyn. If that is why you want to be rid of me. Her protector. After all, what is a cupbearer but a trusted servant to the crown, who at any moment could poison the wine?"

Combe offered a heavy smile.

"How easy it would be for you to lay the blame for all ills at my doorstep," he murmured. "The Cupbearer *is* near at hand, Mistress Duryan. I have no doubt of that. But I am only the Night Hawk." He sat back. "A coach is waiting at the palace gates."

"And where will it take me?"

"Somewhere I can keep a sharp eye on you. Until I have seen where the pieces fall," he said. "You know the greatest secret in Virtudom. One wag of your tongue could bring Inys to its knees."

"So you will silence me with incarceration." Ead paused. "Or do you mean to be rid of me on a more permanent basis?"

The corner of his mouth twitched. "You wound me. Murder is not courteous."

He would keep her somewhere where neither Sabran nor the Priory would be able to find her. She could not get into that coach, or she would never see daylight again.

This time, many pairs of hands were on her. The light waned from her fingers as they escorted her out.

She had no intention of letting Combe lock her away. Or ending her with a knife to the back. As they left the Alabastrine Tower, she slipped a hand beneath her cloak and unlaced her sleeves. The retainers marched her toward the gates of the palace.

Quick as an arrow, she pulled her arms free of her gown. Before the retainers could snare her, she had vaulted over the nearest wall, into the Privy Garden. Shouts of surprise went up.

Her heart battered her ribs. A window was open above her. The Queen Tower was smooth-walled, impossible to climb, but wood-vines snaked up it, thick enough to take her weight. Ead hooked her foot on to a knotted vine.

Wind blew her hair across her eyes as she ascended. The wood-vines creaked darkly. A slender vine snapped between her fingers, and her belly tightened, but she snatched for a new handhold and pressed on. Finally, she slid through the open window, landing in silence.

Into the deserted corridors. Up the stairs to the royal apartments. Outside the darkened Presence Chamber stood a line of armed retainers in black tabards. Each tabard was embroidered with the twin goblets of the Duchess of Justice.

"I wish to see the queen," Ead said breathlessly. "At once."

"Her Majesty is in bed, Mistress Duryan, and night duty has begun," a woman answered.

"Lady Roslain, then."

"The doors to the Great Bedchamber are locked," was the curt reply, "and will not be unlocked until morning."

"I *must* see the queen," Ead cut in, frustrated. "It is a matter of the utmost importance."

The retainers exchanged glances. Finally, one of them, visibly irritated, took a candle and walked into the dark.

Heart thumping, Ead gathered her breath. She hardly knew what she would say to Sabran. Only that she had to make her aware of what Combe was doing.

A blear-eyed Roslain appeared in her bedgown. Strands of hair escaped her braid.

"Ead," she said, her voice taut with impatience, "what in the world is the matter?"

"I need to see Sabran."

Lips pinched, Roslain took her aside.

"Her Majesty has a fever." She looked grim. "Doctor Bourn says that bed rest will resolve it, but my grandmother has stationed her retainers here for additional protection until she is well. I will stay to nurse her."

"You must tell her." Ead grasped her arm. "Roslain, Combe is sending me into exile. You need to—"

"Mistress Duryan!"

Roslain flinched. Retainers wearing the winged book were at the end of the corridor, led by two Knights of the Body.

"Seize her," Sir Marke Birchen shouted. "Ead Duryan, you are arrested. Stop at once!"

Ead flung open the nearest door and rushed into the night.

"Ead," Roslain cried after her, horror-struck. "Sir Marke, what is the meaning of this?"

A line of balconies took Ead to another open door. She ran blindly through the corridors until she slammed through the door of the Privy Kitchen, where Tallys, the scullion, crouched in the corner, eating a custard tart. When Ead burst in, she gasped.

"Mistress Duryan." She looked terrified. "Mistress, I was only—"

Ead raised a finger to her lips. "Tallys," she said, "is there a way out?"

The scullion nodded at once. She took Ead by the hand and led her to a small door, hidden behind a drape.

"This way. The Servant Stair," she whispered. "Are you leaving forever?"

"For now," Ead said.

"Why?"

"I cannot tell you, child." Ead looked her dead in the eye. "Tell no one you saw me. Swear it on your honor as a lady, Tallys."

Tallys swallowed. "I swear it."

Footsteps outside. Ead ducked through the door, and Tallys bolted it behind her.

She hurried down the stair beyond. If she was to leave the palace, she would need a horse and a disguise. There was one person left who might give them to her.

In her quarters, Margret Beck sat in her nightgown. She looked up with a gasp when Ead entered.

"What is the meaning of—" She stood. "Ead?"

Ead shut the door behind her. "Meg, I have no time. I must—"

Almost as soon as the words were out of her mouth, a metallic knock came, the sound of knuckles sheathed in a gauntlet.

"Lady Margret." Knock. "Lady Margret, this is Dame Joan Dale, of the Knights of the Body." Another knock. "My lady, I come on urgent business. Open the door."

Margret motioned Ead toward her unmade bed. Ead pushed herself under it and let the valance fall behind her. She heard Margret walk across the flagstones.

"Forgive me, Dame Joan. I was sleeping." Her voice was slow and hoarse. "Is something the matter?"

"Lady Margret, the Principal Secretary has ordered the arrest of Mistress Ead Duryan. Have you seen her?"

"Ead?" Margret sat down on the bed, as if stunned. "This is impossible. On what grounds?"

She was a consummate actor. Her voice wavered at the cross-roads between shock and disbelief.

"I am not at liberty to speak with you further on the subject." Armored feet crossed the room. "If you do see Mistress Duryan, sound the alarm at once."

"Of course."

The Knight of the Body left, closing the door behind her. Margret slid the bolt across and drew the curtains before she hauled Ead from under the bed.

"Ead," she whispered, "what in damsam have you done?"

"I stepped too close to Sabran. Just like Loth."

"No." Margret stared at her. "You used to tread so *carefully* in this court, Ead—"

"I know. Forgive me." She extinguished the candles and stole a look between the curtains. Guards and armed squires were all over the grounds. "Meg, I need your help. I must return to the Ersyr, or Combe will kill me."

"He wouldn't dare."

"He cannot let me leave the palace alive. Not knowing—" Ead faced her again. "You will hear things about me, things that will make you doubt me, but you must know that I love the queen. And I am certain she is in grave danger."

"From the Cupbearer?"

"And her own Dukes Spiritual. I think they mean to move against her," Ead said. "Combe has some part in it, I am sure. You *must* watch Sabran, Meg. Stay close to her."

Margret searched her face. "Until you return?"

Ead met her expectant gaze. Any promise she made to Margret now, she might not be able to keep.

"Until I return," she finally said.

This seemed to nerve Margret. Jaw set, she went to her press and tossed a woollen cloak, a ruffled shirt, and a kirtle on to the bed. "You won't get far in all that finery," she said. "Fortunate that we are the same height."

Ead stripped to her shift and put on the new clothes, thanking the Mother for Margret Beck. Once the cloak was fastened and the hood up, Margret led her to the door.

"Downstairs is a painting of Lady Brilda Glade. There is a stair to the guardhouse behind it. From there, you can circle around the Privy Garden to the stables. Take Valour."

That horse was her pride and joy. "Meg," Ead said, grasping her hands, "they will know you helped me."

"So be it." She pressed a silk purse on Ead. "Here. Enough to buy you passage to Zeedeur."

"I will remember this kindness, Margret."

Margret embraced her, so tightly Ead could not breathe. "I know there is little chance of it," she said thickly, "but if you should meet Loth on the road—"

"I know."

"I love you like my own sister, Ead Duryan. We *will* meet again." She pressed a kiss to her cheek. "May the Saint go with you."

"I know no Saint," Ead said honestly, and saw her friend's confusion, "but I take your blessing, Meg."

She left the chamber and made haste through the corridors, avoiding the guards. When she found the portrait, she descended the stair beyond and emerged in a passage with a window at its end. She hurdled through it and into the night.

Inside the Royal Mews, all was dark. Valour, a gift to Margret from her father for her twentieth birthday, was the envy of every rider at court. He filled the stall at eighteen hands. Ead placed a gloved hand on his blood-bay coat.

Valour snorted as she saddled him. If rumor had it true, he could outrun even Sabran's horses.

Ead wedged her boot into the stirrup, mounted, and snapped the reins. At once, Valour wheeled out of his stall and charged through the open doors. They were through the gates of Ascalon Palace before Ead heard the cry, and by then there was no catching her. Arrows rained in her wake. Valour let out a whinny, but she whispered to him in Selinyi, urging him on.

As the archers stood down, Ead looked back at the place that had been her prison and her home for eight years. The place where she had met Loth and Margret, two people she had not expected to befriend. The place where she had grown to care for the seed of the Deceiver.

The guards came after her. They hunted a ghost, for Ead Duryan was no more.

She rode hard for six days and nights through the sleet, stopping only to rest Valour. She had to stay ahead of the heralds. If Combe had his way, they would already be taking word of her escape through the country.

Instead of taking the South Pass, she traversed country lanes and fields. The snow began again on the fourth day. Her journey took her through the bountiful county of the Downs, where Lord and Lady Honeybrook had their seat at Dulcet Court, to the town of Crow Coppice. She watered Valour and filled her wineskin before returning to the road under cover of darkness.

She focused on anything but Sabran, but even the swiftest riding left room for thoughts to prey. Now that she was sick, she was even more vulnerable than she had been before.

As Ead urged the gelding across a farmstead, she damned her own folly. The Inysh court had softened her heart.

She could not tell the Prioress how it had been with Sabran. Even Chassar might not understand. She hardly understood herself. All she knew was that she could not leave Sabran at the mercy of the Dukes Spiritual.

When dawn broke on the seventh day, the sea bruised the horizon. To the untaught eye, the cliffs simply fell away, land planing seamlessly into water. One could look at it and never imagine that a city stood between them.

Today, smoke betrayed its presence. A thick, dark cloud of it, billowing skyward.

Ead watched for a long moment. That was more than chimney smoke. She rode to the edge of the cliffs and surveyed the rooftops below.

"Come, Valour," she murmured, and dismounted. She led him to the first set of steps.

Perchling was a mess. Cobblestones splashed with blood. Bone char and melted flesh, oily on the wind. The living wept over the remains of their loved ones, or stood in confusion. No one paid any mind to Ead.

A dark-haired woman was sitting outside the remains of a bakehouse. "You there," Ead said to her. "What happened here?"

The woman was shivering. "They came in the night. Servants of the High Westerns," she whispered. "The war machines drove 'em away, but not before they did ... this." A tear dripped to her jaw. "There will be another Grief of Ages before the year is out."

"Not if I have anything to say about it," Ead said, too softly for her to hear.

She took Valour down the stair to the beach. Catapults and other artillery lay wrecked on the sand. Smoking corpses were littered here and there—soldier and wyrm, tangled in eternal battle, even in death. Cockatrices and basilisks were strewn about in grotesque contortions, tongues lolling, eyes pecked by gulls. Ead walked alongside the gelding.

"Hush," she said when he whickered. "Hush, Valour. The dead have made their beds upon this sand."

From the looks of things, all the Draconic creatures involved in this attack had been killed, either by the war machines or the sword. Sabran would know about it soon. Fortunate for her that her navy was stationed at ports all over Inys, or the whole fleet might have burned.

Ead crossed the beach. The wind blew down her hood, cooling the sweat on her brow. Perchling would ordinarily be full of ships, but each one had been set on fire. Those that were intact would need work before they could sail. Only a rowing boat looked untouched.

"Lost, are you?"

A knife was in her grasp before she knew it, and she spun, poised to throw. A woman held up her hands.

"Easy." She wore a wide-brimmed hat. "Easy."

"Who are you, Yscal?"

"Estina Melaugo. Of the *Rose Eternal*." The woman cocked an eyebrow. "You're a little too late to board a ship."

"So I see. The boat is yours, I presume."

"It is."

"Will you take me?" Ead sheathed her knife. "I seek passage to Zeedeur."

Melaugo looked her up and down. "What do I call you?"

"Meg."

"Meg." Her smile said she knew full well it was an alias. "From your filthy cloak, I'd say you've been riding hard for a few days. Not much sleep, either, by the looks of you."

"You would ride hard if the Night Hawk wanted your head."

Melaugo grinned, showing a tiny gap between her front teeth. "Another enemy of the Night Hawk. He ought to start paying us."

"What do you mean?"

"Oh, nothing." Melaugo motioned to the horizon. "The ship is out there. I'd usually expect coin for safe passage—but perhaps, with so many wyrms in the sky, we should all be kinder to each other."

"Soft words for a pirate."

"Piracy was more of a necessity than a choice for me, Meg." Melaugo eyed Valour. "You can't take that horse."

"The horse," Ead said, "goes where I go."

"Don't make me leave you behind, Meg." When Ead kept her hand on Valour, Melaugo folded her arms and sighed. "We'll have to bring the ship in. The captain will expect compensation for that, if not for you."

Ead tossed her the purse. Inysh money would be useless in the South.

"I take no charity, pirate," she said.

It would not take long to reach Mentendon. Ead lay in her berth and tried to sleep. When she did, she was pierced by unquiet dreams of Sabran and the faceless Cupbearer. When she did not, she padded to the deck and gazed at the crystal stars above the sails, letting them calm her mind.

The captain, Gian Harlowe, stepped from his cabin to smoke his pipe. This was the man who had loved the Queen Mother, according to rumor. Dark eyes, a stern mouth, pockmarks on his brow and cheeks. He looked as if he had been carved by the sea wind.

Their gazes met across the ship, and Harlowe nodded. Ead returned the gesture.

At first light, the sky was a smear of ash, and Zeedeur was on the horizon. This was where Truyde had spent her childhood, where she had first conceived her perilous ideas. It was here that the death of Aubrecht Lievelyn had been written in the stars.

Estina Melaugo joined Ead at the bow.

"Be careful out there," she said. "It's a hard ride from here to the Ersyr, and there are wyrms in those mountains."

"I fear no wyrm." Ead nodded to her. "Thank you, Melaugo. Farewell."

"Farewell, Meg." Melaugo pulled down the brim of her hat and turned away. "Safe travels."

Flanked by the sea and the River Hundert, the Port of Zeedeur was shaped like an arrowhead. Canals hatched the northern quarter, lined with elegant houses and elm trees. Ead had passed through the city only once before, when she and Chassar had sailed for Inys. Here the houses were built in the traditional Mentish style, with bell gables. The crocketed spire of the Port Sanctuary reached up from the heart of the city.

It was the last sanctuary she would see for some time.

She mounted Valour and spurred him past the markets and book peddlers, toward the salt road that would lead her to the capital. In a few days, she would be in Brygstad, and then she would be on her way to the Ersyr—far away from the court she had deceived for so long. From the West.

And from Sabran.

III

A Witch to Live

The bay-trees in our country are all withered,
And meteors fright the fixèd stars of heaven.

—William Shakespeare

38

East

A bell rang full-throated every morning at first light. On hearing it, the scholars of Feather Island folded away their bedding and proceeded to the bathhouse. Once they had washed, they would eat together, and then, before the elders woke, they would have an hour for prayer and reflection. That hour was her favorite time of day.

She knelt before the image of the great Kwiriki. Water trickled down the walls of the underground cavern and dripped into a pool. Only a lantern fended off the dark.

This statue of the Great Elder was not like those she had prayed before in Seiiki. This one showed him with parts of some of the forms he had taken in his lifetime: the antlers of a stag, the talons of a bird, and the tail of a snake.

It was some time before Tané became aware of the *clunk* of an iron leg on rock. She rose to see the learnèd Elder Vara standing at the entrance to the grotto.

"Scholar Tané." He inclined his head. "Forgive me for disturbing your reflection."

She bowed in return.

Elder Vara was thought by most of the residents of Vane Hall to be an eccentric sort. A thin man with weathered brown skin and crow footprints around his eyes, he always had a smile and a kind word for her. His chief duty was to protect and manage the repository, but he also acted as a healer when the need arose.

"I would be honored if you would join me at the repository this morning," he said. "Someone else will see to your chores. And please," he added, "take your time."

Tané hesitated. "I am not permitted in the repository."

"Well, you are today."

He was gone before she could answer. Slowly, she knelt again.

This cavern was the only place where she could forget herself. It was one of a honeycomb of grottos behind a waterfall, shared between the Seiikinese scholars on this side of the isle.

She fanned out the incense and bowed to the statue. Its jewel eyes glinted at her.

At the top of the steps, she emerged into daylight. The sky was the yellow of unbleached silk. She picked her way barefoot across the stepping stones.

Feather Island, lonely and rugged, lay far away from anywhere. Its steep cliff faces and ever-present hood of cloud presented an imposing front to any ship that dared come near. Snakes lazed on its stony beaches. It was home to people from all over the East—and to the bones of the great Kwiriki, who was said to have laid himself to rest at the bottom of the ravine that divided the island, which was called the Path of the Elder. It was also said that his bones kept the island wreathed in fog, for a dragon continued to attract water long after its death. It was why Seiiki was so misty.

Seiiki.

Windward Hall stood on Cape Quill to the north, while Vane Hall, the smaller—where Tané had been placed—was set high on a long-dead volcano, surrounded by forest. There were ice caves just behind it, where lava had once flowed. To get between the hermitages, one had to take a rickety bridge across the ravine.

There were no other settlements. The scholars were alone in the vastness of the sea.

The hermitage was a puzzle-box of knowledge. Each new piece of wisdom was earned with understanding of the last. Ensconced in its halls, Tané had learned first about fire and water. Fire, the element of the winged demons, required constant feeding. It was

408

the element of war and greed and vengeance—always hungry, never satisfied.

Water needed no coal or tinder to exist. It could shape itself to any space. It nourished flesh and earth and asked for nothing in return. That was why the dragons of the East, lords of rain and lake and sea, would always triumph over the fire-breathers. When the ocean had swallowed the world and humankind was washed away, still they would abide.

A fish-hawk snatched a bitterling from the river. A chill wind soughed between the trees. The Autumn Dragon would soon return to her slumber, and the Winter Dragon would wake in the twelfth lake.

As she stepped on to the roofed walkway that led back to the hermitage, Tané wrapped her cloth hood over her hair, which she had cut short before she had left Ginura, so it grazed her collarbones. Miduchi Tané had long hair. The ghost she had become did not.

After reflection, she would usually sweep the floors, help gather fruit from the forest, clear the graves of leaves, or feed the chickens. There were no servants on Feather Island, so the scholars shared the menial duties, with the young and strong-bodied taking the most. Strange that Elder Vara had asked her to come to the repository, where the most important documents were kept.

When she had arrived on Feather Island, she had taken to her room and lain there for days. She had not eaten a morsel or spoken a word. They had stripped her of her weapons in Ginura, so she had torn herself apart within. All she had wanted was to mourn her dream until she breathed no more.

It was Elder Vara who had shaken a semblance of life back into her. When she had grown weak with hunger, he had coaxed her into the sunshine. He had shown her flowers she had never seen. The next day, he had prepared a meal for her, and she had not wanted to disappoint him by leaving it untouched.

Now the other scholars called her the Ghost of Vane Hall. She could eat and work and read like the rest of them, but her gaze was always in a world where Susa still lived.

Tané stepped off the walkway and made for the repository. Only the elders were usually permitted to enter it. As she approached its steps, Feather Island rumbled. She dropped to the ground and covered her head. As the earthshake rattled the hermitage, she hissed through her teeth in sudden pain.

The knot in her side was a knifepoint. Cold pain—the bite of ice against bare skin, freezeburn in her innards. Tears jolted into her eyes as waves of agony pitched through her.

She must have dipped out of consciousness. A gentle voice called her back. "Tané." Paper-dry hands took her arms. "Scholar Tané, can you speak?"

Yes, she tried to say, but nothing came out.

The earthshake had stopped. The pain had not. Elder Vara scooped her into his bony arms. It chagrined her to be lifted like a child, but the pain was more than she could stand.

He took her into the courtyard behind the repository and set her on a stone bench beside the fishpond. A kettle waited at its edge.

"I was going to take you for a walk on the cliffs today," he said, "but I see now that you need to rest. Another time." He poured tea for them both. "Are you in pain?"

Her rib cage felt packed with ice. "An old injury. It is nothing, Elder Vara." Her voice was husky. "These earthshakes come so often now."

"Yes. It is as if the world wants to change its shape, like the dragons of old."

She thought of her conversations with the great Nayimathun. As she tried to steady her breathing, Elder Vara took a seat beside her.

"I am afraid of earthshakes," he confessed. "When I still lived in Seiiki, my mother and I would huddle in our little house in Basai when the ground trembled, and we would tell each other stories to keep our minds off it."

Tané tried to smile. "I do not remember if my mother did the same."

As she spoke, the ground shook again.

"Well," Elder Vara said, "perhaps I could tell you one instead. In keeping with tradition."

"Of course."

He handed her a steaming cup. Tané accepted it in silence.

"In the time before the Great Sorrow, a fire-breather flew to the Empire of the Twelve Lakes and ripped the pearl from the throat of the Spring Dragon, she who brings flowers and soft rains. The winged demons like nothing more than to greedily amass treasure, and no treasure is worth more than a dragon pearl. Though she was badly wounded, the Spring Dragon forbade anyone from pursuing the thief for fear they might also be hurt—but a girl decided she would go. She was twelve years old, small and quick, and so light on her feet that her brothers called her Little Shadow-girl.

"As the Spring Dragon mourned for her pearl, a most unnatural winter fell over the land. Though the cold burned her skin and she had no shoes, the Little Shadow-girl walked to the mountain where the fire-breather had buried its hoard. While the beast was away hunting, she stole into its cave and took back the pearl of the Spring Dragon."

It would have been a heavy treasure to bear. The smallest dragon pearl was as big as a human skull.

"The fire-breather returned just as she had laid hands upon the pearl. Enraged, it snapped its jaws at the thief who had dared enter its lair and tore a piece of flesh from her thigh. The girl dived into the river, and the current whisked her away from the cave. She escaped with the pearl—but when she pulled herself out of the water, she could find nobody who would stitch her wound, for the blood made people fear that she had the red sickness."

Tané watched Elder Vara through tendrils of steam. "What happened to her?"

"She died at the feet of the Spring Dragon. And as the flowers bloomed once more, and the sun thawed the snow, the Spring Dragon declared that the river the Little Shadow-girl had swum in would be named in her honor, for the child had reunited her with the pearl that was her heart. It is said that her ghost wanders its banks, protecting travelers."

Never had Tané heard a tale of such bravery from an ordinary person.

"There are some who find the story sad. Others who find it to be a beautiful example of self-sacrifice," Elder Vara said.

Another shock went through the ground, and inside Tané something called out in answer. She tried to keep the pain from her face, but Elder Vara was too sharp of eye.

"Tané," he said, "may I see this old injury?"

Tané lifted her tunic just enough for him to see the scar. In the daylight, it looked more prominent than usual.

"May I?" Elder Vara asked. When she nodded, he touched it with one finger and frowned. "There is a swelling underneath."

It was hard as a pebble. "My teacher said it happened when I was a child," Tané said. "Before I came to the Houses of Learning."

"You never saw a doctor, then, to see if something could be done?"

She shook her head and covered the scar.

"I think we should open your side, Tané," Elder Vara said decisively. "Let me send for the Seiikinese doctor who attends us. Most growths of this sort are harmless, but occasionally they can eat away at the body from within. We would not want you to die needlessly, child, like the Little Shadow-girl."

"She did not die needlessly," Tané said, her gaze blank. "With her dying breath, she restored the joy of a dragon and, in doing so, restored the world. Is there a more honorable thing to do with a life?"

39

South

A caravan of forty souls was weaving through the desert. In the faint light of sundown, the sand glittered.

Bestriding a camel, Eadaz uq-Nāra watched the sky deepen to red. Her skin had tanned to a deep brown, and her hair, cut to the shoulders, was covered by a white *pargh*.

The caravan she had joined at the Place of Doves was now in the northern reaches of the Burlah—the stretch of desert that rolled toward Rumelabar. The Burlah was the domain of the Nuram tribes. The caravan had already crossed paths with some of their merchants, who had shared their supplies and warned that wyrms had been venturing beyond the mountains, doubtless emboldened by rumors that another High Western had been sighted in the East.

Ead had stopped at the Buried City on her way to Rauca. The Dreadmount, birthplace of wyrmkind, had been as terrible as she remembered it, jutting like a broken sword into the sky. Once or twice, as she walked between crumbled pillars, she had glimpsed the distant flicker of wings at its summit. Wyverns flocking to their cradle of life.

In the shadow of the mountain were the remains of the once-great city of Gulthaga. What little was left on the surface belied the structure beneath. Somewhere inside, Jannart utt Zeedeur had met his end in the pursuit of knowledge.

Ead had considered following him, to see if she could find out more about this Long-Haired Star, the comet that balanced the world. She had scoured the ruins for the route he had used to burrow under the petrified ash. After hours of searching, she had been close to giving up when she saw a tunnel, barely wide enough to crawl in. It was choked by a rockfall.

There would be little point in exploring. After all, she knew no Gulthaganian—but Truyde's prophecy was a worm in her ear.

She had thought her return to the South would breathe life back into her. Indeed, her first step into the Desert of the Unquiet Dream had felt like a rebirth. Having left Valour safe in the Harmur Pass, she trekked alone through the sands to Rauca. Seeing the city again restored her strength, but it was soon lashed away by the winds that blazed off the Burlah.

Her skin had forgotten the touch of the desert. All she was now was another dusty traveler, and her memory was a mirage. Some days she almost believed that she had never worn fine silks and jewels in the court of the Western queen. That she had never been Ead Duryan.

A scorpion made a dash past her camel. The other travelers were singing to pass the time. Ead listened in silence. It had been a lifetime since she had heard anyone sing in Ersyri.

A songbird perched in a cypress tree,
And, lonesome, called out for a mate to wed.
"Dance, dance," it sang, "on the dunes tonight.
"Come, come, my love, and we'll both take flight."

Rumelabar was still so far away. It would take weeks for the caravan to conquer the Burlah in winter, when the bitter nights could kill as swiftly as the sun. She wondered whether Chassar had received word of her departure from Inys, which would have diplomatic ramifications for the Ersyr.

"We will make for the Nuram camp," the caravan-master called. "A storm is coming."

The message was passed down the line. Ead held the reins tighter in frustration. She had no time to waste while a storm blew out of the Burlah.

"Eadaz."

She turned in her saddle. Another camel had fallen into step with hers. Ragab was a grizzled postrider, headed south with a bag of mail.

"A sandstorm," he said, his deep voice weary. "I think this journey will never end."

Ead enjoyed riding with Ragab, who was full of interesting stories from his travels and claimed to have made the crossing nearly a hundred times. He had survived an attack by a basilisk on his village, which had killed his family, blinded him in one eye, and scarred him all over. The other travelers looked at him with pity.

They looked at Ead with pity, too. She had heard them whisper that she was a wandering spirit in the body of a woman, trapped between worlds. Only Ragab had dared to come close.

"I had forgotten how harsh the Burlah is," Ead said. "How desolate."

"Have you crossed it before?"

"Twice."

"When you have made the crossing as many times as I have, you will see beauty in that desolation. Though of all our deserts in the Ersyr," he said, "the one I like best will always be the Desert of the Unquiet Dream. My favorite story, as a child, was how it received its name."

"That is a very sad tale."

"To me, it is beautiful. A tale of love."

Ead reached for her saddle flask. "It has been a long time since I heard it." She removed the stopper. "Perhaps you might tell it to me?"

"If you wish," Ragab said. "We have some way to go."

She let Ragab sip from her flask before she drank herself. He cleared his throat.

"Once there was a king, beloved by his people. He ruled from a blueglass palace in Rauca. His bride, the Butterfly Queen, who he had loved more than anything in the world, had died young, and he grieved for her pitifully. His officials ruled in his stead while he fell into a prison of his own making, surrounded by wealth he despised. No jewels or coins could buy him the woman he had lost. And so he became known as the Melancholy King.

"One night, he rose from his bed for the first time in a year to behold the red moon. When he looked down from his window— why, he could not believe his eyes. There was his queen, in the palace gardens, dressed in the same clothes she had worn on the day he wed her, calling to him to join her on the sands. Her eyes were laughing, and she held the rose he had given her when they first met. Thinking himself in a dream, the king walked from the palace, through the city, and into the desert—without food or water, without a robe, without even his shoes. He walked and walked, following the shadow in the distance. Even as the cold snaked over his skin, even as he grew weak with thirst and ghouls stalked his footsteps, he told himself, *I am only dreaming. I am only dreaming.* He walked after his love, knowing he would reach her, and that he would spend one more night with her—just one more, in his dream, at least—before he woke in his bed alone."

Ead remembered the next part of the story. A shiver coursed through her.

"Of course," Ragab said, "the Melancholy King was not dreaming at all, but following a mirage. The desert had played a trick on him. He died there, and his bones were lost to the sand. And the desert had its name." He patted his camel when it snorted. "Love and fear do strange things to our souls. The dreams they bring, those dreams that leave us drenched in salt water and gasping for breath as if we might die—those, we call unquiet dreams. And only the scent of a rose can avert them."

Gooseflesh freckled Ead as she remembered another rose, tucked behind a pillow.

The caravan arrived at the camp just as the sandstorm crested the horizon. The travelers were hurried into a central tent, where Ead sat down with Ragab on the cushions, and the Nuram, who were fond of guests, shared their cheese and salted bread. They also passed around a water-pipe, which Ead turned down. Ragab, however, was all too pleased to take it.

"None of us will sleep well tonight." He blew out a scented plume. "Once the storm is over, we should reach Gaudaya Oasis in three days, by my reckoning. Then the long road lies ahead of us."

Ead gazed at the moon.

"How long do these storms last?" she asked Ragab.

Ragab shook his head. "Hard to say. It could be minutes or an hour, or more."

Ead halved a round of flatbread with her fingers as a Nuram woman poured a sweet pink tea for them both. Even the desert conspired against her. She burned to leave the caravan and ride for as long as it took to reach Chassar—but she was not the Melancholy King. Fear would not make her take leave of her senses. She was not proud enough to think she could cross the Burlah alone.

While the other travelers listened to the story of the Blueglass Thief of Drayasta, she beat the sand from her clothes and chewed on a soft twig to cleanse her teeth, then found a place to sleep behind a drape.

The Nuram would often sleep under the stars, but now, with a sandstorm roaring overhead, they shut themselves into their tents. Gradually, the nomads and their guests began to retire, and the oil lamps were doused.

Ead covered herself with a woven blanket. Darkness enwrapped her, and she dreamed herself back to Sabran, flesh aching in remembrance of her touch. Then the Mother had mercy, and she slipped into a dreamless sleep.

A *thump* woke her.

Her eyes snapped open. The tent shuddered around her, but beneath the tumult, she could hear something outside. Something sure-footed. She slid a dagger from her pack and stepped into the desert night.

Sand raged through the camp. Ead held her *pargh* over her mouth. When she saw the silhouette, she flicked her dagger up, sure it was a wyverling—but then it stepped, in all its glory, through the dust of the Burlah.

She smiled.

Parspa was the last known *hawiz*. White but for their bronze-tipped wings, the birds could grow as large as wyverns, which had bred with them to create the cockatrice. Chassar, who had a fondness for birds, had found Parspa when she was still in her egg and brought her to the Priory. Now she answered only to him. Ead collected her belongings and climbed onto the bird, and soon they left the camp behind.

They were fleeing from the rising sun. Ead knew they were getting closer when salt cedar fingered through the sand, and then, all at once, they were over the Domain of Lasia.

Her birthplace was a land of red deserts and rugged peaks, of hidden caves and thundering waterfalls, of golden beaches foamed by surf from the Halassa Sea. For the most part, it was a dry country, like the Ersyr—but vast rivers flowed through Lasia, and greenery cleaved to them. Looking at the plains below her, Ead felt the homesickness fade at last. No matter how much of the world she saw, she would always believe this was its most beautiful place.

Soon Parspa was soaring over the ruins of Yikala. Ead and Jondu had gone scavenging there many times as children, eager for trinkets from the days of the Mother.

Parspa banked toward the Lasian Basin. It was this vast and ancient forest, blooded by the River Minara, that cloaked the Priory. By the time the sun had risen, Parspa was above its trees, her shadow coasting over the close-knit canopy.

The bird finally descended, touching down in one of the few clearings in the forest. Ead slid off her back.

"Thank you, my friend," she said in Selinyi. "I know the way from here."

Parspa took off without a sound.

Ead strode between the trees, feeling as small as one of their leaves. Strangler fig clambered up their trunks. Her exhausted feet recalled the way, even if her mind had mislaid it. The mouth of the cave was somewhere close, guarded by powerful wardings, hidden in the thickest foliage. It would take her deep into the ground, to the labyrinth of secret halls.

A whisper in her blood. She turned. A woman stood in a pool of sunlight, her belly great with child.

"Nairuj," Ead said.

"Eadaz," the woman answered. "Welcome home."

———————

Light splintered through arched lattice windows. Ead became aware that she was in bed, her head supported by silk cushions. The soles of her feet were on fire after so many days on the road.

A muffled roar made her sit up. Breathing hard, she groped for a weapon.

"Eadaz." Callused hands cupped hers, startling her. "Eadaz, be still."

She stared at the bearded face before her. Dark eyes that turned up at the corners, like hers.

"Chassar," she whispered. "Chassar. Is this—?"

"Yes." He smiled. "You're home, beloved."

She pressed her face against his chest. His robes soaked up the wet on her lashes.

"You came a long way." His hand moved over her sand-crusted hair. "If you had written before you left Ascalon, I could have sent Parspa much sooner."

Ead grasped his arm. "I had no time. Chassar," she said, "I must tell you. Sabran is in danger—the Dukes Spiritual, I think they mean to fight for her throne—"

"Nothing in Inys matters now. The Prioress will speak with you soon."

She slept again. When she woke, the sky was the red of dying embers. Lasia remained warm for most of the year, but a chill clung to the evening wind. She rose and wrapped herself in a brocaded robe before walking to the balcony. And she beheld it.

The orange tree.

It reached up from the heart of the Lasian Basin, larger and more beautiful than she had dreamed it in Inys. White flowers dotted its branches and the grass. Around it lay the Vale of Blood, where the Mother had vanquished the Nameless One. Ead released her breath.

She was home.

The underground chambers came to an end in this valley. Only these rooms—the sunrooms—had the privilege of looking over it. The Prioress had honored her by allowing her to rest in one. They were usually reserved for prayer and childbirth.

Three thousand feet of unbroken water thundered from high above. That was the roar she had heard. Siyāti uq-Nāra had named the falls the Wail of Galian to mock his cowardice. Far below her, the River Minara crashed through the valley, feeding the roots of the tree.

Her gaze flitted over its labyrinth of branches. Fruit was nestled here and there, rutilant upon the bough. The sight dried her mouth. No water could sate the thirst that throbbed inside her.

As she returned to her chamber, she stopped and pressed her brow against the cool, rose-colored stone of the doorway.

Home.

A low growl lifted the hairs on her nape. She turned to see a full-grown ichneumon in the doorway.

"Aralaq?"

"Eadaz." His voice was low and stony. "You were a pup when I last saw you."

She could not believe the size of him. Once he had been tiny enough to fit in her lap. Now he was massive and deep-chested, standing a head taller than she was. "So were you." Her face softened into a smile. "Have you been guarding me all day?"

"Three days."

The smile faded. "Three," she murmured. "I must have been more exhausted than I thought."

"You have dwelt for too long without the orange tree."

Aralaq padded to her side and nosed her hand. Ead chuckled as he rasped his tongue over her face. She remembered him as a squeaking bundle of fur, all eyes and snuffles, tripping over his long tail.

One of the sisters had found him orphaned in the Ersyr and brought him to the Priory, where she and Jondu had been charged with his care. They had fed him on milk and scraps of snake meat.

"You should bathe." Aralaq licked her fingers. "You smell like camel."

Ead tutted. "Thank you. You have a certain pungent aroma of your own, you know."

She took the oil lamp from her bedside and followed him.

He led her through the tunnels and up flights of steps. They passed two Lasian men—Sons of Siyāti, who attended on the sisters. Both dipped their heads as Ead passed.

When they reached the bathhouse, Aralaq nudged her hip.

"Go. A servant will take you to the Prioress after." Golden eyes looked solemnly at her. "Tread lightly around her, daughter of Zāla."

His tail swept in his wake as he left. She watched him go before stepping through the doorway, into a candlelit interior.

This bathhouse, like the sunrooms, was on the open side of the Priory. A breeze swirled the steam on the surface of the water, like spindrift on the sea. Ead set the oil lamp down and shrugged off her robe before descending into the pool. With each step, it carried away the sand and dirt and sweat, leaving her sleek and new.

She used ash soap to lave her skin. Once she had got the sand from her hair, she let the heat soothe her travel-weary bones.

Tread lightly.

Ichneumons did not give careless warnings. The Prioress would want to know why she had been so insistent upon staying in Inys.

You must always stay with me, Ead Duryan.

"Sister."

She turned her head. One of the Sons of Siyāti was in the doorway.

"The Prioress bids you join her for the evening meal," he said. "Your garments await you."

"Thank you."

In her chamber, she took her time dressing. The garments that had been left for her were not formal, but they befitted her new rank as a postulant. An initiate when she had left for Inys, she had now completed an assignment of consequence for the Priory, making her eligible to be named a Red Damsel. Only the Prioress could decide if she was worthy of this honor.

First was a mantelet of sea silk, which shone like spun gold and covered her to the navel. Next came an embroidered white skirt. A glass band encircled one wrist—the wrist of her sword hand—and strings of wooden beads hung about her neck. She left her hair loose and damp.

This new Prioress had not seen her since she was seventeen. As she poured some wine to nerve herself, she caught sight of her reflection in the flat of her eating knife.

Full lips. Eyes like oak honey, brows set low and straight above them. Her nose was slim at the bridge, broad toward the end. All this she recognized. Yet now she saw, for the first time, how woman-hood had changed her. It had tempted out her cheekbones and pared away the rounds of youth. There was a gauntness about her, too, from the kind of starvation only warriors of the Priory understood.

She looked like the women she had longed to be when she was growing up. Like she was made of stone.

"Are you ready, sister?"

The man was back. Ead smoothed her skirt.

"Yes," she said. "Take me to her."

When Cleolind Onjenyu had founded the Priory of the Orange Tree, she had abandoned her life as a princess of the South and disappeared with her handmaidens into the Vale of Blood. They had named their haven in defiance of Galian. At the time of his coming, knights of the Isles of Inysca had said their vows in build-ings called priories. Galian had planned to found the first Southern priory in Yikala.

I shall found a priory of a different sort, Cleolind had said, *and no craven knight shall soil its garden.*

The Mother herself had been the first Prioress. The second was Siyāti uq-Nāra, from whom many of the brothers and sisters of the Priory, Ead included, claimed descent. After the death of each Prioress, the next one would be chosen by the Red Damsels.

The Prioress was seated at a table with Chassar. Upon seeing Ead, she rose and took her by the hands.

"Beloved daughter." She placed a kiss on her cheek. "Welcome back to Lasia."

Ead returned the gesture. "May the flame of the Mother sustain you, Prioress."

"And you."

Hazel eyes took her in, noting the changes, before the older woman returned to her seat.

Mita Yedanya, formerly the *munguna*—the presumed heir—must now be in her fifth decade. She was built like a broadsword, wide in the shoulder and long in the body. Like Ead, she was of both Lasian and Ersyri descent, her skin like sand lapped by the sea. Black hair, now threaded with silver, was pierced with a wooden pin.

Sarsun chirruped a greeting from his perch. Chassar was midway through a concoction of yogush and braised lamb. He stopped to smile at her. Ead sat beside him, and a Son of Siyāti set a bowl of groundnut stew before her.

Platters of food circled the table. White cheese, honeyed dates, palm-apples and apricots, hot flatbread crowned with pounded chickpeas, rice tossed with onion and plum tomato, sun-dried fish, steaming clams, red plantain split and spiced. Tastes she had craved for nearly a decade.

"A girl left us, and a woman returns," the Prioress said as the Son of Siyāti served Ead as much food as he could fit on her plate. "I am loath to hurry you, but we must know the circumstances under which you left Inys. Chassar tells me you were exiled."

"I fled to escape arrest."

"What happened, daughter?"

Ead poured from a jug of date-palm wine, giving herself a few moments to think.

She began with Truyde utt Zeedeur and her affair with the squire. She told them about Triam Sulyard and his crossing to the East. She told them about the Tablet of Rumelabar and the theory Truyde had drawn from it. A story of cosmic balance—of fire and stars.

"This may have weight, Prioress," Chassar said thoughtfully. "There *are* times of plenty, when the tree gives freely—we are in one now—and periods where it offers less fruit. There have been two such times of scarcity, one of them directly after the Grief of Ages. This theory of a cosmic balance does something to explain it."

The Prioress seemed to contemplate this, but did not voice her thoughts.

"Continue, Eadaz," she said.

Ead did. She told them about the marriage, and the murder, and the child, and the loss of it. About the Dukes Spiritual and what Combe had implied about their intentions toward Sabran.

She left out some things, of course.

"Now she is unable to conceive, her legitimacy is under threat. At least one person in the palace, this Cupbearer, has been trying to murder her, or at least frighten her," Ead finished. "We must send more sisters, or I believe the Dukes Spiritual will move toward the throne. Now they know her secret, she is at their mercy. They could use it to blackmail her. Or simply usurp her."

"Civil war." The Prioress pursed her lips. "I told our last Prioress that this would happen sooner or later, but she would not hear it." She cut into a slice of muskmelon. "We will meddle no more in Inysh affairs."

Ead was sure she must have misheard.

"Prioress," she said, "may I ask what you mean?"

"I mean precisely what I said. That the Priory will no longer interfere in Inys."

Confounded, Ead looked to Chassar, but suddenly he was deeply involved in his meal.

"Prioress—" She fought to keep her voice in hand. "You cannot intend to *abandon* Virtudom to this uncertain fate?"

No reply.

"If Sabran is revealed to be unable to bear a daughter, there will not only be civil war in Inys, but a dangerous schism will split Virtudom. Different factions will be for different members of the Dukes Spiritual. Even the Earls Provincial might try for the throne. Doomsingers will roam the cities. And amidst this chaos, Fýredel will seize power."

The Prioress dipped her fingers into a dish of water, washing away the blood of the muskmelon.

"Eadaz," she said, "the Priory of the Orange Tree is the vanguard against wyrmkind. It has been that for a thousand years." She looked Ead in the eye. "It does *not* exist to hold up failing monarchies. Or to interfere in foreign wars. We are not politicians or bodyguards or mercenaries. We are vessels of the sacred flame."

Ead waited.

"As Chassar said, there are records that indicate periods of scarcity in the Priory. If our scholars have it right, there will be another soon. We are likely to be at war with the Draconic Army up to and throughout that period. Perhaps with the Nameless One himself," the Prioress continued. "We must be ready for the cruelest fight since the Grief of Ages. Consequently, we must concentrate our efforts on the South, and conserve resources wherever possible. We *must* weather the storm."

"Of course, but—"

"Therefore," the Prioress cut across her, "I will not be sending *any* sister into the jaws of a civil war in Virtudom, to save a queen who has all but fallen. Neither will I risk them being executed for heresy. Not when they could be hunting the High Westerns. Or supporting our old friends in the courts of the South."

"Prioress," Ead said, frustrated, "surely the purpose of the Priory is to protect humankind."

"By defeating the Draconic evil in this world."

"If we mean to defeat that evil, there must be stability in the world. The Priory is the first shield against wyrms, but we cannot win alone," Ead stressed. "Virtudom has great military and naval strength. The only way to hold it together, and to prevent it from destroying itself from within, is to keep Sabran Berethnet alive and enthro—"

"Enough."

Ead said no more. There was a stillness in the room that seemed to go on for hours.

"You are strong-willed, Eadaz. Like Zāla was," the Prioress said, softer. "I respected our last Prioress in her decision to station you in Inys. She believed it was what the Mother wanted … but I believe otherwise. It is time to prepare. Time to look to our own, and make ready for war." She shook her head. "I will not see you echoing repugnant prayers in Ascalon for another season."

"Then it was all for nothing. Years of changing sheets," Ead said tartly, "for nothing."

The look the Prioress gave her chilled her to the soul. Chassar cleared his throat.

"More wine, Prioress?"

She gave a slight nod in return, and he poured.

"It was not for nothing." The Prioress stopped him when her cup was almost full. "My predecessor believed the Berethnet claim might be true, and that the possibility made their queens worthy of protection—but whether they are or are not, you have told us that Sabran is now the last of the line. Virtudom *will* fall, whether now or in the near future, when her barrenness is exposed."

"And the Priory will make *no* attempt to soften that fall." Ead could not stomach this. "You mean to let us stand and watch as half the world descends into chaos."

"It is not for us to change the natural course of history." The Prioress picked up her glass. "We must look to the South now, Eadaz. To our purpose."

Ead sat rigid in her chair.

She thought of Loth and Margret. Innocent children like Tallys. Sabran, alone and bereaved in her tower. All lost.

The last Prioress would not have brooked this indifference. She had always believed the Mother had meant for the Priory to protect and support humankind in all corners of the world.

"Fýredel is now awake," the Prioress said, while Ead locked her jaw. "His siblings, Valeysa and Orsul, have also been sighted—the former in the East, the latter here in the South. You have told us of this White Wyrm, which we must assume is a new power, in league with the others. We must dispatch all four to quench the flame in the Draconic Army."

Chassar nodded.

"Where in the South is Orsul?" Ead asked, when she could speak without an outburst.

"He was last seen close to the Gate of Ungulus."

The Prioress dabbed the corner of her mouth with linen. A Son of Siyāti took her plate.

"Eadaz," she said, "you have completed an assignment of import for the Priory. It is time, daughter, for you to take the cloak of a

Red Damsel. I have no doubt that you will be one of our finest warriors."

Mita Yedanya was a blunt woman, brisk in everything. She delivered Ead her dream as if it were a piece of fruit on a platter. Her years in Inys had only ever been meant to bring her closer to that cloak.

Yet the timing of this was purposeful, and it stuck in her craw. The Prioress was using this to conciliate her. As though she were a child to be distracted by a bauble.

"Thank you," Ead said. "I am honored."

Ead and Chassar ate in silence for a time, and Ead sipped the cloudy wine.

"Prioress," she said at last, "I must ask what became of Jondu. Did she ever return to Lasia?"

When the Prioress looked away, her mouth a grim line, Chassar shook his head. "No, beloved." He placed a hand over hers. "Jondu is with the Mother now."

Something died inside Ead. She had been certain, *certain*, that Jondu would find her way back to the Priory. Sure-footed, fierce, dauntless Jondu. Mentor, sister, constant friend.

"Are you sure?" she asked quietly.

"Yes."

Pain flowered sharply in her midriff. She closed her eyes, imagined that pain as a candle, and snuffed it.

Later. She would let the grief burn when there was room for it to breathe.

"She did not die in vain," Chassar continued. "She set out to find the sword of Galian the Deceiver. She did not find Ascalon in Inys—but she did find something else."

Sarsun tapped a talon on his perch. Numbed by the news, Ead looked dully at the object beside him.

A box.

"We do not know how to open it," Chassar admitted as Ead stood. "A riddle stands between us and its secret."

Slowly, Ead approached the box and ran a finger over the grooves on its surface. What the untaught eye would see as mere decoration, she knew to be Selinyi, that ancient language of the

South, the letters wound and intertwined to make them hard to read.

> *a key without a lock or seam*
> *to raise the sea in times of strife*
> *it closed in clouds of salt and steam*
> *it opens with a golden knife*

"I assume you have tried all the knives in the Priory," Ead said.

"Of course."

"Perhaps it refers to Ascalon, then."

"Ascalon was said to have a silver blade." Chasser sighed. "The Sons of Siyāti are searching the archives for an answer."

"We must pray they find it," the Prioress said. "If Jondu was willing to die to put this box into our possession, she must have felt that we could open it. Devoted to the end." She looked to Ead again. "For now, Eadaz, you must go forth and eat of the tree. After eight years, I know your fire is spent." She paused. "Would you like one of your sisters to go with you?"

"No," Ead said. "I will go alone."

Evening turned to night. When the stars were burning over the Vale of Blood, Ead began the descent.

One thousand steps took her to the very foot of the valley. Her bare feet sank into grass and loam. She paused for a moment, to breathe in the night, before she let her robe fall.

White blossom strewed the valley. The orange tree loomed, its branches spread like open hands. Every step she took toward it seared her throat. She had crossed half the world to return here, to the wellspring of her power.

The night seemed to embrace her as she descended to her knees. As her fingers sank into the earth, the tears of relief overran, and each breath came like the drag of a knife up her throat. She forgot about everyone she had ever known. There was only the tree. The giver of fire. It was her one purpose, her reason to live. And it was calling to her, after eight years, promising the sacred flame.

Somewhere nearby, the Prioress, or one of the Red Damsels, would be watching. They needed to see that she was still worthy of this rank. Only the tree could decide who was worthy.

Ead turned up her palms and waited, as the crop waits for rain.

Fill me with your fire again. She held the prayer in her heart. *Let me serve you.*

The night grew too still. And then—slowly, as if it were sinking through water—a golden fruit dropped from on high.

She caught it in both hands. With a gasping sob, she sank her teeth into the flesh.

A feeling like dying and coming to life. The blood of the tree spreading over her tongue, soothing the blaze in her throat. Veins turning to gold. As quickly as it quenched one fire, it sparked another, a fire that torched through her whole being. And the heat cracked her open, like the clay she was, and made her body cry out to the world.

All around her, the world answered.

40

East

Rain sheeted over the Sundance Sea. It was forenoon, but the Fleet of the Tiger Eye kept its lanterns burning.

Laya Yidagé strode across the *Pursuit*. As he followed her, shivering in his sodden cloak, Niclays could not help but glance toward the contused sky, as he had every day for weeks.

Valeysa the Harrower was awake. The sight of her above the ships, crowing and infernal, was seared into his mind forever.

He had seen enough paintings to know her. With scales of burnt orange and golden spines, she was a living ember, as bright as if she had just been retched from the Dreadmount.

Now she was back, and at any moment, she could reappear and reduce the *Pursuit* to cinders. It might, at least, be quicker than whatever gruesome death the pirates would invent for him if he had the misfortune to vex them. He had been on the treasure ship for weeks and had so far managed not to have his tongue cut out or a hand lopped off, but he lived in expectation of it.

His gaze darted to the horizon. Three Seiikinese iron ships had tailed them for days, but just as the Golden Empress had predicted, they had not drawn close enough to engage. Now the *Pursuit* was moving east again, heading for Kawontay, where the pirates would sell the Lacustrine dragon. Niclays wished he knew what they would do to him.

Rain speckled his eyeglasses. He rubbed at them fruitlessly and hurried after Laya.

The Golden Empress had summoned them both to her cabin, where a stove offset the chill. She stood at the head of the table, wearing a padded coat and a hat of otter fur.

"Sea-Moon," she said, "do sit down."

Niclays had scarcely opened his mouth since Valeysa had terrified the wits out of him, but now he found himself blurting out, "You speak Seiikinese, all-honored Captain?"

"Of course I speak fucking Seiikinese." Her gaze was on the table, where a detailed map of the East was painted. "Did you think me a fool?"

"Well, ah, no. But the presence of your interpreter led me to believe—"

"I have an interpreter so my hostages will think me a fool. Did Yidagé do a poor job?"

"No, no," Niclays said, aghast. "No, all-honored Golden Empress. She did excellently."

"So you do think me a fool."

Lost for words, he shut up. She finally looked up at him.

"Sit."

He sat. Eyeing him, the Golden Empress took an eating knife from her belt and ran its tip under her inch-long fingernails, each of which was painted black.

"I have spent thirty years on the high seas," she said. "I have dealt with many manner of people, from fisherfolk to viceroys. I have learned who I need to torture, who I need to kill, and who will tell their secrets, or share their riches, with no bloodshed at all." She spun the knife in her hand. "Before I was taken hostage by pirates, I owned a brothel in Xothu. I know more about people than they know themselves. I know women. I know men, too, from their minds to their cocks. And I know how to judge them almost on sight."

Niclays swallowed.

"If we could leave the cocks out of this." He offered a strained grin. "Old as it is, I am still attached to mine."

The Golden Empress barked a laugh at that.

"You are funny, Sea-Moon," she said. "You people from over the Abyss are always laughing. No wonder you have so many jesters in your courts." Those black eyes bored into him. "I see you. I know what you want, and it has nothing to do with your cock. It has to do with the dragon we took from Ginura."

Niclays deemed it best to remain silent at this point. An armed madwoman was not to be taken lightly.

"What do you want from it?" she asked. "Saliva, perhaps, to perfume a lover? Brains to cure the bloody flux?"

"Anything." Niclays cleared his throat. "I am an alchemist, you see, all-honored Golden Empress."

"An alchemist."

Her tone was scathing. "Yes," Niclays said, with great feeling. "A method-master. I studied the art at university."

"I was under the impression that you had studied anatomy. That was why I gave you a post. Let you live."

"Oh, *yes*," he said hastily. "I *am* an anatomist—an excellent one, I assure you, a giant of my field—but I also pursued alchemy out of passion for the subject. I have sought the secret of eternal life for many years. Though I have not yet been able to brew an elixir, I believe Eastern dragons could help me. Their bodies age over thousands of years, and if I could only re-create that—"

He stopped dead, awaiting her judgment. She had never taken her gaze off him.

"So," she said, "you wish to persuade me that your brain is not as soft as your spine. Doubtless it would be simpler for me to cut off the top of your skull and see for myself."

Niclays dared not answer.

"I think we could strike a bargain, Sea-Moon. Perhaps you are the sort of man who knows how to do business." The Golden Empress reached into her coat. "You said this item was bequeathed to you by a friend. Tell me more about him."

She pulled out a familiar scrap of writing. In her gloved hand was the last piece of Jannart.

"I want to know," she said, "who gave this to you." When he was silent, she held it toward the stove. "Answer me."

"The love of my life," Niclays said, heart pounding. "Jannart, Duke of Zeedeur."

"Do you know what it is?"

"No. Only that he bequeathed it to me."

"Why?"

"Would that I knew."

The Golden Empress narrowed her eyes.

"Please," Niclays said hoarsely. "That fragment of writing is all I have left of him. All that remains."

The corner of her mouth lifted. She laid the fragment on the table. The gentleness with which she handled it made Niclays realize she would never have set it on fire.

Fool, he thought. *Never show your weakness.*

"This writing," the Golden Empress said, "is part of an Eastern text from long ago. It tells of a source of eternal life. A mulberry tree." She patted it. "I have been searching for this missing piece for many years. I expected it to contain directions, but it does not yield the location of this tree. All it does is complete the story."

"Is this not just … a legend, all-honored Golden Empress?"

"All legends have truth in them. I should know," she said. "Some say I ate the heart of a tiger and it sent me mad. Some say I am a water ghost. What is true is that I despise the so-called gods of the East. All rumor that surrounds me stemmed from that." She tapped a finger on the text. "I doubt the mulberry tree grew from the heart of the world, as the tale claims. What I do *not* doubt is that it hides the secret to eternal life. So you see, you will not need to damage a dragon."

Niclays could not quite take this in. Jannart had inherited the key to alchemy.

The Golden Empress considered him. He noticed for the first time that there were notches down the length of her wooden arm. She beckoned to Laya, who had retrieved a gilded wooden box from under the throne.

"Here is my offer. If you can solve this puzzle and find us the route to the mulberry tree," the Golden Empress said, "I will let you drink the elixir of life from it yourself. You will share in our spoils."

Laya brought the box to Niclays and lifted the lid. Inside, nestled in watersilk, lay a thin book. Shining on its wooden cover were the remains of a gold-leaf mulberry tree. Reverently, Niclays took it. It was bound in a Seiikinese style, the leaves stitched into an open spine. Each page was made of silk. Whoever had made it had wanted it to weather many centuries, and so it had.

This was the book Jannart would have dreamed of seeing.

"I have read every possible meaning into each word in Old Seiikinese, yet I have found nothing but a story," the Golden Empress said. "Perhaps a Mentish mind can see it in a different way. Or perhaps the love of your life sent you some message you have yet to hear. Bring me an answer by sunrise in three days, or you may find I grow tired of my new surgeon. And when I grow tired of things, they are not long for this world."

Stomach roiling, Niclays ran his thumbs over the book.

"Yes, all-honored Golden Empress," he murmured.

Laya led him away.

Outside, the air was taut and cold. "Well," Niclays said heavily, "I suspect this will be one of our last meetings, Laya."

She frowned. "Are you giving up hope, Niclays?"

"I will not solve this mystery in *three days*, Laya. Even if I had three hundred, I could not."

Laya took him by the shoulders, and the force of her grasp stopped him. "This Jannart—the man you loved," she said, looking him dead in the eye. "Do you think he would want you to give up, or carry on?"

"I don't *want* to carry on! Do you not understand? Does nobody in this world understand, damn you? Is no one else haunted?" A quiver of wrath entered his voice. "Everything I did—everything I was—everything I am, is because of him. He was someone before me. I am no one without him. I am tired of living without him at my side. He left me for that book and, by the Saint, I resent him for it. I resent him every minute of every day." His voice cracked. "You Lasians believe in an afterlife, don't you?"

Laya studied him.

"Some of us, yes. The Orchard of Divinities," she said. "He may be waiting for you there, or at the Great Table of the Saint. Or perhaps he is nowhere at all. Whatever has become of him, *you* are still here. And you are here for a reason." She held a callused palm to his cheek. "You have a ghost, Niclays. Do not become a ghost yourself."

How many years had it been since anyone had touched his face, or looked at him with sympathy?

"Goodnight," he said. "And thank you, Laya."

He left her.

On his stretch of floor, he lay on his side and pressed one fist over his mouth. He had fled from Mentendon. He had fled from the West. No matter how far he ran, his ghost still followed him.

It was too late. He was mad with grief. He had been mad for years. He had lost his mind the night he had found Jannart dead at the Sun in Splendor, the inn that had been their love nest.

It had been a week since Jannart was supposed to return from his journey, but no one had seen him. Unable to find him at court, and with word from Aleidine that he was not in Zeedeur, Niclays had gone to the only other place he could be.

The smell of vinegar had hit him first. A physician in a plague mask had been outside the room, painting red wings on the door. And when Niclays had shoved past her, into their room, there was Jannart, lying as if asleep, his red hands folded on his chest.

Jannart had lied to everyone. The library where he had hoped to find answers was not in Wilgastrōm, but in Gulthaga, the city razed in the eruption of the Dreadmount. Doubtless he had thought the ruins would be safe, but he must have known there was a risk. Deceived his family and the man he loved. All so he could stitch a single hole in history.

A wyvern had been sleeping in the long-dead halls of Gulthaga. One bite had been all it took.

There was no cure. Jannart had known that, and had wanted to leave before his blood started to burn and his soul was scorched away. And so he had gone to the shadow market in disguise and procured a poison named eternity dust. It gave a quiet death.

Niclays trembled. He could still see the scene now, detailed as a painting. Jannart in the bed, *their* bed. In one hand, the locket Niclays had given him the morning after their first kiss, with the fragment inside. In the other, an empty vial.

It had taken the physician, the innkeeper, and four others to hold Niclays back. He could still hear his own howls of denial, taste the tears, smell the sweetness of the poison.

You fool, he had screamed. *You fucking selfish fool. I waited for you. I waited thirty years . . .*

Did lovers ever reach the Milk Lagoon, or did they only dream of it?

He gripped his head between his hands. With Jannart's death, he had lost one half of himself. The part of him worth living for. He closed his eyes, head aching, chest heaving—and when he fell into a fitful doze, he dreamed of the room at the top of Brygstad Palace.

There is a hidden message in it, Clay.

He tasted black wine on his tongue.

Intuition tells me that it is a vital piece of history.

He felt the heat of the fire on his skin. He saw the stars, richly painted in their constellations, as real as if their love nest opened out on to the sky.

Something about the characters sits oddly with me. Some are larger, others smaller, and they are spaced in a strange manner.

His eyes snapped open.

"Jan," he breathed. "Oh, Jan. Your golden fox still has his cunning."

41

South

Ead lay in her eyrie, glossed with sweat. Her blood ran hot and swift.

This had happened before. The fever. A fog had been around her for eight years, dampening her senses, and now the sun had burned it away. Each breath of wind was like a broad stroke of a finger on her skin.

The sound of the waterfall was crystal-clear. She could hear the calls of honeyguides and sunbirds and mimics in the forest. She could smell ichneumons and white orchids and the perfume of the orange tree.

She missed Sabran. With her skin this tender, the memory of her was torture. She slid a hand between her legs and imagined a cool touch on her body, silken lips, the sweetness of wine. Her hips reared once before she sank into the bed.

After, she lay quiet, burning.

It must be close to dawn by now. Another day that Sabran was alone in Inys, circled by wolves. Margret would only be able to do so much to keep her safe. She was quick-witted, but no warrior.

There had to be a way to convince the Prioress to defend the Inysh throne.

The servants had left a platter of fruit and a knife on her nightstand. For a time, she would burn through enough food for three grown men. She took a pomegranate from the platter.

As she cut away the flower, her hand slipped, made clumsy by her fever. The blade sheared the other wrist, and blood brimmed from the wound. A droplet leaked down to her elbow.

Ead looked at it for a long time, thinking. Then she shrugged on a robe and lit an oil lamp with a snap of her fingers.

An idea was taking form.

The halls were quiet tonight. On her way to the dining chamber, she stopped suddenly next to one of the doors.

She remembered running through these passageways with Jondu, carrying a squeaking Aralaq. How she had feared this corridor, knowing it was where her birthmother had drawn her final breath.

Zāla du Agriya uq-Nāra, who had been the *munguna* before Mita Yedanya. Behind this door was the room she had died in.

There were many legendary sisters in the Priory, but Zāla had made a habit of being legendary. At nineteen, in the second month of her pregnancy, she had answered a call from the young Sahar Taumargam, the future Queen of Yscalin, who was then a princess of the Ersyr. A Nuram tribe had inadvertently woken a pair of wyverns in the Little Mountains. Zāla had found not two, but six of the creatures harrowing the nomads and, against the odds, she had slain them single-handed. Then she had dusted herself off and ridden all the way to the market in Zirin to satisfy her craving for rose candy.

Ead had been born half a year later, too early. *You were small enough to cradle in one hand*, Chassar had once told her, chuckling, *but your cry could have brought down mountains, beloved.* Sisters were not supposed to involve themselves too deeply with their children, for the Priory was one family, but Zāla had often slipped Ead honey pastries and cuddled her close when nobody was looking.

My Ead, she had whispered, and breathed in the baby scent of her head. *My evening star. If the sun burned out tomorrow, your flame would light the world.*

The memory made Ead ache to be held. She had been six when Zāla had died in her bed.

She placed a hand on the door and walked on. *May your flame ascend to light the tree.*

438

The dining chamber was dark and silent. Only Sarsun was there, his head tucked against his chest. When she set foot on the floor, he woke sharply.

"Shh."

Sarsun ruffled his feathers.

Ead placed the oil lamp beside his perch. As if he sensed her intention, he hopped down to scrutinize the riddlebox. Ead took hold of the knife. When she lifted the blade to her skin, Sarsun let out a small hoot. She sliced across her palm, deep enough for blood to flow generously, and placed her hand on the lid of the box.

it closed in clouds of salt and steam—it opens with a golden knife.

"Siyāti uq-Nāra once said that mage blood was golden, you see," she said to Sarsun. "To possess a golden knife, I must draw blood with it."

She would never have believed that a bird could look skeptical until she saw his face.

"I know. It isn't *actually* golden."

Sarsun bowed his head.

The engraved letters gradually filled, as if they were inlaid with ruby. Ead waited. When the blood reached the end of the final word, the riddlebox split down the middle. Ead flinched away, and Sarsun fluttered back to his perch as the box opened like a night-blooming flower.

In it was a key.

Ead took it from its bed of satin. It was the same length as her forefinger, with a bow shaped like a flower with five petals. An orange blossom. The symbol of the Priory.

"Faithless creature," she said to Sarsun.

He pecked her sleeve and flew to the doorway, where he sat and looked at her.

"Yes?"

He gave her a beady-eyed stare, then took wing.

Ead shadowed him to a narrow door, down a flight of winding steps. She had a caliginous memory of this place. Someone had brought her here when she was very small.

When she reached the bottom of the stairs, she found herself in a vaulted, lightless room.

The Mother stood before her.

Ead lifted her lamp toward the effigy. This was not the swooning Damsel of Inysh legend. This was the Mother as she had been in life. Hair shorn close to her skull, an axe in one hand and a sword in the other. Her dress was made for battle, woven in the style favored by warriors of the House of Onjenyu. Guardian, fighter, and born leader—that was the true Cleolind of Lasia, daughter of Selinu the Oathkeeper. Between her feet was a figurine of Washtu, the fire goddess.

Cleolind had never been entombed in the Sanctuary of Our Lady. Her bones slept here, in her own beloved country, in a stone-built coffin beneath the statue. Most effigies lay on their backs, but not this one. Ead reached up to touch the sword before she looked at Sarsun.

"Well?"

He tilted his head. Ead lowered the lamp, searching for whatever she was meant to find.

The coffin was raised on a dais. At the front of this dais was a keyhole with a square groove around it. With a glance at Sarsun, who tapped his talon, Ead knelt and slid the key into place.

When it turned, sweat dampened her nape. She took a deep breath and pulled on the key.

A compartment slid out from beneath the coffin. Inside was another iron box. Ead rotated the orange-blossom clasp and opened it.

A jewel lay before her. Its surface was white as pearl, or fog trapped in a drop of glass.

Sarsun chirruped. Beside the jewel was a scroll the size of her little finger, but Ead hardly saw it. Entranced by the light that danced in the jewel, she reached out to catch it between her fingers.

As soon as she touched its surface, a scream leaped from her lips. Sarsun let out a scream of his own as Ead collapsed before the Mother, her fingers bound to the jewel like a tongue to ice. The last thing she heard was the skirr of his wings.

"Here, beloved."

Chassar handed Ead a cup of walnut milk. Aralaq was lying across her bed, head on his front paws.

The jewel sat on the table. Nobody had touched it since Chassar, alerted by Sarsun and finding her insensible, had carried her back to the sunroom. Her fingers had only released it when she woke.

Now she held the translation of the scroll that had been in the box. The seal had already been broken. Written on brittle paper with an odd sheen to it, the scholars had deemed the message to be Old Seiikinese, interspersed with the odd word in Selinyi.

> *Hail honorable Siyāti, beloved sister of long-honored and learnèd Cleolind.*
>
> *On this the third day of spring in the twentieth year of the reign of all-honored Empress Mokwo, I with Cleolind bound the Nameless One with two sacred jewels. We could not destroy him for his fiery heart was not pierced with the sword. One thousand years he will be held and not one sunrise more.*
>
> *I send to you with sorrow the remains of our dear friend and this her waning jewel to keep until he returns. You will find the other on Komoridu and I enclose a star chart to lead your descendants there. They must use both sword and jewels against him. The jewels will cleave to the mage who touches them and only death can change the wielder.*
>
> *I pray our children, centuries from now, will take up the burden with willing hearts.*
>
> *I am,*
> *Neporo, Queen of Komoridu*

"All these years the warning lay with the Mother. The truth was right beneath our feet," the Prioress said, voice scraped thin. "Why did a sister in the past go to such lengths to conceal it? Why did she hide the key to the tomb and bury it in *Inys*, of all places?"

"Perhaps to protect it," Chassar said. "From Kalyba."

Silence rang out.

"Do not speak that name," the Prioress said very softly. "Not here, Chassar."

Chassar dipped his head in contrition.

"I am certain," he said, "that a sister would have left more for us, but it would have been in the archives. Before the flood."

The Prioress paced back and forth in her red bedgown. "There was no star chart in the box." She stroked a hand over her gold necklet. "And yet . . . we have learned a great deal from this message. If we can believe this Neporo of Komoridu, the Mother failed to pierce the Nameless One's heart. In her lost years, she damaged him enough to somehow *bind* him, but it was not enough to prevent him rising anew."

One thousand years he will be held and not one sunrise more.

His absence had never been anything to do with Sabran.

"The Nameless One will return," the Prioress said, almost to herself, "but we can determine an exact day from this note. One thousand years from the third day of spring in the *twentieth* year of Empress Mokwo of Seiiki—" She made for the door. "I must send for our scholars. Find out when Mokwo ruled. And they may have heard legends about these jewels."

Ead could hardly think. She was as cold as if someone had pulled her from the Ashen Sea.

Chassar noticed. "Eadaz, sleep for a little longer." He kissed the top of her head. "And for now, don't touch the jewel."

"I'm a meddler," Ead muttered, "not a fool."

After he left, Ead curled against the furry warmth of Aralaq, her thoughts a morass.

"Eadaz," Aralaq said.

"Yes?"

"Do not follow stupid birds into dark places again."

She dreamed of Jondu in a dark room. Heard her screaming as a red-hot claw raked away her flesh. Aralaq nosed her awake.

"You were dreaming," he rumbled.

Tears wet her cheeks. He nuzzled her, and she huddled into his fur.

The King of Yscalin was said to have a torture chamber in the bowels of his palace. Jondu would have met with death there. Meanwhile, Ead had been in the shining court of Inys, paid a wage, and decked in finery. She would carry this grief to the end of her days.

The jewel had stopped its glinting. She kept a cautious eye on it as she sipped the sapphire tea that had been left for her.

The Prioress came sweeping into the sunroom.

"We have *nothing* about this Neporo of Komoridu in the archives," she said, without ceremony. "Or this jewel. Whatever it is, it is not our sort of magic." She stopped by the bed. "It is something ... unknown. Dangerous."

Ead put down her glass.

"You will not like to hear this, Prioress," she said, "but Kalyba would know."

Once again, the name stiffened the Prioress. The set of her jaw betrayed her displeasure.

"The Witch of Inysca forged Ascalon. An object imbued with power. This jewel may be another of her creations," Ead said. "Kalyba walked this world long before the Mother drew her first breath."

"She did. And then she walked in the halls of the Priory. She killed your birthmother."

"Nevertheless, she knows a great deal that we do not."

"Has a decade in Inys addled your senses?" the Prioress said curtly. "The witch cannot be trusted."

"The Nameless One may be coming. Our purpose, as sisters of the Priory, is to protect the world from him. If we must treat with lesser enemies to do that, so be it."

The Prioress looked at her.

"I told you, Eadaz," she said. "Our purpose now is to shield the South. Not the world."

"So let me shield the South."

With a sigh through her nose, the Prioress laid her hands on the balustrade.

"There is another reason that I think we should approach Kalyba," Ead said. "Sabran dreamed often of the Bower of Eternity.

She did not know what it was, of course, but she told me she had seen a gateway of sabra flowers and a terrible place beyond. I would like to know why it haunted an Inysh queen."

The Prioress stood by the windows for a long time, stiff as a turret.

"You need not invite Kalyba here," Ead said. "Let me go to her. I can take Aralaq."

The Prioress pursed her lips.

"Go, then," she said, "but I doubt she can or will tell you anything. Banishment has embittered her." She used a piece of cloth to pick up the jewel. "I will keep this here."

Ead felt an unexpected stirring of unease.

"I might need its power," she said. "Kalyba is a stronger mage than I will ever be."

"No. I will not risk this falling into her possession." The Prioress slipped the jewel into a pouch at her side. "You will have weapons. Kalyba is powerful—no one could deny it—but she has not eaten of the tree in years. I have faith that you will overcome, Eadaz uq-Nāra."

42

East

Sweat quivered at the tip of his nose. As Niclays wet his brush and cupped his hand beneath it, unwilling to spill ink on his masterpiece, Laya brought a cup of broth to the table.

"I hate to interrupt, Old Red, but you have not eaten in hours," Laya said. "If you fall flat on your nose, your little chart will be destroyed before the captain can spit on it."

"This *little chart*, Laya, is the key to immortality."

"Looks like madness to me."

"All alchemists have madness in their blood. That, dear lady, is why we get things done."

He had been hunched over the table for what felt like a lifetime, copying the large and small characters from *The Tale of Komoridu* on to a giant roll of silk, ignoring those of middling size. If it proved to be a fruitless endeavor, he would most likely be on the seabed by dawn.

As soon as he remembered the starry vault in Brygstad Palace, he had known. First, he had tried arranging the oddly sized characters in a circle, as Mentish astronomers did, but only nonsense had come out. With a little coaxing, Padar, the Sepuli navigator, had surrendered his own star charts, which were rectangular. Niclays had continued, from that point, to translate each page of text to a pane he had sketched on the silk, keeping them in the order that they appeared in the book.

Once the panes were full of the large and small characters, he was certain they would form a map of part of the sky. He suspected the size of the character was a measure of the radiance of the corresponding star, the larger ones being the brighter.

Somewhere below, the dragon began to thrash about like a beached fish again, rocking the ship.

"Damned creature." Niclays marked the position of the next character. "Won't it be quiet?"

"It must miss being worshipped."

Laya pulled the silk taut for him. As he worked, she scrutinized his face.

"Niclays," she murmured, "how did Jannart die?"

His throat filled with the usual ache, but it was easier to swallow when he had something to occupy his mind.

"Plague," he said.

"I'm sorry."

"Not as sorry as I am."

He had never spoken to a soul about Jannart. How could he, when nobody could know how close they had been? Even now, it made his insides flutter, but Laya was part of no court in Virtudom, and he found that he already trusted her. She would keep his secrets.

"You would have liked him. And he would have liked you." His voice was hoarse. "Jannart adored languages. Ancient and dead ones, especially. He was in love with knowledge."

She smiled. "Aren't all you Ments a little in love with knowledge, Niclays?"

"Much to the distaste of our cousins in Virtudom. They often wonder at how we can question the foundations of our adopted religion, even though its bedrock is a single bloodline of no great exceptionality, which hardly seems sensib—"

The door snapped open then, letting in a gust of wind. They rushed to pin down the pages as the Golden Empress walked in, shadowed by Padar, whose face and chest were dripping in blood, and Ghonra, self-styled Princess of the Sundance Sea and captain of the *White Crow*. Laya had assured Niclays that her rare beauty belied an equally rare bloodlust. The tattoo on her brow was a puzzle they had yet to solve; it simply read *love*.

Niclays kept his head down as she passed. The Golden Empress served herself a cup of wine.

"I hope you are almost finished, Sea-Moon."

"Yes, all-honored Golden Empress," Niclays said brightly. "Soon I will know the whereabouts of the tree."

He concentrated as best he could with Padar and Ghonra breathing down his neck. When he had transferred the last of the characters, he blew lightly on the ink. The Golden Empress brought her cup of wine to the table (Niclays prayed very hard for her not to spill it) and studied his creation.

"What is this?"

He bowed to her. "All-honored Golden Empress," he said, "I believe these characters from *The Tale of Komoridu* represent the stars—our most ancient means of navigation. If they can be matched to an existing star chart, I think they will lead you to the mulberry tree."

She studied him from beneath the frontlet of her headdress. Its beads cast shadows on her brow.

"Yidagé," the Golden Empress said to Laya, "do you know Old Seiikinese?"

"Some, all-honored captain."

"Read the characters."

"I do not think they are supposed to be read as words," Niclays offered, "but as—"

"You *think*, Sea-Moon," said the Golden Empress. "Thinkers bore me. Now, read, Yidagé."

Niclays held his tongue. Laya hovered her finger over each of the characters.

"Niclays." A line creased her brow. "I think they *are* meant to be read as words. There is a message here."

His nerves evaporated. "There is?" He pushed his eyeglasses up his nose. "Well, what does it say?"

"*The Way of the Outcasts*," Laya read aloud, "*begins at the ninth hour of night. The . . . rising jewel—*" She squinted. "Yes, *the rising jewel—is planted in the soil of Komoridu. From under the Magpie's eye, go south and to the Dreaming Star, and look beneath the—*" When she reached the last character of the final pane, she let out a breath. "Oh. These are the characters for *mulberry tree*."

"The star charts," Niclays said, breathless. "Can these patterns be matched to the sky?"

The Golden Empress looked to Padar, who spread his own star charts on the floor. After studying them for a time, he took up the still-wet brush and joined some of the characters on the silk. Niclays flinched at the first stroke, then realized what was forming.

Constellations.

His heart pounded like an axe into wood. When Padar was finished, he set down the brush and considered.

"Do you understand it, Padar?" the Golden Empress asked.

"I do." Slowly, he nodded. "Yes. Each pane shows the sky at a different time of year."

"And this one." Niclays pointed at the last pane. "What do you call that constellation?"

The Golden Empress exchanged a look with her navigator, whose mouth twitched.

"The Seiikinese," she said, "call it the Magpie. The characters for *mulberry tree* form its eye."

From under the Magpie's eye, go south and to the Dreaming Star, and look beneath the mulberry tree.

"Yes." Padar strode around the table. "The book has given us a fixed point. Since the stars move each night, we must begin our course only when we are directly under the Magpie's eye at the ninth hour of night, at the given time of year."

Niclays could hardly keep still. "Which is?"

"The end of winter. After that, we must steer between the Dreaming Star and the South Star."

A silence fell, taut with anticipation, and the Golden Empress smiled. Niclays distinctly felt his knees wobble, either with exhaustion or the sudden discharge of days of fear.

From the grave, Jannart had shown them the star they needed as their point of navigation. Without it, the Golden Empress would never have known how to reach the place.

There was that flicker of doubt again. Perhaps he should never have shown her. Someone had done their best to keep this knowledge from the East, and he had handed it to its outlaws.

"Yidagé, you spoke of a jewel." Ghonra had a gleam in her eye. "A rising jewel."

Laya shook her head. "A poetic description of a seed, I imagine. A stone that rises into a tree."

"Or treasure," Padar said. He exchanged a hungry look with Ghonra. "Buried treasure."

"Padar," the Golden Empress said, "tell the crew to prepare for the hunt of their lives. We make for Kawontay to replenish our provisions, and then we sail for the mulberry tree. Ghonra, inform the crews of the *Black Dove* and the *White Crow*. We have a long journey ahead of us."

The two of them left at once.

"Are—" Niclays cleared his throat. "Are you content with this solution, all-honored captain?"

"For now," the Golden Empress said, "but if nothing waits at the end of this path, I will know who has deceived us."

"I have no intention of deceiving you."

"I hope not."

She reached beneath the table and presented him with a length of what looked like cedar wood. "All of my crew bear arms. This staff will be yours," she said. "Use it well."

He took it from her. It was light, yet he sensed it could deliver a shattering blow.

"Thank you," he said, and bowed. "All-honored captain."

"Eternal life awaits," she said, "but if you still wish to see the dragon, and to claim any part of it, you may go now. Perhaps it can tell us something else about the jewel in *The Tale of Komoridu*, or the island," she said. "Yidagé, take him."

They left the cabin. The moment the door had closed behind them, Laya seized Niclays about the neck and embraced him. His nose smashed into her shoulder, and her beads dug into his chest, but suddenly he was laughing as hard as she was, laughing until he wheezed.

Tears seeped down his face. He was drunk on relief, but also the exhilaration of solving a puzzle. In all his years in Orisima, he had never found the key to the elixir, and now he had unearthed the path to it. He had finished what Jannart had started.

His heart was swelling in his chest. Laya took his head between her hands and grinned in a way that lifted his spirit.

"You," she said, "are a genius, Sea-Moon. Brilliant, just brilliant!"

The pirates were all over the decks. Padar roared his orders at them in Lacustrine. The stars shone bright in a clear sky, beckoning them toward the horizon.

"Not a genius," Niclays admitted, weak-kneed. "Just mad. And lucky." He patted her arm. "Thank you, Laya. For your help, and your belief. Perhaps we will both be supping on the fruit of immortality."

Caution stole into her eyes.

"Perhaps." Hitching up her smile, she placed a hand between his shoulders and guided him through the confusion of pirates. "Come. It is time you claimed your reward."

In the deepest part of the *Pursuit*, a Lacustrine dragon was chained from its snout to the end of its tail. Niclays had thought it magnificent when he first saw it on the beach. Now it looked almost feeble.

Laya waited in the shadows with him. "I must go back," she said. "Will you be all right?"

He leaned on his new staff. "Of course. The beast is bound." His mouth was dry. "You go."

She gave the dragon a last glance before reaching into her coat. From inside, she drew a knife, sheathed in leather.

"My gift." She held it out by the blade. "Just in case."

Niclays took it. He had owned a sword in Mentendon, but the only time he had used a weapon had been in his fencing lessons with Edvart, who had always disarmed him in seconds. Before he could thank her, Laya was making her way back up the steps.

The dragon seemed asleep. A tangled mane flowed around its horns. Its face was wider than the serpentine heads of wyrms, and gaudier, with decorative frills.

Nayimathun, Laya had called it. A name with no clear origin.

Niclays walked toward the beast, staying away from its head. Its lower jaw was loose in sleep, showing teeth the length of a forearm.

The dome on its head was dormant. Panaya had told him about it, the night he had first seen a dragon. When it illuminated, that dome was calling to the celestial plane, lifting the dragon toward the stars. Unlike wyrms, dragons needed no wings to fly.

He had tried to rationalize it for weeks. Months. Perhaps the dome was a kind of lodestone, attracted to particles in the air or the cores of far-off worlds. Perhaps dragons had hollow bones, letting them ride the wind. That was the alchemist in him, theorizing. Yet he had known in his gut that unless he could split a dragon open, to see it through the lens of an anatomist, it would remain inexplicable. Magic, for all intents and purposes.

Even as he studied the beast, its eye snapped open and, in spite of himself, Niclays backed away. In the eye of this creature was a cosmos of knowledge: ice and void and constellation—and nothing close to human. Its pupil was as big as a shield, ringed with a blue glow.

For a long while, they stared at each other. A man of the West and a dragon of the East. Niclays found himself overwhelmed by the urge to fall to his knees, but he only gripped his cane.

"You."

The voice was cool and susurrating. The billow of a sail.

"You are the one who bartered for my scale and blood." A dark blue tongue flickered behind its teeth. "You are Roos."

It spoke in Seiikinese. Each word was drawn out like a shadow at sunrise.

"I am," Niclays confirmed. "And you are the great Nayimathun. Or perhaps," he added, "not so great."

Nayimathun watched his mouth as he spoke. On land, Panaya had told him, dragons heard as humans heard underwater.

"The one who wears the chains is a thousand times greater than the one who wields them," Nayimathun said. "Chains are cowardice." A rumble filled the cavernous hull. "Where is Tané?"

"Seiiki, I assume. I hardly know the girl."

"You knew her enough to threaten her. To try to manipulate her for your own gain."

"This is a cutthroat world, beast. I merely negotiated," Niclays said. "I needed your blood and scale to carry out my work, to unlock the secret of your immortality. I wanted humans to have a chance of surviving in a world ruled by giants."

"We tried to defend you in the Great Sorrow." The eye closed for a moment, darkening their surroundings. "Many of you perished. But we tried."

"Perhaps your kind are not as violent as the Draconic Army," Niclays said, "but you still see to it that humans worship your image and beg you for the rain that swells the crops. As if man is not also enough of a marvel to be adulated."

The dragon huffed cloud through its nostrils.

Niclays decided then. That even if his alchemical tools were lost, and even if he was on his way to a font of eternal life, he would take what he had long been denied.

He laid down his staff and bared the knife Laya had given him. Its handle was lacquer, its blade was serrated down one side. He ran his gaze along the wealth of scale. When he had found an unmarred patch of scale, he placed a hand on it.

The dragon was smooth and cold as a fish. Niclays used the knife to pry the scale up, exposing the sheen of silvery flesh beneath.

"You are not meant to live for eternity."

Niclays flung a withering glance at its head. "As an alchemist, I must disagree," he said. "I believe in possibility, you see. Even if I cannot find the elixir of life in your body, the Golden Empress is on her way to the island of Komoridu. There we will find the mulberry tree, and the jewel that lies beneath it."

The eye flared wide.

"Jewel." A rattle stemmed from the dragon. "You speak of the celestial jewels."

"Jewels," Niclays echoed. "Yes. The rising jewel." He softened his voice. "What do you know of it?"

Nayimathun remained silent. Niclays wrenched the blade upward, biting into scale, and the dragon twitched in its chains.

"I will say nothing to you," it said. "Only that they must not fall into the hands of pirates, son of Mentendon."

According to her journal, my aunt received it from a man who told her to carry it far from the East and never bring it back. Jannart's words kept returning to him, circling in his head like a whipping top. *Never bring it back.*

"I do not expect you to stop your pursuit. It is too late for that," the dragon said, "but do not let the jewel fall into the hands of those who would use it to destroy what little of the world is left. The water in you has grown stagnant, Roos, but it is not beyond cleansing."

Niclays kept his grip on the knife, quaking.

Stagnant.

The dragon spoke true. Everything around him had stilled. His life had stopped, like a clock in water, when Sabran Berethnet had sent him to Orisima. He had failed to solve one mystery since. Not the mystery of eternal life. Not why Jannart had died.

He was an alchemist, the unmaker of mystery. And he would not be stagnant again.

"Enough of this," he hissed, and carved.

43

South

The armorer furnished Ead with a monbone bow, an iron sword, an axe etched with Selinyi prayers, and a slim wood-handled dagger. Instead of the olive cloak of her childhood, she now wore the white of a postulant, a sign of her blossoming into a woman. Chassar, who had come with Sarsun to see her off, set his hands on her shoulders.

"Zāla would be so proud to see you," he said. "Soon the red cloak will be yours."

"If I come back alive."

"You will. Kalyba is a dread creature, but not as strong as she was. She has not eaten of the orange tree, for twenty years, and so will have no siden left."

"She has other magic."

"I trust you to conquer it, beloved. Or to turn back if the risk becomes too great." He patted the ichneumon beside her. "Be sure to return her to me in one piece, Aralaq."

"I am no stupid bird," Aralaq said. "Ichneumons do not lead little sisters into danger."

Sarsun cawed in indignation.

When she had been banished, Kalyba had fled to a part of the forest she had named the Bower of Eternity. It was said that she had put

454

an enchantment on it that tricked the eyes. Nobody knew how she created her illusions.

It was sundown when Ead set out with Aralaq from the Vale of Blood, back into the forest. Ichneumons could run faster than horses, faster even than the hunting leopards that had once lived in Lasia. Ead kept her head low as he crashed through lianas, slithered under roots, and sprang over the many creeks that branched off the Minara.

He tired just before dawn, and they made camp in a cavern behind a waterfall. Aralaq disappeared to hunt, while Ead refreshed herself in the pool below. As she climbed back to the cavern, she recalled the time when Kalyba had been at the Priory.

Ead remembered Kalyba as a redhead with bottomless dark eyes. She had arrived at the Priory when Ead was two years old, claiming to have visited several times before in her many centuries of existence—for she also maintained that she was immortal. Her siden had been granted to her not by the orange tree, but by a hawthorn tree that had once stood on the Inysh island of Nurtha.

The Prioress had welcomed her. Sisters had referred to her as the Hawthorn Sister or Rattletongue, depending on whether they believed her story. Most had kept their distance, for Kalyba had unsettling gifts. Gifts not granted to her by any tree.

Once, Kalyba had come across Ead and Jondu while they played under the sun, and she had smiled at them in a way that had made Ead trust her utterly. *What would you become, little sisters*, she had asked them, *if you could become anything?*

A bird, Jondu had answered, *so I could go anywhere.*

Me, too, Ead had said, because she had always done as Jondu did. *I could strike the wyrms down for the Mother, even as they flew.*

Watch, Kalyba had said.

That was where memory clouded, but Ead was sure that Kalyba had elongated her own fingers into feathers. Certainly she had done something that had charmed Ead and Jondu, enough for them to believe that Kalyba must be the most sacred of handmaidens.

The reasons for her banishment had never been clear, but it was rumored that it was she who had poisoned Zāla as she slept.

Perhaps it was when the Prioress had realized that she was the Lady of the Woods, the terror of Inysh legend, famous for her bloodlust.

As Ead dried her sword, Aralaq came through the waterfall. He gave her a sour look.

"You are a fool to make this journey. The Witch of Inysca will make meat of you."

"From what I hear, Kalyba likes to toy with her prey." She polished the blade on her cloak. "Besides, the witch is nothing if not inquisitive. She'll want to know why I've come to her."

"She will tell you lies."

"Or she will vaunt her knowledge. She has enough of it." With a long-suffering sigh, she reached for her bow. "I suppose I must hunt myself some dinner."

Aralaq growled before he went back through the waterfall, and Ead smiled. He would get her something. Ichneumons had a loyal streak, surly though they were.

She collected what little kindling she could find in the undergrowth and built a fire in the cavern. When Aralaq returned a second time, he threw down a speckled fish.

"This is only because you fed me as a pup," he said, and curled up in the darkness.

"Thank you, Aralaq."

He let out a disgruntled sound.

Ead wrapped the fish in plantain leaf and set it over the fire. As it cooked, her thoughts were drawn back to Inys, carried there as if by the south wind.

Sabran would be sleeping now, with Roslain or Katryen beside her. Fevered, perhaps. Or perhaps she had recovered. She might have already chosen another Lady of the Bedchamber—or rather, had one chosen for her. Now the Dukes Spiritual were circling the throne, it would almost certainly be another woman from one of their families, the better to spy on her.

What had they told the Queen of Inys about Ead? That she was a sorceress and a traitor, no doubt. Whether Sabran had believed it, in her heart, was a different matter. She would not want to accept it—but how could she challenge the Dukes Spiritual when they knew her secret; when they could destroy her with a word?

Did Sabran still trust her? She hardly deserved it. They had shared a bed, shared their bodies, but Ead had never told her the truth of who she was. Sabran had never even known her true name.

Aralaq would wake soon. She lay beside him, close enough to the waterfall that the spray cooled her skin, and tried to get some rest. Facing Kalyba would take all her wits. When Aralaq stirred, she gathered her weapons and hauled herself onto his back again.

They traveled through the forest until noon. When they came to the trunk of the Minara, Ead shielded her eyes against the sun. It was an unforgiving river, swift-flowing and deep. Aralaq bounded between rocks in the shallows, and when there was nothing else for it, he swam, Ead clinging to his fur.

Warm rain began to fall as they reached the other side of the river, plastering her curls to her face and neck. She ate some persimmon as Aralaq moved deeper into the forest. Only when the sun was beginning to sink again did he stop.

"The Bower is close." He sniffed. "If you do not return after an hour, I will come after you."

"Very well."

Ead slid from his back.

"Remember, Eadaz," Aralaq said, "whatever you see in this place is an illusion."

"I know." She sheathed her arm in a bracer. "See you soon."

Aralaq growled his displeasure. Axe in hand, Ead stepped into the mist.

An archway twisted out of boughs, laced with flowers, formed the door. Flowers the color of stormclouds.

I dream of a shaded bower in a forest, where sunlight dapples the grass. The entrance is a gateway of purple flowers—sabra flowers, I think.

Ead raised a hand, and for the first time in years, she conjured magefire. It danced from her fingers and torched the flowers, revealing the thorns beneath the illusion.

She closed her hands. The blue flame of magefire would unknit an enchantment if it burned for long enough, but she would have to use it in moderation if she meant to conserve enough strength to defend herself. With a last glance at Aralaq, she hacked her way through the thorns with her axe and emerged unscathed in the clearing beyond.

She was in the Orchard of Divinities. As she took a step forward, a scent breathed from the greensward, so thick and cloying she could almost roll it on her tongue. Golden light speckled grass deep enough for her to sink to her ankles.

The trees pressed close together here. Voices echoed beyond them—near and far away at once, dancing to the purl of water.

Were they even there, or was this part of the enchantment?

"Min mayde of strore, I knut thu smal,
as lutil as mus in gul mede.
With thu in soyle, corn grewath tal.
In thu I hafde blowende sede."

A great spring-fed pool came into view. Ead found herself walking toward it. With every step, the voices in the trees swelled and her head whirled like a round-wind. The language they sang in was steeped in the unfamiliar, but some of the words were unquestionably an old form of Inysh. Older than old. As ancient as the haithwood.

"In soyle I soweth mayde of strore
boute in belga bearn wil nat slepe.
Min wer is ut in wuda frore—
he huntath dama, nat for me."

Her hand was slick on the axe. The voices spoke of ritual from the dawn of a long-dead age. While she took in the crisscross of branches above her, Ead forced herself to imagine them drenched in blood, and the voices luring her into a trap.

At the end of the path, I find a great rock, and I reach out to touch it with a hand I do not think is mine. Ead turned. There it was, a slab of stone almost as tall as she was, guarding the mouth of a cave. *The rock breaks in two, and inside—*

"Hello."

Ead looked up. A small boy was sitting on a branch above her.

"Hello," he said again in Selinyi. His voice was high and sweet. "Are you here to play with me?"

"I am here to see the Lady of the Woods," Ead said. "Will you fetch her for me, child?"

The boy let out a musical laugh. One blink, and he was there. The next, he was nowhere.

Something made Ead look toward the pool. Sweat prickled on her nape as she watched for any ripple on its surface.

She drew in a breath when the water birthed a head. A woman emerged, sloe-eyed and naked.

"Eadaz du Zāla uq-Nāra." Kalyba stepped into the clearing. "It has been a long time."

The Witch of Inysca. The Lady of the Woods. Her voice was as deep and clear as her pool, with a strange inflection. Northern Inysh, but not quite.

"Kalyba," Ead said.

"Last I saw you, you were no more than six. Now you are a woman," Kalyba observed. "How the years pass. One forgets, when the years leave no indent on the flesh."

Ead remembered her face well now, with its lofty cheekbones and full upper lip. Her skin was tanned, her limbs long and well turned. Auburn hair rolled in waves over her breasts. Anyone who looked at her would swear she was not a day past five and twenty. Beautiful, but clipped by the same hollowness that Ead had seen in her own reflection.

"My last visitor was one of your sisters, come to take my head to Mita Yedanya in punishment for a crime I never committed. I suppose you are here to do the same," Kalyba ruminated. "I would warn you against trying, but the sisters of the Priory have grown arrogant in the years I have been away."

"I am not here to hurt you."

"Why do you come to me, then, sweet mage?"

"To learn."

Kalyba remained still and expressionless. Water trickled down her belly and thighs.

"I have just returned from Inys," Ead said. "The last Prioress sent me there to serve its queen. While I was in Ascalon, I heard tell of the great power of the Lady of the Woods."

"Lady of the Woods." Kalyba closed her eyes and breathed in, as if the name had a rich scent to it. "Oh, it has been a *very* long time since they called me by that name."

"You are dreaded and revered in Inys, even now."

"Doubtless. Strange, as I seldom went to the haithwood, even as a child," the witch said. "The villagers would not set foot in it for fear of me, but I spent most of my years away from my birthplace. It took them far too long to realize that my home was with the hawthorn."

"People fear the haithwood because of you. Only one road leads through it, and those who walk on it speak of corpse candles and screams. Remnants of your magic, they say."

Kalyba smiled faintly.

"Mita Yedanya has called me back to Lasia, but I would sooner pledge my blade to a greater mage." Ead took a step toward her. "I come to offer myself as your student, Lady. To learn the whole truth of magic."

Her voice sounded awestruck even to her own ears. If she could fool the Inysh court for almost a decade, she could also fool a witch.

"I am flattered," Kalyba said, "but surely your Prioress can give you truth."

"Mita Yedanya is not like her predecessors. She looks inward," Ead said. "I do not."

That part, at least, was true.

"A sister who sees beyond her own nose. Rare as silver honey, I should say," Kalyba said. "Are you not frightened of the stories they tell of me in my native land, Eadaz uq-Nāra? There I am a child-stealer, a hag, a murderess. Monster of the tales of old."

"Tales to frighten wayward children. I do not fear that which I do not understand."

"And what makes you think you are *worthy* of the power I have wielded through the ages?"

"Lady, I am not," Ead said, "but with your guidance, perhaps I could be. If you will honor me with your knowledge."

Kalyba considered her for some time, like a wolf considering the lamb.

"Tell me," she said, "how is Sabran?"

Ead almost shivered at the intimate way the witch said that name, as if she spoke of a close friend.

"The Queen of Inys fares well," she replied.

"You ask for truth, yet your own lips lie."

Ead met her gaze. Her face was a carving, its etchings too ancient to translate. "The Queen of Inys is imperiled," she admitted.

"Better." Kalyba tilted her head. "If your offer is sincere, you will do me the kindness of surrendering your weapons. When I lived in Inysca, it was considered a grave insult for guests to bring weapons to the threshold of a hall." Her gaze drifted to the archway of thorns. "Let alone over it."

"Forgive me. I have no wish to insult you."

Kalyba watched her without expression. With the sense that she was signing her own death warrant, Ead divested herself of her weapons and set them on the grass.

"There. Now you have put your trust in me," Kalyba said almost gently, "and in return, I will not harm you."

"My thanks, Lady."

They stood facing one another for a time, with half the clearing between them.

There was no reason for Kalyba to tell her anything. Ead knew that, and so would the witch.

"You say you desire truth, but truth is a weave with many threads," Kalyba said. "You know I am a mage. A sidensmith, like you—or I *was*, before the old Prioress denied me the fruit of the orange tree. All because Mita Yedanya told her I had poisoned your birthmother." She smiled. "As if I would ever stoop to poison."

So Mita was personally responsible for the banishment. The last Prioress had been a kind woman, but easily influenced by those around her, including her *munguna*.

"I am Firstblood. I was first and last to eat of the hawthorn, and it granted me eternal life. But of course," Kalyba said, "you have not come out of curiosity about my siden, for siden is familiar to you. You wish to know the source of my *other* power—the one no sister understands. The power of dream and illusion. The power of Ascalon, my *hildistérron*."

War-star. A poetic term for the sword. Ead had seen it before, in prayer books—but now it plucked a string in her, and the realization came forth like a note of music.

Fire ascends from the earth, light descends from the sky.

Light from the sky.

Hildistérron.

And *Ascalon.* Another name from the ancient tongue of the Isles of Inysca. A corruption of *astra*—another word for *star*—and *lun,* for strength. Loth had told her that.

Strong star.

"When I was in Inys . . . I remembered the text of the Tablet of Rumelabar. It spoke of a balance between fire and starlight." Even as Ead spoke, her mind spun out an explanation that seemed sounder by the moment. "The siden trees grant mages fire. I wondered if your power—your *other* power—comes from the sky. From the Long-Haired Star."

Kalyba did not possess a face that lent itself to shock, but Ead saw it. A flicker in her gaze.

"Good. Oh, *very* good." A little thrum of laughter escaped her. "I had thought its name was lost to time. How ever did a mage hear of the Long-Haired Star?"

"I went to Gulthaga."

Truyde utt Zeedeur had spoken those words. The girl had acted like a fool, but her instinct had been right.

"Clever *and* brave, to venture to the Buried City." Kalyba regarded her. "It would be pleasant to have company in my Bower, since I am denied the sisterhood of the Priory. And since you already have most of the truth . . . I see no harm in telling you the rest."

"I would treasure the knowledge."

"No doubt. Of course," Kalyba mused, "to understand my power, you would have to know the whole truth of siden, and the two branches of magic, and Mita has so little understanding of such things. She keeps her daughters in the dark, draped in the comfort of well-worn books. All of you are soaked in ignorance. My knowledge—*true* knowledge—is a valuable thing."

This was the next move in a game. "One might say it was priceless," Ead agreed.

462

"I paid a price for it. As must you."

At last, Kalyba approached. Water beaded from her hair as she walked around Ead.

"I will take a kiss," she whispered at her ear. Ead stayed rooted in place. "I have been alone for so many years. A kiss from you, sweet Eadaz, and my knowledge is yours."

A metallic scent hung on her skin. For a sudden, eldritch moment, Ead felt something in her blood—something vital—sing in answer to that scent. "Lady," Ead murmured, "how will I know that what you say is the truth?"

"Do you ask the same of Mita Yedanya, or does she receive your unconditional trust?" Receiving no answer, Kalyba said, "I give you my word that I will speak true. When I was young, a word was a sworn oath. It has been many years since then, but I still respect the ancient ways."

There was no choice but to risk it. Steeling herself, Ead leaned close to her and placed a kiss on her cheek.

"There," Kalyba said. Her breath was icy. "The price is paid."

Ead drew back as fast as she dared. She forced down a sudden thought of Sabran.

"There are two branches of magic," Kalyba began. The sunlight picked out threads of gold in her hair and limned each drop of water. "The sisters of the Priory, as you know, are practitioners of *siden*—terrene magic. It comes from the core of the world, and is channeled through the tree. Those who eat of its fruit can wield its magic. Once there were at least three siden trees—the orange, the hawthorn, and the mulberry—but now, to my knowledge, only one remains.

"But siden, dear Eadaz, has a natural opposite. Sidereal magic, or *sterren*—the power of the stars. This kind of magic is cold and elusive, graceful and slippery. It allows the wielder to cast illusions, control water ... even to change their shape. It is far harder to master."

Ead no longer had to feign her look of curiosity.

"When the Long-Haired Star passes, it leaves behind a silver liquid. I named it *star rot*," Kalyba said. "It is in star rot that sterren lives, just as it is in the fruit that siden lives."

"It must be rare."

"Unspeakably so. There has not been a meteor shower since the end of the Grief of Ages—and understand, Eadaz, that the shower *was* the end of the Grief of Ages. It was not coincidence that it came when the wyrms fell. The Easterners believe the comet was sent by their dragon god, Kwiriki." Kalyba smiled. "The shower closed an era when siden was stronger, and forced the wyrms, who are made of it, into their slumber."

"And then sterren was the stronger," Ead said.

"For a time," Kalyba confirmed. "There is a balance between the two branches of magic. They keep one another in check. When one waxes, the other wanes. An Age of Fire will be followed by an Age of Starlight. At present, siden is much stronger, and sterren is a shadow of itself. But when a meteor shower comes ... then sterren will burn bright again."

The world had ridiculed alchemists for their fascination with the Tablet of Rumelabar, but for centuries they had been circling the truth.

And truth it was. Ead felt it in the lining of her belly, in the strings of her heart. She would not have believed it from Kalyba alone, but her explanation formed the thread that held the beads together. The Long-Haired Star. The Tablet of Rumelabar. The fall of the wyrms in the Grief of Ages. The strange gifts of the woman who now stood before her.

All of it connected. All of it stemming to one truth: fire from beneath, light from above. A universe built on this duality.

"The Tablet of Rumelabar speaks of this balance," Ead said, "but also what happens when the balance is unsettled."

"*Too much of one doth inflame the other, and in this is the extinction of the universe,*" Kalyba recited. "A dire warning. Now, what—or who—is the extinction of the universe?"

Ead shook her head. She knew the answer well enough, but best to play the fool. It would keep the witch off her guard.

"Oh, Eadaz, you were doing so well. Still," Kalyba said, "you are young. I must not be too hard a judge."

She turned away. As she moved, her hand came to her right side. It was as smooth and unmarked as the rest of her, but her gait betrayed the pain in it.

"Are you hurt, Lady?" Ead asked.

Kalyba did not reply.

"Long ago, the cosmic duality was . . . upset," was all she said. Ead thought she glimpsed something terrible in those eyes. A shadow of hatred. "Sterren grew too strong in the world and, in return, the fire beneath our feet forged an abomination. A *miscreation* of siden."

The extinction of the universe.

"The Nameless One," Ead said.

"And his followers. They are children of the imbalance. Of chaos." Kalyba seated herself on a boulder. "Successive Prioresses have long seen the connection between the tree and the wyrms, but denied it to themselves and their daughters. Mages can even create Draconic flame during Ages of Fire, like this one . . . but of course, you are forbidden from using it."

All sisters knew they had the potential to make wyrmfire, but it was not taught.

"Your illusions come from sterren," Ead murmured, "so siden burns them away."

"Siden and sterren can destroy each other in particular circumstances," Kalyba conceded, "but they also *attract* one another. Both forms of magic are drawn to themselves most of all, but also to their opposites." Her dark eyes were alight with interest. "Now, my puzzle-solver. If the orange tree is the natural channel of siden, what are the natural channels of sterren?"

Ead thought on it. "The dragons of the East, perhaps."

From what little she knew about them, they were creatures of water. It was a guess, but Kalyba smiled.

"Very good. They were born of sterren. When the Long-Haired Star comes, they can give dreams and change their shapes and knit illusions."

As if to demonstrate, the witch cast a hand down the length of her own body. All at once, she wore an Inysh gown of brown samite and a girdle studded with carnelians and pearls. Jewel lilies opened in her hair. Had the nakedness been the illusion, or was this?

"Long ago, I used my fire to reshape the star rot I had gathered." Kalyba combed her fingers through her hair. "To create the most remarkable weapon ever made."

"Ascalon."

"A sword of sterren, forged with siden. A perfect union. It was when I beheld it—the sword I had made from the tears of a comet—that I knew I was not just a mage." Her mouth flinched. "The Priory calls me *witch* for my gifts, but I prefer *enchantress*. It has a pretty ring to it."

Ead had learned more than she had bargained for, but she had come to ask about the jewel.

"Lady," she said, "your gifts are miraculous indeed. Did you ever forge anything else from sterren?"

"Never. I wanted Ascalon to be unlike anything in this world. A gift for the greatest knight of his time. Of course," Kalyba said, "that is not to say that there *are* no other objects ... but they were not cast by my hand. And if they exist, they are long since lost."

It was tempting to tell her about the jewel, but it was best that Kalyba remained ignorant of it, or she would go out of her way to make it hers.

"I would like nothing better than to lay eyes on the sword. All Inys talks of it," Ead said. "Will you show it to me, Lady?"

Kalyba chuckled low. "If I had it, I would be happy indeed. I searched for Ascalon for centuries, but Galian hid it well."

"He left no clue as to its whereabouts?"

"Only that he meant to leave it in the hands of those who would die to keep it from me." Her smile faded. "The Queens of Inys have also sought it, given that it is sacred to them ... but they will not find it. If I could not, then no one will."

That Kalyba had forged Ascalon for Galian Berethnet was common knowledge in the Priory. It was part of the reason many sisters had distrusted her. The two of them had been born in the same era and had both lived in or around the village of Goldenbirch, but beyond those scant facts, no one understood the nature of their relationship.

"Queen Sabran dreamed of this Bower of Eternity," Ead said. "While I was her lady-in-waiting, she told me so. Only you can weave dreams, Lady. Was it you who sent them to her?"

"That knowledge," Kalyba said, "will require a higher price."

With that, the witch slid from the boulder. Naked once more, she listed on to her side, and the rock beneath her transformed into a bed of flowers. They smelled of cream and honey.

"Come to me." She smoothed a hand over her petals. "Come, lie with me in my Bower, and I will sing to you of dreaming."

"Lady," Ead said, "I desire nothing more than to please you, and to prove my loyalty, but my heart belongs to another."

"The secret of dream-weaving must surely be worth the price of one night. It has been centuries since I felt the soft touch of a lover." Kalyba drew a finger down her own abdomen, stopping just shy of where her thighs met. "But ... I do admire loyalty. So I will accept another gift from you. In exchange for my knowledge of the stars, and *their* gifts."

"Anything."

"Twenty years they have kept me from the orange tree. Once a mage has tasted of the fire, she burns for it evermore. The hunger eats me from within. I would very much like my flame back." Kalyba held her gaze. "Bring me the fruit, and you will be my heir. Swear it to me, Eadaz du Zāla uq-Nāra. Swear that you will bring me what I desire."

"Lady," Ead said, "I swear it by the Mother."

———

"And she said nothing about the jewels," the Prioress said. "Only that she did not make them."

Ead stood in her sunroom, facing her.

"Yes, Prioress," she said. "Ascalon is her only creation. I thought it best not to mention the jewels, for fear she would pursue them."

"Good."

Chassar was grim-faced. The Prioress placed her hands on the balustrade, and her ring glinted in the sun.

"Two strands of magic. I have never heard anything of the sort." She breathed in. "I mislike this. The witch is a liar by nature. There is a reason they called her Rattletongue."

"She might embellish the truth," Chassar said, "but bloodthirsty and cold though she is, she never struck me as a liar. In her day in Inysca, there were brutal punishments for oath-breaking."

"You forget, Chassar, that she lied about Zāla. She claimed she never poisoned her, but only an outsider would have murdered a sister."

Chassar dropped his gaze.

"The jewels must be sterren," Ead said. "Even if Kalyba did not make them. If they are not our kind of magic, they must be the other." The Prioress nodded slowly. "I vowed to her that I would bring her the fruit. Is she like to pursue me when I do not?"

"I doubt she will squander her magic on a hunt. In any case, you are protected here." The Prioress watched the sun descend. "Say nothing of this to your sisters. Our next line of enquiry is this ... Neporo."

"An Easterner," Ead said quietly. "Surely that tells you that the Mother was interested in the world beyond the South."

"I tire of this subject, Eadaz."

Ead bit her tongue. Chassar shot her a cautionary look.

"If Neporo spoke true, then to defeat our enemy, we will need both Ascalon and the jewels." The Prioress rubbed her temple. "Leave me, Eadaz. I must ... consider our course."

Ead inclined her head and left.

In her sunroom, Ead found Aralaq snoozing at the foot of her bed, weary from their journey. She sat on the bed beside him and stroked his silken ears. They twitched in his sleep.

Her mind was a crucible of stars and fire. The Nameless One would return, and the Priory had only one of the three instruments needed to destroy him. With every hour that passed, the danger grew in Virtudom, and Sabran was at greater risk. Meanwhile, Sigoso Vetalda was building his invasion fleet in Quarl Bay. A divided West would not be ready for the Flesh King.

Ead pressed close to Aralaq and closed her eyes. Somehow, she had to find a way to help her.

"Eadaz."

She looked up.

A woman stood in the doorway. Tight curls wreathed her brown face and tumbled into tawny eyes.

"Nairuj," Ead said, rising.

They had been rivals when they were children. Nairuj had always been vying with Jondu for the attention of the Prioress, which Ead, loving Jondu as her elder sister, had taken very much to heart. Now, however, Ead took Nairuj by the hands and kissed her on the cheek.

"It is good to see you," Ead said. "You honor the cloak."

"And you have honored all of us by shielding Sabran for so long. I confess I laughed to see you shipped off to that ludicrous court when I was young and foolish," Nairuj said, with a wry smile, "but I understand now that we all work in different ways for the Mother."

"I see you are serving her as we speak." Ead returned her smile. "You must be close to your time."

"Any day now." Nairuj placed a hand on her belly. "I've come to prepare you for your initiation into the Red Damsels."

Ead felt her smile growing. "Tonight?"

"Yes. Tonight." Nairuj chuckled. "Did you think that after you banished Fýredel, you would not be raised at once when you returned?"

She guided Ead to a chair. A boy came in and set down a tray before retreating.

Ead folded her hands in her lap. Her heart had the wings of a flock of birds.

For one night, she would put aside what she had learned from Kalyba. She would forget everything that had happened outside these walls. Since she was old enough to understand who she was, she had known that she was destined to be a Red Damsel.

Her dream was here. She meant to savor it.

"For you." Nairuj handed her a cup. "From the Prioress."

Ead sipped. "Mother." A weave of sweet flavors unspooled on her tongue. "What is this?"

"Sun wine. From Kumenga. The Prioress keeps a supply," Nairuj whispered. "Tulgus in the kitchen sometimes lets me have a taste. He'll let you have one, too, if you say I sent you. Just don't tell the Prioress."

"Never."

Ead drank again. It tasted exquisite. Nairuj took a wooden comb from the tray.

"Eadaz," she said, "I wanted to give you my condolences. For Jondu. We had our differences, but I respected her very much."

"Thank you," Ead said softly. She shook her head to clear the sadness. "Come, then, Nairuj. Tell me everything that has happened these past eight years."

"I will," Nairuj said, tapping the comb against her palm, "if you promise to me all the secrets of the Inysh court." She reached for a bowl of oil. "I hear life there is like walking on coals. That the courtiers climb over one another to get close to the queen. That there is more intrigue in the court of Sabran the Ninth than there is skystone in Rumelabar."

Ead looked toward the window. The stars were coming out.

"Truly," she said, "you have no idea."

As Nairuj worked on Ead, she told her about the steady waking of wyrms in the South, and how the Red Damsels were working harder by the day to deal with the threat. King Jantar and High Ruler Kagudo—the only sovereigns who knew of the Priory—had asked for more sisters to be posted in their cities and courts. Meanwhile, the menfolk of the Priory, who dealt with domestic matters, might soon have to be trained as slayers.

In return, Ead told her the more preposterous facets of Inys. The petty enmities between courtiers and lovers and poets. Her time as a maid of honor under Oliva Marchyn. The quacks who gave out dung for a fever and leeches for a headache. The eighteen dishes presented to Sabran every morning, of which she ate one.

"And Sabran. Is she as capricious as they say?" Nairuj asked. "I hear that in one morning, she can be as jubilant as a parade, as sad as a lament, and as angry as a wildcat."

Ead did not reply for a long time.

"That is true," she finally said.

A rose behind a pillow. Hands on the virginals. Her laugh as they had raced after the hunt.

"I suppose a little caprice is to be expected of a woman born to sit on such a throne, at such a price." Nairuj patted her belly. "This is heavy enough without the fate of nations perched on top of it."

The hour of the ceremony drew near. Ead let Nairuj and three other sisters help her into her vestures. Once her hair was arranged, they adorned it with a circlet of orange blossoms. They slid bracelets of glass and gold up her arms. Finally, Nairuj took her by the shoulders.

"Ready?"

Ead nodded. She had been ready all her life.

"I envy you," Nairuj said. "The task the Prioress will give you next sounds—"

"Task." Ead looked at her. "What task?"

Nairuj fluttered a hand. "I must not say any more. You will know soon enough." She took Ead by the arm. "Come."

———

They led her to the tomb of the Mother. The burial chamber had been lit with one hundred and twenty candles, the number of people who had been sacrificed by lottery to the Nameless One before Cleolind had ended the rule of blood at last.

The Prioress was waiting in front of the statue. Every sister not posted elsewhere was here to see the daughter of Zāla take her place as a Red Damsel.

Ceremonies were succinct affairs in the Priory. Cleolind had not wanted the pomp and circumstance of courts for her handmaidens. Intimacy was what mattered. The coming together of sisters in support and praise of one another. In the womb-like darkness of the chamber, with the Mother gazing down at them all, Ead felt closer to her than she ever had.

Chassar stood to the left of the Prioress. He looked as proud as if he were her birthfather.

Ead knelt.

"Eadaz du Zāla uq-Nāra," the Prioress said. Her voice echoed. "You have served the Mother faithfully and without question. We welcome you, as our sister and friend, to the ranks of the Red Damsels."

"I am Eadaz du Zāla uq-Nāra," Ead said. "I pledge myself anew to the Mother, as I did once as a child."

"May she keep your blade sharp and your cloak red with blood," the sisters said together, "and may the Nameless One fear your light."

It was traditional for the birthmother to present a sister with her cloak. In the absence of Zāla, it was Chassar who hung it around her shoulders. He fastened it with a brooch at the hollow of her throat, and when he cupped her cheek, Ead returned his smile.

She held out her right hand. The Prioress slid on her silver ring, topped with the five-petalled flower of sunstone. The ring she had imagined herself wearing all her life.

"May you go forth into the world," the Prioress said, "and stand against the ruthless fire. Now and always."

Ead drew the brocade close to her skin. The richness of the red was impossible to fabricate. Only Draconic blood could stain it so.

The Prioress held out both her hands, palms up, and smiled. Ead took them and rose, and applause rang through the burial chamber. As the Prioress turned her to face her sisters, presenting her to them as a Red Damsel, Ead happened to look toward the Sons of Siyāti. And there, standing among them, was a man whose face was familiar.

He was taller than she was. Long, powerful limbs. Deep black skin. When he lifted his head, his features were bared to the candlelight.

She could not be seeing this. Kalyba had addled her senses. He was dead. He was lost. He could not be here.

And yet— and yet, he was.

Loth.

44

South

Ead.

She was staring at him as if at a ghost.

For months he had walked these halls in a half-sleep. He suspected they were putting something into his food, to make him forget the man he had been. He had started to misremember the details of her face—his friend from far away.

Now there she was, cloaked in red, hair thickset with flowers. And she looked ... whole, and full, and fire-new. As if she had gone for too long without water, and now she was in bloom.

Ead shifted her gaze. As if she had never seen him. The Prioress—the head of this sect—guided her from the chamber. Betrayal had stung him at the first sight of her, but he had known, from that instant of flared eyes and parted lips, that she was just as surprised to see him as he was to see her.

No matter what she was, she was still Ead Duryan, still his friend. Somehow, he had to reach her.

Before it was too late to remember.

Chassar was in bed when Ead found him reading by candlelight, spectacles on the bridge of his nose. He looked up as she blew into his chamber like a storm.

"What is Lord Arteloth doing here?" She made no effort to keep her voice low.

His great brows furrowed. "Eadaz," he said, "calm yourself."

Sarsun, who had been snoozing, loosed an indignant caw.

"The Night Hawk sent Loth to Cárscaro," Ead said coolly. "Why is he here?"

Chassar let out a long sigh.

"He was the one who brought us the riddlebox. It was given to him by the Donmata Marosa." He removed his spectacles. "She told him to find me. After meeting Jondu."

"The Donmata is an ally?"

"Apparently." Chassar crossed his nightrobe over his chest and knotted the belt. "Lord Arteloth was not meant to be in the burial chamber tonight."

"Then you purposely kept him out of my way."

The deceit would have hurt from anyone, but it was most hurtful from him.

"I knew that you would not be pleased," Chassar murmured. "I wanted to break it to you myself, after the ceremony. You know that when outsiders find the Priory, they can never leave."

"He has a family. We cannot just—"

"We can. For the Priory." Slowly, Chassar rose from bed. "If we let him go, he would tell all to Sabran."

"You need not fear that. The Night Hawk will never let Loth return to court," Ead said.

"Eadaz, listen to me. Arteloth Beck is a follower of the Deceiver. Perhaps he was kind to you, but he can never *understand* you. Next you will tell me that you came to care for Sabran Bereth—"

"What if I did?"

Chassar scrutinized her face. His mouth was a fess in the depths of his beard.

"You heard the blasphemy of the Inysh," he said. "You know what they have done to the memory of the Mother."

"You told me to get close to her. Is it any wonder if I did?" Ead shot back. "You left me to fend for myself in that court for almost a decade. I was an outsider. A convert. If I had not found people to hold on to, to make the wait endurable—"

"I know. And I will be sorry for it for the rest of my days." He laid a tender hand on her shoulder. "You are tired. And angry. We can speak again in the morning."

She wanted to retort, but this was Chassar, who had helped the Sons of Siyāti raise her, who had made her gurgle with laughter when she was small, who had watched over her when Zāla had died.

"Nairuj told me that the Prioress will give me another task soon," Ead said. "I want to know what it is."

Chassar pressed a finger between his eyes and rubbed. She stood akimbo, waiting.

"You shielded Sabran from Fýredel almost nine years after leaving Lasia. That deep bond with the tree—one that can reach across time and distance—is a rare thing. Very rare." He sank back on to the bed. "The Prioress means to take advantage of it. She intends to send you to the lands beyond the Gate of Ungulus."

Her heart thumped. "For what purpose?"

"A sister brought us rumors from Drayasta. A group of pirates are claiming Valeysa laid an egg somewhere in the Eria during the Grief of Ages," Chassar said. "The Prioress wants you to find and destroy it. Before it can hatch."

"Ungulus." Ead could no longer feel most of her body. "I might be away for years."

"Yes."

The Gate of Ungulus was the edge of the known world. Beyond it, the southern continent was uncharted. The few explorers who had ventured there had spoken of a waste without end, which was named the Eria—glittering salt flats, brutal sun, and not a drop of water. If any of them had made it to the other side, they had never returned to tell the tale.

"There have always been stories circulating Drayasta." Ead walked slowly toward the balcony. "By the Mother, what have I done to deserve *more* exile?"

"This is a mission of true urgency," Chassar said, "but I sense she chose you for it not only because of your endurance, but because this task would return your attention to the South."

"You mean my loyalty is in question."

475

"No," Chassar said, gentler. "She simply believes you might benefit from this journey. It will give you a chance to remember your purpose and cleanse yourself of impurities."

The Prioress wanted her as far away from Virtudom as possible so she would not be able to see the turmoil that would soon break out there. She hoped that by the time Ead returned, she would no longer believe that anywhere but the South mattered.

"There is one other choice."

Ead looked over her shoulder. "Out with it."

"You could offer her a child." Chassar held her gaze. "We must have more warriors for the Priory. The Prioress believes any child of yours will inherit your bond with the tree. Do this, and she may send Nairuj south instead, once she has given birth."

Her jaw hurt from the effort it took to rein in a joyless laugh.

"For me," she said, "that is no choice."

She strode from the room. "Eadaz," Chassar called after her, but she did not look back. "Where are you going?"

"To see her."

"No." He was down the corridor and in front of her in moments. "Eadaz, look at me. The decision is made. Fight her, and she will only extend your time away."

"I am not a child that I need to be sent away to think about what I have done wrong. I am—"

"What is happening?"

Ead turned. The Prioress, resplendent in plum-colored silk, stood at the entrance to the corridor.

"Prioress." Ead went to her. "I beg you not to send me on this assignment beyond Ungulus."

"It is already arranged. We have long suspected that the High Westerns have a nest," the Prioress said. "The sister who goes to destroy it must be able to survive without the fruit. I have confidence that you will do this for me, daughter. That you will serve the Mother once again."

"This is not how I was meant to serve the Mother."

"You will accept nothing but my allowing you to return to Inys. You have your heart set upon this. You must go past the Gate of Ungulus to remember who you are."

476

"I know full well who I am," Ead snapped. "What I do not know is why, in the years I have been absent, this house of ours has become unable to see beyond its nose."

She knew from the silence that followed that she had gone too far.

The Prioress looked at her for a long time, so still she might as well have been cast from bronze.

"If you ask to eschew your duty again," she said at last, "I will have no choice but to take back your cloak."

Ead could not speak. A coldness ran her through.

The Prioress shut herself in her sunroom. Chassar gave Ead a rueful look before he walked away, leaving her to stand and tremble.

A society this old and this secret needed careful handling. She, Eadaz du Zāla uq-Nāra, now knew what it felt like to be handled.

Her journey back to her room was a smear. She strode out onto her balcony and beheld the Vale of Blood once more. The orange tree was as beautiful as ever. Soul-fearing in its perfection.

The Prioress would not stop the fall of Inys. Once civil war took Virtudom apart from within, it would be easy prey for the Flesh King and the Draconic Army. Ead could not stomach it.

The sun wine was still on her nightstand. She drank what was left, trying to steady the quivers of anger. When she had drained the cup, she found herself gazing at it. And as she turned it over in her hands, something woke in her memory.

The twin goblets. The age-old symbol of the Knight of Justice. And her bloodline.

Crest.

Descendant of the Knight of Justice. She who weighed the cups of guilt and innocence, of support and opposition, of virtue and vice. A trusted servant of the crown.

Cupbearer.

Igrain Crest, who had always disapproved of Aubrecht Lievelyn. Whose retainers had seized control of the Queen Tower even as Ead fled from it, ostensibly to protect Sabran.

Ead gripped the balustrade. Loth had sent one warning from Cárscaro. *Beware the Cupbearer.* He had been investigating the disappearance of Prince Wilstan, who in turn had suspected the Vetalda of involvement in the murder of Queen Rosarian.

Had Crest arranged for Rosarian Berethnet to die before her time, leaving a young girl in charge of Inys?

A queen who needed a protector before she came of age. A young princess Crest had stepped in to mold ...

Even as she considered it, Ead knew her instinct had struck true. She had been so blinded by her hatred for Combe, so determined to make him responsible for everything that had happened in Inys, she had missed what had been right before her eyes.

How easy it would be, Combe had said, *for you to lay the blame for all ills at my doorstep.*

If it *was* Crest, then Roslain could be in on it. Perhaps her loyalty to Sabran had gone, along with the child. The entire Crest family could be plotting to usurp her.

And they had the Queen Tower.

Ead paced in the dark. Despite the wet heat of the Lasian Basin, she was so cold that her jaw quaked.

If she returned to Inys, she would be anathema to the Priory. Her name unsaid, her life forfeit.

If she did *not* return to Inys, she would be abandoning all of Virtudom. That seemed to Ead to be a betrayal of all she knew to be right, and all the Priory represented. She was loyal to the Mother, not to Mita Yedanya.

She had to follow the flame in her heart. The flame the tree had given her.

The realization of what she had to do carved pieces from her soul. She tasted salt on her lips. Tears ran down to her chin and fell in fat drops.

This place was where she had been born. It was where she belonged. All she had ever wanted, all her life, was a red cloak. The cloak she would have to leave behind.

She would continue the work of the Mother. In Inys, she could end what Jondu had started.

Ascalon. Without the sword, there was no chance of defeating the Nameless One. The Red Damsels had searched for it. Kalyba had searched for it. To no avail.

None of them had possessed the waning jewel.

Both forms of magic are drawn to themselves most of all, but also to the other.

The jewel had to be sterren. Ascalon might answer to it, and it, in turn, would answer only to her.

Ead gazed out at the tree, throat aching. She sank to her knees, and she prayed that this was the right decision.

Aralaq found her there in the morning, when the sun burned in the pearl-blue sky.

"Eadaz."

She turned her head to look at him, raw and sleepless. His tongue sanded her cheek. "My friend," she said, "I need your help." She took his face between her hands. "Do you remember how I fed you, when you were a pup? How I cared for you?"

His amber eyes seemed to catch the sunlight.

"Yes," he said.

Of course he remembered. Ichneumons did not forget the first hand to feed them.

"There is a man here, among the Sons of Siyāti. His name is Arteloth."

"Yes. I brought him here."

"You were right to save him." She swallowed the thickness in her throat. "I need you to get him out of the Priory, to the mouth of the cave in the forest, after sundown."

He studied her. "You are leaving."

"I must."

His slit nostrils flared. "They will follow."

"Which is why I need your help." She stroked his ears. "You must discover where the Prioress keeps the white jewel from my chamber."

"You are a fool." He nudged her brow with his nose. "Without the tree, you will wither. All sisters do."

"Then wither I will. Better to do that than to do nothing."

A huff escaped him. "Mita has the jewel on her person," he rumbled. "She smells of it. Of the sea."

Ead closed her eyes.

"I will find a way," she said.

479

45

East

The beaches of Feather Island were overrun by seawater. Tané had spent hours with Elder Vara while the island shivered, making it impossible to read.

Elder Vara had managed, of course. The world could end and he would find a way to keep on reading.

After the waters, a terrible hush had fallen. Every bird in the forest had lost its voice. That was when the scholars began to examine the damage wrought by the quake. Most of their number were unscathed, but two men had been tossed from the cliffs. The sea had not returned their bodies—but another body had washed up a day later.

The body of a dragon.

Tané had gone with Elder Vara at sunset to look upon the lifeless god. The steps were hard on his iron leg, and it had taken them a long time to reach the beach, but he had been resolved to go, and Tané had not left his side.

They had found a young Seiikinese dragon twisted across the sand, her jaw slack in death. Birds had already pecked the gleam from her scales, and mist clung to her bones. Tané had shuddered at the sight, and eventually, when she could bear it no more, she had turned away in grief.

She had never seen the carcass of a dragon. It was the most terrible thing she had ever beheld. They had thought at first that the little female had been butchered in Kawontay, and the remains abandoned to the sea—Tané had thought of Nayimathun and sickened—but the body had been whole, with all its scales and teeth and claws.

Gods could not drown. They were one with water. Finally, the elders had concluded that this dragon had been boiled.

Boiled alive by the sea itself.

Nothing was more unnatural. No omen could be more sinister.

Even if all the scholars had combined their strength, they would not have been able to move the dragon. She would be left to thaw out of existence. Eventually, all that remained would be iridescent bone.

The surgeon arrived while Tané was sweeping leaves with three other scholars, who worked in silence. Some shook with tears. The dead dragon had left everyone in a state of shock.

"Scholar Tané," Elder Vara called.

She walked behind him like a shadow, into the corridors.

"The surgeon has come at last. I thought she might examine your side," he said. "The learnèd Doctor Moyaka is a practitioner of Seiikinese and Mentish medicine."

Tané stopped dead.

Moyaka. She knew that name.

Elder Vara turned to face her with a cockled brow. "Scholar Tané, you look distressed."

"I don't want to see this doctor. Please, learnèd Elder Vara. Doctor Moyaka has—" She felt sick. "He knows someone who threatened me. Who threatened my dragon."

She could see Roos again, on the beach. His callous smile as he told her she must mutilate her dragon or lose everything. Moyaka had let that monster stay in his house.

"I know your last days in Seiiki were unhappy, Tané." Elder Vara spoke gently. "I also know how hard it is to let go of the past. But on Feather Island, you *must* let go."

Tané stared at his lined face. "What do you know?" she whispered.

"Everything."

"Who else knows?"

"Only myself and the honored High Elder."

His words made her feel as if she had been stripped naked. Deep down, she had hoped the Governor of Ginura would tell no one why she had been sent away from Seiiki.

"If you are certain you do not want to see learnèd Doctor Moyaka," Elder Vara said, "say it once more, and I will take you to your room."

She had no desire whatsoever to see Doctor Moyaka, but she also had no wish to embarrass Elder Vara by acting like a child.

"I will see him," she said.

"Her," Elder Vara corrected.

A stout Seiikinese woman awaited them in the healing room, where a water fountain burbled. Tané had never seen her before, but she was plainly a relative of the Doctor Moyaka she had met in Ginura.

"Good day, honorable scholar." The woman bowed. "I understand you have an injury to your side."

"An old one," Elder Vara explained, when Tané only bowed in return. "It is a swelling she has had since childhood."

"I see." The learnèd Moyaka patted the mats, where a blanket and a headrest had been placed. "Open your tunic, please, honorable scholar, and lie down."

Tané did as instructed.

"Tell me, Purumé," Elder Vara said to the doctor, "have there been any more attacks in Seiiki by the Fleet of the Tiger Eye?"

"Not since the night they came to Ginura, to my knowledge," Moyaka replied heavily. "But they will soon return. The Golden Empress is emboldened."

It took Tané all her willpower not to shrink from her touch. The lump was still tender.

"Ah, here it is." Moyaka traced the shape of the lump. "How many years have you taken, honorable scholar?"

"Twenty," Tané said softly.

"And you have had this all your life?"

"Since I was a child. My learnèd teacher said my rib was broken once."

"Does it ever hurt?"

"Sometimes."

"Hm." Moyaka probed it with two fingertips. "From the feel of it, it is most likely a bone spur—nothing to be concerned about—but I would like to make a small incision. Just to be sure." She opened a leather case. "Will you need something for the pain?"

The old Tané would have refused, but all she had wanted since arriving here was to feel nothing. To forget herself.

One of the younger scholars brought ice from the caves, wrapped in wool to keep it cold. Moyaka prepared the drug, and Tané drank it in through a pipe. The smoke rubbed her throat raw. When it reached her chest, it blew a dark, sweet comfort through her blood, and her body was half feather and half stone, sinking as her thoughts grew light.

The weight of her shame evaporated. For the first time in weeks, she breathed easy.

Moyaka held the ice to her side. Once Tané could no longer feel much there, the doctor selected an instrument, washed it in boiled water, and glided its edge beneath the lump.

A far-off pain registered. The shadow of pain. Tané pressed her palms to the floor.

"Are you well, child?" Elder Vara asked.

There were three of him. Tané nodded, and the world seemed to nod with her. Moyaka peeled the incision open.

"This is—" She blinked. "Strange. Very strange."

Tané tried to raise her head, but her neck was weak as a blade of grass. Elder Vara placed a hand on her shoulder. "What is it, Purumé?"

"I can't be sure until I remove it," was the puzzled reply, "but ... well, it almost looks like a—"

Her finding was cut off by a shattering crash from outside.

"Another earthshake," Elder Vara said. His voice sounded so far away.

"That did not feel like an earthshake." Moyaka stiffened. "Great Kwiriki save us—"

A glow burst through the window. The floor trembled, and someone shouted *fire*. Moments later, the same voice let out a spine-chilling scream before it cut off sharply.

"Fire-breathers." Elder Vara was already on his feet. "Tané, quickly. We must take shelter in the ravine."

Fire-breathers. But no fire-breathers had been seen in the East for centuries ...

He pulled her arm around his bony shoulders and lifted her from the mats. Tané swayed. Her mind was spindrift, but she had kept enough sense to move. Shoeless and numbed, she went with Elder Vara and Doctor Moyaka through the corridors and into the dining hall, where he slid open the door to the courtyard. Other scholars were making for the forest.

The smells of rain and fire mingled around her. Elder Vara pointed to the bridge.

"Go across. There is a cave on the other side—wait for me inside it, and we will climb down together," Elder Vara said. "Doctor Moyaka and I must see that no one has been left behind." He gave her a push. "Go, Tané. Hurry!"

"And keep pressure on the wound," Doctor Moyaka called after her.

Everything moved as if through water. Tané broke into a loose-footed run, but it felt like she was wading.

The bridge was within sight of Vane Hall. She was closing on it when a shadow winged above her. Heat flared against her back. She tried to go faster, but exhaustion made her blunder and, with every step, the incision wept more blood. Pain beat at the padded armor the drug had wrapped around her.

The bridge crossed the ravine near the Falls of Kwiriki. An elder was already shepherding a cluster of scholars over it. Tané stumbled after them, one hand pressed to her side.

Beneath the bridge was a fatal drop to the Path of the Elder. Treetops rose from a bowl of fog.

Another shadow fell from above. She tried to shout a warning to the other scholars, but her tongue was a wad of cloth in her mouth. A fireball slammed into the roof of the bridge. Seconds later, a spiked tail turned it to an explosion of splinters. Wood groaned and split underfoot. Tané almost fell as she stopped herself running on to it. Powerless, she watched as the structure trembled, a gaping hole ripped through its middle. A third fire-breather smashed one of the pillars that anchored it. Faceless silhouettes cried out as they slid off the edge and plummeted.

Flame ripped through flesh and timber alike. Another section of the bridge crumbled away, like a log that had been ablaze for too long. Wind howled in the wake of wings.

There was no choice. She would have to jump. Tané ran onto the bridge, eyes stinging in the smoke, as the fire-breathers wheeled for a second attack.

Before she could reach the gap, her knees folded. She rolled to break her fall, and her skin ripped open like wet paper. Sobbing in agony, she reached for her side—and the lump, the thing she had carried for years, slipped from the burst seam in her body. Shuddering, she looked at it.

A jewel. Slick with her blood, and no larger than a chestnut. A star imprisoned in a stone.

There was no time to be bewildered. More fire-breathers were flocking. Weak with pain, Tané closed her hand around the jewel. As she struggled across the bridge, dizzier by the moment, something crashed through the roof and landed in front of her.

She found herself face to face with a nightmare.

It looked and smelled like the remnant of a volcanic eruption. Burning coals where there ought to be eyes. Scales as black as cinder. Steam hissed where rain stippled its hide. Two muscular legs took most of its weight, and the joints of its wings ended in cruel hooks—and those *wings*. The wings of a bat. A lizard tail whipped behind. Even with its head lowered, it towered over her, teeth bared and bloodstained.

Tané shivered under its gaze. She had no sword or halberd. Not even a dagger to put out its eye. Once she might have prayed, but no god would hearken to a rider in disgrace.

The fire-breather screamed a challenge. Light scorched in its throat, and Tané came to the detached realization that she was about to die. Elder Vara would find her smoking ruins, and that would be the end of it.

She did not fear death. Dragonriders put themselves in mortal danger every day, and since she was a child, she had known the risks she would face when she joined Clan Miduchi. An hour ago, she might even have embraced this end. Better than the spun-out rot of shame.

Yet when instinct told her to hold out the jewel—to fight to the last with whatever she had—she obeyed.

It burned white-cold against her palm as she thrust it at the beast. Blinding light erupted from inside it.

She held a moonrise in her hand.

With a scream, the fire-breather recoiled from the glare. Throwing up its wing to shield its face, it let out a rasping call, over and over, like a crow greeting the dusk.

The sky came alive with echoing answers.

She stepped closer, still holding out the jewel. With a final look of hatred, the fire-breather roared once more, whipping her hair back from her face, and flung itself skyward. As it veered toward the sea, its kin swerved after it and disappeared into the night.

The other side of the bridge crumbled into the ravine, throwing up a cloud of cinders. Her eyes filled. Weak with pain, she crawled back toward Vane Hall. One half of her tunic was red through.

She buried the jewel in the soil of the courtyard. Whatever it was, she had to keep it hidden. As she had all her life.

The roof of the healing room was staved in. She searched the wet mats for Moyaka's case and found it upturned in the corner. Close to the bottom was a coil of gut-string and a bent needle.

The drugging pipe had been shattered. When she lifted her hand from the wound, blood pulsed out.

With clumsy fingers, she threaded the needle. She cleaned the cut as best she could, but dirt clung to its edges. Touching it made darkness blotch her vision. Head spinning, mouth dry, she groped in the case of oddities again and found an amber bottle.

The worst was yet to come. She had to stay awake, just for a little longer. Nayimathun and Susa had suffered because of her. Now it was her turn.

The needle pierced her skin.

46

South

The kitchens were behind the waterfall, just below the sunrooms. As a child, Ead had loved to sneak in with Jondu and purloin rose candies from Tulgus, the head cook.

The scullery was sun-dappled and always smelled of spices. The servants were preparing jeweled rice, scallions, and chicken in a lime marinade for the evening meal.

She found Loth arranging a platter of fruit with Tulgus. His eyelids looked heavy.

Dreamroot. They must be trying to make him forget.

"Good afternoon, sister," said the white-haired cook.

Ead smiled, trying not to look at Loth. "Do you remember me, Tulgus?"

"I do, sister." He returned the smile. "I certainly remember how much of my food you stole."

His eyes were the pale yellow of groundnut oil. Perhaps he was the one who had gifted Nairuj her eyes.

"I have grown up since then. Now I ask for it." Ead lowered her voice and leaned closer. "Nairuj said you might let me taste a little of the Prioress's sun wine."

"Hm." Tulgus wiped his liver-spotted hands on a cloth. "A small glass. Call it a homecoming gift from the Sons of Siyāti. I will have it brought to your chamber."

"Thank you."

Loth was looking at her as if at a stranger. It took Ead all her strength not to meet his gaze.

As she walked back toward the doorway, she spied the urns where herbs and spices were stored. Seeing that Tulgus was preoccupied, Ead found the jar she needed, took a generous pinch of the powder inside, and dropped it into a pouch.

She snatched a honey pastry from a platter before she left. It would be a long time before she tasted another.

For the rest of the day, she did as any good Red Damsel would when she was about to be sent on a long journey. She practiced her archery under the watchful eyes of the Silver Damsels. Each of her arrows found its mark. Between draws, Ead made certain to look calm, unhurried about nocking her arrows. One bead of sweat could give her away.

When she reached her sunroom, she found it empty of her saddlebags and weapons. Aralaq must have taken them.

A cold feeling came over her. This was it.

The point of no return.

She pulled in a breath, and her spine turned to iron. The Mother would not have watched while the world burned. Crushing the last embers of doubt, Ead changed into her nightrobe and took up her position on the bed, where she pretended to read. Outside, the light of day withdrew.

Loth and Aralaq would be waiting for her by now. When it was full dark and a knock came at her door, she called, "Come in."

One of the menfolk entered, bearing a platter. On it were two cups and a jug.

"Tulgus said you wished to taste the sun wine, sister," he said.

"Yes." She motioned to the nightstand. "Leave it here. And open the doors, if you will."

When he set down the tray, Ead kept her expression clean and leafed past another page in her book. As he shuffled toward the balcony doors, she slipped the pouch of dreamroot from her sleeve and emptied it into one of the cups. By the time the man turned back, she had the other cup in her hand, and the pouch was nowhere to be seen. He took the tray and left.

Wind rushed through the sunroom and blew out the oil lamp. Ead dressed in her travel clothes and boots, still sandy from the

Burlah. The Prioress would be drinking the drugged wine by now.

She took the only knife she had not already packed and sheathed it at her thigh. When she was certain that there was no one outside, she pulled her hood over her eyes and became one with the dark.

The Prioress slept in the highest sunroom in the Priory, close to the crest of the waterfall, where she could see the dawn break over the Vale of Blood. Ead stopped at the arched entrance to the passageway. Two Red Damsels guarded the door.

What she did next was a delicate thing. An ancient skill, no longer taught in the Priory. *Candling*, Jondu had called it. Lighting the smallest flame imaginable within a living body, just enough to cause the loss of breathing. It required a nimbleness of touch.

With the slightest twist of her fingers, she struck one candle in each of the women.

It had been a long time since a sister had turned against her kith. The twins were unprepared to feel the dry heat in their throats. Smoke curled from their mouths and noses and shot black tendrils through their minds, smothering their senses. As they sank, Ead moved past on silent foot and listened at the door. All was quiet.

Inside, moonlight made needles through the windows. She stood in the deep shadows.

The Prioress was in bed, surrounded by veils. The cup was on the nightstand. Ead approached, heart thumping, and looked inside it.

Empty.

Her gaze slid toward the Prioress. Sweat trembled at the very end of a coil of hair above her eyes.

It took moments to find the jewel. The Prioress had pressed it into soft clay and hung it from a cord around her neck.

"You must think me a fool."

A chill took Ead through her gut, like a thrown spear. The Prioress turned onto her back.

"I sensed, somehow, that I should not drink the wine tonight. A premonition from the Mother." Her hand closed around the jewel. "I suppose this . . . rebellion in you is not all your fault. It was inevitable that Inys would poison you."

Ead dared not move.

"You mean to return there. To protect the pretender," the Prioress said. "Your birthmother moves in you. Zāla also believed that we should stretch our limited resources to protect all humankind. She was always whispering in the ear of the old Prioress, telling her that we ought to protect every sovereign in every court—even in the East, where they worship the wyrms of the sea. Where they idolize them as *gods*. Just as the Nameless One would have had us do to him. Oh, yes ... Zāla would have had us protect them, too."

Something about her tone sat wrong with Ead. The hatred in it.

"The Mother loved the South. It is the South she sought to shield from the Nameless One," she continued, "and it is the South I am sworn to protect in her name. Zāla would have had us open our arms to the world and, in doing so, expose our bellies to the sword."

All because Mita Yedanya told her I had poisoned your birthmother. Kalyba had worn a mocking smile. *As if I would ever stoop to poison.*

Mita had banished the witch and never allowed her to return. An outsider, after all, was an easy scapegoat.

"It was not the witch who killed Zāla." Ead closed a hand around her blade, and it nerved her. "It was *you*."

She was cold to her bones. The Prioress raised her eyebrows. "Whatever can you mean, Eadaz?"

"You hated that Zāla looked to defend the world beyond the South. Hated her influence. You knew it would only intensify when she was named Prioress." Gooseflesh tightened her skin. "To control the Priory ... you had to be rid of her."

"I did it for the Mother."

The confession was as blunt as the rest of her.

"Murderer," Ead whispered. "You murdered a *sister*."

Honey pastries. Warm embraces. All her vague memories of Zāla flooded back, and heat swelled to her eyelids.

"To *protect* my sisters, and to ensure the South always had the protection it needed, I was willing to do anything." With a sigh that was almost exasperated, the Prioress sat up. "I gave her a quiet death. Most had condemned Kalyba before I had even opened my mouth. It was an insult to the Mother that she came here—she who loved the Deceiver well enough to forge the sword for him. She is our enemy."

Ead could scarcely hear her. For the first time in her life, she *felt* the Draconic fire in her blood. Rage was a furnace in her belly, and its roar overwhelmed all other sounds.

"The jewel. Give it to me, and I will leave in peace." Her voice was distant to her own ears. "I can use it to find Ascalon. Let me finish what Jondu began, and protect the integrity of Virtudom, and I will not speak a word of your offense."

"Someone will wield the jewel," was the reply, "but it will not be you."

The movement was as quick as a viper bite, too fast to avoid. White heat lashed across her skin. Ead reeled back, one hand beneath her throat, where blood was welling thick and fast.

The Prioress slashed away the remnants of the veil. The blade in her hand was laced with red.

"Only death can change the wielder." Ead looked at the blood on her fingers. "Do you mean to kill birthmother and child both?"

"I will not see a gift from the Mother in the hands of one who would desert her so willingly," Mita said calmly. "The jewel will remain beneath her bones until the Nameless One threatens the people of the South. It will *not* be used to protect a Western pretender."

She lifted the knife in a fluid movement, like a rising note of music.

"No, Eadaz," she said. "It will not do."

Ead looked into those resolute eyes. Her fingers curled around the handle of her blade.

"We both serve the Mother, Mita," she said. "Let us see which of us she favors."

Little moonlight reached the ground in the Lasian Basin, so dense was the canopy of trees. Loth paced the gloaming, wiping the sweat from his hands on his shirt, shivering as if with fever.

The ichneumon had led him through a labyrinth of passageways before emerging here. Loth had only understood that he was being rescued when they were breathing the warm air of the forest. The drink they had been giving him was at last wearing off.

491

Now the ichneumon was curled on a nearby rock, eyes fixed on the mouth of the cave. Loth had buckled on the saddle they had brought outside. Woven bags and saddle flasks were attached to it.

"Where is she?"

He was ignored. Loth wiped his upper lip with one hand and muttered a prayer to the Knight of Courage.

He had not forgotten. They had tried to smoke it out of him, but the Saint had always been there, in his heart. Tulgus had warned him against fighting, so he had prayed and waited for salvation. It had come in the form of the woman he had once known as Ead Duryan.

She was going to get them back to Inys. He believed it as much as he believed in the Knight of Fellowship.

When the ichneumon finally rose, it was with a growl. It bounded off to burrow between the roots of the tree and returned with an exhausted-looking Ead. Her arm was draped around its neck, and she carried another woven bag on her shoulder. Loth ran to her.

"Ead."

She was glossed with blood and sweat, her hair curling thickly around her shoulders. "Loth," she said, "we must leave now."

"Lift her onto me, man of Inys."

The deep voice scared Loth half to death. When he saw where it had come from, he gaped.

"You can *speak*," he spluttered.

"Yes," the ichneumon said. The wolfish eyes went straight back to Ead. "You are bleeding."

"It will stop. We must go."

"The sisters of the Priory will come for you ere long. Horses are slow. And stupid. You cannot outstrip an ichneumon without riding one."

She pressed her face into its fur. "They will butcher you if we are caught. Stay here, Aralaq. Please."

"No." Its ears flinched. "I go where you go."

The ichneumon bent its front legs. Ead looked up at Loth.

"Loth," she rasped, "do you trust me still?"

He swallowed.

"I don't know if I trust the woman you are," he admitted, "but I trust the woman I knew."

"Then ride with me," she said, cupping his cheek, "and if I lose consciousness, keep riding northwest for Córvugar." Her fingers left blood on his face. "Whatever you do, Loth, do not let them take this. Even if you have to leave me behind."

Her hand was clenched around something at the end of a cord. A round, white gemstone, pressed into clay.

"What is it?" he murmured.

She shook her head.

Mustering his strength, Loth hoisted her into the saddle. He swung himself on, curled an arm about her, and pressed her back against his chest, grasping the ichneumon with the other hand.

"Hold on to me," he said against her ear. "I will see us to Córvugar. As you have seen me here."

47

South

Aralaq ran hard through the forest. Loth thought he had known his swiftness in the Spindles, but it was all he could do to hold on as the ichneumon leaped over twisted roots and creeks and between trees, lithe as a stone glancing off water.

He dozed as Aralaq took them farther north, away from the thickness of the forest. His dreams took him first to that accursed tunnel in Yscalin, where Kit must still lie—then farther, back to the map room at the estate, where his tutor was telling him about the history of the Domain of Lasia, and Margret was sitting beside him. She had always been a diligent student, keen to learn about their ancient roots in the South.

He had given up hope of ever seeing his sister again. Now, perhaps, there was a chance.

The rise and fall of the sun. The pounding of paws against earth. When the ichneumon stopped, Loth finally woke.

He rubbed the sand from his eyes. A lake stretched across a dusty expanse of earth, a streak of sapphire under the sky. Water olyphants bathed in its shallows. Beyond the lake were the great rocky peaks that guarded Nzene, all the red-brown of baked clay. Mount Dinduru, the largest, was almost perfect in its symmetry.

By noon, they were in the foothills. Aralaq climbed a brant path up the nearest peak. When they were high enough to make his thighs quake, Loth risked a look down.

Nzene lay before them. The Lasian capital sat in the cradle of the Godsblades, surrounded by high sandstone walls. The mountains—taller and straighter than any in the known world—sliced its streets with shadow. An immense road stretched out beyond it, no doubt a trade route to the Ersyr.

Date-palms and juniper trees lined streets that glistered in the sunlight. Loth spied the Golden Library of Nzene, built of sandstone taken from the ruins of Yikala, connected by a walkway to the Temple of the Dreamer. Towering over it all was the Palace of the Great Onjenyu, where High Ruler Kagudo and her family resided, set high above the houses on a promontory. The River Lase forked around its sacred orchard.

Aralaq sniffed out a shelter beneath a jut of rock, deep enough to protect them from the elements.

"Why are we stopping?" Loth wiped sweat from his face. "Ead told us to keep riding for Córvugar."

Aralaq bent his front legs so Loth could dismount. "The blade she was cut with was laced with a secretion from the ice leech. It stops the blood from clotting," he said. "There will be a cure in Nzene."

Loth lifted Ead from the saddle. "How long will you be?"

The ichneumon did not reply. He licked Ead once across the brow before he disappeared.

When Ead rose from her world of shadows, it was sundown. Her head was a thrice-stirred cauldron. She was dimly aware that she was in a cave, but had no memory of having got there.

Her hand flinched to her collarbones. Feeling the waning jewel between them, she breathed again.

Retrieving it had cost her. She remembered the steel of the blade, and the sting of whatever foulness was on it, as she grabbed the jewel from Mita. Fire had sparked from her fingers, setting the bed ablaze, before she had rolled over the balustrade and into open sky.

She had dropped like a cat and landed on a ledge outside the kitchen. Mercifully, it had been empty, leaving her escape route clear. Still, she had barely made it to Aralaq and Loth before her strength gave out.

Mita deserved a cruel death for what she had done to Zāla, but Ead would not deliver it to her. She would not debase herself by murdering a sister.

A hot tongue licked a curl back from her brow. She found herself almost nose to nose with Aralaq.

"Where?" she said hoarsely.

"The Godsblades."

No. She sat up, biting back a groan when her midriff throbbed. "You stopped." Her voice strained. "You damned fools. The Red Damsels—"

"It was this or let you bleed to death." Aralaq nosed the poultice on her belly. "You did not tell us that the Prioress coated her blade in the glean."

"I had no idea."

She should have expected it. The Prioress wanted her dead, but she could not do it herself without drawing suspicion. Better to slow her with blood loss, then tell the Red Damsels their newly returned sister was a traitor and order them to kill her for it. Her own hands would be clean.

Ead lifted the poultice. The wound was painful, but the mash of sabra flowers had leached the poison from it.

"Aralaq," she said, sliding into Inysh, "you know how quickly the Red Damsels hunt." Having Loth there made the language spring to her tongue. "You were not supposed to stop for anything."

"High Ruler Kagudo keeps a supply of the remedy. Ichneumons do not let little sisters die."

Ead forced herself to breathe, to be calm. The Red Damsels were unlikely to be searching the Godsblades just yet.

"We must move on soon," Aralaq said, with a glance at Loth. "I will check it is safe."

Silence yawned after he left.

"Are you angry, Loth?" Ead finally asked.

He gazed at the capital. Torches had been lit in the streets of Nzene, making it glimmer like embers beneath them.

"I should be," he murmured. "You lied about so much. Your name. Your reason for coming to Inys. Your conversion."

"Our religions are intertwined. Both oppose the Nameless One."

"You never believed in the Saint. Well," he corrected himself, "you *did*. But you think he was a brute and a craven who tried to press a country into accepting his religion."

"And demanded to marry Princess Cleolind before he would slay the monster, yes."

"How can you *say* such a thing, Ead, when you stood in sanctuary and praised him?"

"I did it to survive." When he still refused to look at her, she said, "I confess I am what you would call a sorceress, but no magic is evil. It is what the wielder makes it."

He risked a surly glance at her. "What is it you can do?"

"I can drive away the fire of wyrms. I am immune to the Draconic plague. I can create barriers of protection. My wounds heal quickly. I can move among shadows. I can make metal sing of death like no knight ever could."

"Can you make fire of your own?"

"Yes." She opened her palm, and a flame shivered to life. "Natural fire." Again, and the flame blossomed silver. "Magefire, to undo enchantments." Once more, and it was red, so hot it made Loth sweat. "Wyrmfire."

Loth made the sign of the sword. Ead closed her hand, extinguishing the heresy.

"Loth," she said, "we must decide now whether we can be friends. We both need to be friends to Sabran if this world is to survive."

"What do you mean?"

"There is much you don't know." An understatement indeed. "Sabran conceived a child with Aubrecht Lievelyn, the High Prince of Mentendon. He was killed. I will tell you all later," she added, when he stared. "Not long after, a High Western came to Ascalon Palace. The White Wyrm, they called it." She paused. "Sabran had a miscarriage."

"Saint," he said. "Sab—" His face was tight with sorrow. "I am sorry I was not there."

"I wish you had been." Ead watched his face. "There will be no other child, Loth. The Berethnet line is at an end. Wyrms are rising, Yscalin has all but declared war, and the Nameless One will rise again, soon. I am sure of it."

Loth was beginning to look very sick. "The Nameless One."

"Yes. He will come," Ead said, "though not because of Sabran. It has naught to do with her. Whether there is a queen in Inys or a sun in the sky, he will rise."

Sweat dotted his brow.

"I think I know a way to defeat the Nameless One, but first we must secure Virtudom. Should it fall to civil war, the Draconic Army and the Flesh King will make short work of it." Ead pressed the poultice against her belly. "Certain members of the Dukes Spiritual have abused their power for years. Now they know she will have no heir, I believe they will try to control Sabran, or even to usurp her."

"By the Saint," Loth murmured.

"You warned Meg about the Cupbearer. Do you know who it is?"

"No. All I had from Sigoso was that phrase."

"At first I thought it was the Night Hawk," Ead admitted, "but now I am all but certain that it is Igrain Crest. The twin cups are her badge."

"Lady Igrain. But Sab loves her," Loth said, visibly stunned. "Besides, anyone who takes the Knight of Justice as their patron wears the goblets—and the Cupbearer conspired with King Sigoso to murder Queen Rosarian. Why would Crest do such a thing?"

"I don't know," Ead said frankly, "but she recommended Sabran marry the Chieftain of Askrdal. Sabran chose Lievelyn instead, and then Lievelyn was killed. As for the cutthroats ..."

"It was *you* who killed them?"

"Yes," Ead said, deep in thought, "but I have wondered if they ever meant to kill. Perhaps Crest always planned for them to be caught. Each invasion would have left Sabran more terrified. Her punishment for resisting the call of the childbed was the near-constant fear of death."

"And the Queen Mother?"

"It has long been rumored at court that Queen Rosarian took Gian Harlowe to her bed while she was wed to Prince Wilstan," Ead said. "Infidelity is against the teachings of the Knight of Fellowship. Perhaps Crest likes her queens to be … obedient."

At this, Loth clenched his jaw.

"So you mean for us to take a stand against Crest," he said. "To protect Sabran."

"Yes. And then to take a stand against a far older enemy." Ead glanced toward the mouth of the cave. "Ascalon may lie in Inys. If we can find it, we can use it to weaken the Nameless One."

A bird called out from somewhere above their shelter. Loth passed her a saddle flask.

"Ead," he said, "you do not believe in the Six Virtues." He looked her in the eye. "Why risk everything for Sabran?"

She drank.

It was a question she should have asked herself a long time ago. Her feelings had come like a flower on a tree. A bud, gently forming—and just like that, an undying blossom.

"I realized," she said, after a period of silence, "that she had been spoon-fed a story from the day she was born. She had been taught no other way to be. And yet, I saw that despite everything, some part of her was self-made. This part, small as it appeared at first, was forged in the fire of her own strength, and resisted her cage. And I understood … that this part was made of steel. This part was who she truly was." She held his gaze. "She will be the queen that Inys needs in the days that are to come."

Loth moved to sit beside her. When he touched her elbow, she looked up at him.

"I am glad we found each other again, Ead Duryan." He paused. "Eadaz uq-Nāra."

Ead rested her head on his shoulder. With a sigh, he wrapped an arm around her.

Aralaq returned then, startling them both. "The great bird is on the wing," he said. "The Red Damsels draw near."

Loth got to his feet at once. A strange calm washed over Ead as she took up her bow and quiver.

"Aralaq, we cross the scorchlands to Yscalin. We do not stop," she said, "until we reach Córvugar."

Loth mounted. She handed him the cloak, and when she climbed on, he wrapped it around them both.

Aralaq slid and pawed his way to the foot of the mountain and crept out of its shadow to glimpse the lake. Parspa was circling in silence overhead.

It was dark enough to cover their escape. They moved behind the other Godsblades. When there was nowhere else to hide, Aralaq struck out from the mountains and ran.

The scorchlands of Lasia, where the city of Jotenya had once stood, stretched across the north of the country. During the Grief of Ages, the land had been stripped bare by fire, but new grasses had reclaimed it, and wing-leaved trees, spaced far apart, had risen from the ashes.

The terrain began to shift. Aralaq gathered speed, until his paws were flying over yellow grass. Ead clung to his fur. Her belly still ached, but she had to stay alert, to be ready. The other ichneumons would have picked up on their scent by now.

The stars spiraled and shimmered above them, embers in a sky like char. Different to the ones that peppered the night sky in Inys.

More trees sprang up from the earth. Her eyes were dry from the onslaught of wind. Behind her, Loth was shivering. Ead drew the cloak more tightly around them both, covering his hands, and allowed herself to imagine the ship that would carry them from Córvugar.

An arrow whipped past Aralaq, just missing him. Ead turned to see what they were facing.

There were six riders. Red flames, each astride an ichneumon. The white belonged to Nairuj.

Aralaq growled and pushed himself faster. This was it. Mustering her strength, Ead slipped free of the cloak, grasped Loth by the shoulder, and swung herself behind him, so her back was against his.

Her best chance was to wound the ichneumons. Aralaq was fast even among his own kind, but the white could outrun him. As she nocked an arrow, she remembered a younger Nairuj boasting about how swiftly her mount could cross the Lasian Basin.

First, she allowed herself to adjust to Aralaq. When she knew the cadence of his footfalls, she lifted the bow. Loth reached behind him and grasped her hips, as if he was afraid she would fall.

Her arrow sliced over the grass, straight and true. At the last moment, the white ichneumon jumped over it. Her second shot went awry when Aralaq cleared the carcass of a wild hound.

They could not outrun this. Neither could they stop and fight. Two mages she could take, perhaps three, but not six Red Damsels, not with her injury. Loth would be too slow, and the other ichneumons would make meat of Aralaq. As she drew back her bowstring for the third time, she sent a prayer to the Mother.

The arrow pierced the front paw of an ichneumon. It collapsed, taking its rider with it.

Five left. She was preparing to shoot again when an arrow punched into her leg. A strangled shout tore out of her.

"Ead!"

At any moment, another arrow could lame Aralaq. And that would be the end for all of them.

Nairuj was spurring on her ichneumon. She was close enough now for Ead to see her ochre eyes and the hard line of her mouth. Those eyes had no hatred in them. Just pure, cold resolve. The look of a hunter set on her quarry. She lifted her bow and leveled the arrow at Aralaq.

That was when fire ripped across the scorchlands.

The eruption of light almost blinded Ead. The nearest trees burst into flame. She looked up, searching for its origin, as Loth let out a wordless cry. Shadows were darting above them—winged shadows with whip-like tails.

Wyverlings. They must have strayed from the Little Mountains, hungry for meat after centuries of slumber. In moments, Ead had sent an arrow into the eye of the nearest. With a soul-chilling screech, it crashed headlong into the grass, just missing the Red Damsels, who parted around it.

Three of them rallied against the wyverlings, while Nairuj and another continued their pursuit. As a skeletal beast swooped low and snapped at them, Aralaq stumbled. Ead twisted, heart pitching hard into her throat, fearing a bite. An arrow had skimmed his flank.

"You can make it." She spoke to him in Selinyi. "Aralaq, keep running. Keep going—"

Another wyverling tumbled from above and slammed into a fan tree in front of them. As it fell, the pulled-up roots groaning in protest, Aralaq weaved out of the way and charged past it. Ead smelled brimstone from the flesh of the creature as it let out a long death rattle.

One of the riders was getting closer. Her ichneumon was black, its teeth like knives.

They all saw the wyverling a moment too late. Fire rained from above and consumed the Red Damsel, setting her cloak aflame. She rolled to the ground to smother it. Fire churned the grass and reached for Aralaq. Ead threw out her hand.

Her warding deflected the heat as a shield did a mace. Loth cried out as the flames clawed for him. The wyverling swerved away with a shriek, swallowing its fire. The Red Damsels were in chaos, hunted and harrowed, circled by the creatures. Ead turned, looking for Nairuj.

The white ichneumon lay wounded. A wyvern was bearing down on Nairuj, its jaws flushed with the blood of her mount. Without hesitating, Ead fitted her last arrow to her bowstring.

She hit the wyvern in the heart.

Loth pulled her back down to the saddle. Ead glimpsed Nairuj staring after them, one arm over her belly, before Aralaq spirited them away from the trees, into the darkness.

A smell of burning. Loth wrapped the cloak around Ead again. Even when they were far away, she could still see the tongues of fire in the scorchlands, glowing like the eyes of the Nameless One. Her head rolled forward, and she knew no more.

She woke to Loth saying her name. The grass and fire and trees were gone. Instead, there were houses built from coral rag. Crows on the rooftops. And stillness. Utter stillness.

This was a town that had buried more than it still had living souls. A ship with discolored sails and a figurehead shaped like a seabird in flight was waiting in the harbor—a silent harbor on the edge of the West. Dawn stained the sky a delicate shadow of pink, and the black salt waters stretched before them.

Córvugar.

48

East

The trees of Feather Island had finally stopped burning. Rain fell in fat drops to quench their branches, which hacked a sickly yellow smoke. The Little Shadow-girl walked from her place of exile and sank her hands into the earth.

The comet ended the Great Sorrow, but it has come to this world many times before. Once, many moons ago, it left behind two celestial jewels, each infused with its power. Solid fragments of itself.

She held up the jewel that had been in her side, the jewel she had protected and nurtured with her body, and the rain washed it clean. Mud and water dripped on to her feet.

With them, our ancestors could control the waves. Their presence allowed us to hold on to our strength for longer than we could before.

The jewel shone in the cup of her hands. It was as dark a blue as the Abyss, as her heart.

They have been lost for almost a thousand years.

Not lost. Hidden.

Tané held the jewel to her breast. In the eye of the storm, where unbreakable promises had been sealed before the gods in times long past, she made a vow.

That even if it took her until her dying day, she would find Nayimathun, free her from captivity, and make her a gift of this jewel. Even if it took her a lifetime, she would reunite the dragon with what had been stolen.

IV

Thine is the Queendom

Why do you not inhale
essences of moon and stars,
Con your spirit texts of gold?

—Lu Qingzi

49

West

L oth stood on the deck of the *Bird of Truth*. His heart was leaden as he watched Inys draw closer.

Melancholy. That was the first word that came to mind when he beheld its dowly coast. It looked as if it had never seen the touch of the sun, or heard a joyful song. They were sailing toward Albatross Roost, the westernmost settlement in Inys, which had once been the heart of trade with Yscalin. If they rode hard, rested as little as possible, and met with no brigands, they might make it from here to Ascalon in a week.

Ead kept watch beside him. Already she looked a little less alive than she had in Lasia.

The *Bird of Truth* had sailed past Quarl Bay on its way to Inys. Anchored ships guarded it but, through a spyglass, they glimpsed the fledgling naval arm of the Draconic Army.

King Sigoso would soon be ready to invade. And Inys would need to be ready to repel him.

Ead had said nothing at the sight. Only turned an open hand toward the five ships at anchor—and fire, born of nothing, had roared up their masts. She had watched it devour them all with no expression, orange light flickering in her eyes.

Loth was shaken back to the present as a bitter gust of wind made him huddle deeper into his cloak.

"Inys." His breath steamed white and thick. "I never thought to see it again."

Ead laid a hand on his arm. "Meg never gave up on you," she said. "Neither did Sabran."

After a moment, he covered her hand with his.

A wall had stood between them at the start of their journey. Loth had been ill at ease around her, and Ead had left him to brood. Slowly, though, their old warmth had crept back. In their miserable cabin on the *Bird of Truth*, they had shared their stories of the past few months.

They had avoided any more conversation about religion. Likely they would never agree on the matter. For now, however, they had the same desire to see Virtudom survive.

Loth scratched at his chin with his free hand. He misliked his beard, but Ead had said they ought to disguise themselves when they reached Ascalon, since they were both barred from court.

"Would that I could have burned every one of those ships." Ead folded her arms. "I must be cautious with my siden. It might be years before I taste of the tree again."

"You burned five," Loth said. "Five fewer for Sigoso."

"You look less afraid of me now than you did then."

The blossom ring glinted on her finger. He had seen other sisters of the Priory wearing one.

"All of us have shadows in us," he said. "I accept yours." He placed a hand over her ring. "And I hope you will also accept mine."

With a tired smile, she threaded her fingers between his. "Gladly."

The smell of fish and rotting seaweed soon rode on the wind. The *Bird of Truth* docked with some trouble in the harbor, and its tired passengers decanted on to the quay. Loth held out an arm to help Ead. She had sported a limp for only a few days, even though the arrow had gone clean through her thigh. Loth had seen knights-errant weep for lesser hurts.

Aralaq would leave the ship once everyone had departed. Ead would call for him when the time was right.

They walked down the jetty toward the houses. When Loth saw the sweet-bags swaying in their doorways, he stopped. Ead was looking at them, too.

"What do you suppose is in those?" she asked.

"Dried hawthorn flowers and berries. A tradition from long before the Foundation of Ascalon. To ward away any evil that might taint the house." Loth wet his lips. "I have never seen them hanging in my lifetime."

Clag stuck to their boots as they pressed on. Soon every dwelling they passed had a sweet-bag outside.

"You said these were ancient ways," Ead mused. "What *was* the religion of Inys before the Six Virtues?"

"There was no official religion, but from what little the records tell us, the commons saw the hawthorn as a sacred tree."

Ead withdrew into a brooding silence. They clambered over a drystone wall, on to the cobblestones of the main street.

The only stable in the settlement yielded two sickly horses. They rode side by side. Rain battered their backs as they passed half-frozen fields and sodden flocks of sheep. While they were still in the province of the Marshes, where brigands were rare, they made the decision to keep riding through the night. By dawn, Loth was saddle-sore, but awake.

Ahead of him, Ead held her horse at a canter. Her body seemed wrought with impatience.

Loth wondered if she was right. If Igrain Crest had been manipulating the Inysh court from behind the throne. Whittling Sabran down to her last nerve. Making her afraid to sleep in the dark. Taking a loved one for each of her sins. The thought stoked a fire in his belly. Sabran had always looked to Crest first during her minority, and trusted her.

He spurred his horse to catch up with Ead. They passed a village razed by fire, where a sanctuary coughed gouts of smoke. The poor fools had built their houses with thatched roofs.

"Wyrms," Loth murmured.

Ead brushed at her wind-torn hair. "Doubtless the High Westerns are commanding their servants to intimidate Sabran. They must be waiting for their master before they attack in earnest. This time, the Nameless One will lead his armies himself."

At sunfall, they came upon a dank little inn beside the River Catkin. By now Loth was so tired, he could scarce keep upright in the saddle. They stabled the horses and made their way into the hall, shivering and drenched to the bone.

Ead kept her hood up and went to see the innkeeper. Loth was tempted to stay in the hall by the crackling fire, but there was too great a risk that they would be recognized.

When Ead had secured a candle and a key, Loth took them and went upstairs. The room they were assigned was cramped and drafty, but it was better than the squalid cabin on the *Bird of Truth*.

Ead entered with their supper. Her brow was pinched.

"What is it?" Loth asked.

"I listened to some conversations downstairs. Sabran has not been seen since her public appearance with Lievelyn," she said. "As far as the people know, she is still with child ... but the dearth of news, coupled with the Draconic incursions, has left her subjects uneasy."

"You said she was some way into her pregnancy when she miscarried. Were she still with child, she might have taken her chamber for the lying-in by now," Loth pointed out. "A perfect excuse for her absence."

"Yes. Perhaps she even colluded with it—but I do not think the traitors within the Dukes Spiritual intend to let her continue to rule." Ead set down their supper and hung her cloak to dry over a chair. "Sabran foresaw this. She is in mortal danger, Loth."

"She is still the living descendant of the Saint. The people will not rally behind any of the Dukes Spiritual while she lives."

"Oh, I think they would. If they knew she cannot give them an heir, the commons would believe that Sabran is responsible for the coming of the Nameless One." Ead sat at the table. "That scar on her belly, and what it represents, would strip her of legitimacy in many of their eyes."

"She is *still* a Berethnet."

"And the last of her line."

The innkeeper had provided them with two bowls of gristly pottage and a hunk of stale bread. Loth forced down his share and chased it with the ale.

"I'm going to wash," Ead said.

While she was gone, Loth lay down on his pallet and listened to the rain.

Igrain Crest was a tick on his thoughts. In his childhood, he had seen her as a comforting figure. Stern but kind, she had radiated a sense that everything would be well.

Yet he knew she had burdened Sabran in the four years of her minority. Even before that, when she was a young princess, Crest had hammered into her a need for temperance, for perfection, for devotion to duty. During those years, Sabran had not been permitted to speak with any children but Roslain and Loth, and Crest had always been near at hand, watching her. Though Prince Wilstan had been Protector of the Realm, he had been too deep in mourning to raise his daughter. Crest had taken charge of that.

And there had been one incident. Before the Queen Mother had died.

He recalled a freezing afternoon. Twelve-year-old Sabran on the edge of Chesten Forest, folding a snowball in her gloved hands, her cheeks pink. Both of them laughing until it hurt. After, they had clambered up one of the snow-clad oaks and huddled together on a knotted branch, much to the consternation of the Knights of the Body.

They had climbed almost to the top of that tree. So high they had been able to see into Briar House. And there had been Queen Rosarian in a window, visibly furious, a letter in her fist.

With her had been Igrain Crest, hands behind her back. Rosarian had stormed away. The only reason Loth remembered it so clearly was because Sabran had fallen from that tree a moment later.

It was some time before Ead returned, her hair damp from the river. She removed her boots and settled on the other pallet.

"Ead," Loth said, "do you regret leaving the Priory?"

Her gaze was on the ceiling.

"I have not left," she said. "All I do, I do for the Mother. To glorify her name." She closed her eyes. "But I hope—I pray—that my path will bend southward again someday."

Hating the pain in her voice, Loth reached for her. A careful brush of his thumb along her cheekbone.

"I am glad," he said, "that it bends westward this day."

She returned his smile.

"Loth," she said, "I did miss you."

———

They were riding again before the sun rose in the morning, and on they rode for days. A snowstorm had blown in, slowing their horses, and one night brigands set upon them, demanding all their coin. Alone, Loth would have been overwhelmed, but Ead put up such a spirited fight that they retreated.

There was no more time for sleep. Ead was in her saddle again before the brigands were out of sight; it was all Loth could do to keep up with her. They turned northeast at Crow Coppice and galloped up the South Pass, keeping their heads down as they joined the wagons, packhorses, and coaches moving toward Ascalon. And finally, by owl light, they arrived.

Loth slowed his horse. The spires of Ascalon were black against the evening sky. Even in the rain, this city was the beacon of his heart.

They rode on to Berethnet Mile. Fresh snow was a bordcloth on it, as yet untrampled. At its end, far away, loomed the wrought-iron gates of Ascalon Palace. Even in the gloaming, Loth could see the damage to the Dearn Tower. He had almost not believed that Fýredel had been upon it.

He could smell the River Limber. The bells of the Sanctuary of Our Lady were ringing.

"I want to ride past the palace," Ead said. "To see if there are increased defenses." Loth nodded.

Each ward of the city began at its gatehouse. Queenside, the closest to the palace, had the most impressive, tall and gilded, carved with likenesses of past queens. As they neared it, the street, usually busy at dusk as people flocked to orisons, was quiet.

The snow beneath the gatehouse was stained dark. When Loth looked up, the feeling left his face. High above them, two severed heads were mounted on pikes.

One was unrecognizable. Little more than a skull. The other had been tarred and parboiled, but the features slumped with decay. Ears and nose leaking rot. Flies on pallid skin.

He might not have recognized her if not for the hair. Long and red, streaming like blood.

"Truyde," Ead breathed.

Loth could not tear his gaze from the head. From that swaying hair, grotesquely animate.

Once, he and Sabran and Roslain had all gathered by the fire in the Privy Chamber and listened to Arbella Glenn tell them about Sabran the Fifth, the only tyrant of the House of Berethnet, who had adorned every finial on the palace gates with the heads of those who had displeased her. No queen had dared to raise her ghost by doing it again.

"Quickly." Ead turned her horse. "Follow me."

They rode to the ward of Southerly Wharf, where silk merchants and clothiers reigned. They soon reached the Rose and Candle, one of the finest inns in the city, where they handed their horses to an ostler. Loth stopped to retch. Vomit seethed in his belly.

"Loth." Ead ushered him indoors. "Hurry. I know the innkeeper here. We will be safe."

Loth no longer remembered what it was to be safe. The stench of rot was etched into his throat.

An attendant led them inside and knocked on a door. A ruddy-faced woman in a boxy doublet answered it. When she saw Ead, her eyebrows shot up.

"Well," she said, recovering, "you ought to come in."

She ushered them into her quarters. As soon as the door was closed, she embraced Ead.

"Dear girl. It's been a very long time," she said, her voice hushed. "What in damsam are you doing on the streets?"

"We had no choice." Ead drew back. "Our common friend told me you would give me shelter if I should ever need it."

"The promise stands." The woman inclined her head to Loth. "Lord Arteloth. Welcome to the Rose and Candle."

Loth wiped his mouth. "We thank you for your hospitality, goodwife."

"We need a room," Ead said. "Can you help?"

"I can. But have you only just arrived in Ascalon?" When they nodded, she took a roll of parchment from the table. "Look."

Ead unraveled it. Loth read over her shoulder.

In the name of QUEEN SABRAN, *Her Grace, the* DUCHESS OF JUSTICE, *offers a reward of eighteen thousand crowns for the capture of Ead Duryan, a low-born Southerner in the guise of a lady, wanted alive for Sorcery, Heresy, and High Treason against* HER MAJESTY. *Curling black hair, dark brown eyes. Report any sighting at once to a city guard.*

"The heralds have read your name and description every day," the innkeeper said. "I trust those you met in the yard, but you must speak to no one else. And be gone from this city as soon as you can." She shivered. "Something is not right in the palace. They said that child was a traitor, but I cannot think Queen Sabran would execute one so young."

Ead handed the notice back. "There were two heads," she said. "Whose was the other?"

"Bess Weald. Wicked Bess, they call her now."

The name meant nothing to Loth, but Ead nodded. "We cannot leave the city," she stated. "We are about most important business."

The innkeeper blew out a breath. "Well," she said, "if you want to risk staying, I vowed to the ambassador that I would help you on your way." She picked up a candle. "Come."

She led them up a staircase. Music and laughter echoed from the hall. The innkeeper opened one of the doors and handed Ead the key.

"I shall have your belongings brought up."

"Thank you. I will not forget this, and neither will His Excellency," Ead told her. "We will also need clothes. And weapons, if you can manage it."

"Of course."

Loth took the candle from the innkeeper before he joined Ead, who bolted the door. The chamber boasted one bed, a roaring fire, and a copper bath, full and steaming.

"Bess Weald was the merchant who shot Lievelyn." Ead swallowed. "This is Crest."

"Why would she have murdered Lady Truyde?"

"To silence her. Only Truyde, Sabran, and myself knew that Bess Weald worked for someone called the Cupbearer. And Combe," she added, after a moment. "Crest is covering her spoor. My head would have been up there, too, sooner or later, if I had not left court." She paced the room. "Crest could not have executed Truyde without Sabran knowing. Surely death warrants must have a royal signature."

"No. The signature of whomsoever holds the Duchy of Justice is also valid on a death warrant," Loth said, "but only if the sovereign is unable to sign with her own hand."

The implication settled over them both, heavy with portent.

"We need to get into the palace. Tonight," Ead said, frustration mounting in her voice. "I must speak with someone. In another ward."

"Ead, no. This entire *city* is looking for—"

"I know how to evade discovery." Ead put her hood back up. "Lock the door behind me. When I get back, we will make a plan." She paused to kiss his cheek on the way out. "Fear not for me, my friend."

And she was gone.

Loth undressed and sank into the copper bath. All he could think about was the heads staked on the gatehouse. The promise of an Inys he could not recognize. An Inys without his queen.

He battled sleep for as long as he could, but days of riding in the cold had taken their toll. When he tumbled into bed, he dreamed not of severed heads, but of the Donmata Marosa. She came to him naked, with eyes full of ash, and her kiss tasted of wormwood. *You left me,* she breathed. *You left me to die. Just like you left your friend.*

When a knock finally came, he jerked awake.

"Loth."

He groped for the bolt. Ead was outside. He stood aside to let her into the chamber.

"I have our way in," she said. "We will go with the waterfolk."

They crewed the barges and wherries that crossed the River Limber every day, taking people and goods from one side to the other. "I assume you have more friends among them."

"One," she confirmed. "A shipment of wine is being taken to the Privy Stair for the Feast of High Winter. He has agreed that we can join the waterfolk. That will get us inside."

"And when we are?"

"I mean to find Sabran." Ead looked at him. "If you would prefer to stay here, I will go in alone."

"No," Loth said. "We go together."

They set out dressed like merchants, armed to the chin under their cloaks. Soon they entered the ward of Fiswich-by-Bridge and slipped down the wherry stairs on Delphin Street. The stairs were squeezed alongside a tavern, the Gray Grimalkin, where the water-folk drank after a long day on the Limber.

The tavern faced the east wall of Ascalon Palace. Loth followed Ead. Their riding boots crunched through the shells on the riverbank.

He had never set foot in this part of the city. Fiswich-by-Bridge had a reputation for knavery.

Ead approached one of the men outside the tavern.

"My friend," she said. "Well met."

"Mistress." The man was grubby as a rat, but sharp-eyed. "Do you still wish to join us?"

"If you'll have us."

"I said I would." He glanced at the tavern. "Wait by the barge. Need to fish some of the others from their cups."

Nearby, the barge in question was being loaded with barrels of wine. Loth walked to the edge of the river and watched candles flicker to life in the windows of the Alabastrine Tower. He could only just see the top of the Queen Tower. The royal apartments, benighted.

"Tell me," he muttered to Ead, "what does Ambassador uq-Ispad do to make your friends so agreeable?"

"He pays the innkeeper a pension. As for this man, Chassar covered his gambling debts," she said. "He calls them the Friends of the Priory."

The waterfellow shepherded his associates from the tavern. When the last of the wine was loaded into the barge, Loth and Ead got in and found themselves a place on a bench.

Ead pulled on a flat cap and tucked every curl inside. Each waterfellow grasped an oar and rowed.

The Limber was wide and swift-flowing. It took them some time to reach the landing.

The Privy Stair led up to a postern in the palace wall, designed to be a discreet way for the royal family to leave. Sabran never used her pleasure barge, but her mother had always been out on the river, waving at the people, skimming her fingers through the water. Loth found himself wondering if Queen Rosarian had ever used the stair to escape for trysts with Gian Harlowe.

He was no longer sure if he should give credence to that rumor. His every belief had been bruised and battered. Perhaps nothing he had thought about this court had been true.

Or perhaps this was a test of faith.

They followed the waterfolk up the steps. On the other side of the wall, Loth caught his first glimpse of the three knights-errant who blocked their way. Ead pulled Loth into an alcove to the left, and they crouched behind the well.

"Good evening to you all," one of the knights-errant said. "You have the wine?"

"Aye, sirs." The head waterfellow doffed his cap. "Sixty barrels."

"Take them to the Great Kitchen. But first, your fellows will need to show us their faces. All of you, lower your hoods and remove your caps."

The waterfolk did as they were told.

"Good. Be on your way," the knight-errant said.

The barrels were duly carried up the stairs. Ead crept toward the mouth of the alcove—only to withdraw.

One of the knights-errant was coming down the steps. When he thrust his torch into their hiding place, a voice said, "What's this?"

The flame came closer. "Are we defying the Knight of Fellowship in here?"

Then the knight-errant saw Loth, and he saw Ead, and under the shadow cast by his helm, Loth saw his mouth open wide to raise the alarm.

That was when a knife sliced across his throat. As blood sprayed, Ead threw him into the well.

Three heartbeats, and he hit the bottom.

50

West

She had hoped not to kill anyone in the palace. If there had been more time, Ead might have candled the man.

She retrieved the torch and let it fall into the well. She wiped the blood from her knife.

"Find Meg and hide in her quarters," she said quietly. "I want to scout the palace."

Loth was staring at her as if she were a stranger. She gave him a push up the steps.

"Hurry. They will search everywhere when they find the body."

He went.

Ead followed him before paring away. She crossed the courtyard with the apple tree and pressed her back to the limewashed wall of the Great Kitchen. She waited until a detail of guards had gone past before she slipped into the passage that led to the Sanctuary Royal.

Two more knights-errant, both in black surcoats and armed with partizans, stood outside its doors.

She candled them both. Mother willing, they would wake up too addled to report what had happened. Inside, she hid behind a pillar and gazed into the gloom. As always, many courtiers had gathered for orisons. Voices rang to the vaulted ceiling.

Sabran was nowhere to be seen. Neither was Margret.

Ead took note of how the worshippers were sitting. Usually they would huddle on the benches in the spirit of fellowship. Tonight, however, there was a clear-cut faction. Retainers in full livery. Black and murrey, the twin goblets embroidered on their tabards.

Once, you would have seen Combe's retainers strutting about in his livery, Margret had told her, *as if their first loyalty were not to their queen.*

"Now," the Arch Sanctarian said, once the hymn was finished, "we pray to the Knight of Generosity for Her Majesty, who prefers to pray in seclusion at this most sacred time. We pray for the princess in her belly, who will one day be our queen. And we give thanks to Her Grace, the Duchess of Justice, who tends so vigilantly on them both."

Ead left the sanctuary as soundlessly as she had entered it. She had seen enough.

Carnelian House was not far from the Privy Stair. Loth evaded a brace of retainers, both wearing the badge of the Duchess of Justice, and slipped through the unlocked door.

He chased a winding stair and emerged in a corridor he knew well, decorated with portraits of Ladies of the Bedchamber who had served under long-dead queens. A new likeness of a young Lady Arbella Glenn had appeared at one end.

When he reached the right door, he listened. Silence within. He turned the handle and stepped inside.

Candles lit the chamber. His sister was bent over a book. At the sound of the door opening, she startled to her feet.

"*Courtesy's* name—" She snatched her knife from the nightstand, her eyes wide. "Get you gone, knave, or I will cut out your heart. What sends you to my door?"

"Fraternal duty." He lowered his hood. "And a terrible fear of your wrath if I stayed away a moment longer."

The knife fell from her hand, and her eyes filled. She ran to him and flung her arms around his neck.

"Loth." Her body heaved with sobs. "Loth—"

He drew her into an embrace, close to tears himself. It was only now he held her that he dared believe that he was home.

"I really could cut out your heart, Arteloth Beck. Abandoning me for months, sneaking in here like a vagabond—" Margret laid her hands on his cheeks. Hers were wet with tears. "And *what* is that on your face?"

"I must insist that the Night Hawk shoulders the blame for my absence. Though not for the beard." He kissed her brow. "I will tell you everything later. Meg, Ead is here."

"Ead—" Joy sparked in her eyes, then went out. "No. It's too dangerous for both of you—"

"Where is Sab?"

"The royal apartments, I assume." Margret gripped his shoulder with one hand and used the other to wipe her eyes. "They say she is in confinement because of the pregnancy. Only Roslain is permitted to attend on her, and Crest retainers guard her door."

"Where is Combe in all this?"

"The Night Hawk took wing a few days ago. Stillwater and Fynch, too. I have no idea whether it was of their own volition."

"What of the other Dukes Spiritual?"

"They seem to be helping Crest." She looked at the window. "Did you see there is no light up there?"

Loth nodded, understanding the import well. "Sabran cannot sleep in darkness."

"Aye." Margret moved to shut the curtains. "The thought that she might deliver her bairn in that cheerless room—"

"Meg."

She turned.

"There will be no Princess Glorian," Loth said softly. "Sab is not with child. And will not be with child again."

Margret was very still.

"How?" she finally asked.

"Her belly was . . . pierced. When the White Wyrm came."

His sister groped for her settle.

"Now all this begins to make sense." She sat. "Crest doesn't want to wait until Sabran dies to take the throne."

Her breath shook. Loth came to sit beside her, giving her time to take it all in.

"The Nameless One will return." Margret composed herself. "I suppose all we can do now is prepare for it."

"And we cannot do that if Inys is divided," a new voice said.

Loth rose with his sword drawn to see Ead in the doorway. Margret let out a wordless sound of relief and went to her. They embraced like sisters.

"I must be dreaming," Margret said into her shoulder. "You came back."

"You told me we would meet again." Ead held her close. "I did not want to make you a liar."

"You have a lot of explaining to do. But it can wait." Margret drew back. "Ead, Sabran is in the Queen Tower."

Ead bolted the door. "Tell me everything."

Margret repeated to her exactly what she had told Loth. As she listened, Ead stood like a statue.

"We must reach her," she eventually said.

"The three of us will not get far," Loth murmured.

"Where are the Knights of the Body in all this?"

The loyal bodyguards of the Queens of Inys. Loth had not even thought to ask.

"I have not seen Captain Lintley in a week," Margret owned. "Some of the others are on guard outside the Queen Tower."

"Is it not their duty to protect Her Majesty?" Ead asked.

"They have no reason to suspect the Duchess of Justice of doing her harm. They think Sab is resting."

"Then we need to let them know that Sabran is being held against her will. The Knights of the Body are formidable. With even half of them on our side, we could stamp out the insurrection," Ead said. "We should try to find Lintley. Perhaps they have put him in the guardhouse."

"We could take the secret route I showed you," said Margret.

Ead made for the door. "Good."

"Wait." Margret held out a hand to Loth. "Lend me a weapon, brother, or I shall be as much use as a fire in an ice house."

He surrendered his baselard without complaint.

Margret took a candle and led the way down the corridor. She brought them before a portrait of a woman, and when she dragged one side away from the wall, a passage was revealed. Ead climbed into it and gave Margret a hand. Loth pulled the portrait shut behind them.

A draft blew out the candle, leaving them in darkness. All Loth could hear was their breathing. Then Ead snapped her fingers, and a silver-blue flame jumped like a spark from a firestriker. Loth exchanged a glance with his sister as Ead cupped it in her palm.

"Not all fire is to be feared," Ead said.

Margret appeared to steel herself. "You had better make Crest fear it by dawn."

They followed a flight of steps until they reached a way out. Ead pushed it open just a crack.

"All clear," she murmured. "Meg, which door?"

"The closest," Margret said at once. When Loth raised his eyebrows at her, she stamped on his foot.

Ead stepped into the unlit passageway and tried the door, to no avail. "Captain Lintley?" she said, voice soft. When there was no answer, she knocked. "Sir Tharian."

A pause, then: "Who goes there?"

"Tharian." Margret joined Ead the door. "Tharian, it's Meg."

"Meg—" A muffled oath. "Margret, you must leave. Crest has had me locked in."

She clicked her tongue. "That sounds like a reason to get you out, fool, not to leave."

Loth glanced down the corridor. If anyone opened the door to the guardhouse, they would have nowhere to hide.

Ead knelt beside the door. When she flexed her fingers, the fire drifted to hang beside her like a corpse candle. She studied the keyhole and used her other hand to slide a hairpin from her curls and into the lock. When it clicked, Margret eased open the door, careful not to let the hinges creak.

Inside his chamber, Sir Tharian Lintley stood in a shirt and breeches. Every taper in the room had burned to a stump. He went straight to Margret and cupped her cheek with one hand.

"Margret, you must not—" Catching sight of Loth, he started, and bowed in his soldierly way. "Saint. Lord Arteloth, I had no idea you had returned. And—" His stance changed. "Mistress Duryan."

"Captain Lintley." Ead still held her flame. "Should I expect you to try and arrest me?"

Lintley swallowed.

"I wondered if you were the Lady of the Woods herself," he said. "The Principal Secretary's retainers told stories of your witch-craft."

"Peace." Margret touched his arm. "I don't yet understand it, either, but Ead is my friend. She returned at great risk to her life to help us. And she brought Loth back to me."

A look from her was all it took to soften Lintley.

"Combe ordered us to arrest you that night," he said to Ead. "Is he in league with Crest?"

"That, I do not know. His morals are questionable, to be sure, but he may not be the true enemy." Ead closed the door. "We suspect Her Majesty is being held against her will. And that we have not much time to reach her."

"I have already tried." Lintley looked as if all hope had forsaken him. "And I shall be banished for it."

"What happened?"

"Rumor had it that you were in league with King Sigoso and had returned to him, but it was so soon after Lord Arteloth vanished, I sensed a deliberate attempt to make Her Majesty vulnerable."

"Go on," Ead said.

"Her Majesty had not emerged from the Queen Tower since the White Wyrm came, and there was no light from her window. Dame Joan Dale and I demanded entrance to the Great Bedchamber to reassure ourselves she was well. Crest had us stripped of our armor for disobedience," he said bitterly. "Now I am confined here."

"What of the other Knights of the Body?" Margret asked.

"Three are also here for protesting."

"Not for long," Ead said. "How many retainers would we face, should we make our move tonight?"

"Of the thirty-six retainers Crest has at court, I would guess that about half are armed. She has several knights-errant, too."

The Knights of the Body were among the best warriors in Inys, hand-picked for their skill. They could defeat a rabble of servants.

"Do you think the others are still loyal?" Ead asked.

"Absolutely. Their first allegiance is always to Her Majesty."

"Good," she replied. "Muster them and go after Crest. Once she is apprehended, her retainers will lay down their arms."

They stole out of the chamber. Ead broke the locks on three other doors, and Lintley whispered the plan to his soldiers. Soon they stood with Dame Joan Dale, Dame Suzan Thatch, and Sir Marke Birchen.

"There are not many guards outside the armory." Ead offered Lintley one of her own blades. "Retrieve your weapons, but I would advise against armor. It will make you slow. And loud."

Lintley took the blade. "What will you do?"

"I will find Her Majesty."

"She will be surrounded by retainers in the service of Crest," Lintley reiterated. "They were stationed on almost every floor of the Queen Tower when last I was there."

"I can deal with them."

Lintley shook his head. "I cannot tell if you have lost your wits, Ead, or if you are the Knight of Courage come again."

"Let me go with you," Loth said to her. "I can help."

"If you think a handful of traitors will keep me from her side," came her immediate answer, "you are sorely mistaken." Then, softer, "I can do this alone."

The conviction in her words caught him unawares. He had seen her fell a wyverling. She could handle a few retainers.

"Then I will go with you, Sir Tharian," he said.

Lintley nodded. "It would be my honor to fight alongside you, Lord Arteloth."

"I will go with you, too," Margret said. "If you will have me."

"I will, Lady Margret." Lintley raised a smile. "I will have you."

Their gazes held for a moment longer than necessary. Loth cleared his throat, making Lintley look away.

"I still say you will be arrested before you get to the doors," one of the Knights of the Body said darkly to Ead.

"You speak as if it is a certainty." Ead stood with folded arms. "If any of you wish to turn back, say it now. We can afford no cowardice."

"We number the same as the Saint and his Holy Retinue," Margret said firmly. "If the seven of them managed to found a religion, then I sincerely hope the seven of us can rout a few milk-livered knaves."

Ead climbed the ladder of woodvines up the Queen Tower, as she had before. When she was close to the Privy Kitchen, she pushed off the wall and seized the windowsill. Weakened by her last climb, the woodvines tore away under her boot and collapsed onto the glasshouse far below.

She pulled herself through and fell into a crouch. Somewhere below, a bell began to ring. They must have found the body in the well.

For Lintley, the alarm was good tidings. He and his Knights of the Body could take advantage of the distraction to retrieve their swords from the armory. For Ead, however, the outlook was grim. This commotion would raise every retainer in the Queen Tower from bed.

Only a few more rooms now stood between her and Sabran.

The Gallery of the Blood Royal was empty. She strode past the portraits of the women of the House of Berethnet. Painted green eyes seemed to follow her as she approached the stair. There were differences between the queens—a curl to the hair, a dimple, a well-defined jaw—but each of them looked so much like the others, they might all have been sisters.

Her siden thrummed, and she could hear up to the next floor. Footsteps were approaching. By the time a group of retainers in green stormed down the stair, she was pressed against a tapestry, out of sight.

The bell had drawn them away from the royal apartments. This was her chance to reach Sabran.

Upstairs was the corridor she had lived in as a Lady of the Bedchamber. Ead stopped when she heard a voice from far below.

"To the Queen Tower!" It was Lintley. "Knights of the Body! All swords to the queen!"

They had been seen, and too early. Ead ran to the window and looked down.

With her razor senses, she could see every fine detail of the clash. In the Sundial Garden, Crest retainers were locking swords with the armed Knights of the Body. She saw Loth, sword flashing in his hand. Margret stood back to back with him.

The flame called for release. For the first time since she was a child, Ead conjured a fistful of Draconic fire, red as the morning sun, and hurled it at the Sundial Garden, into the midst of the traitors. Panic reigned. The retainers turned wildly, searching for the source of the fire, no doubt thinking a wyrm was above. Seizing the moment, Loth struck down his adversary with his elbow. Ead saw his face harden, his throat flex, and his fist clench.

"People of the court," he called, "hearken to me!"

The commotion had already roused the palace. Windows were opening in every building.

"I am Lord Arteloth Beck, who was banished from Inys for loyalty to the crown." Loth strode to the middle of the Sundial Garden as he bellowed over the clangor of blades. "Igrain Crest has turned against our queen. She allows her retainers to wear her colors and carry arms. She spits at the Knight of Fellowship by allowing her servants to fight like hounds at court. These are traitorous actions!"

He sounded like a man reborn.

"I urge you, in fellowship and faith, to rise for Her Majesty," he shouted. "Help us reach the Queen Tower and assure her safety!"

Cries of outrage ascended from the windows.

"You. What are you doing in here?"

Ead turned. Twelve more retainers had appeared.

"It's her," one of them barked, and they ran toward her. "Ead Duryan, yield your weapons!"

She could not candle all of them.

Blood it would have to be.

Two swords were already in her hands. She leaped high and landed, catlike, in their midst, slicing fingers and tendons, spilling guts like a cutpurse spilling gold. Death came for them like a desert wind.

Her blades were as red as the cloak she had forsworn. And when the dead lay at her feet, she looked up, tasting iron, hands gloved in wetness.

Lady Igrain Crest stood at the end of the corridor, flanked by two knights-errant.

"Enough, Your Grace." Ead sheathed her blades. "Enough."

Crest appeared unruffled by the carnage.

"Mistress Duryan," she said, eyebrows raised. "Blood, my dear, is never the way forward."

"Rich words," Ead replied, "from one whose hands are soaked in it."

Crest did not flinch.

"How long have you seen yourself as the judge of queens?" Ead took a step toward her. "How long have you been punishing them for straying from whichever path you deemed virtuous?"

"You are raving, Mistress Duryan."

"Murder is against the teachings of your ancestor. And yet ... you judged the Berethnets and found them wanting. Queen Rosarian took a lover outside the marriage bed and, in your eyes, she was stained." Ead paused. "Rosarian is dead because of you."

It was an arrow loosed into the dark, aimed on little more than instinct. And yet Crest smiled.

And Ead knew.

"Queen Rosarian," the Duchess of Justice said, "was removed by Sigoso Vetalda."

"With your approval. Your help from inside. He was scapegoat and weapon, but you were the instigator," Ead said. "I suppose when it all went smoothly, you understood your power. You hoped to mold the daughter into a more obedient queen than the mother. Tried to make Sabran dependent on your counsel, and to make her love you as a second mother." She mirrored that little smile. "But of course, Sabran developed a will of her own."

"I am the heir of Dame Lorain Crest, the Knight of Justice." Crest spoke in a measured tone. "She who ensured that the great duel of life was conducted fairly, who weighed the cups of guilt and innocence, who punished the unworthy, and who saw to it that the righteous would triumph always over the sinners. She who was most beloved of the Saint, whose legacy I have lived to defend."

Her eyes were now afire with fervor.

"Sabran Berethnet," she said softly, "has destroyed the house. She is barren stock. Bastard-born. No true heir of Galian Berethnet. A Crest must wear the crown, to glorify the Saint."

"The Saint would brook no tyrants on the throne of Inys," a voice behind Ead said.

Sir Tharian Lintley appeared at her shoulder with nine of the Knights of the Body. They surrounded Crest and her protectors.

"Igrain Crest," Lintley said, "you are arrested on suspicion of high treason. You will come with us to the Dearn Tower."

"You cannot make an arrest without a warrant from Her Majesty," Crest said, "or from myself." She looked straight ahead, as if all of them were beneath her. "Who are you to draw your swords upon holy blood?"

Lintley did not dignify the question with a retort.

"Go," he said to Ead. "Get to Her Majesty."

Ead needed no urging. She cast a final look at Crest and made for the end of the corridor.

"We can have a peaceful transition now, or war when the truth outs," Crest called after her. "And it will, Mistress Duryan. The righteous will always triumph ... in the end."

Jaw clenched, Ead strode away.

As soon as she was out of sight, she broke into a run. Blood dripped in her wake as she followed the path she had taken countless times.

Into the Presence Chamber she ran. All was cold and dark. She rounded a corner, and there were the doors to the Great Bedchamber. The doors she had walked through so many times to find the Queen of Inys.

Something moved in the darkness. Ead stopped short. Her flame cast a queasy light on the figure crumpled by the doors. Eyes like cobalt glass and a curtain of dark hair.

Roslain.

"Get back." A knife shone in her grasp. "I will cut your throat if you touch her, Grandmother, I swear it—"

"It's me, Roslain. Ead."

The Chief Gentlewoman of the Bedchamber finally saw past the light.

"Ead." She kept the knife up, breathing hard. "I dismissed the rumors about your sorcery … but perhaps *you* are the Lady of the Woods."

"A humbler witch than she, I assure you."

Ead crouched beside Roslain and reached for her right hand, making her flinch. Three of her fingers were bent at a grotesque angle, a splinter of bone jutting out above her love-knot ring.

"Did your grandmother do this?" Ead asked her quietly. "Or are you in league with her?"

Roslain let out a bitter laugh. "*Saint*, Ead."

"You were raised in the shadow of a queen. Perhaps you grew to resent her."

"I am not in her shadow. I *am* her shadow. And that," Roslain bit out, "has been my *privilege*."

Ead studied her, but there was no deceit in that tear-stained face.

"Go to her, but be on your guard," Roslain whispered. "If my grandmother comes back—"

"Your grandmother is arrested."

At this, Roslain let out a breathless sob. Ead squeezed her shoulder. Then she stood, and for the first time in an age, she faced the doors to the Great Bedchamber. Each sinew of her being was a harpstring, pulled taut.

Inside, the darkness yawned sinister. The flame untethered itself from her hand to float like a ghostlight and, by its pallid flicker, Ead made out a figure at the foot of the bed.

"Sabran."

The figure stirred. "Leave me," it rasped. "I am at prayer."

Ead was already beside Sabran, lifting her head. Shivering limbs recoiled from her.

"Sabran." Her voice quaked. "Sabran, look at me."

When Sabran raised her gaze, Ead drew in a breath. Gaunt and listless, wound in the shroud of her own hair, Sabran Berethnet looked more of a carcass than a queen. Her eyes, once limpid, took little in, and the smell of days unwashed clung to her nightgown.

"Ead." Fingers came to her face. Ead pressed the icy hand to her cheek. "No. You are another dream. You come here to torment me." Sabran turned away. "Leave me in peace."

Ead stared at her. Then she laughed for the first time in weeks, a laugh that stemmed from deep in her belly.

"Damn you, intransigent fool." She almost choked on her laughter. "I have crossed the South and the West to get back to you, Sabran Berethnet, and you reward me thus?"

Sabran looked at her a moment longer, her face clearing, and suddenly began to weep. "Ead," she said, her voice splintering, and Ead crushed her close, wrapping her arms around as much of her as she could. Sabran curled like a kitten against her.

There was nothing of her. Ead pulled the coverlet from the bed and enfolded her in it. Explanations could come later. So could vengeance. For now, all she wanted was for her to be safe and warm.

"She killed Truyde utt Zeedeur." Sabran was shivering so badly, she could hardly speak. "She imprisoned my Knights of the Body. Igrain. I tried— I tried—"

"Hush." Ead pressed a kiss to her brow. "I am here. Loth is here. Everything will be well."

51

East

It was just past dawn, and in the courtyard of Vane Hall, Elder Vara was oiling his iron leg. Tané approached him. The cold had turned her knuckles pink.

"Good morning, Elder Vara." She set down a tray. "I thought you might wish to break your fast."

"Tané." His smile was weary. "How kind of you. My old bones would be grateful for the warmth."

She sat beside him. "Does it often need oiling?" she asked.

"Once a day in damp conditions, or rust begins to set in." Elder Vara patted the limb. "Since the metalsmith who made it for me is now dead, I would sooner not chance losing it."

Tané had grown used to reading his expressions. Since the attack, fear had taken up permanent residence in the halls of Feather Island, but the worry etched on his face was fresh.

"Is something amiss?"

Elder Vara glanced at her. "The learnèd Doctor Moyaka wrote to me upon her arrival in Seiiki," he said. "The High Sea Guard suspects the Fleet of the Tiger Eye is holding a dragon hostage. It seems they intend to keep it alive ... to guarantee them safe passage through any waters they desire. A sinister new tactic, to hold our gods as leverage."

Tané made herself pour the tea. Hatred closed her throat.

"There is a rumor that the Golden Empress seeks the fabled mulberry tree," Elder Vara continued. "On the lost isle of Komoridu."

"Do you know anything else about the dragon?" Tané pressed. "Do you know its name?"

"Tané, it grieves me to tell you, but—" Elder Vara sighed. "It is the great Nayimathun."

Tané swallowed, throat aching. "She is still alive?"

"If these rumors are true." Elder Vara gently took charge of the kettle. "Dragons do not do well out of water, Tané, as you know. Even if she *is* alive, the great Nayimathun is not long for this world."

Tané had mourned her dragon. Now there was a possibility, however small, that she lived.

This news changed everything

"We must hope that the High Sea Guard can find a way to free her. I am quite sure they will." Elder Vara passed her a cup. "Please, allow me to change the subject. Did you come out here to ask me something?"

With difficulty, Tané pushed Nayimathun to the back of her mind, but her world was spinning.

"I was wondering," she made herself say, "if I might request your permission to look in the repository. I would like to read about the celestial jewels."

Elder Vara frowned. "That is secret knowledge indeed. I thought only the elders knew of it."

"The great Nayimathun told me."

"Ah." He considered. "Well, if you desire it, of course. There is scant record of the celestial jewels—which were sometimes called the *tide jewels* or *wishing jewels*—but you may examine what little there is." He motioned to the north. "You will need documents from the reign of the long-honored Empress Mokwo, which are stored at Windward Hall. I will send you with a letter to grant you access."

"Thank you, Elder Vara."

———

Tané dressed warmly for the journey. A padded coat over her uniform, a wrap around her head and face, and the fur-lined boots she had been given for winter. Along with a scroll addressed to the High Scholar of Windward Hall, Elder Vara also gave her a satchel of food.

It would be a long trek, especially in the cold. She would have to climb down to the Path of the Elder, scale the rocks on the other side, and walk the warmth of Windward Hall. Tufts of snow began to fall as she set off.

The only way down from this side was to use the craggy rocks beside the Falls of Kwiriki. As she descended, her heart thumped so hard she felt sick. At this very moment, Nayimathun might be fighting for her life in the belly of a butcher-ship.

And surely a celestial jewel—if that *was* what had been stitched into Tané, like a pattern into cloth . . .

Surely that could set a dragon free.

It was almost noon by the time she reached the foot of the ravine, where a driftwood gateway marked the entrance to the most sacred place in the East. Tané washed her hands in the salt water and stepped through, on to a stone-paved path.

On the Path of the Elder, the fog was so thick that it blotted out the sky. Tané could not even see the tops of the cedars that towered into the gray.

It was not quite silent. Every few moments, the leaves rustled, as if unsettled by breath.

Lanterns guided her past the graves of scholars, elders, and leaders of the dragon-fearing East, who had asked for their remains to rest with those of the Great Elder. Some of the stone blocks were so old that the inscriptions had worn away, leaving their occupants unnamed.

Elder Vara had told her not to think of the past. Walking here, however, she could not help but think of Susa. The bodies of the executed were left to rot, the bones discarded.

A head in a ditch, a body uncorked. Darkness stained the edges of her vision.

It took much of the day to cross the burial ground and climb the rock face at its end. By the time she glimpsed Cape Quill—the outstretched arm of the island—the sky had deepened to purple, and the only light was a gold seam on the horizon.

Date-plums hung like tiny suns in the front courtyard of Windward Hall, which overlooked the cape. Tané was greeted at the threshold by a Lacustrine man with a shaven head, proclaiming his role as a bonesinger. These scholars would spend most of their days on the Path of the Elder, tending to the graves of the faithful and singing praise to the bones of the great Kwiriki.

"Honorable scholar." He bowed, and so did Tané. "Welcome to Windward Hall."

"Thank you, learnèd bonesinger."

She removed her boots and stowed them. The bonesinger ushered her into the dimly lit interior of the hermitage, where a charcoal stove kept the cold at bay.

"Now," he said, "what may we do for you?"

"I have a message from the learnèd Elder Vara." She held it out. "He asks that you permit me access to your repository."

With raised eyebrows, the young man took it. "We must respect the wishes of the learnèd Elder Vara," he said, "but you must be tired after your journey. Would you like to visit the repository now, or wait in the guest quarters until morning?"

"Now," Tané said. "If you would be willing to take me."

———

"To our knowledge, Feather Island was the only place in the East to remain untouched during the Great Sorrow," the bonesinger told her as they walked. "Many ancient documents have been sent here to protect them from misfortune. Unfortunately, since the fire-breathers have woken and discovered our whereabouts, those documents are now in danger."

"Were any lost in the attack?"

"A handful," he said. "We organize our archives by reigns. Do you know whose you seek?"

"The long-honored Empress Mokwo."

"Ah, yes. A mysterious figure. It was said she had ambitions to bring the whole East under the rule of the Rainbow Throne. That her face was so lovely that every butterfly wept in envy." His smile dimpled his cheeks. "When history fails to shed light on the truth, myth creates its own."

Tané followed him down a staircase, into a tunnel.

The wheel repository stood like a sentinel in a cave behind the hermitage. Statues of past High Scholars filled alcoves in the walls, and countless teardrops of blue light hung, like wisps of spidersilk, from the ceiling.

"We do not risk flame down here," the bonesinger said. "Fortunately, the cave has its own lamps."

Tané was fascinated. "What are they?"

"Moondrops. Eggs of the lightfly." He turned the repository. "All of our documents are treated with oil of dragon manehair and left to dry out in the ice caves. Scholar Ishari was oil-treating some of our newest additions to the repository when the fire-breathers came."

"Scholar Ishari," Tané echoed. Her stomach knotted. "Is she ... in the hermitage?"

"Sadly, the learnèd scholar was injured in the attack while trying to save the documents. She died of her pains."

He spoke of death the way only bonesingers could, with acceptance and quietude. Tané swallowed the ash of regret. Ishari had taken but nineteen years, and most of them had been spent preparing for a life she had never been given a chance to lead.

The bonesinger opened a door in the repository. "The documents here pertain to the reign of the long-honored Empress Mokwo." There were not many. "I would ask you to handle them as little as possible. Come back inside whenever you please."

"Thank you."

He bowed and left her. In the calm blue glow, Tané took stock of the scrolls. By the flicker of the moondrops, she unraveled the first scroll and began to read, trying hard not to think of Ishari.

It was a letter from a diplomat in the City of the Thousand Flowers. Tané was fluent in Lacustrine, but this was an ancient clerical script. Translating it made her temples ache.

We here address Neporo, self-declared Queen of Komoridu,
whose name we hear for the first time, to thank you for sending
an embassy with tribute. Though we welcome your deference, your
unexpected claim to a land in the Unending Sea has caused some
insult to our neighbor Seiiki, with whose people we are bound in
praise of dragonkind. We regret that we cannot recognize you as
Queen Regnant while the House of Noziken takes issue with the
matter. We confer upon you instead the title Lady of Komoridu,
Friend of the Lacustrine. We expect you to rule your people in peace
and to endeavor to be devoted and obedient to both ourselves and
to Seiiki.

Komoridu. Tané had never heard of such a place. Neither had she heard of any ruler named Neporo.

She opened another scroll. This letter was in archaic Seiikinese, the writing cramped and smeared, but she could just make it out. It seemed to be addressed to the long-honored Noziken Mokwo herself.

Majesty, I address you once again. Neporo is in mourning, for her
friend, the sorceress from across the sea, is dead. It was the two of
them who, using the two objects I described in my last missive—the
waning jewel and the rising jewel—caused the great chaos in the
Abyss on the third day of spring. The body of the Lasian sorceress
will now be returned to her country, and Neporo bids twelve of
her subjects escort it, along with the white jewel the sorceress often
wore at her breast. Since His Augustness, the great Kwiriki in his
mercy has arranged us this opportunity, I will endeavor to do as
you command.

The other documents were all court records. Tané scoured them until the line between her eyebrows felt etched there with a knife.

She almost fell asleep in the glow of the cave, going over every document again, searching for anything she might have missed, checking her translations. Heavy-eyed, she eventually stumbled to the guest quarters, where a meal and a sleep robe had been left for her. She lay on the bedding for a long while, staring into the dark.

It was time to uncover what she had hidden. To unlock whatever power lay inside it.

The great chaos in the Abyss.

But what chaos, and why?

52

West

"If one of you does not speak," the Queen of Inys said, "we shall be here for a very long time."

Loth exchanged a glance with Ead. She was sitting on the other side of the table, wearing an ivory shirt and breeches, her hair half pulled back from her face.

They were in the Council Chamber at the top of the Alabastrine Tower. Buttered light shone through the windows. With only a little help to bathe and dress, the queen had stitched herself back together with as much mettle as any warrior.

Freeing Sabran had been the first victory of the night. The news that the Duchess of Justice had been arrested for high treason had caused most of her retainers to give up their arms. The Knights of the Body, with the help of the palace guards, had worked until the dawn to root out the last of the traitors, and to stop them fleeing the palace.

Nelda Stillwater, Lemand Fynch, and the Night Hawk had arrived at court not long after, each with an affinity of retainers in tow. They had claimed to be coming to liberate the queen from Crest, but Sabran had ordered them all locked away until she could unravel the truth.

Ead had pieced together what had happened. On the night she had been forced to leave Inys, Sabran had grown feverish. She had appeared to recover a few days later, only to collapse.

Crest had ostensibly taken control of her care, but for weeks, behind the doors of the Great Bedchamber, she had pressed her queen to sign a document called the Oath of Relinquishment. Her signature on it would yield the throne of Inys to the Crest family from the drying of the ink until the end of time. Crest had threatened her with exposure of her barrenness, or death, if she refused.

Sabran had remained defiant. Even while she was too weak to feed herself. Even when Crest had shut her up in darkness.

"I see I will not need to bring anyone to pry out your tongues," Sabran said. "You appear to have swallowed them."

Ead was nursing a cup of ale. This was the first time in hours that she had been more than a foot away from Sabran.

"Where should we begin?" she said evenly.

"You can begin, Mistress Duryan, by confessing who you are. They told me you were a witch," Sabran said. "That you had abandoned my court to pledge to the Flesh King."

"And you believed this nonsense."

"I had no idea what to believe. Now, when you return to me, you are drenched in blood and have left a pile of bodies higher than a horse behind you. You are no lady-in-waiting."

Ead rubbed her temple with one finger. Finally, she looked Sabran full in the face.

"My name," she said, "is Eadaz du Zāla uq-Nāra." Though her voice was steady, her eyes betrayed an inner conflict. "And I was brought to you by Chassar uq-Ispad as a bodyguard."

"And what made His Excellency believe that you were better placed to protect me than my Knights of the Body?"

"I am a mage. A practitioner of a branch of magic called siden. Its source is the same orange tree in Lasia that protected Cleolind Onjenyu when she vanquished the Nameless One."

"An enchanted orange tree." Sabran let out a huff of laughter. "Next you will tell me pears can sing."

"Does the Queen of Inys mock what she does not understand?"

Loth glanced from one to the other. Ead had seldom talked to Sabran at all when he had last been at court. Now, it seemed, she could goad the sovereign with impunity.

"Lord Arteloth," Sabran said, "perhaps you can enlighten me as to how *you* came to leave court. And how you met with Mistress Duryan on your journey. It seems she is all addle-brained."

Ead snorted into her cup. Loth reached across the table and poured from the jug of ale.

"Lord Seyton Combe sent Kit and myself to Cárscaro. He believed I was an impediment to your marriage prospects," he said. "In the Palace of Salvation, we met the Donmata Marosa, who had a task for us. And from there, I'm afraid, things only wax stranger."

He told her everything. The Flesh King's confession that he had arranged to murder her mother. The mysterious Cupbearer, whose hands were also bloody in that deed. He told her of Kit's death and the iron box he had taken across the desert, of his imprisonment in the Priory, and the daring escape back to Inys on the *Bird of Truth*.

Ead chimed in here and there. She enriched and broadened the story, telling Sabran about her banishment and her visit to the ruined city of Gulthaga. About the Long-Haired Star and the Tablet of Rumelabar. She went into great depth about the foundation of the Priory of the Orange Tree and its beliefs, and the reason she had been sent to Inys. Sabran did not move once as she listened. Only the flicker of her gaze betrayed her thoughts about each revelation.

"If Sabran the First was not born of Cleolind," she said eventually, "and I am not saying I believe it, Ead—then who *was* her mother? Who was the first Queen of Inys?"

"I don't know."

Sabran raised her eyebrows.

"While I was in Lasia, I learned more about the Tablet of Rumelabar," Ead continued. "To understand its mystery, I paid a visit to Kalyba, the Witch of Inysca." She glanced at Loth. "She is known here as the Lady of the Woods. She created Ascalon for Galian Berethnet."

Ead had not mentioned this on the ship. "The Lady of the Woods is real?" Loth asked.

"She is."

He swallowed.

"And you claim *she* made the True Sword," Sabran said. "The terror of the haithwood."

541

"The very same," Ead said, undaunted. "Ascalon was forged with both siden and sidereal magic—sterren—which comes from a substance left behind by the Long-Haired Star. It was these two branches of power that the Tablet of Rumelabar describes. When one waxes, the other wanes."

Sabran was wearing the same mask of indifference she often wore in the Presence Chamber.

"To recapitulate," she said tautly, "you believe my ancestor—the blessèd Saint—was a power-hungry, lustful craven who tried to press a country into accepting his religion, wielded a sword granted to him by a witch, and never defeated the Nameless One."

"And stole the recognition for the latter from Princess Cleolind, yes."

"You think I am the seed of such a man."

"Fair roses have grown from twisted seeds."

"What you did for me does not give you the right to blaspheme in my presence."

"So you would like your new Virtues Council to tell you only what you want to hear." Ead raised her cup. "Very well, Your Majesty. Loth can be Duke of Flattery, and I'll be Duchess of Deceit."

"Enough," Sabran barked.

"Peace," Loth cut in. "Please." Neither of them spoke. "We cannot quarrel. We must be united now. Because of—" His mouth was dry. "Because of what is to come."

"And what *is* to come?"

Loth tried to say it, but the words fled from him. He gave Ead a defeated look.

"Sabran," Ead said quietly, "the Nameless One will return."

For a long time, Sabran seemed to withdraw into her own world. Slowly, she rose, walked toward the balcony, and stood upon it, limmed by the sun.

"It is true," Ead said eventually. "A letter to the Priory from a woman named Neporo convinced me. Cleolind stood with her to bind the Nameless One—but only for a thousand years. And that thousand years is very close to ending."

Sabran placed her hands on the balustrade. A breeze caught a few strands of her hair.

"So," she said, "it is as my ancestor said. That when the House of Berethnet ends ... the Nameless One will return."

"It has naught to do with you," Ead said. "Or your ancestors. Most likely Galian made the claim to consolidate his new-found power, and to make himself a god in the eyes of his people. He fed his descendants to the jaws of his lie."

Sabran said nothing.

Loth wanted to comfort her, but nothing could soften tidings like these.

"The Nameless One was bound on the third day of spring, during the twentieth year of the reign of Mokwo, Empress of Seiiki," Ead said, "but I do not know when Mokwo ruled. You must ask High Princess Ermuna to find the date. She is Archduchess of Ostendeur, where documents on the East are stored." When Sabran continued in her silence, Ead sighed. "I know this is heresy to you. But if you love the woman you know as the Damsel—if you have any respect for the memory of Cleolind Onjenyu—then you will do this."

Sabran lifted her chin. "And if we discover the date? What then?"

Ead reached under her collar and withdrew the pale jewel she had taken from the Priory.

"This is the waning jewel. It is one of a pair." She placed it on the table. "It is made from sterren. Its sister is most likely in the East. The letter said we need them both."

Sabran looked at it over her shoulder.

The sunshine glowed in the waning jewel. Being close to it gave Loth a sense of cool tranquility—almost the opposite of what he always felt from Ead. She was the living flame of the sun. This was starlight.

"After Cleolind wounded the Nameless One, she appears to have traveled to the East," Ead said. "There she met Neporo of Komoridu, and together they bound the Nameless One in the Abyss." She tapped the jewel. "We must repeat what was done a thousand years ago—but we must finish it this time. And to do that, we also need Ascalon."

Sabran returned her gaze to the horizon. "Every Berethnet queen has searched for the True Sword, to no avail."

"None of them had a jewel that will call to it." Ead hung it around her neck again. "Kalyba told me that Galian meant to leave Ascalon in the hands of those who would die to keep it hidden. We know he had a loyal retinue, but does anyone come to mind?"

"Edrig of Arondine," Loth said at once. "The Saint squired for him before he became a knight himself. Viewed him as a father."

"Where did he live?"

Loth smiled. "As a matter of fact," he said, "he is one of the founders of the Beck family."

Ead raised her eyebrows.

"Goldenbirch," she said. "Perhaps I will begin my search there—with you and Meg, if you will keep me company. Your father has been wanting to speak to her, in any case."

"You truly think it could be in Goldenbirch?"

"It is as good a place as any to begin."

Loth thought of the night before. "One of us should stay," he said. "Meg can go with you."

At last, Sabran turned to face them again.

"Whether this legend is true or not," she said, "I have no choice but to trust you, Ead." Her face hardened. "Our mutual enemy will rise. Both our religions confirm it. I mean for us to stand against him. I mean to lead Inys to victory, as Glorian Shieldheart did."

"I believe you can," Ead said.

Sabran returned to her seat. "Since there are no ships heading north tonight," she said, "I would like you to attend the Feast of High Winter. You, too, Loth."

Loth frowned. "The feast will still proceed?"

"I think there is more need for it than ever. The arrangements ought to be in place."

"People will see that you are not with child." Loth hesitated. "Will you tell them you are barren?"

Sabran dropped her gaze to her belly.

"Barren." A thin smile. "We must think of a different word for it, I think. That one makes me sound like a field stripped of its crop. A waste with nothing left to give."

She was right. It was a cruel way to describe a person.

"Forgive me," he murmured.

544

Sabran nodded. "I will tell the court that I lost the child, but as far as they will know, I might yet conceive another."

It would grieve her subjects, but leave them with a ray of hope.

"Ead," Sabran said, "I would like to make you a member of the Knights Bachelor."

"I want no titles."

"You will accept, or you will be in too much danger to remain at court. Crest told everyone you were a witch. This position will dispel any doubt that I believe you loyal."

"I agree," Loth said.

Ead offered the barest nod of acknowledgment. "Dame I am, then," she said, after a pause.

The silence yawned long between the three of them. Allies now, yet they seemed to sit on a glass in that moment—a glass broken into faultlines of religion and inheritance.

"I will go and tell Margret of our journey," Ead said, and rose. "Oh, and Sabran, I will not be wearing court fashions any longer. I've had more than enough of trying to protect you in a petticoat."

She left without waiting to be dismissed. Sabran looked after her with a strange expression.

"Are you well?" Loth said to her quietly.

"Now you are back."

They both smiled, and Sabran covered his hand with hers. Cold, as always, the nails tinged with lilac. He had teased her about it when they were children. *Princess Snow*.

"I have not yet thanked you for all you did to liberate me," she said. "I understand you were the one who roused the court in my defense."

He squeezed her hand. "You are my queen. And my friend."

"When I heard that you had left, I thought I would go mad ... I knew you would never have gone of your own accord, but I had no proof. I was powerless in my own court."

"I know."

She pressed his hand once more. "For now," she said, "I am entrusting to you the duties of the Duchy of Justice. You will decide whether Combe, Fynch, and Stillwater truly were returning to help me."

"This is a grave obligation. Meant for one with holy blood," Loth said. "Surely one of the Earls Provincial proper would be better."

"I trust it only to you." Sabran pushed a sheet of parchment across the table. "Here is the Oath of Relinquishment pressed upon me by Crest. With my signature, this document would have yielded the throne to her family."

Loth read it. His throat dried out as he took in the wax seal, impressed with the twin goblets.

"The fever and pain made me too weak to understand a great deal of what was happening to me. I was focused on surviving," Sabran said. "Once, however, I heard Crest arguing with Roslain, saying that the Oath of Relinquishment would make her queen some day, and her daughter after that, and that she was an ingrate for resisting. And Ros— Ros said she would die before she took the throne from me."

Loth smiled. He would have expected nothing less from Roslain.

"The night before you arrived," Sabran continued, "I woke unable to breathe. Crest had a pillow over my face. She kept whispering that I was unworthy, like my mother before me. That the line was poisoned. That even Berethnets must answer to the call of justice." Her hand ghosted to her mouth. "Ros broke her fingers prying her off me."

So much suffering, all for naught.

"Crest must die," Sabran concluded. "For their failure to act against her, I will have Eller and Withy confined to their castles to await my pleasure. I will strip them of their duchies in favor of their heirs." Her face closed. "I tell you this. Holy blood or not, I will see Crest burn for what she has done."

Once, Loth would have protested such a brutal punishment, but Crest deserved no pity.

"For a time, I almost believed I *should* yield the throne. That Crest wanted the best for the realm." Sabran lifted her chin. "But we must be united in the face of the Draconic threat. I will cleave to my throne, and we will see what comes of it."

She sounded more a queen than ever.

"Loth," she added, quieter, "you were with Ead in this ... Priory of the Orange Tree. You have seen the truth of her." She held his gaze. "Do you still trust her?"

Loth poured a little more ale for them both.

"The Priory made me question the foundations of our world," he admitted, "but throughout it all, I trusted Ead. She saved my life, at great risk to her own." He handed her a cup. "She wants to keep you alive, Sab. I believe she wants it more than anything."

Something changed in her face.

"I must write to Ermuna. Your chambers await you," she said, "but be sure not to be late for the feast." When she looked up at him, he saw a glint of the old Sabran in her eyes. "Welcome back to court, Lord Arteloth."

———

On the highest floor of the Dearn Tower, in the cell where Truyde utt Zeedeur had spent her final days, Igrain Crest was at prayer. Only an arrow-slit cast light into her prison. When Loth entered, she did not raise her lowered head, nor unclasp her hands.

"Lady Igrain," Loth said.

She was still.

"If it please you, I have come to ask you some questions."

"I will answer for what I have done," Crest said, "only in Halgalant."

"You will not see the heavenly court," Loth said quietly. "So let us begin here."

53

West

The Feast of High Winter began at six of the clock in the Banqueting House of Ascalon Palace. As always, it would be followed by music and dancing in the Presence Chamber.

As the bells chimed in the clock tower, Ead studied her reflection. Her gown was palest blue silk, snowed with seed-pearls, the ruff made of white cutwork lace.

For one more night, she would dress as a courtier. Her sisters would think her even more of a traitor when they discovered that she had accepted a title from the Queen of Inys. If she was to survive here, however, it seemed she had no other choice.

A knock at the door, and Margret let herself in. She wore ivory satin and a silver girdle, and her attifet was studded with moonstones.

"I just came from Sabran," she said. "I am to be made a Lady of the Bedchamber." She set down the candle. "I thought you might not want to go to the Banqueting House alone."

"You thought correctly. As always." Ead met her gaze in the glass. "Meg, what has Loth told you about me?"

"Everything." Margret grasped her by the shoulders. "You know I take the Knight of Courage as my patron. There is courage, I think, in open-mindedness, and thinking for oneself. If you are a witch, then perhaps witches are not so wicked after all." Her face turned serious. "Now, a question. Would you prefer me to call you Eadaz?"

"No. But thank you for asking." Ead was touched. "You may call me Ead, as I call you Meg."

"Very well." Margret linked her arm. "Then let me reintroduce you to court, Ead."

Snow had settled thickly on every ledge and step. Courtiers were emerging from all over the palace, drawn to the light from the windows of the Banqueting House. As they entered, the steward called out, "Lady Margret Beck and Mistress Ead Duryan."

Her old name. Her false name.

The Banqueting House fell almost silent. Hundreds of eyes turned to look upon the witch. Margret tightened her grip on her arm.

Loth was alone at the high table, seated to the left of the throne. He beckoned with one hand.

They walked between the rows of tables. When Margret went to the chair on the other side of the throne, Ead sat beside her. She had never once eaten at the high table, which had always been reserved for the queen, the Dukes Spiritual, and two other guests of honor. In the old days, those guests of honor had usually been Loth and Roslain.

"I've seen more cheer in a charnel garden," Margret muttered. "Did you speak to Roslain, Loth?"

Loth rested his knuckles on his cheek and turned his face toward them, hiding his lips.

"Aye," he said. "After the bonesetter came to tend to her hand." He kept his voice low. "It appears your instinct was right, Ead. Crest believes herself to be the judge of queens."

Ead took no pleasure in it.

"I am not sure when her madness set in," Loth went on, "but when Queen Rosarian was still alive, one of her ladies reported to Crest that she had taken Captain Gian Harlowe as a lover. Crest saw Rosarian as ... a harlot, unfit to be queen. She punished her in several ways. Then decided that she was beyond reform."

Ead could see in his face that he was struggling to swallow this. He had believed for too long in the delicate artifice of court. Now the artfully placed leaves had blown away, revealing the shining jaws of the trap.

"She warned Queen Rosarian," Loth continued, brow pinched, "but the affair with Harlowe carried on. Even—" He glanced toward the doors. "Even after Sab was born."

Margret raised her eyebrows. "So Sabran may be *his* daughter?"

"If Crest speaks true. And I think she does. Once she started talking, she seemed almost desperate to tell me every detail of her ... enterprise."

Another secret to be kept. Another crack in the marble throne.

"Once Sab was old enough to bear children of her own," Loth said, "Crest sought help from King Sigoso. She knew he reviled Rosarian for refusing his hand, so together they conspired to kill her, with Crest hoping the blame would drift toward Yscalin."

"And Crest still considered herself pious?" Margret snorted. "After murdering a Berethnet?"

"Piety can turn the power-hungry into monsters," Ead said. "They can twist any teaching to justify their actions."

She had seen it before. Mita had believed she was serving the Mother when she executed Zāla.

"Crest waited then," Loth said. "Waited to see if Sabran would grow to be more devout than her mother. When Sab resisted the childbed, Crest sensed rebellion. She bribed people to enter the Queen Tower with blades to frighten her. Ead, it is just as you suspected. The cutthroats were supposed to be caught. Crest promised their families would be compensated."

"And she infiltrated Truyde's plan in order to kill Lievelyn?" Margret asked, and Loth nodded. "But *why*?"

"Lievelyn traded with Seiiki. That was the reason she gave me. She also considered him a drain on Inys—but in truth, I think she could not bear that Sabran spurned her choice of companion. That she was becoming influenced by someone other than her."

"Sab did seem to hearken to Lievelyn," Margret conceded. "She went outside her palace for the first time in fourteen years because he asked it of her."

"Just so. An upstart sinner with too much power. Once he had served his purpose, and Sabran was pregnant, he had to die." Loth shook his head. "When the physician told her Sabran would not conceive again, it proved to Crest, once and for all, that she was of tainted seed, and that the House of Berethnet was no longer fit to serve the Saint. She decided that the throne must pass, at last, to the only worthy descendants of the Holy Retinue. To her own heir."

"This confession must be enough to condemn Crest," Ead said.

Loth looked grimly satisfied. "I do believe it is."

At that moment, the steward thumped his staff on the floorboards.

"Her Majesty, Queen Sabran!"

The court fell silent as it rose. When Sabran came into the candlelight, with the silver-clad Knights of the Body behind her, there was a shared intake of breath.

Ead had never seen her look so splendidly alone. Usually she came to the Banqueting Hall with her ladies, or with Seyton Combe or some other person of importance.

She wore no powder on her face. No jewelry but her coronation ring. Her gown was black velvet, its sleeves and forepart mourning gray. It was clear to anyone with sense that she was not with child.

Murmurs of confusion rang through the hall. It was traditional for a queen to be holding her swaddled daughter, the first time she appeared in public after her confinement.

Loth stood to let Sabran take the throne. She lowered herself into it, watched by her court.

"Mistress Lidden," she said, her voice stentorian, "will you not sing for us?"

The Knights of the Body took their places behind the high table. Lintley never removed his hand from his sword. The court musicians began to play, and Jillet Lidden sang.

Silver platters of food were brought out from the Great Kitchen and laid on the tables, displaying all Inys had to offer in the high winter. Swan pie, woodcock, and roasted goose, baked venison in a rich clove sauce, burbot sprinkled with almond snowflakes and silver leaf, white cabbage and honey-glazed parsnip, mussels seethed in butter and red wine vinegar. Conversation stole back into the hall, but nobody seemed able to tear their eyes from the queen.

A page filled their goblets with ice wine from Hróth. Ead accepted a few mussels and a cut of goose. As she ate, she gave Sabran a sidelong glance.

She recognized the look on her face. Fragility with a front of strength. As Sabran lifted her goblet to her lips, only Ead noticed the tremor in her hand.

Jumbles, sugar plums, spiced pear and cranberry pie, pastry horns stuffed with snow cream, and blanched apple tarts, among other delicacies, followed the main course. When Sabran rose, and the steward announced her, a deathly silence fell again.

Sabran did not speak for some time. She stood tall, with her hands clasped at her midriff.

"Good people," she said at last, "we know that things at court have been disquieting in recent days, and that our absence must have troubled you." Somehow, despite the low pitch of her voice, she managed to make herself heard. "Certain people at this court have conspired, of late, to break the spirit of fellowship that has always united the people of Virtudom."

Her face was a locked door. The court waited for revelation.

"It will be a great shock to you that during our recent illness, we were confined in the Queen Tower by one of our own councillors, who was attempting to usurp our Saint-given authority." Murmurs flickered across the hall. "This councillor took advantage of our absence to pursue her own ambition to steal our throne. A person of holy blood."

Ead felt the words in her core, and she knew that everyone else did, too. They struck like a wave. Left no one untouched.

"Because of her actions, we must bring you most grievous news." Sabran placed a hand on her belly. "That during our ordeal ... we lost the beloved daughter we carried."

The silence went on. And on.

And on.

Then one of the maids of honor let out a sob, and it was like a thunderclap. The Banqueting House erupted around her.

Sabran remained still and expressionless. The hall resounded with calls for the perpetrators to pay. The steward banged his staff, shouting to no avail for order, until Sabran raised a hand.

At once, the turmoil ceased.

"These are uncertain times," Sabran said, "and we cannot afford to give way to grief. A shadow has fallen over our realm. More

Draconic creatures are waking, and their wings have brought a wind of fear. We see that fear in all your faces. We have seen it even in our own."

Ead watched the crowd. The words were reaching them. By offering them a glimpse of vulnerability—a fine crack in her armor—Sabran showed that she stood among them.

"But it is in such times that we must look more than ever to the Saint to guide us," Sabran said. "He opens his arms to the fearful. He shelters us with his own shield. And his love, like a sword in the hand, makes us strong. While we stand together in the great Chainmail of Virtudom, we cannot be defeated.

"We mean to reforge with love what greed has broken. On this, the Feast of High Winter, we pardon all those who were so quick to serve their mistress that they neglected, in their haste and fear, to serve their queen. They will not be executed. They will know the balm of mercy.

"But the woman who used them cannot be forgiven. It was her hunger for power, and her wanton abuse of the power she had already been given, that swayed others to her will." The hall flickered with nods. "She has dishonored her holy blood. She has scorned her patron virtue—for Igrain Crest knew no justice in her hypocrisy and malice."

That name sent a ripple of unrest along the tables.

"By her actions, Crest has shamed not only the Knight of Justice, but the blessed Saint and his descendants. Therefore, we expect her to be found guilty of high treason." Sabran made the sign of the sword, and the court mirrored her. "All of the Dukes Spiritual are presently being questioned. It is our fervent hope that the rest are proven innocent, but we shall bow to the evidence."

Each of her words was the skip of a stone across a lake, forming ripples of emotion. The Queen of Inys could not cast illusions, but her voice and bearing on this night had turned her into an enchantress.

"We stand here in love. In hope. And in defiance. Defiance of those would have tried to turn us from our values. Defiance of Draconic hate. We rise to face the winds of fear and, by the Saint, we will turn them back upon our enemies." She walked across the dais, and every eye followed her. "We do not yet have an heir, for our daughter is in the arms of the Saint—but your queen is very much alive. And we will ride into any battle for you, as Glorian Shieldheart rode for her people. Come what may."

Now there were rumbles of agreement. Nods and shouts of *Sabran Queen*.

"We will prove to the entire world," she continued, "that no wyrm will cow the people of Virtudom!"

"Virtudom," voices echoed. "Virtudom!"

They were all on their feet now. Eyes bright in the frenzy of veneration. Cups held up in taut-knuckled fists.

She had led them from the depths of terror to the height of adoration.

Sabran was golden-tongued.

"Now, in the same defiance this realm has professed for a thousand years," she called out, "we celebrate the Feast of High Winter—and prepare for spring, the season of change. The season of sweetness. The season of generosity. And what it gives, we will not hoard, but give in turn to you." She snatched her goblet from the table and thrust it high. "To Virtudom!"

"VIRTUDOM," the court roared back. "VIRTUDOM! VIRTUDOM!"

Their voices filled the hall like song, rising to its very rafters.

The festivities went on late into the night. Though there were balefires outside, the courtiers seemed grateful to be in the Presence Chamber, where Sabran sat on her marble throne, and flames roared in the cavernous hearth. Ead stood with Margret in the corner.

As she sipped her mulled wine, a blaze of red caught her eye. Her hand flicked to the knife on her girdle.

"Ead." Margret touched her elbow. "What is it?"

Red hair. The red hair of the Mentish ambassador, not a cloak— yet Ead did not relax. Her sisters must be biding their time, but they would come.

"Nothing. Forgive me," Ead said. "What were you saying?"

"Tell me what the matter is."

"It is nothing you want to meddle in, Meg."

"I wasn't meddling. Well, perhaps," Margret admitted. "One must be a trifle meddlesome at court, or one has nothing to talk about."

Ead smiled. "Are you ready for our journey to Goldenbirch tomorrow?"

"Aye. Our ship leaves at dawn." Margret paused before adding, "Ead, I don't suppose you were able to bring Valour home."

There was hope in her eyes. "He is with an Ersyri family I trust, on an estate in the Harmur Pass," Ead said. "I could not take him into the desert. You shall have him back, I promise."

"Thank you."

Someone stopped beside Margret and touched her on the shoulder. Katryen Withy, wearing a gown of cloud silk. Pearls inlaid in silver nestled in her wreath of hair.

"Kate." Margret embraced her. "Kate, how do you do?"

"I have been worse." Katryen kissed her on the cheek before turning to Ead. "Oh, Ead. I am very glad you're back."

"Katryen." Ead looked her over. A bruise was fading under her eye, and her jaw was swollen. "What happened to you?"

"I tried to get to Sabran." She touched the mark gingerly. "Crest had me locked in my quarters. Her guard did this when I resisted."

Margret shook her head. "If that tyrant had ever sat the throne ..."

"Thank the Damsel she will not."

Sabran, who had been deep in conversation with Loth, now rose, and the room was quiet. It was time for her to reward those who had proved most faithful to their queen.

The ceremony was no less impressive for its brevity. First, Margret was formally named a Lady of the Bedchamber, while the Knights of the Body were commended for their ceaseless loyalty to the crown. Others who had joined them were given lands and jewels, and then:

"Mistress Ead Duryan."

Ead stepped from the crowd. Whispers and looks dogged her footsteps.

"By the grace of the Six Virtues," the steward read, "it has pleased Her Majesty to name you Dame Eadaz uq-Nāra, Viscountess Nurtha. A member of the Virtues Council."

The Presence Chamber rang with murmurs. *Viscountess* was an honorary title in Inys, used to raise a woman who was not of noble or holy blood. Never had it been bestowed upon one who was not an Inysh subject.

Sabran took the ceremonial sword from Loth. Ead held still as the flat of the blade touched each of her shoulders. This second title would only serve to deepen her treachery in the eyes of her sisters—but she could wear it if it shielded her for long enough to find Ascalon.

"Rise," Sabran said. "My lady."

Ead stood and looked her in the eye.

"Thank you." Her curtsy was brief. "Your Majesty."

She took her letters patent from the steward. People whispered *my lady* as she returned to Margret.

She was Mistress Duryan no more.

There was one last honor to be given. For his courage, Sir Tharian Lintley, who was as much a commoner by blood as Ead, also received a new title. He was made Viscount Morwe.

"Now, Lord Morwe," Sabran said in an arch tone, once Lintley had received his accolade, "we believe you are of appropriate rank to marry a daughter of the Earls Provincial. Pray, do you ... have anyone in mind?"

An outbreak of much-needed laughter followed.

Lintley swallowed. He looked like a man who had just been granted all the wishes of his life.

"Yes." He looked across the room. "Yes, Your Majesty, I do. But I would prefer first to speak to the lady in private. To be certain of her heart."

Margret, who had been watching with pursed lips, raised an eyebrow.

"You have spoken for long enough, Sir Tharian," she called. "Now is the time for action."

More laughter. Lintley chuckled, as did she. Candlelight danced in her eyes. She crossed the room and took his outstretched hand.

"Your Majesty," Lintley said, "I ask your permission, and that of the Knight of Fellowship, to take this woman as my companion in the coming days." The way he gazed at her, she might have been a sunrise after years of night. "So that I might love her as she has always deserved."

Margret looked to the throne. Her throat bobbed, but Sabran had already inclined her head.

"You have our permission," she said. "We give it gladly."

Cheers filled the Presence Chamber. Loth, Ead was pleased to see, clapped as hard as anyone else.

"Now," Sabran said, "we think a dance is in order." She motioned to the consort. "Come, play the Pavane of the Merrow King."

This time, the applause was thunderous. Lintley murmured something to Margret, who smiled and placed a kiss on his cheek. As the dancers took their places, Loth stepped down from his seat and bowed to Ead.

"Viscountess," he said, mock somber. "Would you do me the honor of a dance?"

"I shall, my lord." Ead placed a hand over his, and he led her to the middle of the room. "How do you like the match?" she asked him, seeing him glance toward Margret.

"Very well. Lintley is a good man."

The Pavane of the Merrow King was sedate at first. It began like the ocean on a tranquil day, becoming tumultuous as the music swelled. It was an intricate affair, but Ead and Loth were old hands at it.

"My parents will have heard the news by the time you reach Goldenbirch," Loth said as they skipped with the other couples. "Mama will be even more vexed that I am not betrothed myself."

"I think she will be too relieved that you are alive to care," Ead said. "Besides, you may prefer never to wed."

"As Earl of Goldenbirch, it would be expected of me. And I have always longed for companionship." Loth looked down at her. "But what of you?"

"Me." Ead glided to the right, and he followed. "Would I ever take a companion, you mean?"

"You cannot go home. Perhaps you could ... make a life here. With someone." His gaze was soft. "Unless you already have."

Her chest tightened.

The dance separated them for a moment while they formed a whirlpool with the other pairs. When they reached each other again, Loth said, "Crest told me. I suppose she heard it from the Night Hawk."

Saying it out loud would be dangerous. He knew that.

"I hope you did not keep it from me because you thought I would judge you," Loth murmured. They both turned on the spot. "You are my dearest friend. I want you to be happy."

"Even though it shames the Knight of Fellowship." Ead raised her eyebrows. "We are not wed."

"I would have believed that before," he admitted. "Now I see that there are more important things."

Ead smiled. "You really have changed." They joined hands again as the pavane grew faster. "I did not want to burden you with worry for us both. You care too much."

"It is my way," he said, "but it would be a greater burden to know that my friend felt she could not open her heart to me." He squeezed her hand. "I am here for you. Always."

"And I for you," Ead said. She hoped it could be true.

As the pavane came to its end, she wondered if they would ever lie carefree under the apple tree again, sharing wine and talking until dawn, after everything they had been through. Loth bowed to her, a smile creasing his eyes, and she curtsied back. Then she turned, intending to slip away to her chamber—only to find Sabran waiting.

Ead watched her as the floor cleared. So did the rest of the court.

"Play a candle dance," Sabran said.

This time, there were gasps of delight from the courtiers. The queen had not danced in public once while Ead had lived at court. Loth had confided to her, long ago, that Sabran had stopped dancing the day her mother died.

Many courtiers would never have witnessed this dance, but some of the older servants, who must have seen Queen Rosarian partake, set about plucking candles from the chamber sticks. Soon the other servants followed suit. One candle was given to Sabran, another to Ead. Loth, who was close enough to be caught up in the affair, offered a hand to Katryen.

The consort of instruments struck up an aching tune, and Jillet Lidden began to sing. Three men joined their voices to hers.

Ead curtsied low to Sabran, who mirrored her. Even that small action made her candle flicker.

The circling began. They held the candles in their right hands, and their left hands were held back to back, not quite touching. Six rotations around each other, gazes locked, before they were summoned by the music to opposite sides of the line. Ead circled around Katryen before she returned to Sabran.

Her partner was a magnificent dancer. Every step was precise, yet sleek as velvet. All those years she never danced for her court, she must have trained herself alone. She sailed around Ead like the hand of a clock, drawn closer by the heartbeat, no step faster than the last. When Ead turned her head, their foreheads met, and their shoulders brushed, before they parted again. Ead lost her breath somewhere along the way.

Never had they been this close in public. The scent of her, the short-lived warmth, was a torture no one else could see. Ead circled around Loth before she reunited with Sabran, and her blood was as loud as the music, louder.

It went on for what felt like an eternity. She was lost in a dream of haunting voices, in the lilt of flute and harp and shawm, and in Sabran, half concealed by shadow.

She hardly noticed when the music ended. All she could hear was the drum in her chest. There was an enraptured silence before the court burst into applause. Sabran cupped a hand around her candle and blew it out.

"We will retire for the night." A maid of honor took her candle. "I bid the rest of you to stay and enjoy the festivities. Good evening."

"Good evening, Your Majesty," the court answered, bowing and curtsying as their queen walked away. At the door to the Privy Chamber, Sabran looked over her shoulder at Ead.

That look was a call. Ead snuffed her candle and handed it to a servant.

Her corset felt tighter. A sweet ache blossomed in her belly. She stayed for a little while in the crowd, watching Loth and Margret dance a galliard, before she left the Presence Chamber. The Knights of the Body stood aside for her.

The Privy Chamber was dark and cold. Ead walked through it, remembering the music of the virginals, and opened the doors to the Great Bedchamber.

Sabran waited beside the fire. She wore nothing now but her stiff corset and shift.

"Make no mistake," she said, "I am wroth with you."

Ead stood on the threshold.

"I shared all my secrets with you, Ead." Her voice was hardly there. "You saw me as the night does. As my truest self." She paused. "It was you who drove away Fýredel."

"Yes."

Sabran closed her eyes.

"Nothing in my life was real. Even the attempts to *take* my life were staged, designed to influence and manipulate me. But you, Ead—I believed you were different. I called Combe a liar when he told me you were not what you appeared. Now I wonder if everything between us was part of your act. Your *assignment*."

Ead searched for the right words.

"Answer me," Sabran said, voice straining. "I am your queen."

"You may be *a* queen, but you are not *my* queen. I am not your subject, Sabran." Ead stepped inside and shut the doors. "And that is why you can be certain that what was between us was real."

Sabran gazed into the fire.

"I showed you as much of myself as I could," Ead told her. "Any more would have seen me executed."

"Do you think me a tyrant?"

"I think you a self-righteous fool whose head is harder than a rock. And I would not change you for the world."

Sabran finally looked at her.

"Tell me, Eadaz uq-Nāra," she said softly, "am I a greater fool to want you still?"

Ead crossed the space between them. "No more a fool than I," she said, "to love you as I do."

She reached for Sabran, brushing a lock of her hair behind her ear. Sabran gazed into her eyes.

They stood face to face, barely touching. At last, Sabran took Ead by the hands and placed them on her waist. Ead slid them to her front and set about unravelling her corset.

Sabran watched her. Ead wanted this to be another candle dance, to savor the long climb of their intimacy, but she needed her too much. Her fingers looped beneath the laces and pulled them through the hooks, one after another, and at last the corset opened and fell, leaving Sabran in her shift. Ead slid the silk from her shoulders and held her by her hips.

She stood naked in the shadows. Ead drank in her limbs, her hair, her eyes like foxfire.

The space between them disappeared. Now it was Sabran who did the unlacing. Ead closed her eyes and let herself be stripped.

They embraced like companions on the first night. When Sabran placed a kiss on her neck, just behind the shell of her ear, Ead let her head list to one side. Sabran glided her hands up her back.

Ead lowered her to the bed. Hungry lips came against hers, and Sabran breathed her name. It seemed as if centuries had passed since they had last been here.

They intertwined among the furs and sheets, breathless and fierce. Ead shivered with anticipation as she relearned every detail of the woman she had left behind. Her cheekbones and her tilted-up nose. Her smooth brow. The pillar of her throat and the little chalice at its base. The twin dents low down on her back, like the impressions of fingertips. Sabran unlocked her lips with her own, and Ead kissed her as if this were their last act on earth. As if this one embrace could keep the Nameless One at bay.

Their tongues danced the same pavane as their hips. Ead bent her head and touched her lips to each fine-cut collarbone, the rosebuds at the tips of her breasts. She kissed her belly, where the bruising had at last faded away. The only trace of the truth was a seam beneath her navel.

Sabran cradled her face. Ead looked into the eyes that had haunted her, and called to her still. Her fingers grazed over the scar that led along one thigh, found the dew where it met the other.

Then Sabran rolled her over, mischief in her smile. Her hair eclipsed the candlelight. Ead slid her hands around the cruet of her waist, interlocked her fingers at the small of her back, and dragged her between her legs.

Desire was a banked fire in her. Sabran smoothed a hand beneath her thigh and placed a light kiss on each breast.

Surely this was an unquiet dream. She would throw herself on the mercy of the desert if it meant that she could have this woman.

Sabran worked her way downward. Ead closed her eyes, breath netted in her chest. Her senses splintered to admit each luminous sensation. Fire-warmed skin. Creamgrail and clove. By the time a finger brushed her navel, she was drawn taut, shivering and glazed with sweat. As her hips rose in welcome, soft lips charted the crook of her thigh.

Each sinew of her was a string on a virginal, aching for the stroke of the musician. Her senses wound tight about ever-smaller centers, tensed to the pitch of Sabran Berethnet, and every touch vibrated through her bones.

"I am not your *queen*," Sabran whispered over her skin, "but I am yours." Ead raked her fingers through the dark of her hair. "And you will find that I can also be generous."

They slept only when they were too heavy-limbed and sated to keep their exhaustion at bay. Sometime in the small hours, they woke to the patter of rain against the window, and they sought each other out again, bodies echoing the ember light.

After, they lay interlaced under the coverlets.

"You must remain as my Lady of the Bedchamber," Sabran murmured. "For this. For us."

Ead gazed at the ornate stonework on the ceiling.

"I can play the part of Lady Nurtha," she said, "but it will always be a part."

"I know." Sabran looked into the darkness. "I fell in love with a part you played."

Ead tried not to let the words find her heart, but Sabran had a way of always reaching it.

Chassar had fashioned Ead Duryan, and she had inhabited her so fully that everyone had fallen for the act. For the first time, she understood the depth of betrayal and confusion that Sabran must be feeling.

Sabran took Ead by the hand and traced the underside of her finger. The one that held her sunstone ring.

"You did not wear this before."

Ead was close to falling asleep. "It is the symbol of the Priory," she said. "The ring of a slayer."

"You have slain a Draconic creature, then."

"Long ago. With my sister, Jondu. We killed a wyvern that had woken in the Godsblades."

"How old were you?"

"Fifteen."

Sabran studied the ring for a time.

"I long not to believe your tale of Galian and Cleolind. I prayed to them both all my life," she murmured. "If your version of events is correct, then I never knew either of them."

Ead slid a hand to her back.

"Do you believe me?" she asked. "You know I have no proof of it."

"I know," Sabran said. Their noses touched. "It will take time for me to come to terms with this … but I will not close my mind to the notion that Galian Berethnet was only flesh."

Her breathing grew softer. For a time, Ead thought she had drifted back to sleep. Then Sabran said, "I fear the war Fýredel craves." She entwined their fingers. "And the shadow of the Nameless One."

Ead only stroked her hair with one hand.

"I will address my people soon. They must know that I will stand against the Draconic Army, and that there is a plan in place to end the threat once and for all. If you can find the True Sword, I will show it to them. To lift their spirits." Sabran looked up. "Your ambition is to defeat the Nameless One. If you succeed, what then will you do?"

Ead let her eyelids fall. It was a question she had tried her utmost not to ask herself.

"The Priory was founded to keep the Nameless One at bay," she said. "If I bind him ... I suppose I could do anything."

A strange quiet grew between them. They lay in silence until Sabran shifted away and turned on to her other side.

"Sabran." Ead kept her distance. "What is it?"

"I'm too warm."

Her voice was armored. Faced with the back of her shoulder, Ead tried her best to sleep. She had no right to ask for truth.

It was not yet dawn when she woke. Sabran was asleep beside her, so still, she might have been dead.

Careful not to disturb her, Ead rose. Sabran stirred as she kissed the top of her head. She ought to let her know she was leaving, but even sleeping she looked tired. At least now she was safe, surrounded by people who loved her.

Ead left the Great Bedchamber and returned to her own rooms, where she washed and dressed. Margret was already in the stables in a riding habit and a hat festooned with an ostrich feather, saddling a sleepy-eyed palfrey. When she smiled, Ead embraced her.

"I am so happy for you, Meg Beck." She kissed her cheek. "The soon-to-be Viscountess Morwe."

"I wish he had not needed to be Viscount Morwe to be deemed worthy of me, but things are as they are." Margret withdrew and grasped her hands. "Ead, will you be my giver?"

"It would be an honor. And now you can give your parents the good news."

Margret sighed. Her father sometimes did not know his children. "Aye. Mama will be overjoyed." She smoothed the front of her cream jacket. "Do you think I look all right?"

"I think you look like Lady Margret Beck. A paragon of fashion."

Margret blew out a breath. "Good. I thought I might look like the village fool in this hat."

They rode into the waking streets and crossed the Limber at the Bridge of Supplications, which was carved with the likenesses of every queen of the House of Berethnet. If they made good time, they could be in Summerport, which served the northern counties of Inys, by ten of the clock.

"Your dance with Sab last night set tongues wagging." Margret glanced at her. "Rumor is that the two of you are lovers."

"What would you say if that were true?"

"I would say you and she can do as you please."

She could trust Margret. Mother knew, it would be good to have someone to talk to about her feelings for Sabran—yet something made her want to keep it secret, to keep their hours stolen.

"Rumors are nothing new at court," was all she said. "Come, tell me your plans for the wedding. I think you would look very fine in yellow. What say you?"

———

The grounds of Ascalon Palace were draped in morning fog. A drench of rain had blown in and frozen overnight, turning the paths to frosted glass and dressing every windowsill with icicles.

Loth stood before the ruins of the Marble Gallery, where he and Sabran had often sat and talked for hours. There was a haunting beauty in the way the stone wept to the ground like wax.

No natural fire could have melted it. Only something retched up by the Dreadmount.

"This is where I lost my daughter."

He looked over his shoulder. Sabran was close by, face cold-burned beneath a fur hat. Her Knights of the Body waited at a distance, all in the silver-plated armor of winter.

"I called her Glorian. The grandest name of my lineage. Each of its three bearers were great queens." Her gaze was in the past. "I often wonder what she would have been like. If her name would have been a burden, or if she would have become even more illustrious than the others."

"I think she would have been as fearless and virtuous as her mother."

Sabran managed a tired smile.

"You would have liked Aubrecht." She came to stand beside him. "He was kind and honorable. Like you."

"I am sorry I never met him," Loth said.

They watched the sun rise. Somewhere in the grounds, a lark began to chirrup.

"I prayed this morning for Lord Kitston." Sabran rested her head on his shoulder, and he drew her in close. "Ead does not believe that Halgalant awaits us after death. Perhaps she is right—but I still trust, and always will, that there is a life beyond this one. And I trust that he has found it."

"I must trust in that, too." Loth thought of the tunnel. That lonesome tomb. "Thank you, Sab. Truly."

"I know his death must hurt you still, rightly," Sabran said, "but you must not let it cloud your judgment."

"I know it." He drew in a breath. "I must visit Combe."

"Very well. I will be in the Privy Library, attending to neglected matters of state."

"An invigorating day ahead of you, then."

"Indeed." With another weary smile, Sabran turned back to the Queen Tower. "Good day to you, Lord Arteloth."

"Good day, Your Majesty."

In spite of it all, it was a fine thing to be back at court.

In the Dearn Tower, Lord Seyton Combe was wrapped in a blanket, reading a prayer book with bloodshot eyes. He was shivering, and little wonder.

"Lord Arteloth," the Night Hawk said, when the jailer let Loth in. "How good to see you back at court."

"I wish I could feel as warmly toward you, Your Grace."

"Oh, I expect no warmth, my lord. I had good reasons for sending you away, but you will not like them."

Keeping his face clean of emotion, Loth took a seat.

"For the time being, Queen Sabran has entrusted the investigation of the attempted usurpation of her throne to me," he said. "I would hear everything you know about Crest."

Combe sat back. Loth had always found those eyes unnerving.

"When Queen Sabran was confined to her sickbed," Combe began, "I had no reason, at first, to suspect that anything was amiss with her care. She had agreed to keep to the Queen Tower to conceal her miscarriage, and Lady Roslain was willing to stay with her during her illness. Then, not long after Mistress Duryan left the capital—"

"Fled," Loth corrected. "In fear for her life. Banishing friends of the queen is something of a habit of yours, Your Grace."

"I make a habit of protecting her, my lord."

"You failed."

At this, Combe heaved a long sigh.

"Yes." He rubbed at the shadows under his eyes. "Yes, my lord, I did."

Loth felt, to his exasperation, a flicker of sympathy.

"Continue," he said.

It was a moment before Combe did. "Doctor Bourn came to me," he recounted. "He had been ordered out of the Queen Tower. He confessed his fear that, rather than being cared for, Her Majesty was being *guarded*. Only Lady Igrain and Lady Roslain were attending her.

"I had long been ... uneasy about Igrain. I misliked her rather pitiless species of piety." Combe drew slow circles on his temple. "I had told her what I had learned from one of my spies. That Lady Nurtha, as she is known now, had carnal knowledge of the queen. Something changed in her eyes. She made a comment alluding to Queen Rosarian and her ... marital conduct."

A memory, unbidden, of her portrait in Cárscaro, slashed in a fit of jealous rage.

"I began to fit the pieces together, and I misliked the picture they formed," Combe said. "I sensed Igrain was power-drunk on her own patron virtue. And that she was plotting to supplant her queen with someone else."

"Roslain."

Combe nodded. "The future head of the Crest family. When I attempted to enter the royal apartments, I found myself barred by retainers, who told me the queen was too unwell for visitors. I went away without demur, but that night, I, ah, apprehended Igrain's secretary.

"The duchess is a clever woman. She knew not to keep anything in her own office, but her secretary, under pressure, surrendered documents pertaining to her finances." A grim smile. "I found recurring stipends from the Duchy of Askrdal. A vast payment from Cárscaro, paid after the death of the Queen Mother. Fine cloth and jewels for bribery. A significant number of crowns had been moved from her coffers to those of a merchant named Tam Atkin. I discovered that he is the half-brother of Bess Weald, who shot Lievelyn."

"A conspiracy more than a decade in the making," Loth said, "and you saw none of it." The corner of his mouth flinched. "A hawk has keen eyes. Perhaps they should name you the Night Mole instead. Nosing blindly in the dark."

Combe chuckled humorlessly, but it turned into a cough.

"I would have earned it," he rasped. "You see, Lord Arteloth, while my eyes are everywhere, I closed them to those of holy blood. I *assumed* the loyalty of the other Dukes Spiritual. And so, I did not watch."

He was shivering more than ever.

"I had evidence against Igrain," Combe went on, "but I had to tread carefully. She had occupied the Queen Tower, you understand, and any rash move against her could have endangered Her Majesty. I conferred with Lady Nelda and Lord Lemand, and we decided that the best option would be to go to our estates, return with our retinues, and quench the spark of usurpation. Fortunate, my lord, that you arrived first, or there might have been a great deal more bloodshed."

There was a pause while Loth thought it over. Much as he disliked the man, it had the ring of truth.

"I understand that Igrain grasped for power just as I banished Lady Nurtha, so I may appear complicit in her crimes," Combe said while Loth digested this, "but I call the Saint to witness that I have done nothing unbeseeming an honest man. Nor have I done anything unworthy of my place beside the Queen of Inys." His gaze held steady. "She may be the last Berethnet, but she *is* a Berethnet. And I mean for her to rule for a long time yet."

Loth considered the man who had exiled him to near-certain death. There was something in those eyes that spoke of sincerity, but Loth was no longer the trusting boy who had been sent away. He had seen too much.

"Will you speak against Crest," he finally said, "and surrender your physical evidence?"

"I will."

"And will you send a sum of money to the Earl and Countess of Honeybrook?" Loth asked. "For the loss of their only heir, Kitston Glade. Their beloved son." His throat clenched. "And the kindest friend who ever lived."

"I will. Of course." Combe inclined his head. "May the Knight of Justice guide your hand, my lord. I pray you are kinder than her descendant."

54

East

The Sundance Sea was so crystal-clear that the sunset turned it to pure ruby. Niclays Roos stood at the prow of the *Pursuit*, watching the waves roll and swell.

It was good to be on the move. The *Pursuit* had docked for weeks in the ruined city of Kawontay, where merchants and pirates who defied the sea ban had built a thriving shadow market. The crew had loaded the ship with enough provisions and sweet water for a return journey, and enough gunpowder and other ordnance to flatten a city.

In the end, they had not sold Nayimathun. The Golden Empress had decided to keep her as leverage against the High Sea Guard.

Niclays pressed a hand to his tunic, where a vial of blood and the scale he had carved from the creature was concealed. Every night, he had taken out the scale to examine it, but all he could remember, when his fingers traced its surface, was the way the dragon had looked at him as he cleaved its armor from its flesh.

A rustle pulled his gaze up. The *Pursuit* was flying the crimson sails of a plague ship, purchased to aid its passage through the Sundance Sea. Nonetheless, it remained the most recognizable vessel in the East, and it had soon drawn the vengeful eye of Seiiki. When the High Sea Guard and its dragonriders had come to meet them, the Golden Empress had sent a rowing boat out with a warning. She would gut the great Nayimathun like a fish if so much as an inch of her ship was harmed, or if she caught any of them following. As evidence that she still had the dragon, she had sent one of its teeth.

Every dragon and ship had fallen back. They could hardly have done otherwise. Still, it was likely they were giving chase at a distance.

"There you are."

Niclays turned. Laya Yidagé came to stand beside him.

"You looked pensive," she said.

"Alchemists are supposed to look pensive, dear lady."

At least they were moving. With every star they sailed under, they inched closer to the end.

"I paid a visit to the dragon." Laya pulled her shawl closer. "I think it's dying."

"Has it not been fed?"

"Its scales are drying out. The crew throw buckets of seawater on it, but it needs to be immersed."

Wind gusted across the ship. Niclays hardly noticed its bite. His cloak was heavy enough that he was as snug as a bear in its hide. The Golden Empress had gifted him these clothes after naming him Master of Recipes, a title given to court alchemists in the Empire of the Twelve Lakes.

"Niclays," Laya said under her breath, "I think that you and I ought to make a plan."

"Why?"

"Because if there is no mulberry tree at the end of this path, the Golden Empress will have your head."

Niclays swallowed. "And if there is?"

"Well, then perhaps you won't die. But I have had enough of this fleet now. I have lived as an old salt, but I have no intention of dying one." She looked at him. "I want to go home. Do you?"

The word gave Niclays pause.

Home had been nowhere for so long. His name was Roos after Rozentun—a sleepy town overlooking Vatten Sound, where no one would remember him. Nobody but his mother was left, and she despised him.

Truyde might care whether he lived or died, he supposed. He wondered how she fared. Was she still agitating for an alliance with the East, or quietly mourning her lover?

For a long time, home had been at the Mentish court, where he had royal favor, where he had fallen in love—but Edvart was dead, his household dissolved, his memory confined to statues and portraits. Niclays had no place there now. As for his time in Inys, it had been nothing short of calamitous.

In the end, home had always been Jannart.

"Jan died for this." He wet his lips. "For the tree. I cannot walk away without knowing its secret."

"You are Master of Recipes. Doubtless you will be granted time to study the tree of life," Laya muttered. "If we find the elixir, I suspect the Golden Empress will take us north to the City of the Thousand Flowers. She will try to sell it to the House of Lakseng in return for an end to the sea ban. We could escape into the city, and from there we can flee on foot to Kawontay. You can take a few samples of the elixir with you."

"On foot." Niclays huffed a quiet laugh. "In the unlikely event that we survive *that* journey, what would we do from there?"

"There are Ersyri smugglers in Kawontay who operate in the Sea of Carmentum. We should be able to persuade them to take us across the Abyss. My family would pay them."

There was no one who would pay for his passage.

"They would pay your way, too," Laya said, seeing his face. "I'll make sure of it."

"You're very kind." He hesitated. "What will we do if there is no mulberry tree at the end of the path?"

Laya gave him a look.

"If they find nothing," she said quietly, "then take to the sea, Niclays. It will be kinder than her rage."

He swallowed.

"Yes," he conceded. "I suppose it would."

"We will find something," she said, gentler. "Jannart believed in the legend. I believe he is watching over you, Niclays. And that he will see you home."

Home.

He could give the elixir to any ruler he desired, and they would grant him protection from Sabran. Brygstad was where he most desired to go. He could rent a garret in the Old Quarter and make ends meet teaching alchemy to novices. He could find a little pleasure in its libraries, and the lectures in its university halls. If not there, then Hróth.

And he would find Truyde. He would be a grandfather to her, and he would make Jannart proud.

As the *Pursuit* struck into deeper waters, Niclays stayed beside Laya, and they watched the stars come out. Whatever awaited them, one thing was certain. He or his ghost would be laid to rest.

55

West

The *Flower of Ascalon*, a passenger ship that served the eastern coast of Inys, docked in the ancient trade city of Caliburn-on-Sea at noon. Ead and Margret began their ride across the Leas, following the frozen River Lissom.

Snow had fallen overnight in the north, and it lay across the fields like cream smoothed with a knife. As they rode, the commons doffed their hats and called out greetings to Margret, who smiled and waved at them. She would have made a fine Countess of Goldenbirch, had she been the elder child.

They pared away from the river and through the knee-deep snow. There were no laborers in the fields in high winter, when the land was too cold to till, but Ead kept her hood up nonetheless.

The Beck family had their seat in a great prodigy house named Serinhall. It stood around a mile from Goldenbirch, where Galian Berethnet had been born. The village itself was in ruins, but remained a site of pilgrimage in Virtudom. It lay in the shadow of the haithwood, which separated the Leas from the Lakes.

After hours of riding that left their faces windburned, Margret slowed her horse at the brow of a hill. Ead gazed across a white stretch of parkland. Serinhall towered before them, bleak and magnificent, boasting grand bay windows and high domed rooftops.

"Well, here we are," Margret announced. "Do you want to go straight to Goldenbirch?"

"Not yet," Ead said. "If Galian did hide Ascalon in this province, I think he would have told its keepers. It was his most valuable possession. The symbol of the House of Berethnet."

"And you think my family has kept it secret from their queens all these centuries?"

"Possibly."

Frowning, Margret said, "The Saint did come to Serinhall once, in the year Princess Sabran was born. If there was any evidence that he *did* leave the sword, then Papa would know it. He has made it his life's work to know all there is to know about this estate."

Lord Clarent Beck had been unwell for some time. Once a hale rider, he had taken a fall from his horse, and the injury to his head had left him with what the Inysh called *mind fog*.

"Come, then. No time to lose," Margret said. A wicked glint came into her eye. "Care for a race, Lady Nurtha?"

Ead snapped the reins in answer. As her steed galloped down the hill and across the park, scattering a herd of red deer, Margret shouted something patently discourteous after her. Ead laughed as the wind blew down her hood.

She just beat Margret to the gatehouse. Servants wearing the badge of the Beck family were shoveling the snow.

"Lady Margret!" A reed of a man with a pointed beard bowed to her. "Welcome home, my lady."

"Good day to you, Master Brooke." Margret dismounted. "This is Eadaz uq-Nāra, Viscountess Nurtha. Would you kindly take us to the Countess?"

"Of course, of course." Seeing Ead, the fellow bowed again. "Lady Nurtha. Welcome to Serinhall."

Ead forced herself to nod, but this title would never sit easily on her.

She handed the reins of her horse to another servant. Margret walked with her through the open doors of the house.

In the entrance hall was a wall-length portrait. A man with ebon skin and grave eyes, wearing the tight doublet and hose that had been fashionable in Inys several centuries ago.

"Lord Rothurt Beck," Margret said as they passed. "A figure in one of the tragedies of Inys. Carnelian the Third fell in love with Lord Rothurt, but he was already wed. And this"—Margret motioned to another portrait—"is Margret Ironside, my namesake. She led our forces during the Gorse Hill Rebellion."

Ead raised her eyebrows. "Lord Morwe is marrying into a noble lineage indeed."

"Aye. Pity the man," Margret said wearily. "Mama will never let him forget it."

Master Brooke led them through a veritable labyrinth of wood-paneled corridors and grand oak doors. All this space for two people and their servants.

Lady Annes Beck was reading in the great chamber when they entered. Already a tall woman, she wore an attifet that added several inches to her stature. Her brown skin was unlined, but threads of gray rippled through the spirals of her hair.

"What is it, Master Brooke?" She looked up and removed her eyeglasses. "Saint! Margret!"

Margret curtsied. "Not a saint just yet, Mama, but give me time."

"Oh, my child."

Lady Annes rushed open-armed to her daughter. Unlike her children, she had a southern accent. "I heard only this morning of your betrothal to Lord Morwe," she said, embracing Margret. "I should shake you for accepting without asking our permission, but since Queen Sabran gave hers—" She beamed. "Oh, he has found a rare splendor in you, my darling."

"Thank you, Mama—"

"Now, I've already ordered the finest satin for your gown. A nice rich blue would become you very well. My favorite mercer in Greensward is having the cloth shipped from Kantmarkt. You will wear an attifet, of course, with white pearls and sapphires, and you *must* marry in the Sanctuary of Caliburn-on-Sea, as I did. There is no place lovelier."

"Well, Mama, it seems you have my wedding very much under control." Margret kissed her on the cheek. "Mama, you remember Mistress Duryan. Now she is Dame Eadaz uq-Nāra, Viscountess Nurtha. And my dearest friend. Ead, may I present my mother, the Countess of Goldenbirch."

Ead curtsied. She had met Lady Annes once or twice at court when the countess had come to see her children, but not for long enough for either of them to have left an impression.

"Dame Eadaz," Lady Annes said a little stiffly. "Not four days ago, the heralds said you were wanted for heresy."

"Those heralds were paid by traitors, my lady," Ead said. "Her Majesty gives no credence to their words."

"Hm." Lady Annes looked her over. "Clarent always thought you would marry my son, you know. I do hope there was no improper conduct between you, though perhaps you *are* now a fit consort for the future Earl of Goldenbirch." Before Ead could imagine an answer, the countess had clapped her hands. "Brooke! Ready the evening meal."

"Yes, my lady," came the distant reply.

"Mama," Margret protested, "we can't stay for supper. We need to talk to you about—"

"Don't be silly, Margret. You'll need a little padding if you want to give Lord Morwe an heir."

Margret looked as if she might die of embarrassment. Lady Annes bustled away.

They were left alone in the great chamber. Ead walked to the bay window that looked over the deer park.

"This is a fine home," she said.

"Yes. I miss it terribly." Margret skirted her fingers over the virginals. "I'm sorry for Mama. She is ... candid, but she means well."

"Mothers mostly do."

"Aye." Margret smiled. "Come. We ought to change."

She led Ead through yet more corridors and up a flight of stairs to a guest room in the east wing. Ead peeled off her riding clothes. As she washed her face in the basin, something caught her eye through the window. By the time she reached it, there was nothing there.

She was growing skittish. Her sisters would come for her sooner or later, whether to silence her or to force her back to Lasia.

Shaking herself, she checked that her blades were in reach and readied herself for supper. Margret met her outside, and they proceeded to the parlor, where Lady Annes was already seated. Her servants first filled their cups with perry—a speciality in this province—before they brought a rich game stew and bread with a thick crust.

"Now, tell me, both of you, how court is," Lady Annes said. "I was so terribly sorry to hear that Queen Sabran lost her child."

Her hand drifted to her own midriff. Ead knew that she had miscarried a girl before having Margret.

"Her Majesty is well now, Mama," Margret said. "Now those who would have usurped her have been detained."

"Usurp her," the countess repeated. "Who was it?"

"Crest."

Lady Annes stared. "Igrain." Slowly, she laid down her eating knife. "Saint, I cannot believe it."

"Mama," Margret said gently, "she was also behind the death of Queen Rosarian. She conspired with Sigoso Vetalda."

At this, Lady Annes drew in a breath. A gamut of emotion crossed her face.

"I knew Sigoso would hold a grudge against her. He was relentless in his pursuit." Her voice was tinged with bitterness. "I also knew that Rosarian and Igrain did not get on, for reasons best left unsaid. But for Igrain to have her queen *murdered*, and in such a way—"

Ead wondered if Annes Beck, as a former Lady of the Bedchamber, had known about the affair between Rosarian and Harlowe. Known, perhaps, that the princess was a bastard.

"I am sorry, Mama." Margret took her hand. "Crest will never hurt anyone again."

Lady Annes managed a nod. "At least we can close the door on it now." She dabbed her eyes. "I am only sorry that Arbella did not live to hear this. She always blamed herself."

They ate in silence for a short while. "How is Lord Goldenbirch, my lady?" Ead enquired.

"I'm afraid Clarent is much the same. Sometimes he is in the present, sometimes in the past, and sometimes nowhere at all."

"Is he still asking for me, Mama?" Margret said.

"Yes. Every day," Lady Annes said, sounding tired. "Do go up and see him, won't you?"

Margret looked at Ead across the table.

"Yes, Mama," she said. "Of course I will."

Lady Annes prided herself as a host. This meant that Ead and Margret found themselves still at the dinner table some two hours later.

An inglenook fireplace dried their clothes. Bone-warming food continued to pour from the kitchens. Conversation turned to the impending nuptials, and Lady Annes soon began to counsel her daughter about her wedding night ("You must *expect* to be disappointed, darling, for the act often falls woefully short of the promise"). Throughout, Margret wore the pained smile Ead had seen her wear many a time at court.

"Mama," she said, when she could finally get a word in, "I was telling Ead the family legend. That the Saint visited Serinhall."

Lady Annes washed down her mouthful. "A historian, are you, Dame Eadaz?"

"I have an interest, my lady."

"Well," the countess said, "according to records, Serinhall hosted the Saint for three days shortly after Queen Cleolind died in childbed. Our family were long-standing friends and allies to King Galian. Some say for a time he trusted only them, even above his Holy Retinue."

While curd tart, baked apples and sweetmilk were seamlessly delivered, Ead exchanged a look with Margret.

When the meal was finally over, Lady Annes released them from her presence. Margret led Ead up the stairs, a candle in her hand.

"Saint," she said. "I'm sorry, Ead. She's been waiting for one of us to get married for years so she can plan it all, and Loth has rather disappointed her on that front."

"No matter. She cares about you very much."

When they reached the elaborately carved doors to the north wing, Margret stopped. "What if—" She twisted a ring on her middle finger. "What if Papa does not remember me?"

Ead placed a hand on her back. "He asked for you."

At this, Margret took a deep breath. She handed Ead the candle and opened the doors.

The room beyond was stifling. Lord Clarent Beck was dozing in a wing chair, a coverlet around his shoulders. Only the white of his hair and a line or two set him apart from Loth, such was his likeness to his son. His legs had withered since Ead had last seen him.

"Who is that?" He stirred. "Annes?"

Margret went to him and took his face in her hands. "Papa," she said. "Papa, it's Margret."

His eyes peeled open.

"Meg." His hand came to her arm. "Margret. Is that really you?"

"Yes." A thick laugh escaped her. "Yes, Papa, I'm here. I'm sorry to have left you for so long." She kissed his hand. "Forgive me."

He lifted her chin with one finger.

"Margret," he said, "you are my child. I forgave you all your sins on the first day of your life."

Margret wrapped her arms around him and pressed her face to the crook of his neck. Lord Clarent stroked her hair with a steady hand, his expression one of the utmost serenity. Ead had never known who her birthfather was, but suddenly she wished she had.

"Papa," Margret said, drawing back, "do you remember Ead?"

Dark, heavy-lidded eyes took Ead in. They were just as kind as she remembered them.

"Ead," he said a little hoarsely. "My word. Ead Duryan." He held out a hand, and Ead kissed his signet ring. "How good to see you, child. Have you married my son yet?"

She wondered if he knew Loth had been exiled. "No, my lord," she said gently. "Loth and I do not love each other that way."

"I knew it was too good to be true." Lord Clarent chuckled. "I hoped to see him wed, but I fear I never will."

At this, his brow crimpled, and his face went slack. Margret framed it, keeping his attention fixed on her.

"Papa," she said, "Mama says you have been calling for me."

Lord Clarent blinked. "Calling for you—" Slowly, he nodded. "Yes. I have something important to tell you, Margret."

"I am here now."

"Then you must take the secret. Loth is dead," he said, tremulous, "so now you are heir. Only the heir to Goldenbirch may know." The creases in his brow deepened. "Loth *is* dead."

He must keep forgetting that Loth had returned. Margret glanced at Ead before she looked back at him, her thumbs circling his cheekbones.

They needed him to believe Loth was dead. It was the only way they would learn where the sword was hidden.

"He is ... presumed dead, Papa," Margret said quietly. "I am heir."

His face crumpled between her hands. Ead knew how much it must be hurting Margret to tell him such a painful lie, but summoning Loth from Ascalon would take days they might not have.

"If Loth is dead, then— then you must take it, Margret," Clarent said, eyes wet. "*Hildistérron*."

The word caught Ead in the gut. "*Hildistérron*," Margret murmured. "Ascalon."

"When I became Earl of Goldenbirch, your lady grandmother told me." Clarent kept hold of her hand. "It must be passed down to my children, and to yours. In case *she* should ever return for it."

"She," Ead cut in. "Lord Clarent, who?"

"She. The Lady of the Woods."

Kalyba.

I searched for Ascalon for centuries, but Galian hid it well.

Clarent seemed agitated now. He looked at them both with fear.

"I don't know you," he whispered. "Who are you?"

"Papa," Margret said at once, "it's Margret." When confusion washed into his eyes, her voice quaked: "Papa, I pray you, stay with me. If you do not tell me now, it will be lost to the fog in your mind." She squeezed his hands. "Please. Tell me where Ascalon is hidden."

He clung to her as if she were the embodiment of his memory. Margret held still as he leaned toward her, and his cracked lips came against her ear. Ead watched with a pounding heart as they moved.

At that moment, the door opened, and Lady Annes came into the room.

"Time for your sleepwater, Clarent," she said. "Margret, he must rest now."

Clarent cradled his head in his hands. "My son." His shoulders heaved with sobs. "My son is dead."

Lady Annes took a step forward, her brow furrowing. "No, Clarent, it is good news. Loth is back—"

"My son is dead."

Sobs racked him. Margret pressed a hand to her mouth, eyes brimming. Ead took her by the elbow and ushered her out, leaving Lady Annes to tend to her companion.

"What a thing to tell him," Margret said thickly.

"You had to."

Margret nodded. Dabbing the wet from her eyes, she pulled Ead straight into her own bedchamber, where she fumbled for a quill and parchment and scratched out the message.

"Before I forget what Papa said," she murmured.

You know me from song. My truth is unsung.
I lie where starlight cannot see.
I was forged in fire, and from comet wrung.
I am over leaf and under tree,
my worshippers furred, their offerings dung.
Quench fire, break stone, and set me free.

"Another wretched *riddle*." Perhaps it was the strain of the last few weeks, but Ead felt so threadbare with frustration that the thought pinched at the fraying edge of her sanity. "Mother *curse* these ancients and their riddles. We have no time to—"

"I know exactly what it means." Margret was already stuffing the parchment into her bodice. "And I know where Ascalon is. Follow me."

Margret left word with the steward that they were going for an evening ride, and that Lady Annes should not wait up for them.

She also asked for a spade apiece. The ostler brought these, along with the two swiftest horses in the stables and a saddle lantern each.

Garbed in their heavy cloaks, they galloped away from Serinhall. All Margret would tell Ead was that they were bound for Goldenbirch. To get there, one had to take the old corpse road. It was heaped in snow, but Margret knew her way.

In the days of kings, bodies had been taken from Goldenbirch and other villages on this path to the now-destroyed city of Arondine for burial. During the spring, pilgrims would walk here by candlelight, barefoot and singing. At its end, they would lay offerings at the site where Berethnet Hearth had once stood.

They rode beneath crooked oaks, across grassland, past a standing circle from the dawn of Inys.

"Margret," Ead called, "what does the riddle mean?"

Margret slowed her horse to a canter.

"It came to me as soon as Papa whispered the words. I was only six, but I remember."

Ead dipped her head under a snow-heavy branch. "Pray enlighten me."

"Loth and I grew up apart, as you know—he lived at court with Mama from a young age, and I lived here with Papa—but Loth would come home in the spring for pilgrimage. I hated it when he had to go back. One year, I was so cross with him for leaving me that I swore not to speak to him ever again. To appease me, he promised we would spend the whole last day of his stay together, and I made him promise we would do *anything* I wanted. Then," she said, "I declared that we would pay a visit to the haithwood."

"Brave indeed for a child of the north."

Margret snorted. "Daft, more like. Still, Loth had made the vow, and even at twelve, he was too gallant to break it. At dawn, we slipped out of our beds and followed this very road to Goldenbirch. Then, for the first time in our lives, we kept walking, until we reached the haithwood, home of the Lady of the Woods.

"We stopped at the very edge of the trees. They were like faceless giants to a little girl, but I found it all thrilling. I held Loth by the hand, and we stood trembling in the shadow of the haithwood, wondering if the witch would come to steal us and skin us and chew on our bones the moment we set foot in it. Finally, I lost patience and gave Loth a rather firm push."

Ead bit down a smile.

"Such a scream he let out," Margret recalled. "Still, when he failed to be hauled away to a bloody end, the pair of us grew bold as peacocks, and soon we were picking berries and otherwise larking about. Finally, as dusk fell, we decided to go home. That was when Loth spotted a little hollow. He said it was naught but a coney-hole. I reckoned it must be a wyrm-hole, and that I could kill whatever wyverling was hid in it.

"Well, Loth had a hearty laugh at that, and it stung me into crawling in. It was very small," Margret said. "I had to dig with my hands. Headfirst, I crawled inside it with a candle … and at first, it was just soil. But as I tried to turn around, I slipped and tumbled, and found myself in a tunnel large enough to stand in.

"Somehow my candle had stayed lit, so I dared venture a little farther. It was clear the tunnel had not been made by conies. I don't remember how far I went. Only that my terror was growing by the moment. Finally, when I thought I would fairly wet myself, I ran back and scrambled out and told Loth there was nothing there." Snow caught in her lashes. "I thought I had stumbled on the abode of the Lady of the Woods, and that if I ever told a soul, she would come to steal me back. For years, I had nightmares about that tunnel. Nightmares of being drained of my blood, or buried alive."

It was rare that Margret looked afraid. Even now, eighteen years later, it touched her.

"I suppose I forgot about it, in the end," she said, "but when Papa spoke to me … I remembered. *I am over leaf and under tree, my worshippers furred, their offerings dung.*"

"Conies," Ead murmured. "Kalyba told me she seldom went to the haithwood, but Galian might have. Or perhaps it was your ancestors who told him about the tunnel."

Margret nodded, her jaw tight.

They rode on.

Dark had fallen by the time the ruins of Goldenbirch came into view.

In this hallowed place, the cradle of Virtudom, the silence was absolute. Snow wafted like cinders. As their horses trotted past ruins that had lain untouched for centuries, Ead almost believed the world had ended, and she and Margret were the last people alive. They had gone back in time, to an age when Inys had been known as the Isles of Inysca.

Margret stopped her horse and dismounted.

"This is where Galian Berethnet was born." She hunkered down to brush away some of the snow. "Where a young seamstress gave birth to a son, and his brow was marked with hawthorn ash."

Her gloved hands revealed a slab of marble, set deep into the earth.

HERE STOOD BERETHNET HEARTH

BIRTHPLACE OF KING GALIAN OF INYS

HE WHO IS SAINT OVER ALL VIRTUDOM

"I heard tell that Galian had no earthly remains," Ead recalled. "Is that unusual?"

"Yes," Margret admitted. "Very. The Inyscans should have preserved the remains of a king. Unless—"

"Unless?"

"Unless he died in a way his retainers wanted to conceal." Margret climbed back into her saddle. "No one knows how the Saint perished. The books say only that he joined Queen Cleolind in the heavens and built Halgalant there, as he had built Ascalon here."

She made the sign of the sword over the slab before they spurred their horses on.

The haithwood was dread itself in the north. As it came into sight, Ead understood why. Before the Nameless One had taught the Inyscans to fear the light of fire, this forest had taught them to fear the dark. The bulk of its trees were ancient giantswoods, pressed close enough to form a black curtain wall. To look at it was suffocating.

They rode up to it at a trot and tethered their horses. "Can you find the coney-hole?" Ead kept her voice low. She knew they were alone, but this place unsettled her.

"I imagine so." Margret detached the lantern and tools from her saddle. "Just stay close to me."

The woods beyond consumed all light. Ead retrieved one of the saddle lanterns before she interlocked their fingers and, together, they took their first step into the haithwood.

Snow crunched beneath their riding boots. The canopy was dense—giantswoods never shed their fur of needles—but the snowfall had been heavy enough to leave a deep covering.

As they walked, Ead found herself filled with a profound sense of desolation. It might have been the cold as well as the all-consuming dark, but the fireplace at Serinhall now seemed as far away as the Burlah. She set her chin deep into the fur collar of her cloak. Margret stilled now and then, as if to listen. When a twig snapped, even Ead tensed. Beneath her shirt, the jewel was growing colder.

"There used to be wolves here," Margret said, "but they were hunted to extinction."

If only to keep Margret occupied, Ead asked, "Why is it called the haithwood?"

"We think *haith* was the word the Inyscans used for the old ways. The worship of nature. Hawthorns, especially."

They trudged through the snow for an age without speaking. Loth and Margret had been brave children.

"This is it." Margret approached a snowdrift at the foot of a knotted oak. "Lend me a hand, Ead."

Ead crouched beside her with one of the spades, and they dug. For a time, it seemed Margret had misremembered—but suddenly, their spades broke through the snow, into a hollow.

Ead dislodged the snow from its edges. The coney-hole was by now too small even for a child. They scooped with the spades and their hands until it was big enough to admit them. Margret was eyeing the opening nervously. "I will go first," Ead offered. She kicked loose soil from the hole and slid in, leaving the lantern at the entrance.

It was barely wide enough inside for a well-fed coney, let alone a woman. Ead lit her magefire and pushed herself forward on her belly. She crawled until the tunnel, just as Margret had promised, simply dropped away, into a well of darkness. Unable to turn around, Ead had no choice but to go into it headfirst.

The drop was short and bruising. As she straightened, her magefire flared, unveiling a tunnel with sandstone walls and an arched ceiling, just high enough to stand in.

Margret joined her. She held up her lantern in one hand and a tiny knife in the other.

The walls of the tunnel had alcoves chiseled into them, though only the stumps of candles remained. There was a chill in this secret burrow, but nothing close to the ice on the surface. Margret was still shivering in the swathes of her cloak.

Before long they reached a chamber with a low ceiling, where two iron vats flanked another slab, cut from blackstone. Margret bent to sniff one.

"Eachy oil. A vat this large would burn for a season," she said. "Someone has been tending to this place."

"Remind me how long ago your father took his fall," Ead said.

"Three years."

"Before that, did he ever go to the haithwood?"

"Aye, often. Since the haithwood is in our province, he would sometimes walk with his servants through it, to make sure all was well. Sometimes he would even go alone. I thought it made him the bravest man alive."

By the light of her magefire, Ead read the inscription on the slab.

I AM THE LIGHT OF FIRE AND STAR
WHAT I DRINK WILL DROWN

"Meg," she said, "Loth explained my magic to you, did he not?"

"If I have it right, yours is a magic of fire," Margret said, "and is attracted, in some way, to the magic of starlight—but not as much as the magic of starlight attracts itself. Do I have it right?"

"Just so. Galian must have known the sword would be drawn to sterren, and that Kalyba had a supply of it. He did not want her to hear that call. Whoever buried Ascalon surrounded it with fire. I imagine that for the first few centuries, whoever was the Keeper of the Leas was charged with keeping the entrance open and the braziers lit."

"You think Papa was doing that." Margret nodded slowly. "But when he took his fall—"

"—the secret was almost lost."

The two of them looked down at the slab. Too heavy to pry up with their hands.

"I'll ride back to Serinhall and fetch a greathammer," Margret said.

"Wait."

Ead took the waning jewel from around her neck. It was cold as hoarfrost in her hand.

"It senses Ascalon," she said, "but the pull is not enough to drag it from the stone." She thought. "Ascalon is of starlight, but it was shaped with fire. A union of both."

She held up her magefire.

"And it responds to what is most like itself," Margret said, catching on.

The tongue of flame licked at the jewel. Ead feared her instinct was misplaced until a light glowed in it—white light, the kiss of the moon on water. It sang like a plucked string.

The slab of stone cracked down the middle with a sound like a thunderclap. Ead threw herself back and shielded her face as the blackstone ruptured into pieces. The jewel flew from her hand, and the broken slab vomited a streak of light across the chamber. Something clanged against the wall, loud enough to make her ears ring, and came to rest, steaming, beside the jewel, which quivered in response. Both were glowing silver-white.

When the light dimmed, Margret sank to her knees.

A magnificent sword lay before them. Every inch of it—hilt, crossguard, blade—was a clean, bright silver, with a mirror shine.

I was forged in fire, and from comet wrung.

Ascalon. Made of no earthly metal. Created by Kalyba, wielded by Cleolind Onjenyu, blooded on the Nameless One. A double-edged longsword. From pommel to tip, it was as tall as Loth.

"Ascalon," Margret said hoarsely, her eyes wick with reverence. "The True Sword."

Ead closed a hand around the hilt. Power thrummed within its blade. It shivered at her touch, silver drawn to her golden blood. As she stood, she lifted it with her, speechless with wonder. It was light as air, chill to the touch. A sliver of the Long-Haired Star.

Mother, make me worthy. She pressed her lips to the cold blade. *I will finish all that you began.*

────────

They climbed out of the coney-hole and retraced their steps through the haithwood. By now, the sky was dredged with stars. Ascalon, scabbardless, seemed to drink their light. In the chamber, it had looked almost like steel, but now there was no mistaking its celestial origins.

No ships left during the night. They would have to rest at Serinhall and make for Caliburn-on-Sea at dawn. The thought of another journey weighed on Ead. Even with the sword in hand, the haithwood wound its creepers about her heart and squeezed the warmth from it.

"Hail, who goes there?"

Ead looked up. Margret had stopped beside her, and was holding up her lantern.

"I am Lady Margret Beck, daughter of the Earl and Countess of Goldenbirch, and these are Beck lands. I shall brook no mischief in the haithwood." Margret sounded firm, but Ead knew her voice well enough to hear the fear in it. "Come forth and show yourself."

Now Ead saw it. A figure stood between the trees, its features obscured by the oppressive darkness of the haithwood. A drumbeat later, it had melted into the shadow, as if it had never been there.

"Did you see that?"

"I saw it," Ead said.

A whisper of wind unsettled the trees.

They returned to their horses, moving quickly now. Ead buckled Ascalon on to the saddle.

The wolf moon was high over Goldenbirch. Its light glistered on the snow as they rode back to the corpse road. They had just passed one of the coffin stones that marked it when Ead heard a sharp cry from Margret. She yanked the reins, turning her horse around.

"Meg!"

Her breath snared in her throat. The other horse was nowhere to be seen.

And Margret was standing, a blade at her throat, in the arms of the Witch of Inysca.

This kind of magic is cold and elusive, graceful and slippery. It allows the wielder to cast illusions, control water . . . even to change their shape . . .

"Kalyba," said Ead.

The witch was barefoot. She wore a diaphanous gown, white as the snow, which gathered at her waist.

"Hello, Eadaz."

Ead was tense as a bowstring. "Did you follow me from Lasia?"

"I did. I watched you flee the Priory, and I saw you leave with the Inysh lord on the ship from Córvugar," Kalyba said, expressionless. "I knew then that you had no plans to return to my Bower. No plans to honor your oath."

In her grip, Margret trembled.

"Are you afraid, sweeting?" Kalyba asked her. "Did your milk nurse tell you stories of the Lady of the Woods?" She slid the knife along the nut of Margret's throat, and Margret shuddered. "It seems it was *your* family who concealed my sword from me."

"Let go of her," Ead said. Her horse stamped its hooves. "She has not to do with your grievance against me."

"My grievance." Despite the bitter cold, no gooseflesh had risen on the witch. "You swore to me that you would bring me what I desire. On this isle in ages past, you would have had your lifeblood spilled for breaking such a vow. How fortunate that you have something *else* I desire."

Ascalon was aglow again. Hidden under shirt and cloak, so was the waning jewel.

"It was here all along. In the haithwood." Kalyba watched Ascalon. "My sword, laid to rest in dirt and darkness. Even if it had not been buried too deep for me to hear it calling, I would have had to crawl to it on my belly like an adder. Galian mocks me even in death."

Margret closed her eyes. Her lips moved in silent prayer.

"I suppose he did it just before he went to Nurtha. To his end." Kalyba raised her gaze. "Hand it to me now, Eadaz, and your oath will be fulfilled. You will have given me what I desire."

"Kalyba," Ead said, "I know I broke my oath to you. I will pay for it. But I need Ascalon. I will use it to slay the Nameless One, as Cleolind did not. It will quench the fire within him."

"Yes, it will," Kalyba said, "but you will not wield it, Eadaz."

The witch threw Margret into the snow. At once, Margret began to claw at her own arms, and she retched as if there was water in her chest.

"Ead—" she gasped out. "Ead, the thorns—"

"What are you doing to her?" Ead had dismounted in an instant. "Leave her be."

"Only an illusion," Kalyba said, pacing around Margret. "Still, I suppose mortals do tend to suffer in the grip of my enchantments. Sometimes their hearts give out through fear." She held out a hand. "This is your last chance to give me the sword, Eadaz. Do not let Lady Margret Beck pay the price for your broken oath."

Ead stood her ground. She would not give the sword up. She also had no intention of letting Margret die for it.

The orange tree had not gifted her its fruit for nothing.

She turned her palms outward. Magefire scorched from her hands and consumed both Margret and the witch, burning away the illusion.

Kalyba let out a soul-wrenching cry, and her body contorted. Every auburn tress was cooked from her scalp. Flesh melted from her limbs and cooled again into pale lines. Black hair rushed and rippled to her waist.

Aghast, Ead forced her hands to close. When the flames dwindled, Margret was on all fours, one hand at her throat, eyes bloodshot.

And Sabran Berethnet was standing beside her.

Ead stared at her palms, then back at Kalyba, who was also Sabran. Margret pushed herself away. "*Sabran?*" she coughed out.

Kalyba opened her eyes. Green as willow.

"How?" Ead gasped. "How do you have her face?" She drew one of her blades. "Answer me, witch."

She could not tear her gaze away. Kalyba *was* Sabran, down to the tilt of her nose and the bow of her lips. No scar on the thigh or the belly, and there was a mark Sabran did not have on her right side, under her arm—but otherwise, they might have been twins.

"Their faces are their crowns. And mine is the truth." The voice from those lips belonged to the witch. "You said you wanted to learn, Eadaz, that day in my Bower. You see before you the greatest secret in Virtudom."

"You," Ead whispered.

Who was the first Queen of Inys?

"This is no enchantment." Heart drumming, Ead raised the blade. "This is your true form."

Margret scrambled to her feet and hastened to stand behind Ead, her girdle knife thrust out again.

"Truth you desired. Truth you received," Kalyba said, ignoring their blades. "Yes, Eadaz. This is my true form. My first shape. The shape I wore before I mastered sterren." She clasped her hands at her midriff, making her look, if possible, even more like Sabran. "I never intended to reveal it. Since you have seen, however … I will tell you my tale."

Ead kept her gaze fixed on her, the blade angled toward her throat. Kalyba turned her back, so she faced the moon.

"Galian was my child."

It was not what Ead had expected to hear.

"Not a child born of my womb. I stole him from Goldenbirch when he was a nursling. At the time, I thought the blood of innocents might help me unlock a deeper magic, but he was such a charming baby, with his eyes like cornflower … I confess that I gave way to sentiment, and raised him as my own on Nurtha, in the hollow of the hawthorn tree."

Margret was standing so close, Ead could feel her shivering.

"When he was five and twenty, he left my side to become a knight in the service of Edrig of Arondine. Nine years later, the Nameless One emerged from the Dreadmount.

"I had not seen Galian for many years. But when he heard of the plague and the Nameless One wreaking terror in Lasia, he sought me out again, pleading for my help. His dream, you see, was to unite the warring kings and princelings of Inys under one crown, and to rule a country according to the Six Virtues of Knighthood. To do that, he had to earn their respect with a great deed. He wanted to slay the Nameless One, and to do that, he would need my magic. Like a fool, I gave it him, for by this time I loved him not as a mother. I loved him as companions do. In return, he swore he would be mine alone.

"Blinded by love, I gave him Ascalon, the sword I had forged in starlight and in fire. To Lasia he rode, to the city of Yikala." She let out a huff. "What I had not realized was what else Galian wanted. To unite the Inyscan rulers and strengthen his claim, he desired a queen of royal blood—and when he saw Cleolind Onjenyu, he wanted her. Not only was she unwed and beautiful, but in her veins ran the old blood of the South.

"You know a little of what happened next. Cleolind disdained my knight and took up his sword when he was injured. She wounded the Nameless One and disappeared with her handmaidens into the Lasian Basin, there to bind herself forever in marriage to the orange tree.

"I expected Galian to seek me out, but he broke his promise and my heart. I was sick in love, and oh, I raged." She turned away. "Galian began his journey home without glory or a bride. I followed."

"You do not seem the sort to resent being spurned," Ead said.

"The heart is a cruel thing. His hold on mine was firm." The witch paced around them. "Galian was crushed by his failure, lost to hatred and anger. I did not know then how to change my shape. What I did know well was dreams and trickery." Her eyes closed. "I stepped out of the trees, in front of his horse. His eyes glazed over. He smiled . . . and called me Cleolind."

Ead could not tear her gaze away. "How?"

"I cannot tell you the mysteries of starcraft, Eadaz. All you need know was that sterren gave me a foothold in his mind. Through an enchantment, I made him believe I was the princess who had rebuffed him. Half in dream, his memory blurred, he could not remember what Cleolind had looked like, or that she had banished him, or that I had ever existed. His desire made him malleable. He needed a queen, and there I was. I made him lust for me, as he had for Cleolind on the day he saw her." A smile touched her lips. "He took me back to the Isles of Inysca. There he made me his queen, and I took him to my bed."

"He was like your son," Ead said. Disgust coiled in her belly. "You raised him."

"Love is complex, Eadaz."

Margret pressed a hand to her mouth.

"Soon I was with child," Kalyba whispered. Her hands came to her belly. "Birthing my daughter took a great deal of my strength. I lost too much blood. Finally, as I lay racked with childbed fever, close to death, I could keep hold of Galian no longer. Clear-eyed at last, he threw me into the dungeons." Her voice darkened. "He had the sword. I was weak. A friend helped me escape ... but I had to leave my Sabran. My little princess."

Sabran the First, the first queen regnant of Inys.

All the scattered fragments of the truth were aligning, explaining what the Priory had never understood.

The Deceiver had himself been deceived.

"Galian ripped down every likeness of me that had been painted or carved and forbade any more to be created for the rest of time. Then he went to Nurtha, where I had raised him, and hanged himself from my hawthorn tree. Or what was left of it." At this, the witch grasped her own arms. "He ensured his shame would go with him to the grave."

Ead was silent, sickened.

"I watched a house of queens rise in his place. Great queens, whose names were known throughout the world. All of them had so much of me, and nothing of him. One daughter for each, always with green eyes. An unexpected consequence of the sterren, I suppose."

It was almost too strange a tale to believe. And yet magefire had not burned away that face.

Magefire never lied.

"You wonder why Sabran dreams of my Bower?" Kalyba asked Ead. "If you will not believe the truth from my lips, believe it from hers. My Firstblood lives within her."

"You tormented her," Ead said, voice hoarse. "If all of this is true—if all of the Berethnet queens are your direct descendants—why would you make her dream of blood?"

"I gave her dreams of the childbed so she would know how I suffered birthing her ancestor. And I gave her dreams of the Nameless One, and of me, so she would know her fate."

"And what *is* her fate?"

"The one I made for her."

The witch turned to face them then, and her face fractured. Her skin divided itself into scales, and her eyes became serpentine. The green bled into the whites and burned. A forked tongue lashed between her teeth.

When the last piece of the puzzle fell into place, the very foundations of the world seemed to tremble beneath Ead. She was in the palace again, cradling Sabran, blood slippery on her hands.

"The White Wyrm," she whispered. "That night. It was you. *You* are the sixth High Western."

Kalyba returned to her true, Sabran-shaped form once more, a faint smile on her lips.

"Why?" Ead asked, stunned. "Why would you destroy the House of Berethnet when you made it? Has this all been a game to you—some elaborate revenge on Galian?"

"I have not destroyed the House of Berethnet," Kalyba said. "No. That night—the night I struck down Sabran and her unborn child—I saved it. In ending the line, I earned the trust of Fýredel, who will commend me to the Nameless One." There was no amusement or joy in her now. "He will rise, Eadaz. None can stop him. Even if you were to plunge Ascalon into his heart, even if the Long-Haired Star returns, he will always rise anew. The imbalance in the universe—the imbalance that created him—will always exist. It can never be righted."

Ead tightened her grip on her sword. The jewel was icy cold against her heart.

"The Nameless One will let me be his Flesh Queen in the days to come," Kalyba said. "I shall give him Sabran as a gift and take her place on the throne of Inys. The throne Galian took from me. No one will know the difference. I will tell the people that I *am* Sabran, and that the Nameless One, in his mercy, has allowed me to keep my crown."

"No," Ead said quietly.

Kalyba held out a hand once more. Margret placed hers on Ascalon, still buckled into the saddle.

"Give me the sword," Kalyba said, "and your oath will be fulfilled." Her gaze flicked to Margret. "Or perhaps *you* will return it, child, to undo the wrong your family did me by hiding it."

Margret faced the Lady of the Woods, her childhood fear, and kept her hand on Ascalon.

"My ancestors were brave to keep it from you," she said, "and not for *anything* will I give it to you."

Ead locked gazes with Kalyba. She who had tricked Galian the Deceiver. The White Wyrm. Ancestor of Sabran. If she took the sword, there would be no victory.

"Very well," Kalyba said. "If we must do this the hard way, so be it."

Before their eyes, she began to change.

Limb stretched and bent on itself. Her spine elongated with cracks like gunshots, and her skin was scrolled taut between new bones. In moments, she was as big as a house, and the White Wyrm was before them, towering and terrible. Ead grabbed Margret away just before razor teeth clamped around the horse, smothering the light of Ascalon.

Leathery wings slammed down, bringing with them a hot wind. Horse blood sprayed across the snow as Kalyba launched herself into the night.

As the wingbeats faded into the distance, Ead slid to her knees, shoulders heaving. Spattered with blood, Margret knelt beside her.

"There were thorns," she said, shuddering. "In my— in my throat. In my mouth."

"It was nothing real." Ead leaned against her. "We lost the sword. The *sword*, Meg."

Her hands burned, but she kept them closed. She would need all her siden for the fight that was to come.

"It can't be true." Margret swallowed. "All she said about the Saint. The face she wore was trickery."

"I revealed it with magefire," Ead murmured. "Magefire is revelation. It tells only the truth."

Somewhere in the trees, an owl let out a chilling scream. When Margret flinched, dread in her gaze, Ead reached for her hand and squeezed it.

"Without the True Sword, we cannot kill the Nameless One. And unless we can find the second jewel, we cannot bind him," she said. "But we might be able to raise enough of an army to drive him far away."

"How?" Margret's voice was desolate. "Who can help us now?"

Ead rose, pulling Margret with her, and they stood in the red-stained snow beneath the moon.

"I must speak to Sabran," she said. "It is time to open a new door."

56

West

Loth had spent his morning writing to the Virtues Council, telling them of the imminent threat and calling them to Ascalon. It was an exhausting process, but since Seyton Combe had been released and taken over building a case against Igrain Crest, some of the burden was off his shoulders.

Sabran joined him in the afternoon. A rock dove perched on her forearm, cooing. Its piebald feathers identified it as having come from Mentendon.

"I have received a reply from High Princess Ermuna. She demands justice for the unlawful execution of Lady Truyde." She laid the letter on the table. "She also says that Doctor Niclays Roos has been abducted by pirates, and blames me for withholding his pardon for so long."

Loth unfolded the letter. It had been sealed with the swan of the House of Lievelyn.

"The only justice I can offer for Truyde is the head of Igrain Crest." Sabran unlatched the doors to the balcony. "As for Roos ... I should have relented a long time ago."

"Roos was a swindler," Loth said. "He deserved punishment."

"Not to that extreme."

He sensed there was nothing he could say to deter her. For his part, Loth had never liked the alchemist.

"Fortunately," Sabran said, "Ermuna has agreed, given the urgency of my request, to have the Library of Ostendeur scoured for knowledge about the reign of Empress Mokwo. She has sent one of her servants to find the records, and will send another bird with all speed when she has them."

"Good."

Sabran held up her arm. The rock dove hopped off it and fluttered away.

"Sab."

She looked at him.

"Crest told me something," Loth said. "About ... why she arranged for your mother to die."

"Say it."

Loth let her have a moment without the knowledge. He tried not to think of how Crest had looked throughout the questioning. Her disdainful gaze, her brazen lack of remorse.

"She told me that the Queen Mother committed adultery with a privateer. Captain Gian Harlowe." He hesitated. "The affair began the year before she became pregnant with you."

Sabran closed the doors to the balcony and took the seat at the head of the table.

"So," she said, "I may be a bastard."

"Crest thought so. That was why she took such a great role in your upbringing. She wanted to mold you into a more virtuous queen."

"A more *obedient* queen. A manikin," Sabran said curtly, "to be manipulated."

"Prince Wilstan may have been your father." Loth placed a hand over hers. "The affair with Harlowe might not even have existed. Crest is clearly not in her right mind."

Sabran shook her head. "Part of me has always known. Mother and Father were loving in public, but cold in private." She pressed his hand. "Thank you for telling me, Loth."

"Aye."

She reached in silence for her swan-feather quill. Loth kneaded the stiffness from his neck and continued with his work.

It was peaceful to be alone with her. He found himself glancing at his childhood friend, wondering.

Had Sabran been in love with Lievelyn and turned to Ead for comfort after his death? Or had her marriage to Lievelyn been one of convenience, and it was Ead who was the root of her heart? Perhaps the truth was somewhere between.

"I have a mind," Sabran said, "to make Roslain the new Duchess of Justice. She is heir apparent."

"Is that wise?" When she only continued writing, Loth said, "I have been a friend to Roslain for many years. I know her devotion to you—but can we be sure her part in this was innocent?"

"Combe is as convinced as he can be that she acted only to save my life. Her broken fingers are evidence of her loyalty." She dipped her quill in the inkhorn again. "Her grandmother will lose her head. Ead may have counseled for mercy in the past, but too much of it makes a fool."

Footsteps approached from outside the chamber. Sabran tensed as they heard the clash of partizans.

"Who goes there?" she called.

"The Lady Chancellor, Your Majesty," came the answer.

She relaxed a little. "Send her in."

Lady Nelda Stillwater walked into the Council Chamber, wearing the ruby chain of her office.

"Your Grace," Sabran said.

"Majesty. Lord Arteloth." The Duchess of Courage curtsied. "I have just now been released from the Dearn Tower. I wanted to come in person to tell you of my anger that a fellow duchess would rise against you." Her face was tight. "You have always had my loyalty."

Sabran gave a gracious nod. "I thank you, Nelda, and am very glad to see you released."

"On behalf of my son and granddaughter, I must also beg mercy for Lady Roslain. She has never spoken a word of treason against you in my presence, and I cannot think that she ever meant you harm."

"Be assured that Lady Roslain will be judged fairly."

Loth nodded his agreement. Little Elain, who was but five years old, must be worried for her mother.

"Thank you, Majesty," Stillwater said. "I trust your verdict. Lord Seyton has also asked me to tell you that Lady Margret and Dame Eadaz arrived in Summerport at noonday."

"Send word that they should come to the Council Chamber as soon as they reach the palace."

Stillwater curtsied again and went back through the doors.

"It seems Lord Seyton has already returned to his role as your industrious spymaster," Loth said.

"Indeed." Sabran picked up her quill again. "Are you certain that he had no notion of this plot?"

"*Certain* is a dangerous word," Loth said, "but I am as sure as I can be that everything he does, he does for the crown—and for the queen who wears it. Strangely, I trust him."

"Even though he sent you away. Even though if not for him, Lord Kitston would still be alive." Sabran caught his gaze. "I could still have him stripped of his titles, Loth. Only say the word."

"The Knight of Courage teaches mercy and forgiveness," Loth said quietly. "I choose to take heed."

With a small nod, Sabran returned to her letter, and Loth returned to his.

It was late in the afternoon when a disturbance far below the tower made him raise his head. He went to the balcony and leaned over the balustrade. In the courtyard, at least fifty people, small as emmets from here, had gathered in the Sundial Garden, with more flocking to join them.

"I believe Ead is back." He grinned. "With a gift."

"Gift?"

He was already halfway out of the Council Chamber. Sabran was at his side in moments, chased by her Knights of the Body. "Loth," she said, half-laughing, "what gift?"

"You'll see."

Outside, the sun was bright and heatless, and Margret and Ead were at the center of a commotion. They flanked Aralaq, who stood amid the curious onlookers with a sort of dignified exhaustion. When Sabran appeared, Ead curtsied, and the court followed suit.

"Majesty."

Sabran raised her eyebrows. "Lady Nurtha."

Ead straightened, smiling.

"Madam," she said, "we found this noble creature in Goldenbirch, at the site of Berethnet Hearth." She placed a hand on the ichneumon. "This is Aralaq, a descendant of the very ichneumon who bore Queen Cleolind to Inys. He has come to offer his allegiance to Your Majesty."

Aralaq assessed the queen with his huge, black-rimmed eyes. Sabran took in the miracle before her.

"You are most welcome here, Aralaq." She lowered her head. "As your ancestors were before you."

Aralaq bowed to the queen in return, his nose almost touching the grass. Loth watched how faces changed. To the people of the court, this was further confirmation that Sabran was divine.

"I will guard you as I would my own pup, Sabran of Inys," Aralaq rumbled, "for you are the blood of King Galian, bane of the Nameless One. I pledge my fealty to you."

When Aralaq nuzzled his nose against her palm, the courtiers stared in reverence at their queen and this creature of legend. Sabran stroked between his ears and smiled as she seldom had since she was a girl.

"Master Wood," she said, and the pimpled squire in question bowed, "see to it that Aralaq is treated as our brother in Virtudom."

"Yes, Majesty," Wood said. The knot in his throat bobbed. "May I ask, ah, what Sir Aralaq eats?"

"Wyrm," Aralaq said.

Sabran laughed. "We are a little short of wyrm here, but we have plenty of adders. Consult the cook, Master Wood."

Aralaq licked his chops. Wood looked queasy. Sabran walked back toward the shade of the Alabastrine Tower. Ead spoke to the ichneumon, who nudged her with his nose, before she followed.

Loth embraced his sister. "How were our parents?" he asked.

Margret sighed. "Papa is fading. Mama is pleased that I am to marry Lord Morwe. You must go to them as soon as you are able."

"Did you find Ascalon?"

"Aye," she said, but with no joy. "Loth, do you remember that coney-hole I went down as a child?"

He thought back. "Not that daft game we played as children. In the haithwood," he said. "What of it?"

She took him by the arm. "Come, brother. I will let Ead tell you the unhappy tale."

When they were all back in the Council Chamber, and the doors had shut behind them, Sabran turned to Ead. Margret removed her feathered hat and sat at the table.

"You brought an unexpected gift." Sabran placed her hands on the back of her chair. "Do you also have the True Sword?"

"We found it," Ead said. "It seems the Beck family has guarded it in secret for many centuries, the knowledge passed from heir to heir."

"That's absurd," Loth said. "Papa would never have kept it from his queens."

"He was guarding it for when they needed it most, Loth. He would have told you about it before you inherited the estate."

Loth was thunderstricken. Removing her cloak, Ead took a seat.

"We found Ascalon in a coney-hole in the haithwood," she said. "Kalyba appeared. She had followed me from Lasia."

"The Lady of the Woods," Sabran said.

"Yes. She took the sword from us."

Sabran clenched her jaw. Loth watched his sister and Ead. There was something odd about their expressions.

They were keeping something back.

"I suppose sending mercenaries after a shape-shifter would be an exercise in futility." Sabran sank into the chair. "If Ascalon is lost to us, and there is no guarantee that we will find the second jewel, then we must ... prepare to defend ourselves. A second Grief of Ages will begin the instant the Nameless One rises. I will invoke the holy call to arms, so King Raunus and High Princess Ermuna will be ready to fight."

Her tone was even, but her eyes were haunted. She had more time to prepare than Glorian Shieldheart, who was sixteen and in bed with a fever when the first Grief of Ages began, but it might only be weeks. Or days.

Or hours.

"You will need more than Virtudom to be ready, Sabran," Ead said. "You will need Lasia. You will need the Ersyr. You will need everyone in this world who can lift a sword."

"Other sovereigns will not treat with Virtudom."

"Then you must make a gesture of the love and respect you have for them," Ead said, "by withdrawing the long-standing proclamation that all other religions are heresies. Changing the law to allow those with different values to live at peace in your realms."

"It is a thousand-year tradition," Sabran said curtly. "The Saint himself wrote that all other faiths were false."

"Just because something has always been done does not mean that it *ought* to be done."

"I agree." Loth had spoken before he knew it. The three women looked at him, Margret with raised eyebrows. "I think it would help," he conceded, even as his faith groaned in protest. "During my ... *adventure*, I learned what it was to be a heretic. It felt as though my very existence were under assault. If Inys can be the first to cease using the word, I think it would have done this world a very fine service."

After a moment, Sabran nodded.

"I will put this to the Virtues Council," she said, "but even if the Southern rulers join us, I cannot see that it will do us much good. Yscalin has the largest standing army in the world, and that will be turned against us. Humankind has not the strength to resist the fire now."

"Then humankind will need help," Ead said.

Loth shook his head, lost.

"Tell me," Ead went on, without explaining, "have you heard from High Princess Ermuna?"

"Yes," Sabran said. "She will have the date for me presently."

"Good. The Nameless One will rise from the Abyss on that day, and even if we do *not* unite the sword and jewels, we must still be there to drive him away while he is still weak from his slumber."

Loth frowned. "To where? And how?"

"Across the Halassa Sea, or beyond the Gate of Ungulus. If evil must exist, let it not be in our bosom." She looked Sabran in the eye. "We cannot carry out either of these plans alone."

Sabran sat back.

"You mean for us to call upon the East," she conjectured. "Just as Lady Truyde wanted."

An end to a centuries-long estrangement. Only Ead would have dared propose it to a Berethnet.

"When I first learned of her plan, I thought Lady Truyde reckless and dangerous," Ead said, voice tinged with regret. "Now I see her courage was higher than ours. The Eastern dragons are made of sterren, and while they may not be able to destroy the Nameless One, their powers—however strong or weak—will help us drive him back. To split the Draconic forces, you could also ask your fellow sovereigns to create a diversion."

"They might well help," Loth cut in, "but the Easterners will never parley with us."

"Seiiki trades with Mentendon. And the Easterners may help Inys if you make them an offer they cannot refuse."

"Tell me, Ead." Sabran looked unmoved. "What should I offer the heretics of the East?"

"The first alliance with Virtudom in history."

The Council Chamber fell silent as a crypt.

"No," Loth said firmly. "This is too much. Nobody is going to stand for this. Not the Virtues Council, not the people, and not me."

"You just now advocated for us all to stop thinking of each other as heretics." Margret crossed her arms. "Did you bang your head without my noticing in the last few minutes, brother?"

"I meant people on *this* side of the Abyss. The Easterners venerate wyrms. It is not the same, Meg."

"The Eastern dragons are not our enemies, Loth. I used to believe they were," Ead said, "but I did not understand the duality our world is built on. They are opposite in nature to infernal things like Fýredel."

Loth snorted. "You begin to sound like an alchemist. Have you ever met an Eastern wyrm?"

"No." She cocked an eyebrow. "Have you?"

"I do not need to meet them to know that they have forced the East to worship them. I will not kneel at the altar of heresy."

"They may not force worship," Margret mused. "Perhaps they share a mutual respect with the Easterners."

"Do you hear yourself, Margret?" Loth said, appalled. "They are *wyrms.*"

"The East also fears the Nameless One," Ead said. "Each of our religions agrees that he is the enemy."

"And the enemy of the enemy is a potential friend," Margret agreed.

Loth bit his tongue. If the foundations of his faith were struck once more, they might come tumbling down.

"You do not know what you ask, Ead." When Sabran spoke, her voice sounded too heavy to lift. "We have kept our distance from the East because of their heresy, yes—but to my understanding, the Easterners closed the door first, out of fear of the plague. I will not be able to persuade them to join us without making them a very generous offer in return."

"The banishment of the Nameless One will profit us all," Ead said. "The East did not escape the Grief of Ages, and it will not escape this."

"But its people might buy themselves time to prepare while we lay our heads upon the block," Sabran pointed out.

A bird landed outside. Loth glanced at the balcony, hoping to see a rock dove with a letter. A crow looked back at him.

"I told you that even the countries of Virtudom would not come to the aid of Inys if their own shores were under attack," Sabran said, too concerned with Ead to notice the bird. "You looked surprised."

"I was."

"You should not have been. My grandmother once said that when a wolf comes to the village, a shepherd looks first to her own flock. The wolf bloods his teeth on other sheep, and the shepherd knows it will one day come for hers, but she clings to the hope that she might be able to keep him out. Until the wolf is at her door."

Loth thought that sounded like something Queen Jillian would have said. She had famously argued for tighter alliances with the rest of the world.

"That," Sabran finished, "is how humankind has existed since the Grief of Ages."

"If the Eastern rulers have a whit of intelligence between them, they will see the necessity of cooperation," Ead maintained. "I have faith in the shepherds, even if Queen Jillian did not."

Sabran cast her gaze toward her own right hand, spread on the table. The hand that had once held a love-knot ring.

"Ead, I would speak with you alone." She rose. "Loth, Meg, please see to it that the summons go out to the Virtues Council at once. I need them all here to discuss the future."

"Of course," Margret said.

Sabran walked with Ead from the Council Chamber. When the doors were shut, Margret looked at Loth with an expression he recognized from their music lessons. She had dealt it to him whenever he hit the wrong note.

"I hope you're not intending to argue against this plan."

"Ead is mad to so much as insinuate it," Loth muttered. "An alliance with the East is a remedy for misfortune."

The crow took off again.

"I don't know." Margret reached for a quill and ink. "Perhaps their dragons are nothing like wyrms. These days I feel obliged to question everything I have ever known."

"We are not supposed to *question*, Meg. Faith is an act of trust in the Saint."

"And are you not questioning yours at all?"

"Of course I am." He rubbed his brow with one hand. "And every day I fear I will be damned for it. That I will have no place in Halgalant."

"Loth, you know how I love you, but the sense in your head could fit in a thimble."

Loth pursed his lips. "And you, I suppose, are worldly-wise."

"I was born worldly-wise."

She drew a roll of parchment toward her. Loth asked, "What else happened in Goldenbirch?"

Smile fading, Margret said, "I will tell you tomorrow. And I recommend you have a good, long sleep before you hear it, Loth, because your faith will be tested yet again." She nodded to the pile of letters. "Be quick about it, brother. I must get these to the Master of the Posts."

He did as he was bid. Sometimes he wondered why the Saint had not made Margret the older child.

Night had fallen over Ascalon. Half of the Knights of the Body followed Ead and Sabran to the Privy Garden, but the queen ordered them to wait outside the gate.

Only the stars could see them in the snow-draped dark. Ead remembered strolling with Sabran on these paths in the high summer. The first time she had walked with her alone.

Sabran, the descendant of Kalyba. Kalyba, the founder of the House of Berethnet.

It had haunted her on the way back from Caliburn-on-Sea. It had haunted her as they rode to find Aralaq. The secret that had divided the Priory for centuries.

Drunk on an enchantment, Galian Berethnet had lain with a woman he had seen as a mother and got her with child. He had built his religion like a wall around his shame. And to save his legacy, he had seen no choice but to sanctify the lie.

Tension poured from Sabran like heat off an open flame. When they reached the fountain, with its frozen rivulets of water, they faced each other.

"You realize what a new alliance may entail."

Ead waited for her to finish.

"The East will already have weapons and money. I can add to those," Sabran said, "but remember what I told you. Alliances have ever been forged through marriage."

"Alliances must have been made without marriage in the past."

"This alliance is different. It would have to unite two regions that have been estranged for centuries. Knit two bodies, and you knit two realms. That is why we royals marry—not for love, but to build our houses. That is the way the world is."

"It does not need to be that way. Try, Sabran," Ead urged. "Change the way things are."

"You speak as if nothing was ever easier." Sabran shook her head. "As if custom and tradition have no hold on the world. They are what shapes the world."

"It *is* that easy. A year ago, you would not have believed that you could love someone you considered a heretic." Ead did not look away. "Is that not so?"

Sabran breathed a white mist between them.

"Yes," she said. "It is so."

Snowflakes frosted her eyelashes and caught in her hair. She had stormed outside without a cloak, and now held her own arms to keep in the warmth.

"I will try," she concluded. "I will ... present this as a military alliance only. I am resolved that I will reign without a consort, as I have always desired. It is no longer my duty to marry and conceive a child. But if it is the custom in the East, as it usually is here—"

"It may not be the custom." Ead paused. "But if it is ... perhaps you should reconsider your determination to remain unwed."

Sabran studied her face. Even as her throat ached, Ead did not break her gaze.

"Why do you speak like this?" Sabran said quietly. "You know I never wanted to marry in the first place, and I am not inclined to do it again. That aside, it is you I want. No one else."

"But while you rule, you can never be seen to be with me. I am a heretic, and—"

"Stop." Sabran embraced her then. "Stop it."

Ead drew her close, breathed her in. They sank onto a marble settle.

"Sabran the Seventh, my namesake, fell in love with her Lady of the Bedchamber," Sabran murmured. "After she abdicated in favor of her daughter, they lived together for the rest of their days. If we defeat the Nameless One, my duty will be done."

"As will mine." Ead wrapped her cloak around them both. "Perhaps then I can steal you away."

"Where?"

Ead kissed her temple. "Somewhere."

Another foolish dream but, just for a moment, she allowed herself to inhabit it. A life with Sabran at her side.

"You and Meg kept something from me," Sabran said. "What happened in Goldenbirch?"

It was some time before Ead could bring herself to answer.

"You asked me once if I knew who the first Queen of Inys was, if not Cleolind."

Sabran looked up at her.

"My mother always said it was best to receive bad news in winter, when everything is already dark. So one can heal for spring," she said, while Ead searched for the words. "And I must be at my strongest this particular spring."

Faced with those eyes—the eyes of the witch—Ead knew she could not withhold the revelation any longer. After eight years of lies, she owed Sabran this truth.

Underneath the stars, she gave it.

57

West

In an undercroft in Ascalon Palace, a murderer of hallowed blood awaited execution. Sabran, who had never shown bloodthirst in all the years Loth had known her, had decided she wanted Crest drawn and quartered, but the other Dukes Spiritual had counseled that her people would find it unsettling at such a fragile time. Best to make it quiet and quick.

After a night of pacing the grounds alone, Sabran had relented. The Cupbearer would face the block, and she would face it in private, with only a handful of witnesses.

Crest showed no remorse as she looked at those who had come to watch her die. Roslain stood to one side of the room, a mourning cap over her hair. Loth knew she was not grieving her grandmother, but the treachery that had stained their family name.

Lord Calidor Stillwater kept a comforting hand on her waist. He had ridden from Castle Cordain, the ancestral seat of the Crest family, to be with his companion in her hour of grief.

Loth stood close to them, arm in arm with Margret. Sabran was nearby, wearing the necklace her mother had given her for her twelfth birthday. It was not customary for royals to attend executions, but Sabran had thought it craven to do otherwise.

A low scaffold had been erected and draped with dark cloth. When the clock struck ten, Crest lifted her face into the light.

"I ask for no mercy, and make no apology," she said. "Aubrecht Lievelyn was a sinner and a leech. Rosarian Berethnet was a whore, and Sabran Berethnet is a bastard who will never bear a daughter of her own." She locked gazes with Sabran. "Unlike her, I did not fail in my duty. I served just punishment. I go willingly unto Halgalant, where the Saint will welcome me."

Sabran did not rise to the taunt, but her face was utterly cold.

A cousin of Roslain, also in a mourning cap, divested Crest of her cloak and signet ring and tied the blindfold over her eyes. The executioner stood by, one hand on the haft of the axe.

Igrain Crest knelt before the block, straight-backed, and made the sign of the sword on her brow.

"In the name of the Saint," she said, "I die."

With those words, she lowered her neck into the divot. Loth thought once more of Queen Rosarian, and how her death had not been half as merciful.

The executioner swung up the axe. When it fell, so did the head of the Cupbearer.

No one made a sound. A servant lifted the head by its hair and held it out for the room to see. The hallowed blood of the Knight of Justice trickled down the block, and a servant collected it in a goblet. As the body was shrouded and removed from the scaffold, the Crest cousin walked to Roslain, who stepped away from her companion.

The signet ring would usually be placed on the right hand, but the bonesetter had splinted it. Roslain held out her left hand instead, and her cousin slid on the ring.

"Here is Her Grace, Lady Roslain Crest, Duchess of Justice," the steward said. "May she be rightwise in her conduct, now and always."

***

Igrain Crest was dead. Never again would the shadow of the Cupbearer darken the Queendom of Inys.

Sabran sat in her favorite chair in the Privy Chamber. A lantern clock ticked on the mantelpiece.

She had barely said a word since Ead had told her about Kalyba. Once the story was finished, she had asked to go inside, and they had spent the rest of the night sealed behind the drapes of her bed. Ead had held her in silence while she gazed up at the canopy.

Now she seemed fixated by her own hands. Ead watched her push at her knuckles, roll the pads of her thumbs on her fingers, and rub the polished ruby on her coronation ring.

"Sabran," Ead said, "there is nothing of her power in you."

Sabran clenched her jaw.

"If I have her blood, then I could wield the waning jewel," she said. "Something of her lives in me."

"Without star rot, or a fruit from the orange tree, you can use neither of the two branches of magic. You are not a mage," Ead said, "and you are not about to turn into a wyrm."

Sabran kept worrying at her skin with her fingernails. Ead reached to cover her hand.

"What are you thinking?"

"That I am likely a bastard. That I am descended from a liar and the Lady of the Woods—the same woman who took my child from me—and that no good house could be built on such a foundation." Her hair was a curtain between them. "That everything I am is a lie."

"The House of Berethnet has done many good things. Its origin has no bearing on that." Ead kept hold of her hand. "As to your bastardry—it means your father is alive. Is that not good?"

"I do not know Gian Harlowe. My father, for all intents and purposes, was Lord Wilstan Fynch," Sabran said quietly, "and he is dead. Like my mother, and Aubrecht, and the others."

The grievoushead had her in its vise. Ead tried to knead some warmth into her hand, to no avail.

"I still do not understand why she put the barb in me." Sabran brushed her belly with the other hand. "If she speaks true, then she loved her daughter, Sabran the First. I am her blood."

The barb itself had disappeared. According to the physician who had taken it, all that remained was a lock of hair.

"Kalyba is divorced from her humanity now. You are her blood, but the affinity is not strong enough for her to love you. All she wants is your throne," Ead said. "We may never understand her. What matters is that she is in league with the Nameless One, and that makes her our enemy."

A knock came at the door. A Knight of the Body entered in her silver-plated armor.

"Majesty," she said, bowing, "a bird has just arrived from Brygstad. An urgent message from Her Royal Highness, High Princess Ermuna of the House of Lievelyn."

She handed her the letter and left. Sabran broke the seal and turned to face the window as she read.

"What does she say?" Ead asked.

Sabran drew in a breath through her nose.

"The date is—" The letter fluttered to the floor. "The date is the third day of ... *this* spring."

And so the sandglass turned. Ead had expected the knowledge to fill her with dread, but part of her had already known.

The thousand years are almost done.

"Neporo and Cleolind must have bound the Nameless One six years after the Foundation of Ascalon." Sabran placed her hands on the mantel. "We do not have long."

"Long enough to cross the Abyss," Ead said. "Sabran, you must send your ambassadors to the East with all haste to make the alliance, and I must go with them. To find the other jewel. At least then we could bind him again."

"You cannot run blindly over the Abyss," Sabran said, tensing. "I must write to the Eastern rulers first. The Seiikinese and the Lacustrine will execute any outsider who sets foot on their shores. I must seek their permission to land a special embassy."

"There is no time for it. It will take weeks for a dispatch to get there." Ead made for the door. "I will go ahead on a fast ship and—"

"Have you no care for your own life?" Sabran said hotly. Ead stopped. "I spent *weeks* believing you dead when you left Ascalon. Now you want to go across the sea without protection, without armor, to a place where you could face death or imprisonment."

"I already did that, Sabran. The day I came to Inys." Ead gave her a weary smile. "If I survived once, I can again."

614

Sabran stood with her eyes shut, hands white-knuckled on the mantel.

"I know you must go," she said. "To ask you to stay would be like trying to cage the wind—but please, Ead, wait. Let me arrange the embassy, so you have strength in numbers. Do not go alone."

Ead tightened her grip on the door handle.

Sabran was right. A few days of waiting would be time lost in the East, but it might also save her head.

She turned back and said, "I will stay."

At this, Sabran crossed the room, eyes full, and embraced her. Ead pressed a kiss to her temple and held her close.

Sabran had been dealt a cruel hand. Her Lady of the Bedchamber had died while she slept, her companion in her arms, her mother before her eyes. Her daughter had never drawn breath. Her father—if he had been her father at all—had perished in Yscalin, beyond her reach. Loss had dogged her all her life. Little wonder she was holding on so tightly.

"You remember the first day we walked together. You told me about the lovejay, and how it always knows its partner's song, even if they have been long apart," Ead whispered to her. "My heart knows your song, as yours knows mine. And I will always come back to you."

"I will hold you to that, Eadaz uq-Nāra."

Ead tried to memorize her weight, her scent, the precise tenor of her voice. To lock her into her memory. "Aralaq will stay to guard you. It is why I brought him here," she said. "He is a surly creature, but loyal, and he can tear through a wyvern well enough."

"I will take good care of him." Sabran drew back. "I must meet with the remaining Dukes Spiritual at once to discuss the embassy. Once the rest of the Virtues Council arrives, I will put this … Eastern Proposal to them. If I show them the waning jewel, and explain the significance of the date, I am confident they will vote in my favor."

"They will battle it to the end," Ead said, "but you are golden-tongued."

Sabran nodded, hard with resolve. Ead left her looking out over her city.

She walked down a flight of steps and into the open gallery below the Royal Solarium, where twelve small balconies spilled winter-flowering blossoms. As she strode toward the door to her own chamber, she heard a footstep behind her, soft as felt.

Silently, she turned. A Red Damsel stood in a beam of sunlight. At her lips was a blowpipe, whittled from wood.

The dart had punched through her shirt before Ead could take a breath. Death spread from its bite.

The floor met her knees with bone-jarring force. She lifted a shaking hand to her belly and felt the slender dart in it. Her killer caught and lowered her.

"Forgive me, Eadaz."

"Nairuj," Ead coughed out.

She had known this day would come. A sister of the Priory could avoid her wardings.

The molten glass was setting in her veins. Her muscles cramped around the dart, rejecting the poison. "You had the child," she managed to say.

Ochre eyes looked down at her. "A girl," Nairuj said, after a hesitation. "I did not want this, sister, but the Prioress commands that you are silenced." Ead felt Nairuj twist the ring off her finger, the ring that had been her dream. "Where is the jewel, the white jewel?"

Ead could not reply. The feeling was already trickling from her. She had the curious sense that her ribs were disappearing. As Nairuj felt at her throat for the jewel, Ead gripped the dart in her belly and removed it.

She was so cold. All the fire in her was going out, leaving ashes in its wake.

"Nameless is—" Even breathing was agony. "Spring. The third d-day of spring."

"What is this?"

Sabran. Fear strained her voice.

Nairuj moved like an arrow. Ead watched through watering eyes as her one-time sister pulled a band of silk across her mouth and vaulted over the nearest balustrade.

Footsteps clattered down the corridor. "Ead—" Sabran gathered her into her arms, gasping. "Ead!" Her features were bleeding together. "Look at me. Look at me, Ead, please. T-tell me what she did to you. Tell me which poison—"

Ead tried to speak. To say her name, just one more time. To say she was sorry to break her promise.

I will always come back to you.

Darkness closed around her like a cocoon. She thought of the orange tree. *Not you. Ead. Please.* The voice was fading. *Please don't leave me here alone.* She thought of how it had been between them, from the candle dance to the first touch of her lips.

Then she did not think at all.

The sun was setting over Ascalon. Loth gazed through the window at the candlelit Alabastrine Tower, where the Virtues Council were debating the Eastern Proposal.

Ead lay on her bed. Her lips were as black as her hair, her corset unraveled to reveal a pinhole in her belly.

Sabran had not left her side. She was staring at Ead as if looking away would snap her fragile hold on life. Outside, Aralaq was prowling in the Privy Garden. It had taken a great deal of wheedling to convince him to leave for long enough for the Royal Physician to examine Ead and, even then, he had snapped his jaws when the man had tried to touch her.

Doctor Bourn moved like the hand of a clock around the sickbed. He measured her heartbeat, felt her brow, and studied the wound. When he finally took off his eyeglasses, Sabran raised her head.

"Lady Nurtha has been poisoned," he said, "but by what, I cannot tell. The symptoms are like none I have ever seen."

"The cruel sister," Loth said. "That is its name."

It was supposed to cause death. Once again, Ead had defied her fate.

The Royal Physician frowned at this. "I have never heard of such a poison, my lord. I do not know how to purge it from her." He looked back at Ead. "Majesty, it seems to me that Lady Nurtha has been put into a deep sleep. Perhaps she can be woken from it.

Perhaps not. All we can do is try to keep her alive for as long as we can. And pray for her."

"You *will* wake her," Sabran whispered. "You will find a way. If she dies——"

Her voice broke, and she held her head between her hands. The Royal Physician bowed.

"I am sorry, Your Majesty," he said. "We will do our best for her."

He retreated from the chamber. When the door closed, Sabran began to shiver.

"I was cursed in my cradle. The Lady of the Woods laid a hex upon my head." She never took her eyes from Ead. "Not only is my crown lost, but my loved ones fall like roses in winter. Always before my eyes."

Margret, who had been keeping watch on the other side of the bed, now went to sit beside her.

"Don't think these things. You are not cursed, Sab," she said gently, but firmly. "Ead is not dead, and we will not mourn her. We will fight for her, and for everything she believes in." She looked at Ead. "But I tell you this—I will not marry Tharian until she wakes. If she thinks this foolishness will get her out of giving me away, she is sorely mistaken."

Loth took the seat that Margret had left. He lifted his clasped hands to his lips.

Even when she had been bleeding in Lasia, Ead had never looked this vulnerable. All life and warmth had fled from her.

"I will go to the East." His voice was hoarse. "No matter what the Virtues Council decides, I must go across the Abyss as your representative, Sabran. To broker an alliance. To seek out the other jewel."

Sabran was silent for a very long time. Outside, Aralaq let out a chilling howl.

"I want you to go first to the Unceasing Emperor, Dranghien Lakseng," Sabran said. "He is unwed, and consequently we have more to offer him. If he is convinced to join us, he may persuade the Warlord of Seiiki."

Loth watched her, heartsore.

"I will send with you an entourage of two hundred persons. If you are to reach the Unceasing Emperor, you must display the might of the Queendom of Inys." She met his gaze. "You will bid him meet us on the Abyss with his dragons on the third day of spring. There will not be time for you to come back, or to debate the terms in Inys. I trust that you will seal this alliance with our interests at heart, to achieve the outcome we desire."

"I will, I swear it."

It seemed to Loth that this room was already like a crypt. Shaking off the thought, he went to Ead and brushed a spiral of hair behind her ear. He would not permit himself to think that this was a farewell.

With dignity, Sabran rose from her chair.

"You promised you would return to me," she said to Ead. "Queens do not forget promises made, Eadaz uq-Nāra."

Her stance was rigid. Loth took her by the arm and guided her tenderly from the chamber, leaving Margret to her vigil.

He walked beside his queen. When they reached the end of the corridor, Sabran buckled at last. Loth wrapped her in his arms as she sank to the floor and sobbed as if her soul had been ripped out.

V

Here Be Dragons

Whose word did he fondly follow
That he dared this perilous voyage,
These raging seas?

—Anonymous, from *The Man'yōshū*

58

West

The *Elegant* had been sailing for days, but it felt like centuries. Loth had lost count of exactly how long it had been. All he knew was that he wanted to be off this ship and on dry land.

Sabran had argued with great spirit for the so-called Eastern Proposal. During that time, the Virtues Council had not slept. Their chief worry was how the Inysh people might respond to an alliance with heretics and wyrms, which went against everything they knew.

After hours of debate on how it could be justified from a religious perspective, several consultations with the College of Sanctarians, and fierce arguments for and against, Sabran had moved the vote in her favor. The embassy had been on its way within a day.

The plan, desperate as it was, began to take shape. To raise their chances of victory on the Abyss, they would have to divide the Draconic Army. Sabran had invoked the holy call to arms and written to the sovereigns of both Virtudom and the South, asking them to assist Inys in besieging and reclaiming Cárscaro on the second day of spring. An attack on the sole Draconic stronghold might compel Fýredel and his underlings to remain in Yscalin to defend it.

It would be dangerous. Many would die. It was possible that they would *all* die—but there was no other choice. Either they must smite the Nameless One the hour he rose, or wait for him to annihilate the world. Loth would far sooner die with a sword in his hand.

His mother had been distraught to see him leave again, but at least he had been able to say goodbye this time. She and Margret had sent him off at Perchling, as had Sabran, who had given him her coronation ring to show to the Unceasing Emperor. It hung from a chain around his neck.

Her determination was something to behold. It was clear that she feared this alliance, but Sabran would do anything for her subjects. And he sensed this was her way to honor Ead.

Ead. Every time he woke, he thought she was there, on the road with him.

A knock on the door. Loth opened his eyes.

"Yes?"

The cabin girl entered and bowed.

"Lord Arteloth," she said, "we're in sight of the other ship. Are you ready to leave?"

"We've reached the Bonehouse Trench?"

"Yes, m'lord."

He reached for his boots. The next ship would take him to the Empire of the Twelve Lakes.

"Of course," he said. "A moment. I'll join you on the deck."

The woman bowed again and retreated. Loth reached for his cloak and satchel.

His bodyguards were waiting outside his cabin. Instead of their full armor, the Knights of the Body that Sabran had lent him wore only mail under their surcoats, which were blazoned with the royal badge of Inys. They shadowed Loth as he made his way up to the deck.

The sky was salted with stars. Loth tried not to look too hard at the water as he strode to the prow of the *Elegant*, where the captain stood with her muscular arms folded.

The Abyss was home to many things that other seas were not. He had heard tell of syrens with needles for teeth, of fish that glowed like candles, of baleens that could swallow a ship whole. In the distance, Loth could make out the hulking shape of a man-of-war, winking with lights. When they were close enough to see its ensign and pennant, he raised his eyebrows.

"The *Rose Eternal*."

"The very same," the captain said. She was an Inysh woman of ruddy complexion and towering stature. "Captain Harlowe knows the Eastern waters. He'll see you right from here."

"Harlowe," one of the Knights of the Body said. "Is he not a pirate?"

"Privateer."

The knight snorted.

The *Elegant* drew up alongside the *Rose Eternal*. No ship could drop anchor in the Abyss, so the crews began tying the vessels together. They drifted in the endless black.

"Fuck me, if it isn't Arteloth Beck." Estina Melaugo slapped her hands onto the side and grinned at him. "Didn't think we'd see you again, my lord."

"Good evening to you, Mistress Melaugo," Loth called, pleased to see a face he knew. "I wish we were meeting somewhere more hospitable."

Melaugo clicked her tongue. "Man walks into Yscalin, but he's scared of the Abyss. Dry your eyes and get your noble backside up here, lordling." She dropped a rope ladder and tipped the brim of her hat. "Thank you, Captain Lanthorn. Harlowe sends his regards."

"Send mine in return," the captain of the *Elegant* said, "and good luck to you out there, Estina. Watch yourself."

"Always do."

As his entourage gathered, Loth climbed the ladder. He envied Captain Lanthorn sailing back to blue waters. At the top, Melaugo helped him over and clapped him on the back.

"We all wagered you were dead," she told him. "How in Halgalant did you escape Cárscaro?"

"The Donmata Marosa," Loth replied. "I could not have left without her."

His throat ached as he thought of her. She might be Flesh Queen of Yscalin, eyes full of ash.

"Marosa." Melaugo arched a dark eyebrow. "Well, that's not what I expected you to say. I must hear this story—but Captain Harlowe wants to see you first." She whistled to the privateers as the knights pulled themselves and their heavy armor over the gunwale. "Get Lord Arteloth's people up that ladder and into their cabins. Look lively, now!"

The crew obeyed without question. Some of them even inclined their heads to Loth as they helped the members of the Inysh embassy climb up to the *Rose Eternal*.

Melaugo led him across the deck. In the candlelit interior of his cabin, Gian Harlowe was poring over a map with Gautfred Plume—the quartermaster—and an ashen woman with silver hair.

"Ah. Lord Arteloth." His tone was a trifle warmer than it had been at their last meeting. "Welcome back. Sit." He motioned to a chair. "This is my new cartographer, Hafrid of Elding."

The Northerner placed a hand on her chest in greeting. "Joy and health to you, Lord Arteloth."

Loth sat. "And to you, mistress."

Harlowe glanced up. He wore a jerkin with gold fastenings.

"Tell me," he said, "how do you find the Abyss, my lord?"

"Not to my liking."

"Hm. I'd call you a craven, but these waters unsettle the hardest seafarers—and in any case, none can call you craven when you walked so boldly to your doom." His expression flickered. "I won't ask how you escaped Cárscaro. Whatever a man does to survive is his affair. And I won't ask what happened to your friend."

Loth said nothing, but his stomach twisted. Harlowe beckoned him closer to the map.

"I thought I'd show you where we're going, so you can tell your people, should they squall to you about the crossing."

Harlowe leaned over the map, which showed the three known continents of the world and the constellations of islands that surrounded them. He tapped a thick-knuckled finger on the right side.

"We're heading for the City of the Thousand Flowers. To get there, we'll go through the southern waters of the Abyss so we can catch the westerlies, which will shave a week or two off our journey. We should be in the Sundance Sea within three to four weeks." He rubbed his chin. "The voyage will be harder from there. We'll need to avoid the Seiikinese navy, which sees the *Rose* as an enemy ship— and the wyrms that have been sighted in the East, led by Valeysa."

Loth had seen enough of Fýredel to know that he did not want to meet one of his brethren.

"We're aiming for a closed port on the southwestern coast of the Empire of the Twelve Lakes." Harlowe indicated the place. "There were once several factories there, where the House of Lakseng conducted trade before the sea ban. That was before the Grief of Ages, of course. Arriving at that port should send a potent message to the Emperor."

"That we wish to reopen a closed door," Loth finished. "What do you know of the Unceasing Emperor?"

"Almost nothing. Lakseng lives in a walled palace, comes out for summer progress, and he's marginally softer on trespassers than the salt lords of Seiiki."

"Why?"

"Because Seiiki is an island nation. Once the Draconic plague got its teeth into it, it spread like wildfire. Almost destroyed their population. The Lacustrine had more room to flee from it." Harlowe locked Loth in his unblinking gaze. "You just make sure the Unceasing Emperor is fit for the hand of Queen Sabran, my lord. She deserves a prince who'll love her well."

A muscle started in his cheek as he spoke. He lowered his head back to the map, jaw clenched, and beckoned his cartographer.

"I will do everything I can for Queen Sabran, Captain Harlowe," Loth said quietly. "On my honor."

Harlowe grunted.

"There's a cabin ready for you. If something knocks against the ship, try not to piss yourself. It'll be a baleen." He nodded to the door. "Go on, Estina. Get some drink in the man."

As Melaugo led him across the quarterdeck, Loth took a final look at the retreating *Elegant*. He tried not to dwell on the fact that the *Rose Eternal* was now alone in the middle of the Abyss.

His cabin was finer than the last. Loth suspected he had been elevated not out of a new respect among the crew for his noble blood, but because he had walked into Yscalin and lived to tell the tale.

And tell it he did. He shared his story with Melaugo, who sat on the window seat and listened. He told her of the imprisonment of the Donmata Marosa and the truth about the Flesh King of Yscalin, and described the tunnel where Kit had met his doom.

Out of loyalty to Ead, he left out the parts about the Priory of the Orange Tree. Instead, he said that he had crossed the Spindles and fled back to Inys through Mentendon. When he was finished, Melaugo shook her head.

"I'm sorry, truly. Lord Kitston had a good heart." She drank from her hip flask. "And now you go to the East. I suppose you proved your bravery, but you'll find it hard out there."

"For what I have done," Loth said, "I deserve hardship." He wet his lips. "It's my fault Kit is dead."

"Don't do that, now. He made a choice to go with you. He could have stayed in Yscalin, or aboard our ship, or he could have stayed at home." She handed him the flask. He hesitated before accepting. "You're trying to persuade the Easterners that they need as much help from the West as we need from them, but they've survived on their own for centuries now—and an alliance with Queen Sabran, a gift to any prince on our side of the world, might not tempt the Unceasing Emperor. She's royalty to us, but a blasphemer to him. Her religion is built on a hatred of dragons, while his is built on an adoration of them."

"Not the fiery breeds." Loth sniffed the flask. "The Easterners don't worship *them*."

"No. They fear the Nameless One and his ilk as we do," Melaugo conceded, "but Queen Sabran might still have to sacrifice some principles if she means to go through with this."

Loth drank, and immediately choked the burning liquid out through his nose. Melaugo laughed.

"Try again," she said. "Goes down easier the second time."

He tried again. It still seemed to strip the lining off his cheeks, but it warmed him to his belly.

"Keep it. You'll need it in the Abyss." She got up. "Duty calls, but I'll ask one of our Lacustrine seafarers if they can teach you about their customs, and at least a few words of their tongue. Let's not present you to His Imperial Majesty as a complete idiot."

A thick fog pressed on the *Rose Eternal*, keeping them in darkness even by day. The lanterns cast ghostly light on the waves. To avoid the cold, Loth kept to his cabin, where a Lacustrine gunner named Thim was charged with teaching him about the Empire of the Twelve Lakes.

Thim was eighteen and appeared to have infinite reserves of patience. He taught Loth about his native country, which was divided into twelve regions, each of which housed one of the Great Lakes. It was a vast domain that ended at the Lords of Fallen Night—mountains that closed the way to the rest of the continent, greatest amongst them the merciless Brhazat. Thim told Loth that many Easterners had tried to escape the Great Sorrow by crossing the Lords of Fallen Night, including the last Queen of Sepul, but none had returned. Long-frozen bodies still lay in the snow.

The Unceasing Emperor of the Twelve Lakes was the current head of the House of Lakseng and had been raised by his grand-mother, the Grand Empress Dowager. Thim told Loth the proper way to bow, how to address him, and how to behave in his presence.

He learned that Dranghien Lakseng, though not quite a god, was close to it in the eyes of his people. His house claimed descent from the first human to find a dragon after it fell from the celestial plane. There were rumors among the commons ("which the House of Lakseng does not confirm or deny") that some rulers of the dynasty had been dragons in human form. What was certain was that whenever a Lacustrine ruler was close to death, the Imperial Dragon would choose a successor from among their legitimate heirs.

It unnerved Loth that the court had an Imperial Dragon. How strange to be overseen by wyrms.

"That word is forbidden," Thim said gravely when he used it once. "We call our dragons by their proper name, and the winged beasts from the West, *fire-breathers*."

Loth took note. His life might depend on what he learned now.

When Thim was occupied elsewhere, Loth idled away the hours playing cards with the Knights of the Body and sometimes, in the rare hours she was at liberty, Melaugo. She beat them every time. When night fell, he tried to sleep—but once, he ventured alone to the deck, called from his berth by a haunting song.

The lanterns were extinguished, but the stars were almost bright enough to see by. Harlowe was smoking a pipe at the prow, where Loth joined him.

"Good evening, Captain—"

"Hush." Harlowe was a statue. "Listen."

The song drifted over the black waves. A chill slithered through Loth. "What is that?"

"Syrens."

"Will they not lure us to our death?"

"Only in the stories." Smoke plumed from his mouth. "Watch the sea. It's the sea they call."

At first, all Loth saw was the void. Then a flower of light bloomed in the water, illuminating its surface. Suddenly he could see fish, tens of thousands of them, each full of a rainbow glow.

He had heard tales of the sky lights of Hróth. Never had he thought to see them underwater.

"You see, my lord," Harlowe murmured. The light feathered in his eyes. "You can find beauty anywhere."

59

East

The *Rose Eternal* groaned as the waves heaved beneath it. The storm had blown in a week after they had crossed into the waters of the Sundance Sea, and had not relented since.

Water struck the hull with teeth-rattling force. Wind howled and thunder rumbled, drowning the crew's bellows as they battled with the tempest. In his cabin, Loth prayed to the Saint under his breath, eyes closed, trying to quell his retches. When the next wave came, the lantern above him sputtered and went out.

He could stand it no longer. If he was to die tonight, it would not be in here. He fastened his cloak, his fingers slipping on the clasp, and shouldered his way through the door.

"My lord, the captain said to stay in our cabins," one of his bodyguards called after him.

"The Knight of Courage tells us to look death in the eye," he answered. "I intend to obey."

He sounded bolder than he felt.

When he emerged onto the deck, he could smell the storm. Wind roared into his eyes. His boots slid on the planks as he lurched toward one of the masts and embraced it, already soaked to the bone. Lightning splintered overhead and blinded him.

"Get back to your cabin, lordling," Melaugo shouted. Black paint ran from her eyes. "You want to die out here?"

Harlowe stood on the quarterdeck, his jaw set tight. Plume was at the wheel. When the *Rose* crested a mountainous wave, the sailors cried out. One of the swabbers was pitched over the side, her scream lost to a thunderclap, while another slipped from his handhold and went slithering down the deck. The sails billowed and rattled, twisting the image of Ascalon.

Loth pressed his cheek against the mast. This ship had felt solid as they crossed the Abyss; now he felt its hollowness. He had survived the plague, glimpsed death in the eye of a cockatrice, but it seemed it would be in the waters of the East that he would perish.

Waves battered the *Rose Eternal* from all sides as she crashed back down, soaking her crew. Water poured on to the deck. Rain pummeled their backs. Plume turned the wheel hard to port, but it was as though the *Rose* was taking on a life of her own.

The mast began to splinter. The wind was pulling it too hard. Loth made a break for the quarterdeck. Even if Harlowe was losing control of his ship, Loth felt safer with him than he did anywhere else. This was the man who had fought a pirate lord in a typhoon, who had weathered all the known seas of the world. As he ran, Melaugo screamed a word he couldn't hear.

The rogue wave broke against the ship and took his feet from under him. His mouth and nostrils flooded. He was elbow-deep in water. Plume strained the wheel against it, but suddenly the *Rose* was almost on its side, and the tallest mast skirted the sea. As he slid across the deck, toward the waves, Loth scrabbled for a handhold and found the sinewy arm of the carpenter, who was clinging to the ratlines by his fingertips.

The *Rose* righted herself. The carpenter released Loth, leaving him to cough up water.

"Thank you," Loth choked out. The carpenter waved him off, panting.

"Land ahoy," came a distant shout. "Land!"

Harlowe looked up. Loth blinked sea and rain from his eyes as lightning flashed again. Through a watery smear, he saw the captain open his nightglass and squint into it.

"Hafrid," he bellowed, "what's here?"

The cartographer shielded her face from the rain. "There shouldn't be anything this far south."

"And yet." Harlowe snapped the nightglass closed. "Master Plume, get us to that island."

"If it's inhabited, they'll put us all to the sword," Plume shouted back.

"Then the *Rose* will live, and we'll die faster than we will out here," Harlowe barked at his quartermaster. His eyes were lit by a thunderstroke. "Estina, muster the crew!"

The boatswain took a pipe from a brass chain around her neck and pinched it between her teeth. A high-pitched trill rode the wind. Loth held on to the gunwale, water beading on his lashes, as Melaugo piped orders to the pirates. They danced to the tune of the whistle, scaling the ratlines and heaving at ropes while the ship keened beneath them. It was chaos to Loth's eye—yet soon enough, the island was in sight, drawing closer by the moment. Too close. More whistles, and the courses were taken up.

The *Rose Eternal* did not slow.

Harlowe narrowed his eyes. His ship kept carving its way toward the island, faster than ever.

"This is no natural thing. The tide shouldn't be strong enough to reel us in." His face tightened. "She's going to run aground."

As Loth wiped rain from his brow, a flash came from low down on the island. Bright as a mirror catching the sun.

"What in damsam is that?" Plume squinted as the moonburst of light came again. "Do you see it, Captain?"

"Aye."

"Someone must be signaling us." Melaugo clung to a dripping rope. "Captain?"

Harlowe kept his hands on the balustrade, his gaze on the island. Tines of lightning painted its heights.

"Captain," the leadsman cried, "seventeen fathoms by the mark. We're surrounded by reef."

Melaugo went to the side and looked over. "I see it. Damsel save us, it's everywhere." She held on to the brim of her hat. "Captain, it's almost like she knows her way. She's missing it all by the skin of her barnacles."

Harlowe brazened out the island, his expression set. Loth searched his face for any sign of hope.

"Belay last order," Harlowe commanded. "Let fall all anchors and douse all sails."

"We can't stop now," Plume shouted to him.

"We can try. If the *Rose* runs aground, she's finished. And that, I cannot allow."

"We can avoid it. Risk the storm—"

"Even if we could somehow turn around in this reef, we'll be blown farther south and becalmed when it's done," Harlowe barked. "Would you like to die that way, Master Plume?"

Melaugo traded a frustrated look with Plume before she relayed the command to the crew. Rope was hauled, the sails stowed. Seafarers clung to the yards above, boots planted on footropes, and heaved at the canvas with their bare hands. One of them was lashed off and slammed into the deck. Bone shattered. Blood mingled with seawater. With a calm that belied the chaos around him, Harlowe descended and took the wheel from his quartermaster.

Loth held on. All he could taste was salt. All he could feel was its burn in his eyes. When the first of the *Rose*'s anchors hooked into the seabed, the lurch seemed to unseat his organs.

The crew let fall the second anchor, then the third. Still they did not slow. The leadsman counted down the fathoms. Loth braced himself as three anchors towed in vain at the ship.

Thunder boomed. Lightning flashed. The final anchor plunged beneath the waves, but the sand was too close now, far too close to avoid. Harlowe kept hold of the wheel, his knuckles taut.

It was the reef or the beach. And Loth knew from the look in his eyes that Harlowe would not risk the destruction of the *Rose* by steering her into the teeth of the reef.

Melaugo let out a blast from her whistle. The crew abandoned their work and cleaved to what they could.

The man-of-war shuddered beneath them. Loth clenched his teeth, expecting to feel the hull being shredded. The quake went on for what seemed like eternity—and then, quite suddenly, the *Rose* was almost statue-still. All he could hear was the patter of rain against the deck.

"Six fathoms," the leadsman said, panting.

A riotous cheer went up from the crew. Loth rose, his knees trembling, and joined Melaugo. When he saw the waves around them, still buoying the ship, he pressed his head into his hands and laughed as if he would never stop. Melaugo grinned and crossed her arms.

"There you are, lordling. You've survived your first storm."

"But how did it stop?" Loth watched the sea lap at the hull. "We were going so fast . . ."

"Don't give a fuck, myself. Let's just call it a miracle—from your Saint, if you fancy."

Only Harlowe seemed loath to rejoice. He looked up at the island with a flicker in his jaw.

"Captain." Melaugo had noticed. "What is it?"

His gaze stayed on the island. "I have been a seafarer for many years," he said. "Never have I felt a ship move as the *Rose* just did. As if a god had pulled her out of the storm."

Melaugo seemed not to know what to say. She slapped her sodden hat over her hair.

"Find us dry powder and muster some scouts," Harlowe said. "As soon as we've cleaned up Master Lark's body, we need sweet water and food. I'll take a small party ashore. Everyone else, including those in the Inysh retinue, should stay and help patch up the ship."

"I should like to come with you. If I may," Loth cut in. "Forgive me, Captain Harlowe, but after that experience, I have rather lost my sea legs. I would feel more useful on land."

"I see." Harlowe looked him up and down. "Do you know how to hunt, Lord Arteloth?"

"Indeed. I often hunted in Inys."

"At court, I assume. And I imagine that was with a bow."

"Yes."

"Well, we've no bows here, I'm afraid," Harlowe said, "but we'll teach you how to use a pistol." He clapped Loth on the shoulder as he passed. "I'll make a pirate of you yet."

———

The *Rose Eternal* was left anchored and with all sails furled, but the wind still swayed her dangerously. Loth climbed into a rowing boat with two of the Knights of the Body, who had both refused to carry pistols. Their swords were all they needed in a fight.

Loth held his own pistol with a firm hand. Melaugo had shown him how to prime and fire it.

Rain churned the sea around the boats. They rowed beneath a natural arch, toward a beach that sloped into steep foothills. As they drew closer to the shore, Harlowe raised his nightglass.

"People," he murmured. "On the beach."

He spoke to one of the gunners in another language. The woman took the nightglass from him and peered through it.

"This may be Feather Island, a sacred place, home to the most treasured documents in the East," Harlowe translated. "Only scholars can set foot on it, and they won't be well armed."

"They are still bound by Eastern law." Melaugo cocked her pistol. "We're not privateers to them, Harlowe. We're plague-ridden pirates. Like everyone else on these waters."

"They may not adhere to the sea ban." Harlowe glanced at his boatswain. "Do you have any better ideas, Estina?"

The gunner signaled for her to lower the weapon. Melaugo pursed her lips, but obeyed.

Three people waited for them on the shore. Two men and a woman in robes of darkest red, who watched them with guarded expressions.

Behind them lay what Loth thought, at first, was the wreckage of a ship. Then he saw that it was the skeleton of an enormous beast.

It was close to the length of the beach. Whatever it was that had died here had been larger than a baleen. Now it was picked clean, the bones iridescent under the moonlight.

Loth got out of the rowing boat and helped the other seafarers shove it on to the sand, shaking water from his eyes. Harlowe approached the strangers and bowed. They returned the gesture. He spoke to them for some time before returning to the scouting party.

"The scholars of Feather Island have offered us shelter for as long as the storm continues, and they permit us to collect water. They only have room for forty of us in their house, but they'll let the rest of the crew sleep in their empty storehouses," Harlowe shouted over the wind. "All of this is on the condition that we bring no weapons on to the island, and that we touch none of its residents. They fear we might carry the plague."

"Bit late on the weapons front," Melaugo said.

"I mislike this, Harlowe," one of the Knights of the Body called. "I say we stay on the *Rose*."

"And I say otherwise."

"Why?"

Harlowe turned those cold eyes on him with the lightest touch of contempt. With the storm raging around him, he looked like some chaotic god of the sea.

"I intended to renew our supplies in Kawontay," he said, "but now the storm has blown us off-course, we will be out of food before we can get to it. Most of the water is befouled." He took two hunting knives from their sheaths. "The crew won't sleep on that sea, and I need them on their mettle. There will be a skeleton crew left on watch, of course—and if anyone else wishes to remain on the *Rose*, I won't stop 'em. Let's see how long it takes them to decide that it isn't worth drinking their own piss."

Harlowe approached the strangers again and set the knives, and his pistol, on the sand at their feet. Melaugo clicked her tongue before emptying her clothes of an array of blades. The Knights of the Body laid down their broadswords in the same way a parent might lay down a newborn. Loth ceded his blades and the pistol. The scholars watched them in silence. When all were disarmed, one of the men walked away, and the scouting party followed him.

Feather Island loomed above them. Lightning bared the rough-hewn precipices, lushly green, of breathtaking height. The scholar led them from the beach, beneath another arch, to where a stair had been whittled into a cliff face. Loth craned his neck to see it climbing out of sight.

They were on that stair for a long time. Wind roared at their sides. Rain soaked their boots, making every step perilous. By the time they reached the top, Loth's knees were ready to buckle.

637

The scholar led them over grass and under dripping trees, to a path lined with lanterns. A house was waiting for them, raised from the ground on a platform, with white walls and a tiled roof, supported by pillars of timber. It was like no dwelling Loth had ever seen. The scholar opened the doors and removed his shoes before entering. The newcomers did the same. Loth followed Harlowe into the cool interior of the building.

The walls were unadorned. Instead of carpets, there were sweet-smelling mats. A sunken hearth was surrounded by square cushions. The scholar spoke again to Harlowe.

"This is where we'll stay. The storehouses are nearby." Harlowe eyed the room. "As soon as the storm abates, I'll see if I can't persuade the scholars to sell us some millet. Enough to get us to Kawontay."

"We can give them nothing in exchange," Loth pointed out. "They might need the millet for themselves."

"You'll never be a seafarer if you think that way, my lord."

"I don't want to be a seafarer."

"Of course you don't."

The dark was at its deepest. Tané watched the Inysh ship through the open windows of the healing room.

"They will be gone within a few days," Elder Vara was murmuring to the other elders. "This storm will soon end."

"Vara, they will empty our storehouses," the honored High Elder said, in hushed and angry tones. "They number in the hundreds. We can survive on the fruits of the island for a time, but if they take the rice and millet—"

"They are pirates," another elder cut in. "They may not be from the Fleet of the Tiger Eye, but there are only pirates in these waters. Of course they will take our food—by force, if necessary."

"These are not pirates," Elder Vara soothed. "Their captain says they come from Queen Sabran of Inys. They are bound for the Empire of the Twelve Lakes. I think, for the sake of peace, it would be best to help them on their way."

"By risking the lives of our charges," the same elder hissed. "What if they carry the red sickness?"

Tané was hardly listening to the squabble. Her gaze was on the storm-tossed sea.

The blue jewel was quiet in its prison. She kept it in a watertight lacquer case on her sash, always in reach.

"You are an utter fool," the High Elder barked, drawing her attention back to the room. "You should have refused them shelter. This is sacred land."

"We must show them a little compassion, Elder—"

"Try preaching *compassion* to the people who lost their lives, their families, when the red sickness came to the shores of the East." The elder sniffed. "On your head be it."

He swept out of the room, giving Tané a brief nod as he passed. The other elders followed. Elder Vara pinched the bridge of his nose.

"Do we have any weapons at all on this island?" Tané asked him.

"A handful under the floor in the dining hall, for use if the island is threatened by invaders. The elders, in that case, would secure the archives while the younger scholars fought."

"We ought to keep them close. Most of the scholars are trained in the sword-way," Tané said. "If these pirates try to rob us, we must be ready."

"I have no wish to cause panic among the students, child. The outsiders will remain in the cliffside village. We are too high for them here." He offered her a smile. "You have been a great help to me today, but the night is old. You have earned your rest."

"I am not tired."

"Your face tells me otherwise."

It was true that there was cold sweat on her brow, and that shadow circled her eyes. She bowed and left the healing room.

The corridors of the house were empty. Most of the scholars knew nothing of the pirates, and slept with no cares in the world. Tané kept a hand at her side, close to the case.

It had not taken her long to understand the way her treasure worked. Every day, before reflection and after supper, she had climbed to the top of the dormant volcano, where rainwater pooled in the crater, and attuned herself to the vibrations of the jewel. She found an instinct, buried deep, that showed her how to will those vibrations outward—as if she had done this long ago, and her body was remembering.

At first, she had used the jewel to cast ripples. Next, she had folded an oil-paper butterfly and made it glide away from her. Then, under cover of darkness, she had started to sneak down to the beach.

Days it had taken her to lure in the surf. The tides were set in their ways.

Tané had watched a woman in Cape Hisan embroidering a robe once. The needle dipping in and out, drawing the thread behind it, colors blooming on the silk. Inspired by the memory, Tané had imagined the power in the jewel as a needle, the water as the thread, and herself as a seamster of the sea. *Slowly*, the waves had leaned toward her and wrapped themselves around her legs.

Finally, one night, the jewel as bright as lightning in her grasp, she had hauled the sea onto the beach until there was no sand. It had mystified the scholars before it ebbed away.

That effort had left her almost insensible. But she knew now what she and the jewel could do.

When she had seen the Western ship, embattled by the storm, she had run straight to the cliffs. The great Kwiriki had sent her an opportunity, and she was ready, at last, to seize it.

The sea had answered her willingly this time. Though the ship had strained against it, she had succeeded in guiding it past the coral reef. Now it was almost unguarded in the shallows.

It was time to make her escape. She had wasted away for too long in this place. And she knew exactly where she would go. To the island of the mulberry tree, where the Golden Empress was headed with Nayimathun in the belly of her ship.

Tané hung her gourd of sweet water from her sash and made her way to the empty dining hall. The weapons were hidden beneath a floorboard, just as Elder Vara had said. She tucked the throwing knives into her sash, then took a Seiikinese sword and a dagger.

"I thought I might find you here."

Tané stilled.

"I knew you would try to leave. I saw it in your eyes when I told you about the Fleet of the Tiger Eye." Elder Vara kept his voice low. "You cannot master that ship alone, Tané. You would need a crew of hundreds."

"Or this."

She reached into her case and showed him the jewel, now dull. Elder Vara stared at it.

"The rising jewel of Neporo." His gaze was reverent. "In all my years, I never thought—"

He could not finish. "It was sewn into my side," Tané said quietly. "I have had it inside me my whole life."

"By the light of the great Kwiriki. For centuries Feather Island guarded the star chart to Komoridu, the resting place of the rising jewel," he murmured. "It seems it was never there."

"Do you know where the island is, Elder Vara?" Tané rose. "I meant to search the seas until I found the Golden Empress, but I will have more chance if I know where she is going."

"Tané," Elder Vara said, "you must not go there. Even if you did meet the Fleet of the Tiger Eye, there is no surety that the great Nayimathun is still alive. And if she is, you cannot take on the might of the pirate army to reclaim her. You would die in the attempt."

"I must try." Tané offered a faint smile. "Like the Little Shadow-girl. I took heart from that story, Elder Vara."

She could see the struggle in him.

"I understand," he finally said. "Miduchi Tané died when her dragon was taken. Since then, you have been her ghost. A vengeful ghost—restless, unable to move forward."

Heat pricked her eyes.

"Were I a younger or braver man, I might even have come with you. I would have risked anything," he said, "for my dragon."

Tané stared at him.

"You were a rider," she said.

"You would have known my name. Many years ago, I was called the Driftwood Prince."

One of the greatest dragonriders who had ever lived. Born to a Seiikinese courtier and a pirate from a far-off land, he had been left at the door of the South House and eventually risen to the ranks of the High Sea Guard. One night, he had fallen from his saddle in battle, breaking his leg, and the Fleet of the Tiger Eye had taken him as a hostage.

They had made a trophy of his leg that night. Legend said that they had thrown him into the sea for the bloodfish, but he had survived until dawn, when a friendly ship had found him.

"Now you know," Elder Vara said. "Some riders continue after such injuries, but the memory of it has scarred me. Each time I see a ship, I remember the sound of my bones shattering." A true smile creased his face. "Sometimes my dragon will still come this way. To see me."

Tané felt a surge of admiration such as she had never known.

"It has been peaceful here," she said, "but my blood is the sea, and it cannot be still."

"No. This place was never in your stars." The smile faded. "But perhaps Komoridu is."

He removed a scrap of paper, an inkpot, and a brush from his satchel.

"If the great Kwiriki is good to us, the Golden Empress will never reach Komoridu," he said. "But if she has pieced it together ... she may be almost there." He wrote the instructions. "You must sail east, to the constellation of the Magpie. At the ninth hour of night, make sure your ship is directly under the star representing his eye, and turn southeast. Sail for the midpoint between the South Star and the Dreaming Star."

Tané put the jewel away. "For how long?"

"The chart did not say—but in that direction, you will find Komoridu. Follow those two stars no matter where in the sky they drift. With the jewel, you might be able to catch the *Pursuit*."

"You will let me keep the jewel."

"It was given to you." He handed her the instructions. "Where will you go, Tané, once you find the great Nayimathun?"

She had not yet thought that far ahead. If her dragon was alive, she would free her from the pirates and take her to the Empire of the Twelve Lakes. If not, she would ensure she was avenged.

After that, she did not know what she would do. Only that she might be at peace.

Elder Vara seemed to know from her face that she could give him no answer. "I will send you away with my blessing, Tané, if you promise me one thing," he murmured. "That one day, you will forgive yourself. You are in the spring of your life, child, and have much to learn about this world. Do not deny yourself the privilege of living."

Her jaw trembled.

"Thank you. For everything." She bowed low. "I am honored to have been the student of the Driftwood Prince."

He returned the bow. "I am honored to have been your teacher, Tané." With that, he ushered her toward the doors. "Go, now. Before someone catches you."

The storm still raged around the island, though the thunder was more distant now. Rain drenched Tané as she swung along the rope bridges and picked her way to the hidden steps.

The village was silent. She crouched behind a fallen tree and watched for any movement. There was a flickering light in one of the old houses. A wind bell chimed outside it.

There were two lookouts. Too busy muttering and smoking to see her. She slipped past the buildings and ran over the stiltgrass, making for the stone-cut stair that would take her to the beach.

The steps flew beneath her boots. When she reached the bottom, she faced the sea.

Rowing boats had been pulled on to the sand. There would be more lookouts on the ship, but she could fight them. If she had to shed blood, so be it. She had already lost her honor, her name, and her dragon. There was nothing left to lose.

Tané turned and looked once more at Feather Island, her place of exile. One more home she had gained and lost. She must be destined to be rootless, like a seed tossed on the wind.

She ran and dived beneath the waves. The storm roiled the sea, but she knew how to survive its wrath.

Her heart was rising from the dead. She had worn armor to survive her exile, so thick she had almost forgotten how to feel. Now she savored the warm embrace of salt water, its tang in her mouth, the sense that she could be swept away if she put a hand or foot wrong.

When she came up for breath, she considered the ship. The sails were stowed. A white flag lashed at the stern, emblazoned with a sword and crown. That was the ensign of Inys, the richest nation in the West. Another great breath, and she was under again, deep beneath the waves.

The hull was close enough to touch. She waited for a swell to lift her and grabbed a rope that trailed down its side.

She knew ships. With the jewel as her crew, she could tame this wooden beast.

There was no one on the beach. Elder Vara had not betrayed her to the elders. In the morning, there would be no trace of the ghost she had become.

It was the wind chimes that kept Loth awake. They had not ceased to ring all night. On top of that, he was cold and salt-encrusted, surrounded by the smell and snores of unwashed pirates. Harlowe had told them all to get some sleep before they sought sweet water.

The captain himself had kept a vigil by the hearth. Loth watched the flames dance over his face. They brought out the white tattoo that snaked around his forearm and glinted on the locket he was studying.

Loth sat up and pulled on his shirt. Harlowe glanced at him, but said nothing as he left.

It was still raining outside. Melaugo, who was on watch, looked him up and down.

"Midnight stroll?"

"I'm afraid sleep eludes me." Loth buttoned his shirt. "I won't be long."

"Have you told your shadows?"

"I have not. And I would be grateful if you would leave them to rest."

"Well, they must be very tired in all that mail. Surprised they haven't rusted. I doubt these scholars are going to waylay you," Melaugo said, "but keep your eyes open. And take this." She tossed him her whistle. "We don't know their real feelings toward us."

Loth nodded. He coaxed his sore feet back into his boots.

He walked beneath the canopy of trees, following the few lanterns that still flickered, and took the stair to the beach again. His steps had never been so heavy. When he finally reached the bottom, he found a natural shelter and planted himself on the sand, wishing he had remembered his cloak.

If the storms continued, they might be marooned on this Saint-forsaken island for weeks, and time was running out. He could not fail Sabran now. Lightning splintered the darkness yet again as he pictured the fall of Inys—the certain outcome of his failure.

That was when he saw the woman.

She was halfway across the beach. In the instant she was illuminated, he saw a tunic of dark silk and a curved sword at her side. One smooth dive took her into the sea.

Loth flinched upright. He watched the waves for any sign of her, but no more lightning came.

There were two reasons he could imagine that one of the scholars would swim, under cover of night, to the *Rose Eternal*. One was to slaughter the outsiders, perhaps to prevent an outbreak of plague. The other was to steal the ship. Sanity told him to summon Harlowe, but nobody would hear the whistle over this wind.

Whatever this woman planned to do, he had to stop her.

His feet scuffed through sand. He lurched into the water. It was folly to plunge in when the waves were this rough, but there was no other way.

He swam beneath the arch. When they were children, he and Margret had sometimes paddled in Elsand Lake, but noblemen had little need to swim. On any other night, he might have been too frightened to attempt it.

A wave crashed over his head, thrusting him deep beneath the surface. He kicked hard and broke the surface, spluttering.

Shouts rose from the decks of the *Rose Eternal*. A whistle shrilled. His hands found the rope, then the laths of wood that served as a ladder.

Thim was crumpled by the mast. The woman in red silk was on the quarterdeck. Her sword clashed with that of the carpenter. Black hair whipped around her face.

Loth wavered, his empty hands clutching at air. Three parries and a slash, and the carpenter stumbled, blood on his tunic. The woman kicked him neatly over the gunwale. Another man hurled himself at her back, but she whirled out of his grip and threw him over her shoulder. A moment later, he had followed the carpenter into the sea.

"Stop," Loth shouted.

Her gaze snapped to him. In a blink, she had vaulted the balustrade and landed in a crouch.

Loth turned and ran. He could use a sword well enough, but this woman was no timid scholar. Whoever she was, she fought like the storm. Quick as lightning, lithe as water.

As his boots pounded across the deck, Loth snatched up an orphaned sword. Behind him, the woman unsheathed a knife. When he got to the prow, Loth scrambled on to the gunwale, teeth clenched, hands slippery with rainwater. He would jump before she reached him.

Something struck the base of his skull. He collapsed on to the deck, heavy as a sack of grain.

Hands took hold of him and turned him on to his back. The woman held her knife to his throat. As she did it, he caught sight of what was in her other hand.

It was identical in shape to the one Ead possessed, and glistered in the same unnatural way. Like moonlight on the sea.

"The other jewel," he whispered, and touched it with one finger. "How— how can you have it?"

Her eyes narrowed. She looked at the jewel, then at him. Then she glanced up, toward the sounds of shouting on the beach, and a mask of resolve dropped over her features.

That was the last thing Loth remembered. Her face, and its faint scar, shaped just like a fishhook.

60

East

In the Unending Sea, farther east than most ships dared to sail, and at the ninth hour of night, the *Pursuit* floated beneath the assembly of stars the Seiikinese had named the Magpie.

Padar, their navigator, had stayed true to his word. To him, the celestial bodies were pieces on the gameboard of the sky. No matter how and where they moved, he knew a way to read them. Despite the gyre, he had known well where this star would be at this hour, and how to get there. On the deck beside him, Niclays Roos waited.

Jan, he thought, *I'm almost there.*

Laya Yidagé stood with folded arms beside him. Beneath the shadow of her hood, her jaw had a grim set.

The Southern Star twinkled. Watched by her crew, the Golden Empress rotated the wheel and, as the sails netted the wind, the *Pursuit* began to turn.

"Onward," she called, and her pirates took up the cry. Niclays felt their joy magnified in his own heart.

Onward indeed, to where the maps ended. To the mulberry tree, and to wonders untold.

61

East

When he woke, the cold was brutal, and the sky wore the sickly purple of dusk, casting everything into shadow. It took Loth a moment to realize he was bound.

Spray dampened his face. His head pounded horribly, and his senses were sludge.

He blinked the fur of exhaustion away. In the dim glow of the lanterns, he made out a figure at the helm of the *Rose Eternal*.

"Captain Harlowe?"

No reply. When his vision sharpened, he saw that it was the woman from Feather Island.

No.

They had no time to go off-course. He struggled against his restraints, but there was enough rope around him to hang a giant. Beside him, Thim was also trussed to the mast. Loth nudged him with his shoulder.

"Thim," he whispered.

The gunner did not answer. A bruise was forming on his temple.

Loth turned his head and took their captor in. She was about twenty, perhaps a touch younger, leanly built. Short black hair framed a tanned and windburned face.

"Who are you?" Loth called to her. His throat scorched with thirst. "Why have you taken this ship?"

She ignored him.

"I hope you realize that you have committed an act of *piracy*, mistress," Loth bit out. "Turn back at once, or I shall take this as a declaration of war on Queen Sabran of Inys."

Nothing.

Whoever this silent vagabond was, she had the other jewel. Fate had brought it into his path.

A hand-length case, painted with flowers, hung from a sash at her hip. That must be where she kept it.

Loth dozed for a time. Thirst and exhaustion pulled at him, and one side of his head was pounding. Sometime in the night, he blinked awake and found a gourd at his lips. He drank without question.

Thim, too, was now alert. The woman let him drink and spoke to him in a foreign tongue.

"Thim," Loth muttered, "do you understand her?"

The other man was blear-eyed. "Yes, my lord. She's Seiikinese," he said slowly. "She asks how you know about the jewel."

She stayed crouched in front of them, watching their faces. In the glow of the lantern she had brought with her, Loth could make out the scar on her cheek. "Tell her I know where its twin is," he said. He looked the woman in the eye as Thim translated, and she replied.

"She says that if that is true," Thim said, "you will be able to tell her what color it is."

"White."

When Thim conveyed the words to her, she leaned toward Loth and took hold of his throat.

"Where?" she asked.

So she did speak a little Inysh. Her voice was as cold as her cast-iron expression.

"Inys," he said.

Her mouth pinched shut. A fine-cut mouth that looked as if it seldom smiled.

"You must give the jewel to me," Loth beseeched her. "I have to take it to Queen Sabran, to reunite it with its twin. Together, they can be used to destroy the Nameless One. He will rise again soon, in a matter of weeks. He will come from the Abyss."

Frowning, Thim passed his words to the woman in Seiikinese. Her face hardened before she stood and left them.

"Wait," Loth called after her, frustrated. "For the love of the Saint, did you not hear what I said?"

"We should not provoke her, Lord Arteloth," Thim warned. "The rest of the crew could be stranded on Feather Island for weeks, if not months, without a ship. We are now the only ones who can take word of Queen Sabran's proposal to His Imperial Majesty."

He was right. Their plan was at the mercy of this pirate. Loth sank into his bindings.

Thim tipped back his head and squinted. It took a moment for Loth to realize that he was reading the stars.

"Impossible," Thim murmured. "We cannot have got this far east in so little time."

Loth watched the woman. One of her hands was on the wheel. The other now held a dark stone. For the first time, he became aware of the unbroken roar of water against the ship.

She was using the jewel to drive the *Rose* forward.

"My lord," Thim said under his breath, "I think I know where we are going."

"Tell me."

"We heard a rumor at sea that the Golden Empress—leader of the Fleet of the Tiger Eye—was sailing east in pursuit of the elixir of life. Her butcher-ship, the *Pursuit*, left Kawontay not long ago. They were bound for the Unending Sea."

"What is the Fleet of the Tiger Eye?"

"The largest pirate fleet in existence. They steal and slaughter dragons when they can." Thim glanced at the woman. "If she is chasing the Golden Empress—and I cannot think why else we would be this far east—then we are both dead men."

Loth eyed her. "She seems a very good fighter."

"One fighter cannot best hundreds of pirates, and not even the *Rose* stands a chance against the *Pursuit*. It is a fortress on the sea." Thim swallowed. "We might be able to take the ship back."

"How?"

"Well, when she leaves it, my lord. A man-of-war needs a vast crew, but ... I suppose we have no choice but to try."

They lapsed into silence for a while. All Loth could hear was the crash of the waves.

"Seeing as we have nothing better to do but wait, perhaps we could play a game." He offered the gunner a tired smile. "Are you good at riddles, Thim?"

The stars burned like a host of candles. Tané kept her gaze on them as she steered the Inysh ship, using the west wind as well as the jewel to spur it.

The Inysh lord and the Lacustrine gunner were finally asleep. For quarter of an hour, the former had been straining to solve the easiest of riddles, making Tané grind her teeth in irritation.

I close in the morning, I open at night,
And when I am open, your eye I delight.
I am pale as the moon and live only as long —
For when the sun rises, behold, I am gone.

At least now he had stopped blathering about how clever it was, and she could think. If she timed this right, she would be under the eye of the Magpie tonight.

Using the jewel had left a fine sheen of cold sweat on her. She breathed slow and deep. Though it never drained her strength for long, she sensed that the jewel was drawing on something in her. She was the string, and the jewel was the bow, and only together could they make the ocean sing.

"Loth."

Startled, Tané glanced across the deck. The Inysh man was awake once more.

"Loth," he repeated, and tapped his own chest.

Tané looked back at the stars.

In the South House, she had learned some of every language in the known world. She knew Inysh well enough, but she preferred that the strangers thought otherwise, lulling them into the false belief that they could speak freely.

"May I ask your name?" the Inysh man said.

Great Kwiriki, wash away this fool. Still, he knew about the waning jewel—that was reason enough to keep him alive.

"Tané," she finally said.

"Tané."

He said it gently. She stared him out.

Though he could be no more than thirty, and though he looked presently as if a smile had never been further from his face, there were already laugh lines around his full lips. His skin was the same deep brown as his eyes, which were large and full of warmth. His nose was broad, his jaw strong and unshaven, and his black hair puffed in small, tight curls.

She had the sense that he was kind.

Straight away, she shook off the thought. He hailed from a land that spat on her gods.

"If you cut me loose," Loth said, "perhaps I can help you. You'll have to stop in a day or two. To sleep."

"You misjudge how long I can last without sleep."

He raised his eyebrows. "You do speak Inysh."

"Enough."

The Westerner looked as if he might speak again, but seemed to think better of it. He leaned against the gunner and closed his eyes.

She would have to question him sooner or later. If he knew where the other jewel was, then it had to be returned to dragonkind—but first, she needed to reach Nayimathun.

When Loth finally dozed off, Tané took stock of the stars and turned the wheel. The jewel was like ice in her hand. If she continued like this, she would soon be in Komoridu.

She drank a little from her gourd and blinked the dryness from her eyes.

All she had to do was stay awake.

———

The Unending Sea was an exquisite sapphire blue that turned almost to violet when the sun set. There were no birds in the sky, and emptiness as far as the eye could see.

It was this emptiness that concerned Niclays. The fabled isle of Komoridu had yet to show itself.

He gulped from his flask of rose wine. The pirates had been generous tonight. Their leader had made it clear to them that if they found the riches of the world, they would owe it to the Master of Recipes.

And if they failed to find anything, all of them would know who was to blame.

Death had never held much power over him. He thought of it as he did an old friend that would one day knock again on his door.

For years, he had sought to make the elixir of immortality in the spirit of discovery. He had never meant to drink it. Death, after all, would either end the pain of grief or reunite him with Jannart in whichever afterlife proved to be the right one. Each day, each step, each tick of the clock took him closer to that golden possibility. He was tired of having half a soul.

Yet now death loomed, he did fear it. His hands shook as he gulped more wine. It occurred to him briefly that he ought to stop drinking, to keep his wits about him, but even sober, he would never be able to fight off a pirate. Best he was benumbed.

The ship kept cleaving through the water. Night painted darkness overhead. Soon enough, he was out of wine. He dropped the flask into the sea and watched it bob away.

"Niclays."

Laya was hurrying up the stairs, clutching her shawl around herself. She took him by the arm.

"They've seen something ahead," she said, eyes bright with dread or excitement. "The lookouts."

"What sort of something?"

"Land."

Niclays stared in disbelief. Breathless, he followed her to the prow of the ship, where the Golden Empress stood with Padar.

"You are in luck, Roos," the former said.

She handed him her nightglass. Niclays squinted into it.

An island. Unquestionably. A small one, almost certainly uninhabited, but an island nonetheless. He breathed out as he handed the nightglass back.

"I am glad to see it, all-honored Golden Empress," he said frankly.

She beheld the island with a hunter's intent. As she turned to one of her officers, Niclays glanced at the notches on her wooden arm.

"She's signaling to the *Black Dove* to circle the island," Laya murmured. "The High Sea Guard could still be on our tail. Or rumors could have reached another pirate ship of our quest."

"Surely no pirate captain would be fool enough to confront a ship like this."

"The world is full of fools, Niclays. And they are never more foolish than when they smell eternal life."

Sabran could attest to that.

So could Jannart.

Niclays tapped his fingers on the gunwale. As the island came closer, his mouth turned dry as ashes.

"Come, Roos," the Golden Empress said. Her voice was velvet soft. "You ought to share in the first spoils. After all, you brought us here."

He dared not argue.

When they were anchored, the Golden Empress addressed her pirates. This island, she told them, was home to a bounty that would lay waste to their troubles. The elixir would make them all-powerful. They would be masters of the sea. Her people roared and stamped their feet until Niclays was brittle with fear. They might be triumphant now, but one sniff of failure, one whisper that they had come all this way for nothing, and their joy would turn to murderous ire.

A boat was readied for the scouting party. Laya and Niclays joined the twenty members of the crew, including the Golden Empress, who would set foot on the island before anyone else, and Ghonra, her heir. Though Niclays supposed she would never need an heir if they did find the elixir.

The rowing boat glided out of the shadow of the *Pursuit*. It soon became apparent to Niclays that what they could see of the island was only the pinnacle of it. Much of the rest had been claimed by the sea.

When they could go no farther, they left two of their number with the boat and waded the rest of the way. Niclays stepped onto dry land and wrung the water from his shirt.

This place might be his grave. He had imagined being folded into the dirt of Orisima. Instead, his bones would lie on a hidden island in the vastness of a far-off sea.

Drunkenness made him slow. When Ghonra looked over her shoulder and arched an eyebrow at him, he took a deep breath and trudged after her, up a hummock of slippery rock.

Their footsteps took them into the darkness of a forest. The only hint of civilization was the stone bridge they used to cross a stream. He made out a flight of steps, scarped into the rock. The Golden Empress was the first to mount it.

They climbed the stair for what seemed like hours. It snaked between endless maple and fir trees.

There were no dwellings here. No guardians of the mulberry tree. Just nature, given leave to run its course for centuries. Wasps droned and birds chirruped. A hart bounded across their path and back into the gloaming, startling half the pirates into drawing their swords.

Niclays panted. Sweat drenched his shirt. He mopped his brow fruitlessly as rivulets trickled down his brow. It had been a long time since he had exerted himself like this.

"Niclays," Laya said under her breath. "Are you all right?"

"Dying," he gritted out. "By the grace of the Damsel, I'll expire before we reach the top."

He only realized they had stopped when he walked headlong into Ghonra, who knocked him back with a pointy elbow to the gut. Legs trembling, Niclays looked up to behold a tree. A gnarled and ancient mulberry, larger than any tree he had ever laid eyes on.

Cut down.

Niclays stared at the fallen giant. The feeling bled from his legs. His lips began to shake, and his eyes grew hot.

He was here. At the end of the Way of the Outcasts. This was what Jannart had wanted to see, the secret he had died for. Niclays was standing in the realization of his dream.

His faithless dream.

The mulberry tree bore no flower or fruit. It looked almost grotesque in its mass, stretched beyond its natural proportions, like a body pulled upon a rack. Its trunk was as thick as a baleen. In death, its branches reached for the stars, as if they might hold out silver hands and help it stand again.

The Golden Empress walked slowly among its dead limbs. Laya took Niclays by the arm. He felt her shivering and found himself pressing his hand over hers.

"Yidagé, Roos," the Golden Empress called, "come here."

Laya closed her eyes.

"It's all right." Niclays kept his voice low. "She won't hurt you, Laya. You're too useful to her."

"I have no wish to watch her hurt you."

"I am deeply hurt by how little faith you have in my capacity for battle, Mistress Yidagé." He held up his cane with a weak smile. "I can take them all with this, don't you think?"

She choked back a laugh.

"There are words carved here," the Golden Empress said to Laya, when they were near. "Translate them."

Her face betrayed nothing. Laya let go of Niclays and stepped over a branch and crouched beside the trunk. One of the pirates handed her a torch, and she held it carefully toward the tree. The flames shed light on a cascade of carved words.

"Forgive me, all-honored Golden Empress, but I cannot translate this. Bits of it are familiar, but much of it is not," Laya said. "I fear it is beyond the realm of my knowledge."

"Perhaps I can."

Niclays glanced over his shoulder. The Seiikinese scholar, the one who was never far from the Golden Empress, laid a withered hand on the trunk as if it were the earthly remains of an old friend.

"The torch, if you please," he said. "This will not take long."

There was no moonlight to betray the Western ship. From high in its yards, Tané watched the pirates go ashore.

The *Rose Eternal* was anchored where the pirates could not see. After she had turned the ship southeast at the right moment, they had sailed until her nightglass revealed an island.

Elder Vara believed the rising jewel had come from here. Perhaps this place held the secret of why it had been in her side—or perhaps not. What mattered was Nayimathun.

The wind blew strands of hair across her face. She knew these ships from her days in the South House, where she had learned to identify the most notorious vessels in the Fleet of the Tiger Eye. Both carried the red sails of sickness. The *Black Dove*, which was half the length of the *Pursuit*, was circling the island with its gun ports open.

Tané descended to the deck. She had freed her two captives so they might help her.

"You," Tané said to Thim. "While I am gone, guard the ship."

Thim watched her. "Where are you going?"

"To the *Pursuit*."

"They will tear you apart."

"Help me survive, and I will see to it that you get to the Empire of the Twelve Lakes in one piece. Betray me, and I will leave you here to die," Tané said. "The choice is yours."

"Who *are* you?" Thim asked, frowning. "You fight better than any soldier. None of the crew stood a chance against you. Why were you drafted into the ranks of the scholars, and not the Miduchi?"

Tané handed him the nightglass.

"If they see you," was all she said, "fire one of the cannons as a warning."

But Thim had realized. She watched the deference rise into his eyes. "You *were* Miduchi." Thim studied her face. "Why were you banished?"

"Who I am and who I was are none of your concern." She nodded to Loth. "You. Come with me."

"Into the sea?" Loth stared at her. "We'll freeze."

"Not if we keep moving."

"What do you mean to do on that ship?"

"Free a prisoner."

Tané braced herself before she climbed down the side of the ship, shivering in the chill. Then she let go.

Her body plunged into darkness. The cold knocked the breath from her, bubbles exploding from her lips.

It was worse than she had expected. She had swum every day in Seiiki, whatever the season, but the Sundance Sea had never been this frigid. When she surfaced, her breath came in white puffs. Behind her, Loth made wordless sounds of discomfort. He was at the bottom of the slats.

"Just jump," Tané forced out. "It will b-be over sooner."

Loth squeezed his eyes shut, and his face took on the forbearance of a man who had consigned himself to death before he let go. He sank and surfaced in an instant, gasping.

"*Saint*—" His teeth chattered. "It's f-freezing."

"Then you will need to hurry," Tané said, and swam.

The lanterns on the *Pursuit* were extinguished. The ship was so tall that Tané had little fear of the lookouts. They would never see two heads in the dark water. After all, these nine-masted treasure galleons were larger than any other ship in the world. More than large enough to hold a dragon.

Movement was difficult. The cold stiffened her joints. Tané sucked in a breath and went below the waves again. When she came up beside the *Pursuit*, Loth was close behind, shivering uncontrollably. She had meant to crawl in through the gun ports, but they were closed, and there were no obvious handholds.

The anchor. It was the only link between the water and the deck. She swam beside the hull until she reached the stern.

Salt water mingled with sweat as she lifted herself from the sea and climbed. She could hear Loth struggling up behind her. Every inch of progress felt hard-won. Each limb was fighting to remember its strength.

Close to the top, she lost her grip.

It happened too fast for her to so much as take a breath, let alone scream. One moment she was rising; the next, falling—then she hit something warm and solid. She looked down to see Loth below her. Her foot had landed on his shoulder.

She could tell he was straining to hold them both up, but he smiled. Tané looked away and kept climbing.

Her arms were trembling by the time she reached the defaced carving of the great Imperial Dragon at the stern of the ship. She climbed around it, pulled herself over the side, and landed, light-footed, on the deck. The Golden Empress would be on the island, but she would have left guards behind.

Keeping low, Tané wrung the icy water from her tunic. Loth fell into a crouch beside her. She could just make out the silhouettes of the hundreds of pirates left on board.

The *Pursuit* was a lawless city on the sea. Like all pirate ships, it absorbed miscreants from many parts of the world. In this darkness, provided no one stopped them, they might be able to blend in. Three flights of steps would take them to the lowest deck on the ship.

She straightened and walked out from their hiding place. Loth followed her, keeping his head down.

Pirates surrounded them. Tané could hardly see any of their faces. She heard strains of their conversations.

"—gut the old man if he's betrayed us."

"He's no fool. What purpose would there be in—?"

"He's Mentish. The Seiikinese would have kept him cooped up like a songbird in Orisima," a woman said. "Perhaps he would take death over imprisonment. Like the rest of us."

Roos.

There was no other Ment they could be talking about.

Her fingertips grew hot. She itched to wrap her hands around his throat.

It was not Roos's fault that she had been sent to Feather Island. She alone was to blame for that. Yet he had blackmailed her. He had dared to ask her to hurt Nayimathun. Now he was abetting the pirates who took and slaughtered dragons. For all those things, he deserved death.

She tried to quash the desire for it. There could be no distractions here.

They slipped into the stairway that would take them to the hull. At the bottom, one lantern flickered. Its flame revealed two scarred pirates, both armed with pistols and swords. Tané walked toward them.

"Who goes there?" one of them asked roughly.

One shout would draw a throng of pirates from above. She would have to kill them, and in silence.

Like water.

Her knife slid through the shadows, straight into a beating heart. Before the other guard could react, she had slit his throat. The look in his eyes was like nothing Tané had ever seen. The shock. The realization of his mortality. The reduction of his being to the wetness at his neck. A wordless sound came bubbling from his lips, and he crumpled at her feet.

The taste of iron filled her mouth. She watched the blood throb out of him, black in the lanternlight.

"Tané," Loth said.

Her skin was as chill as the sword in her hand.

"Tané." His voice was hoarse. "Please. We must hurry."

Two corpses lay before her. Her stomach roiled, and blackness hit her like a cloud of flies.

She had killed. Not the way she had killed Susa. This time, she had taken life with her own hand.

Dizzy, she raised her head. Loth removed the lantern that hung above the bodies and held it out to her. She took it, hand unsteady, and walked into the innards of the ship.

She could ask forgiveness from the great Kwiriki in good time. For now, she must find Nayimathun.

At first, all she could see were supplies. Barrels of water. Sacks of rice and millet. Chests that must be filled with plunder. When she caught a glimpse of green, she let out a breath.

Nayimathun.

She was still breathing. Chains held her down, and a wound had festered where scale had been torn from her flesh, but she was breathing.

Loth drew a sign on his chest. He looked as if he had seen his own doom.

Tané sank to her knees before the god who had once been her kin, abandoning her sword and lantern.

"Nayimathun."

No answer. Tané tried to swallow the thickness in her throat. Her eyes brimmed as she took in the damage the chains had wreaked.

A tear ran to her jaw. She boiled with loathing. No one with a soul could do this to a living thing. No one with a shred of shame could treat a god this way. Dragons had sacrificed so much to protect the mortals who shared their world. In return, mortals gave only malice and greed.

Nayimathun kept breathing. Tané stroked a hand down her snout, where the scales were dry as cuttlebone. It was unspeakably cruel of them to have kept her out of water for this long.

"Great Nayimathun." She whispered it. "Please. It's me. It's Tané. Let me take you home."

One eye peeled open. The blue in it was dim, like the last glow of a long-dead star.

"Tané."

She had never truly believed she would hear that voice again.

"Yes." Another tear dribbled down her cheek. "Yes, great Nayimathun. I am here."

"You came," Nayimathun said. Her breaths were labored. "You should not have come."

"I should have come sooner." Tané lowered her head. "Forgive me. For letting them take you."

"Someone took you first," the dragon growled. A tooth was missing from her lower jaw. "You are hurt."

"This is not my blood." With unsteady hands, Tané opened the case at her hip and fumbled out the jewel. "I found one of the jewels you spoke about, Nayimathun. It was sewn into my side." She held it out so the dragon could see it. "This Westerner claims he knows the one who has its twin."

Nayimathun looked for a long time at the jewel, then at Loth, who was shaking in his boots.

"We can speak of this when we are in a safe place," she said, "but by finding these jewels, you have given us a way to fight the Nameless One. For this, Tané, every dragon that draws breath is in your debt." A faint light rippled through her scales. "I am still

661

strong enough to break through the hull, but I must be free. You will need the key to my chains."

"Tell me who has it."

The dragon closed her eyes again.

"The Golden Empress," she said.

62

East

The scholar was surrounded by flaming torches. It seemed to Niclays as if he had been circling the mulberry tree for hours, reading by firelight. During that time, hardly a word had passed between any of the pirates.

When the scholar finally straightened, every head flicked up. The Golden Empress was sitting nearby, sharpening her sword with one hand while her wooden arm weighted it in place. Each rasp of the whetstone down the blade cut Niclays to the quick.

"I am finished," the scholar said.

"Good." The Golden Empress did not deign to look up. "Tell us what you have learned."

Trying not to breathe too hard, Niclays reached into his cloak for his handkerchief and mopped his brow.

"This is written in an ancient script of Seiiki," the scholar said. "It tells the story of a woman named Neporo. She lived over a thousand years ago on this island. Komoridu."

"We are all eager to hear it," the Golden Empress said.

The scholar glanced up at the mulberry tree. Something about his expression still did not sit well with Niclays.

"Neporo lived in the fishing village of Ampiki. She made a paltry living as a pearl-diver, but despite her work, and that of her parents, her family had so little to live on that on some days, they had no choice but to eat leaves and soil from the forest floor."

This was why Niclays had never understood Jannart's obsession. History was miserable.

"When her younger sister died, Neporo decided to end the suffering. She would dive for rare golden pearls in the Unending Sea, where other pearl-divers dared not go. The water there was too cold, too rough—but Neporo saw no other choice. She rowed her little boat out from Ampiki, into the open sea. As she dived, a great typhoon blew away her boat, leaving her stranded among the unforgiving waves.

"Somehow she kept her head above water. With no idea how to read the stars, she could only swim for the brightest in the sky. Finally, she washed up on an island. She found it devoid of human life—but in a clearing, she beheld a mulberry tree of marvelous height. Weak with hunger, she ate of its fruit." He traced some of the words with one finger. "Neporo was *drunk on the thousand-flower wine*. In ancient times, this was a poetic description for the elixir of life."

The Golden Empress continued to sharpen her sword.

"Neporo finally escaped the island and returned home. For ten years, she tried to lead an ordinary life—she wed a kind painter and had a child with him. But her friends and neighbors noticed that she did not age, did not grow weak or sick. Some called her a goddess. Others feared her. Eventually, she left Seiiki and returned to Komoridu, where no one could look upon her as an abomination. The burden of immortality was so great that she considered taking her own life, but for her son, she chose to live."

"The tree granted her immortality," the Golden Empress said, still whetting the blade, "yet she believed herself able to take her own life."

"The tree had granted her protection only from old age. She could still be hurt or killed by other means." The scholar glanced at the tree. "Over the years, many followed Neporo to her island. Black doves and white crows flew to her, for she was mother to the outcasts."

Laya tightened her grip on Niclays, and he tightened his on her.

"We should leave," she breathed against his ear. "Niclays, the tree is dead. There is no elixir."

664

Niclays swallowed. The Golden Empress seemed absorbed; he could slip away unnoticed.

And yet he found himself rooted to the spot, unable to stop listening to the story of Neporo.

"Wait," he said out of the corner of his mouth.

"Around the time the Dreadmount erupted," the scholar continued, "Neporo received two gifts from a dragon. They were called the celestial jewels—and with them, the dragon told Neporo that she would be able to lock the Beast of the Mountain away for a thousand years."

"Answer me this," Padar cut in. "Why did the dragon need to ask a human for help?"

"The tree does not say," came the calm reply. "Though Neporo was willing to stand, she could only control one of the jewels. She needed someone else to wield the second. That was when a miracle came. A princess of the South arrived on the shores of Komoridu. Her name was Cleolind."

Niclays exchanged a stunned glance with Laya. The prayer books said nothing about this.

"Cleolind also possessed eternal life. She had vanquished the Nameless One before, but believed his wounds would soon heal. Determined to end him once and for all, she had gone in search of others who might be able to help her. Neporo was her last hope." The scholar paused to wet his lips. "Cleolind, Princess of Lasia, took up the waning jewel. Neporo, Queen of Komoridu, took up its twin. Together, they sealed the Nameless One in the Abyss—binding him for a thousand years, but not one sunrise more."

Niclays found himself unable to shut his jaw.

Because if this tale was true, then the founding legend of the House of Berethnet was nonsense. It was not a line of daughters that kept the Nameless One chained, but two jewels.

Oh, Sabran was going to be *most* upset.

"Cleolind had been weakened by her first encounter with the Nameless One. Facing him a second time destroyed her. Neporo returned the body to the South, along with the waning jewel."

"And the other jewel—the rising jewel." The Golden Empress spoke softly. "What became of it?"

The scholar placed a bony hand on the tree again.

"A section of the story is lost," he said. Niclays saw that the bark had been viciously hacked. "Fortunately, we can read the end."

"And?"

"It seems that somebody wanted the jewel for themselves. To keep it safe, a descendant of Neporo stitched the rising jewel into his own side, so it might never be taken from him. He left Komoridu and started a humble life in Ampiki, in the same pit-house Neporo had once lived in. When he died, it was taken from his body and placed into that of his daughter. And so on." Pause. "The jewel lives in a descendant of Neporo."

The Golden Empress looked up from her sword. Niclays listened to his own heartbeat.

"This tree is dead," she said, "and the jewel is gone. What does this mean for us?"

"Even if it had not died, it says here that the tree only granted immortality to the very first person who ate of its fruit. After that, it withheld the gift of eternal life," the scholar murmured. "I am sorry, all-honored one. We are centuries too late. There is nothing on this island but ghosts."

Niclays began to feel very sick. The feeling intensified when the Golden Empress rose, her gaze pinned to his face.

"All-honored captain," he said tremulously, "I brought you to the right place. Did I not?"

She walked toward him, sword held loosely in her hand. He grasped his cane until his knuckles blanched.

"Your prize may not be lost. Jannart had other books, in Mentendon," he pleaded, but his voice was cracking. "For the love of the Saint, I was *not* the one who gave you the bloody map in the first place—"

"Indeed," said the Golden Empress, "but it was you who brought me here, on this futile pursuit."

"No. Wait— I can make you an elixir from the dragon's scale, I am *sure* of it. Let me help you—"

She kept coming.

That was when Laya seized Niclays by the arm. His cane fell as she hauled him into the trees.

Her sudden move had taken the pirates by surprise. Ignoring the stairs, she crashed through the undergrowth, dragging Niclays with her. Behind them, the scouting party bellowed their fury. Terrible as the horn before the hunt.

"Laya," Niclays gasped out, "this is very heroic, but my knees will never outrun a pack of bloodthirsty pirates."

"Your knees will manage, Old Red, or you will not have knees," Laya called back. Her voice had a razor edge of panic, but there was laughter there, too. "We're going to beat them to the boat."

"They left guards!"

As she dropped to a lower scarp of rock, Laya grasped the dagger in her belt with one hand. "What?" she said, extending the other hand to him. "Do you think all this time on pirate ships has taught me nothing about fighting?"

Niclays hit the ground with knee-jarring force. Laya pulled him down against a tree.

They lay still in the hollow of the tree. His knees screamed, and his ankle throbbed. Three pirates ran past them. As soon as they had disappeared into the foliage, Laya was on her feet again, helping Niclays up.

"Stay with me, Old Red." She kept a firm hold of his hand. "Come on. We're going home."

Home.

They forged on, slithering where the mud was slack, and running when they could. Before Niclays knew it, the beach was in sight. And there was the rowing boat, with only two guards.

They were going to make it. They would row northward until they reached the Empire of the Twelve Lakes, and from there they would cast off from the East once and for all.

Laya let go of his hand, drew her dagger, and ran across the sand, cloak billowing behind her. She was fast. Before she could strike at the first guard, hands fell upon Niclays. The pirates had caught up with them. "Laya," he shouted, but it was too late. They had her. She cried out as Ghonra twisted her arm.

Padar forced Niclays to his knees. "Padar, Ghonra," Laya pleaded, "don't do this. We've known each other so long. Please, have mercy—"

"You know us better than that." Ghonra wrenched the knife from her hand and held it to her throat. "I gave this blade to you," she bit out, "as a kindness, Yidagé. Beg again, and it will have your tongue."

Laya clamped her mouth shut. Niclays wanted desperately to tell her it was all right, to look away, to say nothing. Anything so they might not kill her, too.

His bladder was threatening to give out. Clenching every muscle in his body, he tried to divorce his mind from his flesh. To float away from himself, into memory.

He quaked as the Golden Empress, unperturbed by the fleeting chase, crouched in front of him. And he imagined himself as a notch on her arm.

And he realized.

He wanted to feel the sun on his face. He wanted to read books and walk through the cobbled streets of Brygstad. He wanted to listen to music, to visit museums and art galleries and theatres, to marvel at the beauty of human creation. He wanted to travel to the South and the North and drink in all they had to offer. He wanted to laugh again.

He wanted to *live*.

"I brought my crew over two seas," the Golden Empress said to him, so softly only he could hear, "for nothing but a story. They will need someone to blame for this disappointment—and I assure you, Master of Recipes, that it will not be me. Unless you would like Yidagé to take the fall on your behalf, it must be you." She touched him under the chin with her knife. "They may not kill you. But I think you will be pleading for that mercy."

Her face blurred. Close by, Ghonra gripped Laya by the throat, poised to spill her life.

"I can find some means of making it her fault." The Golden Empress looked at her interpreter, who had sailed with her for decades, without remorse. "Lies cost nothing, after all."

Once, Niclays had allowed a young musician to be tortured to spare himself the same fate. The act of a man who had forgotten how to serve anyone but himself. If he was to die with any pride, he would not let Laya suffer for him any more than she had already.

"You will do no such thing," he said quietly.

Laya shook her head. Her face crumpled into a look of grief.

"Take him back to the *Pursuit*, and tell the crew what we found." The Golden Empress rose. "Let us see what they will—"

She stopped. Niclays looked up.

The Golden Empress dropped her blade. A curved sword was across her throat, and Tané Miduchi was standing behind her.

Niclays could hardly believe who he was seeing. He gaped at the woman he had tried to blackmail.

"You," he stammered.

Wherever she had been, the last few months had not been kind to her. She was thinner, her eyes smeared with shadow. Fresh blood on her hands. "Give me the key," she said in Lacustrine, her voice deep and thick with hatred. "The key for the chains."

None of the pirates moved. Their captain was just as still, her eyebrows raised.

"Now," the dragonrider said, "or your leader dies." Her hand was steady. "The key."

"Somebody give it to her," the Golden Empress said, sounding almost irritated by this interruption. "If she wants her beast, let her take it."

Ghonra stepped forward. If her adoptive mother died here, she would be the next Golden Empress, but Niclays had sensed a filial loyalty from her. She reached under her collar and held up a bronze key.

"No," the dragonrider said. "The key is made of iron." The blade drew blood. "Take me for a fool again, and she dies."

Ghonra smirked. She produced another key and tossed it.

"For you, dragon-lover," she purred. "Best of luck getting back to the ship."

"Let me leave unharmed, and I may not have to use this."

The dragonrider threw the Golden Empress aside and held up her free hand. In it was a jewel the size of a walnut, blue as smalt.

Surely not.

Niclays started to laugh. A climbing, unhinged sort of laugh.

"The rising jewel," the scholar breathed, staring. "You. *You* are the descendant of Neporo."

The dragonrider stared back in silence.

Tané Miduchi. Heir of the Queen of Komoridu. Heir to an empty rock and a dead tree. It was clear from her expression that she had no idea. Riders were often taken from deprived homes. She must have been separated from her family before they could tell her the truth.

"Take my friend with you," Niclays said to her suddenly, hot tears of laughter still in his eyes. He nodded to Laya, whose lips were moving in prayer. "I beg you, Lady Tané. She is innocent in all of this."

"For you," the dragonrider said, with the utmost contempt, "I do *nothing*."

"And what of me?" the Golden Empress asked. "Do you not wish me dead, rider?"

The younger woman clenched her jaw. Her fingers wrung the hilt of her sword.

"Come. I am old and slow, child. You can put an end to the slaughter of dragons, here and now." The Golden Empress tapped the flat of her own blade against her palm. "Cut my throat. Earn back your honor."

With a cold smile, the dragonrider closed her fist around the rising jewel.

"I will not kill you this night, butcher," she said, "but what you see before you is a ghost. When you least expect it, I will return to haunt you. I will hunt you to the ends of the earth. And I vow to you that if we meet again, I will turn the sea red."

She sheathed her sword and walked into the darkness. With her walked the only chance of escape.

That was when one of the pirates fired his pistol after her.

Tané Miduchi stopped. Niclays saw her fist tighten around the jewel, and he felt the slightest tremor.

A wet roar filled the sky. Laya screamed. Niclays barely had time to look up, and to stare at the wall of water that was churning up the beach, before it swept them all into icy darkness.

Niclays went head over heels. His nostrils burned as he breathed salt water straight into his chest. Blind with dread, he grappled with the flood, bubbles swarming from his mouth. All he could see was his hands. When he broke the surface, his eyeglasses were lost.

From what little he could make out, the pirates had been flung far and wide, the boat that had brought them here was empty, and Tané Miduchi had disappeared.

"Find her," the Golden Empress roared. Niclays coughed up water. "Back to the ship. Bring me that jewel!"

The sea withdrew in a rush, as if sucked into the belly of a god. Niclays found himself on all fours on the sand, spluttering, hair dripping into his eyes.

A sword lay before him. His hand closed around it. If he could find Laya, they still had a chance. They could fight their way on to the boat and be gone . . .

As he called her name, he became aware of a shadow. He raised the sword, but the Golden Empress knocked it away.

A flash of steel, and another.

Blood on the sand.

A frothing gargle escaped him. He buckled, one hand locked over his throat. The other hand was gone. Somewhere in the chaos, Laya was shouting his name.

"My crew must have flesh." The Golden Empress scooped up his hand as if it were a dead fish. He retched at the sight of it. Still flushed with life. Liver-spotted with his years. "Consider this mercy. I would take the rest of you, but my cargo is in danger, and carrying you would slow us down. You understand, Roos. You know good business."

Darkness pumped from the screaming mouth of his arm. The pain was like nothing he had ever felt. Boiling oil. A sun in the stump. He would never hold a quill in this hand again. That was all he could think, even as his lifeblood welled from his throat. Then Laya was at his side, pressing the wound.

"Hold on," she said, voice cracking. "Hold on, Niclays." She gathered him close. "I'm here. I'm going to stay with you. You are going to sleep in Mentendon, not here. Not now. I promise."

A ringing drowned her words. Just before his world turned black, he looked toward the sky and saw, at last, the form of death.

Death, as it turned out, had wings.

The *Pursuit* was such an enormous ship that the waves hardly disturbed it. One could almost dream that it was not on water at all. Loth sat in its hull, listening to the commotion on the deck, all too aware that he was deep inside a nest of criminals. He dared not let go of his baselard, but he had doused the lantern, just in case. It was a miracle that no one had come down here yet. Tané had been gone for what felt like an eternity.

The wyrm—no, *dragon*—observed him with a fearsome blue eye. Loth looked staunchly at the floor.

It was true that this creature did not look, or act, like the Draconic beasts of the West, though it was just as large. The horns were not unlike those of a High Western, but that was where the similarities ended. A mane like riverweed flowed down its neck. Its face was broad, its eyes round as bucklers, and its scales reminded Loth more of a fish than a lizard. He still had no intention of trusting or talking to it. One glimpse of its teeth, white and razor-sharp, and he knew it was just as capable as Fýredel of tearing him to shreds.

Footsteps. He shifted behind a crate and gripped the baselard.

His brow was damp. He had never killed. Not even the cocka-trice. After all this madness, he was somehow free of that stain—but he would, to survive. To save his country.

When Tané appeared, her breathing was labored, her footsteps wove drunkenly, and she was soaked to the skin. Without a word, she took a key from her sash and undid the first of the padlocks. Loth helped her heave the chains away.

The dragon shook itself and let out a low growl. Tané stepped back, motioning for Loth to do the same, as it lifted its head and stretched to its full and formidable length. Loth was only too happy to oblige. For the first time, the beast looked angry. Its nostrils flared. Its eyes were on fire. It splayed its toes, found its balance, and, with one great swing, smashed its tail against the side of the ship.

The *Pursuit* shuddered. Loth almost lost his footing as the floor quaked beneath him.

Shouts came from above. The dragon was panting. If it was too weak to break through, they would all die here.

Tané called out to it. Whatever she said, it worked. The dragon steadied itself. Baring its teeth, it slammed its tail again. Wood splintered. Again. A chest slid across the floor. Again. The shouts from the pirates were closer now, their footsteps on the stair. With a snarl, the dragon rammed its body against the hull, gave it a mighty butt with its head—and this time, water came roaring in. Tané ran to the dragon and climbed onto its back.

Mortal sin or certain death. Death was the option the Knight of Courage would have taken, but the Knight of Courage had never needed to get to the Empire of the Twelve Lakes as badly as Loth did. Abandoning all hope of Halgalant, Loth waded after the murderous wyrm-lover. Desperately, he tried to climb her beast, but its scales were slick as oil.

Tané thrust out a hand. He grasped it, tasting salt, and she hoisted him up. As he looked for something to grip, he fought to blot out the rising dread. He was *on* a wyrm.

"Thim," he shouted. "What about Thim?"

His words were lost as the dragon clawed from its prison. In panic, Loth grabbed on to Tané, who had lowered her head and grasped the wet mane that surrounded them. With a last push, the dragon writhed through the gaping hole in the *Pursuit*. Loth screamed as they plunged into the sea.

A roar in his ears. Salt on his lips. A freezing slap of air. Pistols were firing from the decks of the *Pursuit*, the gun ports were opening, and Loth was still astride the dragon. It slithered through the roiling waves, avoiding every shot. Tané gasped out desperate-sounding words, hands still wrapped in its mane.

It rose, like a feather caught by the wind. Water streamed from its scales as it left the sea behind. Thighs aching with the effort of remaining seated, Loth tightened his arms around Tané and watched the pirates turn to specks.

"Saint have mercy." His voice cracked. "Blessèd Damsel, protect your poor servant."

A flare of light made him look west. Now the sails of the *Black Dove* were on fire—and suddenly, wyrms were flocking. The Draconic Army. Loth searched the dark, heart booming.

There was always a master.

The High Western announced its presence with a jet of fire. It winged above the *Black Dove* and smashed through one of its masts with its tail.

Valeysa. The Flame of Despair. Harlowe had said she was near at hand. Her scales, hot as live coals, seemed to drink in the fire that now raged across the fleet. As her followers swarmed over the listing *Pursuit*, she let out a roar that shook Loth to his bones.

Tané urged her dragon onwards. The *Rose Eternal* was in sight. If they descended now, Valeysa would certainly mark them. If they fled, Thim would be on his own. Loth thought his stomach would drop out as their mount arced into a graceful dive.

Thim was in the crow's nest. When he saw rescue coming, he scrambled even higher, to the top of the mainmast, and crouched there precariously. As it passed, the dragon scooped him up with its tail. He shouted, legs wheeling, as it yanked him from the *Rose Eternal*.

The dragon was on the rise again, toward a mantelshelf of cloud. It moved through the air as if it were swimming. Thim crawled painfully up its body, using its scales as handholds. When he was near enough, Loth reached out and helped him clamber on to its neck.

A shriek raised every hair on his arms. A wyvern was flying after them, spouting flame.

The dragon seemed as disturbed by the threat as it would be by a fly. The next jet of flame came so close that Loth smelled brimstone. Thim cocked his pistol and fired at the creature. It screamed, but kept coming. Loth squeezed his eyes shut. Either he was going to fall to his death, or he was going to be cooked like a goose.

Before either thing could happen, a powerful wind came from nowhere, almost unseating them all. The howl of it was deafening. When he could peel one eye open, Loth realized that the dragon was *breathing* the wind, as Draconic things breathed fire. Its eyes glowed welkin blue. Cloud smoked from its nostrils. Water beaded on its scales, only to be caught up and scattered like rain.

The wyrm screeched in rage. Its hide steamed and its jaws gaped open, but its flame was quenched, gusted back into its throat—and at last, the wind folded its wings and sent it tumbling toward the sea.

Rain battered Loth's face. He spat water. Lightning flashed as the dragon entered the clouds, victorious, draping itself in fog as it ascended.

That was when Tané keeled to one side. As she fell, some merciful instinct made Loth snap out a hand. His fingers snared the back of her tunic, not a heartbeat too soon. The dragon growled. Breathing hard, Loth scooped Tané close, and Thim hooked an arm around them both.

Tané was lifeless, head lolling. Loth checked that the case was still on her sash. If it came undone now, the jewel would be forever lost to the sea.

"I hope you know how to talk to dragons," he called to Thim. "Can you tell it where to go?"

No reply. When he looked over his shoulder, Loth saw that Thim was staring in wonder at the sky.

"I am seated on a god," he said, moonstruck. "I am not worthy of this."

At least somebody saw this nightmare as a blessing. Loth steeled himself and addressed the dragon.

"Well met, great dragon of the East," he tried, shouting over the wind. "I don't know if you can understand me, but I must speak to the Unceasing Emperor of the Twelve Lakes. It is of the utmost importance. Might you be able to take us to his palace?"

A rumble went through its body.

"Hold on to Tané," it said in Inysh, "and yes, son of the West, I will take you to the City of the Thousand Flowers."

63

East

When Tané woke, she found herself looking at a window. The sky beyond was pale as bone ash.

She lay in a canopy bed. Someone had dressed her in clean silk, but her skin was gritty with salt. A bowl of embers sat nearby, casting a lambent red glow on the ceiling.

When she remembered, her hand flinched to her side.

Her sash was gone. Seized by dread, she scrabbled through the quilts, almost scalding herself on a copper bedwarmer, only to find her case on a stand beside the bed.

The rising jewel glistened inside. Tané sank into the pillows and held the case to her chest.

For a long time, she remained in bed, imprisoned in a doze. Finally, a woman came into the room. She wore layers of blue and white, and the hem of her skirt touched the floor.

"Noble rider." She curtsied to Tané with clasped hands. "This humble one is relieved to find you awake."

The room swam. "Where is this?"

"This is the City of the Thousand Flowers, and you are in the home of His Imperial Majesty, the Unceasing Emperor of the Twelve Lakes, who rules beneath the gracious stars. He who is pleased to have you as his guest," the woman replied with a smile. "I will bring you something to eat. You have had a long journey."

"Wait. Please," Tané said, sitting up. "Where is Nayimathun?"

"The shining Nayimathun of the Deep Snows is resting. As for your friends, they are also guests in the palace."

"You must not punish the Westerner for breaching the sea ban. He has knowledge I need."

"Neither of your companions have been harmed," the woman said. "You are safe here."

She retreated from the room.

Tané took in the ornate ceiling, the nightwood furniture. It was as if she were a rider again.

The City of the Thousand Flowers. Ancient capital of the Empire of the Twelve Lakes. Its palace was home not only to the honored Unceasing Emperor and the honored Grand Empress Dowager, but to the Imperial Dragon herself. The dragons of Seiiki looked to their eldest for guidance, but their Lacustrine cousins answered to one ruler.

Her thigh was throbbing. She pushed back the sheets and saw that it was bandaged.

She remembered the Seiikinese man, clad in robes of mulberry red. Another scholar who had run from his fate. He had called her the descendant of the long-honored Neporo.

Impossible, surely. Neporo had been a queen. Her descendants could hardly have ended up in a fishing village, scratching out a living in the farthest reaches of Seiiki.

The servant returned and set down a tray. Red tea, porridge, and boiled eggs with a helping of winter melon.

"I will have a bath filled for you."

"Thank you," Tané said.

She picked at the meal while she waited. The Unceasing Emperor would not have her as his guest for long when he found out what she was. A fugitive. A murderer.

"Good morning."

Thim was in the doorway, clean-shaven, wearing Lacustrine clothing. He lowered himself into the chair beside her bed.

"The servant told me you were awake," he said in Seiikinese.

His tone was cool. Even if they had worked together on the ship, she had still stolen it from his crew.

677

"As you see," Tané said.

"I wanted to thank you," he added, with a dip of his head, "for saving my life."

"It was the great Nayimathun who saved you." Tané put down her teacup. "Where is the Westerner, honorable Thim?"

"Lord Arteloth is in the Twilight Gardens. He wants to speak to you."

"I will come when I am dressed." She paused before saying, "Why did you sail with people from over the Abyss?"

Thim furrowed his brow.

"They are not only raised to hate fire-breathers, but our dragons," Tané reminded him. "Knowing this, why would you sail with them?"

"Perhaps you should ask yourself a different question, honored Miduchi," he said. "Would the world be any better if we were all the same?"

The door closed behind him. Tané reflected on his words and realized that she had no answer.

The servant soon returned to take her to the bath. With her assistance, Tané rose from her bed and limped into the next room.

"There are clothes in the closet," the servant said. "Will you need help to dress, noble rider?"

"No. Thank you."

"Very well. You are free to explore the palace grounds, though you must not enter the interior court. His Imperial Majesty desires your presence in the Hall of the Fallen Star tomorrow."

With that, Tané was alone again. She stood in the shade of the bathing room and listened to the birdsong.

The bath was brimful with hot water. Tané slid her robe from her shoulders and unwrapped her thigh. If she craned her neck, she could see the stitches where someone had sealed the bullet graze. She would be fortunate to avoid a fever.

Bird skin stippled her arms as she lowered herself into the bath. She sluiced the salt out of her hair, then lay in the water, tired to her bones.

She did not deserve to be addressed as a lady, or given fine chambers. This peace could not last.

When she was clean, Tané dressed. An undershirt and a black silk tunic, then trousers, socks, and snug cloth boots. A sleeveless blue coat, trimmed with fur, came next, and finally the case on a new sash.

Her heart stumbled when she thought of facing Nayimathun. Her dragon had seen the blood on her hands.

Someone had left a crutch by the door. Tané took it and stepped out of her bedchamber, into a passageway of latticed windows and richly paneled walls. Painted constellations glinted at her from the ceiling. Dark stone paved the floors, heated from beneath.

Outside, she beheld a courtyard of such immensity that it could have housed a shoal of dragons. Lanternlight burned through an ashen mist. She could just see the great hall, raised on a terrace of layered marble, each tier a darker shade of blue.

"Soldier," Tané said to a guard, "may this humble one ask how to find the Twilight Gardens?"

"Lady," he said, "the Twilight Gardens are in that direction." He motioned to a distant gateway.

It took an eternity for her to traverse the courtyard. The Hall of the Fallen Star loomed above her. Tomorrow, she would be inside it, standing before the head of the House of Lakseng.

More guards directed her through the grounds. Finally, she reached the correct gate. The snow had been shoveled from the courtyard, but here it had been left untouched.

The Twilight Gardens were a legend in Cape Hisan. At dusk, they were said to come alive with lightflies. Night-blooming flowers would sweeten the paths. Mirrors stood here and there to direct the moonlight, and the ponds were still and limpid, the better to reflect the stars.

Even by day, this retreat was like a painting. She walked slowly, watched by statues of past Lacustrine rulers and their consorts, some of them accompanied by young dragons. Each consort held a pot of creamy yellow-pink roses. There were season trees, too, dressed in white for winter, reminding Tané of Seiiki. Of home.

She crossed a bridge over a stream. Through the fog, she could see pine trees and the shoulder of a mountain. Walking between those trees for long enough would take her to the Lake of Long Days.

Nayimathun was coiled in the snow on the other side of the bridge, the end of her tail swirling through a lotus pond. Loth and Thim were deep in conversation in a nearby pavilion. Tané collected herself. When she was close, Nayimathun huffed cloud through her nostrils. Tané laid down the crutch and bowed.

"Great Nayimathun."

A low growl. Tané closed her eyes.

"Rise, Tané," the dragon said. "I told you. You must speak to me as you would to a friend."

"No, great Nayimathun. I have been no friend to you," Tané raised her head, but there was a stone in her throat. "The honored Governor of Ginura was right to exile me from Seiiki. You were on the beach that night because of me. All of this happened because you chose me, and not one of the others, as your kin." Her voice quavered. "You should not speak kindly to me. I have killed and lied and served myself. I ran from my punishment. The water in me was never pure."

The dragon tilted her head. Tané tried to stay facing her, but a rush of shame made her drop her gaze.

"To be kin to a dragon," Nayimathun said, "you must not only have a soul of water. You must have the blood of the sea, and the sea is not always pure. It is not any one thing. There is darkness in it, and danger, and cruelty. It can raze great cities with its rage. Its depths are unknowable; they do not see the touch of the sun. To be a Miduchi is not to be pure, Tané. It is to be the living sea. That is why I chose you. You have a dragon's heart."

A dragon's heart. There could be no greater honor. Tané wanted to speak, to deny it—but when Nayimathun nuzzled her as though she were a hatchling, she broke. Tears dripped down her cheeks as she wrapped her arms around her friend and shook.

"Thank you," she whispered. "Thank you, Nayimathun."

A contented rumble answered her. "Let go of your guilt now, rider. Do not spend your salt."

They stayed like that for a long time. Shudders racked Tané as she pressed her cheek against Nayimathun. She had carried a nameless weight on her shoulders since Susa had died, but it was no longer too heavy to bear. When she could breathe without weeping, she moved her hand to where Nayimathun had been wounded. A metal scale now covered the flesh, engraved with wishes for healing.

"Who did this?"

"It no longer matters. What happened on the ship is in the past." Nayimathun bumped her with her snout. "The Nameless One will rise. Every dragon in the East can feel it."

Tané dried her tears and reached into the case. "This belongs to you."

She held out the rising jewel in the palm of her hand. Nayimathun gave it a delicate sniff.

"You say it was sewn into your side."

"Yes," Tané said. "I always had a swelling there." Her throat felt tight again. "I know nothing of my family, or why they would have put it into my side, but on the island, one of the *Pursuit*'s crew saw the jewel. He said I was the descendant of ... Neporo."

Nayimathun puffed more cloud. "Neporo," she echoed. "Yes ... that was her name. She wielded this jewel the first time."

"But, Nayimathun, I cannot be descended from a queen," Tané said. "My family were very poor."

"You have her jewel, Tané. It may be the only explanation," Nayimathun said. "The Grand Empress Dowager was a temperate ruler, but her grandson is young and impulsive. It would be best for us to keep the true nature of the jewel between us, lest it be taken from you." Her gaze flicked to Loth. "This one knows where it is, but he is afraid of me. Perhaps he will confide in another human."

Tané followed her line of sight. When he saw them both watching him, Loth stopped talking to Thim.

"You must support his appeal tomorrow. He means to propose an alliance between the Unceasing Emperor and Queen Sabran of Inys," Nayimathun said.

"The honored Unceasing Emperor will never agree." Tané was stunned. "It would be madness even to propose it to him."

"He may be tempted. Now the Nameless One is coming, it is of paramount importance that we stand together."

"He is coming, then?"

681

"We have felt it. The diminishing of our power, and the rise of his. His fire burns ever hotter." Nayimathun nudged her. "Go, now. Ask her envoy about the waning jewel. We must have it."

Tané put the rising jewel away. Whatever Loth knew about the twin, it was unlikely that he would agree to yield it to dragonkind, or to her, without a fight.

She walked across the bridge and joined the two men in the pavilion.

"Tell me where the waning jewel is," she said to the Westerner. "It must be returned to dragonkind."

Loth blinked before his face set. "That is quite out of the question," he said. "My dear friend in Inys is the possessor of the jewel."

"Which friend is this?"

"Her name is Eadaz uq-Nāra. Lady Nurtha. She is a mage."

Tané had never heard the word. "I think he means *sorceress*," Thim said to Tané in Seiikinese.

"The jewel does not belong to this Lady Nurtha," Tané said, irked. "It belongs to dragonkind."

"They choose their own wielders. And only death can sever the link between Ead and the waning jewel."

"Is she able to come here?"

"She is gravely ill."

"Will she recover?"

Something flickered in his eyes. He rested his arms on the balustrade and gazed out at the pine trees.

"There may be one way to heal her," he murmured. "In the South there is an orange tree, guarded by wyrm-slayers. Its fruit can offset the effects of poison."

"Wyrm-slayers." Tané misliked this revelation. "And is this Eadaz uq-Nāra a wyrm-slayer, too?"

"Yes."

Tané tensed. "I am aware," she said, "that over the Abyss, you consider our dragons to be evil. That you consider them as cruel and frightening as the Nameless One."

"It is true that there have been … misunderstandings, but I am quite sure Ead has never harmed one of your Eastern dragons." He turned to look at her. "I need your help, Lady Tané. To carry out my task."

"And what is that?"

"Several weeks ago, Ead found a letter from an Eastern woman named Neporo, who once wielded your jewel."

Neporo again. Her name was all over the world, haunting Tané like a faceless ghost.

"Do you know that name?" Loth said, studying her.

"Yes. What did the letter say?"

"That the Nameless One would return a thousand years after he was bound in the Abyss with the two jewels. He was bound on the third day of spring, in the twentieth year of the reign of Empress Mokwo of Seiiki."

Tané calculated. "This spring." Beside her, Thim cursed under his breath.

"Queen Sabran wishes us to meet him when he rises. We cannot destroy him, not without the sword Ascalon—but we can bind him anew with the jewels." Loth paused. "We do not have much time. I know I have little evidence of what I claim, and that you may not believe me. But will you trust me?"

His gaze was open and sincere.

Making the decision was easy, in the end. She had no choice but to reunite the jewels.

"The great Nayimathun says we should not tell anyone else about the jewels, for fear others might seek to take them," she said. "When we meet His Imperial Majesty tomorrow, you will put your queen's proposal to him. If he agrees to the alliance ... I will ask if I can fly to Inys with Nayimathun to inform your queen of his decision. On our way there, we will go South. I will find the healing fruit, and we will take it to Eadaz uq-Nāra."

Loth smiled then, and his breath came out in a fur of white. "Thank you, Tané."

"I do not like keeping this from His Imperial Majesty," Thim muttered. "He is the chosen representative of the Imperial Dragon. Does the great Nayimathun not trust him?"

"It is not for us to question gods."

His mouth became a thin line, but he nodded.

"Be sure to make a persuasive case to the honored Unceasing Emperor, Lord Arteloth Beck," Tané said to Loth. "Leave the rest to me."

———

First light spilled like oil over the palace. Loth considered his reflection. Instead of his breeches and a doublet, he now wore a blue tunic and flat boots in the style of the Lacustrine court. He had already been examined by a physician, who had found no evidence of the plague.

The plan Tané had proposed might just work. If she had mage blood, like Ead, then she might be able to retrieve an orange. The thought nerved him for the meeting ahead.

The dragon, Nayimathun, was nothing like Fýredel, except in her great size. Terrifying as she appeared, with her mountain-tops of teeth and firework eyes, she seemed almost gentle. She had cradled Tané with her tail like a mother. She had saved Thim. Seeing that the creature was capable of compassion toward a human made Loth doubt his religion all over again. This year was either a test from the Saint, or he was on the verge of apostasy.

A servant soon came to take him to the Hall of the Fallen Star, where the Unceasing Emperor would receive his unexpected visitors. The others were already outside. Thim was dressed almost the same as Loth, while Tané had been given another fur-lined surcoat that struck Loth as a mark of status. Dragonriders must be held in very high regard.

"Remember," she said to him, "say nothing of the jewel."

She touched the case at her side. Loth looked up at the hall and took a deep breath.

Armed guards led them through a set of studded blue doors, which were flanked by statues of dragons. More guards stood on either side of the track of dark wood, polished to a high shine, that would lead them to the middle of the hall. Loth gazed up at pillars of midnight stone.

A latticed ceiling soared above, the panels arranged around a carving of a dragon. Each panel showed a phase of the moon.

Lanterns hung one under the other, so they looked like ever-falling stars.

Dranghien Lakseng, the Unceasing Emperor of the Twelve Lakes, sat on a raised throne of what looked like moulded silver. He cut an arresting figure. Black hair, bound in a knot at the crown of his head, ornamented with pearls and silver-leaf flowers. Eyes like shards of onyx. Thick brows. Lips as sharply cut as his cheekbones, set in an arch smile. His robe was black, embroidered all over with stars, so it seemed as if he wore the night. He was no more than thirty.

Tané and Thim both knelt. Loth did the same.

"Rise," said a clear, smooth voice.

They rose.

"I hardly know which of you to address first," the Unceasing Emperor remarked, after several moments had passed in silence. "A woman of Seiiki, a man of the West, and one of my own subjects. A fascinating combination. I suppose we must make do with Inysh, since I am told, Lord Arteloth, that you do not speak anything else. Fortunately, I challenged myself, as a boy, to learn a language from each of the four parts of the world."

Loth cleared his throat.

"Your Imperial Majesty," he said. "You speak the Inysh language very well."

"There really is no need for flattery. I receive more than enough of that from my Grand Secretariat." The Unceasing Emperor gave them an arch smile. "You are the first Inysh man to set foot in the Empire of the Twelve Lakes in centuries. My officials tell me that you come with a message from Queen Sabran of Inys, yet you arrived on dragonback, looking rather more disheveled than official ambassadors generally do."

"Ah, yes. I apologize for—"

"If this one who stands beneath your throne may speak, Your Majesty," Thim chimed in. The Unceasing Emperor inclined his head. "I am a privateer in the employ of Queen Sabran."

"A Lacustrine seafarer in the employ of the Inysh queen. This is indeed a day of surprises."

Thim swallowed.

"We were stranded by a storm on Feather Island, where my captain and crewmates are still marooned," he continued. "Our ship was captured by the noble rider of Seiiki, who chased the *Pursuit* eastward. We freed Nayimathun, the exalted dragon, and she carried us to you."

"Ah," the Unceasing Emperor murmured. "Tell me, Lady Tané, did you find the so-called Golden Empress?"

"Yes, Majesty," Tané said, "but I left her alive. My purpose was to free my esteemed friend, the shining Nayimathun of the Deep Snows."

"Majesty." Thim went to his knees again. "This humble one pleads with you to send the Lacustrine navy to assist Captain Harlowe, and to retrieve his warship, the *Rose*—"

"We will speak of your crew later," the Unceasing Emperor said, with a wave of one hand. A broad ring encircled his thumb. "For now, I will hear the message from Queen Sabran."

Skin prickling, Loth drew in a deep breath through his nose. His words would dictate what happened next.

"Your Imperial Majesty," he began, "the Nameless One, our mutual enemy, will soon return."

No reply.

"Queen Sabran has evidence of it. A letter from one Neporo of Komoridu. He was bound with the celestial jewels, which I believe are known to the dragons of the East. The binding will end a thousand years after it was made, on the third day of the coming spring."

"Neporo of Komoridu is a figure of myth," the Unceasing Emperor stated. "Do you mean to mock me?"

"No." Loth dipped his head. "It is the truth, Majesty."

"Do you have this letter?"

"No."

"So I am to trust your word that it exists." The corner of his mouth gave a humorless twitch. "Very well. If the Nameless One *is* coming, what do you want from me?"

"Queen Sabran wishes us to face the beast on the Abyss on the day he rises," Loth said, trying not to rush his words. "If we are to do this, we will need help, and to set aside centuries of fear and suspicion. If Your Imperial Majesty will consent to intercede with the dragons of the Empire of the Twelve Lakes on her behalf, Queen Sabran offers a formal alliance between Virtudom and the East. She begs you to look to what is best for the world, for the Nameless One seeks to destroy us all."

The Unceasing Emperor was silent for a very long time. Loth tried to keep his expression clear, but there was sweat under his collar.

"This is ... not what I expected," the Unceasing Emperor finally said. His gaze was piercing. "Does Queen Sabran have a plan?"

"Her Majesty has proposed an attack on two fronts. First," Loth said, "the rulers of the West, North, and South would join their armies to take back the Draconic stronghold of Cárscaro."

Even as Loth said it, the face of the Donmata Marosa rose unbidden from his memory.

Would she survive if the city was stormed?

"It will draw the eye of Fýredel, right wing of the beast," he continued. "We hope that he will send at least some of the Draconic Army, to defend it, leaving the Nameless One more vulnerable."

"I presume she also has a plan to drive back the beast itself."

"Yes."

"Queen Sabran is indeed ambitious," the Unceasing Emperor remarked, one eyebrow rising, "but what is it she offers my country in return for the labor of its gods?"

As their gazes met, Loth suddenly remembered the glassblower in Rauca. Bargaining had never been his strong point. Now he would have to barter for the fate of the world.

"First, the chance to make history," he began. "With this act, you would be the emperor who bridged the Abyss. Imagine a world where we can trade freely again; where we can benefit from our shared knowledge, from—"

"—*my* dragons," the Unceasing Emperor cut in. "And those of my brother-in-arms in Seiiki, I presume. The world you paint is beautiful, but the red sickness is still as much a threat to our shores as ever."

"If we defeat our common enemy, and stamp out Draconic support, then the red sickness will ebb away."

"We can only hope. What else?"

Loth made the offers the Virtues Council had permitted him to make. A new trading partnership between Virtudom and the East. Guarantees that the Inysh would support the Lacustrine, both financially and militarily, in the event of conflict or disaster for as long as the alliance endured. A tribute in jewels and gold for the Eastern dragons.

"This all sounds very reasonable," the Unceasing Emperor remarked, "but I note that you have not mentioned marriage, Lord Arteloth. Her Majesty *does* offer her hand?"

Loth wet his lips.

"My queen would be honored to strengthen this historic alliance through matrimony," he began, smiling. Even Margret had admitted that his smile could soften any heart. "However, she is latterly widowed. She would prefer that this be a military alliance only. Of course," he added, "she understands if Lacustrine tradition forbids this without marriage."

"I am saddened for Her Majesty, and pray she finds strength in her grief." The Unceasing Emperor paused. "Admirable of her, to think we can overcome those differences *without* marriage, and the heir that would follow. Indeed, all this is a step toward modernity."

He drummed his fingers on the arms of his throne again, studying Loth with mild interest.

"I can tell that you are no diplomat, Lord Arteloth, but your attempts to flatter me are good-natured, if clumsy. And these are desperate times," the Unceasing Emperor concluded. "In the name of a modern alliance ... I will not make marriage a prerequisite of the arrangement."

"Really?" Loth blurted. "Your Imperial Majesty," he added, hot in the face.

"You are surprised by my swift agreement."

"I did expect more difficulty," Loth admitted.

"I like to imagine that I am a forward-looking ruler. And it happens that I am in no mood to marry." His face tightened for a moment. "I should clarify, Lord Arteloth, that I am only agreeing to the stand against the Nameless One. Other matters, such as trade, will take far more time to resolve. Given the continued threat of the red sickness."

"Yes, Your Imperial Majesty."

"Of course, my *personal* consent to a battle on the sea, while valuable to you, is not a guarantee that this will proceed. I must consult with my Grand Secretariat first, for my people will expect an alliance to come with an empress, and I imagine that the more old-fashioned of them will argue for it. Either way, it must be framed wisely."

Loth was too overwhelmed with relief to worry. "Of course."

"I must also consult with the Imperial Dragon, who is my guiding star. The dragons of this country are her subjects, not mine, and will only be persuaded if she finds this alliance to her liking."

"I understand." Loth bowed low. "Thank you, Majesty." He straightened and cleared his throat. "There is great risk for us all, I know. But what ruler made history by avoiding it?"

At this, the Unceasing Emperor permitted himself the ghost of a smile.

"Until we come to an agreement, Lord Arteloth, you will remain here as my honored guest," he said. "And unless my ministers raise any concerns that require further discussion, you will have an answer by dawn."

"Thank you." Loth hesitated. "Your Majesty, might— might Lady Tané go on dragonback to take this news to Queen Sabran?"

Tané looked at him. "Lady Tané is not my subject, Lord Arteloth," the Unceasing Emperor said. "You will have to discuss the matter with her yourself. But first," he said, "I should like Lady Tané to join me for breakfast."

When he rose, the guards flinched to attention. He spoke to Tané in another language and, with a nod, she left with him.

Loth walked with Thim back to the Twilight Gardens. Thim skimmed a stone across the pond.

"It doesn't matter what the ministers say."

Loth frowned. "What do you mean?"

"The only counsel His Imperial Majesty heeds, apart from that of the shining Imperial Dragon, is that of his grandmother, the Grand Empress Dowager." Thim watched the ripples spread. "He respects her above all others. She will already know every word that passed between us in that throne room."

689

Loth glanced over his shoulder.

"If she advises him against the alliance—"

"On the contrary," Thim said, "I think she will encourage it. So that he might live up to his reign-name. How can a mortal be *unceasing*, after all, except through memorable and historic actions?"

"Then there may be hope." Loth loosed a breath. "You will have to excuse me, Thim. If this is to work, I must do my part and pray for it."

When she was a child, Tané had imagined many possible futures for herself. In her dreams, she had thrown down the fire-breathing demons on the back of her dragon. She had become the greatest rider in Seiiki, greater even than Princess Dumai, and children had prayed that they would be like her one day. Her image had been painted on the walls of great houses, and her name had been enshrined in history.

In all that time, she had never dreamed that she would one day walk with the Unceasing Emperor of the Twelve Lakes in the City of the Thousand Flowers.

The Unceasing Emperor wore a cloak lined with fur. As they followed the paths, which had been cleared of snow, his bodyguards shadowed them. When they reached a pavilion beside a pond, the Unceasing Emperor motioned to one of the chairs.

"Please," he said. Tané sat, and so did he. "I thought that you could join me while I break my fast."

"This humble one is honored, Majesty."

"Do you know what kind of bird that is?"

Tané looked in the direction he was indicating. Close by, a swan was tending to its nest.

"Yes, of course," she said. "A swan."

"Ah, not just any swan. In Lacustrine, these ones are called *silent* swans. It was said that the Nameless One burned their voices from their throats, and they will only sing again when a ruler is born who will see the end of that fiend once and for all. They say the night I came into this world, they sang for the first time in centuries." He

690

smiled. "And people wonder why we sovereigns form such a high opinion of ourselves. They try to make us think that even birds care what we do."

Tané smiled a little in return.

"I find your story intriguing. I understand that you were once a promising sea guardian, but a misunderstanding in Ginura led to your exile to Feather Island."

"Yes, Majesty," Tané said.

"I have a great love for stories. Will you humor me and tell me all that has happened to you?"

Her palms were sweating.

"A great deal has happened to me," she finally said. "It may take some of Your Majesty's morning."

"Ah, I have nothing to do but watch my councillors wring their hands over Lord Arteloth's proposal."

Servants came to pour them tea and offer platters of food: dates soaked in red mountain-honey, sun pears, plum-leaved apples, steamed nuts, mounds of black rice. Each dish was covered with a square of silk embroidered with stars. She had sworn never to speak of her past, but his easy smile put her at ease. While he ate, she told him about how she had broken seclusion and witnessed the arrival of Sulyard, and how Susa had paid for her reckless attempt to conceal it, and everything that had occurred since.

Everything but the jewel stitched into her side.

"So you defied your banishment to free your dragon, with little hope of success," the Unceasing Emperor murmured. "For that, I commend you. And it seems you also found the lost island." He dabbed his mouth. "Tell me, now—did you happen to come across a mulberry tree on Komoridu?"

Tané looked up and met his bright gaze.

"There was a dead tree," she said. "Dead and twisted, covered in writing. I did not have time to read it."

"They say the spirit of Neporo is in the tree. Anyone who eats of its fruit absorbs her immortality."

"The tree bore no fruit, Majesty."

A flicker of some nameless emotion crossed his face.

"No matter," he said, and held out his cup for more tea. A servant refilled it. "Now I know your past, I am curious about your future. What do you intend to do next?"

Tané interlocked her fingers in her lap.

"First," she said, "I wish to play a part in destroying the Nameless One. After that, I wish to return to Seiiki." She hesitated. "If Your Imperial Majesty could help me do that, I would be grateful."

"How might I help you?"

"By writing to the all-honored Warlord on my behalf. If you tell him that I retrieved Nayimathun, a subject of the shining Imperial Dragon, he may hear my case and allow me to return."

The Unceasing Emperor sipped his tea.

"It is true that you reclaimed a dragon from the Fleet of the Tiger Eye, risking your own life. No easy feat," he conceded. "To reward your courage, I will do as you request—but know that I cannot permit you to return to Seiiki before I have an answer. It would be remiss of me to allow a fugitive to return there without permission."

"I understand."

"Very well."

He stood and walked to the balustrade. Tané joined him.

"It seems Lord Arteloth desires you to take word to Inys if I agree to his proposal," the Unceasing Emperor said. "Are you so eager to be my ambassador?"

"It would expedite matters, Majesty. If you would permit a citizen of Seiiki to be your messenger on this occasion."

The jewel felt heavy at her side. If he refused, she would not be able to make the detour to the South.

"It would be unconventional. You are not my subject, and you are in disgrace," the Unceasing Emperor mused, "but it seems we are destined for a change in the way of things. Besides, I like to defy convention now and then. No ruler made progress by playing a safe hand. And it keeps my officials on their toes." Sunlight gleamed in the darkness of his hair. "They never expect us to actually rule, you know. If we do, they call us mad.

"They raise us to be soft as silk, distract us with luxury and wealth beyond measure, so we never rock the boat that carries us.

692

They expect us to be so bored by our power that we let them do the ruling in our stead. Behind every throne is a masked servant who seeks only to make a puppet of the one who sits on it. My esteemed grandmother taught me this."

Tané waited, unsure of what to say.

The Unceasing Emperor clasped his hands behind his back. A great breath made his shoulders rise.

"You have proven your ability to see difficult tasks to their end, and we have no time to lose," he said. "If you are willing to be my messenger to the West, as Lord Arteloth wishes, I see no reason to deny it. Since this is a year for breaking tradition."

"It would be my honor, Your Imperial Majesty."

"I am pleased to hear it." He glanced at her. "You must be weary after your journey. Please, go back to your chambers and rest. You will know when I have come to a decision to carry to Sabran."

"Thank you, Your Imperial Majesty."

She left him to his breakfast and made her way back into the spiderweb of corridors. With little to do but wait, she took to her bed.

It was deep night when a knock woke her. She opened the door and ushered Loth and Thim inside.

"Well?"

"The all-honored Unceasing Emperor has made his decision," Thim said in Seiikinese. "He agrees to the proposal."

Tané shut the door.

"Good," she said. Loth sank into a chair. "Why does he look so dismayed?"

"Because he has been asked to remain in the palace. I have also been asked to remain, to help direct the navy to where we left the *Rose Eternal.*"

A small chill went through Tané. For the first time in her life, she would be leaving the East. That thought would have daunted her once, but at least she would not be alone. With Nayimathun beside her, she could do anything.

"Tané," Loth said, "will you go south before you go to Inys?"

She needed to save Lady Nurtha from the poison. Both jewels must be used against the Nameless One.

693

"I will," she said. "Tell me where to find the house of dragonslayers."

He told her, as best he could.

"You must be careful," Loth said. "The women there will likely slaughter your dragon if they see her."

"They will not touch her," Tané said.

"Ead told me that their present Prioress is not to be trusted. If they catch you, you must speak *only* to Chassar uq-Ispad. He cares for Ead. I am quite sure he will help you if he knows you mean to heal her." Loth lifted a chain from around his neck. "Take this."

Tané took the proffered object. A silver ring. A red jewel was mounted on it, enwheeled by diamonds.

"It belongs to Queen Sabran. If you give it to her, she will know you come from me." Loth held out a sealed letter. "I ask that you also give her this. So she knows I am well."

Tané nodded, tucked the ring into her case, and rolled the letter small enough to fit beside it.

"The honored Chief Grand Secretary will meet you in the morning to give you a letter for Queen Sabran from His Imperial Majesty. You will leave this city under cover of darkness," Thim said. "If you can see this through, Lady Tané, we will all be in your debt."

Tané looked out of the window. Another journey.

"I will see it done, honorable Thim," she said. "You can be sure of it."

64

East

In the morning, the honored Chief Grand Secretary handed Tané the letter she would take to Inys. There would be no embassy sent across the sea, no pomp or ceremony. One dragon and one woman would carry the news.

Her weapons were returned to her. In addition, she received a Seiikinese pistol and a finer sword, as well as a pair of Lacustrine bladed wheels.

She had enough food to last her for two weeks on dragonback. Nayimathun would hunt fish and birds.

When darkness fell over the City of the Thousand Flowers, Tané met Nayimathun in the courtyard. A saddle of black leather, edged with wood and gold lacquer, had been secured on her back, though *saddle* was far too unassuming a word for it—it was more of an open palanquin, enabling the rider to sleep during a long flight. Such was the secrecy of their assignment that no Lacustrine courtiers or officials were here to witness them leave. Only Thim and Loth had been permitted.

"Good evening, Tané," Nayimathun said.

"Nayimathun." Tané patted her neck. "Are you sure you feel strong enough for this journey?"

"I am certain. Besides," the dragon said, and nudged Tané with her snout, "you seem to have a habit of stumbling into trouble without me."

A smile warmed her lips. It felt good to smile.

Thim stayed where he was, but Loth approached her. Tané busied herself with securing the pouches that hung from the saddle.

"Tané," he said, "please tell Queen Sabran that I am safe and well." He paused. "And if you do wake Ead ... tell her that I've missed her, and I will see her soon."

Tané turned to him. There was tension in his face. He was trying, just as she was, not to look afraid.

"I will tell her," she said. "Perhaps when I return, I can bring her with me."

"I doubt Ead would ever consent to ride a dragon, even in the service of peace," Loth said with a chuckle, "but I have been surprised many times this year." His smile was tired, but true. "Goodbye, and good luck. And"—he hesitated—"goodbye to you, too, Nayimathun."

"Farewell, man of Inys," Nayimathun said.

The last light of dusk withdrew from the city. Tané climbed into the saddle and made sure her cloak was wrapped all the way around her body. Nayimathun took off. Tané watched the City of the Thousand Flowers fall away until the palace was a flicker in the sleeping white labyrinth. Cloaked in the darkness of the new moon, they left another capital behind.

They flew over the pearly lakes and the pine trees dressed in white, following the River Shim. The cold kept Tané awake, but made her eyes water.

Nayimathun stayed above the clouds during the day, and avoided settled areas at night. Sometimes they would spot a pillar of smoke in the distance, and they would know that fire-breathers had attacked that settlement. The further west they traveled, the more of these dark columns they saw.

On the second day, they reached the Sleepless Sea, where Nayimathun landed on a small island to rest. There would be nowhere to land when they flew over the Abyss, not unless they veered into the North. Dragons could go for a long time without sleep, but Tané knew the journey would be hard for Nayimathun. She had been underfed by the pirates.

They slept in a tidal cave. When Nayimathun woke, she immersed herself in the shallows while Tané filled her gourds with water from a stream.

"If you grow hungry, tell me. I will pass you something to eat," she said to Nayimathun. "And if you need to swim in the Abyss, you must not fear for me. My clothes will dry in the sun."

Nayimathun rolled over lazily. Suddenly she lashed her tail, spraying water, and Tané was drenched to the bone.

For the first time in an eternity, she laughed. She laughed until her stomach hurt. Nayimathun snapped playfully as Tané used the jewel to fling water back at her, and the sun made rainbows in the spray.

She could not remember the last time she had laughed. It must have been with Susa.

By sunset, they were flying again. Tané held on to the saddle and breathed in the clean wind. In spite of all that lay before them, she had never felt more at peace than she did now.

The black of the Abyss spread like a stain into the Sundance Sea. As soon as Nayimathun left the green waters behind, Tané felt a chill. A vault of darkness now lay below them—the vault in which Neporo of Komoridu had once imprisoned the Nameless One.

Days passed. Nayimathun spent most of the journey above the clouds. Tané chewed on cuts of ginger root and tried to stay awake. Mountain sickness was common in riders.

Her heart thumped heavily. Sometimes Nayimathun would descend to swim, and Tané would relieve herself and stretch her limbs in the water, but she only relaxed when she was back in the saddle. This ocean did not welcome her.

"What do you know of Inys," the dragon asked.

"Queen Sabran is the descendant of the warrior Berethnet, who defeated the Nameless One long ago," Tané said. "Each queen has a daughter, and each daughter looks the same as her mother. They live in the city of Ascalon." She pushed back a wet strand of hair. "They also believe the people of the East are blasphemers, and see our way of life as the opposite of theirs—as sin to their virtue."

"Yes," Nayimathun said, "but if she seeks our help, Queen Sabran must have learned the difference between fire and water. Remember to be compassionate when you judge her, Tané. She is a young woman, responsible for the welfare of her people."

Nights above the Abyss were colder than any Tané had ever felt. A harsh wind cracked her lips and scourged her cheeks. One night, she woke with the clouds in her breath, and she looked down at the sea and saw that there were stars there, mirrored in the water.

When she woke next, the sun was high, and a golden haze made a ribbon across the horizon.

"What place is this?"

Her voice was rough. She reached for a gourd and drank enough water to moisten her tongue.

"The Ersyr. The Golden Land," Nayimathun said. "Tané, I must swim before we enter the desert."

Tané gripped the horn of the saddle. Her head grew light as Nayimathun descended.

The sea stung her face. It was warm here, and clear as glass. She glimpsed rubble and flotsam strewed among the sills of coral. Metal glinted at her from the seabed.

"All of that is from the Serene Republic of Carmentum, after which this sea is named," Nayimathun said when they surfaced. Her scales glittered like gems under the sun. "Much of that country was destroyed by the fire-breather Fýredel. Its people flung many of its treasures into the sea to protect them from his fire. Pirates dive for them and sell them."

She swam until the shore was close, then took to the sky again. A desert stretched before them, vast and barren, rippling in the heat. Tané felt thirsty just looking at it.

There was no cloud to hide in. They would have to stay higher than ever to avoid wandering eyes.

"This desert is called the Burlah," Nayimathun said. "We must fly across it to reach Lasia."

"Nayimathun, you are not made for this climate. The sun will dry your scales."

"We have no choice. If we do not awaken Lady Nurtha, we may never find another person who can wield the waning jewel."

The moisture on her scales was drying almost as quickly as it appeared. Dragons could make their own water for a time, but in the end, this beating sun would overwhelm Nayimathun. She would be weaker over the next few days than she had ever been.

They flew. And they flew. Tané shed her cloak and used it to cover the metal scale, to prevent it from growing too hot.

The day went on for eternity. Her head ached. The sun burned her face and scorched the skin at the parting of her hair. There was nowhere to hide from it. By sunset, she was shivering so hard that she had to reach for her cloak again, even though her skin was hot.

"Tané, you have the sun quake," Nayimathun said. "You must keep your cloak on in the day."

Tané dabbed her brow. "We can't carry on like this. We'll both be dead before we reach Lasia."

"We have no choice," Nayimathun said again. Then, "The River Minara runs through that land. We can rest there."

Tané wanted to answer. Before she could, she slipped back into a fitful sleep.

The next day, she wrapped the cloak around her body and head. Sweat drenched her, but it kept the sun off her skin. She removed it only to tend to Nayimathun, and to cool the metal scale with water, making it sizzle and sputter.

The desert did not end. Her gourds ran dry as bone. She sank into the cradle of the saddle and let go of her thoughts.

———

When she opened her eyes again, she was falling.

Branches lashed at her cloak and hair. She had no time to scream before the water seized her.

Panic thrummed along her limbs. Blind, she kicked. Her head broke the surface. In the blackness of night, she could just make out a fallen tree jutting over the water, almost too high to reach. As the current gulped her toward it, she grabbed one of its branches. The river tore at her legs. She hauled herself onto the tree and keeled over it, shuddering.

For a long time, she clung there, too bruised and shaken to move. Warm rain drummed on her scalp. When she finally came to her senses, she pushed her weight onto her hands and pinched the tree with her knees. It shook as she moved inch-meal along it.

As she fought to stay calm, she remembered Mount Tego. How she had weathered the freezing wind and knee-deep snow and the agony in her limbs. How she had climbed a sheer rock with bare hands, breathing flimsy air, one slip from death. How she had not let herself turn back. After all, dragonriders had to be able to remain nimble-fingered and strong at great heights. They could not fear the fall.

She had stood on the pinnacle of the world. She had ridden a dragon across the Abyss.

She could do this.

Her fear crushed, she moved faster. When she reached the end of the tree, her boots sank into mud.

"Nayimathun," she shouted.

Only the roar of the water answered.

The case with the jewel was still on her sash. She was on the bank of a river, close to where it frothed into white rapids. If she had not been shocked awake in time, she would have been washed to her death. She pressed her back against a tree and slid to the ground.

She had fallen from the saddle. Either Nayimathun was looking for her, or she had fallen, too. If that was the case, she could not be far away.

This had to be the River Minara, which meant they had reached the Lasian Basin. She searched her memory for the maps she had seen as a child. The west of the country, she remembered, was covered by forest. That was where Loth had told her she would find the Priory.

Tané swallowed and blinked the water from her eyes. If she was to survive this, she would have to keep a clear head. The pistol was useless now it was wet, and her bow and sword had been attached to the saddle, but she still had a knife and the bladed wheels.

A few of her possessions had fallen with her. Tané crawled to the nearest bag and opened it with aching fingers. When she felt the compass in her hand, she let out a sigh of relief.

She gathered up as much as she could carry. Using a strip of her cloak, a branch, and a little sap, she fashioned a torch and kindled it with a spark from two stones. It might attract a few animals, but better to risk discovery than step on a snake, or fail to see a hunter in the dark.

The trees pressed close as conspirators. Just looking at them almost made her courage fail.

You have a dragon's heart.

She paced into the forest, away from the roar of the Minara. Her boots sank into loam. It smelled the way Seiiki did after the plum rain. Rich and earthy. Comforting.

Her body was a half-drawn knife. Despite the familiar scent, the first steps were the hardest she had ever taken. She walked light-footed as a crane. When a twig snapped beneath her, birds of many colors took off from the trees. Before long, she found the damage to the canopy. Something large had fallen nearby. A few steps more, and her torch revealed a pool of silver blood.

Dragon blood.

The forest seemed set on hampering her progress. Hidden roots snared at her ankles. Once a branch crumbled beneath her, and she found herself up to her waist in swamp. She only just kept her grip on the torch, and it took far too long to prize herself free.

Her hand shook as she limped onward, following the trail of blood. From the amount that had been shed, Nayimathun was injured, but not badly enough to kill her. Her blood might still entice predators. The thought made Tané break into a run. In the East, tigers were sometimes bold enough to attack dragons, but the scent of Nayimathun would be strange to the animals of this forest. She prayed that would be enough to keep them at bay.

When she heard voices, she smothered the torch. An unfamiliar language. Not Lasian. She held her knife between her teeth and climbed a nearby tree.

Nayimathun was lying in a clearing. An arrow was embedded in her crown—the part of her that gave her the means to fly. Six figures were gathered around her, all in scarlet cloaks.

Tané tensed. One of the strangers was handling her bow, running her fingers over its limb. These must be the Red Damsels, the warriors of the Priory—and now they knew a dragonrider was close.

At any moment, one of them could plunge a sword into Nayimathun. She would be no match for them in this state.

After what seemed like hours, all but two of the Red Damsels disappeared into the trees. Now they were hunters, and Tané was their prey. Their sorcery might put her at a disadvantage, but even that did not make them all-powerful.

She dropped in silence from the tree. Her best weapon now was the element of surprise. She would get Nayimathun to safety, and then she would track one of the Red Damsels to the Priory.

Nayimathun opened one eye, and Tané knew that she had seen her. The dragon waited for her to creep nearer before she lashed her tail. In the precious moments the Red Damsels were distracted, Tané moved like a shadow toward them. She caught sight of dark eyes beneath a hood—eyes as dark as her own—and for the strangest moment, she felt as if the sun was on her face.

The feeling died as soon as she got close. She attacked with every drop of her strength. The first swing of her wheel nicked skin, but a blade snapped up to deflect the second, jarring her arm to the shoulder. The force of the collision rang through her teeth. As the hunters circled her, cloaks spinning around them, she fended them off with a wheel in each hand. They were quick as two fish eluding the hook, but it was clear that they had never encountered bladed wheels. Tané gave herself over to the fight.

The fleeting calm soon fled from her. As she swerved away from their swords, she had the chilling realization that she had never been in a fight to the death. The Western pirates had been easy—brutal, but undisciplined. She had scrapped with other apprentices as a child, trained with them when she was older, but her knowledge of battle was little practice and no end of theory. These mages had been locked in a war for most of their lives, and they moved like partners in a dance. A warrior forged in the schoolroom, alone and wounded, would be no match for them. She should never have confronted them in the open.

Thirst and exhaustion made her slow. With every step, their swords flashed closer to her skin, while her wheels were nowhere near theirs.

Her steps grew drunken. Her arms ached. She hissed as a blade sliced her shoulder, then her jaw. Two more scars for her collection. The next blow set fire to her waist. Blood soaked into her tunic. When the Red Damsels attacked together, she only just lifted the wheels in time to parry.

She was going to lose this fight.

A feint caught her off-guard. Metal bit open her thigh. One knee gave way, and she dropped the wheels.

That was when Nayimathun reared her head. With a roar, she clamped one of the mages between her teeth and hurled her across the clearing.

The other woman turned so quickly that Tané almost missed it. Her palms were full of flame.

Nayimathun flinched from the light. As the woman walked toward her, she recoiled, snapping. Tané aimed true and plunged her knife through red brocade, between two struts of rib. When the woman fell, Tané stepped around her and went to her dragon.

Once it would have shamed her that Nayimathun had seen her kill. It was against the way—but her life had been in danger. Both of their lives. Now she had killed for Nayimathun, and Nayimathun had killed for her. After all they had survived already, she had no regrets.

"Tané." Nayimathun lowered her head. "The arrow."

Even looking at it made Tané feel queasy. As gently as she could, she reached up and eased the arrow from the yielding flesh. It took enough force to make her arms shake.

Nayimathun shuddered as it came free. Blood dribbled down her snout. Tané placed a hand on her jaw.

"Can you fly?"

"Not while this heals," Nayimathun panted. "They were from the Priory. Follow the others. Find the fruit."

"No," Tané said at once, chest tight. "No. I will *not* leave you again."

"Do as I say." The dragon bared her teeth. They were tipped with blood. "I will fly again, but I will not be able to reach Inys yet. Find another way. Save this Lady Nurtha. Carry the message to Queen Sabran."

"And leave you here alone?"

"I will follow the river to the sea and heal. When I can fly again, I will find you."

Days after their reunion, and now they had to part again. "How will I reach Inys without you?" Tané said thickly.

"You will make a path," Nayimathun said, gentler. "Water always does." She gave Tané a soft nudge. "We will see each other again soon."

Tané shivered. She clung to her dragon for as long as she dared, face pressed into her scales.

"Go, Nayimathun. Go now," she whispered, and made for the trees.

The other Red Damsels had gone north. Tané kept low as she chased their footprints. There was no time to make a torch, but her eyes were used to the darkness now.

Even when she lost the trail, she knew where the women had gone. She was following a feeling. It was as if her quarry had left warmth in their wake, a warmth that called to her very blood.

It ended in another clearing. She paused for breath, holding her damp side. There was nothing here. Just trees, countless trees.

Her eyelids grew heavy. She swayed on her feet. Now a woman in white was standing before her, and the sun was shining from her fingers.

That was the last that she remembered of the forest.

65

South

They had taken the rising jewel. It was the first thing she knew when she woke: the empty feeling of its absence. She was lying in a room of salmon-colored stone, and her hands were tied behind her back.

A woman with a shaved head and warm brown skin stood in the doorway.

"Who are you?"

She spoke in Ersyri. Tané knew a little of the language, but said nothing.

The woman watched her. "You were carrying a ring belonging to Queen Sabran of Inys," she said. "I would like to know if she sent you here." When Tané only looked away, her lips tightened. "You were also carrying a blue jewel. Where did you find it?"

She knew how to withstand interrogation. Pirates would do all manner of things to their enemies to bleed them of their secrets. To prepare for the worst, all apprentices had to prove that they could suffer a beating from a soldier without revealing their name.

Tané had not made a sound in hers.

When no reply was forthcoming, the woman changed her tone. "You and your sea beast injured one of our sisters and slew another," she said. "If you cannot give some justification for your crime, we will have no choice but to execute you. Even if you had not spilled our blood, consorting with a wyrm is punishable by death."

She could not reveal the truth. They would never yield a fruit from their sacred tree to a dragonrider.

"At least tell me who you are," the woman said, softer. "Save yourself, child."

"I will speak to Chassar uq-Ispad," Tané said. "No one else."

With a small frown, the woman left.

Tané tried to clear her head. From the light, it would not be long until sunset. She fought to stay awake, but she found herself drifting as her body chased the rest she had denied it.

Nayimathun would get away. She could swim downriver faster than any human could run.

A man entered her prison, jolting her from a doze. A knife was tucked into a crimson sash around his middle. A robe of purple brocade, embellished with silverwork, crossed over his massive chest.

"I am Chassar uq-Ispad," he said. His voice was deep and gentle. "I am told you speak Ersyri."

Tané watched him sit in front of her.

"I have come here for a fruit of the orange tree," she said, "to take to Eadaz uq-Nāra."

"Eadaz." Surprise jumped into his eyes, then pain. "Child, I do not know what you have heard of Eadaz, or how you know her name, but the fruit cannot bring back the dead."

"She is not dead. Poisoned, but alive. With the fruit, I can save her."

He froze as if she had struck him.

"Who told you about me?" he asked hoarsely. "About the Priory?"

"Lord Arteloth Beck."

At this, Chassar uq-Ispad looked very tired.

"I see." He knuckled his temple. "I suppose you also meant to take the blue jewel to Eadaz. The Prioress has it now, and she intends to execute you."

"Why?"

"Because you murdered a sister. And because you rode here on the back of a sea wyrm. And lastly," Chassar said, "because killing you would allow her to control the rising jewel."

"You could help me escape."

706

"Eadaz was able to steal the waning jewel from Mita Yedanya, the Prioress. She will not let its twin be taken," Chassar said heavily. "I would have to take her life first. And that, I cannot do."

Tané waited as he sat in silence.

"I trust that you will think of something, Ambassador uq-Ispad," she said, "or Eadaz *will* die." He looked at her. "Let me go, and she may not. The choice belongs to you."

Chassar uq-Ispad did not return. He must have chosen loyalty to the Prioress.

All was lost.

Two women came at twilight. Their cloaks were pale brocade. Tané allowed them to lead her over tiled floors, through corridors that must never have seen sunlight. In every nook and alcove, there were cast-bronze figures of a woman holding an orb.

Tané knew she needed to fight, but suddenly she felt too weak to so much as bend a blade of grass. Her captors escorted her through an archway, on to a slim ledge of rock. A waterfall formed a veil on her right. The roar was so loud, she could no longer discern her own footsteps.

At least she would hear water at the end. The thunder of the falls reminded her of Seiiki.

"Sisters."

Tané looked up. Chassar uq-Ispad was walking toward them.

"The Prioress has asked that I interrogate this one again," he called in Ersyri. "I will not be long."

The two women exchanged glances before letting Tané go. Chassar waited until they were out of sight, then took Tané by the arm and marched her back along the ledge.

"We have not long," he said against her ear. "Do what you must, then leave and do not look back. All that awaits you here is a noose."

"Will they not know you helped me?"

"That need not concern you." Chassar showed her a stair carved into the rock. "That will take you to the valley. Only the tree can decide if you are worthy of a fruit." He reached into his robe and withdrew her lacquer case. "This is yours. The coronation ring and the letter are still inside." Next he produced a length of silk. "Carry the fruit in this."

With his help, Tané knotted it around her body. "How will I get to Inys?" she asked him. "My dragon is gone."

"Follow the River Minara until it forks and turn right. That way will take you north. I will send help, but you must not stop. The sisters will be on the hunt the moment they realize you are gone." He squeezed her shoulder. "I will do what I can to delay them."

"I cannot leave here without the rising jewel," she bit out. "It answers only to me."

Chassar looked grim.

"If I can get it from her, I will send someone after you with it," he said, "but you must leave."

He was gone before she could thank him.

There was no handhold on the stair. She cleaved to the stone on her left, watching the steps, mindful of the placement of her feet. Then the stair wound around the cliff side, and she saw it.

When Loth had spoken of an orange tree, she had imagined it as one of those that grew on Seiiki, small and unassuming. This was as tall as a cedar, and the scent of it made her mouth water. A living sister of the mulberry tree on Komoridu.

White flowers peppered its branches. Its leaves were polished green. Gnarled roots fanned around its trunk, snaking over the floor of the valley like patterning on silk. The Minara flowed around and beneath them.

There was no time to marvel. A shadow winged past, so close it ruffled her hair. Tané pressed her back against the rock face, watching the sky, still as prey in the eye of a hunter.

For a long time, there was silence. Then, out of the night, a firestorm.

Her body reacted before her mind could. She threw herself out of the way, but the stair was narrow and precarious, and suddenly she was tumbling, out of control, and the steps were a hammer on her back. Half-blind with panic, she grappled for something to break her fall as her body rolled toward a sheer drop.

At the last, she threw out a hand and caught the stair. She hung there, breathless.

She imagined herself on Mount Tego again. Steadying her nerves, she turned to see what had happened.

Fire-breathers. They were everywhere. Not pausing to question where they had come from, Tané dared look down. She was closer to the valley floor than she had thought, and time was running out. She let go of the stair, slithered on her back down the rock, and hit the grass with knee-jarring force.

The roots. The roots were thick and dense enough to protect her. As she delved into them, a fire-breather shrieked and crashed into the river, so close to Tané that she felt the spray of water from the impact. An arrow, fletched with a pale feather, was buried in its throat.

Chaos was unfolding in the valley. The trees around it were already on fire. Tané crawled on her belly, tensing whenever a hot wind blistered overhead. When she found an opening in the roots, she clambered back on to the grass and staggered to the foot of the tree.

Somehow, she knew what to do. She sank to her knees and turned her palms upward.

Cinders fell like snow on to her hair. She thought she had failed until a gentle *snap* came from above, and an orb, round and golden, dropped from on high. It missed her hands and tumbled into the tangle of giant roots. Cursing under her breath, she chased it.

The fruit rolled toward the rushing waters of the Minara. Tané threw herself forward and stopped it with one hand.

A flicker caught her eye. Between the roots, she saw a bird land, and as she watched, entranced, it turned into a naked woman.

Feather stretched to limb. The beak became a pair of red lips. Copper hair poured to the small of a slim back.

A shape-shifter. Everyone in Seiiki knew that dragons had once been able to change their forms, but it had been a long time since anyone had seen proof of it with their own eyes.

Another woman was approaching across the valley. A dark braid snaked over her shoulder. She wore a gold necklace and a scarlet robe with long sleeves, darker and more richly embroidered than those of the other women. When a fire-breather dived for her, she swept its flame aside as if it were a fly. Around her neck, on a chain, was the rising jewel.

"Kalyba," she said.

"Mita," the redhead answered.

They bandied words for a time, circling each other. Even if Tané could have understood their exchange, its content was of little consequence. All that mattered was which of them triumphed.

The Prioress moved toward the other woman. Her face was taut with hatred. The sun glinted off her sword as she swung it. Kalyba turned back into a hawk and swooped over her head. A heartbeat later, she wore a human shape again. Her laugh chilled Tané to the core. With a shout of frustration, the Prioress hurled a fistful of red fire.

Their battle brought them nearer and nearer to the roots. Tané withdrew into the shadows.

The women fought with fire and wind. They fought for an eternity. And when it seemed as if neither of them would ever best the other, Kalyba disappeared, as if she had never been there at all. The Prioress was so close now, Tané could hear her breathing.

It was then that the witch rose silently from the deep grass. She must have taken the form of something too small to see—an insect, perhaps. The Prioress turned a moment too late.

A sound like a foot crunching a shell, and she folded at the knees. Kalyba placed a hand on her head, as one might comfort a child. Mita Yedanya collapsed on to the grass.

Kalyba held up the heart of her enemy. Blood seeped from between her fingers. When she spoke, it was in a language Tané had never heard. Her voice rang through the valley.

Tané pulled her hand from her mouth. The body was close enough to touch. One last risk, and she could leave this madness behind her. She shifted back onto her belly and crawled toward the dead Prioress.

An arrow whistled from somewhere in the clearing, just missing Kalyba. Tané flinched back. Sweat ran down her cheek as she reached for the corpse, but her fingers were too clumsy. Hardly daring to breathe, she bent over the body, the crater where a heart had been. Her fingers shook as she pulled at the chain, passed it over her own head, and tucked the jewel underneath her tunic.

When Kalyba looked back, both she and Tané froze. Recognition sparked in her eyes.

"Neporo."

Tané watched her expression flicker. Kalyba began to laugh.

"Neporo," she exclaimed. "I wondered— all these centuries, I wondered so often if you had survived, my sister. How wonderfully strange that it should be here that I find my answer." A smile twisted her mouth, beautiful and terrible. "Look upon my work. All this destruction is because of *you*. And now you come on your hands and knees to beg the orange tree for mercy."

Tané scrambled back, boots sliding through mud. She had never been afraid to fight in her life, but this woman, this *creature*, made something ring in her blood like a sword out of a sheath.

"You're too late. The Nameless One will rise, and no starfall will weaken him. He would welcome you, Neporo." Kalyba walked toward her, blood dripping from the heart in her palm. "Flesh Queen of Komoridu."

"I am not Neporo," Tané found her voice in a dark hollow. "My name is Tané."

Kalyba stopped.

She was *wrong*. Like a cockroach wrapped in amber, preserved in the wrong time.

Yet Tané felt irresistibly drawn to her. Her blood called to this woman even as her flesh recoiled.

"I almost forgot that she had a child," Kalyba said. "How could it be possible that her descendants have not only lasted this long without my knowledge, but that you are here on the very same day as I am?" This little quirk of fate seemed to amuse her. "Know this, blood of the mulberry tree. Your ancestor is responsible for this. You are born of wicked seed."

The rush of the river was closer now. Kalyba watched her go deeper into the roots.

"You look ... so much like her." The witch softened her voice. "A ghost of her."

An arrow sailed across the clearing then and struck Kalyba in the back of her shoulder, making her turn in fury. A woman with golden eyes had emerged from the caves, a second arrow already nocked. She looked straight at Tané, and her gaze was a command.

Run.

Tané wavered. Honor told her to stand and fight, but instinct pulled harder. All that mattered now was that she reached Inys, and that Kalyba stayed ignorant of what she carried there.

She threw herself into the river, and the river took her back into its arms.

For a long time, all she knew was the fight to keep her head above water. As the river carried her from the valley, she crossed one arm over the fruit and used the other to swim. Smoke followed her all the way to the fork, where she hauled herself, dripping, from the rush, so bruised and tired and footsore that she could only lie and shudder.

Twilight turned to dusk, and dusk to moonless night.

Tané stood, her legs shaking, and walked.

Instinct made her take the jewel from its case, and it lit her way. Between the boughs of the canopy, she found the right star and followed its glimmer. Once, she saw the eyes of an animal watching her from the trees, but it kept its distance. Everything did.

At some point, her boots found a path of hard-packed earth, and she walked until the trees began to thin. When she was out of the forest, under the sky, she fell at last.

Her own hair was her pillow. She breathed through the clenched fist of her throat, and she wished on everything she loved that she was home in Seiiki, where the trees grew sweet.

An earth-shaking *thump* made her open her eyes. Wind unsettled her hair, and Tané looked up to see a bird looming over her. White as moonshine, with wings of bronze.

Ascalon Palace glistened in the first glow of sunrise. A ring of high towers at the crook of a river. Tané limped toward it, past the city-dwellers who had risen from their beds.

The great white bird had found a gap in the coastal defenses and taken her to a forest north of Ascalon. From there, she followed a well-trodden road until the horizon birthed a city.

The gates of the palace were threaded with flowers. When she got close, a throng of guards in silver plate blocked her way.

"Hold." Spears pointed at her chest. "No farther, mistress. State your business here."

She raised her head so they could see her face. The spears flinched higher as the guards stared at her.

"By the Saint," one of them murmured. "An Easterner."

"Who are you?" another asked her.

Tané tried to form words, but her mouth was dry, and her legs quaked.

Frowning, the second man loosened his grip on his sword. "Get the Resident Ambassador to Mentendon," he said to the woman beside him.

Her armor rattled as she left. The others kept their spears trained on the stranger.

It was some time before another woman approached the gates. Her braided hair was a deep red, and she wore a black garment that flattened her breasts and waist, with skirts that belled out from her hips. Lace covered her brown skin to the throat.

"Who are you, honorable stranger?" she said in perfect Seiikinese. "Why have you come to Ascalon?"

Tané did not give her name. Instead, she held the ruby ring into the light.

"Take me to Lady Nurtha," she said.

VI

The Keys to the Abyss

For whatsoever from one place doth fall,
is with the tide unto an other brought:
For there is nothing lost, that may be
found, if sought.

—Edmund Spenser

66

West

Her world had become a night without stars. It was sleep, but not-sleep; a boundless darkness, settled by one soul. She had been chained here for a thousand years, but now, at last, she stirred.

A golden sun seared to life within her. As the fire sloughed off her skin, she remembered the bite of the cruel sister. She could see the outlines of faces all around her, but their features were unclear.

"Ead."

She felt sculpted from marble. Her limbs cleaved to the bed, as an effigy was bound forever to the tomb. In the dark spots in her vision, somebody was praying for her soul.

Ead, come back to us.

She knew that voice, the scent of cicely, but her lips were stone and would not part.

Ead.

New warmth fired deep in her bones, burning away the bounds that imprisoned them. The calyx that surrounded her cracked and, at last, the heat opened her throat.

"Meg," she whispered, "I believe this is the second time I have found you nursing me."

A choked laugh. "Then you should stop giving me cause to nurse you, silly goose." Margret folded her into her arms. "Oh, Ead, I feared this wretched fruit might not work—" She turned to her servants. "Send word at once to Her Majesty that Lady Nurtha is awake. Doctor Bourn, too."

"Her Majesty is in council, Lady Margret."

"I assure you that Her Majesty will have you all gelded if this is kept from her. Go, now."

Wretched fruit. Ead realized what Margret had said and looked over her shoulder. On the nightstand was an orange with a bite taken out of it. Drunken sweetness roiled her senses.

"Meg." Her throat was so dry. "Meg, tell me you did not go to the Priory on my account."

"I'm not fool enough to think I could fight my way through a house of dragonslayers." Margret kissed the top of her head. "You might not believe in the Saint, but a higher power must have a care for you, Eadaz uq-Nāra."

"Indeed. The higher power of Lady Margret Beck." Ead grasped her hand. "Who brought the fruit?"

"That," Margret said, "is a wondrous tale. And I will tell it to you as soon as you've had some caudle."

"Is there anything you think that foul stuff doesn't cure?"

"Cankers. Otherwise, no."

It was Tallys who brought the caudle to her bed. Upon seeing Ead, she burst into tears.

"Oh, Mistress Duryan," she sobbed. "I thought you were going to die, m'lady."

"Not quite yet, Tallys, despite efforts to the contrary." Ead smiled. "How lovely it is to see you again."

Tallys curtsied several times before retreating. Margret closed the door behind her.

"Now," Ead said to Margret, "I am drinking my caudle. Tell me everything."

"Three more mouthfuls, if you please."

Ead grimaced and obeyed. When she had forced it down, Margret made good on her word.

She told her how Loth had volunteered to be the Inysh ambassador in the East, and how he had gone across the Abyss to make the proposal to the Unceasing Emperor. How weeks had passed. How wyverns had burned the crops. How a Seiikinese girl had stumbled to the palace with bloody hands, carrying a golden fruit and the Inysh coronation ring, which Loth had last possessed.

"And that was not all she carried." Margret glanced at the door. "Ead, she has the other jewel. The rising jewel."

Ead almost dropped the cup.

"That cannot be," she said hoarsely. "It is in the East."

"No more."

"Let me see it." She tried to sit up, arms quavering with the effort. "Let me see the jewel."

"Enough of that." Margret wrestled her back into the pillows. "You have taken little but drops of honey for weeks."

"Tell me *exactly* how she found it."

"Would that I knew. As soon as she had handed me the fruit, she fell down with exhaustion."

"Who knows she is here?"

"Myself, Doctor Bourn, and a few of the Knights of the Body. Tharian feared that if anyone saw an Easterner in Ascalon Palace, they would haul the poor child to the stake."

"I understand his caution," Ead said, "but, Meg, I must speak to her."

"You can speak to whoever you like once I am satisfied that you will not fall on your face while doing so."

Ead pursed her lips and drank.

"Dearest Meg," she said, quieter, and touched her hand, "did I miss your wedding?"

"Of course not. I delayed it for you." Margret took back the cup. "I had no idea what a tiring affair it would be. Mama wants me to wear white now. Who in the world wears *white* on their wedding day?"

Ead was about to remark that she would look very well in white when the door flew open—and then Sabran was in the bedchamber, dressed in crimson silk, breast heaving.

Margret stood.

"I will see to it that Doctor Bourn also received my message," she said, with the slightest smile.

She closed the door softly behind her.

For a long time, neither of them spoke. Then Ead held out a hand, and Sabran came to the bed and embraced her, breathing as if she had run for leagues. Ead held her close.

"Damn you, Eadaz uq-Nāra."

Ead released a breath, half sigh and half laugh. "How many times have we damned each other now?"

"Not nearly enough."

Sabran remained by her side until a harassed-looking Tharian Lintley came to take her back to the Council Chamber. The Dukes Spiritual were poring over the letter from Loth, and her presence was required.

At noon, Margret let Aralaq into the bedchamber. He licked Ead's face raw, told her that she should never walk into poisonous darts ("Yes, Aralaq, I wonder that I never thought of that before"), and spent the rest of the day draped across her like a fur coverlet.

Sabran had insisted that the Royal Physician examine her before she rose, but by sundown, Ead yearned to stretch her limbs. When Doctor Bourn finally came, he wisely judged that she was well enough to stand. She eased her legs from under Aralaq, who had lapsed into a doze, and dropped a kiss between his ears. His nose twitched.

Tomorrow, she would pay a visit to the stranger.

This night was for Sabran.

The highest room in the Queen Tower was taken up by an immense sunken bath. Water was drawn up from a spring and stove-heated in the Privy Kitchen so the queen might have hot baths all year round.

A slow-burning candle was the only light. The rest of the chamber was steam and shadow. Through its large windows, Ead could see the glittering stars above Ascalon.

Sabran sat on the edge of the bath in a petticoat, hair strung with pearls. Ead shed her robe and stepped into the steaming water. She savored its warmth as she poured from a jar of creamgrail, lathered it between her palms, and worked it into her hair.

She dipped her head under and washed the sweet foam away. Submerged to her shoulders, she floated to Sabran and laid her head on her lap. Cool fingers untangled her curls. The heat loosened her limbs, made her feel alive again.

"I feared you had left me for good this time," Sabran said to her. The walls reflected her voice.

"The poison I was given comes from the fruit of the tree when it rots. It is meant to kill," Ead said. "Nairuj must have given me a diluted measure on purpose. She spared me."

"Not only that, but the other jewel has come to us. As if brought by the tide." Sabran ghosted her fingers through the water. "Even you must see that as divine intervention."

"Perhaps. I will speak to our Seiikinese guest in the morning." Ead drifted backward and let her hair fan out across the water's surface. "Is Loth well?"

"Apparently so. He has had yet more adventures, this time involving pirates," Sabran said dryly, "but yes. The Unceasing Emperor has asked him to remain in the City of the Thousand Flowers. He says he is unharmed."

No doubt Loth would be kept there until Sabran paid what she had promised. A common enough arrangement. He would manage; he had navigated far more devious courts.

"So the last stand of humanity will take place betwixt and between the two sides of the world," Sabran murmured. "We will not last long on the Abyss. Not in wooden ships. The Lord Admiral assures me that there are ways to protect our vessels from flame, and we will have water aplenty to quench the fires, but I cannot think that these methods will buy more than minutes." Sabran met her gaze. "Do you think the witch will come?"

It was almost a certainty.

"I wager she will try to end your life with the True Sword. The sword Galian revered will be used to end his bloodline. *Their* bloodline," Ead said. "She would relish the poesy of it."

"What a loving ancestor I have," Sabran said calmly.

"You accept what I told you, then." Ead studied her face. "That you have mage blood in you."

"I have accepted many things."

Ead saw in her eyes that it was the truth. There was a new and cold resolve about them.

It had been a year of hard realities. The walls they had built to protect their beliefs had crumbled at their feet, and Sabran had watched her faith begin to decay with them.

"I have spent my life believing that in my blood was the power to keep a monster chained. Now I must face it knowing otherwise." Sabran closed her eyes. "I am afraid of what that day will bring. I am afraid that we will not see the first light of summer."

Ead waded to her and framed her face between her hands.

"We have nothing to fear," she said, with more conviction than she felt. "The Nameless One was defeated before. He can be defeated again."

Sabran nodded. "I pray so."

Her petticoat soaked up the water. Ead felt her every limb turn boneless as Sabran pulled her out of the bath, smiling.

Their lips came together in the darkness. Ead gathered Sabran to her, and Sabran kissed the droplets from her skin. They had been parted twice, and Ead knew, as she had always known, that they would be divided anew before long, whether by war or by fate.

She slipped her hands beneath the satin of the petticoat. When her palms found burning flesh, she drew back.

"Sabran," she said, "you're on fire."

She had thought it was the heat from the bath, but Sabran was a splinter of kindling.

"It's nothing, Ead, truly." Sabran smoothed a thumb over her cheek. "Doctor Bourn says the inflammation will flare from time to time."

"Then you need to rest."

"I can hardly take to my bed at a time like this."

"You can take to your bed or your bier. The choice is yours."

Making a face, Sabran sat up. "Very well. But you are not to play nursemaid." She watched Ead rise and dry herself. "You must speak with the Easterner on the morrow. Everything depends on our being able to coexist in peace."

Ead pulled on her bedgown.

"I make no promises," she said.

722

In her years of study at the South House, Tané had been taught only what were considered to be the necessary facts about the Queendom of Inys. She had learned about their monarchy and their religion of Six Virtues. She knew their capital was called Ascalon, and that they had the largest and best-armed navy in the world. Now she also knew that they lived in damp and cold, kept idols in their bedchambers, and forced their sick to drink a lumpy gruel that set her teeth on edge.

Fortunately, nobody had tried to coax it into her this morning. A servant had brought her a jug of ale, thick-cut slices of sweet bread, and a stew of brown meat. All of it had clotted in her stomach. She had only tried ale once before, when Susa had stolen a cup for her from Orisima, and she had thought it foul.

In the South House, there had been minimal furniture and sparing artwork. She had always liked that simplicity; it left her room to think. Castles were more ornate, of course, but the Inysh seemed to revel in *things*. In *adornment*. Even the curtains were dolorous. Then there was the bed, which was so laden with covers, it seemed to swallow her.

Still, it was good to be warm. After such a long journey, all she had been able to do for a day was sleep.

The Resident Ambassador to Mentendon returned when the sun was high.

"Lady Nurtha is here, honorable Tané," she said in Seiikinese. "Should I let her in?"

At last.

"Yes." Tané set the meal aside. "I will see her."

When she was alone, Tané folded her hands on the covers. Eels were twisting in her stomach. She had wanted to meet Lady Nurtha on her feet, but the Inysh had put her in a lace-trimmed garment that made her look a fool. Better to maintain a semblance of dignity.

A woman soon appeared in the doorway. Her riding boots made no sound.

Tané studied the slayer. Her skin was smooth and golden-brown, and her hair curled to her shoulders, thick and dark. There was something of Chassar, the man who had saved

723

her, in the lines of her jaw and brow, and Tané wondered if they were kin.

"The Resident Ambassador tells me you speak Inysh." She had a Southern lilt. "I had no idea it was taught in Seiiki."

"Not to everyone," Tané said. "Only to those in training for the High Sea Guard."

"I see." The slayer folded her arms. "I am Eadaz uq-Nāra. You may call me Ead."

"Tané."

"You have no family name."

"It was Miduchi once."

There was a brief silence.

"I am told you made a perilous journey to the Priory to save my life. I thank you for it." Ead went to the window seat. "I assume Lord Arteloth told you what I am."

"A wyrm-killer."

"Yes. And you are a wyrm-lover."

"You would slay my dragon if she were here."

"A few weeks ago, you would have been right. My sisters once slaughtered an Eastern wyrm that thought it shrewd to fly over Lasia." Ead spoke without apparent remorse, and Tané wrestled with a surge of hatred. "If you will oblige me, I would like to hear how you started this journey, Tané."

If the slayer was going to be civil, so would Tané. She told Ead how she had come to have the rising jewel, her skirmish with the pirates, and her brief and violent detour to the Priory.

It was at this point that Ead began to pace back and forth. Two small lines appeared between her eyebrows.

"So the Prioress is dead, and the Witch of Inysca has possession of the orange tree," she said. "Let us hope that she seeks only to keep it to herself, and not to gift it to the Nameless One."

Tané allowed her a moment. "Who is the Witch of Inysca?" she finally asked, quietly.

Ead closed her eyes.

"It is a long tale," she said, "but if you wish, I will tell it to you. I will tell you everything that has happened to me over the last year. After your journey, you deserve the truth."

While rain drizzled down the window, she did. Tané listened without interrupting.

She listened to Ead tell her the history of the Priory of the Orange Tree, and the letter she had found from Neporo. About the Witch of Inysca and the House of Berethnet. About the two branches of magic, and the comet and the sword Ascalon, and how the jewels fit into it all. A servant brought them hot wine while Ead talked, but by the time she was finished, both cups had turned cold, untouched.

"I understand if you find this difficult to believe," Ead said. "It all sounds quite ridiculous."

"No." Tané released her breath for what felt like the first time in hours. "Well, yes, it does. But I believe you."

She realized she was shivering. Ead flicked her fingers, and a fire sprang up in the hearth.

"Neporo had a mulberry tree," Tané said, even as she took in this evidence of magic. "I may be her descendant. It is how I came to have the rising jewel."

For a time, Ead seemed to digest this. "Is this mulberry tree alive?"

"No."

Ead visibly clenched her jaw.

"Cleolind and Neporo," she said. "One mage of the South. One of the East. It seems that history is to repeat itself."

"I am like you, then." Tané watched the flames dance behind a grate. "Kalyba also had a tree, and Queen Sabran is her descendant. Does that make us both sorceresses?"

"Mages," Ead corrected, though she sounded distracted. "Having mage blood does not make you one. You must eat of the fruit to call yourself that. But it *is* why the tree yielded you a fruit in the first place." She lowered herself on the window seat. "You said my sisters grounded your wyrm. It never occurred to me to ask how you reached Inys."

"A great bird."

Ead's gaze snapped to her.

"Parspa," she said. "Chassar must have sent her."

"Yes."

725

"I am surprised he trusted you. The Priory does not take kindly to wyrm-lovers."

"You would not despise the Eastern dragons if you knew anything about them. They are nothing like the fire-breathers." Tané stared her out. "I despise the Nameless One. His servants threw down our gods in the Great Sorrow, and I mean to throw him down in punishment for it. In any case," she said, "you have no choice but to trust me."

"I could kill you. Take the jewel."

From the look in her eyes, she would do it. There was a knife in a sheath at her hip.

"And use both jewels yourself?" Tané said, undaunted. "I assume you know how." She took her case from under the pillows and tipped the rising jewel into her palm. "I have used mine to guide a ship through a windless sea. I have used it to draw the waves onto the sand. So I know that it drains you—slowly at first, so you can bear it, like the ache from a rotten tooth. Then it turns your blood cold, and your limbs heavy, and you long only to sleep for years." She held it out. "The burden must be shared."

Slowly, Ead took it. With her other hand, she eased a chain from around her neck.

The waning jewel. A little moon, round and milky. The steady glow from a star was inside it, calm where its twin was always sparkling. Ead held one jewel in each palm.

"The keys to the Abyss."

Tané felt a chill.

It seemed impossible that they had united them.

"There is a plan in place to defeat the Nameless One. I assume Loth told you." Ead handed back the blue jewel. "You and I will use these keys to bind him forever in the deep."

Just as Neporo had a thousand years ago, with a fellow mage beside her.

"I should warn you," Ead said, "that we cannot kill the Nameless One without Ascalon. Someone must drive it into his heart before we use the jewels. To quench his fire. My hope is that the Witch of Inysca will bring it to us, and that we can take it from her. If not, it is possible that your Eastern wyr— dragons ... will be able to weaken him enough for us to use the jewels without the sword. Perhaps then we can bind him for another thousand years. I mislike that option, for it means that another generation will have to take up this mantle."

"I agree," Tané said. "It must end here."

"Good. We will practice with the jewels together."

Ead reached into a pouch at her side and withdrew the golden fruit Tané had brought to Inys.

"Take a bite of this," she said. "Siden may help you in this battle. Especially if Kalyba comes." Tané watched her place it on the nightstand. "Do it soon. It will rot today."

After a moment, Tané nodded.

"Binding the Nameless One may be the end of us both," Ead said, softer. "Are you willing to take that risk?"

"To die in the service of a better world would be the highest honor."

Ead gave her a faint smile. "I believe we understand each other. On this one thing, at least."

To her surprise, Tané found herself smiling in return.

"Come and find me when you feel stronger," Ead said. "There is a lake in Chesten Forest. We can learn to use the jewels. And see how long we can last without killing each other."

With that, she took her leave. Tané slipped the rising jewel, still glinting, back into its case.

The golden fruit was glowing. She cupped it in her hands for a long time before she tasted of its flesh. Sweetness burst beneath her teeth and washed over her tongue. When she swallowed, it was hot.

The fruit fell to the floor, and she erupted into flame.

In the Great Bedchamber, the Queen of Inys burned. Doctor Bourn had watched her all day, but now Ead went to her side, against her word.

Sabran slept in the vise of her fever. Ead sat on the bed and soaked a cloth with water.

The Prioress was dead, and the Priory in the hands of the witch. The thought of the Vale of Blood filled with wyrms, brought there by a mage, was as bitter to Ead as wormwood.

At least Kalyba would not harm the orange tree. It was her only source of the siden she craved.

Ead cooled Sabran's hot brow. She could not mourn for Mita Yedanya, but she did for her sisters, who had lost their second matriarch in as many years. With the Prioress dead, they would either flee elsewhere and elect a new leader—likely Nairuj—or submit to Kalyba so they might stay close to the tree. Whatever they chose, Ead prayed Chassar would be safe.

Sabran had fallen still by dusk. Ead was trimming the wicks on the candles when the silence broke.

"What did the Easterner say?"

Ead looked over her shoulder. Sabran was watching her.

Quietly, so no one outside the door could eavesdrop, Ead recounted her meeting with Tané. When she was finished, Sabran gazed with glassy eyes at the canopy.

"I will address my people the day after tomorrow," she said. "To tell them about the alliance."

"You are not well. Surely you can delay for a day or two."

"A queen does not abandon her plans for a trifling fever." She sighed as Ead covered her with the mantle. "I told you not to play nursemaid."

"And I told you I was not your subject."

Sabran muttered into her pillow.

When she had drifted back to sleep, Ead took out the waning jewel. It had sensed *other* magic, and latched on to it, even though its nature was the opposite of hers.

A knock had her tucking the jewel away. She opened the door and found Margret on the threshold.

"Ead." She looked nervous. "The rulers of the South have just arrived at Summerport. What do you suppose they want?"

67

West

Damp skin moved against his own, and a hand gentled his hair. Those were the first things he knew before the agony broke into his sleep, sharp and vengeful.

The air burned his mouth, reeking of brimstone. A whimper escaped his lips.

"Jan."

"Shh, Niclays."

He knew that voice. "Laya," he tried to say, but only a groan came out.

"Oh, Niclays, thank the gods." She pressed a cloth to his brow when he whimpered. "You must be quiet."

The events of Komoridu came back to him in a flash. Ignoring her pleas for him to be still, he groped for his throat. Where a second mouth had been, he could feel shiny, tender skin—the scar of cautery. He raised his arm and saw that it now ended in a puffy stump, webbed with black stitches. Tears squeezed from his eyes.

He was an anatomist. Even now, he knew this wound would almost certainly kill him.

"Shh." Laya stroked his hair. Her cheeks were damp, too. "I'm so sorry, Niclays."

A sickening throb filled his arm. He took the piece of leather she offered and bit with all his might to keep from screaming.

A strained creak came to his attention. Slowly, he realized that the swaying was not the result of pain, but the fact that he and Laya were suspended in an iron cage.

If he had been seized by fear before, he was losing his mind to it now. His first thought was that the Golden Empress had taken them ashore and left them to starve—then he remembered the last thing he had heard before fainting. The drumbeat of Draconic wings.

"Where?" he forced out. Vomit threatened to follow his words. "Laya. Where?"

Laya swallowed, hard enough for him to see the movement of her throat. "Dreadmount." She held him close. "The red veins in the rock. No other mountain has them."

Birthplace of the Nameless One. Niclays knew he ought to be pissing himself with fear, but all he could think was how close he was to Brygstad.

He wadded down his gasps. The bars were wide enough to squeeze through, but the fall would kill them both. In the sunless cavern, he could just make out the mass of scales.

Red scales.

Not on a living beast. No—painted on the wall of this cavern was a memory. It showed a woman in a Lasian war cap facing the Nameless One, sword piercing his breast.

The sword was unmistakably Ascalon. And its wielder was Cleolind Onjenyu, Princess of the Domain of Lasia.

So many lies.

Red scales. Red wings. The immensity of the beast covered most of the wall. Delirious, Niclays began to count its scales while Laya dabbed his brow. Anything to distract him from the agony. He had counted them twice over before he fell into a doze, and dreamed of swords and blood and a redheaded corpse. When Laya stiffened against him, he opened his eyes.

A woman had appeared in the cage, dressed all in white. That was when he knew he was delirious.

"Sabran," he gasped.

A fever dream. Sabran Berethnet was standing in front of him, hair black against waxen skin. The supposed beauty that had always given him a chill, as if he had put a foot through ice.

Her face came closer. Those eyes, the creamy green of jade.

"Hello, Niclays," she said. "My name is Kalyba."

He could not even summon a croak. His body was a nerveless thing, unmoving and cold.

"I suppose you must be confused." Her lips were red as apples. "I am sorry to have brought you so far, but you were very close to dying. I find the loss of life distasteful." She laid a glacial hand on his head. "Let me explain. I am of the Firstblood, like Neporo, whose story you read in Komoridu. I ate of the hawthorn tree when Inys had no queen."

Even if Niclays had been able to speak in more than whimpers, he would not have known what to say in the presence of this being. Laya held him tighter, shivering.

"I suppose you know where you are. I imagine it frightens you, but this is a safe place. I have been preparing it, you see. For spring." Kalyba teased a wisp of hair back from his eyes. "The Nameless One came here after Cleolind wounded him. He bid me find an artist to paint the story, to show how it was on that day in Lasia. So he might always remember."

Niclays might have thought her mad, had he not felt mad himself. All this had to be a nightmare.

"Immortality is my gift," Kalyba whispered. "Unlike Neporo, I learned to share it. Even restore the dead to life."

Jannart.

Her breath was the chill of high winter. Niclays gazed at her, mesmerized by her eyes.

"I know you are an alchemist. Let me share the gift with you. Show you how to unknit the seams of age. I could teach you how to build a man from the ashes of his bones."

Her face began to change. The green in her eyes drained to gray, and her hair turned red as blood.

"All I need," said Jannart, "is one small favor in return."

It was the first time in many decades that the House of Berethnet had received the rulers of the South. Ead was on Sabran's right, watching them.

Jantar Taumargam, who was called the Splendid, was as much of a presence as his epithet implied. He was not imposing in the physical sense; he was fine-boned, slim as a feather, almost delicate at first glance—but his eyes were dungeons. Once he had you in his gaze, you were his until he let it go. He wore a brocaded sapphire robe with a high collar, closed with a gold belt. His queen, Saiyma, was already on her way to Brygstad.

Beside him was the High Ruler of Lasia.

At five and twenty, Kagudo Onjenyu was the youngest monarch in the known world, but her bearing made it clear that those who took her lightly would pay a heavy toll. Her skin was a deep brown. Cowry shells encircled her neck and wrists, and each of her fingers gleamed with gold. A shawl of sea silk, knitted in the Kumenga fashion, draped her shoulders. Four sisters of the Priory had been assigned to defend her since the day she was born.

Not that Kagudo needed much defending. Rumor had it she was as great a warrior as Cleolind had been.

"As you know, the Mentish land army is small," Sabran was saying. "The wolfcoats of Hróth will be a great help, as will their navy on my side of this battle, but more soldiers are needed." She paused to breathe. Combe gave her a concerned look. "You both have soldiers and weapons at your disposal, strong enough to damage Sigoso's armies."

There were dark circles under her eyes. She had insisted on rising to greet the Southern rulers, but Ead knew her skin was still on fire.

Tané was bed bound with her own fever. She had eaten of the fruit. Sabran had wanted the Easterner present, but it was best that she slept. She would need her strength for the task ahead.

"The Ersyr does not hold with conflict," Jantar said. "The Dawnsinger spoke against war. But if the rumors spreading across my country are true, it seems we have no choice but to take up arms."

The Southern monarchs had arrived under cover of night. Next they would join Saiyma in Brygstad to confer with High Princess Ermuna. It was too much of a risk to discuss strategy by letter.

None of the rulers wore their crowns. At this table, they faced each other as equals.

"Cárscaro has never been taken," Kagudo commented. There was a richness to her voice that made everyone sit up a little straighter. "The Vetalda built it in the mountains with good reason. An approach across the volcanic plain would be madness."

"I agree." Jantar leaned forward to study the map. "The Spindles are riddled with wyrms." He tapped a finger on it. "Yscalin has natural defenses on all sides but one. Its border with Lasia."

Kagudo looked at the map without changing her expression.

"Lord Arteloth Beck was in the Palace of Salvation in the summer," Sabran said. "He learned that the people of Cárscaro are not willing servants of the Nameless One. If we can remove King Sigoso, Cárscaro will fall from within, perhaps bloodlessly." She pointed to the city on the map. "There is a siege passage that runs underneath the palace. The Donmata Marosa is apparently an ally, and she may be able to help from inside. If a small group of soldiers could fight their way to the passage and enter the palace before the main assault begins, you could put an end to Sigoso."

"That will not kill the wyrms that defend Cárscaro," Kagudo said.

A servant came to pour them all more wine. Ead declined. She needed a clear head.

"You should know, Sabran," Kagudo continued, "that I would not affix my seal to this siege were it not crucial to Lasia. Frankly, the idea that we should sacrifice our soldiers to a grand diversion while you face the Nameless One is questionable. You have decided that we will fight the kittens, and you the cat, though he would come for me just as quickly as you."

"The diversion was my suggestion, Majesty," Ead said.

It was at this point that the High Ruler of Lasia looked at her for the first time. Ead felt a tingle at her nape.

"Lady Nurtha," Kagudo said.

"Queen Sabran was the one who proposed an assault on Cárscaro, but I suggested that she meet the Nameless One on the Abyss."

"I see."

"Of course," Ead said, "you are blood and heir of the House of Onjenyu, whose land the Nameless One threatened before any other. If you wish to avenge his cruelty toward your people, leave one of your generals to oversee the siege of Cárscaro. Join us on the sea."

"I would be grateful for your sword, Kagudo," Sabran said. "If you chose my battle front."

"Indeed." Kagudo sipped her wine. "I imagine you would enjoy the company of a heretic very much."

"We call you heretics no more. As I promised in my letter, those days are at an end."

"I see it only took the House of Berethnet a thousand years and a crisis of this magnitude to follow its own teachings on courtesy."

Sabran had the wisdom to let her consider. Kagudo looked for some time at Ead.

"No," she finally said. "Let Raunus go with you. He is a seafarer, and my people take precedence over an ancient grudge. They will want to see their ruler on the battlefield closest to home. In any case, Cárscaro has threatened our domain for too long."

From there, all talk was of strategy. Ead tried to listen, but her mind was elsewhere. The Council Chamber seemed to press in on her, and at last she said, "If Your Majesties will excuse me."

They all stopped talking.

"Of course, Lady Nurtha," Jantar said, with a brief smile.

Sabran watched her go. So did Kagudo.

Outside, night was on the turn. Ead used her key to enter the Privy Garden, where she sat on the stone bench and gripped its edge.

It must have been hours that she sat there, lost in thought. For the first time, she could feel the weight of her responsibility like a boulder on her back.

Everything now depended on her ability to use the jewels with Tané. Thousands of lives and the very survival of humankind hung on that requisite. There was no other plan. Only the hope that two fragments of a legend would be able to bind the Beast of the Mountain. Every moment he remained alive would be another moment of soldiers dying on the foothills of Cárscaro. Every moment would be another ship burned.

"Lady Nurtha."

Ead looked up. The sky held its first light, and Kagudo Onjenyu stood before her.

"Your Majesty," she said, and rose.

"Please," Kagudo said. She wore a fur-lined cloak now, fastened with a brooch over one shoulder. "I know the sisters of the Priory know no sovereign but the Mother."

Ead gave her obeisance nonetheless. It was true that the Priory answered to no ruler but its Prioress, but Kagudo was the blood of the Onjenyu, the dynasty of the Mother.

Kagudo regarded her with apparent interest. The High Ruler was beautiful in a way that stopped the heart for an instant. Her eyes were long and narrow, slicing upward at the corners, set deep above broad cheekbones. Now she was standing, Ead could see the rich orange barkcloth of her skirt. The cap of a royal warrior had been placed over her hair.

"You seemed to be deep in thought," she said.

"I have a great deal to consider, Majesty."

"As do we all." Kagudo glanced back at the Alabastrine Tower. "Our council of war is over, for now. Perhaps you would care to walk with me. I find myself in need of air."

"I should be honored."

They took to the gravel path that snaked through the Privy Garden. Kagudo's guards, who wore circlets of gold on their upper arms and carried deadly looking spears, walked a short way behind them.

"I know who you are, Eadaz uq-Nāra." Kagudo spoke in Selinyi. "Chassar uq-Ispad told me years ago about the young woman whose duty was to guard the Queen of Inys."

Ead hoped she looked less surprised than she felt.

"I suspect you know by now that the Prioress is dead. As for the Priory, it appears that it has been occupied by a witch."

"I prayed it was not true," Ead said.

"Our prayers do not always bear fruit," Kagudo said. "Your people and mine have long had an understanding. Cleolind of Lasia was of my house. Like my ancestors, I have honored our relationship with her handmaidens."

"Your support has been instrumental to our success."

Kagudo stopped and turned to face her. "I will speak plainly," she said. "I asked you to walk with me because I wanted to make myself known to you. To meet you in person. After all, the time will soon come for the Red Damsels to choose another Prioress."

A weight dropped into her belly. "I will have no say in that. The Priory considers me a traitor."

"That may be, but it is possible that you are about to face its oldest enemy. And if you could slay the Nameless One ... your crimes would surely be forgiven." If only that were true. "Mita Yedanya, unlike her predecessor, looked inward. Now, a little inwardness is reasonable, even necessary—but if your climb to this position at the Inysh court is anything to go by, Eadaz, you also look outward. A ruler should know how to do both."

Ead let these words take root inside her. They might never grow into anything, but there the seed lay.

"Did you never dream of being Prioress?" Kagudo asked. "You are a descendant of Siyāti uq-Nāra, after all. The woman Cleolind deemed worthy to succeed her."

Of course she had dreamed of it. Every girl in the Priory wanted to be a Red Damsel, and every Red Damsel hoped that she would one day be the representative of the Mother.

"I do not know that looking outward has served me well," Ead said quietly. "I have been banished, named a witch. One of my own sisters was sent to dispatch me. I gave eight years to protect Queen Sabran, believing she might be the blood of the Mother, only to find that she never was." Kagudo smiled thinly at that. "You never believed it?"

"Oh, not for a moment. You and I both know that Cleolind Onjenyu, who was willing to die for her people, would never have abandoned them for Galian Berethnet. You knew it, too, even if you had no proof ... but the truth has a way of always surfacing."

The High Ruler raised her face. The moon was fading from the sky.

"Sabran has promised me that after our battles, she will ensure the world knows who really vanquished the Nameless One a thousand years ago. She will restore the Mother to prominence."

The truth would shake Virtudom to its foundations. It would ring out like a bell across the continents.

"You look just as surprised as I was," Kagudo said, with a not-quite-smile. "Centuries of lies will not be undone in a day, of course. The children of the past died believing that Galian Berethnet wielded the sword, and that Cleolind Onjenyu was no more than his adoring bride. That can never be undone, nor mended ... but the children of tomorrow will know the truth."

Ead knew what pain this would cause Sabran. To finally, publicly sever her ties to the woman she had known as the Damsel. The woman whose truth she had never known.

But she would do it. Because it was the right thing—the only thing—to do.

"I trust in the Priory. As I always have," Kagudo said, and placed a hand on her shoulder. "The gods walk with you, Eadaz uq-Nāra. I hope very much that we meet again."

"I hope the same."

Ead bowed to the blood of the Onjenyu. She was surprised when Kagudo returned the gesture.

They parted at the gates to the Privy Garden. Ead pressed her back to its wall as dawn blanched the horizon. Her head was a spinning top of new and uncertain possibilities.

Prioress. If she could defeat the Nameless One, the High Ruler would support any claim she made to the position. That was no small thing. Few Prioresses of the past had been honored with the backing of the Onjenyu.

She returned with a start to the present when a voice called her name. Margret was running to her as fast as her skirts would allow.

"Ead," she said, taking her by the hands, "King Jantar received my letter. He brought Valour."

Ead winched up a smile. "I am glad of it."

Margret frowned. "Are you well?"

"Perfectly."

They both turned to face the palace gates, where courtiers were flocking to hear Sabran make her speech. Margret linked their arms.

"I was sure this day would never come," she said as they slowly followed the rest of the court. "The day a Berethnet queen would have to announce that we are once again at war with the Draconic Army."

The palace gates were not yet open. The city guards were out in force beyond them, while the court assembled behind. Lords and peasants faced each other through the bars.

"You asked about my wedding. I meant to marry Tharian as soon as you woke," Margret said, "but I can hardly do it now, without Loth."

"When, then?"

"After the battle."

"Can you wait that long?"

Margret elbowed her. "The Knight of Fellowship *commands* I wait that long."

The crowd outside grew larger and louder, calling for their queen. As the hands of the clock edged toward six, Tané came to stand beside them. Someone had combed the knots out of her hair and garbed her in a shirt and breeches.

Ead returned her nod. She could sense the siden in the Easterner now, bright as a hot coal.

Bells chimed in the tower. When the royal fanfare began, the crowd at last fell silent. The sound of hooves soon broke it. Sabran rode forth on a white horse in full barding.

She wore the silver-plated armor of winter. Her cloak was crimson velvet, arranged so the ceremonial sword could be seen at her side, and her lips were red as a new rose. Her hair was braided in the ramshorn style that Glorian the Third had favored. The Dukes Spiritual rode behind her, each carrying their family banner. Tané watched them pass with an opaque expression.

The war horse stopped outside the gates. Sabran gripped its reins as Aralaq prowled out from behind and took up a defensive stance beside her. He growled low in his throat. With her head held high, the Queen of Inys faced the stunned eyes of her city.

"My loving people of Virtudom," she said, and her voice was her power, "the Draconic Army has returned."

68

East

It had been centuries since an Eastern fleet had crossed the Abyss. Armed to the hilt with harpoons, swivel guns and siege crossbows, the forty ships were covered by great plates of iron. Even their sails were coated with an iridescent wax, made from the bile of Seiikinese wyrms, that made the cloth harder to burn. The colossal *Dancing Pearl* was at the front, with the *Defiance*, which carried the Warlord of Seiiki, beside it.

And all around, the dragons swam.

Loth watched one of them from the staterooms of the *Dancing Pearl*. Every so often, its head broke the surface so its rider, who bestrode it on a saddle, could breathe. The woman wore facial armor and a helm with lames to protect her neck. She could be warm and dry on a ship, but instead she chose to stay in that black water with her wyrm.

If the two sides of the world could reconcile, this might soon be a common sight in all seas.

The Unceasing Emperor nursed a glass of Lacustrine rose wine. They were deep in a game of Knaves and Damsels, which Loth had taught him the day before.

"Tell me about your queen."

Loth looked up from his hand of cards. "Majesty?"

"You wonder why I ask." The Unceasing Emperor smiled. "I know very little of the rulers from over the Abyss, my lord. If

Queen Sabran is to be an ally to my country, it would behoove me to know something more of her than her famous name. Do you not agree?"

"Yes, Your Imperial Majesty." Loth cleared his throat. "What do you wish to know?"

"You are her friend."

Loth considered for some time. How to paint a portrait of Sabran, who had been in his life since he was six. Since a time when all they had worried about was how many adventures they could fit into a day.

"Queen Sabran is loyal to those who are loyal to her. She is kind-hearted," he finally said, "but hides it well to protect herself. To seem untouched. Her people expect that of their queen."

"You will find that people expect that of all rulers."

That must be true.

"Sometimes a great melancholy comes upon her," Loth continued, "and she takes to her bed for days. She calls them her shadow hours. Her mother, Queen Rosarian, was murdered when she was fourteen. Sabran was there. Since then, she has never been truly happy."

"And her father?"

"Wilstan Fynch, who was once Duke of Temperance, is also dead."

The Unceasing Emperor sighed. "I'm afraid we share in our orphanhood. My parents fell prey to smallpox when I was eight, but my grandmother hurried me away to our hunting lodge in the north while they sickened. I resented not being able to say good-bye. Now I see it was a mercy." He drank. "What age was Her Majesty when she was crowned?"

"Fourteen."

The coronation had taken place in the Sanctuary of Our Lady on a dark and snowy morning. Unlike her mother, who had famously gone to her coronation in a barge, Sabran had ridden through the streets in her carriage, cheered by two hundred thousand of her subjects-to-be, who had traveled from all over Inys to see their princess become a young queen.

"I assume there was a regent," the Unceasing Emperor said.

"Her father was Lord Protector, supported by Lady Igrain Crest, the Duchess of Justice. Later, we discovered that Crest had a part in the death of Queen Rosarian. And ... other atrocities."

The Unceasing Emperor raised his eyebrows. "Another thing we have in common. After I was enthroned, there were almost nine years years of regency. And one of those regents grew too power-hungry to remain at court." He put down his cup. "What else?"

"She likes to hunt and play music. When she was a child, she loved to dance. Every morning, she would dance six galliards." His chest tightened when he thought of those days. "After her mother died, she stopped dancing for many years."

The Unceasing Emperor watched his face. In the light from the bronze lantern on the table, his eyes looked infinite.

"Now tell me," he said, "if she has a lover."

"Majesty," Loth began, unsure of what he was about to say.

"Peace. I'm afraid you would not make a good ruler, with a face that easy to read." The Unceasing Emperor shook his head. "I wondered. When she withheld her hand. I cannot blame her." He drank again. "Perhaps Her Majesty is braver than I was, to try to change tradition."

Loth watched him pour more of the drink.

"You see, once, I fell in love myself. I was twenty when I met her in the palace. I could tell you of her beauty, Lord Arteloth, but I doubt the greatest writer in history could do justice to it, and alas, I never was a writer of much skill. But I can tell you that I could talk to her for hours; as I could with no one else."

"What was her name?"

The Unceasing Emperor closed his eyes for a moment. Loth saw the lines of his throat shift.

"Let us just call her ... the Sea Maiden."

Loth waited for him to continue.

"Of course, others were talking, too. The Grand Secretariat soon learned of our relationship. They were not pleased, given her low rank and the fact that I had not yet married a suitable woman, but I knew my power. I told them I would do as I liked." He let out a sharp breath through his nose. "Such arrogance. I had great power, but I owed it to the Imperial Dragon, my guiding star. I begged her, but though she saw my pain, she would not approve the match. She said there was a shadow in my lover that no one could control. She said that power would unleash it. For both our sakes, I must let her go.

"At first, I resisted. I lived in denial, and I would not stop the affair. Would not stop taking her to swim in the sacred lakes when she asked, or lavishing her with gifts in my palaces. But the stability of my land rested on the alliance of human and dragon. I could no more break it than I could stop a comet in its tracks . . . and I feared that, if I wed the woman I loved, the Grand Secretariat might find a way to make her disappear. Unless I was to treat her like a prisoner, to surround her with bodyguards, I would have to submit."

Loth thought of how the Virtues Council had exiled Ead. All for the crime of love.

"I told her to leave me. She refused. Finally, I said I had never wanted her; that she would never be my empress. This time, I saw pain in her. And rage. She told me that she would build her own empire in defiance of me, and that one day she would drive her blade into my heart, as I had done to her." His jaw flexed. "I never saw her again."

Now it was Loth who poured himself a drink.

All his life, he had intended to find a companion. Now he wondered if he was fortunate to have never fallen in love.

The Unceasing Emperor lay on his bed, head pillowed on one arm, and gazed at the ceiling, heavy-eyed.

"In the Empire of the Twelve Lakes, there lives a bird with purple feathers." The drink had stolen into his voice. "If you saw it in flight, you would think it was a jewel with wings. Many have hunted it . . . but seize it, and your hands will burn. Those feathers, precious as they are, are poison." His eyes closed. "Thank your knights, Lord Arteloth, that you were not born to sit a throne."

69

West

Far away, beyond the Abyss, the shores of Seiiki called to her. She
had dreamed for days of its plum rain, its black sand, the kiss
of its sun-warmed sea on her skin. She missed the scent of sinking
incense and the fog that crowned the mountains. She missed walks
through the cedar forests in the depths of winter. More than any of
that, she missed her gods.

It was the second day of spring, and Nayimathun had not come.
Tané had known it would take time for her to fly again, but if she
had reached the sea, it would have helped to knit the wound. That
left the possibility that she had never got there. That the mages had
hunted down and butchered her.

Let go of your guilt now, rider.

She wanted to obey, but her mind would not. It picked at her old
wounds until they bled again.

A knock interrupted her pacing. She found Ead outside, hair
sparkling with raindrops.

In the cabin, Tané lit what was left of the tallow candle. "How do
you feel?" Ead asked, shutting the door behind her.

"Stronger."

"Good. Your siden has settled." Ead met her gaze. "I just wanted
to check you were all right."

"I am fine."

"You don't look it."

Tané sat on her berth. She wanted to pretend otherwise, but she felt as if she could speak her mind around Ead.

"What if we fail?" she asked. "What if we cannot use the jewels as Cleolind and Neporo did?"

"You have the blood of Neporo, and weeks of practice to commend you." The smile was brief. "Whatever happens, I think we will have Ascalon, Tané. I think we will be able to defeat him for good."

"Why?"

"Because sterren calls to sterren. When we use the jewels, they will cry out to Kalyba. I imagine they have been calling to her ever since the two of us began to use them." Her face was hard. "She will come."

"I hope you are right." Tané toyed with a tress of her own hair. "How are we to defeat her?"

"She is very powerful. Ideally, both of us will avoid single combat with her. But if it comes to that, I have a theory," Ead said. "Kalyba draws her ability to change shape from star rot, and her stores of it must be low. Taking a form that is not her own drains it, and the more she *changes* forms, I suspect, the worse the drain. Forcing her to change shape many times may weaken her. Trap her in one shape."

"You do not know this for sure."

"No," Ead admitted, "but it is all I have."

"How comforting."

With another smile, Ead sat on the chest at the end of the bed.

"One of us must wield Ascalon. Drive it into the Nameless One," she said. "You were exposed to the sterren in the rising jewel for years. The sword may answer more willingly to your hands."

It took Tané a moment to understand. Ead was offering an artefact she had fought to obtain, a keystone of her religion, to a dragonrider. Someone she should still, by rights, consider an enemy.

"Princess Cleolind used it first," Tané said, after a hesitation. "One of her handmaidens should wield it now."

"We cannot quarrel about this. He must die tomorrow, or he will destroy us all."

744

Tané glanced down at her hands. Stained with the blood of her closest friend. Unworthy of Ascalon.

"If there is opportunity," she said, "I will take it."

"Very well." Ead smiled a little. "Goodnight, rider."

"Goodnight, slayer."

The door shut out an icy gust of wind.

Outside, the stars were bright above the Abyss. The eyes of dragons fallen and unborn. Tané asked them now for one more boon. *Let me do what I must*, she prayed, *then let me ask no more.*

The *Reconciliation* was a colossal man-of-war. Except for the *Rose Eternal*, which had been lost in the East, it was the largest and best-armed ship in the Inysh navy.

In the royal staterooms, Ead lay beneath a pile of fur coverlets. Sabran drowsed beside her. It was the first time in days that she had looked peaceful.

Ead nestled into the bedding. The cruel sister had left an imprint somewhere inside her, and it chilled her to the bone.

Tomorrow night, they would be in sight of the other ships. The thought of seeing Loth again was not quite enough to stop the ache in her chest when she thought of his sister. Margret would be in Nzene by now.

Before they had left Ascalon, the Southern rulers had asked Sabran to send willing Inysh with healing skills to the Spindles. Though she was a Lady of the Bedchamber, Margret had asked Sabran for her leave to answer the call. *I'll only get in the way on the ship*, she had told her. *I cannot use a sword, but I can mend the wound it leaves.*

Ead had expected Sabran to deny the request, but she had finally held Margret tightly and ordered her to be safe, and to return. In another break with protocol, she had commanded Sir Tharian Lintley to escort his betrothed and lead the Inysh soldiers. Even her Captain of the Knights of the Body could not protect his queen from the Nameless One. Lintley had not left her willingly, but he could not refuse an order.

Sabran stirred. She looked over her shoulder as Ead pressed a kiss to it.

"You said once that you would take me away," Sabran said softly. "Somewhere."

Ead traced the high slope of her cheekbone. Sabran turned to face her.

"I want you to," she continued. "One day."

Sabran slid a leg over hers. Ead drew her in, so they shared their warmth.

"We said our duties would be done," Ead murmured, "but we both knew it was an airy hope." She sought her gaze. "You are a beloved queen, Sabran. A queen Inys needs. You cannot give up your throne tomorrow, whether or not the Nameless One falls. And I cannot give up on the Priory."

"I know." Sabran shifted closer. "Even as we both whispered in the snow, I knew. We are both wed to our callings."

"We will find a way," promised Ead. "Somehow."

"Let us not think of the future this night," Sabran said softly. "It is not yet dawn." She cupped Ead's face with a faint smile. "We still have time for airy hopes."

Ead touched their brows together. "Now it is you who speaks the comely words."

It was a distraction, but Ead welcomed it. As the candle burned to nothing, she slid her fingers between their bodies, and Sabran kissed her with abandon and tenderness by turns.

Soon they would face the Nameless One. In the light-headed comfort of their joining, with Sabran in her arms and her flesh ablaze with desire, Ead let herself forget it. The arch in her back brought them closer together. Closer to that elusive *somewhere*. She quaked at the gentle touches on her skin, unable to foresee them in the darkness, and savored the shivers that coursed through Sabran as she gave them in return.

After, they both lay still, intertwined.

"You can light another candle," Ead said to her. "Light does not keep me awake."

"I do not need it." Sabran slid a hand to Ead's nape. "Not with you."

Ead tucked her head under Sabran's chin and listened to her heartbeat. She prayed that sound would never cease.

It was still pitch-black when she woke in the same position, to knocking on the cabin door.

"Your Majesty."

Sabran reached for her bedgown. At the door, she conferred in a low voice with one of her Knights of the Body.

"The crew has rescued someone from the water," she said to Ead when she returned.

"How could anyone possibly have swum this far into the Abyss?"

"He was in a rowing boat." She lit a new candle. "Will you come with me?"

Ead nodded and rose to dress.

Six Knights of the Body led them across the *Reconciliation* to the captain's cabin. At present, it was occupied by one man.

Someone had wrapped a coverlet around him. He was pallid and clammy, wearing a travel-soiled Lacustrine tunic, with a head of gray hair, matted with salt water. His left arm was missing below the elbow. From the smell, the loss was recent.

He looked up with bloodshot eyes. Ead recognized him at once, but it was Sabran who spoke first.

"Doctor Roos," she said, and her voice was ice.

Sabran the Ninth. Thirty-sixth queen of the House of Berethnet. Close to a decade of despising her from afar, and now here she was.

Beside her was the person he had been sent here to kill.

During his days at court, she had been known as Ead Duryan. An Ersyri with a relatively minor position in the Upper Household. Clearly not so minor now. He remembered her eyes, dark and piercing, and the proud way that she held herself.

"Doctor Roos," Sabran said.

She might have been addressing a rat.

"Your *Majesty*," Niclays said, his own voice dripping with disdain. He bent his head in a bow. "What a very great pleasure to see you again."

747

The Queen of Inys took the seat on the other side of the table.

"I am sure you remember Mistress Ead Duryan," she said. "She is now known as Dame Eadaz uq-Nāra, Viscountess Nurtha."

"Lady Nurtha," Niclays said, inclining his head. He could not imagine what this young chamberer had done to acquire such high titles.

She remained standing, arms folded. "Doctor Roos."

Her face betrayed none of her feelings toward him, but he suspected, from the way she took an almost protective stance beside Sabran, that they were not particularly warm.

Niclays tried not to meet her gaze. He could mask his intentions well enough, but something about her eyes made him think that they could see right through him.

The blade was cold in his palm. Kalyba had warned him that Ead Duryan was much faster than an ordinary woman, but she would also have no idea that he was carrying something that could harm her. He must strike hard and fast. And with the wrong hand.

Sabran placed her hands on the table, fingertips just touching. "How did you come to be this far into the Abyss?"

Now for the lie.

"I was trying, madam," he said, "to escape from the exile you imposed on me."

"You believed you could cross the Abyss in a rowing boat."

"Desperation will drive any man to folly."

"Or woman. Perhaps that explains why I engaged your services all those years ago."

One corner of his mouth crooked up. "Your Majesty," he said, "you impress me. I had not thought that one heart could hold such rancor."

"My memory is long," Sabran said.

He was sick with hatred. Seven years of imprisonment in Orisima meant nothing to her. She would still deny him a return to Mentendon, all because he had embarrassed her. Because he had made a queen feel small. He saw it in those ruthless eyes.

Kalyba could make them weep. The witch had promised that the death of Ead Duryan would break Sabran Berethnet and, once she was broken, Kalyba would give her to the Nameless One. As he looked at her, Niclays wanted it. He wanted to see her suffer. To be sorry. All he need do was kill her lady-in-waiting and take the white jewel she carried.

Kalyba would resurrect him if the guards ran him through. He would be allowed to return to Mentendon not only with riches, but with Jannart. She would give Jannart back to him.

If he did not do as she said, Laya would die.

"I want you to know something, Sabran Berethnet," Niclays whispered. The pain in his arm was making his eyes water. "I loathe you. I loathe every lash of your eyes, every finger on your hands, and every tooth in your mouth. I loathe you to the very marrow of your bones."

Sabran met his gaze without flinching.

"You cannot fathom the depth of the enmity I have felt for you. I have cursed your name with every sunrise. The thought that I might one day create the elixir of life, then deny it to you, has driven my every action. All I longed to do was thwart your ambition."

"You will not speak to Her Majesty in this manner," one of her shining knights interrupted.

"I will speak to Her Majesty however I please. If she wants me to stop, let her stop me herself," Niclays said curtly, "rather than letting her metal-clad manikin do it for her."

Still Sabran said nothing. The knight in question looked at her before desisting, tight-lipped.

"Years I spent on that island." Niclays spoke through gritted teeth. "Years on a scrap of land clinging to Cape Hisan, watched and mistrusted. Years of walking the same few streets, aching for home. All because I had promised you a gift that had never been given, and you, the Queen of Inys, were naïve enough to swallow it whole. Yes, I deserved chastisement. Yes, I was a cur, and a year or two away might have done me good. But *seven* ... by the Saint, madam, death by burning would have been a mercy in comparison."

His hand clenched around the blade so hard that his nails bit into his palm.

"I could forgive your theft of my money. I could forgive your lies," Sabran whispered, "but you preyed on me, Roos. I was young and afraid, and I confided my deepest fear to you. That fear was something I concealed even from my Ladies of the Bedchamber."

"And that warrants seven years in exile."

"It warrants something. Perhaps I will apologize when you consent to make even the slightest reparation for your lies."

"I wrote to you, *groveling*," Niclays spat, "after Aubrecht Lievelyn refused to allow me to return home. He was so desirous of your sacred cunt that he prized it over—"

Sabran stood, her face bloodless, and every partizan in the room snapped toward his chest.

"You will not speak of Aubrecht Lievelyn again," she said, deadly soft, "or I will have you thrown off this ship in pieces."

He had gone too far. The Knights of the Body wore no visors indoors; he could see the shock written on their faces, a disgust that ran far deeper than it would at a crude insult.

"He's dead," Niclays deduced. "Isn't he?"

The silence confirmed it.

"I received no letter." Sabran kept her voice low. "Why not disclose its contents to me now?"

He chuckled darkly. "Oh, Sabran. Seven years have not changed you. Shall I tell you why I am really here?"

The blade was ice in the heat of his hand. Behind Sabran, Ead Duryan was none the wiser. Just one lunge, and he could get it into her throat after all. He could hear Sabran scream. Watch that mask of a face crack open.

That was when the door swung open, and none other than Tané Miduchi strode into the cabin.

His jaw dropped. The Knights of the Body crossed their partizans in front of her at once, but she shoved against them, looking more than ready to claw his throat open.

"You cannot trust this man," she barked at Sabran. "He is a blackmailer, a *monster*—"

"Ah, Lady Tané," Niclays said dryly. "We meet again. The strings of our fates appear to be tangled."

In truth, he was shocked to see her. He had assumed that she had drowned, or that the Golden Empress had hunted her down. What she was doing with the Queen of Inys was beyond him.

"I let you live on Komoridu," she hissed at him, "but no more. You always come back. Like a weed." She wrestled against the Knights of the Body. "I will gut you with my own blade, you soulless—"

"Wait." Ead grasped her shoulder. "Doctor Roos, you said you would tell us why you were *really* here. I recommend you do so now, before your trail of destruction catches up with you."

"He is here to do us ill, for his own gain," Miduchi said, staring him out. "He always is."

"Then let him confess it."

Miduchi shrugged off her hand, but stopped pushing against the guards. Her narrow shoulders heaved.

Niclays sank back into his seat. His arm was full of fire. His head throbbed.

"The Miduchi is right," he said, between heavy breaths. "I was sent here by some … sorceress, or shape-shifter. Kalyba."

Ead turned sharply to face him. "What?"

"Damned if I knew such things existed, but I suppose I should stop being surprised at this rate." A stab of pain in his stump. "In telling you this, I condemn a friend to death." His jaw trembled. "But … I think that friend would want me to do this."

He removed the shard of metal and laid it on the table. One of the Knights of the Body made toward it, but Ead warded him away with one hand.

"Kalyba gave it to me. It was sh-she who left me in the boat. She told me I was to reach the ship to get close to you, Lady Nurtha," Niclays said. "To d-drive this into your heart."

"A sterren blade," Ead said, eyeing it. "Like Ascalon. Not large enough to use against the Nameless One, but it would have pierced *my* skin well enough." Her gaze flicked up. "I can only assume she fears me more than she did before. Perhaps she has heard the jewels calling."

"Jewels." Niclays raised his eyebrows. "You have them both?"

With a nod, Ead sat beside Sabran.

"The Witch of Inysca is persuasive," she said to him. "She must have promised you all the riches you desired. Why confess?"

"Oh, she offered me something far greater than riches, Lady Nurtha. Something for which I would gladly sacrifice what little wealth remains to me," Niclays said, with a bitter smile. "She showed me the face of my only love. And she promised to return him to me."

"And yet you do not do her bidding."

"Once," he said, "I would have. If she had not worn his face—if she had only promised that I would see him again—I might well have become her little homunculus. But seeing him ... I was repulsed. Because Jannart—" The name snared in his throat. "Jannart is dead. He chose the manner of his death, and by resurrecting him like that, Kalyba dishonored his memory."

Ead watched him.

"I am an alchemist. All my life, I believed that the end goal of alchemy was the glorious transformation of imperfection into purity. Lead into gold, disease into wellness, decay to eternal life. But now I understand. I see. Those were false destinations."

His professor had been right, as always. She had often said that the true alchemy was the work, not its completion. Niclays had thought it was her way of comforting those who never made any progress.

"Sounds foolish, I know," he continued. "Like the ravings of a madman ... but it was just what Jannart always knew, and what I failed to see. For him, the pursuit of the mulberry tree in the East was his great work. He had the final piece, but not the rest."

"Jannart utt Zeedeur," Ead said softly.

He looked at her through burning eyes. "Jannart was my midnight sun," he rasped. "The light I have followed. My grief drove me to Inys, and that step took me to the East. There, I tried to finish his work in the hope that it would bring me closer to him. By doing all this, I completed, unbeknownst to me, the first stage of alchemy, of *my* work. The putrefaction of my soul. With his death, my work began. I faced the shadows in myself."

Nobody moved or spoke. Ead was looking at him with a strange expression. Something like pity, but not quite. Niclays pressed on, trying not to notice the burning in his brow. He was on fire, body and mind.

"So you see," he said, "the work lies in myself. I fell into shadow, and now I must rise, so I might be a better man."

"That would take a long time," the dragonrider said.

"Oh, it will," Niclays agreed, fevered as much by excitement as the wound, "but that is the *point*. Don't you see?"

"I see that you are raving mad."

"No, no. I am approaching the next stage of transmutation. The white sun. The cleansing of impurities, the illumination of the mind! Any fool could tell that nothing can bring Jannart back," Niclays ploughed on, "so I will *resist* Kalyba. She represents my past impurities, the one who comes to undo my progress and return me to my old instincts. To earn the white sun, I will give you the key to destroying all darkness."

"Which is?" Ead said.

"Knowledge," he finished, triumphant. "The Nameless One has a weakness. The twentieth scale of his chest armor is the one that Cleolind Onjenyu damaged all those years ago. She failed to hit the mark, but perhaps she opened the door. A door into his armor."

Ead studied his face, her eyes narrowed a little.

"You can't trust him," Miduchi said. "He would sell his soul for a handful of silver."

"I have no soul to sell, honored Miduchi. But I may yet earn one," Niclays said. Saint, he was hot. "You see, Jan did leave someone behind, someone who I still care for. Truyde utt Zeedeur, his granddaughter. I want to be what he was to her, and to do that, I must be better. I must be *good*. And this is the way."

He finished, staring around in wall-eyed excitement, but all was still. Sabran lowered her gaze, and Ead closed her eyes for a moment.

"She is still in Inys. A maid of honor." As Niclays looked between them, his smile faded. "Isn't she?"

"Leave us," Sabran said to her Knights of the Body. "Please."

They obeyed their queen.

"No," Niclays whispered, trembling. "No." His voice cracked. "What did you do to her?"

"It was Igrain Crest." It was Ead who spoke. "Truyde plotted with her companion, Triam Sulyard, to bring about a reunion between East and West. She staged an assault on Queen Sabran, which Crest infiltrated to cause the death of Aubrecht Lievelyn."

Niclays tried to take it in. Truyde had never expressed strong political views, but when he had last seen her, she had been no more than ten years old.

As he listened, numbness enveloped him. His ears rang. Everything turned dark at the corners, and a chain twisted around him and cut away his breath. By the time Ead had finished speaking, he could no longer feel anything but the dull throb at the end of his arm.

The fires within him had suddenly died. The shadows had returned.

"You left her in the Dearn Tower." He forced it out. "She should have been sent to Brygstad and tried fairly. But no. You drew it out, just as you did to me." A tear seeped into the corner of his mouth. "Her bones lie on one side of the world, and Triam Sulyard's on the other. How much suffering might have been avoided if they had felt safe enough to broach their ideas with you, Sabran, rather than take matters into their own hands."

Sabran did not look away.

"It is not only you who seeks a white sun," she said.

Slowly, Niclays rose. Cold sweat dotted his brow. The pain in his arm was now so great, he could hardly see.

"Is Crest dead?"

"Yes," Sabran said. "Her reign in the shadow of the throne is at an end."

It should comfort him. Perhaps one day it would. But it would not bring her back.

He pictured Truyde, the granddaughter he had never and would never have. Her eyes and freckles had come from her mother, but her red hair, that had been a gift from her grandsire. All gone. He remembered how her face had lit up when he had visited the Silk Hall, and how she had run to him with her arms full of books and begged him to help her learn from them. *Everything*, she had said. *I want to know everything.* Above all things, it was her bright mind, ever-curious, that had made her most like Jannart.

"High Princess Ermuna has extended you an invitation to return home," Sabran said quietly. "She seeks no permission from Inys, and even if she had, I have no further quarrel with it."

It was all he had wanted to hear for seven years. Victory had never tasted so much like ashes.

"Home. Yes." A hollow laugh escaped him. "Take my gift of knowledge. Destroy the Nameless One, so there might be other children who strive to change the world. And then, I pray you, Your Majesty, leave me to my shadows. I'm afraid they are all I have left."

70

Abyss

The *Reconciliation* was a ghost ship in the distance. Loth watched other vessels emerge behind it from the fog.

It was the end of the second day of spring, and they were above the Bonehouse Trench, the deepest part of the Abyss. In Cárscaro, a group of mercenaries would be making their way through the mountain pass to kill King Sigoso and secure the Donmata Marosa.

If she was still alive. If the Flesh King had already died, his daughter might be a puppet now.

The ensigns of every country, save one, rippled among the ships. The Unceasing Emperor was gazing at them, hands behind his back. He wore a scaled cuirass over a dark robe, a heavy surcoat on top, and an ornate iron helmet, inlaid with silver moons and stars.

"So," he said, "it begins." He glanced at Loth. "I thank you, Lord Arteloth. For the pleasure of your company."

"The pleasure was mine, Majesty."

It took time for the ships to be tied to each other. Finally, Sabran came to the *Dancing Pearl* with Lady Nelda Stillwater and Lord Lemand Fynch on either side of her, followed by most of her Knights of the Body and a throng of Inysh naval officers and soldiers.

Befitting the situation, her attire struck a delicate balance between splendor and practicality. A gown that was more like a coat, lacking a framework and cutting off above the ankle, with riding boots beneath. A crown of twelve stars, interspersed with dancing pearls, sat atop her braided hair. And though she was no warrior, she wore the Sword of Virtudom, the stand-in for Ascalon, at her side.

When Loth saw Ead in the party, wrapped in a cloak with a fur collar, he breathed without strain for the first time in days. She was alive. Tané had kept her word.

Tané herself was also among those who came across, though her dragon was nowhere to be seen. When their gazes met, she inclined her head. Loth returned the gesture.

The Unceasing Emperor stopped a short distance from Sabran. He bowed, while Sabran curtsied.

"Your Majesty," the Unceasing Emperor said.

Her face was cast in marble. "Your Imperial Majesty."

There was a moment in which they regarded one another, these two rulers who governed with irreconcilable mandates, who had lived out their lives in the shadow of giants.

"Forgive our ignorance of your language," Sabran said at last. "We understand you speak ours."

"Indeed," the Unceasing Emperor said, "though I assure you that I am ignorant of Inysh matters on most other fronts. Language was one of my passions as a boy." He offered a gracious smile. "I see you have a passion from my side of the world, too. Dancing pearls."

"We are very fond of them. This crown was made before the Grief of Ages, when Inys still traded with Seiiki."

"They are exquisite. We have fine pearls in the Empire of the Twelve Lakes, too. Freshwater pearls."

"We should like to see them," Sabran said. "We must thank Your Imperial Majesty, and the all-honored Warlord, for your swift acquiescence to our request for aid."

"My brother-in-arms and I could hardly have refused, Your Majesty, given the urgency of our situation. And how passionately Lord Arteloth argued for this alliance."

"We expected no less." Loth caught her eye, and she gave him the faintest smile. "May we ask if the dragons of the East are close?" she added. "We rather expected to be able to see them. Or perhaps they are smaller than we have always assumed."

A few nervous chuckles rose.

"Well," the Unceasing Emperor said, "the legends say they could once make themselves smaller than a plum. For now, however, they are as large as you have imagined." The corner of his mouth twitched. "They are beneath the waves, Your Majesty. Immersing themselves in water, gathering their strength. I hope very much that you will be able to meet the Imperial Dragon, my guiding star, after this battle."

Sabran maintained a neutral expression. "We are sure it would be an honor," she said. "Does Your Imperial Majesty"—her voice strained a little—"ride on this ... being?"

"When I am on progress. And perhaps tonight." He leaned toward her, just slightly. "I must confess, however, to a trifling fear of heights. My virtuous grandmother tells me I am unlike all my predecessors in the House of Lakseng in this respect."

"Perhaps that is a favorable sign. After all," Sabran said, "this is a day for new traditions."

At this, he smiled. "It is."

Another fanfare, and the Warlord of Seiiki joined the meeting. Silver-haired, with a thin moustache, Pitosu Nadama had the build and bearing of a man who had once been a warrior, but had not had occasion to take up arms in many years. A sleeveless coat of gold covered his armor. With him were thirty of the dragonriders of Seiiki, who bowed to the foreign rulers.

The rider Loth had seen in the water was among them. She had removed her helm and mask, revealing a sun-beaten face and hair in a topknot. She was looking at Tané, who looked straight back at her.

Nadama hailed the Unceasing Emperor in his own language before turning to Sabran.

"Your Majesty." Even his voice was military, clipped and clear. "My fellow riders will fight alongside you this day. Despite our differences." He glanced at the Unceasing Emperor. "This time, we will ensure the Nameless One does not return to plague us."

"Be assured that Inys stands with you, all-honored Warlord," Sabran answered. White breath fluttered from her mouth. "This day, and for the rest of time."

Nadama nodded.

Trumpets sounded then, announcing King Raunus of the House of Hraustr. A pale giant of a man with golden hair, eyes like iron, and great knotted muscles. He greeted Sabran with a bone-crushing embrace before introducing himself brusquely to the Eastern rulers. His hand stayed close to the gold-plated rapier at his side.

Despite the friendly opening, the tension between the four of them was a low-burning fire. One errant breath of wind could fan it. After centuries of estrangement, Loth supposed it was of little wonder that each side should be wary of the other.

When they had conferred in low voices for a time, the rulers withdrew to their own ships. The dragonriders marched after the Warlord. The moment they began to leave, Tané turned on her heel and strode in the other direction.

Ead followed Sabran into her cabin, but motioned to Loth to join them. Loth waited for most of the guests to clear the deck. As soon as he was past the Knights of the Body and through the door, he scooped Ead right off her feet.

"Being your friend is quite a strenuous affair, you know," he said, feeling her smile against his own cheek. He gathered Sabran close with the other arm. "That applies to both of you."

"Rich words from the man who sailed into the East with pirates," Sabran said into his shoulder.

He chuckled. When he set Ead down, he saw that the stain was gone from her lips, though she looked tired. "I'm all right," she told him. "Thanks to Tané. And to you."

He cupped one of her hands between his. "You still feel cold."

"It will pass."

Loth turned to Sabran and straightened her crown of pearls, which had gone awry in the embrace. "I remember your mother wearing this. She would be proud of this alliance, Sab."

She raised a smile. "I hope so."

"We have an hour before the third day of spring begins. I had better see Meg."

"Meg is not here," Ead said.

Loth stilled. "What?"

She told him everything that had happened since she had woken from her sleep of death. How Tané had eaten the fruit, and how the rulers of the South had come to broker an alliance. When she revealed exactly where his sister was, Loth took a deep breath.

"You let her go to Cárscaro." He said it to them both. "To a siege."

"Loth," Ead said, "Meg made her own choice."

"She was determined to play her part, and I saw no reason to take that from her," Sabran explained. "Captain Lintley is with her."

He imagined his sister on the barren plain, hunkered in a field hospital among the filth and blood of battle. He thought of Margret with the bloodblaze and felt sick.

"I must address the Inysh seafarers," Sabran murmured. "I pray we see the dawn."

Loth swallowed the cork of dread in his throat. "May Cleolind watch over us all," he said.

On the deck of the *Dancing Pearl*, Tané stood among the soldiers and archers who had gathered to await the hour.

The Unceasing Emperor was on the upper deck. Behind him, like an immense shadow, the Imperial Dragon loomed. Her scales were darkest gold, eyes blue as glaciers. Long tendrils matched the white of her horns. At the stern were three of the Seiikinese dragon elders. Even after all the time Tané had spent in the company of dragons, these ones were the most colossal she had ever seen.

Close to the elders, the Warlord of Seiiki kept watch beside the Sea General. Tané knew her former commander was more than aware of her presence. Every time she looked away from him, she sensed his attention snap to her face.

Onren and Kanperu were among the dragonriders. The latter had gained a scar across one eye since Tané had last seen him. Their dragons waited behind the *Defiance*.

A touch on her arm made her look back. A figure emerged from the shadows behind her, wearing a hooded cloak.

Ead.

"Where is Roos?" Tané asked her softly.

"The fever has set in. His fight today will be for his life." Ead never took her gaze from Sabran. "Has your dragon arrived?" Tané shook her head. "Could you ride another?"

"I am no longer a rider."

"But surely today—"

"You do not seem to understand," Tané said shortly. "I am disgraced. They will not even speak to me."

Finally, Ead nodded. "Keep the jewel close," was all she said before she returned to the shadows.

Tané tried to concentrate. A breath of wind caressed her spine, unsettled her hair, and rose to fill the sails of the *Dancing Pearl*.

Deep in the Abyss, there was movement. No more than the flicker of butterfly wings, or the quickening of a child in the womb.

"He comes," the Imperial Dragon said. Her voice quaked through the ships.

Tané reached for her case. The jewel was so cold that she could feel it through the wood and lacquer.

The wind howled against the sails. This was it. Clouds gathered above the ships. The Imperial Dragon called out to her brethren in the language of her kind. The Seiikinese dragons joined their voices to hers. Water bubbled on their scales. The mist grew thick as they brought the storm, and with it, their strength. As they took off from the sea, water streamed off them, soaking the humans below. Tané shook it from her eyes.

It happened so quickly. One moment, all was silent, save the rain.

Then, madness.

The first thing she thought was that the sun had risen, such was the light that ignited in the north. Then came a heat that sucked the breath from her. Fire exploded across the Seiikinese warship *Chrysanthemum*, moments before a second eruption tore through the fleet of the Northern king, and a full-throated roar announced the arrival of the enemy.

When the black High Western appeared, the downwind from its flight extinguished every lantern on every ship. "Fýredel," someone bellowed.

Tané choked on the hot stench from his scales. Screams rang out. In the light from the fire, she saw Loth rushing Queen Sabran to her Knights of the Body and the Imperial Guard encircling the Unceasing Emperor before a shoulder slammed into her chest, knocking her flat.

A war conch sounded in the darkness. The riders disappeared with their dragons into the sea. Even as chaos sparked around her, Tané ached to be among them.

The black High Western circled the fleet. Its servants came tearing above the ships. They tangled with the Eastern dragons. Wings, endless wings, flocking like bats. Tails whipped lightning across the sky.

A wyvern flew straight at the mainmast of the *Reconciliation*. It groaned and buckled, bringing down the highest sail. An agonized cry went up from the deck.

The sails of the iron-armored *Chrysanthemum* were engulfed in flame. Tané ran with the crowd, pistol in hand. The force of the power inside her—her siden—throbbed in her blood like a second heartbeat.

A fire-breather landed in front of her. Bigger than a stallion. Two legs. A scarlet tongue rattled in its mouth.

Wyvern.

All her life she had prepared for this. It was what she had been born to do.

Tané took out the rising jewel. White light flared out of it, and the wyvern screamed in rage, shielding itself from the glow with its wing. She drove it back, away from the archers.

Another wyvern crashed down behind her, shaking the deck, eyes like live coals in its head. Caught between them, Tané stuffed the jewel back into its case with one hand and drew her Inysh sword from its scabbard with the other. The weight of it unbalanced her, and the first swing went wide, but the second found its mark. Red-hot blood spurted as the blade hewed through scale and flesh and bone. The wyvern struck the deck, headless, its body still thrashing.

And just for a moment, she saw Susa in that pool of blood, a head of dark hair rolling into a ditch, and she could not move an inch. The first wyvern vomited flame at her back.

She twisted just in time. Of its own accord, her hand flew up, and golden light discharged from her palms. The Draconic fire glanced off her, burning up the shoulder of her shirt and making her cry out as blisters formed, but the rest of the flames petered into the fog.

The wyvern cocked its head, pupils slitted, before it let out a hideous snarl and erupted with more blue-tinged fire. Tané backed away, sword at the ready. She needed a Seiikinese blade. No one could move like water with this dead weight in their hands.

Her enemy spat its fire in bursts. Rain hammered its hide. When it was close enough, Tané ducked a bite from its rotting teeth and slashed at its legs. Her next move was too slow—a burly tail snapped across her midriff, its spines just missing her. She went flying across the deck.

The sword clattered out of her hand just before she hit one of the masts and thumped down again, bashing her head. The shock of the impact held her in place. At least one of her ribs was cracked. Her back felt shredded. As the wyvern stalked toward her, nostrils smoking, a Seiikinese soldier thrust his blade into its flank. In the first moment of its rage, he circled the wyvern and aimed for its eye. It clapped its jaws over his leg and slammed him into the deck, over and over, back and forth, as if he were a scrap of meat. Tané heard his bones shatter, his screams bubbling away. The beast hurled what was left over the side.

A charred soldier lay nearby, clad in blue and silver armor. Tané took up a shield emblazoned with the heraldry of the Kingdom of Hróth and hefted it on to her left arm, clenching her jaw against the pain in her ribs. With her other hand, she lifted her bloody sword.

The heat from the fires drew sweat to the surface. The sword was slippery in her hand.

She was no longer aware of the other fire-breathers that flocked above the ships, tearing at sails and breathing great clouds of fire, or the soldiers battling around her. All she knew was the wyvern, and all the wyvern knew was her.

When it lunged for her, she rolled away from its bite and hurdled the tail that whipped toward her knees. Its lack of front limbs made it too cumbersome to fight at close quarters with something as small and quick as a human. This fiend had been bred for swooping and snatching. Like a bird of prey. As it pursued her, her sword gouged the wound the soldier had left. Her shield blocked a flame. The wyvern wrenched it out of her grip. She thrust the sword up, crunching through the underside of its jaw and deep into the roof of its mouth, and the fire in its eyes was extinguished. She backed away from the corpse.

The siden replenished her before exhaustion could set in. Nothing could touch her. Not even death. As the black High Western smashed down the mast of the *Water Mother*, Tané snatched up a fallen spear.

Her eyes ached. She could see the fire-breathers as if they were motes of dust in a sunray. With one swing of her arm, the spear flew at a bird-headed monster and impaled its wing, pinning it to its body. Flapping wildly with the other, it plummeted into the waves.

The *Reconciliation* had pulled away from the *Dancing Pearl*. So had the *Defiance* and the *Chrysanthemum*. Their cannons were slanting upward. She heard the crump of a swivel gun before the *Reconciliation* released everything it had. Chainshot swiveled skyward and snagged on wings and tails. A deafening *whump-whump* began as the cannons fired. Crossbow bolts shivered from the Lacustrine ships, splinters of bronze catching the firelight. She could hear captains bellowing orders and pistols discharging from the decks of the *Defiance* and the twang of bowstrings across the fleet.

The clamor was too much. Her head was spinning. She was drunk on siden, seeing the whole battle like a vision.

A weapon. She needed another weapon. If she could reach the *Defiance*, she could find something. One step took her onto the gunwale, and she dived into the sea.

The quiet beneath the water cooled the fire within. She surfaced and swam hard for the *Defiance*. Nearby, one of the Ersyri ships had been overcome by flame, and it shed its crew from every side.

There would be black powder on that ship. Lots of it. She took a huge breath and swam downward.

When the ship exploded, she felt the flash of heat through the water. Foul orange light stained the Abyss. The force of it took hold of her and spun her off-course. She kicked back, blinded by her own hair. As she neared the *Defiance*, she surfaced.

Black smoke swelled from the flaming carcass of the ship. For a moment, Tané could only stare at the destruction.

The black High Western settled on the ruins as though they were a throne. Flesh-fed and banded with muscle, it was a grotesque size. The spikes on its tail were each ten feet long.

Fýredel.

"Sabran Berethnet." His voice bled with hatred. "My master comes for you at last. Where is the child that will keep him at bay?"

As he mocked the Queen of Inys, a Seiikinese elder dragon, glowing all over, shattered the surface of the Abyss. One great leap took him high over the *Dancing Pearl* to catch a wyvern in his mouth. Lightning flashed between his teeth. His eyes shone blue-white. Tané saw the wyvern erupt into white flame before the dragon plunged back into the sea, taking his trophy with him. Fýredel watched the display with bared teeth.

"Dranghien Lakseng." The name boomed across the water. "Will you not show your face?"

Tané kept swimming. The cannons of the *Defiance* seemed as loud as the thunder. She found the handholds and climbed.

"Behold the Roar of Hróth, who hides in the snow," Fýredel sneered, exposing his teeth again. Cannons barked from the *Bear Guard* in answer. "Behold the Warlord of Seiiki, who preaches unity between human and sea-slug. We will throw down your guardians and scatter them like sheep, as we did centuries ago. We will leave black sand from shore to shore."

Tané reached the deck of the *Defiance*. Seiikinese soldiers wielded longbows and pistols. An arrow skittered off a wyvern. She pulled a sword from the hand of a dead woman. Somewhere in the night, a dragon was keening.

"Gone are the days of heroes," Fýredel said. "From North to South and West to East, your world will burn."

Tané took the rising jewel from its case. If Kalyba was close, she would be drawn to its power.

Sterren punched through the waves like a needle through silk and drew them like a shroud over Fýredel. He launched himself skyward with a snarl, droplets raining off his wings, scales billowing steam.

"Black sails, west sou'west!" came a shout.

In the distance, through the haze of smoke, Tané could see them.

"Yscali ensign," the captain of the *Reconciliation* bellowed. "The Draconic Navy!"

Tané counted them. Twenty ships.

Another wyvern swooped, and she rolled behind a mast. A full line of archers fell to its tail. A soldier hurled his halberd at the creature, straight into its haunch.

An archer was slumped over the gunwale, bones shattered. Tané shoved the jewel away and took his bow and quiver. Four arrows left.

"Fire-breather," the lookout above her roared. "Port, port!"

The remaining archers turned and drew while matchlocks were reloaded. Tané nocked an arrow of her own.

A second High Western, pale as a crane, came out of the night. Tané watched the wings fold inward, the scales change seamlessly to skin, the green eyes gain their whites, and black hair flow where horns had been. By the time it landed on the *Defiance*, the wyrm had become the same woman Tané had seen in Lasia. Red lips closed over the last flicker of a forked tongue.

"Child," Kalyba said in Inysh, "give me that jewel."

Something in Tané urged her to obey.

"It is not a weapon. It is the imbalance." The witch stalked toward her. "*Give* it to me."

Shaken, Tané pulled back her bowstring and forced herself not to look at what Kalyba held. The blade was the bright, pure silver of a star.

Ascalon.

"A bow. Oh, dear. Eadaz should have warned you that you cannot kill a witch with a splinter of wood. Or fire." Kalyba kept striding toward her, naked, eyes wild. "I should have expected this defiance from the seed of Neporo."

With every step Kalyba took across the deck, Tané took one away from her. Soon she would run out of ship. The bow was useless—her enemy could shape-shift away from an arrow in a heartbeat, and it was clear the sword could transfigure with her. When it was in her hand, it was like another limb.

"I wonder," Kalyba said, "if you could best me in combat. After all, you are Firstblood." Her mouth curved. "Come, blood of the mulberry tree. Let us see who is the greater witch."

Tané set down her bow. Planting her feet apart, she let her siden rise like the sun into her hands.

71

Abyss

On the *Reconciliation,* Loth stood guard beside his queen in the shadow beneath the quarterdeck, surrounded by twelve of the Knights of the Body.

One of the topsails was afire. Bodies strewed the decks. Cannons hawked barshot and chainshot, cut with cries of *Fire* from the boatswain, while siege engines from Perchling hurled grappling hooks that tangled around legs and wings.

It was all the gunners could do to avoid the Eastern dragons. Though some of them were in flight, strangling the fiery breeds the way snakes crushed their quarry, others had adopted a different way to kill. They would dive beneath the waves, then swim up with all their might and breach. One clap of their jaws, and they would drag their prey back to the deep.

Water streamed from their scales as they soared over the *Reconciliation.* Fires sputtered out beneath them.

Sabran kept one hand on the Sword of Virtudom. They watched the pale wyrm transform into a woman and land on the *Defiance.*

Kalyba.

The Witch of Inysca.

"Ead will go to her," Sabran shouted to him over the clangor. "Someone must distract the witch so she can strike."

The Draconic Navy was drawing closer by the moment. A square-rigger with red sails bore down on the *Reconciliation.*

"Hard to port," the captain bawled. "Gun crew, belay last order. Fire on that ship!"

A terrible shriek of wood and metal. The ship rammed straight into the nearby *Merrow Queen*.

"All right," Loth called to Sabran. "To the *Defiance*."

The Knights of the Body were already moving. Keeping Sabran between them, they struck out across the deck. As they ran, they shed their heaviest armor. Breastplates, greaves, and pauldrons clattered in their wake. Cannons ripped into the enemy ship.

"Swords!" The captain drew his cutlass. "Get Her Majesty to the boat!"

"There's no time," Loth shouted.

The captain gritted his teeth. His hair clung to his face. "Take her, then, Lord Arteloth, and don't look back," he replied. "Hurry!"

Sabran climbed over the side of the ship. Loth joined her, and she took his hand.

The waves swallowed them all.

Tané hurled fire at Kalyba across the *Defiance*. Flames danced along the deck, catching in pools of Draconic blood. When the witch countered the attack with lurid red fire of her own, so hot it roasted the moisture from the air, Tané gripped the rising jewel. Seawater crashed onto the ship, which pitched beneath them, and the fires were smothered.

Every soldier and archer had fled from the duel. The ship was their battleground.

Kalyba moved lithely from bird to woman, quick as lightning. Tané screamed in frustration as a beak ripped her cheek open and a talon almost took out her eye. Each time the witch changed, Ascalon changed with her. When she was in her human guise, she swung with the sword, and when Tané parried, and their blades locked, the rising jewel sang in answer.

"I hear it," Kalyba breathed. "Give it to me."

Tané slammed her forehead into hers and struck with a concealed knife, catching the witch across the cheek. Kalyba reeled, eyes flared wide, red lacing her face. Then antlers erupted from her skull, and she was a bleeding white stag, ghastly and *massive*, and the sword was gone again.

Tané used the jewel to throw back a cockatrice. The siden sharpened her senses, made her limbs move quicker than she would have thought possible as the stag thundered across the deck. She saw that one of the antlers was tipped with silver, and as it lowered its head to skewer her, she brought her sword up, severing it.

Kalyba collided with the deck in human form. Blood jeweled from her shoulder, where a chunk of flesh had been hacked away, and Ascalon lay beside her, glazed with ruby. Tané lunged for it, but the witch already had fire in her hands.

Tané threw herself behind the mainmast. Red fire blazed off her thigh, so hot—like molten iron on her flesh—that it made her cry out. Eyes full of brine, she crushed the pain and struck out across the deck. She was almost at the stern when she stopped in her tracks.

Queen Sabran was on the *Defiance*. Loth stood beside her, broadsword drawn, and twelve bodyguards fanned out around them. All of them were dripping wet.

"Sabran," Kalyba breathed.

The queen gazed at her forebear. Their faces were identical.

"Your Majesty," one of the guards stammered. All of them were looking between their queen and her double. "This is sorcery."

"Stand back," Sabran said to her guards.

"Yes, *do*, gallant knight. Do as my offspring decrees." Kalyba curled her fingers around the flame in her palm. "Do you not see that I am your Damsel, foremother of Inys?"

The knights did not move. Neither did the queen. Her left hand strangled the hilt of her sword.

"You are an imitation of me," Kalyba said to her, venomous. "Just as your sword is a cheap imitation of this one."

She held up Ascalon. Sabran flinched.

"I did not want to believe Ead," she replied, "but I see that my affinity with you cannot be denied." She stepped toward Kalyba. "You took my child from me, Witch of Inysca. Tell me, after you went to so much trouble to found the House of Berethnet, why would you destroy it?"

Kalyba closed her fist, and the flame was snuffed.

"One shortcoming of immortality," she said, "is that everything you build seems too small, too transient. A painting, a song, a book—all of them rot away. But a masterwork, made over many years, many centuries ... I cannot tell you the fulfilment it brings. To see your actions, in your lifetime, made into a legacy." She lifted up Ascalon. "Galian lusted after Cleolind Onjenyu the moment he laid eyes on her. Though I had nursed him at my breast, though I gave him the sword that was the sum of all my achievements, and though I was beautiful, he wanted her above all things. Above me."

"So it was unrequited love," Sabran said. "Or was it jealousy?"

"A little of both, I suppose. I was younger then. Caged by a tender heart."

Tané saw a flicker in the shadows.

Sabran moved a little to the left. Kalyba circled with her. Here, on this stretch of the ship, it was as if they were in the eye of the storm. No wyrms breathed fire near the witch.

"I watched Inys grow into a great nation. At first, that was enough," Kalyba confessed. "To see my daughters thrive."

"You still could," Sabran told her softly. "I have no mother now, Kalyba. I would welcome another."

Kalyba paused. Just for a moment, her face looked as naked as the rest of her.

"No, my *lykyn*," she said, just as softly. "I mean to be a queen, as I once was. I will sit on the throne you can no longer hold." She walked toward Sabran. The Knights of the Body pointed their swords at her. "I watched my daughters rule a country for a thousand years. I watched you preach against the Nameless One. What you failed to see is that the only way forward is to join with him.

"When I am queen, Inys will never burn again. It will be a Draconic place, protected. The people will never know you are gone. Instead they will rejoice to know that Sabran the Ninth, after reconciling her differences with the Nameless One, was blessed with his immortality. That she will reign forever."

Sabran tightened her grip on her sword.

She was waiting for something, Tané realized. Her gaze flicked past her forebear, toward the bow of the ship.

"I misbelieve your grand talk," the queen said, her tone pitying. "I think that this is simply the last act in your revenge. Your desire to destroy all trace of Galian Berethnet." Her smile was pitying. "You are as beholden to your heart as you ever were."

Suddenly Kalyba was right in front of her. The Knights of the Body started toward her, but she was already too close, close enough to kill their queen if they moved against her now. Sabran held very still as the witch pushed a wet strand of hair from her brow.

"It will hurt me," Kalyba whispered, "to hurt you. You are mine … but the Nameless One will bring great things to this world. Greater things than even you could bring." She kissed her forehead. "When I give you to him, he will know, at last, that I cherish him above all things."

Sabran suddenly wrapped her arms around the witch. Tané stiffened, taken aback.

"Forgive me," the queen said.

Kalyba wrenched away, eyes flared. Quick as a scorpion, she turned, fire igniting in her hand again.

A narrow blade ran her through. The sterren blade.

A sliver of the comet.

Kalyba drew in a sharp breath. As she stared at the shard of metal in her breast, her hooded killer revealed her face.

"I do this for you." Ead twisted the blade deeper. There was no malice in her expression. "I will take you to the hawthorn tree, Kalyba. May it bring you the peace you did not find here."

Dark lifeblood flowed from the witch, down her breast and past her navel. Even immortals bled.

"Eadaz uq-Nāra." The name left her like a curse. "You are so very like Cleolind, you know." Blood speckled her lips. "After all this time, I see her spirit. Somehow … she outlived me."

As she sank over her mortal wound, the Witch of Inysca let out a scream. It echoed across the water, far into the Abyss. Ascalon fell from her hand, and Sabran seized it. At the last, Kalyba grabbed her by the throat.

"Your house," she whispered to the queen, "is built on barren ground." Sabran strained to break her grip, but her hand was a vise. "I see chaos, Sabran the Ninth. Beware the sweet water."

Ead pulled her blade free, and more blood pulsed from Kalyba, like wine from a gourd. By the time she had fallen to the deck, her eyes were cold and dead as emeralds.

Sabran gazed in silence at the naked body of her forebear, one hand at her throat, where finger marks had already blossomed. Ead removed her cloak and covered the witch, while Tané picked up another sword.

A bell rang from the Inysh fleet. The sails of the *Defiance* stirred. Tané watched as the same wind set the Seiikinese flag aflutter. Even the cannon fire seemed to grow softer as a preternatural hush descended.

"This is it," Ead said, her voice calm. "He is coming."

In the sky, the fire-breathers moved the way starlings did, whirling in great clouds of wing. A dance of welcome.

In the distance, the sea exploded upward.

The waters of the Abyss convulsed. Shouts of panic spiked the night as waves crested the ships. Tané hit the gunwale as the *Defiance* lurched, unable to wrest her gaze from the horizon.

The eruption of water rose high enough to obliterate the stars. Amidst the chaos, a shape took form.

She had heard stories of the beast. Every child had grown up hearing about the nightmare that had crawled out of the mountain to ravage all the world. She had seen images of him, richly painted in gold-leaf and red lacquer, with blots of soot-ink where eyes ought to be.

No artist had captured the magnitude of the enemy, or the way the fire inside him made him smoulder. They had never seen it for themselves. His wingspan was the length of two Lacustrine treasure ships. His teeth were as black as his eyes. The waves crashed and the thunder rolled.

Prayers in every language. Dragons rising from the sea to meet their enemy, letting out haunting calls. Soldiers on the *Defiance* brandished their weapons, and on the *Lord of Thunder*, archers exchanged their arrows for longer ones, fletched with purple feathers. Poison arrows might fell a wyvern or a cockatrice, but nothing would get under those scales. Only one sword had a chance.

Ead retrieved Ascalon.

"Tané," she shouted over the din, "take it."

Tané took its weight in her clammy hands. She had expected it to be heavy, but it felt as if it could be hollow.

The sword that could slay the true enemy of the East. The sword that could earn back her honor.

"Go." Ead gave her a push. "Go!"

Tané scraped up all her fear and crushed it into a dark place inside her. She made sure her borrowed sword was secure at her side. Then, keeping Ascalon in hand, she made for the closest sail. She scaled the battens, fighting through wind and rain, until she reached the top.

"Tané!"

She turned. A Seiikinese dragon with silver scales was rising from the waves.

"Tané." The rider beckoned her. "Jump!"

Tané had no time to think. She threw herself from the beam, into nothing.

A hand sheathed in a gauntlet took hold of her arm and hauled her into the saddle. Ascalon almost slipped from her embrace, but she pinned it with her elbow.

"It's been a while," Onren called.

The saddle was just big enough for two, but there was nothing to hold a second rider in place. "Onren," Tané started, "if the honored Sea General finds out you let me ride with—"

"You are a rider, Tané." Her voice was muffled by the mask. "And this is no place for rules."

Tané pushed Ascalon into a sheath on the saddle and secured it. Her fingers were wet and icy, clumsy on the hilt. The sheath had not been made for such a long blade, but it would hold the sword better than she could. Seeing her struggle, Onren reached into one of the pouches and passed Tané a pair of gauntlets. She slipped them over her hands.

"I assume you found a way to kill the Nameless One on your travels," Onren said.

"A scale of his chest armor is loose." Tané had to shout to be heard over the clash of weapons and the roars of wyrms and fire. "We have to tear it off and pierce the flesh beneath with this sword."

"I think we can manage that." Onren gripped the horn of the saddle. "Don't you, Norumo?"

Her dragon hissed his agreement. Cloud frothed from his nostrils. Tané held on to Onren, her hair flying about her face.

The Seiikinese dragons were coming together. Most of their riders held longbows or pistols. At the same time, the fire-breathers flocked to protect their master, forming an appalling swarm in front of him. Tané felt Onren freeze. After all they had learned, all they had sacrificed, none of their schooling had prepared them for this. This was war.

They were close to the front of the formation, behind the elders. The great Tukupa the Silver led the charge, with the Sea General buckled into the saddle on her back. The Imperial Dragon flew beside her, leading the Lacustrine dragons. Tané shielded her eyes against the rain, straining to see. The Unceasing Emperor was a small figure astride his fellow ruler.

Bracing herself, Tané locked her arms around Onren. With a growl, the great Norumo lowered his head.

When they hit the flock, the collision almost threw Tané from the saddle. She clung to Onren, who hacked with her sword at wings and tails while Norumo rammed his horns into anything in his path. All was uproar and thunder, screaming and death, rain and ruin. She had the short-lived sensation that this was a terrible dream.

Lightning flashed through her eyelids. When she looked up, she met the eyes of the Nameless One. He stared into her soul. And when he opened his mouth, she saw doom.

Fire and smoke blasted from his jaws.

It was as if a volcano had erupted into the night. The dragon elders parted around the Nameless One and snapped at his sides, but Norumo, like his rider, had a taste for breaking rules.

He dived beneath the inferno and rolled. Tané tightened her arms around Onren as the world turned on its head. Another dragon tried to avoid that cavernous mouth, but the Nameless One bit her in two. Scales glittered as his teeth scattered them, like a fistful of coins tossed into the air. Tané watched, sickened, as the two halves of the dragon sank toward the sea.

Smoke was in her chest and eyes. Blood surged to her head. They passed beneath the Nameless One, close enough for the heat from his belly to parch her skin and steal what was left of her breath. As Norumo spiraled, Onren thrust out her sword. It sparked over red scales, but made no mark. Norumo swerved between the spikes of an endless tail—and then they were flying even higher, above the beast, back toward the flock.

I see you, rider.

Tané stared at the Nameless One. His eye was upon her.

You carry a blade I know well. The voice rang in every crevice of her mind. *It was last in the possession of the White Wyrm. Did you slay her for it, as you now hope to slay me?*

Her hand flinched to her temple. She could feel his rage in her very bones, in the hollows of her skull.

"We need to get closer," Onren said, panting.

Norumo was moving back into formation, but his breathing was just as labored as hers. The heat had baked the moisture from his scales.

I smell the fire inside you, daughter of the East. Soon your ashes will scatter the sea. I suppose that befits one who swims with the slugs of the water.

Tears streamed down her face. Her head was going to burst open.

"Tané, what is it?"

"Onren," she gasped, "do you hear his voice?"

"Whose voice?"

She cannot hear me. Only those who have tasted of the trees of knowledge can, the Nameless One said. Tané sobbed in agony. *I was born out of the hidden fire, forged in the vital furnace that gave you but one spark. For as long as you live, I will live inside you, in your every thought and memory.*

One of the Seiikinese dragons that had separated from the rest of the formation slammed into his neck. The vise on her mind sprang open. She fell against Onren, shuddering.

"Tané!"

The flock tore at Norumo. The Imperial Dragon, who was almost as large as the monster, forced a path through the swarm, let out a mighty roar, and scourged the Nameless One with her claws. Gold sparks flew and, for the first time, gouges appeared in that age-old armor. The Nameless One twisted his head, teeth bared, but the Imperial Dragon was already out of reach.

Onren punched the air. "For Seiiki!" she cried out. Other riders echoed her.

Tané shouted it until her throat was raw.

The Sea General blew through his war conch, summoning the dragons for a second foray. This time, the flock they faced was even larger, a wall of wings. Fire-breathers everywhere were abandoning their clashes with the ships and flying to defend their master. Their ranks closed around the Nameless One, who was moving ever closer to the fleet.

"We can't get through that." Onren grasped the saddle. "Norumo, take us to the front."

He growled low and drew up alongside the elders. Tané tensed as the Sea General turned his face toward them. Onren snapped open a fan and signaled for him to cease the charge.

The Sea General signed with a fan in return. He wanted them to approach from above. Other riders passed the message along.

Upward they flew, toward the moon. When they dived, in perfect unison, Tané narrowed her eyes. The wind tore back her hair. She reached for Ascalon and drew it from the sheath.

This time, she would strike him.

One moment, the fire-breathers rose to meet them. The next, all Tané could see was darkness.

Norumo let out a roar. A blue glow vented between his scales before lightning splintered from his mouth. Every hair on Tané stood on end. As Norumo skewered an amphiptere on his horns, another bolt flashed out of the turmoil. It whipped past Onren, glanced off her armor, and caught Tané across the bare skin of her arm.

She felt her heart stop.

The lightning hit a wyvern, but not before it set her clothes on fire. Onren screamed her name just before Tané was thrust from dragonback, into the chaos of the sky.

The wind smothered her shirt, but not the white-hot flame beneath her skin. For a moment, she felt weightless. She could hear nothing, see nothing.

When she became aware again, the fire-breathers were high above her, the black sea rushing up below. Ascalon was wrenched from her hand. One flash of silver, and it vanished.

She had failed. The sword was gone. Nothing but death awaited them at the end of this day.

Hope was lost, but her body refused to give up the fight. Some long-buried instinct made her heed her training. All students of the Houses of Learning had been taught how to raise their chances of survival if they should ever fall from dragonback. She faced the Abyss and opened her arms, as if to embrace it.

Then a banner of misty green rushed beneath her. She was caught in the coil of a tail.

"I have you, little sister." Nayimathun lifted Tané on to her back. "Hold on."

Her fingers splayed over wet scales.

"Nayimathun," Tané gasped.

Livid red branches had spread from her shoulder, down her right arm, and across her neckline.

"Nayimathun," she said, panting, "I lost Ascalon."

"No," Nayimathun said. "This is not over. It fell to the deck of the *Dancing Pearl*."

Tané looked down at the ships. It seemed impossible that the sword had avoided the endless black water.

Another ship fractured into pieces as its black powder combusted. Bleeding, his wing injured, Fýredel threw back his head and let out a long sound that stemmed from deep within. Even Tané knew what it was. A rallying cry.

The herd above their heads was thrown into disarray. As she watched, half of the fire-breathers dropped away from the Nameless One, to Fýredel.

"Now," Tané shouted. "Now, Nayimathun!"

Her dragon did not hesitate. She flew toward the enemy.

"Aim for his chest." Tané unsheathed the sword at her side. Rain lashed her face. "We have to break through his scales."

Nayimathun bared her teeth. She rammed through what remained of the vanguard. The other dragons were calling to her, but she paid them no heed. As fire roared to meet them, she swept over the Nameless One and wrapped herself around his body, so her head was beneath his, out of the reach of his teeth and flame. Tané heard her scales begin to sizzle.

"Go, Tané," she forced out.

Forgetting her fear, Tané leaped from dragonback and grabbed on to a scale. The heat burned through her gauntlets, but she kept climbing up the Nameless One, stretching up to each plate of his armor, using their razor-sharp edges as handholds, counting down from the top of his throat. When she reached the twentieth scale, she saw the imperfection, the place where it had never fitted smoothly back over the scar beneath. Holding on with one hand, she jammed the blade of her sword beneath the scale, planted her boots on the one below, and pulled on the haft with all her might.

The Nameless One opened his jaws and let out an inferno, but though the fire soaked her in sweat and made it hard to breathe, Tané kept craning. Screaming with the effort, she threw all her weight behind the pull.

The blade of her sword snapped. She dropped ten feet before she flung out a hand and caught herself on another scale.

Her arms were trembling. She was going to slip.

Then, with a war cry that rang in her bones, Nayimathun reared. The haft of the sword caught between two of her teeth. With one jerk of her head, she ripped the scale free.

Steam vented from the flesh of the Nameless One. Tané threw out an arm to stop it scalding her—and fell from his armor.

Her fingers caught in a riverweed mane. She hauled herself back onto Nayimathun. At once, her dragon uncoiled herself, scales burnt dry, and plunged toward the ocean. Tané choked on the stench of hot metal. The Nameless One came after them, jaws gaping to show the spark in his throat. Nayimathun keened as razor teeth closed on her tail.

The sound screamed through Tané. She flicked her knife into her hand, twisted at the waist, and hurled it into the depths of a black eye. His jaws unlocked, but not before flesh and scale tore asunder. Nayimathun tumbled away from him, toward the Abyss, blood spraying from her.

"Nayimathun—" Tané choked on her name. "Nayimathun!"

The rain turned silver.

"Find the sword," was all her dragon said. Her voice was fading. "This must end here. It must be now."

The soldier stabbed for Ead with his partizan, almost catching her cheek. His face was clammy, he had pissed himself, and he was shaking so hard his jaw rattled. "Stop fighting, you witless fool," Ead shouted at him. "Drop your weapon, or you give me no choice."

He wore a mail coat and a scaled helmet. His eyes were bloodshot with exhaustion, but he was in the grip of something beyond reason. When he swung for Ead again, the blow pendulous, she ducked beneath his arm and drew her sword upward, opening him from belly to shoulder.

The man had come from the Draconic Navy. Its soldiers fought as if possessed, and perhaps they were. Possessed by fear of what would happen to their families in Cárscaro if they lost this fight.

The Nameless One circled high above the ships. Ead watched as he thrashed, and a ribbon of pale green fell away from him. The sound of the Draconic tongue echoed across the waves.

"The sword," Fýredel bellowed. "Find the sword!"

Half the Yscali soldiers scrambled to obey, while others took to the sea. Blood was spreading through the water, along with the wax that had protected the ships.

A wyvern winged overhead and set fire to a trail of debris. Howls rose as soldiers and seafarers were broiled alive.

Ead cupped a bloody hand over the waning jewel. There was a hum inside it. A tiny heartbeat.

Find the sword.

The jewel was calling to itself. Seeking out the stars.

She stepped over another body, toward the prow. The hum faded. When she backtracked to the stern, it grew stronger. The *Dancing Pearl* was the nearest ship, straight ahead of her, still afloat.

She dived. Her body sliced deep into the water. A flare of light lit her way as more gunpowder ignited.

Daughter of Zāla.

She knew the voice was in her head. It was too clear, too soft, as if the speaker was close enough for her to feel his breath—but under the water, it seemed as if it stemmed from the Abyss itself.

The voice of the Nameless One.

I know your name, Eadaz uq-Nāra. My servants have whispered it in voices filled with dread. They speak of a root of the orange tree, a root that can stretch far into the world and still burn golden as the sun.

I am the handmaiden of Cleolind, serpent. Somehow she knew how to speak to him. *This night I will complete her work.*

Without me, you will have nothing to unite you. You will fall to wars of wealth and religion. You will make enemies of each other. As you always have. And you will end yourselves.

Ead swam. The white jewel rang against her skin.

You need not give your life. Her head broke the surface, and she kept swimming. *Another fire burns in your heart. Become my handmaiden instead, and I will spare Sabran Berethnet. If you do not do this*, the voice said, *I will break her.*

You will have to break me first. And I have proven difficult to break.

She climbed onto the ship and rose.

So be it.

And so the Nameless One, the blight upon the nations, plunged toward the ship.

Every fire in the Abyss went out. All Ead could hear were cries of fear as death came as a shadow from above. Only starlight pierced the darkness, but in that light, Ascalon shone.

She ran across the *Dancing Pearl*. Her world darkened until there was only the beat of her heart and the blade. She willed the Mother to give her the strength that had filled her on that day in Lasia.

Unearthly metal, alive to her touch. The Nameless One opened his jaws, and a white sun rose inside his mouth. Ead saw the place where his armor had been torn away. She lifted the sword that Kalyba had made, that Cleolind had wielded, that had lived in song for a thousand years.

She buried it to the hilt in flesh.

Ascalon glowed until it blinded her. She had a moment to see the skin of her hands simmering with heat—a moment, an age, something between—before the sword was wrenched from them. She was thrown high across the deck, over the gunwale, into the sea. Scale crashed through the *Dancing Pearl*, carving it fesswise.

The strength left her as quickly as it had come.

She had driven the blade into his heart, as the Mother had not, but it was not enough. He must be chained to the Abyss to die. And she carried a key.

The jewel drifted in front of her. The star inside it lit the dark. How she longed to sleep for eternity.

Another light flickered in the shadows. Lightning, glowing in a vast pair of eyes.

Tané and her dragon. A hand reached through the water and Ead grasped it.

They rose from the ocean, toward the stars. Tané held the blue jewel in one hand. The Nameless One thrashed in the Abyss, head thrown back, fire spraying from his mouth like lava from the mantle of the earth, with Ascalon still buried in his breast.

Tané locked her right hand over Ead's and pushed her fingers between her knuckles, so they both held the waning jewel. It pressed against the dying beat of her heart.

"Together," Tané whispered. "For Neporo. For Cleolind."

Slowly, Ead reached up with her other hand, and their fingers interlocked around the rising jewel.

Her thoughts waxed faint with every breath, but her blood knew what to do. It was instinct, deep-rooted and ancient as the tree.

The ocean rose to their command. They played this final game by turns, never breaking their hold on each other.

They spun him a cocoon, two seamsters weaving with the waves. Steam filled the air as they knitted the Nameless One into the sea, and the darkness quenched the hot coal of his heart.

He looked up at Ead one last time, and she looked into him. A flash of light blinded her where Ascalon had torn him open. The Beast of the Mountain let out a scream before he disappeared.

Ead knew that she would hear that sound for as long as she drew breath. It would echo through her unquiet dreams, like a song across the desert. The dragons of the East dived after him, to see him to his grave. The sea closed over all their heads.

And the Abyss was still.

72

West

In the foothills of the Spindles, the wyrm Valeysa was dead, brought down by a harpoon. All around her, the ground was strewn with the earthly remains of human and wyrm.

Fýredel had not stayed to defend his Draconic territory. Instead, he had summoned his brother and sister to rout the combined armies of North and South and West. They had failed. As for Fýredel himself, he had taken wing as soon as the Nameless One had disappeared beneath the waves, and his followers had scattered once more.

The sun was rising over Yscalin. Its light fell on the blood and the char, the fire and the bones. A Seiikinese woman named Onren had brought Loth here on dragonback so he could find Margret. Standing on the wretched plain, he strained his gaze to Cárscaro.

Smoke rose from the once-great city. No one had been able to tell him whether the Donmata Marosa had survived the night. What *was* known was that King Sigoso, murderer of queens, was dead. His wasted corpse hung from the Gate of Niunda. Seeing it had caused his soldiers to desert.

Loth prayed the princess lived. With all his soul, he prayed she was up there, ready to be crowned.

The field hospital was a league from where the fight had begun. Several tents had been erected near a mountain stream, and the flags of all nations flew outside them.

The wounded were crying in agony. Some had burns that went deep into their flesh. Others were so covered in blood, they were unrecognizable. Loth spotted King Jantar of the Ersyr among those who were gravely hurt, lying with his warriors, tended to from all sides. One woman, whose leg had been shattered, was biting down on a leather strap while the barber-surgeons sawed it off below the knee. Healers brought in pails of water.

He found Margret in a tent for Inysh casualties. Its flaps were open to let out the reek of vinegar.

A bloodstained apron was tied over her skirts. She was kneeling beside Sir Tharian Lintley, who lay still and bruised on a pallet. A deep wound stretched from his jaw to his temple. It had been stitched with care, but he would be scarred for life.

Margret looked up at Loth. For a moment, she was blear-eyed, as if she had forgotten who he was.

"Loth."

He crouched beside her. When she leaned into him, he enveloped her in his arms and rested his chin on the top of her head.

"I think he'll be all right." She smelled of smoke. "It was a soldier. Not a wyrm."

His sister curled against his chest.

"He is dead." Loth kissed her brow. "It's over, Meg."

Her face was smeared with ash. Tears washed into her eyes, and she pressed a trembling hand to her mouth.

Outside, a finger of light broached the horizon, pink as a wild rose. As a new spring dawn crested the Spindles, they held each other close and watched it gild the sky.

73

West

Brygstad, capital of the Free State of Mentendon, crown jewel of learning in the West. Years he had dreamed of returning to its streets.

There were the tall and narrow houses, each with a bell gable. There were the sugared roofs. There was the crocketed spire of the Sanctuary of the Saint, towering from the heart of the city.

Niclays Roos sat in a heated coach, wrapped in a fur-lined cloak. During his convalescence at Ascalon Palace, High Princess Ermuna had written to request his presence at court. His knowledge of the East, she had told him in her letter, would help enrich the relationship between Mentendon and Seiiki. He might even be called upon to help open negotiations for a new trade deal with the Empire of the Twelve Lakes.

He wanted none of it. That court was haunted. If he walked there, all he would see were the ghosts of his past.

Still, he had to show his face. One did not refuse a royal invitation, especially if one was intending not to be banished again.

The coach trundled over the Sun Bridge. Through the window, he looked out at the frozen River Bugen and the snow-capped spires of the city he had lost. He had crossed this bridge on foot when he had first come to court, having traveled from Rozentun on a haywain. In those days, he had not been able to afford coaches. His mother had withheld his inheritance, pointing out, not erroneously, that it amounted to the cost of his degree. All he had possessed was a sharp tongue and the shirt on his back.

It had been enough for Jannart.

His left arm now ended just below the elbow. Though it ached at times, the pain was easy to ignore.

Death had kissed his cheek on the *Dancing Pearl*. The Inysh physicians had assured him that now he was through the worst, what was left of the limb would heal. He had never trusted Inysh physicians—pious quacks, the lot of them—but he supposed he had no choice but to believe them.

It was Eadaz uq-Nāra who had mortally wounded the Nameless One with the True Sword. And *then*, as if that were not sufficient heroism for one night, she and Tané Miduchi had finished him off with the jewels. It was the stuff of legend, a tale destined to be enshrined in song—and Niclays had slept through the whole damned thing. The thought made a smile pull at the corner of his mouth. Jannart would have laughed his guts out.

Somewhere in the city, bells were ringing. Someone had been wed today.

The coach passed the Free State Theatre. On some nights, Edvart had disguised himself as a minor lord and slipped out with Jannart and Niclays to watch an opera or concert or play. They had always gone drinking in the Old Quarter after so Edvart could let go of his cares for a while. Niclays closed his eyes, remembering the laughs of friends long dead.

At least some of his friends had managed not to die. After the Siege of Cárscaro, a search party had been sent for Laya. As he had lain abed on the *Dancing Pearl*, racked with fever, he had remembered certain things about that cavern that had been their prison—namely the red veins that had snaked through its walls.

They had found her in the Dreadmount. Close to death from thirst, she had been nursed back to health in a field hospital, and High Ruler Kagudo had taken her back to Nzene on her own ship. After decades away, she was home, and had already written to invite him to visit her.

He would go soon, when he had taken in enough of Mentendon to be certain it was there. To be sure that this was real.

The coach stopped outside the gates of Brygstad Palace—an austere structure of dark sandstone, hiding an interior of white marble and gilt. A footman opened the door.

"Doctor Roos," he said, "Her Royal Highness, High Princess Ermuna, welcomes you back to Mentish court."

Heat prickled in his eyes. He saw the stained-glass dormer window of the highest room.

"Not yet."

The footman looked baffled. "Doctor," he said, "Her Royal Highness expects you at noon."

"At noon, dear boy. Noon is not now." He sat back. "Do take my belongings, but I shall go to the Old Quarter."

Reluctantly, the footman gave the order.

The coach trundled through the north of the city, past bookshops and museums and guildhalls and bakehouses. Hungry for the sights, Niclays leaned out on his elbow. Scents wafted from the open market, scents he had dreamed about so often in Orisima. Gingerbread and sugared quinces. Pies to crack open with the flat of a knife, revealing the spiral of pear and cheese and cuts of hard-boiled egg inside. Pancakes drizzled with sugar-brandy. The apple tarts he had loved to eat on strolls along the river.

On every corner, stalls sold pamphlets and tracts. The sight made Niclays think of Purumé and Eizaru, his friends on the other side of the world. Perhaps, when and if the sea ban was lifted, they could walk these streets with him.

The coach stopped outside a shabby-looking inn in a lane that branched off Brunna Square. The golden paint had flaked from its sign, but inside, the Sun in Splendor was just as he remembered it.

There was something he had to do before he faced the court. He would seek the ghosts before they found him.

It was traditional for the people of Mentendon to be laid to rest in their birthplaces. Only in rare cases was it permitted for them to be entombed elsewhere.

Jannart had been one of those rare cases. Custom dictated that he should be buried in Zeedeur, but Edvart, torn by grief, had given his dearest friend the honor of a tomb in the Silver Cemetery, where members of the House of Lievelyn were interred. Not long after, Edvart had caught the sweat and joined him there, along with his infant daughter.

The cemetery was a short walk from the Old Quarter. Snow lay thick and untouched over its grounds.

Niclays had never visited the mausoleum. Instead he had fled to Inys, racked with denial. Not believing in an afterlife, he had never seen the point of talking at a slab of stone.

It was icy cold in the mausoleum. An effigy, sculpted from alabaster, lay upon the tomb.

As he approached it, Niclays breathed in deeply. Whoever had captured his likeness had known Jannart well when he was in his early forties. On the shield of the statue, representing the protection of the Saint in death, was an inscription.

> JANNART UTT ZEEDEUR
> SEEK NOT THE MIDNIGHT SUN ON EARTH
> BUT LOOK FOR IT WITHIN

Niclays spread his hand over the words.

"Your bones lie behind me. Nothing lies ahead. You are dead, and I an old man," he murmured. "I resented you for such a long time, Jannart. I had been comfortable in the belief that I would die before you did. Perhaps I even tried to ensure it. I hated you—hated the memory of you—for leaving first. Leaving me."

With a lump in his throat, he turned away. He sank to the floor, his back to the tomb.

"I failed her, Jan." His voice grew almost too soft to hear. "I lost myself, and I lost sight of your grandchild. When the wolves encircled Truyde, I was not there to beat them back.

"I thought—" Niclays shook his head. "I thought of dying. When they brought me up from inside the *Dancing Pearl*, I watched the sea burning. Light from darkness. Fire and stars. I looked into the Abyss, and I almost let myself fall." A dry chuckle.

"And then I stepped back. Too heartsore to live, too craven to die. But then ... you sent me on that journey for a reason. The only way I could think to honor you was by continuing to live.

"You loved me. Without condition. You saw the person I could be. And I will be that person, Jan. I will endure, my midnight sun." He touched the stone face one more time, the lips that were so like they had been in life. "I will teach my heart to beat again."

It hurt to leave him in the dark. Still, leave he did. Those bones had long since let him go.

Outside, the snow had eased a little, but a frigid chill remained. As he walked back through the cemetery, tears icy on his cheeks, a woman came through its wrought-iron gates, wearing a cloak lined with sable. When she looked up, her lips parted, and Niclays froze.

He knew her well.

Aleidine Teldan utt Kantmarkt was standing in the cemetery.

"Niclays," she whispered.

"Aleidine," he replied in disbelief.

She was still a handsome woman in her august years. Her russet hair, as thick as ever, was streaked with white and gathered into a coiffure. The love-knot ring was still on her hand, though not on the forefinger, where it ought to be. No ring had replaced it.

They stared at each other. Aleidine recovered first. "You truly are back." She let out a sound, almost a laugh. "I heard rumors, but I dared not believe them."

"Yes, indeed. After some trials." Niclays tried to compose himself, but his throat had shrunk. "I, er— do you live here now, then? In Brygstad, I mean. Not the cemetery."

"No, no. Still in the Silk Hall, but Oscarde lives here now. I came to visit him. I thought I would visit Jannart, too."

"Of course."

There was silence between them for a moment.

"Sit with me, Niclays," Aleidine said, with a brief smile. "Please."

He considered the wisdom of following her, but did it anyway, to a stone bench by the cemetery wall. Aleidine dusted the snow from it before she sat. He remembered how she had insisted on doing things the servants would usually manage, like polishing the marquetry and dusting the portraits Jannart hung about the house.

For a long while, the silence continued, unbroken. Niclays watched the snowflakes falling. Years he had wondered what he would say if he ever saw Aleidine again. Now the words eluded him.

"Niclays, your arm."

His cloak had fallen back, revealing the stump. "Ah, yes. Pirates, believe it or not," he said, forcing a smile.

"I do believe it. People talk in this city. You already have a reputation as an adventurer." She smiled a little in return. It deepened the fine wrinkles around her eyes. "Niclays, I know we ... never spoke properly after Jannart died. You left for Inys so quickly—"

"Don't." His voice was hoarse. "I know you must have realized. All those years—"

"I don't seek to reprimand you, Niclays." Aleidine spoke gently. "I cared very deeply for Jannart, but I had no claim on his heart. Our families arranged our marriage, as you know. It was not his choice." Snowflakes caught in her lashes. "He was an extraordinary man. All I wanted for him was happiness. You were that happiness, Niclays, and I bear no grudge against you. In fact, I thank you."

"Jannart swore to give nobody else but you his favor. He swore it in a sanctuary, before witnesses," Niclays said tautly. "You were always a pious woman, Ally."

"I was, and am," she conceded, "and that is why, though Jannart broke that vow to me, I refused to break mine to him. I swore, first and foremost, to love and defend him." She laid a delicate hand over his. "He needed your love. The best way I could honor the promises I made him was to let him have it in peace. And to let him love you in return."

She meant it. The sincerity of her belief was carved deep into her face. Niclays tried to speak, but the words, whatever they were, stuck in his throat. He turned his hand and held hers in return.

"Truyde," he finally said. "Where was she laid to rest?"

The pain in her eyes was unbearable. "Queen Sabran had her remains sent to me," she said. "She lies in our family plot at Zeedeur."

Niclays tightened his grip on her hand.

"She missed you terribly, Niclays," she said. "She was so very like Jannart. I saw him in her smile, her hair, her cleverness ... I wish you could have seen her as a woman."

Something was pushing in his chest, making it hard to breathe. His jaw quaked with the effort of keeping it inside.

"What will you do now, Niclays?"

He swallowed the taste of grief. "Our young princess wants to offer me a place at court," he said, "but I should sooner take up a professorship. Not that anyone would give me one."

"Ask her," Aleidine said. "I am sure the University of Brygstad would welcome you."

"A former exile who dabbles in alchemy and spent weeks in the employ of pirates," he said dryly. "Yes, that sounds like someone they would want to mold the minds of the next generation."

"You have seen more of the world than others have written of it. Imagine the insight you could bring, Niclays. You could shake the dust from the lecterns, breathe life into the textbooks."

The possibility warmed him. He had not given it serious consideration, but perhaps he *would* ask Ermuna if she could intercede with the university on his behalf.

Aleidine looked toward the mausoleum. Her breath shivered out in a white plume.

"Niclays," she said, "I understand if you would rather live your life here as a different man. But ... if you would favor me with your company from time to time—"

"Yes." He patted her hand. "Of course I will, Aleidine."

"I'd be so glad. And of course, I could reintroduce you into society. You know, I have a very dear friend at the university, about our age, who I know would be delighted to meet you. Alariks. He teaches astronomy." Her eyes were sparkling. "I am *quite* sure you would like him."

"Well, he sounds—"

"And Oscarde— oh, Oscarde will be overjoyed to see you again. And of course, you'd be welcome to stay with me for as long as you liked—"

"I certainly wouldn't wish to intrude, but—"

"Niclays," she said, "you are family. You could never intrude."

"You're very kind."

They looked at each other, slightly breathless from the outpouring of courtesy. Finally, Niclays managed a smile, and so did Aleidine.

"Now," she said, "I hear you have an audience with our High Princess. Ought you not to get ready?"

"I ought to," Niclays admitted, "but first, perhaps I could ask a small favor."

"Of course."

"I want you to tell me, in"—he checked his pocket watch—"two hours, everything that has happened since I left Ostendeur. I have years of politics and news to catch up on, and don't want to look a fool in front of our new princess. Jannart was the historian, I know," he said lightly, "but you were the one in the know when it came to gossip."

Aleidine chuckled. "I should be delighted," she said. "Come. We can walk by the Bugen. And you can tell me all about your adventure."

"Oh, dear lady," Niclays said, "there is enough of a story there to fill a book."

74

West

In Serinhall, Lord Arteloth Beck worked in a study, a stack of letters and a leather-bound notebook beside him. His parents had gone away for a week, ostensibly for a change of scene, but Loth knew his mother was trying to prepare him for the future. To be Earl of Goldenbirch, with a seat on the Virtues Council, responsible for the largest province in Inys.

He had hoped that, as the years passed, something would shift in him, like clockwork into motion, and that he would be ready for it. Instead he longed to be at court.

One of his dearest friends was dead. As for Ead, he knew she would not stay in Inys forever. News that she had slain the Nameless One had spread, and she wanted none of the renown that would come with it. Sooner or later, her path would bend southward.

Court would never be the same without the two of them. And yet it was where he thrived. It was where Sabran would rule for many years. And he wanted to be there with her, at the heart of their country, to help usher in a new and golden age for Inys.

"Good evening."

Margret walked into the study.

"I do think one should knock," Loth said, stifling a yawn.

"I did, brother. Several times." She laid a hand on his shoulder. "Here. Hot wine."

"Thank you." He took a grateful sip. "What time is it?"

"Past the time we both ought to have been asleep." Margret rubbed her eyes. "Strange to be on our own. Without Mama and Papa. What have you been doing up here for hours?"

"Everything."

He felt her watching him as he closed the notebook. It was full of the household expenses.

"You would sooner be at the palace," Margret said gently.

She knew him too well. Loth only drank the wine, letting it warm the hollow in his belly.

"I have always loved Serinhall. And you have always loved court. And yet I was born the second child, and you the first, so you must be Earl of Goldenbirch." Margret sighed. "I suppose Mama thought you deserved a childhood away from Goldenbirch, since you would be rooted to it when you were older. In fact, she made us both fall in love with the wrong place."

"Aye." He had to smile at the absurdity of it. "Well. Nothing to be done about it."

"I don't know. Inys is changing," Margret said, a sparkle in her eye. "These next few years will be difficult, but they will give this country a new face. We should allow ourselves to broaden our horizons."

Loth looked up at her with a knitted brow. "You do say the strangest things, sister."

"The wisest are seldom appreciated in their time." She squeezed his shoulder before placing a letter in front of him. "This arrived this morning. Try to get some sleep, brother."

She left. Loth turned the letter over and saw the wax seal. Impressed with the pear of the House of Vetalda.

His heart clenched like a fist. He broke the seal and unfolded the letter inside, swirled with an elegant hand.

As he read, a breeze rushed through the open window. It smelled of fresh-cut grass and hay and the life he had craved when he had been far from home. The scents of Goldenbirch.

Now something had changed. Other scents rushed like surf into his dreams. Salt and tar and cold sea wind. Mulled wine, spiced with ginger and nutmeg. And lavender. The flower that had perfumed his dream of Yscalin.

He picked up his quill and began to write.

The fire burned low in the Privy Chamber at Briar House. Frost trimmed every window as if with lace. In the gloom, Sabran lay on her back on a settle, wine-softened, looking as if she could fall asleep. Beside the hearth, long past the cusp of exhaustion, Ead drank her in.

Sometimes, when she looked at Sabran, she almost believed she was the Melancholy King, chasing a mirage across the dunes. Then Sabran would touch her lips to hers, or come to her bedside by moonlight, and she would know that it was real.

"I have something to tell you."

Sabran looked at her.

"Sarsun came to me a few days ago," Ead murmured. "With a letter from Chassar."

The sand eagle had swept into Ascalon Palace and onto her arm, carrying a note. It had taken Ead a long time to work up the courage to read it, and still longer to unravel her feelings when she did.

Beloved—

I have no words to express my pride in what we have heard of your deeds on the Abyss, nor my relief that your heart beats as strong as it always has. When the Prioress sent your sister to silence you, I could do nothing. Craven as I am, I failed you, as I promised Zāla I never would.

And yet I am reminded—as I so often am—that you never needed my protection. You are your own shield.

I write to you with long-awaited tidings. The Red Damsels wish you to return to Lasia to take up the mantle of the Prioress. If you accept, I will meet you in Kumenga on the first day of winter. They could use your steady hand and level head. Most of all, they could use your heart.

I hope you can forgive me. Either way, the orange tree awaits.

"Word that I was the slayer has spread," she said. "It is the greatest honor they could bestow."

Slowly, Sabran sat up.

"I am happy for you." She took Ead by the hand. "You slew the Nameless One. And this was your dream." Their gazes met. "Will you accept?"

"If I go," Ead said, "I would be able to shape the future of the Priory." She interlocked their fingers. "Four of the High Westerns are dead. That means their wyverns, and any progeny they sired, have lost their fire—but even without it, they pose a danger to the world. They must be hunted and slain wherever they hide. And of course ... a great enemy remains at large."

"Fýredel."

Ead nodded. "He must be hunted," she said, "but as Prioress, I could also ensure that the Red Damsels work to protect the stability of this new world. A world outside the shadow of the Nameless One."

Sabran poured them both another cup of perry.

"You would be in Lasia," she said, her tone guarded.

"Yes."

The air between them was suddenly taut.

Ead had never been naïve enough to think they could make a life together in Inys. As a viscountess, she was fit to marry a queen, but she could not be princess consort. She wanted no more titles or graces, no place beside the marble throne. Marriage to a queen required loyalty only to her realm, and Ead claimed no loyalty to anyone but the Mother.

Yet what was between them could not be denied. It was Sabran Berethnet who sang to her soul.

"I would visit," Ead said. "Not ... often, you understand. The Prioress belongs in the South. But I would find a way." She took a cup. "I know I have said this to you once before, Sabran, but I would not blame you if you would prefer not to live that way."

"I would live alone for fifty years to have one day with you."

Ead unfolded herself and went to her. Sabran shifted up, and they sat with their legs intertwined.

"I have something to tell you, too," Sabran said. "In a decade or so, I mean to abdicate the throne. I will use this period to ensure a smooth transition of power from the House of Berethnet to another ruler."

Ead raised her eyebrows.

"Your people believe in the divinity of your house," she said. "How will you explain this to them?"

"I will say that now the Nameless One is dead, the age-old vow of the House of Berethnet—to keep him at bay—is fulfilled. And then I will honor the promise I made to Kagudo," she said. "I will tell my people the truth. About Galian. About Cleolind. There will be a Great Reformation of Virtudom." A long breath escaped her. "It will be very difficult. There will be years of denial, of anger—but it must be done."

Ead saw the steel in her gaze. "So be it." She dropped her head onto Sabran's shoulder. "But who will rule after you?"

Sabran rested her cheek against Ead's brow. "I think at first it must be one of the next generation of Dukes Spiritual. The people will find it easier to embrace a new ruler from the nobility. But in truth ... I do not think it well that the future of any country rests on the begetting of children. A woman is more than a womb to be seeded. Perhaps I can go further in this Great Reformation. Perhaps I can shake the very foundations of succession."

"I believe you could." Ead traced her collarbone. "You can be persuasive."

"I suppose I inherited that gift from my ancestor."

Ead knew how Kalyba haunted her. Kalyba and the prophecy she had made. Often Sabran would wake in the night, remembering the witch, whose face had been the mirror of hers.

After she was healed, Ead had taken Kalyba's body to Nurtha. Finding someone who would row her to the island had been difficult, but eventually, when she had recognized Ead as Viscountess Nurtha, a young woman had sculled her across the Little Sea.

The few people who lived on Nurtha spoke only Morgish and hung wreaths of hawthorn on their doors. None had spoken to her as she made her way through the woods.

The hawthorn tree was felled, but not rotted. Ead could see that it had once been as magnificent as its sister in the South. She had stood among its branches and imagined a young Inysh girl plucking a red berry from its branches, a berry that had changed her forever.

She had laid the Witch of Inysca to rest beneath it. The only Firstblood that now remained was what lived in Sabran, and in Tané.

For a time, only the snap of the fire broke the silence. Finally, Sabran moved to sit on the footstool in front of Ead, so they could face each other, and laced their fingers.

"Don't laugh at me."

"Are you about to say something foolish?"

"Possibly." Sabran paused as if to collect herself. "In the days before Virtudom, the people of Inysca would make a trothplight to the one they loved. A promise that they would make a home together." She held her gaze. "You must do your duty as Prioress. I must do mine as Queen of Inys. For a time, we must go our separate ways ... but ten years from now, I will meet you on the sand of Perchling. And we will find our somewhere."

Ead looked down at their joined hands.

Ten years without being with her each day. Ten years of separation. The thought hollowed her.

But she knew how to ache for something far away. She knew how to endure.

Sabran watched her face. At last, Ead leaned close and kissed her.

"Ten years," she said, "and not one sunrise more."

75

East

The Imperial Palace was much the same as it had been the last time Lady Tané of Clan Miduchi had set foot in its halls. As the sun went down, she walked away from the Hall of the Fallen Star, past servants clearing paths with shovels, blowing warmth into her hands.

While she regained her strength in preparation for her formal return to the High Sea Guard, she had acted as an unofficial ambassador between Seiiki and the Empire of the Twelve Lakes. The Unceasing Emperor had been courteous, as always. He had given her a letter to take back to Ginura, as he often did, and they had spoken for a time about what was happening on the other continents.

All seemed quiet in the world, yet Tané was restless. Something called to her from a distant past.

Nayimathun waited in the Grand Courtyard, surrounded by well-dressed Lacustrine courtiers, who carefully touched her scales for a blessing. Tané climbed into the saddle and pulled on her gauntlets.

"Do you have the letter?" the dragon asked.

"Yes." Tané patted her neck. "Are you ready, Nayimathun?"

"Always."

She took to the sky and, soon enough, they were over the Sundance Sea. Pirates still roamed its waters. Although discussions with Inys were under way, the red sickness was not yet abated, and for now, the Great Edict stood, as Tané suspected it would for some time.

The Golden Empress was out there somewhere. She would live for as long as the sea ban did, and while she drew breath, the trade in dragonflesh would endure. Tané meant to make good on the vow she had made to her on Komoridu, in the shadow of the mulberry tree. Once she had recovered from her injuries, she had begun the climb back to strength with Onren and Dumusa. Soon she would be ready to return to the waves.

The Warlord of Seiiki had rewarded her for her actions on the Abyss. She had been given a mansion in Nanta and her life back.

Except Susa. That loss would remain an arrowhead in her, buried too deep to dig out. Each day, she expected another water ghost to come out of the sea. A ghost without its head.

Nayimathun returned her to Ginura, where she delivered the letter and returned to Salt Flower Castle. As she combed her hair, she cast her gaze toward the bronze mirror and traced the scar on her cheekbone. The scar that had set her on the path to the Abyss.

She changed out of her travel-soiled clothes and slung on her cloak. At dusk, she walked to Ginura Bay, where Nayimathun was bathing on the same beach where she had been captured. Tané walked into the shallows.

"Nayimathun," she said, placing a hand on her scales, "I would like to go now. If you will take me."

That wild gaze locked on hers.

"Yes," the dragon said. "To Komoridu."

———

Not long before, Tané had returned to the village of Ampiki—her first visit since she was a child—to search for any trace of Neporo of Komoridu. It had never been rebuilt after the fire. The only people there had been the young men and women who collected seaweed from its shore.

She had gone back to Feather Island to speak to Elder Vara, who had welcomed her with open arms. He had told her all he knew about Neporo, though it was precious little. There were records of her marriage to a painter, several more letters that pertained to the rise of a new ruler in the East, and some fanciful drawings of what the Queen of Komoridu might have looked like.

In the end, there was only one place to find her.

Light pulsed through Nayimathun as she flew. When Komoridu came into sight—a drop of ink on the face of the sea—she descended onto its sand, and Tané slid out of the saddle.

"I will wait here," Nayimathun said.

Tané patted her in return. She lit her lantern and walked into the trees.

This was her inheritance. The island for outcasts.

One fateful day, as a child in Ampiki, Tané had followed a butterfly to the sea. Elder Vara had told her that in some tales, butterflies were the spirits of the dead, sent by the great Kwiriki. Like dragons, they changed their shape, and so the great Kwiriki in his wisdom had chosen them as his messengers from the celestial plane. If not for that butterfly, Tané would have perished with her parents, and the jewel might have been lost.

Hours she walked the silent forest. Here and there, she found glimpses of what must once have stood a thousand years before. Foundations of houses long since fallen. Shards of cord-marked pottery. The blade of an axe. She wondered if, beneath the ground, the soil was packed with bones. Unsure of what she was looking for, or why, she walked until she found a cave. Inside was a statue of a woman, whittled into the rock, her face weathered but whole.

Tané knew that face. It was her own.

She set the lantern down and knelt before the Firstblood. In her mind, she had thought of all the things she had wanted to say to her, but now she was here, she had only one.

"Thank you."

Neporo gazed back at her, unblinking.

Tané watched her, feeling as if she were in a dream. She stayed until the lantern had burned out. In the darkness, she took the stair she had taken once before, up to the ripped-up mulberry tree that had died beneath the stars. Tané lay beside it and fell asleep.

In the morning, a white butterfly was cupped in her hand, and her side was damp with blood.

76

West

The *Rose Eternal* skirted the western coast of Yscalin. Since
Fýredel had disappeared, its people had begun to rebuild the
damage wrought in the Draconic Years. Prayer houses and sanctuaries rose from the wreckage. Lavender was planted in the fields
that had been burned. And soon enough, red pear trees would
sweeten the streets of Cárscaro again.

Mereswine leaped together from the waves, spraying water.
Dusk had fallen, but Ead had never felt more awake. The salt
wind danced through her hair, and she breathed it deep into her
lungs.

Prioress. She who stood where the Mother once had. Guardian
of the orange tree.

All her life she had been a handmaiden. She had never known
what it was to rule. She had also spent enough time with Sabran to
know that a crown was a heavy weight to bear—but the Priory of
the Orange Tree did not possess a crown. She was not an empress
or a queen, but one cloak among many.

She would find out where Fýredel had hidden, and she would
slay him as she had his master. She would not rest until the only fire
that ascended came through the orange tree, and the mages who ate
of its fruit. And when the Long-Haired Star came once more, the
balance would be restored.

Gian Harlowe came to join her at the stern, clay pipe in hand.

He lit it with a taper, breathed in deeply, and puffed out a wreath of blue-tinged smoke. Ead watched it drift away.

"Queen Marosa will invite the foreign sovereigns to her court in the spring, I hear," he said. "To open Yscalin again."

Ead nodded. "Let us hope that this peace holds."

"Aye."

For a time, the only sound was the waves.

"Captain," Ead said, and Harlowe grunted, "at the Inysh court, there are rumors about you, spoken deep in the shadows. Rumors that you courted Queen Rosarian." She watched his brow darken. "They say you meant to take her to the Milk Lagoon."

"The Milk Lagoon is a fable," he said curtly. "A tale whispered to children and lovers without hope."

"A wise young woman told me once that all legends grow from a seed of truth."

"Is it you or the Queen of Inys who desires the truth?"

Ead waited, watching his face. Those eyes were in a distant past.

"She was never much like Rose." His voice softened. "She was night-born, you know. They say that makes a child grave ... but Rose came into the world at the lark's calling."

He drew on his pipe again.

"Some truths," he said, "are safest buried. Some castles best kept in the sky. There's promise in tales that are yet to be spoken. In the shadow realm, known only to the few." He glanced at her. "You ought to know, Eadaz uq-Nāra. You whose secrets will one day be a song."

With the faintest smile, Ead cast her gaze toward the stars.

"One day, perhaps," she said. "But not today."

The Persons of the Tale

Eastern names are listed by family name first.
Western, Northern, and Southern names are listed by given name first.

✛

THE STORYTELLERS

❖ **Arteloth "Loth" Beck**: Heir apparent to the wealthy northern province of the Leas in Inys and the estate of Goldenbirch. Elder child of Lord Clarent and Lady Annes Beck, brother of Margret Beck, and closest friend of Sabran IX of Inys.

❖ **Eadaz du Zāla uq-Nāra** (*also known as* Ead Duryan): An initiate of the Priory of the Orange Tree, currently posing as an Ordinary Chamberer in the Upper Household of Sabran IX of Inys. She is a descendant of Siyāti uq-Nāra, who was the closest friend of Cleolind Onjenyu.

❖ **Niclays Roos**: An anatomist and alchemist from the Free State of Mentendon and former friend of Edvart II. He was banished by Sabran IX of Inys to Orisima, the last Western trading post in Seiiki.

❖ **Tané**: A Seiikinese orphan who was drafted into the Houses of Learning as a child to train for the High Sea Guard. Principal apprentice from the South House.

❖ **Chief Officer**: The official responsible for security for the Mentish trading post of Orisima.

❖ **Dranghien VI**: Unceasing Emperor of the Twelve Lakes, current head of the House of Lakseng. Like all his bloodline, he claims descent from the Carrier of Light, who the Lacustrine believe was the first human to befriend a dragon when it fell from the heavens.

❖ **Dumusa**: Principal apprentice from the West House, of Miduchi descent. Her paternal grandfather was a Southern explorer, executed for defying the Great Edict.

❖ **Elder Vara**: Healer and archivist at Vane Hall on Feather Island.

❖ **Ghonra**: Heir to the Fleet of the Tiger Eye, adopted daughter of the Golden Empress, and captain of the *White Crow*. She styles herself "Princess of the Sundance Sea."

❖ **The Golden Empress**: Leader of the Fleet of the Tiger Eye—the most formidable pirate fleet in the East, comprising some 40,000 pirates—and captain of its largest treasure ship, the *Pursuit*. She drives the illegal trade in dragonflesh.

❖ **Governor of Cape Hisan**: The official in charge of administrating the Seiikinese region of Cape Hisan. He is responsible for ensuring that the Lacustrine and Mentish settlers adhere to Seiikinese law.

❖ **Governor of Ginura**: The official in charge of administrating the Seiikinese capital of Ginura. She is also the chief magistrate of Seiiki. Traditionally, this post is always held by a member of the House of Nadama.

❖ **Grand Empress Dowager**: A member of the House of Lakseng through marriage. She was official regent for her grandson, the Unceasing Emperor of the Twelve Lakes, during his minority.

- ❖ **Ishari**: An apprentice from the South House. Roommate to Tané.

- ❖ **Kanperu**: An apprentice from the West House.

- ❖ **Laya Yidagé**: Interpreter to the Golden Empress. She was taken prisoner by the Fleet of the Tiger Eye after attempting to follow her adventurous father to Seiiki.

- ❖ **Moyaka Eizaru**: A physician from Ginura. Father of Purumé. Friend and former student of Niclays Roos.

- ❖ **Moyaka Purumé**: An anatomist and botanist from Ginura. Daughter of Eizaru. Friend and former student of Niclays Roos.

- ❖ **Muste**: Assistant to Niclays Roos in Orisima. Companion of Panaya.

- ❖ **Nadama Pitosu**: Warlord of Seiiki and current head of the House of Nadama. He is descended from the First Warlord, who took up arms to avenge the fallen House of Noziken.

- ❖ **Onren**: Principal apprentice from the East House.

- ❖ **Padar**: Navigator on the *Pursuit*.

- ❖ **Panaya**: A resident of Cape Hisan and interpreter to the settlers of Orisima. Companion to Muste.

- ❖ **Sea General**: Commander of the High Sea Guard of Seiiki. Head of Clan Miduchi. Current rider of Tukupa the Silver.

- ❖ **Susa**: A resident of Cape Hisan and childhood friend of Tané. A street urchin until she was adopted by an innkeeper.

- ❖ **Turosa**: Principal apprentice from the North House, of Miduchi descent, famed for his skill with blades. Long-time rival of Tané.

- **Viceroy of Orisima**: The Mentish official who oversees the trading post of Orisima.

DECEASED AND HISTORICAL
PERSONS OF THE EAST

- **Little Shadow-girl**: A mythical figure. A peasant who sacrificed her life to reunite the Spring Dragon with the pearl that had been stolen from her.

- **Neporo**: Self-declared Queen of Komoridu. Very little is known about her.

- **Noziken Mokwo**: A former Empress of Seiiki. Head of the House of Noziken during her reign.

- **Snow-Walking Maiden**: A semilegendary figure. She nursed Kwiriki back to health when he was injured and in the guise of a bird. To thank her, Kwiriki carved her the Rainbow Throne and gave her power over Seiiki. She was the founding member of the House of Noziken and the first Empress of Seiiki.

THE SOUTH

- **Chassar uq-Ispad**: A mage of the Priory of the Orange Tree and its chief link to the outside world. He poses as an ambassador to King Jantar and Queen Saiyma of the Ersyr to allow him access to foreign courts. He helped raise Eadaz uq-Nāra after the sudden death of her birthmother. Chassar has a gift for taming birds, often using Sarsun and Parspa to carry out his work.

- **Jantar I** (the Splendid): King of the Ersyr and current head of the House of Taumargam. Spouse to Queen Saiyma and an ally of the Priory of the Orange Tree.

- **Jondu du Ishruka uq-Nāra**: Childhood friend and mentor to Eadaz uq-Nāra. She was sent to Inys to find Ascalon. Like Eadaz, she is a descendant of Siyāti uq-Nāra.

❖ **Kagudo Onjenyu**: High Ruler of the Domain of Lasia and current head of the House of Onjenyu. She is a descendant of Selinu the Oathkeeper through his son, the half-brother of Cleolind Onjenyu. Kagudo is an ally of the Priory of the Orange Tree and has been guarded by Red Damsels since the day she was born.

❖ **Mita Yedanya**: Prioress of the Orange Tree. She was formerly the *munguna*, or heir presumptive.

❖ **Nairuj Yedanya**: A Red Damsel of the Priory of the Orange Tree and its presumed *munguna*.

❖ **Saiyma Taumargam**: Queen consort of the Ersyr and spouse of Jantar I.

DECEASED AND HISTORICAL
PERSONS OF THE SOUTH

❖ **Butterfly Queen**: A semimythical figure. She was a beloved queen consort of the Ersyr, but died young, plunging her king into unending grief.

❖ **Cleolind Onjenyu** (the Mother *or* the Damsel): Crown princess of the Domain of Lasia and daughter of Selinu the Oathkeeper. Founder of the Priory of the Orange Tree. The religion of the Virtues of Knighthood professes that she wed Sir Galian Berethnet and became queen consort of Inys after he defeated the Nameless One to save her. Members of the Priory believe it was Cleolind who vanquished the beast, and most believe she did not leave with Galian. Cleolind died after leaving the Priory on unknown business not long after its foundation.

❖ **Dawnsinger**: A prophet of the ancient Ersyr. Among his predictions, he claimed that the sun would rise from the Dreadmount and sweep away Gulthaga, which was locked in a bitter war with his people.

- **Melancholy King**: A semimythical figure, said to have been an early king of the House of Taumargam. He wandered into the desert, following a mirage of his wife, the Butterfly Queen, and died of thirst. Ersyris use him as a cautionary tale, most often to warn against blind love.

- **Selinu the Oathkeeper**: High Ruler of Lasia and head of the House of Onjenyu when the Nameless One settled in Yikala. He organized a lottery of lives to placate the beast, which ended only when his own daughter, Cleolind, was chosen as the sacrifice.

- **Siyāti uq-Nāra**: The beloved friend and handmaiden of Cleolind Onjenyu. She became Prioress of the Orange Tree after Cleolind died abroad. Many sisters and brothers of the Priory are descended from Siyāti through her seven children.

- **Zāla du Agriya uq-Nāra**: A sister of the Priory of the Orange Tree and birthmother to Eadaz du Zāla uq-Nāra. She was poisoned when Eadaz was six.

VIRTUDOM

- **Aleidine Teldan utt Kantmarkt**: A member of the wealthy Teldan family, she was ennobled upon her marriage to Lord Jannart utt Zeedeur, the future Duke of Zeedeur. She is now known as the Dowager Duchess of Zeedeur. Grandmother of Truyde

- **Annes Beck** (Lady Goldenbirch): Daughter of the Baron and Baroness of Greensward. Countess of Goldenbirch through her marriage to Lord Clarent Beck. Mother to Arteloth and Margret. Former Lady of the Bedchamber to Rosarian IV of Inys.

- **Arbella "Bella" Glenn** (Viscountess Suth): One of the three Ladies of the Bedchamber to Sabran IX of Inys and Keeper of the Queen's Jewels. She was also Lady of the

Bedchamber, milk nurse, and Mistress of the Robes to the late Rosarian IV. Since Rosarian's death, she has never spoken.

- **Aubrecht II** (the Red Prince): High Prince of the Free State of Mentendon, Archduke of Brygstad, and current head of the House of Lievelyn. Grand-nephew of the late Prince Leovart and nephew of the late Prince Edvart. Brother to Ermuna, Bedona, and Betriese. He is the eldest of the siblings.

- **Bedona Lievelyn:** Princess of the Free State of Mentendon. Sister to Aubrecht, Ermuna, and Betriese.

- **Betriese Lievelyn:** Princess of the Free State of Mentendon. Sister to Aubrecht, Ermuna, and Bedona. She is the youngest of the siblings, born just after Bedona, her identical twin.

- **Calidor Stillwater:** Second son of Nelda Stillwater, the Duchess of Courage. Companion of Lady Roslain Crest and father of Lady Elain Crest.

- **Chieftain of Askrdal:** Highest-ranking nobleman in the ancient Duchy of Askrdal in Hróth. A friend of Lady Igrain Crest.

- **Clarent Beck** (Lord Goldenbirch): Earl of Goldenbirch and Keeper of the Leas. Companion of Lady Annes Beck. Father to Arteloth and Margret.

- **Elain Crest:** Daughter of Lady Roslain Crest and Lord Calidor Stillwater. She is expected to inherit the Duchy of Justice after her mother, who is next in line.

- **Ermuna Lievelyn:** Crown princess of the Free State of Mentendon and Archduchess of Ostendeur. Sister to Aubrecht, Bedona, and Betriese.

- **Estina Melaugo:** Boatswain on the *Rose Eternal*.

- **Gautfred Plume:** Quartermaster on the *Rose Eternal*.

- ❖ **Gian Harlowe**: An Inysh privateer and captain of the *Rose Eternal*. Rumored to have been the lover of Rosarian IV of Inys, who gifted him the ship.

- ❖ **Grance Lambren**: A member of the Knights of the Body.

- ❖ **Gules Heath**: Longest-serving member of the Knights of the Body.

- ❖ **Hallan Bourn**: Royal Physician to Sabran IX of Inys.

- ❖ **Helchen Roos**: Mother of Niclays Roos. She has been estranged from her son for decades.

- ❖ **Igrain Crest**: Duchess of Justice, Lady High Treasurer of Inys, and current head of the Crest family. She was regent in all but name during the minority of Sabran IX of Inys and remains her trusted advisor on the Virtues Council.

- ❖ **Jillet Lidden**: A maid of honor in the Upper Household of Sabran IX of Inys. She often sings at court.

- ❖ **Joan Dale**: A member of the Knights of the Body and second-in-command to Sir Tharian Lintley. She is a distant relative of Sir Antor Dale.

- ❖ **Kalyba** (the Lady of the Woods *or* the Witch of Inysca): A mysterious figure in Inysh history. Creator of Ascalon. She is said to have lived in the haithwood in the north of Inys, and to have abducted and murdered children.

- ❖ **Katryen "Kate" Withy**: Mistress of the Robes and one of the three Ladies of the Bedchamber to Sabran IX of Inys. She is the favorite niece of Lord Bartal Withy, the Duke of Fellowship.

- ❖ **Kitston Glade**: Poet at the court of Sabran IX of Inys and friend of Lord Arteloth Beck. Sole heir of the Earl and Countess of Honeybrook. Heir apparent to the province of the Downs.

- ❖ **Lemand Fynch**: Acting Duke of Temperance and Lord Admiral of Inys in place of his missing uncle, Lord

Wilstan Fynch, whose position he fills on the Virtues Council. Acting head of the Fynch family.

❖ **Linora Payling**: Daughter of the Earl and Countess of Payling Hill. She is an Ordinary Chamberer in the Upper Household of Sabran IX of Inys.

❖ **Margret "Meg" Beck**: Daughter and younger child of Lord Clarent and Lady Annes Beck. She is an Ordinary Chamberer in the Upper Household of Sabran IX of Inys and Keeper of the Privy Library. Sister to Arteloth Beck.

❖ **Marke Birchen**: A member of the Knights of the Body.

❖ **Marosa Vetalda**: Donmata of Yscalin. Daughter of Sigoso III and his late companion, Queen Sahar.

❖ **Nelda Stillwater**: Duchess of Courage and Lady Chancellor of Inys. Current head of the Stillwater family.

❖ **Oliva Marchyn**: Mother of the Maids, who oversees the maids of honor.

❖ **Oscarde utt Zeedeur**: Duke of Zeedeur and Mentish ambassador to the Queendom of Inys. Son of Lord Jannart utt Zeedeur and Lady Aleidine Teldan utt Kantmarkt.

❖ **Priessa Yelarigas**: First Lady of the Bedchamber to the Donmata Marosa of Yscalin.

❖ **Ranulf Heath the Younger**: Earl of Deorn and Keeper of the Lakes. His father, Ranulf Heath the Elder, was prince consort to Jillian VI of Inys, grandmother of Sabran IX.

❖ **Raunus III**: King of Hróth and current head of the House of Hraustr.

❖ **Ritshard Eller**: Duke of Generosity and current head of the Eller family. A member of the Dukes Spiritual.

❖ **Roslain Crest**: Chief Gentlewoman of the Bedchamber to Queen Sabran IX of Inys and heir apparent to the

Duchy of Justice. Her mother, Lady Helain Crest, held the same position in the household of Rosarian IV. Roslain is the companion of Lord Calidor Stillwater, mother of Lady Elain Crest, and granddaughter of Lady Igrain Crest.

❖ **Sabran IX** (the Magnificent): Thirty-sixth queen of Inys and current head of the House of Berethnet. Daughter of Rosarian IV. Like all members of her dynasty, she claims descent from Sir Galian Berethnet and Princess Cleolind of Lasia.

❖ **Seyton Combe** (the Night Hawk): Duke of Courtesy, Principal Secretary, and spymaster to Sabran IX of Inys.

❖ **Sigoso III**: King of Yscalin and current head of the House of Vetalda, presently styling himself *Flesh King*. Once loyal to Virtudom, he has renounced the Virtues of Knighthood and now pledges his allegiance to the Nameless One. Father of Marosa Vetalda, his daughter with Sahar Taumargam.

❖ **Tallys**: A scullion in the Lower Household of Sabran IX of Inys.

❖ **Tharian Lintley**: Captain of the Knights of the Body, the personal guard of Sabran IX of Inys. A commoner by blood, he became a member of the Virtues Council when he was knighted.

❖ **Thim**: A deserter from the *Black Dove*, now a gunner on the *Rose Eternal*.

❖ **Triam Sulyard**: A former page in the Lower Household of Sabran IX of Inys, then squire to Sir Marke Birchen. He is secretly wed to Lady Truyde utt Zeedeur.

❖ **Truyde utt Zeedeur**: Heir apparent to the Duchy of Zeedeur. Daughter of Oscarde utt Zeedeur and his late companion. She is serving as a maid of honor in the Upper Household of Sabran IX of Inys.

❖ **Wilstan Fynch**: Duke of Temperance, Lord Admiral of Inys, and prince consort to the late Rosarian IV of Inys. He became the Inysh ambassador-in-residence to the Kingdom of Yscalin after her death. His nephew, Lord Lemand Fynch, holds his position on the Virtues Council in his absence.

DECEASED AND HISTORICAL PERSONS OF VIRTUDOM

❖ **Antor Dale**: A knight who wed Rosarian I of Inys after he played a public game of love with her. Her father, Isalarico IV of Yscalin, gave special permission for the marriage to proceed, since it was popular with the people. Sir Antor embodies the ideals of chivalry.

❖ **Brilda Glade**: Chief Gentlewoman of the Bedchamber to Sabran VII of Inys, who eventually became her companion.

❖ **Carnelian I** (the Flower of Ascalon): Fourth queen of the House of Berethnet.

❖ **Carnelian III**: Twenty-fifth queen of the House of Berethnet. She caused a stir when she refused to hire a milk nurse for her daughter, Princess Marian. She fell in love with Lord Rothurt Beck, but was unable to marry him.

❖ **Carnelian V** (the Mourning Dove): Thirty-third queen of the House of Berethnet, famed for her beautiful voice and periods of sadness. Great-grandmother of Sabran IX of Inys.

❖ **Edrig of Arondine**: Trusted friend of Sir Galian Berethnet, who served as his knight. When Galian was crowned King of Inys, Edrig was named Keeper of the Leas and given the family name *Beck*.

❖ **Edvart II**: High Prince of the Free State of Mentendon. Edvart and his infant daughter died not long after Jannart utt Zeedeur during the Brygstad Terror, when half the Mentish court died of the sweating sickness. He was succeeded by his uncle, Leovart.

❖ **Galian Berethnet** (the Saint *or* Galian the Deceiver): The first King of Inys. Galian was born in the Inyscan village of Goldenbirch, but rose to squire for Edrig of Arondine. The religion of the Virtues of Knighthood, which Galian based on the knightly code, professes that he vanquished the Nameless One in Lasia, married Princess Cleolind of the House of Onjonyu, and with her founded the House of Berethnet. Worshipped in Virtudom, but reviled in many parts of the South, Galian is thought by his followers to rule in Halgalant, the heavenly court, where he awaits the righteous at the Great Table.

❖ **Glorian II** (Glorian Hartbane): Tenth queen of the House of Berethnet. A gifted hunter. Her marriage to Isalarico IV of Yscalin brought his country into Virtudom.

❖ **Glorian III** (Glorian Shieldheart): Twentieth queen of the House of Berethnet, arguably its best-known and most beloved monarch. She led Inys during the Grief of Ages and famously took her newborn daughter, Sabran VII, on to the battlefield. This action inspired her soldiers to fight to the end.

❖ **Haynrick Vatten**: Steward-in-Waiting to Mentendon during the Grief of Ages. He was betrothed to the future Sabran VII of Inys when he was four years old. The Vatten, who ruled Mentendon for centuries on behalf of the House of Hraustr, were eventually overthrown and exiled back to Hróth, but their descendants still wielded power in Mentendon.

❖ **Isalarico IV** (the Benevolent): King of Yscalin and prince consort of Inys. He pledged his country to Virtudom upon his marriage to Glorian II of Inys.

- ❖ **Jannart utt Zeedeur**: The late Duke of Zeedeur, previously Marquess of Zeedeur. He was a close friend to Edvart II of Mentendon, the secret lover of Niclays Roos, and companion to Lady Aleidine Teldan utt Kantmarkt. Jannart was a passionate historian.

- ❖ **Jillian VI**: Thirty-fourth queen of the House of Berethnet. Maternal grandmother to Sabran IX of Inys. Jillian was musically gifted, religiously tolerant, and argued for closer ties between Virtudom and the rest of the world.

- ❖ **Leovart I**: High Prince of the Free State of Mentendon. He was not supposed to sit on the throne, but persuaded the Privy Council to let him hold it for his grand-nephew, Aubrecht, who Leovart declared was too gentle and inexperienced to rule. He was notorious for proposing to countless noble and royal women.

- ❖ **Lorain Crest**: One of the six members of the Holy Retinue, friend to Sir Galian Berethnet. Dame Lorain is remembered in Inys as the Knight of Justice.

- ❖ **Never Queen**: The sobriquet of Princess Sabran of Inys, daughter of Marian IV. She was the twenty-fourth royal woman of the House of Berethnet, but died giving birth to the future Rosarian II before she could be crowned.

- ❖ **Rosarian I** (the Apple of All Eyes): Eleventh queen of the House of Berethnet. Her popular reign integrated traditions from Yscalin—the kingdom of her father, Isalarico IV.

- ❖ **Rosarian II** (the Architect of Inys): Twenty-fourth queen of the House of Berethnet. She was a gifted architect who traveled extensively in her youth, while she was still a princess. Rosarian personally designed many buildings in Inys, including the marble-faced clock tower of Ascalon Palace.

- ❖ **Rosarian IV** (the Merrow Queen): Thirty-fifth queen of the House of Berethnet, mother to Sabran IX of Inys. She was assassinated by means of a poisoned gown.

- ❖ **Rothurt Beck**: An earl of Goldenbirch. Carnelian III of Inys fell in love with him, but he was already wed.

- ❖ **Sabran V**: Sixteenth queen of the House of Berethnet. Her reign marked the beginning of the Century of Discontent, which saw three unpopular queens in a row. She was notorious for her cruelty and extravagant lifestyle.

- ❖ **Sabran VI** (the Ambitious): Nineteenth queen of the House of Berethnet. Most famous for bringing Hróth into Virtudom through her love marriage to Bardholt Hraustr. Her coronation ended the Century of Discontent. Sabran and Bardholt were slain by Fýredel, leaving their daughter, Glorian III, to weather the Grief of Ages.

- ❖ **Sabran VII**: Twenty-first queen of the House of Berethnet. Daughter of Glorian III of Inys. She was betrothed to Haynrick Vatten, Steward-in-Waiting to Mentendon, on the day she was born. After his death, and her own abdication, Sabran wed her principal Lady of the Bedchamber, Lady Brilda Glade.

- ❖ **Sahar Taumargam**: A princess of the Ersyr who became queen consort of Yscalin upon her marriage to Sigoso III. Sister of Jantar I of the Ersyr. She died under suspicious circumstances.

- ❖ **Wulf Glenn**: Friend and bodyguard of Glorian III of Inys. One of the most famous knights in Inysh history, an ideal of courage and gallantry. He is an ancestor of Lady Arbella Glenn.

NONHUMAN CHARACTERS

- ❖ **Aralaq**: An ichneumon, raised in the Priory of the Orange Tree by Eadaz and Jondu uq-Nāra.

- ❖ **Orsul**: One of the five High Westerns that led the Draconic Army during the Grief of Ages.

- ❖ **Fýredel**: Leader of the Draconic Army, loyal to the Nameless One and known as his *right wing*. He led a ruthless campaign against humankind in 511 CE. Some say he emerged from the Dreadmount at the same time as the Nameless One, while others believe he emerged at the same time as his siblings, during the Second Great Eruption.

- ❖ **Valeysa**: One of the five High Westerns that led the Draconic Army during the Grief of Ages.

- ❖ **Imperial Dragon**: Leader of all Lacustrine dragons, elected by arcane means. The current Imperial Dragon is a female who was hatched in the Lake of Golden Leaves in CE 209. The Imperial Dragon traditionally councils the human royal family of the Empire of the Twelve Lakes and chooses which of its heirs will inherit the throne.

- ❖ **Kwiriki**: Believed by the Seiikinese to have been the first dragon to take a human rider, worshipped as a deity. He carved the Rainbow Throne—now destroyed—out of his horn. The Seiikinese believe Kwiriki left for the celestial plane, and that he sent the comet that ended the Great Sorrow. Butterflies are his messengers.

- ❖ **The Nameless One**: An enormous red wyrm, created from a proliferation of *siden* in the core of the world. He is thought to have been the first creature to emerge from the Dreadmount and is the overlord of the Draconic Army, which was created for him by Fýredel. Little is known about the Nameless One, but it is assumed that his ultimate goal was to sow chaos and conquer humankind. His confrontation with Cleolind Onjenyu and Galian Berethnet in Lasia in BCE 2 became a fundament of religion and legend the world over.

- ❖ **Nayimathun of the Deep Snows**: A Lacustrine dragon who fought in the Great Sorrow. A wanderer by nature, she is now a member of the High Sea Guard of Seiiki.

- ❖ **Norumo**: A Seiikinese dragon and a member of the High Sea Guard of Seiiki.

- ❖ **Parspa**: The last known *hawiz*—a species of giant, plant-eating bird, native to the South. She answers only to Chassar uq-Ispad, who tamed her.

- ❖ **Sarsun**: A sand eagle. Friend of Chassar uq-Ispad and messenger to the Priory of the Orange Tree.

- ❖ **Tukupa** (the Silver): A Seiikinese elder dragon descended from Kwiriki. Traditionally, the Sea General of Seiiki is her rider, but she may also carry the Warlord of Seiiki and members of his family.

Glossary

Attifet: A headdress worn by women in the northern provinces of Inys. It dips in the middle, lending it a heartlike shape.

Baldachin: An ornate canopy that stands over the *boss* of a *sanctuary*.

Barding: Horse armor.

Bodmin: A wildcat, known to roam the moors of Inys. Its fur is warm and, due to its rarity, expensive.

Boss: The raised center of a shield. In Inys, this name is given to the platform at the heart of a *sanctuary*, where the sanctarian preaches and ceremonies take place.

Buckler: A small shield.

Carcanet: A jeweled chain or necklace.

Charnel garden: A place where bones are buried, usually attached to a *sanctuary*.

Comfit: Fennel seeds coated in sugar.

Coney: A wild rabbit.

Creamgrail: An Inysh flower. The sap it produces is a valuable commodity—when combined with water, it forms a thick cream that cleans and scents the hair. When prepared correctly, its root induces sleep.

Cupshotten: Drunk.

Damsam: A mild Inysh oath. Contraction of "Damsel's name."

Dipsas: Venom from a tiny snake native to the Ersyr.

Doublet: A close-fitting jacket with long sleeves and a high collar.

Dowry: A transfer of money upon marriage.

Eachy: A sea cow.

Emmet: An ant.

Eria: A colossal salt desert beyond the Gate of Ungulus. No one living has ever been known to cross it.

Farthingale: A hoop skirt stiffened with whalebone, worn beneath Inysh and Yscali gowns to give them a distinctive bell-like shape.

Fesswise: Horizontally, in the manner of a heraldic fess.

Foxfire: Bioluminescence, caused by rotting fungi.

Fustian: A heavy cover for a bed, made of twilled cloth.

Garth: A small courtyard.

Girdle: A jeweled chain, worn around the hips as a belt.

Grievoushead: An Inysh term for depression or dejection of the spirits. It runs in the House of Berethnet.

Gurnet: A bottom-feeding sea fish. The word is used in Inys as an all-purpose insult.

Haithwood: A primeval forest in the north of Inys, which divides the provinces of the Leas and the Lakes. It is associated with the legend of the Lady of the Woods.

Halberd: A two-handed Seiikinese weapon with a broad, curved blade at one end.

Halgalant: The afterlife of the religion of the Virtues of Knighthood, said to have been built in the heavens by Sir Galian Berethnet after his demise. A beautiful castle in a bountiful land where King Galian holds court at the Great Table with the righteous.

Hellburner: A type of Mentish fireship that uses a clockwork mechanism to ignite a fuse, causing a massive explosion.

Herigaut: A garment worn by sanctarians in Inys, usually made of green and white cloth. Some believe the colors represent the leaves and blossoms of the hawthorn.

Intelligencer: A spy.

Jerkin: A sleeveless jacket.

Kirtle: A one-piece sleeveless gown. May be worn on its own or as an extra layer beneath a more formal garment.

Mangonel: A catapult-like device. Once used as a siege engine, it was repurposed for use against the Draconic Army in the Grief of Ages.

Marchpane: Marzipan.

Mereswine: A dolphin or porpoise.

Merrow: A gender-neutral Old Morgish term for one of the legendary merfolk.

Midnight sun: In the school of alchemy taught to Niclays Roos, the midnight sun (also known as the red sun or Rosarian's Sun) represents the final stage of the Great Work. The white sun, which precedes the red, is a symbol of purification after the first stage, the putrefaction.

Monbone: Ichneumon bone. It is used by the Priory of the Orange Tree to make bows.

Morgish: A language originating from the Inysh isle of Morga.

Munguna: The presumed heir to the Priory of the Orange Tree.

Oakmouse: A squirrel.

Orchard of Divinities: The afterlife in the dominant polytheistic religion of Lasia.

Orisons: Prayers.

Orris: Iris.

Page: An attendant in an Inysh royal palace, usually aged between six and twelve. They pass messages and carry out assignments for persons of noble birth.

Palanquin: An enclosed litter.

Pargh: A cloth wrapped around the face and head to keep sand away from the eyes, most often used in the Ersyr.

Partizan: A spear-like Inysh weapon.

Perry: A sweet pear cider. The city of Córvugar in Yscalin produced a famous red perry, which inspired the Inysh drink.

Pestilence: Bubonic plague. Once a serious threat, it has all but died out.

Poppet: A doll.

Priory: A building where knights of the Isles of Inysca would gather in ancient times. They were succeeded by the *sanctuary*.

Quarl: A jellyfish.

Rail: A floor-length garment worn over a nightgown for additional warmth, usually sleeveless and tied with a sash.

Rock dove: A homing pigeon, used for carrying letters.

Rose cold: Hay fever.

Samite: An expensive and heavy material, used in garments and drapery.

Sanctuary: A religious building in Inys, where those who believe in the Six Virtues of Knighthood can pray and hear teachings. Sanctuaries developed from earlier *priories*, where knights would seek comfort and guidance. The main chamber of a sanctuary is round, like a shield, and the center is known as the *boss*. A *charnel garden* is usually nearby.

Selinyi: An ancient language of the South, thought to originate from beyond the *Eria*. It was eventually incorporated into the various dialects of Lasian, but is still spoken in its original form by the House of Onjenyu and by the handmaids of the Priory of the Orange Tree.

Settle: An upholstered wooden seat, not unlike a sofa. May not be upholstered in poorer households.

Setwall: Valerian.

Shawm: A woodwind instrument.

Shellblood: A bluish dye, extracted from sea snails in the Sundance Sea. Used in Seiikinese paint and cosmetics.

Siden: Another name for terrene magic. It comes from the *Womb of Fire* and is channeled through the siden trees. Siden is kept in check by *sterren*.

Skep: Beehive.

Smalt: Cobalt glass. A rich dark blue in color.

Sodden-witted: Drunk.

Sorrower: A black Seiikinese bird with a call like a grizzling infant. Legend has it that an empress of Seiiki was driven insane by its cry. Some say sorrowers are possessed by the spirits of stillborn children, while others believe their song can bring on a miscarriage. This has resulted in them being sporadically hunted throughout Seiikinese history.

Squire: An attendant in the service of a knight or knight-errant, usually aged between fourteen and twenty.

Sterren: Another name for sidereal magic. It comes from the Long-Haired Star in the form of a substance called "star rot."

Suns: The main currency of the Ersyr.

Sunstone: A colorless crystal mined in Hróth, used by seafarers of the ancient world to locate the sun on an overcast day. Sunstone is traditionally cut into the shape of an orange blossom and mounted on the rings given to Red Damsels of the Priory of the Orange Tree. It symbolizes the draw between a Red Damsel and the light of the tree, and her ability always to find it.

Vestures: Ceremonial garments.

Visard: A silk-lined velvet mask. The wearer must bite on a bead to hold it in place, preventing speech.

Warding: A protective magic that requires *siden* to create. Wardings take two forms: earth-wardings and wind-wardings. An earth-warding can be drawn on earth, wood, or stone and alerts a mage when anyone approaches. A wind-warding, which uses more siden, is a barrier against Draconic fire.

Womb of Fire: The core of the world. It is the wellspring of *siden* and the birthplace of the Nameless One and his followers, the High Westerns. Siden is drawn up naturally from the Womb of Fire through the siden trees as part of the universal balance, but its Draconic miscreations—a result of imbalance—come up through the Dreadmount.

Woodvine: Wisteria. It flowers thickly in the summer.

Wyverling: A young or small *wyvern.*

Wyvern: A two-legged, winged Draconic creature. Like the High Westerns, the wyverns came from the Dreadmount. Fýredel bred them with a number of animals to create the foot-soldiers of his Draconic Army, such as the cockatrice. Each wyvern is bound to one High Western. Should the High Western die, the flame in its wyverns will go out, as will the flame in every creature descended from those wyverns.

Timeline

CE 512: The House of Noziken falls. The Grief of Ages, or Great Sorrow, ends with the arrival of the Long-Haired Star

CE 960: Niclays Roos arrives at the court of Edvart II of Mentendon and meets Jannart utt Zeedeur

CE 974: Princess Rosarian Berethnet is crowned Queen of Inys

CE 991: Queen Rosarian IV dies. Her daughter, Princess Sabran, is crowned queen and enters her period of minority. Tané officially begins her education and training for the High Sea Guard

CE 993: Jannart utt Zeedeur dies, leaving his companion, Aleidine Teldan utt Kantmarkt, a widow. Edvart II of Mentendon and his daughter die of the sweat a few months later. Edvart is succeeded by his uncle, Leovart

CE 994: Queen Sahar of Yscalin dies, leaving Princess Marosa Vetalda as the sole heir of King Sigoso

CE 995: Queen Sabran's minority ends. Niclays Roos becomes her court alchemist

CE 997: Ead Duryan arrives at court. Tané meets Susa.

CE 998: Niclays Roos is banished from court to the Mentish outpost of Orisima in Cape Hisan

CE 1000: The celebration of 1,000 years of Berethnet rule

CE 1003: Truyde utt Zeedeur arrives at the Inysh court. Fýredel wakes beneath Mount Fruma and seizes control of Cárscaro. Under his orders, Yscalin declares allegiance to the Nameless One

CE 1005: *The Priory of the Orange Tree* begins. Tané is nineteen, Ead is twenty-six, Loth is thirty, and Niclays is sixty-four

Acknowledgments

The Priory of the Orange Tree is my longest published book and has taken more than three years to finish. I wrote its first words in April 2015 and edited it for the last time in June 2018. When you go on a quest like that, you need an army to help you reach the end.

To you, my readers, for stepping into this world with me. Without you, I'm just a girl with a skullful of curious ideas. Remember that whoever and wherever you are, the realm of adventure will never be closed to you. You are your own shield.

To my agent, David Godwin, who believed in *Priory* as much as he believed in *The Bone Season* and is always there to reassure and support me. To Heather Godwin, Kirsty McLachlan, Lisette Verhagen, Philippa Sitters, and the rest of DGA for continuing to be fantastic.

To my Holy Retinue of editors: Alexa von Hirschberg, Callum Kenny, Genevieve Herr, and Marigold Atkey. You've each been extraordinary in drawing out the best in *Priory*. Thank you so much for your patience, wisdom, and commitment, and for understanding everything I wanted to achieve with this story.

To the worldwide team at Bloomsbury: Alexandra Pringle, Amanda Shipp, Ben Turner, Carrie Hsieh, Cesca Hopwood, Cindy Loh, Cristina Gilbert, Francesca Sturiale, Genevieve Nelsson, Hermione Davis, Imogen Denny, Jack Birch, Janet Aspey, Jasmine Horsey, Josh Moorby, Kathleen Farrar, Laura Keefe, Laura Phillips, Lea Beresford, Marie Coolman, Meenakshi Singh, Nancy Miller,

Sarah Knight, Phil Beresford, Nicole Jarvis, Philippa Cotton, Sara Mercurio, Trâm-Anh Doan, and everyone else—thank you for continuing to publish the outpourings of my peculiar imagination. It remains such a privilege and a dream to work with you.

To David Mann and Ivan Belikov, the talents behind the magnificent jacket. Thank you both for your attention to detail, for capturing the essence of the story so well, and for listening so readily to my suggestions.

To Lin Vasey, Sarah-Jane Forder and Veronica Lyons, who went pearl-diving into this sea of a book for all the things I'd missed.

To Emily Faccini for the maps and illustrations that have made *Priory* such a thing of beauty.

To Katherine Webber, Lisa Lueddecke, and Melinda Salisbury—I vividly remember you telling me to just hurry up and *show* you this dragon book I kept making enigmatic comments about. Your fierce encouragement and relentless enthusiasm for *Priory* fueled me to keep going for months, and then years. It would have taken me far longer to finish if I hadn't known you were there, waiting for the next part. Thank you. I love you.

To Alwyn Hamilton, Laure Eve and Nina Douglas, my West London squad. Thank you for all the coffee, laughs, and ~~procrastination~~ writing days, and for giving me the willpower to climb the never-ending mountain of structural edits on my laptop.

To the wonderful people—among them Dhonielle Clayton, Kevin Tsang, Molly Night, Natasha Pulley, and Tammi Gill— who gave me feedback on and assistance with various aspects of *Priory*. Thank you for your insight and generosity.

To Claire Donnelly, Ilana Fernandes-Lassman, John Moore, Kiran Millwood Hargrave, Krystal Sutherland, Laini Taylor, Leiana Leatutufu, Victoria Aveyard, Richard Smith, and Vickie Morrish, who have all been incredible friends and supporters.

To Doctor Siân Grønlie, who introduced me to Old English and sparked my interest in etymology.

To all fans of my ongoing *Bone Season* series, including the ever-incredible advocates—thank you for being so patient while I was elsewhere, and for joining me on a new journey.

To booksellers, librarians, reviewers and bloggers on all platforms, my fellow authors, and bookwyrms in general. I am so proud and lucky to be a member of this big-hearted community.

Priory contests, incorporates, reimagines, and/or was influenced by elements of a number of myths, legends, and historical works of fiction, including the tale of Hohodemi as told in *Kojiki* and *Nihongi*, *The Faerie Queene* by Edmund Spenser, and various versions of Saint George and the Dragon, including those in *The Golden Legend* by Jacobus de Voragine, *The Renowned History of the Seven Champions of Christendom* by Richard Johnson, and the *Codex Romanus Angelicus*.

I owe a significant debt of inspiration to true events and situations of the past. I am deeply grateful to the historians and linguists whose publications helped me decide how to weave these events into *Priory*, how to construct its world, and how best to name its places and characters. The British Library provided me with access to many of the texts I required during my research. We must never underestimate the value of libraries, or the urgency of the need to protect them, in a world that often appears to forget the importance of stories.

My final acknowledgment is for my incredible family, especially to my mum, Amanda Jones—my best friend—who inspired me to build this world as high as it was wide.

Note on the Author

Samantha Shannon was born in west London in 1991. In 2013 she published *The Bone Season*, the first in a seven-book series. *The Mime Order* followed in 2015 and *The Song Rising* in 2017. The series is internationally bestselling, and her books have been translated into twenty-six languages. The film rights have been optioned by the Imaginarium Studios. *The Priory of the Orange Tree* is her fourth novel.

samanthashannon.co.uk / @say_shannon